S0-CFN-289

READER'S DIGEST

CONDENSED BOOKS

ROSA RUGOSA
by Carolyn Bucha

READER'S DIGEST CONDENSED BOOKS

VOLUME 3 1994

THE READER'S DIGEST ASSOCIATION, INC.
Pleasantville, New York

Reader's Digest Condensed Books are published every two to three months at Pleasantville, N.Y.

FIRST EDITION: Volume 213

Library of Congress Catalog Card Number: 50-12721
Printed in the United States of America

CONTENTS

A Dangerous Fortune

Ken Follett

They belong to one of the most powerful banking families in the world. Nations rise and fall at their bidding. Lives and livelihoods hang in the balance. But behind a veil of Victorian propriety, each is vying to gain fortune's favor.

Augusta, the cunning matriarch, greedy for a title as well as wealth.

Hugh, the clever nephew, in love with the wrong woman.

Micky, the suave outsider, willing to do anything to achieve his ambitions.

Maisie, the lowborn beauty, risen to high society and eager to stay there.

For each of them, everything depends on a tip of the scales.

PROLOGUE

1866

1

On the day of the tragedy the boys of Windfield School had been confined to their rooms.

It was a hot Saturday in May, and they would normally have spent the afternoon playing cricket, but a crime had been committed. Six gold sovereigns had been stolen from the desk of Mr. Offerton, the Latin master, and the whole school was under suspicion. The boys were to be kept in until the thief was caught.

Micky Miranda sat at a table scarred with the initials of generations of bored schoolboys. In his hand was a publication called *Equipment of Infantry.* Swords and rifles usually fascinated him, but he was too hot to concentrate. On the other side of the table his roommate, Edward Pilaster, looked up from a Latin exercise book. He was copying Micky's translation of a page from Plutarch, and now he pointed an inky finger and said, "I can't read this word."

Micky looked. "Decapitated," he said. Micky found Latin easy. Many of the words were similar in Spanish, his native language.

Edward's pen scratched on. Micky got up restlessly and went to the open window. He looked wistfully across the stable yard to the woods. There was a shady swimming hole in a disused quarry at the north end of Bishop's Wood. The water was cold and deep.

"Let's go swimming," he said suddenly.

"We can't," Edward said.

"We could go out through the synagogue." The "synagogue" was the room next door, which was shared by three Jewish boys. Windfield School was tolerant of religious differences, which was

why it appealed to Jewish parents, to Edward's Methodist family, and to Micky's Catholic father. "We can go through their window and drop onto the washhouse roof."

Edward looked scared. "It's the striper if you're caught."

The striper was the ash cane wielded by the headmaster, Dr. Poleson. The punishment for breaking detention was twelve agonizing strokes. But the chance of getting caught was remote, and Micky could almost feel the cold water on his sweaty skin.

He looked at his roommate. Edward was not well liked at school. He was too lazy to be a good student, too clumsy to do well in games, and too selfish to make many friends. Micky was the only friend he had, and Edward hated Micky to spend time with other boys. "I'll see if Pilkington wants to go," Micky said, and he went to the door.

"No, don't do that," said Edward anxiously. "I'll go."

Micky opened the door. There was no one in the corridor. He darted into the next room. Edward followed.

"Hello, Hebrews," Micky said.

Two of the boys were playing cards. They glanced up without speaking. The third, Fatty Greenbourne, was eating a cake. "Hello, you two," he said amiably. "Want some cake?"

"By heaven, Greenbourne, you eat like a pig," Micky said.

Fatty shrugged. He suffered a good deal of mockery, being fat as well as Jewish, but none of it seemed to touch him. His father was said to be the richest man in the world, and perhaps that made him impervious to name-calling. Micky looked out the window. The stable yard was deserted. Fatty said, "What are you fellows doing?"

"Going swimming," said Micky. He sat on the windowsill, rolled over onto his stomach, wriggled backwards, then dropped the few inches onto the sloping roof of the washhouse. He glanced up and saw Edward looking anxiously out. "Come on," Micky said. He scrambled down the roof and used a drainpipe to ease himself to the ground. A minute later Edward landed beside him.

Micky peeked around the corner of the washhouse wall. There was no one in sight. Without further hesitation he darted across the stable yard and into the woods. Edward came up beside him. "We did it!" Micky said. "Nobody spotted us."

"We'll probably be caught going back in," Edward said morosely.

Micky smiled at him. Edward was very English looking, with straight fair hair and blue eyes and a nose like a broad-bladed knife.

A big boy with wide shoulders, he had no sense of style, and wore his clothes awkwardly. He and Micky were the same age, sixteen, but in other ways they were different: Micky had curly dark hair and dark eyes, and he was meticulous about his appearance. "Trust me, Pilaster," Micky said. "Don't I always take care of you?"

They followed a path through the wood. It was cooler under the beech and elm trees, and Micky began to feel better. "What will you do this summer?" he asked Edward.

"We usually go to Scotland in August."

"Do your people have a shooting box there?" Micky had picked up the jargon of the English upper classes, and he knew shooting box was the correct term even if the house was a fifty-room castle.

"They rent a place," Edward replied. "But we don't shoot over it. My father's not a sportsman, you know."

Micky heard a defensive note in Edward's voice and pondered its significance. He knew that the English aristocracy liked to shoot birds in August and hunt foxes all winter. He also knew that aristocrats did not send their sons to this school. The fathers of Windfield boys were businessmen, not earls, and such men did not have time to waste hunting and shooting. The Pilasters were bankers, and when Edward said "My father's not a sportsman," he was acknowledging that his family was not in the very highest rank of society.

It amused Micky that Englishmen respected the idle more than people who worked. In his own country, people respected nothing but power. If a man had the power to control others—to feed or starve them, imprison or free them, kill them or let them live—what more did he need?

"What about you? How will you spend the summer?"

Micky had wanted Edward to ask that. "Here at school," he said. "I can't go home. It takes six weeks one way. I'd have to start back before I got there."

"By Jove, that's hard."

In fact, Micky had no wish to go back. He had loathed his home since his mother died. There were only men there now—his father, his older brother Paulo, some uncles, and four hundred cowboys. Papa was a hero to the men, and a stranger to Micky—cold, unapproachable, impatient. But Micky's brother was the real problem. Paulo was stupid but strong. He never missed a chance to prove to everyone that Micky could not rope steers or break horses. No,

Micky did not want to go home for the vacation. But he did not want to remain at school, either. What he really wanted was to be invited to spend the summer with the Pilaster family.

They clambered over a picket fence and walked up a hill. As they breasted the rise, they came upon the swimming hole. The chiseled sides of the quarry were steep, but agile boys could scramble down. At the bottom was a deep pool of murky green water that contained toads, frogs, and the occasional water snake.

To Micky's surprise there were also three boys in it. He peered at them. All three were in the lower fourth at Windfield.

The mop of carrot-colored hair belonged to Antonio Silva, who, despite his coloring, was a compatriot of Micky's. They came from a South American country called Cordova. Tonio's father did not have as much land as Micky's, but the Silvas lived in the capital and had influential friends.

The second boy was Hugh Pilaster, a cousin of Edward's. There was no resemblance between them; Hugh had black hair and small, neat features and usually wore an impish grin. Edward resented Hugh for being a good scholar and making Edward look like a dunce.

The other was Peter Middleton, a timid boy who attached himself to the more confident Hugh. All three had white, hairless thirteen-year-old bodies with thin arms and legs.

Then Micky saw a fourth boy, at the far end of the pool. He was older than the other three and did not seem to be with them. Micky could not see his face well enough to identify him.

Edward was grinning evilly. He had seen an opportunity to make mischief. He put his finger to his lips in a hushing gesture, then started down the side of the quarry. Micky followed.

They reached the ledge where the small boys had left their clothes. Tonio and Hugh were diving underwater investigating something, while Peter swam quietly on his own. Peter was the first to spot the newcomers. "Oh, no," he said.

"Well, well," said Edward. "You boys are breaking bounds."

Hugh Pilaster noticed his cousin and shouted, "So are you!"

"You'd better go back before you're caught," Edward said. He picked up a pair of trousers from the ground. "But don't get your clothes wet, or everyone will know where you've been." He threw the trousers into the pool and cackled with laughter.

"You cad!" Peter yelled as he made a grab for the trousers.

As Edward continued to throw clothes into the water, Hugh scrambled out of the pool. Micky expected him to escape, but he ran straight at Edward and gave him a mighty shove. Although Edward was much bigger, he was caught off balance. He staggered, then toppled over and fell into the pool with a terrific splash.

It was done in a twinkling, and Hugh snatched up an armful of clothes and went up the quarry side like a monkey. Peter and Tonio shrieked with mocking laughter.

Micky chased Hugh a short way, but he could not catch the smaller, nimbler boy. Turning back, he saw that Edward had surfaced. Edward got hold of Peter Middleton and started ducking his head again and again, punishing him for that mocking laugh.

Tonio swam to the edge of the pool, clutching a bundle of sodden clothing. "Leave him alone, you big ape!" he yelled back at Edward. Then he went farther along the side and turned with a stone in his hand. Micky yelled a warning to Edward, but it was too late. Tonio threw the stone, and it hit Edward on the head. A bright splash of blood appeared on his brow. Edward gave a roar of pain and, leaving Peter, struck out across the pool after Tonio.

2

HUGH raced naked through the wood, clutching his clothes. Coming to a place where the path was crossed by another, he dodged to the left, ran a little way, then dived into the bushes and hid. His cousin Edward and Edward's crony, Micky Miranda, were the worst bullies in school. He felt sure Edward would come after him. Edward had always hated Hugh.

Their fathers had quarreled, too. Hugh's father, Tobias, had taken his capital out of the family business and started his own enterprise, trading in dyes for the textile industry. Even at thirteen, Hugh knew that the worst crime in the Pilaster family was to take your capital out of the bank. Edward's father, Joseph, had never forgiven his brother Tobias.

Hugh wondered what had happened to his friends. The older boy, Albert Cammel, nicknamed Hump, had been swimming alone at the far end of the pool. Hump had left his clothes in a different place, so he had probably escaped.

Hugh, too, had escaped, but he was not yet out of trouble. He would have to sneak into school in his soaking wet clothes and hope he would not be seen. He groaned miserably at the thought.

He had been in and out of trouble since he came to Windfield eighteen months before. He had no trouble studying; he came top of his class in every test. But the petty rules irritated him. He ran when he should have walked, read when he was supposed to go to sleep, and talked during prayers. And he always ended up guilty and scared.

The wood was silent for several minutes while he reflected gloomily on his destiny. At last he decided that Edward was not coming after him. He stood up and pulled on his wet trousers and shirt. Then he heard someone crying. Cautiously he peeped out and saw Tonio's shock of carrot-colored hair. His friend was walking slowly along the path, carrying his clothes and sobbing.

"What happened?" Hugh asked. "Where's Peter?"

"I'll never tell. Never!" Tonio said fiercely. "They'll kill me."

"All right, don't tell me," Hugh said. Tonio was usually brave to the point of recklessness, but he was terrified of Micky Miranda. Whatever had happened, Tonio would keep quiet about it. "You'd better get dressed," Hugh said practically.

Tonio looked blankly at the sodden garments in his arms. Hugh helped him put them on; then they walked toward the school.

Tonio stopped crying, though he still looked shaken. Hugh wondered why his friend was so disturbed. After all, bullying was nothing new at Windfield. What had happened at the pool after Hugh had escaped? But Tonio said nothing more about it all the way back.

The school was a collection of buildings that had once been a large farm, and their dormitory was in an old dairy near the chapel. To get there, the two boys had to climb a wall and sprint across a courtyard. They had just reached their door when disaster struck. A familiar voice rang out, "Pilaster Minor, is that you?" And Hugh knew the game was up.

He turned. Mr. Offerton had chosen that very moment to come out of the chapel. Hugh stifled a groan. Mr. Offerton, whose money had been stolen, was the least likely of all the masters to show mercy. It would be the striper.

"Come here, Pilaster," Mr. Offerton said.

Hugh shuffled over to him, with Tonio following behind.

"Headmaster's study, right away," said Mr. Offerton.

"Yes, sir," Hugh said miserably. When the headmaster saw how he was dressed, he would probably be sacked, too. And how would he explain it to his mother? The two boys turned away, but Mr. Offerton said, "Not you, Silva."

Hugh and Tonio exchanged a quick mystified look. Why should Hugh be punished and not Tonio?

Hugh made for the headmaster's house, on the far side of the school compound. He met Dr. Poleson in the hall. For some reason the headmaster did not look angry. Instead of demanding to know why Hugh was out of his room and dripping wet, he simply opened the study door and said quietly, "In here, young Pilaster."

Hugh went in.

He was astonished to see his mother sitting there. Worse yet, she was weeping. "I only went swimming!" he blurted out. Then he began to understand that this had nothing to do with his breaking detention. He had a dreadful feeling it was much worse than that.

"Mother, what is it?" he said. "Why have you come?"

"Oh, Hugh," she sobbed, "your father's dead."

3

SATURDAY was the best day of the week for Maisie Robinson. On Saturday, Papa got paid. Tonight there would be meat for supper, and new bread. She sat on the front doorstep with her brother, Danny, waiting for Papa to come home from work. Danny was thirteen, two years older than Maisie.

The house was one of a row of damp dwellings in the dockland neighborhood of a town on the northeast coast of England. It belonged to Mrs. MacNeil, a widow. She lived in the front room downstairs. The Robinsons lived in the back room, and another family lived upstairs. When Papa arrived home, Mrs. MacNeil would be on the doorstep waiting to collect the rent.

Their name was not really Robinson; it was Rabinowicz. Mrs. MacNeil had hated them ever since she discovered they were Jews. There were no other Jews in town. The Robinsons had never intended to come here. They had paid for passage to Manchester, where there were lots of Jews, but the ship's captain had cheated them. When they discovered they were in the wrong place, Papa said they would save up enough money to move to Manchester. But then Mama had fallen ill. She was still ill, and they were still here.

Papa worked on the waterfront, in a warehouse with the words "Tobias Pilaster & Co" over the gate. Papa worked as a clerk, keeping records of the barrels of dyes that came in and out of the building. He was a careful man—a taker of notes and a maker of lists. Mama was the reverse. She was the daring one. Mama loved to meet new people, dress up, and play games. That was why Papa loved her so much, Maisie thought.

Mama was not spirited anymore. She lay all day on an old mattress, drifting in and out of sleep. The doctor had said she needed building up, with plenty of fresh eggs and cream and beef every day; and then Papa had paid him with the money for that night's dinner. Now Maisie felt guilty every time she ate, knowing she was taking food that might save her mother's life.

Maisie and Danny had learned to steal. They would pilfer potatoes and apples from the stalls in the square. Maisie knew Mama would be ashamed, but Maisie was hungry.

She looked up and saw some men from Pilasters coming along the street. They were talking angrily, waving their arms and shaking their fists. As they came closer, she saw Papa among them. A thin man with a black beard and soft brown eyes, he was walking with his head bowed. He looked so hopeless that Maisie wanted to cry.

"Papa, what's happened?" she said. "Why are you home early?"

"Come inside." His voice was so low Maisie could only just hear.

The two children followed him into the back of the house. He knelt by the mattress and kissed Mama's lips. She smiled at him. He did not smile back. "The firm's bust," he said, speaking Yiddish. "Tobias Pilaster went bankrupt. There's been a financial crash. A big bank in London failed yesterday. So I've got no work and no pay."

"They must pay you," Mama whispered. "You worked all week."

"They've no money. That's what bankrupt means. It means you owe people money and can't pay them."

"But Mr. Pilaster is a good man, you always said."

"Tobias Pilaster's dead. He hanged himself last night in his office in London. He had a son Danny's age."

"But how are we to feed our children?"

"I don't know," Papa said, and he began to cry. He leaned forward and buried his wet face in Mama's breast.

Maisie was appalled. Papa never cried. It seemed to mean the end of any hope. No money meant no food.

Danny stood up, looked at Maisie, and jerked his head toward the door. Together they tiptoed out of the room. Maisie sat on the front step and began to cry. "What are we going to do?" she said.

"We'll have to run away," Danny said. "If we stay, we'll die."

Maisie didn't care if she died, but a different thought occurred to her: Mama would surely starve herself to feed them. "You're right," Maisie said to Danny. "If we go, perhaps Papa will be able to find enough food for Mama." Hearing herself say the words, she was awestruck by what was happening to her family. It was worse even than the day they had left Viskis—with the village houses still burning behind them—and got on a cold train with all their belongings in two sailcloth bags. For then she had known that Papa would always look after her, no matter what else happened, and now she had to take care of herself. "Where will we go?" she said in a whisper.

"I'm going to America. There's a ship in the harbor that's bound for Boston on the morning tide. I'll hide on deck in one of the boats."

Looking at her brother, Maisie saw for the first time that there was the shadow of a mustache on his upper lip. He was becoming a man. One day he would have a full black beard like Papa's. She understood she was not included in his plans, and she felt miserable. "We're not going together, then," she said sadly.

He looked guilty, but he did not contradict her. "Go to Newcastle. It's a huge city. No one will notice you. Cut your hair, steal a pair of trousers, and pretend to be a boy. Go to a stable and help with the horses. You've always been good with horses."

Maisie could not imagine being alone. "I'd rather go with you."

"You can't. It's going to be hard enough, anyway, to hide myself on the ship. I couldn't look after you, too."

She saw that his mind was made up. With dread in her heart she said, "When should we go?"

"Now. I'll need to get aboard the ship as soon as it's dark."

She stood up. She had no spare clothes, no possessions. There was no food to take. "I want to kiss Mama good-bye," she said.

"Don't," said Danny harshly. "If you do, you'll stay."

It was true. If she saw Mama, she would break down. She swallowed hard. "All right," she said, fighting back tears, "I'm ready."

When they got to the end of the street, she wanted to turn around and take a last look at the house, but she was afraid she would weaken. So she walked on and never looked back.

4

CHARACTER OF THE ENGLISH SCHOOLBOY

The deputy coroner for Ashton, Mr. H. S. Wasbrough, held an inquest yesterday at the Station Hotel, Windfield, on the body of Peter James St. John Middleton, aged 13. The boy had been swimming in a pool at a disused quarry near Windfield School when two older boys saw him apparently in difficulties, the court was told. One of the older boys, Miguel Miranda, a native of Cordova, gave evidence that his companion, Edward Pilaster, aged 16, dived in to try to save the younger boy, but to no avail. The jury returned a verdict of accidental death by drowning. The deputy coroner then called attention to the bravery of Edward Pilaster and said the character of the English schoolboy, as formed by such institutions as Windfield, was a thing of which we might justifiably feel proud.

—*The Times*

MICKY Miranda was captivated by Edward's mother.

Augusta Pilaster was a tall, statuesque woman in her thirties. She had black hair and black eyebrows and a haughty, high-cheekboned face with a straight, sharp nose and a strong chin. She wore a black coat and hat to the inquest, and that made her even more dramatic. Micky could hardly take his eyes off her.

Beside her sat her husband, Joseph, Edward's father—an ugly, sour-faced man of about forty. He had the same big blade of a nose as Edward and the same fair coloring, but his blond hair was receding, and he had bushy side-whiskers, as if to compensate for his baldness. Micky wondered what had made such a splendid woman marry him. He was very rich; perhaps that was it.

Mr. and Mrs. Pilaster, Edward and Micky, and the headmaster, Dr. Poleson, were returning to the school in a carriage hired from the Station Hotel. The inquest had gone well. Micky had put on his most honest expression to tell the story he and Edward had made up.

He and Edward were the only boys asked to the inquest. Hugh had been taken away from the school on the day of the drowning because of the death of his father. Tonio was not asked to give evidence, because nobody knew he had witnessed the death; Micky had scared him into silence. The other witness, the unknown boy at the far end of the pool, had not come forward.

Peter Middleton's parents were too grief-stricken to attend. They sent their lawyer, a sleepy-eyed old man whose only object was to get the whole thing over, with a minimum of fuss. Peter's older brother, David, was there and became agitated when the lawyer declined to ask Micky or Edward any questions. But to Micky's relief the old man waved aside his protests.

In the headmaster's dusty drawing room, Mrs. Pilaster embraced Edward and kissed the wound on his forehead where Tonio's stone had hit him. Micky and Edward had told everyone that Edward banged his head when he dived in to rescue Peter.

As they drank their tea, Micky saw a new side to Edward. His mother, sitting beside him on the sofa, touched him constantly. Instead of being embarrassed, as most boys would, he seemed to like it. She's stupid about him, Micky thought, and he loves it.

After some small talk Mrs. Pilaster stood up abruptly. The men scrambled to their feet. "I should like a few minutes in the chapel," she said. "Perhaps Micky would show me the way."

"By all means," the headmaster replied. "Off you go, Miranda."

Micky was impressed. How effortlessly she made them all do her bidding. Feeling pleased to be her escort, he led her to the chapel. It was empty. She took a back pew and invited him to sit beside her. Looking straight into his eyes, she said, "Now tell me the truth."

AUGUSTA saw a flash of fear in the boy's expression. However, he recovered in an instant. "I've told you the truth," he said.

She shook her head. "You have not."

He smiled, and it took her by surprise. Few men could resist the force of her will, but it seemed he was exceptional. "How old are you?" she said.

"Sixteen."

She studied him. He was outrageously good looking, although there was already a hint of decadence in the heavy-lidded eyes and full lips. He reminded her of the Earl of Strang, but she pushed that thought aside with a guilty pang. "Peter Middleton was not in difficulties when you arrived at the pool," she said.

"What makes you say this?" he said coolly.

He was scared, she sensed, but he maintained his composure.

"You're forgetting that Hugh Pilaster was there," she said. "He is my nephew. He has spoken to his mother, who is my sister-in-law."

"What did he say?"

Augusta frowned. "He said that Edward threw Peter's clothes into the water."

"And then?"

Augusta smiled. This boy was taking control of the conversation. He was interrogating her. "Just tell me what really happened."

He nodded. "Very well."

When he said that, Augusta was relieved, but worried as well. She wanted to know the truth, but she feared what it might be. Poor Teddy. He had almost died as a baby because there had been something wrong with her breast milk. Ever since then, he had needed her special protection.

"Edward didn't mean any harm," Micky said. "He threw the clothes into the water as a joke. Then Hugh pushed Edward in."

"That little Hugh has always been a troublemaker," Augusta said.

"The other boys laughed, and Edward pushed Peter's head under to teach him a lesson. Hugh ran off. Then Tonio threw a stone at Edward, and he went chasing after Tonio. I was watching them. No one was looking at Peter Middleton. Tonio got away from Edward eventually. That was when we noticed Peter. Perhaps Edward's ducking exhausted him. Anyway, he was floating face down. We got him out of the water right away, but he was dead."

It was hardly Edward's fault, Augusta thought. All the same, she was deeply grateful that this story had not come out at the inquest. "What about the other boys? They must know what happened."

"It was lucky that Hugh left the school that very day."

"And the other one— Did you call him Tony?"

"Antonio Silva. Tonio for short. Don't worry about him. He's from my country. He'll do as I tell him. He knows that if he gets me into trouble, his family will suffer back home."

There was something chilling in the boy's voice as he said this, and Augusta shivered. "No other boys saw what happened?"

Micky frowned. "There was another boy swimming in the pool when we got there. I don't know who it was, and I'm not sure at what point he left. But he hasn't come forward as a witness, so I suppose he's no danger to us."

No danger to us. It struck Augusta that she was involved with this boy in something dishonest, possibly criminal. She looked hard at him and said, "What do you want?"

Looking bewildered, he said, "What do you mean?"

"You covered up for my son." He was unbalanced by her directness. That pleased her; she was in control again. "I think you want something in return. Why don't you just tell me what it is."

She saw his gaze drop to her bosom, and for a wild moment she thought he was going to make an indecent suggestion. Then he said, "I want to spend the summer with Edward."

She had thought he would ask for money or a job at Pilasters Bank. This seemed such a small, almost childish request. "You shall stay with us for the summer, and welcome," she said. The thought did not displease her—his manners were perfect, and he was good-looking; it would be no hardship to have him as a guest. And perhaps some of his strength of will would rub off on Edward.

Micky smiled. He got up from the pew, where they were sitting. "Thank you," he said, and offered his hand.

She took it. "I'm grateful to you for protecting Teddy."

He bent down as if he were going to kiss her hand, and then, to her astonishment, he kissed her lips. A moment later he was gone.

She sat in the cool chapel for a long time, staring at the bare walls, realizing she had entered into a criminal conspiracy with a mere schoolboy. She began to wonder, with a distinct feeling of apprehension, how this handsome, knowing boy would use his power.

PART I

1873

Chapter One: May

1

WHEN Micky Miranda was twenty-three, his father came to London to buy rifles. Senor Carlos Raul Xavier Miranda, known always as Papa, was a short man with massive shoulders. His tanned face was carved in lines of brutality. In leather chaps and a broad-brimmed hat, seated on a chestnut stallion, he made a commanding figure. But here in Hyde Park, wearing a frock coat and a top hat, he felt foolish, and that made him dangerously bad-tempered.

Father and son were not alike. Micky was tall and slim, with regular features, and he got his way by smiling rather than by frowning. He was deeply attached to the refinements of London life—beautiful clothes, polite manners, linen sheets, and indoor plumbing. His great fear was that Papa would want to take him back to Cordova. He could not bear the prospect of being under the thumb of his older brother, Paulo. Perhaps Micky would go home one day, but it would be as an important man in his own right. Meanwhile, he had to persuade his father that he was useful here in London.

They were walking along South Carriage Road on a sunny Saturday afternoon. The park was thronged with well-dressed Londoners enjoying the warm weather. But Papa was not enjoying himself. "I must have those rifles," he muttered in Spanish.

"You could buy them back home," Micky said tentatively.

"Two thousand of them?" Papa said. "Perhaps I could. But everyone would know about it."

So he wanted to keep it secret. Micky had no idea what Papa was up to. There had been no war in Cordova since the now legendary March of the Cowboys, when Papa had led his men across the Andes to liberate Santamaria Province from its Spanish overlords. Micky was afraid to ask who the guns were for. Instead he said, "Anyway, you couldn't get such high-quality weapons at home."

"That's true," said Papa. "The Westley Richards is a fine rifle. But how can they ask for the money before the guns are delivered?"

Micky had been able to help Papa with his choice of rifles. Micky had always been fascinated by weapons of all kinds, and he kept up with the latest technical developments. Papa needed short-barreled rifles that would not be too cumbersome for men on horseback. But Papa knew nothing about international trade, and he had assumed the manufacturer would deliver the rifles in Cordova and accept payment there. On the contrary, the payment was required before the weapons left the factory.

"We'll solve this problem, Papa," Micky said soothingly. "That's what merchant banks are for. The bank will pay the manufacturer. It will arrange for the guns to be shipped to Cordova. When they arrive, the bank will accept payment from you at their office there."

"How do they make a living?"

"They take a cut of everything. They will pay the rifle manufacturer a discounted price, take a commission on the shipping and insurance, and charge you extra for the guns."

Papa nodded. He was trying not to show it, but he was impressed.

They left the park and walked to the home of Joseph and Augusta Pilaster.

In the seven years since Peter Middleton drowned, Micky had spent every vacation with the Pilasters. After school he had toured Europe with Edward for a year, and he had roomed with Edward during the three years they spent at Oxford University, drinking and gambling and raising Cain.

Micky had never again kissed Augusta. He would have liked to—and he sensed that she might have let him—but he had held back out of prudence. He had achieved something priceless by being accepted almost as a son in one of England's richest families. It would be insane to jeopardize that by seducing Joseph Pilaster's wife.

Edward's parents had recently moved into a new house on Kensington Gore, across from Hyde Park and the gardens of Kensington Palace. It was the perfect location for the home of a rich commercial family, and the house was certainly striking. It was of red brick and white stone, with big leaded windows on the first and second floors. Above the second floor was a huge gable, its triangular shape enclosing three rows of windows—six, then four, then two at the apex. The sides of the gable were stepped, and on the steps were perched stone animals—lions and dragons and monkeys. At the very top of the gable was a ship in full sail.

"I'm sure there's not another house like this in London," Micky said as he and his father stood outside staring at it.

"No doubt that is what the lady intended," Papa replied.

Micky nodded. Papa had not yet met Augusta, but he had her measure already. The door was open, and they went in.

Augusta was having a tea party to show off her house. The hall was jammed with people. Micky and his father handed their hats to a footman, then pushed through the crowd to the vast drawing room at the back of the house. The French doors were open, and the party spilled out onto a flagged terrace and a garden.

Papa did not need Micky to point out Augusta to him.

She stood in the center of the room, draped in a royal-blue silk dress with a low square neckline. As Papa shook her hand, she gazed at him with her hypnotic dark eyes and said in a deep velvet voice, "Senor Miranda, what a pleasure to meet you. Micky has told me of your splendid ranch."

Papa was immediately entranced. He bowed low over her hand. "You must come and visit us one day."

God forbid, Micky thought. Augusta in Cordova would be as out of place as a flamingo in a coal mine. "What a tempting prospect," she said to Papa. Then, withdrawing her hand from his without missing a beat, she looked over his shoulder and cried, "Why, Captain Tillotson, how kind of you to come." And she turned away to greet the latest arrival.

Papa was bereft. It took him a moment to regain his composure. Then he said abruptly, "Take me to the head of the bank."

"Certainly," Micky said. He looked around for old Seth. The entire Pilaster clan was here, including aunts, in-laws, and cousins. Most of the other guests were business connections, Micky judged—and rivals, too, he thought as he saw the thin, upright figure of Ben Greenbourne, head of Greenbournes Bank. Ben was the father of Solomon, the boy Micky had known as Fatty. They had lost touch since school. Fatty had not studied at a university, but had gone straight into his father's business.

The aristocracy thought it vulgar to talk about money, but this group had no such inhibitions. Micky kept hearing the word "crash." In the newspapers it was sometimes spelled "Krach" because it had started in Austria. Share prices were down and the bank rate was up, according to Edward, who was now working at the family bank. Some people were alarmed, but the Pilasters felt confident that London would not be pulled down with Vienna.

Micky took Papa out through the French doors onto the terrace. There they found old Seth sitting with a rug over his knees, despite the warm spring weather. He was weak from some unspecified illness, and he looked as frail as an eggshell, but he had the Pilaster nose—a big curved blade—that made him formidable still.

"Mr. Pilaster, may I present my father, Senor Carlos Miranda, who is over from Cordova for a visit."

Seth shook Papa's hand. "Cordova, eh? My bank has an office in your capital city, Palma."

"I go to the capital very little," Papa said. "I have a ranch."

"So, you're in the beef business. Look into refrigeration."

Papa was baffled. Micky explained: "Someone has invented a

machine for keeping meat cold. If they can find a way to install it in ships, we will be able to send fresh meat without salting it."

Papa frowned. "This could be bad. I have a big salting plant."

"Knock it down," said Seth. "Go in for refrigeration."

Papa did not like people telling him what to do, and Micky felt a little anxious. Out of the corner of his eye he spotted Edward. "Papa, I want you to meet my best friend," he said. He eased his father away from Seth. "Allow me to present Edward Pilaster."

After Papa and Edward shook hands, Micky said, "May we talk business for a moment?"

They stepped off the terrace onto the newly laid lawn. The borders were freshly planted with tiny shrubs. "Papa has made a large purchase here, and he needs to arrange shipping and finance."

Edward looked keen. "I'll gladly handle it. What is the cargo?"

"Rifles," Micky said.

Edward's face fell. "Oh. Then I can't help you."

Micky was mystified. "Why?"

"Because of old Seth. He's a Methodist, you know—well, the whole family is—but he's more devout than most. Anyway, he won't finance arms sales, and as he's Senior Partner, that's bank policy."

Micky had a sinking feeling in his stomach. "The damned old hypocrite is practically dead. Why should he interfere?"

"He is about to retire," Edward pointed out. "But I think Uncle Samuel will take over, and he's the same, you know."

Worse. Samuel was Seth's bachelor son, fifty-three years old and in perfect health. "We'll have to go to another bank," Micky said.

Edward said, "That should be straightforward, provided you can give a couple of sound business references."

"References? Why?" Micky asked.

"A bank needs some assurance that they're dealing with a respectable businessman."

In South America, Papa was a caudillo—a provincial landowner with a workforce of cowboys that doubled as his private army. He wielded power in a way the British had not known since the Middle Ages. It was like asking William the Conqueror for references.

Micky pretended to be unperturbed. "No doubt we can provide something," he said. In fact, he was stumped. But if he was going to stay in London, he had to bring this deal off.

They strolled back toward the crowded terrace, Micky hiding his anxiety. Papa had not understood the conversation, but Micky would explain it later—and then there would be trouble.

Augusta appeared on the terrace and spoke to Edward. "Find Hastead for me, Teddy darling." Hastead was her obsequious butler. "There's no cordial left, and the wretched man has disappeared." Edward went off. She favored Papa with a warm smile, then looked at Micky. Always quick to sense other people's moods, she said, "You're not enjoying the party. What's the matter?"

He did not hesitate to confide in her. "I was hoping Papa could help Edward by bringing new business to the bank, but it involves guns, and Edward just explained that Seth won't finance weapons."

"Seth won't be Senior Partner much longer," Augusta said.

"Apparently Samuel feels the same as his father."

"Does he?" Augusta said, and her tone was arch. "And who says that Samuel is to be the next Senior Partner?"

2

Hugh Pilaster was wearing a new sky-blue ascot-style cravat, slightly puffed at the neckline and held in place with a pin. He really should have been wearing a new suit, but he could not afford one, so he had to brighten up his old clothes with a new tie.

It was a bit embarrassing, living with Augusta and being so poor, but at Pilasters Bank everyone started at the bottom. Hugh was doing the work of an apprentice clerk—and was paid accordingly.

Many of the people here at the party were his relations, inevitably. His father Tobias and Edward's father Joseph had been brothers. But Hugh's father had withdrawn his capital from the family business, started his own enterprise, gone bankrupt, and killed himself. That was why Hugh had left the expensive Windfield boarding school and become a day boy at the Folkestone Academy for the Sons of Gentlemen; it was why he started work at nineteen instead of going to university; and it was why he lived with his aunt. He was a relation, but a poor one—an embarrassment to the family.

His father had been the victim of a financial crisis, but that made no difference. He had failed on May 11, 1866, a date known to bankers as Black Friday. A bill broker called Overend & Gurney

Ltd. had gone bankrupt for five million pounds, and many firms were dragged down, including Tobias Pilaster & Co. But there were no excuses in business, according to the Pilaster philosophy.

Well, I'm a Pilaster, too, Hugh thought. There was a rage that boiled in his heart sometimes when he brooded about what had happened to his father, and it made him all the more determined to become the richest and most respected of the whole crew.

Then he saw Augusta bearing down on him with a girl in tow. "Dear Hugh," she said, "here's your friend Miss Bodwin."

Hugh groaned inwardly. Rachel Bodwin was a tall, intellectual girl of radical opinions. She was not pretty—she had dull brown hair, and light eyes set rather close together—but she was lively and interesting, and Hugh had liked her a lot when he first came to London to work at the bank. But Augusta had decided he should marry Rachel, and that had ruined the relationship.

"How lovely you look, Miss Bodwin," he said automatically.

"You're very kind," she replied in a bored tone.

Augusta was turning away when she caught sight of Hugh's sky-blue tie. "Heavens, what is that? You look like an innkeeper."

Hugh blushed. "It's a new tie. It's called an ascot."

"You shall give it to the bootboy tomorrow," she said, and she turned away.

Resentment flared in Hugh's breast. "Women ought not to comment on a man's clothes," he said moodily. "It's not ladylike."

Rachel said, "I think women should comment on what interests them, so I shall say that I like your tie. It matches your eyes."

Hugh smiled at her, feeling better. She was very nice, after all. However, it was not her niceness that caused Augusta to want him to marry her. Rachel was the daughter of a lawyer specializing in commercial contracts. On the social ladder they were several rungs below the Pilasters. Indeed, they would not be at this party at all except that Mr. Bodwin had done useful work for the bank. By marrying Rachel, Hugh would confirm his status as a lesser breed of Pilaster, and that was what Augusta wanted.

Rachel touched his arm. "Hugh, listen to me for a moment. I like you. You're one of the few people in London society who aren't unspeakably dull. But I don't love you, and I will never marry you, no matter how often your aunt throws us together. And I know you feel the same about me, so please don't pretend to be heartbroken."

After a stunned moment, Hugh grinned. This directness was what he liked about her. But he supposed she was right: liking was not loving. He was not sure what love was, but she seemed to know. "Does this mean we can go back to quarreling about women's suffrage?" he said cheerfully.

"Yes, but not today." And with that, she left him.

3

THE party was going well, to judge by the cacophony of talk, laughter, and a hundred silver teaspoons clinking in bone china saucers. Augusta briefly checked the dining room, where the servants were dispensing lobster salad, fruitcake, and iced drinks. She moved through the hall, speaking a word or two to each guest.

Underneath her smooth demeanor she was worried about her conversation with Micky Miranda. He assumed that when old Seth died or retired, his son, Samuel, would take over as Senior Partner of Pilasters Bank. Micky would not have made that assumption on his own; he must have picked it up from the family. Augusta wanted the job for her husband, Joseph, who was Seth's nephew.

She glanced through the drawing-room window and saw the four partners together on the terrace. Three were Pilasters: Seth, Samuel, and Joseph—the early nineteenth-century Methodists had favored biblical names. The fourth partner was Major George Hartshorn, husband of Joseph's sister, Madeleine. A former army officer, he had joined the bank when he married Madeleine. Although he was an amiable man, he was not clever enough to run the bank, and anyway, they had never had a Senior Partner whose name was not Pilaster. The only serious candidates were Samuel and Joseph. Technically, the decision would be made by a vote of the partners. In reality, Augusta was determined to have her way.

The Senior Partner of Pilasters Bank was one of the most important people in the world. Along with a handful of others—J. P. Morgan, the Rothschilds, Ben Greenbourne—he held the prosperity of nations in his hands. He was consulted by prime ministers and courted by diplomats, and his wife was fawned upon by all. Joseph wanted the job, but he had no subtlety. It would not occur to him that there were things he should do to make sure he won the contest. For instance, he would never try to discredit his rival.

Augusta would have to find ways to do that for him.

She had no trouble identifying Samuel's weakness. At the age of fifty-three, he was a bachelor and lived with a young man who was blithely referred to as his secretary. Until now the family had paid no attention to Samuel's domestic arrangements, but Augusta was planning to change all that.

Samuel had to be handled carefully. He was a fussy, finicky man, but he was not weak and would not be intimidated.

As she moved among her guests, she spotted her sister-in-law Madeleine Hartshorn. Poor Madeleine. You could tell she was Joseph's sister, for she had the Pilaster nose. No woman could look anything but plain with a beak like that.

Augusta took Madeleine's arm, saying, "Come upstairs and see my room. I think you'll like it."

Augusta had furnished her bedroom in the latest Japanese style, with fretwork chairs, peacock-feather wallpaper, and a display of porcelain over the mantelpiece. The window seat was partly concealed by dragonfly curtains.

"Augusta, how daring!" said Madeleine.

Augusta was happy with the effect. "Come and see Joseph's room." She took Madeleine through a door. Joseph's bedroom was furnished in a more moderate version of the same style, with brocade curtains and dark leather paper on the walls. Augusta was especially proud of a lacquered display cabinet that held his collection of jeweled snuffboxes.

"Joseph is so eccentric," said Madeleine, looking at the boxes.

Augusta smiled. "He says they're an investment."

While Madeleine admired them, Augusta remembered her purpose. "Madeleine dear," she said softly, "what *are* we going to do about cousin Samuel and his 'secretary'?"

Madeleine looked puzzled. "Ought we to do something?"

"If Samuel is to become Senior Partner, we must. The Senior Partner must be quite *quite* irreproachable in his private life."

Comprehension dawned, and Madeleine flushed. "Surely you're not suggesting that Samuel is in some way . . . depraved?"

"I trust that I shall never know," Augusta said evasively. "The important thing is what people think."

Madeleine looked worried, but before she could reply, Augusta ushered her out of the room, saying, "Now I must return to my guests." At this stage all she wanted was to plant the seed of doubt. Anything more might be too heavy-handed.

4

MICKY and his father left the party and set out to walk back to their lodgings. Their route lay entirely through parks—first Hyde Park, then Green Park and St. James's Park—until they reached the river. They stopped on Westminster Bridge to look at the river. Small pleasure boats made a pretty sight in the evening sun.

Micky was still cursing old Seth for frustrating his plans. "We will solve this problem about the rifles, Papa," he said. "Don't worry."

Papa shrugged. "Who is standing in our way?" he asked.

It was a simple question, but it had a deep meaning in the Miranda family. It really meant, Whom do we have to kill to get this done? In Cordova, Papa's reckless brutality had made him a man to be feared. In England, it would get him thrown in jail. "I don't anticipate the need for drastic action," Micky said, trying to cover his nervousness with an air of unconcern.

"For now, there is no hurry," Papa said. "Winter is beginning at home. There will be no fighting until the summer." He gave Micky a hard look. "But I *must* have the rifles by the end of October."

"I'll see to it, Papa."

Then, out of the blue, Papa said, "I want you to stay in London."

Micky felt his shoulders slump with relief. "I think it might be a good idea," he said, trying to hide his eagerness.

Then Papa dropped his bombshell. "But your allowance will stop. The family can't keep you. You must support yourself."

Micky was appalled. Papa's meanness was as legendary as his violence, but still this was unexpected. The Mirandas were rich. Papa had thousands of head of cattle, monopolized all horse dealing, and owned most of the stores in Santamaria Province.

It was true their money did not buy much in England. When Micky went to Windfield School, he had managed to supplement his allowance by playing cards, but he had found it hard to make ends meet until he befriended Edward. Even now Edward paid for all the expensive entertainments they shared—the opera, visits to racecourses, hunting, and whores. Still, Micky needed to pay his rent, tailor bills, subscriptions to gentlemen's clubs. How did Papa expect him to do that? Take a job? The idea was appalling. No member of the Miranda family worked for wages.

Papa abruptly changed the subject. "I will now tell you what the rifles are for. We are going to take over the desert."

Micky did not understand. Bordering the Miranda land was a smaller property owned by the Delabarca family. To the north of both was land so arid that neither Papa nor his neighbor had ever bothered to claim it. "What do we want the desert for?" Micky said.

"Beneath the dust there is a mineral called nitrate. It's used as a fertilizer. It can be shipped all over the world. Delabarca has started mining it, and it has made his family rich. The Delabarcas will soon be stronger than we are. We have to destroy them."

Chapter Two: June

1

THE Argyll Rooms, just off Piccadilly Circus, were the most popular place of entertainment in London, but Hugh had never been in them before. Although not actually a brothel like the famous Nellie's, the place had a low reputation. However, Edward had casually invited Hugh to join him and Micky for the evening, and somehow they had ended up here. They wore evening dress, a sign that they were upper-class people going slumming.

The ballroom was an extravagantly gaslit arena, with huge mirrors intensifying the brilliant light. The dance floor was crowded with couples, and behind an elaborate gold trelliswork screen an orchestra was playing a vigorous polka. The girls were dressed in evening gowns with bustles, many of the gowns cut very low at the neckline, and the most amazing hats. Micky and Edward had assured Hugh that they were not prostitutes, but ordinary girls—shop assistants and parlormaids. The atmosphere was a curious but exciting mixture of respectability and license.

Hugh felt dazzled. All around him were girls who had come here for the sole purpose of flirting.

The polka ended, and some of the dancers returned to their tables. Edward pointed and cried, "There's Fatty Greenbourne!"

Hugh followed his finger and saw their old schoolmate, bigger than ever, bulging out of his white waistcoat. On his arm was a stunningly beautiful girl. Fatty and the girl sat down at a table. Micky said, "Why don't we join them for a while?"

Hugh was keen for a closer look at the girl, and he assented readily. The three young men threaded their way through the tables. "Good evening, Fatty," Edward said cheerily.

"Hullo, you lot," he replied. "People call me Solly nowadays," he added amiably. Though he was still fat, he had acquired an air of authority in his middle twenties. He turned to his companion. "Miss Robinson, may I present some old school friends—Edward Pilaster, Hugh Pilaster, and Micky Miranda."

Miss Robinson's reaction was startling. She went pale beneath her rouge. "Pilaster? Not the same family as Tobias Pilaster?"

"My father," said Hugh. "How do you know the name?"

She recovered her composure quickly. "My father used to work for Tobias Pilaster and Co. As a child, I wondered who Co was." They laughed, and the moment of tension passed. She added, "Would you lads like to sit down?"

There was a bottle of champagne on the table. Solly called for more glasses. "Well, this is a real reunion of old Windfield chums," he said. "Guess who else is here. Tonio Silva. He's on the dance floor with Miss Robinson's friend Miss April Tilsley."

Miss Robinson said, "You could call me Maisie. I'm not a *formal* girl." And she threw a lascivious wink at Solly.

Hugh studied her. She was quite short, but added about a foot to her height by piling her tawny hair into a high chignon and topping it with a huge hat decorated with artificial leaves and fruit. Underneath the hat was a small, impudent face with a wicked twinkle in the green eyes. Hugh could hardly take his eyes off her. After a while Maisie felt his stare and returned it. He turned away with an apologetic smile.

The dance ended, and Tonio Silva came to the table with April Tilsley. Hugh had run into Tonio several times since school, but even if he had not seen him for years, he would have recognized him instantly by his shock of carrot-colored hair. They had been best friends until that awful day in 1866.

Hugh had often wondered over the years what had really happened that day at the swimming hole. He had never believed the newspaper story about Edward's trying to rescue Peter Middleton. Edward did not have the courage. But Tonio still would not speak of it.

Hugh studied Tonio's face as he shook hands with Micky. "How are you, Miranda?" Tonio said in a normal voice, but his expression showed a mixture of fear and admiration.

Tonio's companion, April, was a little older than Maisie, and there was a pinched, sharp look about her that made her less attractive. Maisie, however, was vivacious and the prettiest woman in the room. Hugh searched for something to say and finally blurted out, "Have you always lived in London, Miss Robinson?"

"Only for three days," she said.

"So recently," he said. "Where were you before?"

"Traveling," she said, and turned away to speak to Solly.

"Maisie's been with a circus for four years," said April.

"Heavens! Doing what?"

Maisie turned around again. "Bareback horse-riding. Standing on the horses, jumping from one to another—all those tricks."

April added, "In tights, of course."

The thought of Maisie in tights was unbearably tantalizing. "How did you get into that line of work?" Hugh asked.

She hesitated, then faced Hugh directly, and a dangerous glint came into her eyes. "It was like this," she said. "My father worked for Tobias Pilaster and Co. Your father cheated my father out of a week's wages. At that time my mother was sick. Without that money either I would starve or she would die. So I ran away from home. I was eleven years old at the time."

Hugh felt his face flush. "I don't believe my father cheated anyone," he said. "And if you were eleven, you can't possibly have understood what happened. Your father shouldn't have had children if he couldn't afford to feed them."

"He could feed them!" Maisie blazed. "He worked like a slave, and then your father stole his money!"

"My father went bankrupt, but he never stole."

"It's the same thing when you're the loser!"

"It's not the same, and you're insolent to pretend that it is." Hugh knew he should stop, but he was angry. "Ever since I was thirteen, I've had to listen to the Pilaster family running my father down, but I'm not going to take it from a circus performer."

Maisie stood up, her eyes flashing like cut emeralds. For a moment Hugh thought she was going to slap him. Then she said, "Dance with me, Solly. Perhaps your rude friend will have gone when the music stops."

2

HUGH'S quarrel with Maisie broke up the party. Solly and Maisie went off on their own, and the others decided to go ratting. Ratting was against the law, but Micky Miranda knew half a dozen pits.

It was dark when they emerged from the Argyll into the district of London known as Babylon. Here, out of sight of the palaces of Mayfair but conveniently close to the gentlemen's clubs of St. James's, was a warren of narrow streets dedicated to gambling, blood sports, opium smoking, and prostitution.

Micky led his friends into a narrow alley. Checking that they were in tow, he entered a dingy pub, walked through the bar and out the back door. He crossed a yard and opened the door of a ramshackle wooden building. A man in a long, greasy coat demanded fourpence as the price of admission. Edward paid, and they went in.

The place was brightly lit and full of tobacco smoke. Forty or fifty men and a few women stood around a circular pit. Several of the men had dogs with them, carried in their arms or tied to chair legs.

Micky pointed out a bearded man who held a muzzled dog on a chain. It was a squat, muscular animal with a big head and a powerful jaw. "He'll be on next," Micky said.

Edward went off to buy drinks from a woman with a tray. Ignoring Hugh and April, Micky turned to Tonio and addressed him in Spanish. "What are you doing these days?"

"I'm an attaché to the Cordovan minister in London."

"Really?" Micky was intrigued. No doubt Tonio had got the post of attaché because his family were well connected in the Cordovan capital, Palma. By contrast, Micky's Papa was a provincial baron and had no such strings to pull. "What's the work like?"

"I answer letters from British firms that want to do business in Cordova." Tonio lowered his voice. "Don't tell a soul, but I have to write only two or three letters a day."

"Do they pay you?" Many diplomats were men of independent means who worked for nothing.

"No. But I have a room at the minister's residence and all my meals, plus an allowance for clothing. They also pay my subscriptions to clubs."

Micky was envious. It was just the kind of job that would suit him. He wondered if Tonio could be eased out of the post.

Edward came back with five tots of brandy and handed them around. Micky swallowed his at once. It was cheap and fiery.

Suddenly the muzzled dog growled and started to run in frantic circles, pulling on its chain. Micky looked around to see two men carrying in a cage of huge rats. The rats were even more frenzied than the dog, running over one another and squeaking with terror. The entrance was locked from the inside, and the man in the greasy coat started to take bets. Hugh had never seen such big rats.

"How many this contest?" Edward said to one of the handlers.

"Six dozen," the man replied.

Tonio said, "How does the betting work?"

"You can bet on the dog or the rats," Edward explained, "and if you think the rats will win, you can bet on how many will be left when the dog dies."

The dirty man was calling out odds and taking money in exchange for scraps of paper on which he scribbled numbers with a thick pencil. Edward put a sovereign on the dog, and Micky bet a shilling on six rats surviving, for which he got odds of five to one. Micky noticed that Hugh declined to bet, like the dull stick he was.

The pit was four feet deep, surrounded by a wood fence another four feet high. Candles threw light into the hole. The dog was unmuzzled and let into the pit. The rat handlers picked up the cage. There was a quiet moment of anticipation.

Suddenly Tonio said, "Ten guineas on the dog."

Micky was surprised. Tonio had talked as if he had to be careful how he spent money. Was he making bets he could not afford?

The bookmaker hesitated. It was a big bet for him, too. Then he scribbled a slip, handed it over, and pocketed Tonio's money.

The handlers swung the cage back, then forward, as if they were going to throw the whole thing into the pit. Then a hinged flap at one end opened, and the rats were hurled through the air. April screamed with shock, and Micky laughed.

The dog went to work with lethal concentration. As the rats rained down on him, his jaws snapped rhythmically. He would pick one up, break its back with one shake of his huge head, and drop it for another. The smell of blood became nauseating. All the dogs in the room barked madly, and the spectators added to the noise, shrieking and shouting. Micky laughed and laughed.

For a few seconds the dog had it all his own way and killed a dozen or more. Then the rats turned all at once, as if they had heard a signal. They began to fly at the dog, biting his legs and his short tail. Some got on his back and bit his neck and ears.

The dog kept turning around in dizzying circles, catching rat after rat, killing them all. But there were always more behind him. Half the rats were dead when he began to tire. Sensing the dog's fatigue, the rats became bolder. When he had one in his jaws, another would spring for his throat. Others attacked his rear end. Wearily he snapped them up in his jaws; wearily he broke their backs; wearily he dropped them on the bloody ground. Finally his legs buckled under him and his head drooped.

Micky counted: there were six rats left.

He looked at his companions. Hugh looked ill. Edward said to him, "A bit strong for your stomach, eh?"

"The dog and the rats are simply behaving as nature intended," Hugh said. "It's the humans who disgust me."

April's eyes were sparkling as she looked up at Tonio, a man—she thought—who could afford to lose ten guineas in a bet.

Micky looked at Tonio and saw in his face a hint of panic. I don't believe he *can* afford to lose ten guineas, Micky thought.

Micky collected his winnings from the bookmaker: five shillings. He had made a profit on the evening. But he had a feeling that what he had learned about Tonio could be worth a great deal more.

Chapter Three: July

1

As a little boy, Hugh had thought Pilasters Bank was owned by the walkers. These personages were in fact lowly messengers, but they all wore immaculate morning dress with silver watch chains across their ample waistcoats, and they moved about the bank with such ponderous dignity that to a child they appeared the most important people there.

Hugh had been brought here at the age of ten by his grandfather, old Seth's brother. The marble-walled banking hall on the first floor had seemed like a church—huge, silent, and mysterious. The mystery had gone out of it now. He knew that the massive leather-bound ledgers were not arcane texts, but simple lists of financial transactions, and his own fingers had become cramped and ink-stained by days of writing in them. A bill of exchange was no longer a magic spell, but merely a promise to pay money at a future date. Discounting, which, as a child, he had thought must mean counting backwards, turned out to be the practice of buying bills of exchange at a little less than their face value, keeping them until their due date, then cashing them at a small profit.

Hugh was an assistant to Jonas Mulberry, the principal clerk. A bald man of about forty, Mulberry was good-hearted but a little sour. He would always take time to explain things to Hugh, but he was quick to find fault if Hugh was in the least careless.

This morning he had asked Hugh to count the applications for the Russian loan issue. The bank was raising a loan of two million pounds for the government of Russia. It had issued one-hundred-pound bonds that paid five pounds' interest per year. But Pilasters was selling the bonds for ninety-three pounds, so the true interest rate was over five and three eighths. Most of the bonds had been bought by other banks, but some had been offered to the public.

Counting the applications took most of the day. It was a few minutes before four o'clock when Hugh added the last column of figures. A little more than one hundred thousand pounds' worth of bonds remained unsold. The partners would be disappointed.

He wrote the tally on a clean sheet of paper and went in search of Mulberry. The banking hall was quiet now. A few customers stood at the long, polished counter. Behind the counter, clerks lifted big ledgers on and off the shelves. Pilasters did not have many private accounts. It was a merchant bank, lending money to traders to finance their ventures. But all the family kept accounts at the bank, and the facility was extended to a small number of very rich clients. Hugh spotted one of them now: Sir John Cammel. Hugh had known his son at Windfield. A thin man with a bald head, Sir John earned vast incomes from coal mines and docks on his lands in Yorkshire. Now he was pacing the marble floor, looking impatient. Hugh said, "I hope you're being attended to, Sir John."

"No, I'm not, lad. Doesn't anyone do any work in this place?"

Hugh glanced around. None of the partners was in sight. He decided to use his initiative. "Come upstairs to the Partners' Room, sir. I know they will be keen to see you."

Hugh led him upstairs. The partners all worked together in the same room. The room was furnished with leather sofas and bookcases. In framed portraits on the walls ancestral Pilasters looked down their beaklike noses at their descendants.

The room was empty. "One of them will be back in a moment," Hugh said. "May I offer you a glass of Madeira?" He went to the sideboard and poured a generous measure while Sir John settled himself in a leather armchair. "I'm Hugh Pilaster, by the way."

"Oh, yes?" Sir John was somewhat mollified to find he was talking to a Pilaster rather than an ordinary office boy. "Did you go to Windfield?"

"Yes, sir. I was there with your son Albert. I haven't seen him since . . . since then."

"He went to the Cape Colony. He raises horses there."

Albert Cammel had been at the swimming hole on that fateful day in 1866. Hugh had never heard his version of how Peter Middleton drowned. "I'd like to write to him," Hugh said.

"I daresay he'll be glad of a letter from an old school friend. I'll give you his address." Sir John moved to the table, dipped a quill into the inkwell, and scribbled on a sheet of paper. "There you are."

"Thank you." Sir John was mollified now, Hugh noted with satisfaction. "Is there anything I can do for you while you're waiting?"

"Well, perhaps you can deal with this." He took a check out of his pocket. Hugh examined it. It was for a hundred and ten thousand pounds—the largest personal check Hugh had ever handled. "I've just sold a coal mine," Sir John explained.

"I can certainly deposit it for you."

"What interest will I get?"

"Four percent at present."

"That'll do, I suppose."

Hugh hesitated. If Sir John could be persuaded to buy Russian bonds, the loan issue could be transformed from being slightly undersubscribed to slightly oversubscribed. Should he mention it? He had already overstepped his authority by bringing a guest into the Partners' Room. He decided to take a chance. "You could get five and three eighths by buying Russian bonds."

Sir John narrowed his eyes. "Are they safe?"

"As safe as the Russian government." Then, afraid he was sounding too eager, he backed off. "I'll place this check to your account. If you wish, you can talk to one of my uncles about the bonds."

"All right, young Pilaster, off you go."

Hugh went out and met Samuel Pilaster in the hall. "Sir John Cammel is in there, Uncle," Hugh said. "I found him in the banking hall looking bad-tempered, so I've given him a glass of Madeira. I hope I did the right thing."

"I'm sure you did," said Samuel. "I'll take care of him."

"He brought this check for a hundred and ten thousand. I mentioned the Russian loan."

Samuel raised his eyebrows. "That was precocious of you. It's not a bad idea."

Hugh returned to the banking hall, pulled out Sir John's ledger and entered the deposit, then took the check to the clearing clerk. Next he went up to Mulberry's office. He handed over the tally of Russian bonds and sat down at his own table.

A little later Samuel came in and handed some papers to Mulberry. "Sir John bought the bonds," he said to Hugh. "Good work."

When he had gone, Mulberry said to Hugh, "Did you advise Sir John Cammel to buy the surplus Russian bonds?"

"I just mentioned it," said Hugh.

"Well, well," said Mulberry. "Well, well."

2

IT WAS a sunny Sunday afternoon, and all London was out for a stroll. Maisie Robinson and April Tilsley were strolling down Piccadilly, looking at the palaces of the rich and trying to pick up men.

They shared a single room in Soho, in a slum house on Carnaby Street. They would get up around midday, dress carefully, and go out on the streets. By evening they generally found a couple of men to pay for their dinner; if not, they went hungry. When the rent was due, April would ask a boyfriend for a "loan." Maisie always wore the same clothes and washed her underwear every night. Sooner or later, she hoped, one of the men who bought her dinner would want to marry her or set her up as his mistress.

"Where did the rest of you go after I shouted at that boy Hugh?" Maisie asked April as they strolled.

"Ratting. Then me and Tonio went to Batt's Hotel."

"To play whist?"

They giggled.

"It brought back bad memories, meeting people called Pilaster," Maisie said.

April nodded. "Bosses. I hate their guts."

"My brother and me left home the day Tobias Pilaster went bankrupt," Maisie said. She smiled ruefully. "You could say it's because of the Pilasters that I'm here today."

"What did you do after you left? Join the circus straightaway?"

"No." Maisie felt a tug at her heart as she remembered how frightened and lonely she had been. "My brother stowed away on a ship going to Boston. I've not seen him or heard from him since. I slept at a rubbish tip for a week. After that I walked to Newcastle. I dressed as a lad and worked at a stable. I stayed there three years."

"Why did you leave?"

"I grew these," Maisie said, and jiggled her breasts. "When the head stable hand found out I was a lass, he tried to rape me. I smacked him across the face with a riding crop, and that was the end of the job. That's when I joined the circus. I started as a stable hand and eventually became one of the riders. I liked the circus, but the pay was unreliable. And here I am." Maisie sighed. "I can't lie to you, April. I'm not cut out for this life."

"You're perfect for it," April protested. "You've got that twinkle in your eye that men can't resist. Listen, persist with Solly Greenbourne. Give him a bit more each time; then ask him to buy you a little house in Chelsea."

Maisie knew April was right, but her soul revolted against it. She was not sure why. It was partly because she was not attracted to Solly. Paradoxically, another reason was that he was so nice. She could not bring herself to manipulate him heartlessly. But worst of all, she felt she would be giving up all hope of real love—a real marriage with a man she really burned for.

April said, "What about one of the others?"

"I liked Hugh, but I offended him."

"He's got no money. Solly's your man. If you let him slip through your fingers, you'll end up with a nasty little middle-aged grocer who keeps you short of money and expects you to launder your own sheets."

Maisie brooded on that prospect as they came to the western end of Piccadilly and turned north into Mayfair. Cutting through a mews, they passed a big livery stable, and Maisie stopped to pet a tall chestnut stallion. The horse nuzzled her hand.

A man's voice said, "Redboy don't generally allow strangers to touch him."

Maisie turned to see a middle-aged man in a yellow waistcoat. She smiled. "He doesn't mind me, do you, Redboy?"

"I don't suppose you could ride him, now, could you?"

"Ride him? Yes, I could ride him—without a saddle, and stand upright on his back, too. Is he yours?"

The man bowed and said, "George Sammles, proprietor, at your service." He pointed to his name painted over the door.

Maisie said, "I shouldn't boast, Mr. Sammles, but I can probably ride anything you have in your stables."

"Is that a fact," he said thoughtfully. He hesitated. "This may seem a mite sudden, but I'm asking myself whether you might be interested in a business proposition."

Maisie wondered what was coming next. "Go on."

"You see, Redboy's for sale," the man began. "But you don't sell horses by keeping them indoors. Whereas, if you was to ride him around the park for an hour or so, looking, if I may be so bold, as pretty as a pitcher, you'd attract attention. Sooner or later someone would ask you how much you wanted for the horse."

"And then I'd tell the person, 'Away and see Mr. Sammles in the Curzon Mews, for the nag's his.' Is that what you mean?"

"Exackly so, except rather than call Redboy a nag, you might term him 'this fine specimen of horseflesh,' or such. What do you think the job's worth?"

Maisie picked a ridiculous sum. "A pound a day."

"Too much," he said promptly. "I'll give you half that."

She could hardly believe her luck. Ten shillings a day was an enormous wage. Girls of her age who worked as housemaids were lucky to get a shilling a day. "Done," she said. "When do I start?"

"Come tomorrow at half past ten."

3

Traffic in the Park

To the Editor of *The Times:*

Sir—There has been noted in Hyde Park, at about half past eleven o'clock each morning, a jam of carriages so large that there has been no getting forward for up to an hour. The fault lies with a lady whose name is unknown, but whom men term the Lioness—doubtless on account of the tawny color of her hair—a charming creature, who rides horses that would daunt many males. The fame of her beauty and equestrian daring is such that all London migrates to the park at the hour when she is expected and, once there, cannot move. Could not you, sir, prevail upon her to desist so that the park may return to its normal state of decorum?

An observer

The letter had to be a joke, Hugh thought as he put down the newspaper. But the Lioness was real enough. He had heard the clerks at the bank talking about her, and he was intrigued. He gazed through the leaded windows of his aunt's house to the park. The sun was shining, and it was a holiday. Hugh thought he might just go to the park to see what the fuss was all about.

Aunt Augusta was also planning to go to the park. She went at this time most mornings, as did all upper-class women and idle men. It was a place to see and be seen. The real cause of congestion was people stopping their carriages to gossip.

Hugh heard his aunt's voice. He got up from the breakfast table and went into the hall. As usual, Aunt Augusta was beautifully dressed. Today she wore a purple day gown with a tight jacket bodice and yards of ruffles below. She was talking to Uncle Joseph, who had the harassed air he often wore when Augusta was speaking to him. Hugh wondered whether there was any affection between them. There must have been at one time, he supposed.

Augusta carried on speaking as if Hugh were not there, which was her usual way. "The whole family is worried," she was saying insistently to Joseph. "There could be a scandal."

"But the situation—whatever it may be—has been going on for years, and no one has ever thought it scandalous."

"Because Samuel is not the Senior Partner. An ordinary person can do many things without attracting notice. But the Senior Partner of Pilasters Bank is a public figure."

"Well, the matter may not be urgent. Uncle Seth is still alive and shows every sign of hanging on indefinitely."

"I know," Augusta said with a note of frustration. "But sooner or later he will hand over the reins. You must make Samuel understand that unless he gives way, Seth will have to be told the facts."

Hugh could not help admiring her ruthlessness. She was sending Samuel a message: give up your secretary, or we'll force your father to confront the reality that his son is more or less married to a man.

In truth she did not care a straw about Samuel and his secretary. She just wanted to make it impossible for him to become Senior Partner, so that the mantle would fall on her husband.

Now Joseph said uneasily, "I should like to resolve matters without such drastic action."

Augusta lowered her voice to an intimate murmur. When she did this, Hugh always thought she was transparently insincere, like a dragon trying to purr. "I'm sure you'll find a way to do just that. Will you drive with me today? I should so like your company."

He shook his head. "I must go to the bank." He turned to Hugh. "Drive in the park with your aunt. She needs an escort." With that, he put on his hat and left.

Hugh did not really want to drive with Augusta, but he was curious to see the Lioness, so he did not argue.

Augusta's daughter, Clementine, appeared, dressed to go out. Twenty years old, she looked like her mother; but where Augusta was overbearing, Clementine was sly.

They all went out. The footman handed them up into the carriage. Augusta and Clementine sat facing forward, and Hugh settled himself opposite them. The ladies opened their parasols, the coachman flicked his whip, and they set off.

A few moments later they were on South Carriage Road. It was as crowded as the writer of the letter to *The Times* had claimed. There were hundreds of horses ridden by top-hatted men and sidesaddle women, dozens of carriages of every type, plus children on ponies, nurses with baby carriages, and people with dogs.

A carriage pulled alongside them, and Hugh saw his aunt Madeleine Hartshorn. Both carriages stopped, and the ladies exchanged

greetings. Augusta said, "Take a turn with us, Madeleine. I want to talk to you."

Madeleine's footman helped her down from her own carriage and into Augusta's, and they drove off.

"They're threatening to tell old Seth about Samuel's secretary," Augusta said.

"Oh, no," said Madeleine. "They mustn't."

"I've spoken to Joseph, but they won't be stopped." Augusta's tone of sincere concern took Hugh's breath away. How did she manage to lie so convincingly?

Their carriage slowed almost to a halt. There was a knot of vehicles ahead. Suddenly a smart little victoria broke through, pulled by a pair of high-stepping ponies and driven by a woman.

"It's the Lioness!" Clementine squealed.

Hugh looked at the woman driving the victoria and was astonished to recognize her. It was Maisie Robinson.

She cracked a whip, and the ponies picked up speed. She was wearing a brown merino costume with a mushroom-colored bow at her throat. On her head was a perky little top hat with a curly brim.

Hugh felt angry with her all over again for what she had said about his father. All the same, there was something irresistibly charming about the set of that small, neat body in the driving seat.

So, the Lioness was Maisie Robinson. But how come she suddenly had horses and carriages? What was she up to?

While Hugh was still marveling, there was an accident.

A nervous thoroughbred trotted past Augusta's carriage and was startled by a small, noisy terrier. It reared up, and the rider fell off into the path of Maisie's victoria.

Quickly she changed direction, showing impressive control of her vehicle. Her evasive action took her right in front of Augusta's horses. The coachman hauled on his reins and let out an oath.

Maisie brought her carriage to an abrupt stop. Everyone looked at the thrown rider. He appeared unhurt. He got to his feet, dusted himself down, and walked off, cursing, to catch his horse.

Maisie saw Hugh. "Hugh Pilaster, I do declare!" she cried.

Hugh blushed. "Good morning," he said, and realized he had made a serious error of etiquette. He ought not to have acknowledged Maisie while he was with his aunts, for he could not possibly introduce such a person to them.

However, Maisie made no attempt to address the ladies. "How do you like these ponies?" she said. "They're for sale."

Hugh was completely thrown by this beautiful, surprising woman. "They're very fine," he said without looking at them.

Aunt Augusta said icily, "Hugh, tell this *person* to let us pass!"

Maisie looked at Augusta for the first time. "Shut your gob, you old cow," she said casually.

Clementine gasped, and Aunt Madeleine gave a small scream of horror. Hugh's mouth dropped open. Maisie's gorgeous clothes and expensive equipage had made it easy to forget that she was an urchin from the slums. Her words were so splendidly vulgar that for a moment Augusta was too stunned to reply, and Maisie gave her no time to recover. Turning back to Hugh, she said, "Tell your cousin Edward he should buy my ponies!" Then she cracked her whip and drove away.

4

Cape Colony, South Africa

Dear Hugh,

Jolly nice to hear from you! One is rather isolated out here, and you can't imagine the pleasure we get out of a long, newsy letter from home. Mrs. Cammel, who used to be the Hon. Amelia Clapham until she married me, was especially amused by your account of the Lioness.

I'm glad you asked me about the drowning of Peter Middleton. I have felt guilty ever since that day. I didn't actually see the poor chap die, but I saw enough to guess the rest.

Your cousin Edward was, as you so colorfully put it, more rotten than a dead cat. You managed to get your clothes and scarper, but Peter and Tonio weren't so quick.

I was on the other side, and I don't think Edward and Micky even noticed me. Or perhaps they didn't recognize me. At any rate, they never spoke to me about the incident.

Anyway, after you had gone, Edward proceeded to torment Peter, pushing his head under the water and splashing his face while the poor boy struggled to retrieve his clothes.

I could see it was getting out of hand, but I was a complete coward, I'm afraid. I should have gone to Peter's aid, but I was no match for Micky Miranda and Edward. I don't mind admitting I was frightened. Anyway, I grabbed my clothes and sneaked away.

I looked back once from the lip of the quarry. Tonio was scrambling up the side, clutching a bundle of wet clothes, and Edward was swimming across the pool after him, leaving Peter spluttering in the middle.

I thought Peter would be all right, but obviously I was wrong. He must have been at the end of his tether. While Edward was chasing Tonio and Micky was watching, Peter drowned without anyone's noticing.

As the ghastly story emerged, I never had the guts to admit that I had seen what happened. Not a tale to be proud of, Hugh. But telling the truth at last has made me feel a bit better.

Hugh put down Albert Cammel's letter. It explained both more and less than Cammel imagined. It explained how Micky Miranda had insinuated himself into the Pilaster family. No doubt Micky had told Augusta that Edward had virtually killed Peter. But in court Micky said Edward had tried to rescue the drowning boy. In telling that lie, Micky had saved the Pilasters from public disgrace. Augusta would have been powerfully grateful—and perhaps also fearful that Micky might one day turn against them and reveal the truth. It gave Hugh a cold, scared feeling in the pit of his stomach.

But another puzzle remained. For Hugh knew something about Peter Middleton that almost no one else was aware of. Peter had been something of a weakling. Embarrassed, he had embarked on a training program, and his main exercise was swimming. He stroked across that pool hour after hour, trying to build his physique. As a result, he was like a fish in the water, able to dive to the bottom and hold his breath for several minutes. It would have taken more than Edward Pilaster to drown him.

So why had he died?

Albert Cammel had told the truth, as far as he knew it, Hugh was sure. But something else had happened on that hot afternoon in Bishop's Wood. Casual horseplay could not have killed Peter. And if his death was not accidental, it was deliberate. It was murder.

Hugh shuddered. There had been only three people there: Edward, Micky, and Peter. Peter must have been murdered by Edward or Micky—or both.

5

AUGUSTA was already dissatisfied with her decor. The drawing room was full of Oriental screens and Japanese fans and vases in black-lacquered cabinets. But the look was no longer exclusive.

The drawing room was where Augusta held court at teatime every weekday. The women usually came first—her daughter Clementine and her sisters-in-law Madeleine and Beatrice. Beatrice was married to Joseph's brother William, who was always called Young William because he was born twenty-three years after Joseph. The partners—Joseph, old Seth, Madeleine's husband George Hartshorn, and Samuel—would arrive from the bank at about five. If business was quiet, Edward and Hugh would come, too. The only nonmember of the family who was a regular teatime guest was Micky Miranda. It was at these gatherings that Augusta found out what was going on at the bank.

A few minutes before four o'clock on an afternoon in late July, she was standing in the drawing room, feeling discontented with her furniture, when Samuel walked in. All the Pilasters were ugly, but Samuel was the worst, she thought. He had the big nose, but he also had a weak, womanish mouth. He was a fussy man, immaculately dressed, fastidious about his food, a lover of cats.

But what made Augusta dislike him was that of all the men in the family, he was the most difficult to persuade. She could charm old Seth, who was susceptible to an attractive woman even at his advanced age; she could generally get around Joseph by wearing down his patience; George Hartshorn was under Madeleine's thumb and so could be manipulated indirectly. Nothing worked on Samuel—least of all her feminine charms. He had an infuriating way of laughing at her when she thought she was being subtle and clever. She was much more wounded by Samuel's quiet mockery than she was at being called an old cow by a trollop in the park.

Today, however, Samuel did not wear that amused, skeptical smile. He looked angry, so angry that for a moment Augusta was alarmed. He had obviously come early in order to find her alone. It struck her that for two months she had been conspiring to ruin him and that people had been murdered for less than that. He did not shake her hand, but stood in front of her, wearing a pearl-gray morning coat and a deep wine-red tie, smelling faintly of cologne. Augusta held up her hands in a defensive gesture.

Samuel gave a humorless laugh and moved away. "I'm not going to strike you, Augusta," he said. "Though heaven knows, you deserve a whipping."

Of course he would not touch her. He was a gentle soul who refused to finance the export of rifles. Augusta's confidence came back in a rush, and she said, "How dare you criticize me!"

"Criticize? I don't stoop to criticize you. I despise you."

Augusta would not be intimidated. "Have you come here to tell me that you are willing to give up your vicious ways?" she said.

"My vicious ways," he repeated. "You're willing to destroy my father's happiness and make my own life miserable, all for the sake of your ambition, and yet you can talk about *my* vicious ways!"

"I'm only concerned for the bank," she said coldly.

"Is that your excuse for blackmailing me?"

"I'm doing my duty." Now that she felt in control again, she began to wonder why he had come here. Was it to concede defeat—or to defy her? If he gave in, she could rest assured that soon she would be the wife of the Senior Partner. If he defied her, there was a long, difficult struggle ahead, with no certainty of the outcome.

He went to the window and looked out. "It's not for myself that I'm worried," he went on. "I'd like to be Senior Partner, and I'd be a good one. But Joseph isn't up to the job. He's bad-tempered and impulsive, and he makes poor decisions. He'll harm the bank."

For a moment Augusta wondered if he was right. But there was nothing very difficult about what the partners did: they loaned people money and collected the interest. Joseph could do that as well as any of them. "You men always pretend that banking is complex and mysterious," she said. "But you don't fool me."

"Would you really go to my father, as you have threatened?"

She hesitated only for an instant. "There is no alternative."

He stared at her for a long time, then spoke with obvious distaste. "Very well. I'd like to be Senior Partner when my father retires, but I can live without it. I shall tell the others. But remember, we all have secrets. One day someone will use your secrets against you this way, and you'll remember what you did to me."

Augusta was mystified. What was he referring to? "I have no secrets to be ashamed of," she said.

"Don't you?" He gave her a peculiar look. "A young lawyer called David Middleton came to see me yesterday."

Suddenly Augusta felt cold. Middleton—that was the name of the boy who had drowned.

Samuel said, "David Middleton believes that his brother, Peter, was killed—by Edward."

Augusta wanted desperately to sit down, but she refused to give Samuel the satisfaction of seeing her rattled. "Why on earth is he making trouble now, after seven years?"

"Middleton told me he remained silent for fear of causing his parents more distress. However, his mother died soon after Peter, and his father died this year."

"Why did he approach you, not me?"

"He belongs to my club. Anyway, he has reread the inquest records, and he says several eyewitnesses were never called to give evidence. He's not going to let this rest." Samuel went to the door. "I won't stay for tea. Good afternoon, Augusta."

Augusta sat down heavily on a sofa. She had not foreseen this. That old business ought to have been completely forgotten! She was dreadfully frightened for Edward.

Hastead, her butler, came in, followed by two parlormaids with trays of tea and cakes. "With your permission, madam," he said. At her nod they began to set out the china. Augusta could sometimes be soothed by Hastead's obsequious manner, but today it did not work. She got up and went to the open French doors. The view of the sunny garden did nothing for her, either. How was she going to stop David Middleton?

She was still agonizing over the problem when Micky Miranda arrived. He looked as fetching as always, in his black morning coat and striped trousers. When he saw that she was distressed, he came across the room with the grace and speed of a jungle cat, his voice like a caress. "Mrs. Pilaster, what on earth has upset you?"

She was grateful he was the first to come. She grabbed him by the arms. "Something frightful has happened."

His hands rested on her waist, and she felt a shiver of pleasure. "Tell me about it," he said soothingly.

She began to feel calmer. She was very fond of Micky. Again he reminded her of the young Earl of Strang—his graceful manners, his beautiful clothes, the way he moved.

She saw the maids staring, and realized that it was mildly indecent for Micky to stand there with both hands on her hips. She took his arm and led him through the French doors into the garden. They sat together on a wooden bench in the shade. Augusta spoke quietly, and Micky leaned close to hear her. "Samuel came to tell me he will not seek the position of Senior Partner."

"Good news!"

"Yes. It means that the post will certainly go to my husband."

"And Papa can have his rifles."

"As soon as Seth retires."

"It's maddening the way old Seth hangs on!" Micky exclaimed. "But that's not what has upset you."

"No. It's that wretched boy who drowned—Peter Middleton. Samuel told me that Peter's brother, a lawyer, is asking questions."

Micky's fine face darkened. "After all these years?"

"Apparently he kept quiet for his parents' sake, but now they're dead." Augusta hesitated. There was a question she had to ask, but she was afraid of the answer. She screwed up her nerve. "Micky, do you think it was Edward's fault the boy died?"

"Well . . ." Micky paused, then said, "Yes. Peter was a poor swimmer. Edward didn't drown him, but he did exhaust him. Peter was alive when Edward left him to chase Tonio. But he was too weak to swim to the side, and he drowned while no one was watching."

Augusta closed her eyes. "Teddy didn't want to kill him."

"Of course not."

"So it's not murder."

"I'm afraid it is. If a thief throws a man to the ground intending only to rob him, but the man suffers a heart attack and dies, the thief is guilty of murder, even though he did not intend to kill."

"How do you know this?"

"I checked with a lawyer years ago." He held her hands. "Heaven forbid that Middleton should discover the truth."

Augusta shuddered as she imagined the consequences. There would be a scandal; the police would be brought in; poor Teddy might have to go on trial; and if he should be found guilty . . .

Augusta realized it was time to take action. Thank heavens, Edward had a true friend in Micky. "We must make sure Middleton's inquiries lead nowhere. How many people know the truth?"

"Six," Micky said immediately. "Edward, you, and me make three, but we aren't going to tell Middleton anything. Then there is Hugh."

"He wasn't there when the boy died."

"No. But he saw enough to know that the story we told the coroner was false. And the fact that we lied makes us look guilty."

"Hugh is a problem, then. The others?"

"Tonio Silva saw it all."

"He never said anything at the time."

"He was too frightened of me then. But I'm not sure he is now."

"And the sixth?"

"We never found out who that was."

Augusta felt a fresh tremor of fear. The unknown witness might reveal himself, but there was nothing they could do about him now. "Two people we can deal with, then—Hugh and Tonio."

There was a thoughtful silence. Then Micky said, "Tonio has a weakness. He's a bad gambler. He loses more than he can afford."

The thought crossed Augusta's mind that Micky might know how to cheat at cards. "Perhaps you could arrange a game?"

Micky said, "It might be expensive. Would you stake me?"

"How much would you need?"

"A hundred pounds, I fear."

Augusta did not hesitate. "Very well," she said.

That left Hugh. Something had to be done about him. But what? Just then she heard voices in the house; other teatime guests were arriving. She gave Micky's hand a conspiratorial squeeze as they stood up, and they went inside.

Chapter Four: August

1

LONDON was hot and sticky, and the population longed for fresh air and open fields. On the first day of August everyone went to the races at Goodwood. They traveled by trains from Victoria Station in south London. The divisions of British society were mirrored in the transport arrangements: high society in the upholstered luxury of the first-class coaches, shopkeepers and schoolteachers crowded but comfortable in second class, factory workers and domestic servants crammed together on hard wooden benches in third.

Maisie Robinson and April Tilsley had gone with Solly Greenbourne and Tonio Silva. Their position in the social hierarchy was dubious. Solly and Tonio clearly belonged in first class, but Maisie and April should have gone third. Solly compromised by buying second-class tickets. However, he was too fond of his food to settle for a lunch bought off a stall, so he had sent four servants ahead with a vast picnic of cold salmon and white wine packed in ice.

They spread a tablecloth on the ground and sat around it on the springy turf. Maisie fed Solly tidbits. She was growing more and more fond of him. He was kind to everyone and full of fun. Gluttony was his only real vice. She knew she should be taking more from him. It drove April mad. It was crazy to be walking out with one of the richest men in the world and living in one room in Soho. Maisie still had not let him have his way with her, but it seemed that the more she refused him, the more devoted to her he became.

The racing began after lunch. A bookmaker in a loud checked suit was standing on a box and shouting odds. Tonio and Solly bet on every race. Maisie got bored. One horse race was the same as another if you didn't gamble. She decided to look around.

The horses were not the only attraction. The downs around the racecourse were crowded with tents, stalls, and carts. There were gambling booths, freak shows, and Gypsies telling fortunes. People were selling gin, cider, meat pies, and Bibles. Barrel organs and bands competed with one another, and through the crowds wandered jugglers and acrobats. It reminded Maisie of the circus.

She passed a puppet show as it was reaching its climax, with the irascible Mr. Punch being knocked about by his wife. She studied the crowd and spotted a boy at the back robbing a man in a top hat. Everyone but Maisie was watching the show, and no one else saw the small grubby hand sliding into the man's waistcoat pocket.

Maisie had no intention of doing anything; wealthy and careless young men deserved to lose their pocket watches. But when she looked more closely at the victim, she recognized the black hair and blue eyes of Hugh Pilaster. She recalled April's telling her Hugh had no money. He could not afford to lose his watch. She decided on impulse to save him from his own carelessness.

She made her way quickly around to the back of the crowd. The pickpocket was a ragged boy of about eleven years—just the age Maisie had been when she ran away from home. He was delicately drawing Hugh's watch chain out of his waistcoat. There was a burst of laughter from the audience watching the show, and at that moment the pickpocket edged away with the watch in his hand.

Maisie grabbed him by the wrist. "Give it to me, and I'll say nothing," she hissed.

He hesitated for a moment, then dropped the watch onto the ground. She released his hand, and he was gone in a twinkling.

She picked up the watch. It was a gold hunter. On the back was inscribed TOBIAS PILASTER, FROM YOUR LOVING WIFE, LYDIA, 23RD MAY 1851. It had been a gift from Hugh's mother to his father. Maisie was glad she had rescued it. She tapped Hugh on the shoulder.

He turned around, and his blue eyes widened. "Miss Robinson!"

"What's the time?" she said.

He reached automatically for his watch and found his pocket empty. "That's funny." He looked around as if he might have dropped it.

She held it up. "I saw you being robbed, and rescued it."

"By Jove!" he said. "Where's the thief?"

"I let him go. He was only a wee lad. I'd have let him take the watch, only I know you can't afford to buy another."

"You don't really mean that."

"I do. I used to steal when I was a child."

"How dreadful."

Maisie was once again annoyed by him. There was something sanctimonious in his attitude. She said, "I remember your father's funeral. It was a cold day. Your father died owing my father money, yet you had a coat that day and I had none. Was that honest?"

"I was thirteen years old when my father went bankrupt," he said with sudden anger. "Does that mean I have to turn a blind eye to villainy all my life?"

Maisie did not want to quarrel with him again. She touched his arm. "I'm sorry," she said. "I didn't mean to criticize your father. I just wanted you to understand why a child might steal."

He softened immediately. "And I haven't thanked you for saving my watch. It was my mother's wedding gift to my father, so it's more precious than its price. Would you like a beer? It's so hot."

It was just what she felt like. "Yes, please."

A few yards off, there was a cart loaded with huge barrels. Hugh bought two pottery tankards of warm, malty ale. Maisie took a long draught. It tasted better than Solly's French wine.

"Are you here on your own?" Hugh asked.

"No. I'm with . . . friends." For some reason she did not want him to know she had been brought by Solly. "And you? Are you with your awful aunt?"

He grimaced. "No. Methodists don't approve of race meetings."

"It must be hard, living with her."

"Eventually I'll get promoted, and then I'll be independent." He grinned. "And then I'll tell her to shut her gob, like you did."

"I hope you didn't get into trouble."

"I did, but it was worth it to see the expression on her face." On impulse he added, "Come out with me tonight. We'll go to Cremorne Gardens and dance."

She was tempted, but she thought of Solly. "No, thank you."

"Why not?"

She asked herself the same question. She was not in love with Solly, and she was taking no money from him. I'm eighteen years old, she thought, and if I can't go dancing with a boy I like, what's the point in living? "All right, then. Let's meet somewhere." She did not want him to see the Soho slum where she lived.

"Westminster Pier at eight o'clock," he said. "We'll take the steamer to Chelsea."

She made a rapid calculation. Solly would want to stay until the last race. Then they had to get the train back to London. She would say good-bye to him at Victoria Station and walk to Westminster. She thought she could make it. "But if I'm late, you'll wait?"

"All night if necessary."

Maisie walked away knowing she would have to invent a reason for leaving Solly. He was expecting to take her out to dinner. She would try to think of something convincing.

She found her friends where she had left them, between the white-painted rail that bounded the track, and the bookmaker in the checked suit. April and Tonio were looking triumphant. As soon as April saw Maisie, she said, "We've won a hundred and ten pounds. Isn't it wonderful?"

Maisie was happy for April. As she was congratulating them, Micky Miranda appeared, strolling along with his thumbs in the pockets of his dove-gray waistcoat. He had Edward Pilaster in tow, as always. Maisie was curious about their relationship. They were so different: Micky—slim, immaculate, confident; Edward—big, clumsy, hoggish. Why were they so inseparable?

They all talked about their winnings. Both Edward and Tonio had made a lot on a horse called Prince Charlie. Solly had won money, then lost it again, and seemed to enjoy both equally. Micky did not say how he had fared, and Maisie guessed he had not bet much. He seemed too calculating a person to be a heavy gambler.

However, with his next breath Micky surprised her. He said to Solly, "We're having a heavyweight card game tonight at the club, Greenbourne. A pound minimum. Will you join in?"

Solly would go along with anything. "I'll join in," he said.

Micky turned to Tonio. "Would you care to join us?"

That surprised Maisie. At the Argyll Rooms she got the impression that Micky disliked Tonio. Why was he now inviting him to a card game?

"Count on me," Tonio said excitedly. "I'll be there."

"Shall we all dine together at the club?"

Solly looked at Maisie, and she realized she had been provided with a ready-made excuse for not spending the evening with him. "Dine with the boys, Solly. I don't mind. I've had a lovely day."

"That's settled, then," said Micky.

He and Edward took their leave, and Tonio and April went to place a bet on the next race. Solly offered Maisie his arm, and they strolled alongside the track. After a while Solly said, "Do you like me, Maisie?"

She stood on tiptoe and kissed his cheek. "I like you a lot."

Solly looked into her eyes, and Maisie was mystified to see

tears behind his spectacles. "Solly dear, what is it?" she said.

"I like you, too," he said. "More than anyone I've ever met."

"Thank you." She was touched. It was unusual for Solly to show any emotion stronger than mild enthusiasm.

Then he said, "Will you marry me?"

She was flabbergasted. Men of Solly's class did not propose to girls like her. They kept them as mistresses and had children by them, but did not marry them. She was too astounded to speak.

Solly went on. "I'd give you anything you want. Please say yes."

Marriage to Solly! She would be unbelievably rich for ever and ever. A soft bed every night, a blazing fire in every room of the house. She would never be cold again, never hungry, never weary.

He said, "I love you so much. I'm just desperate for you."

He really did love her, she could tell. And that was the trouble. She did not love him. He deserved better. He deserved a wife who really loved him. She said, "You're the kindest, most gentle man I've ever met—"

"Don't say no, please," he interrupted. "If you can't say yes, say nothing. Think about it—at least for a day, perhaps longer."

Maisie sighed. "I'll think about it," she said.

2

Hugh and Maisie took the penny ride on the pleasure steamer from Westminster Pier to Chelsea. There they disembarked and walked up the wharf to the magnificent gilded gateway of Cremorne Gardens. The gardens consisted of twelve acres of groves and grottoes, flower beds and lawns, between the river and the King's Road. It was dusk when they arrived, and the place was packed. Many of the younger people who had been at the races had decided to finish the day here. They sauntered carefree through the gardens, laughing and flirting, the girls in pairs, the young men in larger groups, the couples arm in arm.

The weather had been fine all day, but now it was becoming a hot, thundery night that threatened a storm. Hugh felt elated and nervous. He was thrilled to have Maisie on his arm, but he had the insecure sense that he did not know the rules of the game he was playing. What did she expect? Would she let him kiss her?

Maisie was wearing a blue-green gown with a low neckline and a bustle behind, and a sailor hat poised jauntily on her piled-up hair. She attracted a lot of admiring glances.

They passed a ballet theater, an Oriental circus, and several shooting galleries, then went into a restaurant to dine. Their dinner was quite expensive, but Hugh had brought the money he had been saving for his next suit of clothes, so he had plenty of cash.

When they left the restaurant, the people in the gardens seemed more boisterous than they had earlier—no doubt because they had consumed a good deal of beer and gin in the interim.

Hugh and Maisie came upon a dance floor. Hugh led her onto the floor and took her in his arms. His fingertips tingled as he rested his right hand on the small of her back. With his left hand he held hers, and she gave it a squeeze. The sensation thrilled him.

At the end of the first dance he smiled at her, and to his surprise she reached up and touched his mouth with her fingertip. "I like it when you grin," she said. "You look boyish."

Boyish was not exactly the impression he was trying to give, but at this point, anything that pleased her was all right with him.

They danced again. They were good partners: although Maisie was short, Hugh was only a little taller, and they were both light on their feet. He had danced with dozens of girls, but he had never enjoyed it this much.

They stayed on the floor until midnight, when the music stopped. All the couples left the dance floor and moved on to the garden paths. Hugh noticed that many of the men kept their arms around their partners, so with some trepidation he did the same. Maisie did not seem to mind.

The festivities were becoming unruly. Beside the paths, there were occasional cabins, like boxes at the opera, where people could sit and dine and watch the crowds walk by. Some of the cabins had been rented by groups of undergraduates who were now drunk. A man walking in front of Hugh had his top hat knocked off his head, and Hugh himself had to duck to avoid a flying loaf of bread. He held Maisie closer to him protectively. A few minutes later they had to detour around a scuffle involving six or seven young men, all shouting, punching, and knocking one another down.

Then a group of thirty or forty came charging along, pushing women aside and throwing men to the ground. There was no escaping them; they spread out across the lawns on either side of the path. Hugh acted quickly. He stood in front of Maisie with his back to the onslaught, then took off his hat and put both arms around her, holding her tight. The mob swept by. A heavy shoulder hit Hugh in the back, and he staggered, still holding Maisie, but he managed to remain upright. Then the hooligans were gone.

Hugh relaxed his grip and looked down at Maisie. She looked back at him expectantly. Hesitantly he leaned down and kissed her lips. They were deliciously soft. He closed his eyes. It was his first kiss. And it was as delightful as he had dreamed.

She broke the kiss, looked hard at him, then hugged him tight. "You could spoil all my plans," she said quietly.

He was not sure what she meant.

Suddenly she froze. "Listen," she said.

Hugh had been vaguely aware that the gardens were getting very noisy, and now he was hearing shouting, and everyone on the footpath was running in different directions. "There must be a fight," he said. Then he heard a police whistle.

"We'd better leave," Maisie said. "There'll be trouble."

"Let's cut across the lawns to the King's Road entrance. It might be quicker."

The gaslights went out. Hugh and Maisie pressed forward in the dark. Now there was a continuous clamor of men shouting and women screaming, punctuated by police whistles. It suddenly occurred to Hugh that he might be arrested. Then everyone would find out what he had been up to. Augusta would say he was too dissolute to be given a responsible post at the bank. He groaned; then he recalled how it had felt to kiss Maisie, and he decided he did not care what Augusta said.

As they approached the gate to exit the gardens, a troop of thirty or forty policemen entered. Fighting against the flow of the crowd, they started indiscriminately clubbing men and women. The crowd turned and began to run in the opposite direction.

Hugh thought fast. "Let me carry you," he said to Maisie. "Pretend you've fainted."

He picked her up, and she closed her eyes and went limp. He walked forward against the press of the crowd, shouting, "Make way, there! Make way!" in his most authoritative voice, and people tried to get out of the way. He came up against the advancing policemen, and for a brief moment he thought his bluff would be called. Just then a sergeant shouted, "Let the gentleman pass!"

Hugh walked through the line of police and suddenly found himself in the clear.

Maisie opened her eyes, and he smiled at her. "You all right?"

She nodded. She seemed tearful. "Put me down."

He put her down gently. "I say, don't cry. It's over now."

She shook her head. "It's not the riot," she said. "I've seen fights before. But this is the first time anyone ever took care of me. All my life I've had to look after myself. It's a new experience."

He did not know what to say. All the girls he had ever met assumed that men would take care of them. Being with Maisie was a constant revelation.

3

MICKY Miranda had begun to cheat at cards while he was at Windfield School, to supplement his inadequate allowance. Later a professional cardsharp had taught him all the basic principles of the craft. It was most dangerous when the stakes were high. Suspicion mounted with the size of the bets.

If he were caught tonight, it would not just mean the failure of his scheme to ruin Tonio. Cheating at cards was the worst crime a gentleman could commit in England. He would be asked to resign from his clubs, and no one would speak to him. He would be forced to go back to Cordova, endure the taunts of his older brother, and spend the rest of his life raising cattle. The thought made him ill.

But the rewards were as dramatic as the risks. He was doing this not just to please Augusta. He wanted Tonio's job. It would enable him to live like a gentleman while doing hardly any work.

Micky, Edward, Solly, and Tonio dined early at the Cowes, the club they all favored. By ten o'clock they were in the cardroom, joined at the baccarat table by two other club gamblers—Captain Carter and Viscount Montagne. There was a white line drawn around the table, ten or twelve inches from the edge. Each player had a pile of gold sovereigns in front of him, outside the white square. Once money crossed the line into the square, it was staked.

Micky licked his lips nervously, caught himself, and tried to relax.

Baccarat might have been invented, he thought, to enable the smart to steal from the rich. In the first place, it was a game purely of chance. A player received two cards and added up their values. If the total came to more than nine, only the last digit counted, so fifteen was five, twenty was zero, and the highest possible score was nine. A player with a low score could draw a third card, which would be dealt face up, so everyone could see it.

The banker dealt just three hands—one to his left, one to his right, one to himself. Players and bystanders bet on either the left or right hand. The banker paid out to any hand higher than his own.

The second advantage of baccarat, from the cheat's point of view, was that it was played with a pack of at least three decks of cards. This meant the cheat could use a fourth deck and confidently deal a card out of his sleeve without worrying whether another player already had the same card in his hand.

While the others were making themselves comfortable, Micky asked a waiter for three new decks of cards. When the man came back, he naturally handed the cards to Micky.

In order to control the game, Micky had to deal, so his first challenge was to make sure he was banker. This involved two tricks: neutralizing the cut, and second-card dealing.

He broke the seals. The cards were always packed with the jokers on top and the ace of spades at the bottom. Micky took out the jokers and shuffled, enjoying the slippery feel of the new cards. It was the simplest of operations to move an ace from the bottom to the top of the pack, but then he had to let another player cut the cards without moving the ace from the top.

He passed the pack to Solly, sitting on his right. As Micky put it down, he contracted his hand a fraction so the top card—the ace of spades—stayed in his palm. Solly cut. Keeping his palm down to conceal the ace, Micky picked up the pack, replacing the hidden card on top. He had successfully neutralized the cut.

"High card gets the bank?" he said, forcing himself to sound indifferent as to whether they said yes or no.

There was a murmur of assent.

Holding the pack firmly, he slid the top card back a fraction of an inch and began to deal fast, keeping the top card back and dealing the second until he came to himself, when he dealt the ace. They all turned over their cards. Micky's was the only ace, so he was banker.

He managed a casual smile. "I think I'm going to be lucky tonight," he said, and he dealt the first hand.

Tonio was playing on his left, with Edward and Viscount Montagne. On his right were Solly and Captain Carter. Micky did not want to win; he just wanted Tonio to lose.

He played fair for a while, losing a little of Augusta's money. When the time was right, he lit a cigar. In the inside pocket of his coat, next to his cigar case, was another deck of cards, bought at the stationer's where the club's playing cards came from. He had arranged the extra deck in winning pairs, all giving a total of nine.

Returning his cigar case to his pocket, he palmed the extra deck. Then, picking up the pack from the table with his other hand, he slid the new cards to the bottom of the old pack. While the others mixed their brandy and water, he shuffled, carefully bringing to the top of the pack, in order, one card from the bottom and two cards at random, another from the bottom, and another two at random. Then, dealing first to his left, then to his right, then to himself, he gave himself the winning pair.

Next time around he gave Solly's side a winning hand. For a while he continued the same way, making Tonio lose and Solly win. No suspicion attached to Micky, for the pile of sovereigns in front of him remained about the same.

Tonio had started by putting on the table most of the money he had won at the races—about a hundred pounds. When it was down to about fifty, he stood up and said, "This side is unlucky. I'm going to sit by Solly."

That won't help you, Micky thought. It was no more difficult to make the left side win and the right side lose from now on. It was not enough that Tonio should be cleaned out. Micky wanted him to play with borrowed money and be unable to repay his debts. Only then would he be thoroughly disgraced.

When Tonio's money was almost gone, Micky took out his cigar case again. "Try one, Tonio," he said. To his relief Tonio accepted. Tonio would not leave before finishing his cigar.

After they had lit up, Micky moved in for the kill. A couple of hands later Tonio was broke. "Well, that's everything I won at Goodwood," he said despondently.

"We ought to give you a chance to win it back," Micky said. "Pilaster will lend you a hundred pounds, I'm sure."

Edward looked a little startled, but it would be ungenerous to refuse, and he said, "By all means."

Solly intervened. "Perhaps you should retire, Silva, and be grateful that you've had a great day's gambling at no cost."

Micky silently cursed Solly for being a good-natured nuisance. If Tonio did the sensible thing now, the whole scheme would be ruined. But Tonio could not resist the temptation to carry on. "I might as well play until I finish my cigar," he said. He beckoned to a waiter and ordered pen, paper, and ink. Edward counted out a hundred sovereigns, and Tonio scribbled an IOU. Micky knew that if Tonio lost, he could never repay the debt.

The game went on until Tonio was down to fifty pounds again. "I only win when I gamble high," he said. "I'm putting the lot on this next hand."

It was a big bet. If Tonio lost, he was finished.

Micky dealt the cards. He looked at Edward, on the left, who tapped his cards, indicating that he wanted a third. Micky dealt him a four of clubs and turned to Solly, who was playing the hand on which Tonio had staked his future. Solly passed.

Micky turned over his cards and showed a five and a four. Edward had a four showing, and turned over a worthless king and another four, making eight. His side had lost. Solly turned up a two and a four. The right side had also lost to the banker.

And Tonio was ruined.

He turned pale and muttered something that Micky recognized as a Spanish curse.

Micky suppressed a smile of triumph.

4

In the early hours of the morning, Maisie and Hugh walked hand in hand through the new suburbs of Fulham and South Kensington. Maisie felt bewildered but happy. In the past when men had kissed her, she felt it was part of a transaction, something she gave in return for whatever she needed from them. Tonight had been different. She had *wanted* Hugh to kiss her, and when he had, it had been delicious. Yet he was not skillful or experienced. Quite the reverse. So why had she enjoyed it so much?

They reached Kensington Gore and turned right, heading for the city center, where she lived. Hugh stopped opposite a huge house whose front was illuminated by two gaslights. He put his arm around her shoulders. "That's my aunt Augusta's house," he said.

She put her arm around his waist and stared at the vast mansion. It reminded her that she and Hugh lived on separate islands in society, divided by an ocean of money and privilege. The thought troubled her. "I was born in Russia in a one-room hut," she said.

"Really? Maisie Robinson doesn't sound like a Russian name."

"I was born Miriam Rabinowicz."

"Miriam—I like it." He drew her to him and kissed her. Her anxiety evaporated, and she gave herself up to the sensation.

Then it started to rain. It happened not gradually, but all at once. There was a flash of lightning, a clap of thunder, and an instant downpour. By the time they broke the kiss, their faces were wet. Hugh seized her hand. "Let's take shelter in the house," he said.

They ran across the road. Hugh led her down the steps, to the tradesmen's entrance in the basement area. By the time they reached the doorway, she was soaked to the skin. Hugh unlocked the door. Putting a finger to his lips, he ushered her inside.

They tiptoed through a kitchen the size of a small church. She followed him to a back staircase and up three long flights, where they passed through another door and emerged on a landing. He glanced into a bedroom where a night-light burned. He said, "Edward's still out. There's no one else on this floor. Aunt and Uncle's rooms are on the floor below us, and the servants' above. Come."

He led her into his bedroom and turned up the gaslight. "I'll fetch towels," he said, and he went out again.

She took off her hat and looked around the room. It was furnished simply: the room of a poor relation. There was a single bed, a dresser, a plain wardrobe, and a small desk. On the desk was a framed photograph of a woman and a girl about six years old.

Hugh came back with a pile of towels. Maisie took one and buried her wet face in it gratefully. "Who's the picture of?"

"My mother and my sister. My sister was born after my father died. Her name is Dorothy. I call her Dotty. I'm very fond of her."

"Where do they live?"

"In Folkestone, by the sea."

Maisie wondered if she would ever meet them.

Hugh removed his coat and boots, then drew up the chair from the desk and made her sit down. He knelt in front of her, took off her shoes, and dried her feet.

Her dress was wet through, and she shivered. She could not get dry without taking it off. Underneath she was quite decent. She had on a full-length petticoat and a chemise. Impulsively she stood up, turned her back to Hugh, and said, "Will you undo me?"

She could feel his hands shaking as his fingers fumbled with the hooks and eyes that fastened her dress. When he was done, she thanked him, stepped out of the dress, and turned to face him.

His expression was a touching mixture of embarrassment and desire. He stood like Ali Baba staring at the thieves' treasure. She had thought that she would simply dry herself with a towel and put her dress back on later when it dried, but now she knew it was not going to be like that. And she was glad.

She put her hands on his cheeks, pulled his head down, and kissed him. She felt as if she were melting inside. She wanted more of this, now and always.

"Maisie," he said, "I want to . . ."

She smiled. "So do I." She had no doubts. She wanted him more than she had ever wanted anything.

He stroked her hair. "I've never done it before," he said.

"Nor have I."

He stared at her. "But I thought—" He stopped.

She felt a spasm of anger, then controlled herself. It was her own fault if he had thought she was promiscuous. "Let's lie down."

He sighed happily, then said, "Are you sure?"

"Am I sure?" she repeated. Men never thought about how she felt. She took his hand in hers and kissed the palm. "If I wasn't sure before, I am now."

She lay down on the narrow bed. He lay beside her, and she sensed him fumbling with his trousers. Then he lowered his face to hers and kissed her, gently at first and then passionately. She pulled him to her, and she gave herself up to him.

Distantly, above the noise of his breathing and hers, she heard a door open.

Suddenly a harsh voice shattered the mood like a stone through a window. "Well, well, Hugh. What's all this?"

Maisie froze.

Hugh gave a despairing groan.

The sneering voice came again. "What do you think this house is, a brothel?"

Hugh rolled off the bed, and Maisie saw his cousin Edward standing in the doorway, smoking a cigar. Hugh quickly covered her with a big towel. She sat upright and pulled it up to her neck.

Edward grinned. "If you've finished, I might give her a go."

Hugh wrapped a towel around his waist. Controlling his anger with a visible effort, he said, "You're drunk, Edward. Get out."

Edward ignored him and approached the bed. "Why, it's Greenbourne's dolly-mop! I won't tell him, so long as you're nice to me."

Maisie saw that he was in earnest. She shuddered with loathing.

Hugh was enraged. "Get out of here, you damn fool," he said.

"Be a sport," Edward persisted. "After all, she's only a whore."

Hugh took two strides and hit Edward a mighty punch on the nose. Blood spurted, and Edward let out a roar of agony. Hugh hit him again. Edward screamed in pain and fell to the floor. Then Hugh was on top of him, still hitting him. Maisie cried, "Hugh, stop. You'll kill him!" She jumped off the bed and tried to grab Hugh's arms, but he was in a fury, and it was hard to restrain him.

A moment later she glimpsed a movement out of the corner of her eye. She looked up and saw Hugh's aunt Augusta standing at the door in a black silk peignoir. In her eyes was a look of triumph.

5

As soon as Augusta saw the half-naked girl, she sensed that this was her chance to get rid of Hugh once and for all. She recognized her immediately. This was the trollop who had insulted her in the park.

The outlines of a plan were forming in Augusta's mind when suddenly she saw Edward lying on the floor with blood all over his face. "Teddy!" She fell to her knees beside him. "Speak to me!" she yelled. All her old fears rose up in force, and she was taken back twenty-three years, to when he nearly died as a baby.

Edward sat up and groaned, and her terror eased.

"I caught Hugh with his whore, and he went mad," Edward said.

She reached out and touched Edward's nose. He gave a yelp but permitted her to press delicately. Nothing broken, she thought.

She heard her husband say, "What the deuce is going on?"

She stood up. "Hugh has attacked Edward," she said.

Joseph turned to Hugh. "What do you mean by it, sir?"

"The silly fool asked for it," Hugh said defiantly.

That's right, Hugh, make it worse, Augusta thought. Whatever you do, don't apologize. I want your uncle to stay angry with you.

She began to think rapidly. How could she best exploit this situation? Hugh had to be silenced, for he knew too much about the death of Peter Middleton. Now was the moment to strike.

First she had to separate him from the girl.

Some servants had appeared in their nightclothes and were hovering in the doorway that led to the back stairs. Augusta saw her butler. "Hastead, help Mr. Edward to his bed, will you?" He bustled forward and got Teddy to his feet.

Next Augusta spoke to her housekeeper. "Mrs. Merton, cover this girl with something and take her to my room." Mrs. Merton took off her own dressing gown and draped it around the girl.

Augusta said, "Hugh, run to Dr. Humbold's house in Church Street. He'd better have a look at poor Edward's nose."

"I'm not leaving Maisie," Hugh said.

Augusta said sharply, "Since you've done the damage, it's the least you can do to fetch a doctor!"

Maisie said, "I'll be all right, Hugh. I'll be here when you get back."

He was still reluctant to go, but he could think of no good reason to refuse. After a moment he said, "I'll put my things on."

Augusta concealed her relief. She had separated them. Now if her luck held, she would be able to seal Hugh's fate. She turned to her husband. "Come. Let's go to your room and discuss this."

They went down the stairs and entered his bedroom. As soon as the door was closed, Augusta said, "Hugh can't continue to live here. You must discharge him from the bank."

Joseph hesitated. "I suppose I better," he said after a moment. "I imagine he will go back to his mother in Folkestone, but I don't know what he'll do for work."

Augusta realized she had made a mistake. Hugh would be even more dangerous if he were unemployed and resentful. David Middleton had not yet approached him, but sooner or later he would. She became flustered, wishing she had thought more before insisting Hugh should be dismissed. "Perhaps we're being harsh," she said.

He raised his eyebrows, surprised at this display of mercy.

Augusta went on. "Well, you keep saying that Hugh has great potential as a banker. Maybe it's unwise to throw that away." She sat down to think. Suddenly she was inspired. "Send him abroad."

"Eh?"

The more she thought about the idea, the better she liked it. "The Far East or South America," she went on. "Someplace where his behavior will not reflect on my house."

"It's not a bad idea," Joseph said reflectively. "There's an opening in the United States. The old boy who runs our Boston office needs an assistant."

America would be perfect, Augusta thought. "Let him go as soon as possible," she said. "I don't want him in the house another day."

"He can book his passage in the morning," Joseph said, "and stay with his mother until his ship sails."

And he won't see David Middleton for years, Augusta thought with satisfaction. Were there any other snags? She remembered Maisie. Did Hugh care for her? It seemed unlikely, but anything was possible. She stood up. "I must get rid of that girl," she said, and went to her bedroom.

Maisie was clothed again and pinning her hat to her hair. Mrs. Merton was cramming a rather flashy blue-green gown into a cheap bag. "I've loaned her a dress of mine, as hers is soaked, mum," said the housekeeper.

That answered a question that had been nagging Augusta. It was unlike Hugh to do something as blatantly stupid as to bring home a trollop. Now she saw how it had come about. They had been caught in the sudden storm, and Hugh had brought the woman inside to get dry. Then one thing had led to another.

"What is your name?" she said to the girl.

"Maisie Robinson. I know yours."

Augusta found that she loathed Maisie Robinson. She was not sure why; the girl was hardly worthy of such strong feelings. It had something to do with the way she looked—proud, voluptuous, independent. "I suppose that you want money," Augusta said disdainfully.

"You hypocritical cow," Maisie said. "You didn't marry that rich, ugly husband of yours for love."

It was the truth, and the words took Augusta's breath away. She had underestimated this young woman. She swallowed hard and forced herself to sound neutral. "Will you sit down for a moment?"

After some hesitation Maisie took a chair.

Augusta sat opposite her. The girl had to be made to give Hugh up. Augusta sensed that money would not work with her, and she was clearly not the type to be bullied, either. It would work best if Maisie thought that giving Hugh up was her own idea. And that might be best achieved by Augusta's arguing the opposite.

Augusta said, "If you want to marry him, I can't stop you." The girl looked surprised, and Augusta congratulated herself on having caught her off guard.

"What makes you think I want to marry him?" Maisie said.

Augusta almost laughed. She wanted to say, *The fact that you're a scheming little gold digger,* but instead she said, "What girl wouldn't want to marry him? He's personable and good-looking, and he comes from a great family."

"It almost sounds as if you want me to marry him."

Augusta intended to give exactly that impression, but she had to tread delicately. Maisie was too bright to be easily hoodwinked. "Let's not be fanciful, Maisie," she said. "No woman of my class would wish a man of her family to marry quite so far below him."

"She might if she hated him enough," Maisie said.

Feeling encouraged, Augusta continued to lead her on. "But I don't hate Hugh," she said. "Why would I want to ruin his career?"

"Because he shows up that ass of a son of yours—Edward."

A wave of anger engulfed Augusta. Once again Maisie had come uncomfortably close to the truth. "I think you had better not mention the name of my son," Augusta said in a low voice.

Maisie grinned. "I seem to have touched a sore place." She immediately became grave again. "So, that's your game. Well, I won't play it. I like Hugh too much to ruin him."

Augusta was surprised and pleased by the strength of Maisie's passion. "What are you going to do?" Augusta asked.

Maisie struggled not to cry. "I shan't see him anymore. You may yet destroy him, but you won't have my help."

"He might come after you."

"I shall disappear. He doesn't know where I live." There were tears in Maisie's eyes. She stood up. "I'll go now, before he comes back. Thank you for lending me your dress, Mrs. Merton."

The housekeeper opened the door for her. "I'll show you out."

Augusta let out a long breath. She had done it. She had stunted Hugh's career, neutralized Maisie Robinson, and averted the danger from David Middleton—all in one night.

6

MICKY Miranda lived in two rooms of a house in Camberwell, a modest south London suburb. At nine o'clock each morning the landlady brought coffee and hot rolls for him and Papa. Over breakfast Micky explained how he had caused Tonio Silva to lose a hundred pounds he did not have.

"When I was your age—"

"You would have slit his throat, I know. But there are times when it's better to tread softly, Papa. Think of Samuel Pilaster and his objections to dealing in guns. I got him out of the way without bloodshed, didn't I?" In fact, Augusta had done it, but Micky had not told Papa that.

"When do I get the rifles?" Papa said stubbornly.

It was a sore point. It was August, and in September the winter snow would start to melt on the mountains of Santamaria. Papa wanted to go home with his weapons. As soon as Joseph became Senior Partner, Edward would put the deal through and the guns would be shipped. But old Seth clung to his post and his life.

"You'll get them soon, Papa. Seth can't last much longer."

Micky turned his mind to the day ahead. Tonio now owed money he could never pay. The next step was to turn a problem into a crisis. He wanted Edward and Tonio to quarrel publicly. Tonio's disgrace would then become general knowledge, and he would be obliged to resign from his job and go home to Cordova. That would put him comfortably out of reach of David Middleton.

While Micky was brooding over this tricky problem, there was a knock at the door, and the landlady announced a visitor. A moment later Tonio came in. "Sit down. Have some coffee," Micky said cheerfully. "Bad luck last night."

Tonio bowed to Papa and sat down. He looked as if he had not slept. "I lost more than I can afford," he said. "You know what it means. In this country a man who doesn't pay his gambling debts isn't a gentleman. And a man who isn't a gentleman can't be a diplomat. I might have to resign and go home."

Exactly, thought Micky, but he said, "I do see the problem."

"Will you give me the money?" Tonio pleaded. "You're Cordovan. You don't condemn a man for one mistake. And I would pay you back eventually."

"If I had the money, I'd give it to you," said Micky.

Tonio looked at Papa, who stared at him coldly and said simply, "No." Papa despised the Silva family as lily-livered city dwellers who lived by patronage and corruption.

Tonio hung his head. "I don't know what to do," he said. "If I go home in disgrace, I won't be able to face my family."

Micky said thoughtfully, "Perhaps there is a way I can help."

Tonio brightened. "Oh, please, anything!"

"Edward and I are good friends. I could ask him to wait for his money. I don't say he'll agree to it, mind you, but I'll try."

Tonio looked hopeful. "I don't know how to thank you."

"Don't thank me," Micky said. "It's unlucky. Just meet me at the club at lunchtime."

"Right." Tonio stood up and bowed again to Papa. "Good-bye, Senor Miranda." He went out.

"Stupid boy," Papa muttered.

"A complete fool," Micky agreed.

Micky went into the next room and dressed in his morning clothes. Then, leaving Papa to his own devices, he walked across the bridge to the financial district, which was called the City because it covered the square mile of the original Roman city of London.

Pilasters Bank was a big, new building with an imposing entrance flanked by massive fluted pillars. It was a few minutes past noon when Micky went through the double doors into the banking hall. He approached one of the walkers and said, "Be good enough to tell Mr. Edward Pilaster that Mr. Miranda has called."

After a few minutes Edward appeared, with a bruised nose and a black eye. Micky raised his eyebrows. "My dear fellow, what happened to you?"

"I had a fight with Hugh. I told him off for bringing a whore into the house, and he lost his temper. You won't see him again for a long time. He's being sent to Boston."

Well done, Augusta, thought Micky. It would be neat if both Hugh and Tonio could be dealt with on the same day. He said, "You look as if you might benefit from champagne and lunch."

They left the bank, hailed a hansom cab, and directed it to the Cowes Club on Pall Mall. As soon as they were on their way, Micky began his prepared speech. "I hate a chap who spreads reports about another chap's bad behavior," he said. "But when it affects one's friends, one is more or less obliged to say something."

"I'm not sure I follow you," Edward said.

"I'm talking about Tonio Silva. I'm afraid he has no intention of paying his debt to you. Worse, he's been boasting about it, saying you aren't man enough to make him pay."

Edward reddened. "Has he, by the devil! We'll see about that."

Micky was pleased. Edward was in just the right mood to quarrel. Everything was working out.

At last the cab pulled up outside the club. Micky waited while Edward paid the driver. They went inside. In the cloakroom, in a knot of people hanging up their hats, they met Tonio.

Micky tensed. He had put everything in place; now he could only hope that the drama would play itself out as he had planned.

Tonio caught Edward's eye, looked awkward, and said, "By Jove. Good morning, you two."

Micky looked at Edward, whose face turned pink. "See here, Silva," Edward said loudly. "About that hundred pounds."

The room went suddenly quiet. It was bad behavior to talk about money, and a gentleman would do so only in extreme circumstances. Bystanders sensed a scandal. Tonio went white.

Edward said brutally, "You can let me have it today, if it would suit your convenience."

A challenge had been issued. As a gentleman, Tonio had only one option. He had to say, *By all means. If it's important, you shall have your money right away.* If he did not do that, everyone would know he could not pay, and he would be ostracized.

Micky watched with horrid fascination. A look of panic came over Tonio's face. He opened his mouth in protest, but no words came out. Then his face crumpled, and he turned and ran.

Micky was elated; it had all gone perfectly. "Order a brandy for me, Edward. I'd better go after Silva and make sure he doesn't throw himself under a horse bus." He dashed out.

This was the most subtle part of his plan: he now had to convince the man he had ruined that he was his best friend.

Tonio was hurrying along in the direction of St. James's. Micky caught up with him. "I say, Silva, I'm dreadfully sorry," he said.

Tonio stopped. There were tears on his cheeks. "I'm finished," he said. "It's all over."

"Pilaster turned me down flat," Micky said. "I did my best."

"I know. Thank you for trying. I wish there was something I could do to show my appreciation."

"Well . . ." Micky feigned embarrassment. "I suppose the Cordovan minister will be looking for someone to replace you."

"He'll need someone right away." Comprehension showed on Tonio's tearstained face. "Of course. You'd be perfect!"

"If you could put in a word . . ."

"I'll do more than that. I'll tell him how you tried to get me out of this mess. I'm sure he'll want to appoint you." Tonio took Micky's hand in both of his. "You're a true friend."

Chapter Five: September

1

HUGH'S six-year-old sister, Dorothy, was folding his shirts and packing them into his trunk. As soon as she went to bed, he would have to do them again, because her folding was hopelessly untidy. But he pretended she was very good at it. He was feeling wistful; he would not see his baby sister again for years.

September rain drummed on the windows, and down in the bay the wind lashed the waves. Hugh began to fold his two new suits. The bank had paid for them. He had a suspicion his mother had persuaded Seth to authorize that. She had also insisted Hugh be allowed a few weeks off before leaving for America, to give him time to get ready. The old man was as tightfisted as the rest of the Pilasters, but he had a soft spot for Hugh's mother. It was the small allowance Seth gave her that she had been living on all these years.

While Hugh was thinking about Mother, she came into the room.

"It's almost bedtime, Dorothy," she said. "Go and put on your nightdress." As soon as Dotty was out of the room, Mother began to refold Hugh's shirts.

He wanted to talk to her about Maisie, but he felt shy. Augusta had written to her, he knew. The story she had heard might be a long way from the truth. After a moment he said, "Mother, Aunt Augusta doesn't always say quite what is true."

"No need to be so polite," she said with a bitter smile. "Augusta has been telling lies for years."

Hugh was startled by her frankness. "Why?"

His mother put down the shirt she was folding and thought for a minute. "Augusta was a very beautiful girl," she said. "She was an only child, willful and spoiled. Her parents were nothing special—her father had three little grocery stores in the west London suburbs. But Augusta was clearly destined for higher things. When she was seventeen, the Earl of Strang fell for her. Naturally his parents were horrified at the prospect that he should marry a grocer's daughter."

"Did they become engaged?" Hugh asked.

"Not formally, but everyone assumed it was a foregone conclusion. Then there was a scandal. Her father was accused of systematically giving short weight in his shops. He denied it vehemently, and in the end nothing came of it. But Strang dropped Augusta."

"She must have been heartbroken."

"She was wild with rage. All her life she had had her own way. Now she wanted Strang, and she couldn't have him."

"And she married Uncle Joseph on the rebound, as they say."

"I'd say she married him in a fit of temper. He was older than she by seven years and even richer than Strang."

"What happened to Strang?"

"He married a French countess and died in a hunting accident. Augusta still yearns for what Strang could have given her—the title, the ancestral home. But that isn't what Strang offered her, in truth. He offered her love. That's what she's really lost."

Hugh had never had such an intimate conversation with his mother. He felt encouraged to open his heart to her. "Mother," he began, "about Maisie Robinson . . ."

"Were you fond of her, Hugh?"

"Rather." He felt tears in his eyes. "I don't understand why she disappeared. I never knew her address. I've inquired at the livery stables she worked for and at the Argyll Rooms, where I met her. Solly Greenbourne was fond of her, too, and he's as baffled as I am."

"How mysterious."

"I'm sure Aunt Augusta arranged this somehow," Hugh said.

"I have no doubt of it. I can't imagine how, but she is appallingly devious. However, you must look to the future now, Hugh. Boston will be such an opportunity for you. You must work hard and conscientiously. In time you'll forget the girl."

"I wonder if I ever shall."

Mother kissed his forehead. "You will. I promise."

2

THERE was only one picture on the wall in the attic room Maisie shared with April. It was a garish circus poster showing Maisie in spangled tights, standing on the back of a galloping horse. Underneath in red letters were the words "The Amazing Maisie." Otherwise the room contained only a narrow bed, a washstand, and one chair. The girls' clothes hung from nails banged into the wall, and the dirt on the window served instead of curtains.

Maisie was getting dressed when April burst into the room with a newspaper in her hand. "It's you, Maisie. It's you!" she said. "In the *Lloyd's Weekly News*. Listen. 'If Miss Maisie Robinson will contact Messrs. Goldman and Jay, solicitors, at Gray's Inn, she will learn something to her advantage.' It must be you."

Maisie's heart beat faster, but she made her expression stern. "It's Hugh," she said. "I'll not go." She thought about Hugh every day and every night, and she was miserable. She hardly knew him, but it was impossible to forget him. Nevertheless, she was determined to try. She loved him too much to ruin him.

She put her arms into her corset. "Help me with my stays."

April began pulling the laces. "I've never had my name in the paper. You have twice, if you count the 'Lioness' as a name."

"And how much good has it done me? Heavens, I'm getting fat."

April tied the laces and helped her into her gown. They were going out tonight. April had a new lover, and he and a friend were taking April and Maisie to a music hall. In order to hide from Hugh, Maisie had been obliged to give up working for Sammles—much to Sammles' regret, for she had sold five horses—and the money she had saved was rapidly running out.

Maisie's gown was tight across her bosom, and she winced as April did it up. April gave her a curious look and said, "Maisie, when did you last have the curse?"

Maisie thought for a moment, and a chill descended on her. "Oh, dear. I think it was before we went to Goodwood. Am I pregnant?"

"Your waist is bigger, and you haven't had the curse for almost two months. Yes, you're pregnant," April said in an exasperated voice.

"Oh, my God." Maisie began to cry. "What am I going to do?"

"We could go to that lawyer's office for a start."

SUDDENLY EVERYTHING WAS different. Maisie realized that she was now obliged to get in touch with Hugh, for the sake of the child inside her. And when she admitted this to herself, she felt more glad than frightened. She longed to see him again. All the same, she was nervous as she and April climbed the staircase to the lawyers' rooms.

The clerk in the outer office was a young man who seemed disposed to flirt. "Ladies," he said, "how could two such goddesses have need of the services of Messrs. Goldman and Jay?"

Maisie had no patience with gallantry today. "My name is Maisie Robinson," she said.

"Aha! The advertisement. By a happy chance, the gentleman in question is with Mr. Jay at this very minute."

Maisie felt faint with trepidation. "Tell me something. The gentleman in question . . . Is he by any chance Mr. Hugh Pilaster?"

"Good Lord, no! As a matter of fact, I know Hugh Pilaster. We were at school together in Folkestone. He's gone to America. Took ship a couple of weeks ago."

Maisie was stunned. Gone to America. And she had his child inside her. She was too horrified to cry.

April said aggressively, "Who is it, then?"

The clerk realized he was out of his depth. He said nervously, "I'd better let him tell you himself. Excuse me." He disappeared through an inner door.

When the door opened again, a different man came out. Not much older than Maisie, he had the face of a biblical prophet, with dark eyes staring out from under black eyebrows, a big nose with flaring nostrils, and a bushy beard. He looked familiar, and after a moment she decided he reminded her a little of her father.

"Maisie?" he said. "Don't you recognize me?"

Suddenly she remembered a wire-thin boy with the first shadow of a mustache on his lip. "Oh, good heavens!" she yelped. "Danny!" She ran to his arms. "Danny, is it really you?"

He hugged her so hard it hurt. "Sure, it's me," he said.

"Who?" April was saying. "Who is he?"

"My brother. The one that ran away to America." Maisie stared at him. "What have you been doing for the last seven years?"

"Building railways. It happened I arrived at a good time. The War Between the States had ended, and the railway boom was beginning. They were so desperate for workers that even a skinny thirteen-year-old could get a job. I worked on the first-ever steel bridge, over the Mississippi at St. Louis; then I got a job building the Union Pacific Railroad in Utah and joined a union and led a strike."

"Why did you come back?"

"There's been a stock market crash. The railroads have run out of money, and the banks financing them have gone bust. Thousands of men are looking for work. I decided to make a new start."

"What will you do, build railroads here?"

He shook his head. "I've got a new idea. Twice, my life has been wrecked by a financial crash. The bankers make the same mistakes again and again, and it's the workingmen who suffer. Nobody ever helps them; nobody ever will. They have to help each other. I'm going to start a kind of club for workingmen. They'll pay sixpence a week, and if they're thrown out of work through no fault of their own, the club will pay them while they look for a new job."

Maisie stared at her brother in admiration. The plan was formidably ambitious. But she had thought the same when at the age of thirteen he stowed away on a ship bound for Boston. He had done what he said then, and he probably would now. He said he had led a strike. He seemed to be the kind of person other men would follow.

"What about Papa and Mama?" he said. "Have you seen them?"

Maisie shook her head, and then, surprising herself, she began to cry. Suddenly she felt again the pain of losing her family, a pain she had refused to acknowledge all these years.

Danny put a hand on her shoulder. "I'll go up north and see if I can trace them."

"I hope you find them," Maisie said. "I miss them so much." She caught the eye of April, who was staring at her in astonishment. "I'm so afraid they'll be ashamed of me."

"And why should they?" he said.

"I'm pregnant."

His face reddened. "And not married?"

"No."

"Who is the swine? I'd like to break his neck."

"Shut up, Danny," Maisie said angrily. "You left me alone seven years ago, and you've no business to come back and act as if you own me." He looked abashed, and she went on in a quieter voice. "It doesn't matter. He would have married me, but I didn't want him to, so forget about him. Anyway, he's gone to America."

Danny calmed down. "You can have what money I've got."

"I don't want it." She was sounding ungracious, but she could not help it. "There's no need for you to take care of me, Danny. I managed when I was eleven years old, so I suppose I can now."

3

MICKY Miranda and Papa were in a small eating house in Soho, a few minutes from the Cordovan ministry in Portland Place, where Micky now sat at a writing table for an hour or two every morning, dealing with the minister's mail.

Papa wiped his bowl with a chunk of bread and pushed it aside. "I must explain something to you," he said. "I need rifles to fight the Delabarca family and take over their nitrate mines. But that is only the first step. I plan to become governor of the province."

Governor! Micky had not realized Papa's aspirations were so high.

But Papa had not finished. "When we control the province, we will look to the nation. We will become fervent supporters of President Garcia. You will be his envoy in London. Your brother will become his minister of justice. Your uncles will be generals. And then, when the time is right, we will move the Garcia family aside and step in."

"You mean we will take over the government?" Micky said.

"Yes. In twenty years' time, my son, either I will be president of Cordova . . . or you will."

Papa surprised Micky by his subtle strategy: to become a fervent supporter of the current ruler and then to betray him. And Micky might be president one day. Why not? He was clever, ruthless, and well connected. "President," he said dreamily. "I like it."

Papa reached across the table with both hands and grabbed him by the lapels. "This entire plan has been put at risk because you have completely failed in the small task allotted to you!"

Micky was terrified. "Papa, you'll get your rifles," he said.

"In one more month it will be spring in Cordova. We have to take the Delabarca mines this season. Next year will be too late. I have booked passage on a freighter bound for Panama. The captain has been bribed to put me and the weapons ashore on the Atlantic coast of Santamaria." Papa stood up, dragging Micky upright, tearing his shirt by the force of his grip. "The ship sails in five days' time. Now get out of here and buy me those guns!"

Augusta was alone in the drawing room when Micky arrived. She looked pleased to see him. She held his hand in both of hers.

Normally Micky enjoyed flirting with Augusta, but today he was too desperately worried to dally with her. "How is Seth?" he asked, hoping to hear of a sudden relapse. The old man was quite weak now. He had moved into Augusta's house and spent most days in bed. But he stubbornly refused to resign.

Augusta let go of Micky's hand. "Come close to the fire." She sat on a sofa and patted the seat beside her. "Seth is much better. He may be with us for years yet." She could not keep the irritation out of her voice. "You shall visit him when you have had some tea."

There were voices in the hall. "There's something I must tell you before the others come in," she said. "I met David Middleton. He said he did not believe that the truth about his brother's death had been told, and asked if I could put him in touch with Hugh Pilaster or Antonio Silva. I told him they were abroad."

"I wish we could solve the problem of old Seth as neatly as we solved that one," Micky said as the door opened.

Edward came in, then his sister, Clementine. Augusta poured tea, and Hastead brought in hot buttered muffins. Edward ate several, but Micky had no appetite. More family members arrived—Young William, Madeleine, and her husband, Major Hartshorn.

One by one they went up to visit Seth; one by one they came down and said how marvelous he was. Micky went up last. A nurse sat outside. Micky went in and closed the door.

Seth was sitting up in bed reading *The Economist.* Micky said, "Good afternoon, Mr. Pilaster. How are you feeling?"

The old man put his journal aside with obvious reluctance. "I'm feeling well, I thank you. How is your father?"

"Impatient to be home." Micky stared at the frail old man. The skin of his face was translucent, but there was lively intelligence in the eyes. He looked as if he could run the bank for another decade.

Micky seemed to hear his father's voice in his ear, saying, *"Who is standing in our way?"* Micky's heart filled with loathing.

"What's the matter?" Seth said. "You look sicker than I."

"Are you comfortable?" Micky said. "Let me adjust your pillows."

"Please, don't trouble. They're all right," said Seth. But Micky reached behind Seth and pulled out a big feather pillow.

Micky looked at the old man and hesitated.

Fear flashed in Seth's eyes, and he opened his mouth to call out.

Before he could make a sound, Micky pushed the pillow over his face. Unfortunately, Seth's arms were outside the bedclothes, and now his hands grasped Micky's forearms with surprising strength. Micky stared in horror at the aged talons clamped to his coat sleeves, but he held on with all his might. He suppressed the hysterical laughter that bubbled to his lips.

At last all movement ceased. Micky cautiously removed the pillow and stared at the white, still face. The old man looked dead. Micky lowered his head to Seth's chest to check for a heartbeat. There was none.

A wave of nausea engulfed him. He felt himself shaking with fear and disgust. He grabbed the bedpost to steady himself. I killed him, he thought. I killed him.

There was a voice on the landing. Micky looked at the body on the bed. Seth's dead eyes were open and staring.

The door opened. Augusta walked in. She looked at the still face of Seth and the pillow in Micky's hands. The blood drained from her cheeks.

Micky stared at her, silent and helpless, waiting for her to speak.

Slowly and quietly she closed the door. She took the pillow from Micky. She lifted Seth's lifeless head and replaced the pillow; then she straightened the sheets. She picked up *The Economist* from the floor, placed it on his chest, and folded his hands over it so that he looked as if he had fallen asleep reading it. Then she closed his eyes.

She came to Micky. "You're shaking," she said. She took his face in her hands and kissed his mouth. For a moment he was too stunned to react. Then he put his arms around her and embraced her. They clung together. Micky was too bewildered to think.

Augusta broke away. "This never happened," she said in a fierce whisper. "Do you understand me? *None of it ever happened!*" She smoothed her dress, then turned and went to the door. Automatically he followed her out.

The nurse looked an inquiry at them. Augusta put a finger to her lips. "He's just dropped off to sleep," she said quietly.

"Best thing," said the nurse. "I'll leave him for an hour or so."

Augusta nodded agreement. "I should, if I were you. Believe me, he's quite comfortable now."

PART II

1879

Chapter One: January

1

HUGH returned to London after six years. In that period the Pilasters had doubled their wealth, and Hugh was partly responsible. He had done extraordinarily well in Boston. Transatlantic trade was booming, and Hugh had made sure Pilasters Bank was financing a healthy chunk of that business. He had guided the partners into a series of lucrative issues of North American stocks and bonds. Then he had developed an expertise in the chaotic market for railway stocks. Uncle Joseph had been wary at first, but Hugh's judgment had proved sound. Now Pilasters led the world in raising capital for the industrial development of North America. Hugh was being paid a thousand pounds a year, and he knew he was worth more.

He had told the partners he wanted to come home on furlough to see his mother and sister, but he also had another reason for returning to London. He was about to drop a bombshell: a proposal to merge Pilasters' North American operation with the New York bank of Madler and Bell. It would make a lot of money for the bank, and it would mean the end of his period of exile.

After spending a day with his mother and sister in Folkestone, he took the train to London, then made his way to Pilasters Bank.

They were all waiting for him in the Partners' Room—Uncle Joseph, sitting at the Senior Partner's desk, looking older and balder and more like old Seth; Aunt Madeleine's husband, Major Hartshorn, reading *The Times* beside the fire; Samuel, beautifully dressed as ever in a charcoal-gray double-breasted cutaway jacket, frowning over a contract; and the newest partner, Young William, now thirty-one, sitting at his desk and writing in a notebook.

Hugh shook hands with all of them and accepted a glass of sherry. "Six years ago in this room I sold Sir John Cammel a hundred and ten thousand pounds' worth of Russian government bonds. Pilasters' commission on that sale was more than I've been paid in the eight years I've worked for the bank," he said with a smile.

Joseph said tetchily, "I hope you're not asking for a rise in salary. You're already the highest-paid employee in the entire firm."

"Except the partners," said Hugh.

"Naturally," Joseph snapped.

Hugh perceived that he had got off to a bad start. Too eager, as always, he told himself. Slow down. "I'm not asking for a rise," he said. "However, I do have a proposition to put to the partners."

He gathered his thoughts. His proposition would bring in more business at one stroke than most partners could attract in a year. If they agreed to it, they'd surely make him a partner.

"Boston is no longer the financial center of the United States," he began. "New York's the place now. We really ought to move our office. But there's a snag. I've done a good deal of business in the last six years with the New York house of Madler and Bell. Sidney Madler took me under his wing when I was green. If we moved to New York, we'd be in competition with them."

"Nothing wrong with competition," Major Hartshorn asserted.

"Perhaps. But I've got a better idea. Why not merge our North American operation with Madler and Bell? Set up a joint venture. Call it Madler, Bell, and Pilaster. The new house would deal with all the import-export financing currently done by both houses, and the profits would be shared. I'd handle the business from London."

"I don't like it," said Joseph. "It's just handing over our business to someone else's control."

"But you haven't heard the best part," Hugh said. "All of Madler and Bell's European business, currently distributed among several agents in London, would be handed over to Pilasters."

Joseph grunted in surprise. "That must amount to . . ."

"More than fifty thousand pounds a year in commissions."

Hartshorn said, "Good heavens!"

They were all startled. The prospect was irresistible.

Young William said, "You would supervise the venture from London?"

Hugh saw that William regarded him as a rival. "Why not?" he said. "After all, London is where the money is raised."

"And what would your status be?"

"Mr. Madler and Mr. Bell would expect to deal with a partner."

"You're too young to be a partner," Joseph said immediately.

"I'm twenty-six, Uncle," Hugh said. "You were made a partner when you were twenty-nine."

"Three years is a long time."

"And fifty thousand pounds is a lot of money." Hugh realized he was sounding cocky—a fault he was prone to—and he backed off. "I know you'll want to talk it over. Perhaps I should leave you."

Samuel nodded. "Whether this works out or not, Hugh, you're to be congratulated on a jolly enterprising proposition."

AT FOUR o'clock that afternoon Hugh stood outside Augusta's enormous house in Kensington Gore. Six years of London soot had darkened the red brick and smudged the white stone, but it still had the ship in full sail at the apex of the roof.

It was a house full of memories for him. Here he had suffered Augusta's persecution, punched Edward's nose, and made love to Maisie Robinson. The recollection of Maisie was the most poignant. He had not heard anything of her since that night, but he still thought about her every day of his life.

He crossed the street and knocked on the door. It was opened by Hastead, Augusta's oily butler. "Good afternoon, Mr. Hugh," he said, but his voice was frosty, which indicated that Hugh was still out of favor in this house.

Hugh passed through the lobby and into the hall. There, like a reception committee, stood the three harridans of the Pilaster family: Augusta, her sister-in-law Madeleine, and her daughter Clementine. Augusta, at forty-seven, was as striking as ever. If she was a little heavier than six years ago, she had the height to carry it.

"Well, Hugh," she said, "I trust your foreign experiences have made you a wiser young man."

She was not going to let anyone forget that he had left under a cloud. Hugh replied, "I trust we all grow wiser as we age, Aunt," and he had the satisfaction of seeing her face darken with anger.

Clementine said, "Let me present my fiancé, Sir Harry Tonks."

Hugh shook hands. Hugh did not envy him marriage to Clementine. She had always had a mean streak. "What part of England are you from, Sir Harry?" he asked.

"I've a place in Dorsetshire. Most of my tenants grow hops."

Landed gentry, Hugh concluded. If he has any sense, he will sell his farms and put the money into Pilasters Bank. In fact, Harry did not seem very bright, but he might be biddable. The Pilaster women liked to marry men who would do as they were told.

"Come into the drawing room," Augusta commanded. "Everyone's waiting to see you."

Hugh followed her in. The familiar room, with the French doors leading to the long garden, had been redecorated in a profusion of bold floral patterns. "You've changed this room, Aunt."

Augusta said, "The carpet has to be changed. It's not right."

She was never satisfied, Hugh recalled.

Most of the family were here. Hugh had gone away in disgrace, but he returned a hero. Now they were keen to take a second look.

The first person he shook hands with was his cousin Edward. He was twenty-nine, but he looked older. He was already stout, and his face had the flushed look of a glutton. "So you're back," Edward said. He tried a smile, but it turned into a resentful sneer. Hugh could hardly blame him. Hugh's success drew attention to Edward's lack of achievement at the bank.

Micky stood next to Edward. Still handsome and immaculately dressed, Micky seemed even more self-assured. Hugh said, "Hullo, Miranda. Are you still working for the Cordovan minister?"

"I *am* the Cordovan minister," Micky replied.

Somehow Hugh was not surprised. He moved on and shook hands with Young William and his wife, Beatrice.

Hastead interrupted them to give Hugh an envelope. "This just arrived by messenger," he said. It contained a formal note.

123, PICCADILLY
LONDON, W.
Mrs. Solomon Greenbourne requests the pleasure
of your company at dinner tonight.

Below, in a familiar scrawl, was written, "Welcome home!—Solly." Hugh was pleased. Solly was always amiable and easygoing.

Hastead said, "The messenger is waiting for a reply, Mr. Hugh."

Hugh said, "My compliments to Mrs. Greenbourne, and I shall be delighted to join them for dinner."

Hastead bowed and withdrew. Beatrice said, "My goodness, are you dining with the Solomon Greenbournes? How marvelous!"

Hugh was surprised. "I've always liked Solly, but an invitation to dine with him was never a coveted privilege."

"It is now," said Beatrice. "They're part of the Marlborough set—friends with the Prince of Wales."

"Solly married a fireball," William explained. "Mrs. Greenbourne loves to entertain, and her parties are the best in London."

"Well," said Hugh, "I can't wait to meet Mrs. Greenbourne."

PICCADILLY was a street of palaces. At eight o'clock on a chilly January evening the wide road was hectic with carriages and cabs, the gaslit pavements thronged by men dressed like Hugh, in white tie and tails, and by women in velvet cloaks and fur collars.

Solly's house was just down the street from his father's place and not much smaller. Hugh passed through an imposing doorway, into a vast hall lined with green marble. A butler took his hat, and a footman led him up the staircase to an extravagant drawing room.

Other guests had arrived already, and stood around drinking champagne. Solly detached himself from a group of laughing people to come over. "Pilaster, how are you, for goodness' sake?"

Solly was still fat and bespectacled, and jollier than ever. "I'm very well, thanks, Greenbourne," Hugh said.

"I know. I've been watching your progress. I hope the Pilasters are paying you a fortune. You deserve it."

"And you've become a socialite, they say."

"None of my doing. I got married." He tapped the bare shoulder of a short woman in a green dress. She was facing the other way, but her back was oddly familiar. Solly said to her, "My dear, do you remember my old friend Hugh Pilaster?"

She finished what she was saying to her companions; then she turned slowly, like a door opening into the past, and Hugh's heart stopped as he saw her face.

"I remember him," she said. "How are you, Mr. Pilaster?"

Hugh stared, speechless, at the woman who had become Mrs. Solomon Greenbourne. It was Maisie.

2

AUGUSTA sat at her dressing table and put on the pearls she always wore at dinner parties. Then she took from her open jewelry box the ring Strang had given her thirty years ago. It was in the form of a gold serpent with a diamond head and ruby eyes. She put it on her finger and brushed the raised head against her lips.

She would never be the Countess of Strang; she had accepted

that years ago. But she was determined to have a title. And since Joseph did not have one, she would have to get him one.

She had brooded over the problem for years. Now the time was right. She would begin her campaign tonight over dinner. Among her guests were three people who would play a crucial part in having Joseph made an earl.

He might take the title Earl of Whitehaven, she thought. Whitehaven was the port where the Pilaster family had begun in business, four generations ago. She imagined herself and Joseph entering a grand drawing room as a butler announced, *The Earl and Countess of Whitehaven,* and the thought made her smile.

She knew exactly what she had to do, but all the same she felt uneasy. She would need to be very surefooted tonight. If she had misjudged her people, she would be doomed.

A maid knocked and said, "Mr. Hobbes has arrived, madam."

She put Strang's ring away, got up from her dressing table, and went through the communicating door into Joseph's room. He was dressed for dinner, sitting at the cabinet where he kept his collection of jeweled snuffboxes, looking at one of them in the gaslight. Augusta wondered whether to mention Hugh to him now.

Hugh continued to be a nuisance. Six years ago she thought she had dealt with him once and for all, but he was once again threatening to overshadow Edward. There was talk of his becoming a partner; Augusta could not tolerate that. However, this was not the moment to confront Joseph about Hugh. She wanted him in a good mood for the dinner party.

"Stay up here a few more minutes if you like," she said to him. "Only Arnold Hobbes has arrived."

"Very well, if you don't mind," he said.

It would suit her to have Hobbes alone for a while.

Hobbes was the editor of a political journal called *The Forum.* It generally sided with the Conservative Party, which was now in power. Hobbes was in a curious position. He was powerful because his journal was widely read, yet he did not make much money out of it. The combination was perfectly suited to Augusta's purpose. He had the power to help her, and he might be bought.

She entered the drawing room, and he stood up eagerly to greet her. He was a nervous, quick-witted man, birdlike in his movements. "What mischief have you been at today?" she said playfully.

He peered at her through smeared spectacles. "I've been writing about the City of Glasgow Bank," he said. "It failed a little while ago. Many of the Scottish trade unions have been ruined."

"I seem to remember hearing talk of it," she said. "My husband said the City of Glasgow had been known for years to be unsound."

"I don't understand this," he said excitedly. "People know a bank is no good, yet it is allowed to continue in business until it crashes and thousands of people lose their life savings."

Augusta saw her chance. "Perhaps the worlds of commerce and government are too widely separated."

"It must be so. Better communication between businessmen and statesmen might prevent such catastrophes."

"I wonder. . . ." Augusta hesitated as if considering an idea that had just struck her. "I wonder whether someone such as yourself would consider becoming a director of one or two companies."

He was surprised. "Indeed, I might."

"The rewards are not great—a hundred or two a year." His eyes lit up; that was a lot of money to him. "But the obligations are small. My husband could arrange it, if you were interested. Do think it over, and tell me if you would like me to mention it."

"Very well, I shall."

So far, so good, Augusta thought. But showing him the bait was easy. Now she had to get him on the hook. She said, "And the world of commerce should reciprocate, of course. More businessmen should serve their country in the House of Lords, I feel."

His eyes narrowed, and she guessed that his quick mind was beginning to understand the bargain he was being offered. She developed her theme. "Both Houses of Parliament would benefit from the knowledge of senior businessmen. Yet there is a curious prejudice against a businessman's being elevated to the peerage."

"There is, and it is quite irrational," Hobbes admitted. "Our merchants, manufacturers, and bankers are responsible for the nation's prosperity, much more so than landowners and clergymen, yet it is the latter who are ennobled for their services to the nation."

"You should write an article about the question." She gave him her warmest smile.

There was a long pause; then he said, "Perhaps we should take this up. Closer links between commerce and government."

"Peerages for businessmen," Augusta said.

"And company directorships for journalists," he added.

The rest of the party arrived in a bunch, and Joseph appeared at the same time. A few moments later dinner was announced.

Augusta had arranged for Edward to walk in to dinner with Emily Maple, a shy, pretty girl of nineteen who was with her father—a Methodist minister—and her mother. They hardly fitted in, but Augusta was getting desperate in her search for a suitable bride for Edward. He was now twenty-nine years old and had never shown a spark of interest in any eligible girl. The trouble was, he saw no reason to marry. He enjoyed his life with his male friends—going to his club and so on. Settling down had little appeal. For a while she had assumed this was just a normal phase in a young man's life, but it had gone on too long, and lately she had begun to worry.

On her left at the table, Augusta had placed Michael Fortescue, a personable young man with political aspirations. He was said to be close to the prime minister, Benjamin Disraeli. Fortescue was the second of the three people Augusta needed to help her get Joseph a peerage. As the consommé was served, she smiled warmly at him and said in a low, intimate voice, "When are we going to see you in Parliament?"

"I wish I knew," he said.

"Everyone speaks of you as brilliant," she went on. "Why don't you stand in a by-election?"

"You're very kind, but by-elections are expensive, Mrs. Pilaster, and I am not a wealthy man."

"I didn't know that," she lied. "You should find a sponsor, then."

"A banker, perhaps?" he said in a half-playful, half-wistful tone.

"It's not inconceivable. Mr. Pilaster is keen to take a more active part in government."

"In what way would Mr. Pilaster like to serve the nation—other than by sponsoring a candidate?"

"Perhaps in the House of Lords. Do you think it is possible?" She was enjoying this, and so was he.

"Possible? Certainly. Likely is another question. Shall I inquire?"

"It would be most kind," she said with satisfaction. "And if a suitable by-election should be called . . ."

"You're very good."

She touched his arm. He was a very attractive young man, she thought. She enjoyed plotting with him.

She was feeling good. She had dealt with two of the three key people, and she had not yet slipped.

Throughout the next course Augusta made polite conversation with Lord Morte, who was sitting on her right. It was his wife she wanted to influence, and for that she had to wait until after dinner.

The men stayed in the dining room to smoke, and Augusta took the ladies upstairs to her bedroom. There she got Lady Morte alone for a few minutes. Fifteen years older than Augusta, Harriet Morte was a lady-in-waiting to Queen Victoria. Like Hobbes and Fortescue, she had influence, and Augusta hoped that like them she would be corruptible. Although Lord and Lady Morte had plenty of money, they spent more than they had. Lady Morte's jewelry was magnificent, and Lord Morte believed—against the evidence of forty years—that he had a good eye for a racehorse.

Augusta began: "Mr. Pilaster and I are such admirers of the queen. If ever we could help you with your noble duties, we'd be thrilled."

"How very nice. But what could you possibly do?"

"What do bankers do? They lend." Augusta lowered her voice. "Court life must be cripplingly expensive, I imagine."

Lady Morte stiffened. There was a taboo on talking about money in her class, but Augusta plowed on. "If you were to open an account with Pilasters, there would never be any problems in that area."

Lady Morte hesitated. Her instincts told her to snub Augusta, but greed held her back. Finally she said, "You're very kind."

Augusta had cleared the third hurdle. If she had assessed the woman correctly, Lady Morte would be hopelessly in debt to Pilasters Bank within six months. Then she would find out what Augusta wanted from her.

3

KINGSBRIDGE Manor was one of the largest houses in England. Maisie had stayed there three or four times, and she still had not seen half of it. The young Duke of Kingsbridge, known as Kingo, had owned a hundred thousand acres of Wiltshire farmland. On Solly's advice he had sold half of it and bought a big chunk of South Kensington with the proceeds. Consequently, the agricultural depression that had impoverished many great families had left Kingo untouched, and he was still able to entertain his friends in the grand style.

The Prince of Wales had been with them for the first week. Solly and Kingo and the prince shared a taste for boisterous fun, and Maisie had helped to provide it. She had substituted soapsuds for whipped cream on Kingo's dessert, and she had glued together the pages of *The Times* so that it could not be opened. By hazard, the prince himself had been the first to pick up the newspaper, and as he fumbled with the pages, there had been a moment of suspense when everyone wondered how he would take it. But he began to chuckle as he realized what had happened, and the others all laughed uproariously, from relief as much as amusement.

The prince had left, and Hugh Pilaster arrived—and then the trouble started.

It had been Solly's idea to get Hugh invited here. Solly liked Hugh. Maisie could not think of a plausible reason to object. It had been Solly who asked Hugh to dinner in London, too.

Hugh had recovered from the shock of their meeting, but Maisie had not. She would never forget his expression when he first saw her. He had shown his feelings quite nakedly, and Maisie had been dismayed to see the hurt in his eyes. She had wounded him deeply six years ago, and he had not got over it.

The look on his face had haunted her ever since. She had been upset when she learned he was coming here. She was married to Solly, who was a good husband, and she could not bear the thought of hurting him. And there was Bertie, her reason for living.

Their child was named Hubert, but they called him Bertie, which was also the nickname of the Prince of Wales. Bertie Greenbourne would be five years old on May first, but that was a secret; his birthday was celebrated in September to hide the fact that he had been born only six months after the wedding. Solly's family knew the truth, but no one else did. Bertie had been born in Switzerland during their honeymoon. Since then, Maisie had been happy.

Solly's parents had not welcomed Maisie. They were stiff-necked, snobbish German Jews who had been living in England for generations, and they looked down on Yiddish-speaking Russian Jews just off the boat. The fact that Maisie was carrying another man's child gave them an excuse for rejecting her. However, Solly's sister, Kate, who was about Maisie's age and had a seven-year-old daughter, was nice to Maisie when her parents were not around.

Solly loved Maisie, and he loved Bertie, too, although he did not know whose child he was; and that was enough for Maisie—until Hugh came back.

She got up early as always and went along to the nursery wing of the great house. Bertie was having breakfast with Kingo's children. She kissed his sticky face and said, "What are you having?"

"Porridge with honey." He spoke with the drawling accent of the upper classes—an accent and a manner that Maisie had been at pains to learn and from which she still occasionally slipped.

Anyone with the least instinct for class differences could tell she was not a born lady. However, she played the part so well and she was so pretty and charming that society accepted her.

"I think I'll have some porridge, too," she said, sitting down.

Bertie did not take after Hugh. As a baby, he had resembled Solly—for all babies looked like Solly—and now he was like Maisie's father, with dark hair and brown eyes. She would have liked to have had more children, but something had gone wrong inside her when Bertie was born, and she could not conceive again.

When Maisie returned to their room, Solly was getting ready to go out for a walk. She kissed him and helped him put on his ankle boots. Then she put on a fur coat and hat and he donned a plaid inverness coat with a cape, and they went down to meet the others.

It was a bright, frosty morning. Maisie walked with Kingo on one side of her and Solly on the other. Hugh was behind with Kingo's wife, the duchess. Maisie could feel his presence.

After about half a mile they came to the main gate, and Maisie saw a familiar tall, black-bearded figure approaching from the village. It was her brother, Danny.

Danny had returned to their hometown six years ago to find that their parents no longer lived in the old house and had left no other address. Disappointed, he traveled farther north, to Glasgow, and founded the Working Men's Welfare Association, which not only insured workingmen against unemployment but also campaigned for safety rules in factories. His name started appearing in the newspapers. Papa read about him and came to his office, and there was a joyful reunion. It turned out that Papa and Mama had met other Jews soon after Maisie and Danny ran away. They borrowed money to move to Manchester, where Papa found another job. Mama survived her illness and was now quite healthy.

Maisie was married to Solly by the time the family was reunited.

Solly would cheerfully have given Papa a house and an income for life, but Papa did not want to retire, and instead asked Solly to lend him the money to open a shop. Now Mama and Papa sold caviar and other delicacies to the wealthy citizens of Manchester.

Seeing Danny here at Kingsbridge, Maisie immediately feared something had happened to their parents, and she ran to him, her heart in her mouth, saying, "Danny, what's wrong? Is it Mama?"

"Papa and Mama are fine," he said in his American accent. "I just came to spend a few hours with you."

Danny was dressed like a clerk, in a worn black suit and a bowler hat. Kingo looked at him askance, but Solly rose to the occasion with his usual social grace. He shook Danny's hand and said, "How are you, Robinson? This is my friend the Duke of Kingsbridge. Kingo, allow me to present my brother-in-law Dan Robinson, general secretary of the Working Men's Welfare Association."

"How do you do, Duke," Danny said with easy courtesy.

Then Solly said, "And this is our friend Hugh Pilaster."

Maisie tensed. Danny knew secrets about Hugh that Maisie had never told her husband. He knew that Hugh was Bertie's father, and Danny had once wanted to break Hugh's neck. However, he was six years older now. He shook hands coolly but civilly.

Hugh, who did not know he was a father and had no inkling of these undertones, spoke to Danny in a friendly way. "Are you the brother who ran away from home and went to Boston?"

"I sure am."

Solly said, "Fancy Hugh knowing that!"

Maisie felt bewildered by the conversation; it was skating over the surface of too many secrets, and the ice was thin. She hastened to get back onto firm ground. "Danny, why are you here?"

His face took on an expression of bitterness. "I'm ruined for the third time in my life by incompetent bankers."

"Danny, please!" Maisie protested. He knew perfectly well that both Solly and Hugh were bankers.

But Hugh said, "Don't worry. We hate incompetent bankers, too. What exactly has happened, Mr. Robinson?"

"I spent five years building up the welfare association," Danny said. "It was a big success. We paid out hundreds of pounds every week in benefits and took in thousands in subscriptions. And where do you think we put the surplus?"

Solly said, "In a bank, I trust."

"In the City of Glasgow Bank, to be exact."

"Oh, no!" Maisie cried. It made her want to weep.

Danny nodded. "All those shillings paid in by hardworking men—lost by fools in top hats." He sighed. "I tried to rescue the association, but the task was hopeless."

Kingo said abruptly, "Mr. Robinson, I am sorry for you and your members. Will you take some refreshment? You must have walked seven miles if you came from the railway station."

"I will, and thank you."

Maisie said, "I'll take Danny indoors and leave you to finish your walk." She felt her brother was wounded, and she wanted to get him alone and do what she could to ease his pain.

The others obviously felt the tragedy, too. Kingo said, "Will you stop for the night, Mr. Robinson?"

Maisie winced. Kingo was being too generous. It was easy enough to be civil to Danny for a few minutes out here in the park, but if he stayed overnight, Kingo and his lotus-eating friends would soon get fed up with Danny's coarse clothes and working-class concerns; then they would snub him, and he would be hurt.

But Danny said, "I have to be back in London tonight. I just came to spend a few hours with my sister."

Kingo said, "In that case, allow me to have you driven to the station in my carriage whenever you're ready."

"That's real kind of you."

Maisie took her brother's arm. "Come. I'll get you some lunch."

AFTER Danny left for London, Maisie joined Solly for an afternoon nap. Solly lay on the bed in a red silk bathrobe.

"I can't rescue Dan's welfare association," he said as he watched her undress. "Even if it made financial sense to me—which it doesn't—I couldn't persuade the other partners."

Maisie felt a surge of affection for him. She had not asked him to help Danny. "You've already done so much for my family, you never have to apologize. Besides, Danny won't take anything from you. He's too proud."

"But what will he do?"

Maisie stepped out of her petticoats. "Tomorrow Danny is meeting with the Amalgamated Society of Engineers. He wants to be a member of Parliament, and he hopes that they will sponsor him."

Solly rolled on his side and propped his head up on his elbow to get a better view of his wife. "I wish I weren't leaving you tonight."

Maisie wished the same. A part of her was excited at the prospect of being with Hugh when Solly was away, but that made her feel more guilty still. "I don't mind," she said.

"I feel so ashamed of my family."

"You shouldn't." It was Passover, and Solly was going home to celebrate the ritual seder with his parents. Maisie was not invited. She understood Ben Greenbourne's dislike of her and half felt she deserved the way he treated her, but Solly was deeply upset by it.

"Are you sure you don't mind?" he said anxiously.

"I'm sure. Listen, if I felt strongly about it, I could go to Manchester and spend Passover with my own parents." She became thoughtful. "The fact is that I've never felt part of all that Jewish stuff—not since we left Russia. When we came to England, there were no Jews in the town. Even when I married a Jew, your family made me feel unwelcome. I'm fated to be an outsider."

"I'll miss you tonight," he said.

She sat on the bed and leaned over to kiss him. "I'll miss you, too."

THEY were eighteen around the long dinner table that evening. Maisie found herself seated next to Hugh, and as the meal progressed, she felt his presence more and more. She made an effort to keep the conversation light, and took care to talk as much to the man on her other side, but the past seemed to stand at her shoulder waiting to be acknowledged. They had never spoken of what had happened six years ago. All Hugh knew was that she had disappeared without a trace, only to surface as Mrs. Solomon Greenbourne. Sooner or later she was going to have to give him some explanation.

A moment came when several people around them were talking noisily. Maisie decided she should speak now. She turned to Hugh. "I would have ruined your career, you know."

He understood what she was talking about. "Who told you that?"

"Your aunt Augusta. And she was right."

"You didn't ruin Solly's career," he said, suddenly angry.

"Even so, it was difficult enough. His family hate me still."

"Why didn't you simply tell me what you were doing and why?"

"I couldn't." Remembering those awful days, she felt choked up.

"It broke my heart to cut myself off like that. I couldn't have done it if I'd had to justify myself to you as well."

Still he would not let her off the hook. "You could have sent me a note. It was awful not knowing, not understanding."

"I'm sorry," she said feebly. "I didn't want to hurt you. I wanted to save you from unhappiness. I did it for love." As soon as she heard herself say the word love, she regretted it.

He picked up on it. "Do you love Solly now?" he said abruptly.

"Yes. The way we live . . . it isn't difficult to be contented."

He had not finished being angry. "You got what you wanted."

That was hard, but she felt she deserved it, so she just nodded.

"What happened to April?" he asked.

This was going too far. "You class me with April, do you?"

He smiled ruefully. "No. You were never like April. All the same, I'd like to know what became of her. Do you still see her?"

"Yes—discreetly." April was a neutral topic that would get them off emotional ground. "Do you know a place called Nellie's?"

He lowered his voice. "It's a brothel."

"Well, April owns it."

"Goodness! How did that happen?"

"First she became the mistress of a famous novelist and lived in a little cottage in Clapham. He tired of her at about the time Nell was thinking about retirement. So April sold the cottage and bought Nell out."

"Fancy that," said Hugh.

The table had suddenly gone quiet, and his words were heard by several people nearby. Someone said, "Fancy what?" Hugh just grinned and made no reply.

When dinner was over, Kingo announced that he wanted to dance. The drawing-room carpet was rolled up, and a footman who could play polkas on the piano was summoned and set to work.

Maisie danced with everyone except Hugh; then it was obvious she was avoiding him, so she danced with him, and it was as if six years had rolled back and they were in Cremorne Gardens again. He hardly led her; they seemed instinctively to do the same thing.

Afterwards the duchess suggested they all take a turn around the garden. Out in the darkness, Maisie took Hugh's arm. She was interested in what he had been doing for the past six years. "In Boston . . . was there a girl you liked?"

"I tried, Maisie," he said. "There were girls in Boston who would make wonderful wives and mothers. I paid attention to some of them. But when it came to the point where I had to make a proposal or back off, I realized each time that what I felt was not enough. It was not what I felt for you. It wasn't love."

Now he had said it. "Stop," Maisie whispered.

"Two or three mothers got rather cross with me. Then my reputation spread around, and the girls became wary. They knew I wasn't serious. And if a girl did fall for me, I would discourage her. I don't like to break people's hearts. I know too well what it feels like."

Her face was wet with tears, and she was glad of the tactful dark.

"Anyway, I know what's wrong with me now. I guess I always knew, but the last two days have removed any doubts."

They had fallen behind the others, and now he stopped and faced her. "I still love you."

It was out, and everything was ruined, her happiness destroyed.

"I think you love me, too," he went on mercilessly. "Don't you?"

She looked up at him. He inclined his head and kissed her lips, and she did not turn away. "Salt tears," he said. "You do love me. I knew it." He mopped her face gently with his handkerchief.

She had to put a stop to this. "We must catch up with the others," she said. "People will talk." She turned and began to walk.

When they reentered the house, the tall clock in the hall was striking midnight. Maisie suddenly felt drained by the tensions of the day. "I'm going to bed," she announced.

She saw the duchess look reflexively at Hugh, then back at her, and suppress a little smile; and Maisie realized they all thought Hugh would sleep with her tonight. The ladies went upstairs together, leaving the men to drink a nightcap.

Maisie went into her bedroom and closed the door. They might all be wrong; perhaps Hugh would not come to her tonight. The thought stabbed her like a pain.

After a while she heard the men coming up the stairs, heavy-footed and laughing at some joke. None of them would be shocked by a little adultery at a country-house party. Did they not feel disloyal to their friend Solly? she thought derisively. And then it hit her that she was the one who ought to feel disloyal.

She had put Solly out of her mind all evening, but now he came back to her in spirit. Kind, generous Solly—the man who loved her to distraction, the man who cared for Bertie, knowing he was another man's child. Now Maisie was about to let another man come into her bed. What kind of woman am I? she thought.

The idea of forgoing this night with Hugh made her want to weep. But she went to the door and locked it.

A moment later there was a soft tap.

"Maisie," a voice called softly. "It's me, Hugh. Let me in."

She leaned her back against the wall, and the tears streamed down her face, dripping off her chin.

"At least let us talk!"

She knew that if she opened the door, there would be no talking; she would take him in her arms in a frenzy of desire.

"Say something. Are you there? I know you're there."

She stood still, crying silently.

After a while he went away.

4

THE Cordovan ministry was busy. Tomorrow was Cordovan Independence Day, and there would be a big reception for members of Parliament, diplomats, and journalists. But when Edward Pilaster arrived, Micky Miranda dropped everything. Micky needed half a million pounds, and he was hoping to get the money from Edward.

Micky brought Edward into the minister's chamber and spread out a map of Cordova on the table. "Here is Santamaria Province, in the north of the country," he began.

"I do know the geography of Cordova," Edward said peevishly.

"Of course you do," said Micky in a soothing voice. Pilasters Bank did a healthy volume of business with Cordova, financing its exports of nitrate, salt beef, and silver and its imports of mining equipment, guns, and luxury goods. Edward handled all that, thanks to Micky, and he was now the leading London expert on Cordova. "And you know that all the nitrate mined by my father has to be transported to Palma by mule train. But what you may not know is that it is possible to build a railroad along the route." Micky took a bound volume from his desk. "We commissioned a survey. The details are in here, including costs. Take a look."

"How much?" Edward said.

"Five hundred thousand pounds."

Edward riffled through the report. "What about politics?"

Micky glanced up at the big portrait of President Garcia on the wall. "The president favors the idea." Ever since Papa had become governor of Santamaria Province—with the help of two thousand Westley Richards rifles—the Mirandas had been the president's close allies. Garcia did not suspect Papa's motive for wanting a railway to Palma: it would enable the Mirandas to attack the capital within two days instead of two weeks.

"How will it be paid for?" said Edward.

"We'll raise the money on the London market," Micky said. "I thought Pilasters Bank might like to have the business."

Edward shook his head. "Cordova isn't the same as Canada or Russia. Investors don't like your political setup, with every provincial caudillo having his own personal army."

Micky fought down panic. "Surely if a bank with the prestige of Pilasters were to back the project, people would conclude that Cordova must be a good place to invest."

"If one of the partners really wanted to push it through, it could probably be done," Edward said. "But I'm not a partner."

Micky had underestimated the difficulty of raising half a million pounds. But he was not beaten. He would find a way.

That night Micky and the Pilasters went to see *H.M.S. Pinafore* at the Opera Comique. Micky got there a few minutes early. While he was waiting in the foyer, he ran into the Bodwin family, who were Pilaster hangers-on. Albert Bodwin was a lawyer who did a lot of work for the bank, and Augusta had once tried to get the daughter, Rachel Bodwin, to marry Hugh.

Micky's mind was on the problem of raising the money for the railroad, but he flirted with Rachel Bodwin automatically. She was not exactly pretty, but she had a good figure—long legs, a narrow waist, and a deep bust. She was attracted to him, but then so was almost everyone—old and young, male and female. Micky liked it when rich and influential people fell for him, for it gave him power. But Rachel was nobody, and her interest in him was valueless.

The Pilasters arrived, and Micky turned his attention to Augusta. She was wearing a striking evening gown in deep raspberry-pink. "You look . . . delicious, Mrs. Pilaster," he said, and she smiled with pleasure. Then it was time to take their seats in their box.

Micky worried over his railroad loan throughout the first act. It had not occurred to him that Cordova's primitive political setup might be seen by investors as risky. That meant he could not get the railroad project financed by any other bank. The only way to raise the money would be to use his inside influence with Pilasters.

During the first interval he found himself alone in the box with Augusta for a few moments, and he tackled her immediately. "When will Edward be made a partner in the bank?"

"That's a sore point," she said sourly. "My husband has promised to make Edward a partner as soon as he marries. We have even agreed on a bride—Emily Maple, the daughter of Deacon Maple. But somehow Edward never quite gets around to asking her."

This did not surprise Micky. He could not imagine Edward's marrying, no matter how suitable the girl. But now there was an incentive: the partnership. Even if Edward did not care about that, Micky did. "What can we do to encourage him?"

Augusta gave Micky a sharp look and said, "I have a funny feeling that he might go ahead if you were married."

Micky looked away. That was perceptive of her. He, too, felt that if he married first, Edward might be more willing. "Me marry?" he said with a little laugh. Naturally, he would marry sooner or later, but he saw no reason to do so yet.

However, if it was the price of financing the railroad . . .

Throughout the next act Micky thought about Edward. They had been friends for fifteen years. Edward was weak and insecure, eager to please but without initiative or drive. His life's project was to get people to encourage and support him. Now Edward needed to be pushed into a marriage that was necessary for his career—and for Micky's.

During the second interval Micky said to Augusta, "Edward needs someone to help him at the bank—a clever clerk to look after his interests."

Augusta thought for a moment. "That's a very good notion indeed," she said. "Do you have someone in mind?"

"I have a cousin working for me at the ministry—Simon Oliver. It was Olivera, but he anglicized it. He's completely trustworthy."

"Bring him to tea," Augusta said. "If I like the looks of him, I'll speak to Joseph."

The last act began. He and Augusta often thought alike, Micky mused. It was Augusta he should be married to; together they could conquer the world. He pushed that fantastic notion out of his head. Who was he going to marry? She should not be an heiress, for he had nothing to offer such a girl. No, he needed a girl of modest background, one who liked him already and would accept him with alacrity. His eye roamed idly around the stalls of the theater—and lit on Rachel Bodwin.

An hour later Micky and Edward were eating supper in a private room at Nellie's, served by two women. Apart from the table, the room contained a sofa, a wardrobe, a washstand, and a big bed. April Tilsley had redecorated the place, but already the wallpaper was torn and the carpet ripped. However, low candlelight hid the tawdriness of the room.

Micky looked across the table at Edward. Theirs had been a fruitful friendship, he mused. There were times when he felt almost fond of Edward. He had helped Edward, Edward had helped him, and together they had enjoyed all the vices of the most sophisticated city in the world.

When they finished eating, Micky poured another glass of wine and said, "I'm going to marry Rachel Bodwin."

Edward stared at him. "I don't believe it."

Micky shrugged. "It's true, all the same."

"You swine!"

Micky stared at his friend in surprise. "What the devil has got into you?" he said. "Aren't you going to marry Emily Maple?"

"I'm not marrying anyone!" Edward roared, and he overturned the table. Micky sprang back as crockery smashed and wine spilled. The two women cringed away.

Micky was baffled by Edward's fury. He had to calm the man. "It's not a disaster," he said in a reasonable tone. "It's not going to make any difference to us. We'll still come here."

Edward looked suspicious. In a quieter voice he said, "Will we?"

"Yes. When we are first married, we should spend a few evenings at home and give the occasional dinner party. But after a while we'll go right back to normal."

"So nothing will change," Edward said with a foolish grin.

"Oh, yes," said Micky. "One thing will change. You'll be a partner in the bank."

Chapter Two: April

1

THE music hall was as hot as a Turkish bath. The air smelled of beer and shellfish. Onstage, a woman in rags was holding a doll, to represent a newborn baby, and singing about how she had been seduced and abandoned. The audience, sitting at long trestle tables, joined in the chorus, *"And all it took was a little drop of gin!"*

Hugh sang at the top of his voice. He had drunk several glasses of warm beer, and he was pressed up against Nora Dempster, a pleasant person to be squashed by. She had a soft, plump body and a beguiling smile, and she had probably saved his life.

After his visit to Kingsbridge Manor he had fallen into a black depression. Seeing Maisie had raised old ghosts, and since she rejected him again, the ghosts had haunted him without respite.

He had been able to live through the daytime, for work took his mind off his grief. He was busy organizing the joint enterprise with Madler and Bell, which the Pilasters partners had finally approved. And he was soon to become a partner himself. But in the evenings he had no enthusiasm for anything. He sat in his rooms thinking about Maisie, or walked the streets hoping to bump into her.

Instead he had bumped into Nora as she was coming out of a store in Oxford Street one Saturday afternoon. She stumbled, and he caught her in his arms. Then she dropped her purchase—a pottery vase—and it smashed on the pavement. She gave a cry of dismay. Hugh naturally insisted on buying a replacement.

She had a pretty, round face, with sandy-blond curls poking out from a bonnet, and her clothes were cheap but pleasing—a pink wool dress embroidered with flowers and worn over a bustle, and a tight-fitting French navy velvet jacket trimmed with rabbit fur. She spoke with a broad cockney drawl.

After buying the replacement vase, Hugh had taken her home in a hansom. She lived with her father, a traveling salesman of patent medicines. Her mother was dead. The neighborhood was poor working class rather than middle class.

Hugh had assumed he would never see her again, and all day Sunday he had brooded about Maisie. On Monday at the bank, he had got a note from Nora, thanking him for his kindness. Her handwriting was small and neat, he had noticed before discarding the note.

Next day he had stepped out of the bank for lunch and saw her walking toward him. He had doffed his hat, and she had stopped to talk. She worked as an assistant to a corset maker, she had told him with a blush, and she was on her way to the shop after visiting a client. A sudden impulse had made him ask her to go dancing that night.

She said she would like to go, but she did not have a respectable hat, so he took her to a milliner's shop and bought her one.

Much of their romance was conducted while shopping. She had never owned much, and she took delight in Hugh's affluence.

Maisie did not disappear from his mind. He still thought of her every day, but the memories no longer plunged him into despair. He had something to look forward to now—his next rendezvous with Nora. In a few weeks she had given him back his *joie de vivre.*

On one of their shopping expeditions they met Maisie in a furrier's store in Bond Street. Feeling rather bashful, Hugh introduced the two women. Nora was bowled over to meet Mrs. Solomon Greenbourne. Maisie invited them to tea at the Piccadilly house. That evening Hugh saw Maisie again at a ball, and to his surprise Maisie was quite ungracious about Nora. "I'm sorry, but I don't like her," Maisie had said. "She strikes me as a hard-hearted, grasping woman, and I don't believe she loves you one bit."

Hugh had been hurt and offended; Maisie was just jealous, he decided.

Now, when the music-hall show ended, they went outside into a fog and set off for Nora's home in Camden Town. In the thick fog all sound was muffled and people loomed without warning—a drunk staggering out of a pub, a policeman on patrol. Hugh and Nora held hands and stopped every now and again to kiss. The fog made everything hushed and secret and romantic.

Hugh had not felt so good for years. He realized he had been alone too long. Maisie was thoroughly settled with Solly; she would never be his. It was time he had someone warm and soft to share his bed and his life. Why not Nora?

He took her hand. "Nora, will you marry me?"

She went slightly pale. "Do you mean it?"

He asked himself the same question. From the start he had thought of this as a dalliance, not a serious courtship. Yet now he realized that he would like nothing better than to spend the rest of his life with Nora. There would be trouble, of course; the family would say he was marrying beneath him. They could go to the devil. He was twenty-six years old, he earned a thousand pounds a year, and he was about to be made a partner in one of the most prestigious banks in the world. He could marry whom he liked.

He looked at Nora, pink and pretty and lovable. He kissed her, and she kissed him back passionately.

2

THE Duchess of Tenbigh's costume ball was the first great event of the 1879 London season. Everyone was talking about it weeks in advance, and people would go to any length to get an invitation.

Augusta and Joseph Pilaster were not invited. That was hardly surprising; they did not belong in the very highest echelon of London society. But Augusta wanted to go, and she mentioned it to Harriet Morte, who looked embarrassed and said nothing. As a lady-in-waiting to the queen, Lady Morte had great social power, but she did not offer to get Augusta invited.

Augusta checked Lord Morte's account with Pilasters Bank and found that he had an overdraft of a thousand pounds. The next day he got a note asking him when he hoped to regularize the account. Augusta called on Lady Morte the same day. She apologized, saying that the note had been an error and the clerk who sent it had been sacked; then she mentioned the ball again.

Lady Morte's normally impassive face was momentarily animated by a glare of hatred. She knew she must exert her influence to get Augusta invited to the ball or find a thousand pounds to pay off her overdraft. The invitations arrived the following day.

Augusta was going as Queen Elizabeth, and Joseph as the Earl of Leicester. On the night of the ball they had dinner at home and changed afterwards. When she was dressed, Augusta went into Joseph's room to help him dress and talk to him about Hugh.

She was incensed that Hugh was to be made a partner at the same time as Edward. Worse, everyone knew that Edward had been made a partner only because he had married and been given a two-hundred-fifty-thousand-pound investment in the bank, whereas Hugh had brought off a spectacularly profitable deal with Madler and Bell of New York.

Their promotion was to take place at the end of April, but earlier in the month, to Augusta's delight, Hugh made the unbelievably foolish mistake of marrying a plump little working-class girl. Clearly he had a weakness for girls from the gutter.

As Augusta adjusted Joseph's Elizabethan ruff, she said, "I presume you'll have to think again about Hugh's being made a partner. A partner can hardly have a shopgirl as a wife. She will embarrass him. She won't know how to act."

"She can learn." He hesitated, then added, "I sometimes think you forget your own background, my dear."

Augusta was outraged. "I never worked in my father's shops," she said. "I was brought up to be a lady."

The ball began at half past ten, and the Pilasters arrived with Edward and Emily in tow. There was already a queue from the hall up the curving staircase to the landing where the Duke and Duchess of Tenbigh, dressed as Solomon and Sheba, were greeting their guests. The hall was a mass of flowers, and a band played.

The Pilasters were followed in by Micky Miranda—invited because of his diplomatic status—and his new wife, Rachel. Micky looked more dashing than ever in a Cardinal Wolsey outfit.

Up ahead of them Augusta spotted another pair of newlyweds, Hugh and Nora. Because of his friendship with the Greenbournes, Hugh was invited everywhere. He was dressed as an Indian raja, and Nora as a snake charmer, in a sequined gown cut to reveal harem trousers. Artificial snakes were wound around her arms and legs, and one laid its papier-mâché head on her ample bosom.

Augusta shuddered. "Hugh's wife really is impossibly vulgar," she murmured to Joseph. "I just don't think she's fit to be the wife of a partner in Pilasters Bank."

"Nora won't have to make any financial decisions."

Augusta could have screamed with frustration. Nora would have to do something unforgivable before Joseph and his partners would turn against Hugh. Now, there was a thought. Augusta's anger died down. Perhaps there was a way she could get Nora into trouble.

She looked up the stairs again and studied her prey. Nora and Hugh were talking to the Hungarian attaché, Count de Tokoly, a man of doubtful morals, who was appropriately dressed as Henry VIII. Nora was just the kind of girl the count would be charmed by, Augusta thought biliously.

"Nora is talking to Count de Tokoly," Augusta murmured to Joseph. "She had better take care of her reputation."
"Now, don't you be rude to him," Joseph replied brusquely. "We're hoping to raise two million pounds for his government."
Augusta continued to brood. If Nora could be brought to disgrace herself tonight, preferably in front of the Prince of Wales . . .
Just then the royal party arrived. The band stopped in the middle of a waltz and struck up the national anthem. All the guests bowed and curtsied as the Prince of Wales and Princess Alexandra, dressed as King Arthur and Queen Guinevere, came up the staircase. At the top of the stairs, the duke and duchess welcomed their royal guests.
Inside the ballroom, the prince and princess moved to a dais. It had been arranged that some of the more spectacular costumes should pass in front of the royal party in procession. A crush formed near the dais, and Augusta found herself shoulder to shoulder with Count de Tokoly.
"What a delightful girl your nephew's wife is, Mrs. Pilaster," he said. "I shall ask her to dance. Do you think she will accept?"
Augusta could not resist an acid retort. "I am sure of it. She is not fastidious." She turned away. No doubt it was too much to hope that Nora would cause some kind of incident with the count.
Augusta was suddenly inspired. The count and Nora—the combination could be explosive. She looked around, spotted Micky, and went over to him. "I want you to do something for me," she said. "Do you know Count de Tokoly?"
"Indeed. All we diplomats know one another."
"Tell him that Nora is no better than she ought to be."
Micky's mouth curled in a smile. "You know what he will do?"
"I trust he will make an indecent suggestion to her."
Micky nodded. "I am your slave, in this as in all things."
Augusta waved the compliment aside impatiently. She looked for Nora and saw her staring in wonderment at the lavish decor. Without further reflection Augusta made her way through the crowd to Nora's side and spoke into her ear. "A word of advice."
"Much obliged for it, I'm sure," Nora said.
Augusta said, "I noticed you talking to Count de Tokoly. Be careful. If you value your reputation, don't let him take any liberties. If he is not set straight immediately, he can be very embarrassing."
Nora nodded. "Don't worry. I know how to deal with his type."

Hugh was standing nearby talking to the Duke of Kingsbridge. Now he noticed Augusta. He looked at her suspiciously and came to his wife's side. Augusta turned away to watch the procession. She had done her work; the seeds were planted.

Passing in front of the prince were some of the Marlborough set, including Solly and Maisie Greenbourne. They were dressed as Eastern potentates, and instead of bowing and curtsying, they knelt and salaamed, which drew a laugh from the portly prince.

The procession ended. The band struck up a waltz. The prince led the duchess onto the floor, and the duke took the princess. Others rapidly followed suit, and suddenly Micky was at Augusta's side asking her to dance.

As soon as she was in his arms, it was like being seventeen again and dancing with Strang. She felt young and beautiful and carefree. Then Micky said, "Look over there."

She followed the direction of his nod and saw Nora dancing with Count de Tokoly. "Did you speak to him?"

"I did."

She tensed. "Let's get closer," she said.

It was not easy, for the royal group was in that corner, but Micky skillfully steered her through the crush. So far Nora and the count looked like any other dancing couple. He made occasional remarks; she nodded and smiled. Augusta was just wondering whether she had misjudged her victims when the explosion came.

Augusta was the only person to see how it started. The count put his lips close to Nora's ear and spoke. She stopped dancing abruptly and pushed him away. The count spoke again, his face creasing with a lascivious grin. At that second the music stopped, and in the momentary silence that followed, Nora slapped him.

The smack sounded throughout the ballroom like a gunshot. It was the kind of blow that would deter a drunk in a saloon bar. The count staggered back—and bumped into the Prince of Wales.

There was a collective gasp from the people around. In the horrified silence Nora's cockney accent rang out loud and clear: "Don't you ever come near me again, you filthy old reprobate!"

For a second they formed a still tableau—the outraged woman, the humiliated count, and the startled prince. Then Hugh appeared at Nora's side. The count drew himself up and stalked out.

Augusta looked triumphantly at Micky.

"Brilliant," he murmured with real admiration. "You're brilliant, Augusta." He squeezed her arm and led her off the dance floor.

Joseph was waiting for her. "That wretched girl!" he expostulated. "She's brought disgrace on the family and lost us a major contract, too!"

It was just the reaction Augusta had hoped for. "Now perhaps you'll believe that Hugh can't be made a partner," she said.

"You're right, my dear. You've been right all along."

Hugh was steering Nora to the door. "We're leaving, of course," he said as they passed.

"We'll all have to leave now," Augusta said. However, she did not want them to go immediately. If no more was said tonight, there was a danger that tomorrow, when people cooled off, they might say that the incident was not as bad as it had seemed. Augusta wanted a row now—hot tempers, angry words, accusations that could not easily be forgotten. She put a detaining hand on Nora's arm. "I tried to warn you about Count de Tokoly," she said accusingly.

Hugh said, "When such a man insults a lady on the dance floor, there isn't much she can do other than cause a scene."

"Don't be ridiculous," Augusta snapped. "Any well-bred young girl would have said she felt unwell, and sent for her carriage."

"Heaven knows the damage you've done to the family and the bank tonight," Joseph said to Hugh. "We've certainly lost the Hungarian account, and we'll never again be invited to a royal event."

Hugh spoke with controlled fury. "Let me get this straight. A Pilaster wife must suffer insult rather than jeopardize a business deal, is that your philosophy?"

Joseph was mightily offended. "You insolent pup," he raged. "What I'm saying is that by marrying beneath yourself, you have disqualified yourself from ever becoming a partner in the bank."

He said it! Augusta thought jubilantly. He said it!

Hugh was jolted into silence. Unlike Augusta, he had not thought ahead. Now the significance of what had happened was sinking in.

"So that's it." Hugh looked at Augusta. "Very well, you win. I don't know how it was done, but I've no doubt you provoked this incident." He turned to Joseph. "But you ought to reflect on it, Uncle Joseph. Think about who genuinely cares for the bank"—he looked again at Augusta—"and who are its real enemies."

3

THE news of Hugh's fall spread around the City in hours. By the following afternoon, people who had clamored to see him with moneymaking schemes for railways, shipyards, and suburban housing were canceling their appointments. Within the Partners' Room there was a row. Samuel had been indignant when Joseph announced that Hugh could not be made a partner. However, Young William had sided with his brother Joseph, and Major Hartshorn did the same, so Samuel was outvoted.

Hugh's resentment grew inside him like cancer, but he now had a wife and a new house to support, so he had to stay on at the bank.

On the second Monday after the Duchess of Tenbigh's ball, Hugh met a stranger in the office. He was a dark-haired man of about twenty-one. Hugh smiled and said, "Hullo. Who are you?"

"Simon Oliver, Mr. Edward's clerk," he said in a Spanish accent.

Hugh made a connection. "Are you from South America?"

"Yes. Cordova."

That made sense. As Edward's specialty was South America in general, and Cordova in particular, it could be useful to have a native of that country to work with him. "I was at school with the Cordovan minister, Micky Miranda," Hugh said.

"He is my cousin."

"Ah. Well, I hope you enjoy working with us."

Hugh was thoughtful as he returned to his office. Edward needed all the help he could get, but Hugh was a little bothered at having a cousin of Micky's in such a potentially influential position.

His unease was vindicated a few days later. Jonas Mulberry told him what was going on in the Partners' Room. "I don't like it, Mr. Hugh," he said. "South American bonds have never been good."

"We're not launching a South American bond, are we?"

Mulberry nodded. "Mr. Edward proposed it, and the partners agreed. It's for a new railroad from the capital city, Palma, to Santamaria Province."

Hugh shook his head. "Investors who like railroads can get six percent on their money in the States. Why go to Cordova?"

"Exactly."

"I'll try to find out what their thinking is," Hugh said.

Only Samuel and Joseph were in the Partners' Room when Hugh came in. He put a report on Samuel's table.

"Thank you." Samuel looked up. "Something on your mind?"

"Yes. I wonder why we're backing the Santamaria railroad."

Samuel said, "Your uncle Joseph feels South America may be ready for revival."

Hearing his name, Joseph joined in. "This is a toe dipped into the water to feel the temperature."

Hugh frowned. His instinct had been right: the investment did not make commercial sense, and Joseph could not justify it. So why had they done it? As soon as he put the question that way, he saw the answer. "You've done it for Edward, haven't you?"

"It's not your place to question my motives," said Joseph.

"It's not your place to risk other people's money as a favor to your son. Small investors will put up the money for this railroad, and they will lose everything if it fails."

Uncle Joseph was now beyond civility. "Don't you dare stand here in my bank and lecture me, you insolent whippersnapper."

Hugh stared at his uncle for a long moment. Then, boiling with frustration, he turned and left the room, slamming the door.

Ten minutes later he went to ask Solly Greenbourne for a job. He was not certain Greenbournes would take him on. Bankers felt it was not quite gentlemanly to pirate top managers from their rivals. But Hugh was an asset any bank would covet. They made him an offer that very morning.

WHEN Hugh got back to Pilasters Bank, there was a note waiting for him. It read:

> 10:30 a.m.
> My dear Pilaster,
> I must see you right away. You will find me in Plage's Coffee House around the corner. I will wait for you.
> Your old friend, Antonio Silva

So Tonio was back! He had left the country in disgrace at about the same time as Hugh. What had happened to him since? Full of curiosity, Hugh went straight to the coffeehouse. He found an older, shabbier, more subdued Tonio sitting in a corner. He still had a shock of carrot-colored hair, but otherwise there was nothing left of the mischievous schoolboy. Although he was only twenty-six, there were tiny lines of worry around his eyes.

"I made a big success of Boston," Hugh said in answer to Tonio's first question. "I came back in January. But now I'm having trouble with my family all over again. How about you?"

"There have been a lot of changes in my country. My family is not as influential as it once was. The Mirandas are now the favorites of President Garcia. They took over the nitrate mines in the north, and that has made them rich." Tonio took a sheaf of papers from inside his coat. "Read this. It's an article I've written."

The article described conditions at a Miranda nitrate mine. Because the trade was financed by Pilasters Bank, Tonio held the bank responsible for the ill-treatment of the miners. At first Hugh was unmoved; long hours, poor wages, and child labor were features of mines all over the world. But as he read on, he saw this was worse. At the Miranda mines the overseers were armed with whips and guns. Laborers—including women and children—were flogged for being too slow, and if they tried to leave before they had worked out their contracts, they could be shot. Tonio had eyewitness accounts.

Hugh was horrified that his family's bank was financing such a brutal industry, but he tried to put aside his feelings and think about consequences. The article was just the kind of material *The Times* liked to publish. There would be speeches in Parliament and letters in the weekly journals. It would be bad for the bank.

Do I care? thought Hugh. The bank had treated him badly, and he was about to leave it. But he owed Pilasters his loyalty until then. The fact that Tonio was showing him the article before publishing it suggested he wanted to make a deal. "What's your objective?" Hugh asked. "Do you want us to stop financing the nitrate trade?"

Tonio shook his head. "If Pilasters pulled out, another bank would take over. No. We must be more subtle. The Mirandas are planning a railway. It will make Papa Miranda the most powerful man in the country. I want the railway stopped."

"And that's why you're going to publish this article."

"Several articles. And I'll make speeches, lobby members of Parliament—whatever it takes to undermine the financing of this railway."

It might work, too, Hugh thought. Investors would shy away from anything controversial. "So why have you come to me?"

"We could shortcut the process. If the bank decides not to underwrite the railway bonds, I won't publish the article."

"I admire your spirit," said Hugh. "But the consequences for the bank don't affect me. I'm about to resign."

"Really." Tonio was astonished. "Why?"

"It's a long story. I'll tell you another time. However, the upshot is that all I can do is tell the partners about your proposition." He was still holding Tonio's manuscript. "May I keep this?"

"Yes. I have a copy."

The sheets of paper bore the letterhead of the Hotel Russe, Berwick Street, Soho. It was not one of London's fancy establishments. "I'll let you know what the partners say."

Hugh left the coffeehouse and walked back to the bank. In the Partners' Room, he found Samuel, Joseph, and Edward. He handed Tonio's article to Samuel, who read it and passed it on to Edward.

Edward became apoplectic with rage. He pointed his finger at Hugh. "You've cooked this up with your old school friend. You're trying to undermine our South American business! You're just jealous of me, because you weren't made a partner!"

Hugh sighed. "The question is whether the bank wants to be responsible for increasing the power of Papa Miranda, a man who apparently thinks nothing of murdering children."

"I don't believe that," Edward said. "The Silva family are enemies of the Mirandas. This is just malicious propaganda."

"I'm sure that's what your friend Micky will say. But is it true?"

Samuel stepped in. "We don't have to find out whether this tale is true or not," he said. "We're bankers, not judges. The fact that the Santamaria railroad is going to be controversial makes the bond issue riskier. We have to reconsider."

Uncle Joseph said aggressively, "I won't be bullied. Let this South American popinjay publish his article and go to the devil."

"That's one way to handle it," Samuel mused. "We can wait and see what effect the article has on the price of existing South American stocks. If they crash, we'll cancel the Santamaria railroad."

Joseph, somewhat mollified, said, "I don't mind submitting to the decision of the market."

"There is one other option," Samuel went on. "We could get another bank to join us on the issue of bonds. That way, any hostile publicity would be enfeebled by having a divided target."

That made sense, Hugh thought. He would prefer to cancel the issue, but Samuel's strategy would minimize the risk.

"All right," Joseph said. "Find us a partner. Try Greenbournes."

Hugh wondered whether he should advise Solly to turn Pilasters down, and immediately thought better of it; Hugh was being hired as an expert on North America, and it would seem presumptuous if he started out by passing judgment on a completely different area. He decided to have one more try at persuading Uncle Joseph to cancel the issue completely. "Why don't we just wash our hands of the Santamaria railroad?" he said. "The risk has always been high, and now we're threatened with bad publicity on top."

Edward said petulantly, "The partners have made their decision, and it's not for you to question them."

Hugh gave up. "You're right. I'm not a partner, and soon I won't be an employee. I'm resigning. I shall be working at Greenbournes."

Uncle Joseph's eyes looked as if they would pop out. "But you're the one who knows all the North Americans!"

"I imagine that's why Greenbournes was so keen to hire me." He could not help being pleased that Uncle Joseph was so irate.

"But you'll take business away from us."

"You should have thought of that when you decided to go back on your offer of a partnership."

"How much are they paying you?"

Hugh stood up to leave. "That's not for you to ask," he said.

Edward shrieked, "How dare you speak to my father that way!"

Joseph's indignation burst like a bubble, and to Hugh's surprise he calmed down. "Oh, shut up, Edward," he said mildly. "There are times I wish you were more like Hugh. At least he's got spunk." He turned back to Hugh. "Go on, clear off," he said without malice. "I hope you'll come a cropper, but I'm not betting on it."

"No doubt that's the nearest to good wishes that I'm likely to get from your branch of the family," Hugh said. "Good day to you."

4

AUGUSTA and Micky were having tea and discussing his marriage to Rachel when Edward came bursting into the drawing room. "Antonio Silva's back," he said before he closed the door behind him.

Augusta paled. "How do you know?"

"Hugh saw him. Tonio's trying to sabotage the Santamaria railroad bond issue." Edward handed her a sheaf of papers. "Read that."

Micky said, "What is it?"

"An article Tonio plans to publish about your family's mines."

"What has this to do with your bond issue?" asked Augusta.

"Investors don't like controversy. This could scare them off."

Micky was shaken. "What does your father say about it?"

"We're trying to get another bank to come in with us, but basically we're going to let Tonio publish. If the publicity causes a crash in South American stocks, we'll abandon the Santamaria railroad."

Damn Tonio, Micky thought. He had to be silenced.

Micky pretended to be calm. "May I see the article, please?"

Augusta handed it to him.

He noticed the hotel address at the top of the paper. Putting on an air of insouciance, he said, "Why, this is no problem at all. Now that we know where to find him, we can deal with him."

Chapter Three: May

1

SOLLY and Maisie Greenbourne went out most evenings. The only time they stayed home was when they were giving a party. Tonight they were going to a dinner, then on to a ball afterwards.

Solly came in at half past six to watch Maisie getting dressed. Her hair was decorated with yellow silk flowers, and he helped her into a gown of yellow-and-white-striped silk taffeta.

She opened her jewelry box and took out an emerald necklace and matching earrings Solly had given her on their first wedding anniversary. As she was putting them on, he said, "We're going to be seeing a lot more of our old friend Hugh Pilaster from now on."

"Why, what's happened?" she said neutrally.

"He's coming to work at the bank. They refused him a partnership at Pilasters."

"Oh, no." She knew Hugh better than anyone, and she could guess how broken he was. "They are a mean-spirited family."

"It's because of his wife."

"I'm not surprised." She had witnessed the incident at the Duchess of Tenbigh's ball, and knowing the Pilasters, she wondered if

Augusta had stage-managed the whole incident to discredit Hugh.

"You have to feel sorry for Nora."

"Mmm." Maisie's dislike of Nora had not changed since their first meeting, before the wedding. She still considered Nora a heartless gold digger.

"Anyway, I thought that you might help her."

"What?" Maisie said sharply.

"Rehabilitate her. You know what it's like to be looked down on because of your background. You overcame all that prejudice."

"And now I'm supposed to work the same transformation on every other guttersnipe who marries into society?"

"I've obviously done something wrong," Solly said worriedly. "I thought you'd be glad to help. You've always been so fond of Hugh."

Maisie suddenly felt ashamed of herself. "Oh, Solly, how can I be so ungrateful? You've been so kind and generous to me and my family. Of course I'll do this for you if you wish."

She knew what had really made her cross. In her innermost heart she still wanted to be Hugh's wife, and she hated Nora for winning what she had lost. It was a shameful attitude, and Maisie resolved to throw herself energetically into the task of bringing Nora Pilaster into the good graces of London's high society.

She was able to begin her campaign that very night. When they entered the drawing room of their dinner host, the first person she saw was Count de Tokoly. She knew him quite well, and he always flirted with her, so she felt free to be direct. "I want you to forgive Nora Pilaster for slapping you," she said.

"Forgive?" he said. "I'm flattered! To think that at my age I can still make a young woman slap my face. It's a great compliment."

That wasn't how you felt at the time, Maisie thought. However, she was glad he had decided to make light of the whole incident. "Tell me," she said. "Did anyone encourage you?"

He looked at Maisie through narrowed eyes. "You're clever, Mrs. Greenbourne. I've always respected you for that. The Cordovan minister, Senor Miranda, told me that Nora was . . . what shall we say . . . susceptible."

So that was it. "And Micky Miranda was put up to it by Augusta. I'm sure of it. Those two are as thick as thieves."

De Tokoly was miffed. "I hope I haven't been used as a pawn."

"That's the danger of being predictable," Maisie said waspishly.

THE NEXT DAY SHE TOOK NORA to her dressmaker. As Nora tried on styles and fabrics, Maisie found out more about the incident at the Duchess of Tenbigh's ball. "Did Augusta say anything to you beforehand about the count?" she asked.

"She warned me not to let him take any liberties."

"And if Augusta had said nothing, would you have behaved the same way?"

Nora looked thoughtful. "I probably wouldn't have slapped him, but Augusta made me think it was important to take a stand."

Maisie nodded. "There you are. She wanted this to happen. She also got someone to tell the count you were easy. Never underestimate Augusta's capacity for treachery."

"She doesn't scare me," Nora said defiantly. "I haven't got too many scruples myself."

Maisie believed her—and felt sorry for Hugh.

A polonaise was the perfect dress style for Nora, Maisie thought as the dressmaker pinned a gown around Nora's generous figure. The fussy details suited her pretty looks; the pleated frills and the tieback skirt with flounces looked sweet on her.

"Looking pretty is half the battle," Maisie said as Nora admired herself in the mirror. "As far as men are concerned, it's really all that matters. But you have to do more to get accepted by women."

Nora said, "I've always got on better with men than women. You must be the same. That's why we've got where we are."

Are we the same? wondered Maisie.

"Not that I put myself on the same level as you," Nora added. "Every ambitious girl in London envies you."

Maisie winced at the thought that she was looked up to as a hero by fortune-hunting women, but she said nothing, because she probably deserved it. Nora had married for money, and she was quite happy to admit it to Maisie, because she assumed that Maisie had done the same. And she was right.

Nora said, "I'm not complaining, but I did pick the black sheep of the family—the one with no capital. You married one of the richest men in the world."

How surprised you would be, Maisie thought, if you knew how willingly I'd swap. She put the thought out of her mind. All right, she and Nora were two of a kind. She would help Nora to win the acceptance of the snobs and shrews who ruled society.

2

Micky Miranda stood in a doorway in Berwick Street—a narrow, filthy passage of cheap pubs and lodging houses—wearing a light overcoat and smoking a cigar. There was a gas lamp nearby, but he stood in the shadow so that his face could not easily be seen. He had been there since nightfall; now it was almost midnight.

The Hotel Russe was across the street. There was a light over the door, and inside, Micky could see the lobby. However, there did not appear to be anyone there. Two other men loitered on the far pavement, one on either side of the hotel entrance. All three of them were waiting for Antonio Silva.

A few minutes after midnight a familiar figure appeared at the far end of Berwick Street. There was no doubt it was Tonio. Micky could even see the carroty color of the side-whiskers. Micky gestured to his two accomplices.

They moved fast. Before Tonio reached the door of his hotel, the two men seized him and bundled him into an alley. He shouted once, but after that his cries were muffled.

Throwing away the remains of his cigar, Micky crossed the road and entered the alley. They had stuffed a scarf into Tonio's mouth, and they were beating him with iron bars. His head and face were already covered with blood.

The sight made Micky feel ill. "Stop it, you fools," he hissed at them. He did not want them to kill Tonio. The incident must look like a robbery. A murder would create a great deal more fuss.

With apparent reluctance the two thugs stopped hitting Tonio, who slumped to the ground and lay still.

"Empty his pockets," Micky whispered.

Tonio did not move as they took from him a watch and chain, a pocketbook, some coins, a silk handkerchief, and a key.

"Give me the key," Micky said. "The rest is yours."

The older of the two men—Barker, humorously known as Dog—said, "Give us the money."

He gave them each ten pounds in gold sovereigns.

Dog gave him the key. Tied to it with a thread was a card with the number 11 scrawled on it. Micky turned and made for the Hotel Russe. To his relief the desk in the little lobby was still unoccupied.

He went up the stairs and let himself into room number 11. Micky put his hat and cane on a chair and began to search methodically. In the writing desk he found a copy of the article for *The Times,* which he took. However, it was not worth much. Tonio either had copies or could rewrite it from memory. But in order to get the article published, he would have to produce some kind of evidence, and it was the evidence that Micky was looking for.

He tipped Tonio's shirts and underwear out of the chest of drawers. There was nothing hidden there. He looked behind and underneath the chest, the bed, and the wardrobe. Nothing. He finally found what he wanted, under the mattress.

Inside a large envelope was a wad of papers tied together with lawyers' ribbons. He untied the ribbons and scanned the documents. They were sworn affidavits of witnesses who had seen floggings and executions at his family's nitrate mines.

Micky lifted the sheaf of papers to his lips and kissed them. They were the answer to his prayers. He would send the names of the witnesses to Papa, and Papa would silence them.

Without proof, Tonio's article was worthless.

3

JOSEPH Pilaster finished off a large plate of grilled lamb's kidneys and scrambled eggs and began to butter a slice of toast. Augusta wondered whether the bad temper of middle-aged men had to do with the amount of meat they ate. The thought of kidneys for breakfast made her feel quite ill.

"Sidney Madler has come to London from New York," he said. "He's angry about Hugh's not being a partner."

"What is it to do with him?" Augusta said.

"There was an understanding that the London end of our joint operation would be run by Hugh. Now Hugh has resigned, as you know. I'll have to tell Madler something. When Hugh goes to Greenbournes, he's likely to take most of the business with him."

"Tell him Hugh has married an impossible wife. He can hardly fail to understand that."

"Of course." Joseph stood up. "Good-bye, dear."

When he had gone, she sat at the table wondering how serious this threat was. She was surprised to hear that Hugh's departure would cost the bank a lot of money. For a moment she wondered whether she might be endangering the bank, which was the foundation of all her hopes and schemes. But that was ridiculous. Pilasters was hugely wealthy. Nothing she could do would threaten it.

While she was finishing her breakfast, Hastead sidled in to tell her that Mr. Fortescue was in the drawing room. She immediately put Madler out of her mind. This was much more important. Having won the Deaconridge by-election with financial help from Joseph, Fortescue was now a member of Parliament and indebted to Augusta.

Her campaign had gone according to plan so far. Arnold Hobbes had published a series of articles in *The Forum* calling for peerages for commercial men. Lady Morte had talked to the queen about it and had sung Joseph's praises. And Fortescue had told Prime Minister Disraeli that there was a groundswell of public opinion in favor of the idea. Now perhaps the whole effort was about to bear fruit.

As she entered the drawing room, her head was full of the phrases she hoped soon to hear: *Lady Whitehaven . . . the Earl and Countess Whitehaven . . . as Your Ladyship pleases . . .*

Fortescue looked a little tense. "I've just been with the prime minister," he said. "I've convinced him that it is time the banking industry was represented in the House of Lords."

"Wonderful!" said Augusta. "But why do you look so glum?"

"There's also bad news," Fortescue said. "I'm afraid he wants to give the peerage to Ben Greenbourne."

"No!" Augusta felt as if she had been punched. "I didn't go to all this trouble for Ben Greenbourne!"

"I agree it's ironic," Fortescue said. "But I did my best."

"Don't be so smug," she snapped. "Not if you want my help in future elections. We must find a way to change the prime minister's mind. What are Ben Greenbourne's weaknesses? His son is married to a guttersnipe, but that's not enough." It occurred to her that if Greenbourne got a title, it would be inherited by his son, Solly, which would mean that Maisie would be a countess. The thought was sickening. "He's a Jew," she said suddenly. "That's the key."

Fortescue looked dubious. "The prime minister himself is a Jew by birth, and he has now been made Lord Beaconsfield."

"I know. But Disraeli is a practicing Christian."

Later that morning, when Augusta went to call on Lady Morte, she raised the religious issue.

"It might make a difference," Lady Morte mused. "The queen is constantly criticizing the prince for having so many Jewish friends."

"Then if you were to mention to her that the prime minister is proposing to ennoble one of them . . ."

"I can bring it up in conversation. I'm not sure it will be enough to effect your purpose."

Augusta thought hard. "Is there anything we can do to make the whole question a matter of more concern to Her Majesty?"

"If there were to be some public protest—questions in Parliament, perhaps, or articles in the press . . ."

"The press," Augusta said. She thought of Arnold Hobbes. "Yes," she said, "I think that could be arranged."

Hobbes was discombobulated by Augusta's presence in his cramped, inky office. But he fetched her a chair, then sat down to listen as she told him about Ben Greenbourne's peerage.

"Most regrettable," he blabbered nervously. "However, I don't think *The Forum* could be accused of lack of enthusiasm in promoting the cause which you so kindly suggested to me."

For which you got two lucrative directorships, Augusta thought. "I know it's not your fault. But the point is, what can you do about it?"

"My journal is in a difficult position," he said worriedly. "Having campaigned so vociferously for a banker to get a peerage, it's hard for us to turn around and protest when it actually happens."

Augusta pondered. "When Disraeli took his seat in the House of Lords, he took the oath of loyalty on a Christian Bible?"

"Indeed."

"Old and New Testament?"

"I begin to see your drift, Mrs. Pilaster. Would Ben Greenbourne swear on a Christian Bible? I doubt it."

Augusta shook her head dubiously. "He might if nothing were said about it. But if there were to be a noisy public demand . . ."

Hobbes warmed to the idea. "I see the headline already. 'Blasphemy in the House of Lords.' Mrs. Pilaster, you're quite brilliant."

Augusta nodded. She was beginning to feel better. Lady Morte would turn the queen against Greenbourne, Hobbes would make an issue of it in the press, and Fortescue would be standing by to whisper into the ear of the prime minister the name of a blameless alternative: Joseph. Once again, the prospects looked good.

Chapter Four: June

1

MAISIE Greenbourne's midsummer ball was one of the fixtures of the London season. She always had the best band, the most delicious food, and endless champagne. But the main reason everyone wanted to go was that the Prince of Wales always came. This year Maisie decided to use the occasion to launch the new Nora Pilaster.

It was a high-risk strategy, for while Maisie was fairly sure she could predict the prince's reactions, now and again he turned on his friends if he felt he was being used. She was amazed that she had allowed herself to take that risk. But it was for Hugh.

It was now two months since Hugh had resigned. Solly was impatient for him to start at Greenbournes, but the partners had insisted on three months' notice. No doubt they wanted to postpone the moment when Hugh went to work for their rivals.

The guests began to arrive at ten thirty. Maisie did not normally invite Augusta Pilaster, but she had this year, wanting Augusta to see Nora's triumph—if triumph it should be. Maisie had also invited Hugh's New York mentor, Sidney Madler.

Maisie and Solly stood shaking hands with their guests for an hour; then the prince arrived. They escorted him into the ballroom and presented Solly's father. Ben Greenbourne bowed from the waist as stiffly as a Prussian guardsman. Then Maisie danced with the prince.

"I've a splendid tidbit of gossip for you, sir," she said as they waltzed. "Although I hope it won't make you cross. It's about the incident at the Duchess of Tenbigh's ball. It seems someone deliberately provoked it. De Tokoly was told, quite falsely, that the young woman was open to invitation."

"Cunning. Who was behind it?"

Maisie hesitated. She had never used her friendship with the prince to put someone down. But Augusta deserved it.

"It was Augusta Pilaster. The girl, Nora, is married to her nephew, Hugh. Augusta did it to spite Hugh, whom she hates."

"What a snake she must be. I rather feel like punishing her."

This was the moment Maisie had been leading up to. "All you would have to do is notice Nora, to show everyone that she is

forgiven," she said. The dance ended. "Shall I present her to you?"
He said shrewdly, "Did you plan all this, you little minx?"
She had been afraid of this. He was not stupid, and he could guess that she had been scheming. She did her best to blush. "You have found me out. How foolish of me to think I might pull the wool over *your* eagle eyes." She changed her expression and favored him with a direct, candid gaze. "What shall I do for a penance?"
A lascivious smile passed over his face. "Don't tempt me. Come, I forgive you. Where is this Nora?"
She was hovering close by, as instructed. Maisie caught her eye, and she approached instantly, looking quite bewitching in a gauzy sky-blue gown covered with little satin bows. The off-the-shoulder style made the most of her voluptuous figure. Maisie said, "Your Royal Highness, may I present Mrs. Hugh Pilaster."
Nora curtsied and batted her eyelashes.
"Charming," the prince said enthusiastically. "Quite charming."

HUGH watched in delight as Nora chatted happily with the Prince of Wales. Yesterday she had been a social outcast. Now she was the envy of every woman in the room—her clothes were perfect, her manners charming, and she was flirting with the heir to the throne. And the transformation had been brought about by Maisie.
Hugh glanced at his aunt Augusta, standing next to him with Uncle Joseph. She was staring at Nora and the prince. How it must gall her, Hugh thought, to know that Maisie, the working-class girl she derided six years ago, is now so much more influential than she is.
With perfect timing Sidney Madler came over. Looking incredulous, he said to Joseph, "Is *that* the woman you say is unsuitable to be a banker's wife?"
Before Joseph could answer, Augusta spoke. In a deceptively mild voice she said, "She did lose the bank a major contract."
Hugh replied, "As a matter of fact, she didn't. That loan is going through. Count de Tokoly got over his pique."
Madler said, "Financial need generally outweighs social prejudice in the end."
"Yes," said Joseph, "so it does. I think I may have been too hasty."
Augusta interrupted. "Joseph, what are you saying?"
"This is business, dear—men's talk. You need not concern yourself." He turned to Hugh. "We certainly don't want you working for

Greenbournes and taking your North American business with you."

Hugh tried to steady his nerves. "There's only one thing you can offer me to make me change my mind, and that's a partnership."

Joseph sighed. "You're the very devil to negotiate with."

Madler put in, "As every good banker should be."

"Very well," Joseph said at last. "I'm offering you a partnership."

Hugh glanced at Augusta. Her face was a rigid mask of self-control. "In that case," he said, savoring the moment, "I accept."

Augusta finally lost her composure. "You're going to regret this for the rest of your lives!" she spat. Then she stalked off, cutting a swath through the crowd in the ballroom as she headed for the door.

She left the party, taking the carriage. Her husband could go home in a hansom. She fumed all the way to Kensington, where Hastead was waiting in the hall. "Mr. Hobbes is in the drawing room, ma'am," he said sleepily. "He insisted on waiting."

Augusta was in no mood to see the editor of *The Forum.* What was he doing here in the early hours of the morning? She found him asleep by the dying fire. "Good morning!" she said loudly.

He sprang to his feet. "Mrs. Pilaster! Good—ah, yes, morning."

"What brings you here so late?"

"I thought you would like to be the first to see this," he said, and he handed her a journal. It was a new issue of *The Forum,* still smelling of the printing press. She opened it and read the headline of the lead article: CAN A JEW BE A LORD?

Her spirits lifted. Tonight's fiasco was only one defeat, she reminded herself. There were other battles to be fought.

2

ON THE morning after the ball Hugh woke up feeling jubilant. His wife had been accepted into high society, and he was going to be made a partner in Pilasters Bank. He would make not just thousands of pounds but, over the years, hundreds of thousands.

With his morning mail there was a letter from Tonio Silva.

Tonio had vanished shortly after Hugh met him in the coffeehouse. No article had appeared in *The Times.* Hugh had felt rather foolish, having made such a fuss about the danger to the bank.

He had written to Tonio at the Hotel Russe, but got no reply. Now he opened Tonio's letter anxiously. It came from a hospital, asking Hugh to visit. The letter finished, "Whatever you do, tell no one where I am."

Mystified and concerned, Hugh went straight to the hospital. He found Tonio in a dark, bare ward of thirty close-packed beds. His ginger hair had been shaved, and his face and head were scarred. "Dear God," Hugh said. "What happened?"

"I was attacked in the street more than a month ago."

"You should have contacted me before. We must get you out of here. I'll send my doctor to you and arrange a nurse—"

"I appreciate your generosity, but it's safer here. The people who attacked me were not just thieves. My hotel key was taken, and they used it to get into my room. Nothing was stolen but the papers pertaining to my article, including affidavits signed by witnesses."

Hugh was horrified. It chilled his heart to think that Pilasters might have any link with violent crime. "It almost sounds as if the bank is under suspicion."

"Not the bank," Tonio said. "Pilasters is a powerful institution, but I don't believe it could organize murders in Cordova."

"Murders? Who has been murdered?"

"All the witnesses whose names were on the affidavits stolen from my hotel room. They nearly killed me, too."

"Who is behind all this?"

"Micky Miranda."

Hugh shook his head incredulously. "I'm not fond of Micky, as you know, but I can't believe he's a killer."

"He is," Tonio said. "I know it for sure. I haven't always acted as if I knew. In fact, I've been a damn fool about Miranda. For a while he made me think he was my friend. The truth is that he's evil through and through, and I've known it since school."

"How could you?"

Tonio shifted in the bed. "I know what really happened the afternoon Peter Middleton drowned."

Hugh was electrified. He had been wondering about this for years. "Go on, man," he said. "I can't wait to hear this."

Tonio hesitated. "Could you give me a little wine?" There was a bottle of Madeira beside the bed. Hugh poured some into a glass. While Tonio sipped it, Hugh recalled the heat of that day, the scarred rock walls of the swimming hole, and the cold, cold water.

"The coroner was told that Peter was in difficulty in the pool.

But he was never told that Edward was ducking him repeatedly—"

"I knew that much," Hugh interrupted. "I had a letter from Hump Cammel in the Cape Colony. He was watching from the far side of the pool. But he didn't stay to see the end."

"That's right. You escaped, and Hump ran away. That left me, Peter, Edward, and Micky."

"What happened after I left?" Hugh said impatiently.

"I got out and threw a stone at Edward. It was a lucky shot. It hit him square in the middle of the forehead and drew blood. He left off tormenting Peter and came after me. I scrambled up the side of the quarry. Halfway up I looked back. Peter had swum to the side and was trying to get out of the water, but Micky kept pushing him under. I only glanced at them for a moment; then I continued to climb."

He took another sip of the wine. "When I got to the rim of the quarry, I looked back again. Edward was still coming after me, but he was a long way behind." Tonio paused, and an expression of revulsion crossed his scarred face. "By this time Micky was in the water with Peter. What I saw—and I can see it in my memory now as if it were yesterday—was Micky holding Peter's head under the water. Peter was thrashing about, but he couldn't break the hold. Micky was drowning him. There is absolutely no doubt about it. It was straightforward murder."

"But why did you never tell anyone?" Hugh asked.

"I was afraid of Micky—afraid he'd do to me what he did to Peter. I'm still afraid of Micky. You should be, too."

"I am. Don't worry." Hugh was thoughtful. "You know, I don't believe Edward and his mother know the truth about this. They had no reason to cover up for Micky. Edward might have, out of friendship. But in those days Augusta didn't even know him."

"So what do you think happened?"

Hugh frowned. "Imagine this. Edward gives up chasing you and goes back to the swimming hole. He finds Micky dragging Peter's body out of the water. As Edward arrives, Micky says, 'You fool, you've killed him!' Remember, Edward hasn't seen Micky holding Peter's head under. Micky pretends that Peter was so exhausted by Edward's ducking that he drowned. 'What am I going to do?' says Edward. Micky says, 'Don't worry. We'll say it was an accident. In fact, we'll say you jumped in and tried to rescue him.' Micky thereby covers up his own crime and earns the undying gratitude of Edward and Augusta. Does that make sense?"

Tonio nodded. "By heaven, I think you're right."

"We must go to the police," Hugh said.

"You're forgetting something. Micky has diplomatic immunity."

"He could still be disgraced and sent home," said Hugh.

Tonio shook his head. "I'm the only witness. Micky and Edward will both tell a different story. And it's well known that Micky's family and mine are enemies. We couldn't convince anyone."

A new thought struck Hugh, and he frowned in puzzlement. "You know, you've solved a mystery for me. I couldn't understand how Peter drowned when he was such a good swimmer. But your answer is an even greater mystery."

"I'm not sure I follow you."

"Micky Miranda murdered Peter Middleton. . . . But why?"

Chapter Five: July

1

AUGUSTA was triumphant on the day Joseph's peerage was announced. Micky went to the house at teatime, as usual, and found the drawing room crowded with people congratulating her on becoming Countess Whitehaven.

She was amazing, Micky thought; she had planned her campaign like a general. At one point there had been a rumor that Ben Greenbourne was to get the peerage, but that had been killed by an eruption of anti-Jewish sentiment in the press. Augusta was not admitting even to Micky that she had been behind the press coverage, but he was sure of it. In some ways she reminded him of his father; Papa had the same remorseless determination.

The only person who had ever defeated her ingenuity was Hugh Pilaster. It was astonishing how difficult he was to crush. He was like a persistent garden weed.

Happily for Micky, Hugh had been unable to stop the Santamaria railroad. "By the way," Micky said to Edward over teacups, "when are you going to sign the contract with Greenbournes?"

"Tomorrow."

"Good." Micky would be relieved when the deal was finally sewn up. It had dragged on for half a year.

That evening, Edward and Micky dined at the Cowes Club. Throughout the meal Edward was interrupted every few minutes by people congratulating him; one day he would inherit the title.

After the meal they moved to the smoking room. For a while they had the room to themselves. Their marriages were not going well. Rachel had left Micky and gone home to her parents; Emily was spending all her time at the country house Edward had bought. So he and Micky were both bachelors again.

Micky glanced across the empty room and saw the bulky form of Solly Greenbourne in the doorway. "Here comes another friend to congratulate you," Micky said to Edward. But when Solly was closer, Micky realized he was not wearing his usual amiable smile. In fact, he looked positively angry.

Micky felt intuitively that there was some problem with the Santamaria railroad deal. Anxiety made him fatuously amicable. "Hello, Solly, old boy. How's the genius of the City?"

Solly was not interested in Micky, however. He faced Edward. "Pilaster, you're a damned cad," he said.

Edward was mystified. "What the devil are you talking about?"

Solly reddened. "I've discovered that you and that witch you call Mother are behind those filthy articles in *The Forum.*"

Oh, no! Micky said to himself. This was a catastrophe. He had suspected Augusta's involvement, but how had Solly found out?

The same question occurred to Edward. "Who's been filling your fat head with such rot?"

"One of your mother's cronies is a lady-in-waiting to the queen," Solly replied. Micky guessed he meant Harriet Morte. "She told the Prince of Wales. I've just been with him."

Solly must be insane with anger to speak so indiscreetly about a private conversation with royalty, Micky thought. He did not see how a quarrel such as this could be patched up in time for the signing of the contract tomorrow. He tried desperately to cool the temperature. "Solly, you can't be sure this story is true—"

Solly rounded on him. "Can't I? When I read in today's paper that Joseph Pilaster got the peerage that was to go to my father?"

Micky began to understand how the armor of Solly's amiability had been breached. It was not for himself that he was angry, but for his father. Ben Greenbourne's grandfather had arrived in London with a bale of furs, a five-pound note, and a hole in his boot. For Ben to take a seat in the House of Lords would be the ultimate badge of acceptance into English society, a triumph not just for himself and his family but for the entire Jewish community in Britain.

Edward said, "I can't help it if you're a Jew."

Micky butted in. "You two shouldn't let your parents come between you. After all, you're partners in a major business deal."

"Don't be a fool, Miranda," Solly said. "You can forget about the Santamaria railroad. After our partners hear this story, Greenbournes Bank will never do business with the Pilasters again."

Micky tasted bile in his throat as he watched Solly leave the room. With one simple sentence he had wiped out all Micky's hopes. Was there anything he could do to prevent Solly's canceling the deal? If there was, it would have to be done quickly, before Solly told the other Greenbournes. He stood up abruptly.

"Where are you going?" Edward said.

Micky decided not to tell Edward what he had in mind. "To the cardroom," he replied. "Don't you want to play?"

"Yes, of course." Edward heaved himself out of his chair.

At the foot of the stairs, Micky turned toward the toilets, saying, "You go on up. I'll catch you."

Edward went upstairs. Micky stepped into the cloakroom, grabbed his hat and cane, and dashed out through the front door.

He looked up and down Pall Mall. It was dusk, and the gaslights were being lit. Micky could not see Solly anywhere. Then, a hundred yards away, he spotted him—a big figure in evening dress and a top hat—heading toward St. James's at a brisk waddle.

Micky went after him. He would explain to Solly how important the railroad was to Cordova. He would say that Solly was punishing millions of peasants on account of something Augusta had done. Solly was softhearted; he might yet be talked around.

Solly turned up a side street, heading toward his house in Piccadilly. Micky broke into a run. "Greenbourne," he called, "wait!"

Solly stopped and turned, breathing hard. He recognized Micky and turned away again.

Micky grabbed his arm. "I must talk to you."

Solly was so breathless he could hardly speak. "Take your hands off me," he panted. He broke away and walked on.

Several steps later he came to a cross street and was forced to stop at the curb as a carriage went by. Micky spoke to him again.

"Solly, calm down," he said. "I only want to reason with you."

"Go to the devil!" Solly shouted.

The road cleared. To stop his moving away again, Micky grabbed Solly's lapels. Solly struggled to free himself, but Micky held on. "Listen to me!" he yelled.

"Let me go!" Solly got a hand free and punched Micky's nose.

The blow stung, and Micky tasted blood. He lost his temper. "Damn you!" he cried. He let go of Solly's coat and punched him back, hitting him on the cheek.

Solly turned and stepped into the road. At that moment they both saw a carriage coming toward them, being driven very fast. Solly jumped back to avoid being hit.

Micky saw a chance. If Solly were dead, Micky's troubles would be over. There was no time to reckon the odds, no room for hesitation. Micky gave Solly a shove, pushing him in front of the horses.

The coachman yelled and hauled on the reins. Solly stumbled, saw the horses almost on top of him, fell to the ground, and screamed. For a frozen moment Micky saw the charging horses, the heavy carriage wheels, the terrified coachman, and the huge, helpless form of Solly, flat on his back on the road. Then the horses charged over him.

Micky turned away. He felt faint and had to lean on the wall. He forced himself to look at the motionless body in the road. Solly's head was smashed, his face unrecognizable. He was dead.

And Micky was saved. Now Ben Greenbourne need never know what Augusta had done to him; the deal could go ahead, the railroad would be built, and Micky would be a hero in Cordova.

He felt a warm trickle on his lip. His nose was bleeding. He pulled out a handkerchief and dabbed at it. He looked up and down the street. There was no one around. Only the coachman had seen what happened.

The carriage juddered to a halt thirty yards down the road. The coachman leaped down. Micky turned and walked quickly away. The coachman called after him, "Hey, you!"

Micky rounded the corner without looking back. By God, I did it, he thought. He hurried up the steps of the club. With luck nobody would have noticed his absence. But as he entered the front door, he had the bad fortune to bump into Hugh Pilaster going out.

Hugh nodded to him and said, "Evening, Miranda."

"Evening, Pilaster," said Micky, cursing Hugh under his breath. He went to the cloakroom. His nose was red from Solly's punch, but otherwise he just appeared a little rumpled. He straightened his clothing and hurried up the stairs to the cardroom.

2

HUGH went to see Maisie two days after Solly died. He found her alone, neatly dressed in a black gown, in the drawing room of the palatial Piccadilly house. Her face was lined with grief, and she looked as if she had not slept. His heart ached for her.

"Why do such things happen?" Maisie said miserably.

Hugh hesitated. He could not help wondering whether Micky had had something to do with the death of Solly. The police were looking for a well-dressed man who had been arguing with Solly just before he was run over. Hugh had seen Micky entering the Cowes Club at around the time Solly died. But there was no motive; quite the reverse. Solly had been on the point of closing the Santamaria railroad deal that was so close to Micky's heart. Why would he kill his benefactor? Hugh decided to say nothing to Maisie about his unfounded suspicions. "It seems to have been a tragic accident," he said.

"The coachman thinks Solly was pushed. Why would the witness run away if he wasn't guilty?"

"He may have been attempting to rob Solly. That's what the newspapers are saying." It was a sensational case: the grisly death of a prominent banker, one of the richest men in the world.

"If you had only waited a little longer, you could have married me instead of Nora," Maisie said.

Hugh was startled by her frankness. He was not sure how to respond, so he made a foolish joke. "If a Pilaster married a Greenbourne, it would be not so much a wedding as a merger."

She shook her head. "I'm not a Greenbourne. Solly's family never really accepted me."

"You must have inherited a big chunk of the bank, though."

"I've inherited nothing, Hugh."

"But that's impossible."

"It's true. Solly had no money of his own. His father gave him a huge monthly allowance, but he never settled any capital on him, because of me. Even this house is rented. I own my clothes and jewelry, but I'm not the heir to the bank, and neither is little Bertie."

Hugh was astonished. "The old man won't provide for your son?"

"Not a penny. I saw my father-in-law this morning."

As her friend, Hugh felt personally affronted. "It's disgraceful."

"Not really. I gave Solly five years of happiness, and in return I had five years of the high life. I can go back to normal. I'll sell my jewelry, invest the money, and live quietly on the income."

It was hard to take in. "Will you live with your parents?"

"In Manchester? No. I'll stay in London. Rachel Miranda is opening a hospital for unwed mothers. I might work with her."

Hugh was worried by Ben Greenbourne's ill-treatment of his daughter-in-law. He decided he would try to change the man's mind. But he would not mention it to Maisie beforehand. He did not want to raise her hopes. "You're very philosophical," he said.

Maisie shrugged. "I've no regrets—except that you married Nora."

"I'm very fond of her," he said unconvincingly.

"You were angry because I wouldn't have an affair with you," Maisie said brutally. "You picked Nora because she reminded you of me. But she never loved you. She married you for your money."

It was true. Nora was only happy when he gave her gifts. But Maisie's scorn made him defensive. "She's not as bad as that."

"All the same, you're not happy."

Feeling confused, Hugh fell back on what he knew to be right. "Well, I've married her now, and I won't leave her," he said. "That's what the vows mean."

Maisie smiled tearfully. "I knew you would say that." She stood up. "Thank you for coming, dear Hugh," she said.

He intended to shake her hand, but instead he bent to kiss her cheek, and then somehow he found himself kissing her lips. It was a long, tender kiss, and it almost destroyed Hugh's resolve. But he tore himself away and left without another word.

BEN Greenbourne's house was another palace a few yards along Piccadilly. Hugh went straight there after seeing Maisie. The butler showed him into the library.

Greenbourne looked old and worn, but he showed no sign of tears. Formal as ever, he shook hands, then waved Hugh to a chair.

Greenbourne had an old letter in his hand. "Listen to this," he said, and he began to read.

"Dear Papa,

"We have a new Latin teacher, and I am getting on much better. Waterford caught a rat, and he is training it to eat out of his hand. The food here is too little. Can you send me a cake?

"Your loving son,

"Solomon"

He folded the letter. "He was fourteen when he wrote that. How I wish I could turn back the years," Greenbourne said, and Hugh saw that the old man's self-control was weakening.

"I must be one of Solly's oldest friends," Hugh said. "But I've come here not just as Solly's friend but as Maisie's, too."

Greenbourne stiffened immediately.

Hugh went on. "I met her soon after Solly did. I fell in love with her myself, but Solly won her."

"He was richer."

"Mr. Greenbourne, allow me to be frank. Maisie was a penniless girl looking for a rich husband. But after she married Solly, she kept her part of the bargain. She was a good wife to him."

"And she has enjoyed the life of a lady for five years."

"Funnily enough, that's what she said. But what about Bertie? Surely you don't want to leave your grandson destitute?"

"Grandson?" said Greenbourne. "Hubert is no relation to me."

Hugh had an odd premonition that something momentous was about to happen. "I don't understand. What do you mean?"

"That woman was already with child when she married my son."

Hugh gasped.

"Solly knew it, and he knew the child was not his," Greenbourne went on. "He took her all the same—against my will, I might add."

Hugh felt as if his heart had stopped. "Who was the father?"

"She would never say," Greenbourne said. "Solly never knew."

But Hugh did. The child was his. Maisie had never been promiscuous, despite appearances. She had been a virgin when he seduced her. He had made her pregnant on that first night.

"It is appalling, of course," Greenbourne said, seeing his consternation, and misunderstanding the reason for it.

I have a child, Hugh thought. A son, Hubert, called Bertie. The thought wrenched at his heart. He stood up. "I must go. My condolences, Mr. Greenbourne. Solly was the best man I ever knew."

Hugh went out into the sunshine and headed home. Everything was different now. Nora was his legal wife, but Maisie was the mother of his son. A child needed a father. Suddenly the question of what to do with the rest of his life was open again.

He tried to consider the practicalities. He felt sure that Nora would be willing to divorce him if she were offered enough money. The Pilasters would ask him to resign from the bank; the social stigma of divorce was too great to allow him to continue as a partner. But what was that, balanced against the joy of being with the woman he had always loved?

He found himself outside his house. Nora would be in her over-decorated bedroom, dressing for lunch. What was to stop him walking in and announcing that he was leaving her? That was what he wanted to do. He went into the house and ran up the stairs.

She was in front of the mirror, putting on a pendant of rubies and sapphires he had given her. She spoke before he did. "I've got some news," she said. "The inevitable has happened."

Suddenly Hugh guessed. It was too late; he could never leave her now. He felt revulsion and the pain of loss—of Maisie, of his son.

He looked into her eyes. There was defiance there, almost as if she had guessed what he had been planning. Perhaps she had. Then she said it. "I'm going to have a baby."

PART III

1890

Chapter One: September

1

JOSEPH Pilaster died in September 1890, having been Senior Partner of Pilasters Bank for seventeen years. During that period Britain had grown steadily richer and so had the Pilasters. Joseph's estate came to more than two million pounds, including his collection of sixty-five antique jeweled snuffboxes—one for each year of his life—which was worth a hundred thousand pounds on its own.

The Pilasters were now almost as rich as the Greenbournes. As well as the interest on their invested capital, the partners shared out the profits among them, and after a decade of such profit shares, Hugh was halfway to being a millionaire.

On the morning of the funeral, Hugh inspected his face in the mirror, looking for signs of mortality. He was thirty-seven, and his hair was going gray. Mustaches were fashionable, and he wondered whether he should grow one to make himself look younger.

Hugh and Nora had moved to a bigger house when the children started coming. They had three sons: Tobias, named for Hugh's father; Samuel, for Samuel Pilaster; and Solomon, for Solly Greenbourne. Nora produced babies with little difficulty, but once they were born, she lost interest in them. Hugh gave them a lot of attention to compensate for their mother's coldness.

Hugh's secret child, Bertie, now sixteen, was a prizewinning scholar at Windfield School and star of the cricket team. Hugh paid the boy's fees and visited the school on Speech Day. Perhaps this led a few cynical people to suspect that he was Bertie's real father. But most people assumed Hugh was simply being generously faithful to the memory of his friend Solly.

When Hugh went down to breakfast, his mother was already there. She and Dotty had come up from Folkestone yesterday for the funeral, which was today at eleven.

Hugh kissed his mother and sat down, and she said without preamble, "Do you think he really loves her, Hugh?"

Dotty, now twenty-three, was engaged to Lord Ipswich, eldest son of the Duke of Norwich. Nick Ipswich was heir to a bankrupt dukedom, and Mama was afraid he only wanted Dotty for her money—or rather her brother's money.

Hugh looked fondly at his mother. She still wore black twenty-four years after the death of his father. Her hair was now white, but she was as beautiful as ever. "He loves her, Mama," he said.

Nick had come to Hugh to ask formal permission to marry Dotty. "I've told Miss Pilaster that I'm a poor man," he had said to Hugh. "She says she has known both affluence and poverty, and she thinks happiness comes from the people you are with, not the money you have." It was all very idealistic, and Hugh would certainly give his sister a generous dowry; but he was happy to know that Nick genuinely loved her for richer or poorer.

Dotty came down a few minutes later. Hugh's shy, giggly little sister had become a sultry woman, dark-haired and strong-willed. A lot of young men were intimidated by her. But Nick Ipswich had a quiet strength that did not need the prop of a compliant wife.

Nick called by appointment at ten, while they were still sitting around the breakfast table. He sat next to Dotty and took a cup of coffee. He had typically English good looks—fair hair and blue eyes—and Dotty looked as if she wanted to eat him with a spoon.

Hugh had asked for this meeting, so he plunged right in. "Dotty, your fiancé and I have had several discussions about money. We've worked out that the finances of the dukedom can be transformed permanently with about a hundred thousand pounds. So that is what I'm going to give you as a dowry."

Dotty threw her arms around her fiancé and kissed him, then came around the table and kissed Hugh. Hugh felt a little awkward, but all the same, he was glad to be able to make them so happy.

Nora came down dressed for the funeral in purple-and-black bombazine. She had taken breakfast in her room, as always. She had become very plump, and her face was rounder than ever. "Where are those boys?" she said irritably, looking at the clock. "I told that wretched governess to have them ready—"

She was interrupted by the arrival of the governess and the children—ten-year-old Toby; Sam, who was six; and Sol, four. They were all in black morning coats, and each carried a miniature top hat. Hugh felt a glow of pride. "My little soldiers," he said.

Sam, the middle one, was bursting with news. "Mama, I've got a pet," he said excitedly. He took a matchbox from his pocket, held it out to his mother, and opened it. "Bill the Spider!"

Nora screamed, knocked the box from his hand, and jumped away. "Horrible boy!" she yelled.

Sam scrabbled on the floor for the box. "Bill's gone," he cried, and burst into tears.

Nora turned on the governess. "How could you let him do this!"

Hugh intervened. "There's no harm done." He put an arm around Nora's shoulders. "You were taken by surprise, that's all." He ushered her out into the hall. "Come on, everyone. It's time to leave."

As they left the house, he put a hand on Sam's shoulder. "Now, Sam, I hope you've learned that you must not frighten ladies."

KENSINGTON Methodist Hall was packed to the galleries. Representatives had come from every important financial institution in the City. The family were ushered to reserved seats in the front row. Hugh sat next to Samuel, who was in his seventies but still alert.

Samuel was the obvious choice as Senior Partner now that Joseph was dead. He was the oldest and most experienced. However, Augusta would oppose him fiercely. She would probably back Joseph's brother, Young William, now forty-two.

Among the other partners, two would not be considered, because they did not bear the Pilaster name: Major Hartshorn and Sir Harry Tonks, husband of Clementine. The remaining partners were Hugh and Edward.

Hugh wanted to be Senior Partner. He wanted it with all his heart. However, Augusta would oppose him even more bitterly than she would oppose Samuel. But he could not bear to wait until Augusta was dead before he took control. She was only fifty-eight; she could be around in another fifteen years, as vigorous and spiteful as ever.

Edward was sitting next to Augusta in the front row. His wife, Emily, sat on his other side, which was a rare event. They led quite separate lives. Edward was heavy and red-faced in middle age, and he had recently developed some kind of skin rash. He was neither intelligent nor hardworking, and he relied on his clerk, Simon Oliver, to keep him out of trouble. The idea of his being Senior Partner was unthinkable.

Next to Emily was Micky Miranda, fiendishly debonair in a gray coat with a black mink collar. He and Edward were still as thick as thieves, and Micky was involved in many of the risky South American investments the bank had backed in recent years.

The service was long and tedious. Then the procession to the cemetery, in the September rain, took more than an hour.

Hugh studied Augusta as her husband's coffin was lowered into the ground. She stood under a big umbrella held by Edward. Her proud face was carved in stern lines, and she showed no grief.

After the burial, there was a lunch at Whitehaven House for the whole Pilaster family, including all the partners with their wives and children. Hugh had not been inside the house—which now belonged to Edward—for a year or two. It had been redecorated yet again. Moorish arches had been inserted in the doorways, and here in the dining room were a Cairo screen and a Koran stand.

Augusta sat Edward in his father's chair. Hugh thought that was a bit tactless. Putting him at the head of the table cruelly emphasized how incapable he was of filling his father's shoes.

However, Augusta had a purpose, as always. Toward the end of

the meal she said with her customary abruptness, "There must be a new Senior Partner, and obviously it will be Edward."

Hugh was horrified. It was unnerving that she would even make the suggestion. "I think the partners should discuss the question tomorrow," he said.

"I'll thank you not to tell me what I may and may not discuss in my own house, young Hugh," said Augusta.

"If you insist." He collected his thoughts. "You, dear Aunt, don't understand the subtleties of the decision, perhaps because you have never worked at the bank. The oldest surviving partner is Samuel. I'm sure we would all agree that he would be a wise choice. However, Samuel has declined the honor once before. If he should do so again, the eldest Pilaster would be Young William, who is also widely respected in the City."

Augusta said impatiently, "It is not the City that has to make the choice; it is the Pilaster family. We may choose whom we like."

"We can't do what we like," Hugh said emphatically. "We're entrusted with other people's money. We have duties to them."

Augusta was indignant. "Edward is as good as anyone!"

Hugh looked around the table. "Is there anyone here who will say that Edward is the most able banker among us?"

The other partners were silent. Suddenly Hugh realized Augusta must have spoken to them beforehand. But surely she could not have persuaded them to accept Edward as Senior Partner.

"What has she said to you?" he said abruptly. "William? George? Harry? Come on, out with it."

They all looked a little foolish. Finally William said, "Augusta and Edward have made it clear that unless Edward becomes Senior Partner, they will withdraw their capital from the business."

"What?" Hugh was stunned. Between them, Augusta and Edward controlled about forty percent of the bank's capital. If they withdrew the money, the bank would be crippled.

It was startling that Augusta would make such a threat—and even worse that the partners were ready to give in to her. "You're surrendering all authority to her," he said. "If you let her get away with it this time, she'll do it again."

Edward blustered, "Don't you dare speak of my mother like that. Mind your manners!"

"Manners be damned," Hugh said. "You're about to ruin a great bank." He pushed back his chair and stood up, throwing his napkin down on the table like a challenge. "Well, here's one person who won't be bullied. I resign." As he turned from the table, he caught Augusta's eye, and saw on her face a victorious smile.

SAMUEL came to see him that evening. He looked weary and sad. Hugh offered him a drink, and he asked for port. Hugh called his butler and ordered a bottle decanted.

"I shall resign, too," Samuel said. "I shall go at the end of the year. I told them so after you made your dramatic exit."

"What did they say?"

"Well, that's why I'm here, dear boy. I regret to say I'm a messenger from the enemy. They asked me to persuade you not to resign."

"Then they're fools."

"That they are. However, there is one thing you ought to think about. If you resign immediately, everyone in the City will know why. People will say that if Hugh Pilaster believes Edward can't run the bank, he's probably right. It could cause a financial crisis."

Hugh had not thought of that. A crisis might bring down other, perfectly sound businesses, the way the collapse of Overend & Gurney had destroyed Hugh's father's firm in 1866.

"Perhaps you ought to stay until the end of the financial year, like me," Samuel said. "It's only a few months. By then Edward will have been in charge for a while and people will be used to it."

The butler came back with the port. Hugh sipped it thoughtfully. "All right," he said at last. "I'll stay until the end of the year."

Samuel nodded. "I thought you would," he said. "It's the right thing to do, and you always do the right thing in the end."

2

BEFORE Maisie Greenbourne finally said good-bye to high society eleven years ago, she had gone to all her friends—who were many and rich—and persuaded them to give money to Rachel Miranda's Southwark Female Hospital. Consequently, the hospital's costs were covered by the income from its investments.

The money was managed by Rachel's father, the only man involved in the running of the hospital. At first Maisie had wanted to handle the investments herself, but she had found that bankers and stockbrokers refused to take her seriously.

Rachel never saw Micky Miranda, but he would not divorce her. For ten years she had been carrying on a discreet affair with Maisie's brother, Dan Robinson, who was now a member of Parliament. The three of them lived together in Maisie's suburban house.

The hospital was in a working-class area in the heart of the city. They had taken a long lease on a row of four houses and had knocked internal doors through the walls on each level. Instead of cavernous wards, they had small, comfortable rooms, each with only two or three beds.

Maisie's office was a cozy sanctuary near the main entrance. It had two chairs, a faded rug, and bright curtains. On the wall was the framed poster of "The Amazing Maisie."

The woman sitting opposite her was barefoot, ragged, and nine months pregnant. In her eyes was the wary, desperate look of a starving cat. Maisie said, "What's your name, dear?"

"Rose Porter, mum."

Maisie poured Rose a cup of tea. "You look tired."

"I've walked all the way from Bath, mum."

It was a hundred miles. "It must have taken a week," said Maisie. "You poor thing."

Rose burst into tears.

This was normal, and Maisie was used to it. She sat on the arm of Rose's chair, put her arm around her shoulders, and hugged her.

"Tell me how you were living before you fell pregnant."

"I was cook for a Mrs. Freeman in Bath."

"And how did you meet your young man?"

"He came up and spoke to me in the street," Rose said. "It was my afternoon off, and I had a new yellow parasol. I looked a treat, I know I did. That yellow parasol was the undoing of me."

Maisie coaxed the story out of her. It was typical. The man was an upholsterer. He had courted her, and they had talked of marriage. Then he had lost his job. He moved to another town, looking for work—and vanished. Then she found she was pregnant.

Rose winced, and Maisie said, "What's the matter?"

"My back hurts. It must be all the walking."

Maisie smiled. "It's not backache. Your baby's coming." She took Rose upstairs and handed her over to a nurse, then stopped beside the bed of the woman they called Miss Nobody, who refused to give any details about herself, not even her name. She was a dark-haired girl of about eighteen. Her accent was upper class, and Maisie was fairly sure she was Jewish. "How do you feel?" Maisie asked.

"I'm comfortable—and so grateful to you, Mrs. Greenbourne."

She was as different from Rose as could be, but they were both in the same predicament.

Maisie returned to her office and glanced at the clock. She would have to hurry, she realized. It was the first day of term at Windfield School, and she had to take Bertie.

WHEN Maisie took Bertie to school, she was always accompanied by Hugh, and she always attracted a lot of attention. At thirty-five, she was still pretty enough to turn men's heads. Today she wore a tomato-red outfit—a dress with a short jacket over it, and a hat with a feather. She knew she looked pretty and carefree. In fact, these visits to the school with Bertie and Hugh broke her heart.

It was seventeen years since she had spent a night with Hugh, and she loved him as much as ever. Most of the time she immersed herself in the troubles of the poor girls who came to the hospital, and forgot her own grief. But two or three times a year she had to see Hugh, and then the pain came back.

He had known for eleven years that he was Bertie's real father. After his meeting with Ben Greenbourne, Hugh had confronted Maisie with his suspicions, and she finally told him the truth. Since then he had done everything he could for Bertie. Bertie still believed his father was the late, lovable Solomon Greenbourne; to tell him the truth would just cause unnecessary pain. Maisie told her son that Hugh was his dead father's best friend. Luckily there was no likeness between Bertie and Hugh. In fact, Bertie was like Maisie's father, with soft dark hair and sad brown eyes. He was a good athlete and a hardworking student, and Maisie was proud of him.

On these school occasions, Hugh was scrupulously polite to Maisie, but she could tell that he felt the bittersweetness of the situation. The only aspect of Hugh's homelife he talked about was his three sons, whom he loved to distraction. But Maisie had gathered that Nora was not a loving mother. Over the years she had watched Hugh resign himself to a cold, frustrating marriage.

Today he had on a silver-gray tweed suit that matched his silver-streaked hair. She took his arm as they walked into the school, and she thought she would give her soul to be with him every day.

They helped Bertie unpack his trunk; then Bertie made them tea in his study.

"My boy Toby will be coming here next half," Hugh said. "I wonder if you'd keep an eye on him for me."

"I'll be glad to," Bertie said. "I'll make sure he doesn't go swimming in Bishop's Wood." Maisie frowned at him, and he said, "Sorry. Bad joke."

"They still talk about that, do they?" Hugh said.

"Every year the headmaster tells the story of how Peter Middleton drowned, to try and frighten chaps. But they still go swimming."

After tea they said good-bye to Bertie, walked back into the town, and took the train to London. As they watched the scenery flash by, Hugh said, "Edward is going to be Senior Partner at the bank."

Maisie was startled. "I didn't think he had the brains."

"He hasn't. I shall resign at the end of the year."

"Oh, Hugh!" Maisie knew how much he cared for that bank. All his hopes were tied up in it. He had had so much bad luck, while Edward had far too much good. "Edward is Lord Whitehaven, too," she said. "Do you realize that if the title had gone to Ben Greenbourne, Bertie would be in line to inherit it?"

"Yes."

"But Augusta put a stop to it. She was behind all that rubbish in the newspapers about 'Can a Jew be a peer?' Do you remember?"

"I do. But how can you be so sure that Augusta was behind it?"

"The Prince of Wales told us."

Hugh shook his head. "Augusta never ceases to amaze me."

Maisie sat in silence for a while thinking of Hugh. Now that he was leaving the bank, what was left in his life? He did not love his wife, and his wife did not love their children. Why should he not find happiness in the arms of the woman he had always loved?

At Paddington Station, he helped her into a hansom. As they said good-bye, she held his hands and said, "Come home with me."

He looked sad and shook his head.

"We love each other—we always have," she pleaded. "Come with me, and to hell with the consequences. People should grab happiness where they can. You only have one life."

"But when you grab happiness, you may let go of something even more valuable—your integrity. That night at Kingo's house I would have betrayed Solly if you had let me. But over the years I have come to value integrity more than anything."

"But what is it?"

"Telling the truth, keeping promises, taking responsibility for your mistakes. It's a matter of being what you claim to be."

He withdrew his hands and stepped back. "Good-bye, Maisie."

She stared at him helplessly. Years of suppressed yearning caught up with her. She would have stayed there forever, but Hugh nodded to the cabbie and said, "Drive on."

A moment later Hugh was gone from her sight.

3

HUGH slept badly that night. He kept waking up and running over his conversation with Maisie. He wished he had given in and gone home with her. But something else was bothering him, too. He had a feeling she had said something momentous, the significance of which eluded him. He ran over the conversation: *"Come home with me. . . . Do you realize that if the title had gone to Ben Greenbourne, Bertie would be in line to inherit it?"*

Hugh had not realized Augusta had been behind the nasty propaganda about whether a Jew could be a lord. But the Prince of Wales had known somehow, and he had told Maisie and Solly.

Suddenly Hugh sat up, staring into darkness. Solly had known.

If Solly knew that the Pilasters were responsible for a campaign of racial hatred against his father, he would never again do business with Pilasters Bank. In particular, he would have canceled the Santamaria railroad issue. He would have told Edward that he was canceling it. And Edward would have told Micky.

"Good heavens," Hugh said aloud. If Solly had been about to cancel, Micky might have killed him to save the deal. Had Micky murdered *two* of his friends—Peter Middleton and Solly Greenbourne? And if he had, what was Hugh going to do about it?

HE WAS still agonizing over the question the next day when something happened that gave him the answer.

His clerk, Jonas Mulberry, reported that he had seen some papers being drawn up by Edward's clerk, Simon Oliver. It was a proposal for a loan issue to Cordova for two million pounds, to build a new harbor in Santamaria Province.

Hugh was appalled. The bank needed less exposure in South America, not more. But what could he do about it? Edward was Senior Partner now, and completely under the influence of Micky Miranda. Could Hugh weaken that influence? He had to try.

Edward had already left for lunch. Guessing his destination, Hugh took a hansom to the Cowes Club. It was still early, and he found Edward alone in the smoking room, drinking a large glass of Madeira. Edward's skin rash was getting worse, he noticed.

Hugh sat down and ordered tea. Edward made no bones about showing that he had no wish for his cousin's company. "You didn't come this far for a cup of tea," he said. "What do you want?"

It was a bad start. Feeling pessimistic, Hugh began. "I have something to say that will shock and horrify you. You'll have trouble believing it, but all the same it's true. I think Micky is a murderer."

"Oh, come now," Edward said angrily. "That's nonsense."

"Listen to me before you dismiss the idea out of hand. Yesterday I learned that Solly Greenbourne knew your mother was behind the campaign to stop Ben Greenbourne's getting a peerage."

Edward gave a start, as if what Hugh had said chimed with something he already knew. Hugh felt more hopeful. "I'm on the right track, am I not?" he said. Guessing, he went on. "Solly threatened to cancel the Santamaria railroad deal, didn't he?"

Edward nodded. "I was sitting at this very table with Micky when Solly came in, angry as the devil. But—"

"And that night Solly died."

"Yes. But Micky was with me all night. We played cards here, then went on to Nellie's."

Hugh sat forward in his chair. "He must have left you just for a few minutes. I saw him coming into the club about the time Solly died."

"That must have been earlier." Edward's face settled into an expression of decided skepticism. "Micky's not a murderer."

"He is. He killed Peter Middleton, too."

"This is ridiculous!"

"You think you killed him. I know that. You ducked him repeatedly, then went chasing after Tonio; and you think that Peter was too exhausted to swim to the side and drowned. But there's something you don't know. Peter was a very strong swimmer. He had been practicing swimming every day that spring. He swam to the side without difficulty. Tonio saw it."

"What—" Edward swallowed. "What else did Tonio see?"

"While you were climbing up the side of the quarry, Micky held Peter's head under the water until he drowned."

To Hugh's surprise Edward did not spurn the idea. Instead he said, "Why have you waited so long to tell me this?"

"I didn't think you'd believe me." He studied Edward's expression. "But you do believe me, don't you?"

Edward nodded. "I know why he did it."

"Why?" said Hugh. "Why did Micky kill Peter?"

Edward took a long swallow of Madeira. "In Cordova the Mirandas are a wealthy family, but their dollars don't buy much here. When Micky came to Windfield, he spent his entire allowance in a few weeks. When he ran out of money, he stole."

Hugh remembered the scandal that had rocked the school in May of 1866. "The six gold sovereigns that were stolen from Mr. Offerton," he said wonderingly. "Micky was the thief?"

"Yes. And Peter knew. He saw Micky coming out of Offerton's study. When the theft was reported, he guessed the truth. He said he would tell unless Micky owned up. We thought it was a piece of luck to catch him at the pool. When I ducked him, I was trying to frighten him into silence. But I never thought . . ."

"That Micky would kill him."

"And all these years he's let me think it was my fault."

Hugh stood up to go. "I'm sorry to have given you such a blow."

Edward said nothing. He seemed to have forgotten Hugh's existence. He was staring into his glass. Hugh looked hard at him and saw with a jolt that he was crying.

Hugh went out quietly and closed the door.

Chapter Two: October

1

MICKY Miranda was worried. He sat in the lounge of the Cowes Club smoking a cigar, wondering what he had done to offend Edward. Edward was avoiding him. He stayed away from the club, he did not go to Nellie's, and he did not even appear in Augusta's drawing room at teatime. Micky had not seen him for a week.

Every now and again Edward would go into a sulk, but it never lasted more than a day or two. This time it was serious, and it could jeopardize the Santamaria harbor money.

In the last decade Pilasters Bank had issued Cordovan bonds about once a year. Some of the money had been capital for railways, waterworks, and mines; some had been simple loans to the government. Micky had taken a commission on everything, and he was now personally very rich. More significantly, his ability to raise the money had made him the unquestioned heir to his father's power.

And Papa was about to start a revolution. The plans were laid. The Miranda army would dash south by rail and lay siege to the capital. But revolutions cost money. Papa had instructed Micky to raise the biggest loan yet—two million pounds sterling—to buy weapons and supplies for a civil war. And Papa had promised a matchless reward: when Papa was president, Micky would be prime minister, and he would become president himself when Papa died. But now it had been put at risk by Edward.

While Micky sat smoking and worrying, he spotted Hugh Pilaster. Micky did not like Hugh, and he knew the feeling was mutual. However, he went over to Hugh's table. "Evening, Pilaster. Have you seen Edward lately? He seems to have vanished."

"He comes to the bank every day."

"Ah." Micky hesitated, then sat down. In a lower voice he said, "Would you happen to know whether I've offended him?"

Hugh looked thoughtful for a moment. "I can't think of why I shouldn't tell you. Edward has discovered that you killed Peter Middleton and you've lied to him about it for twenty-four years."

Micky almost jumped out of his chair. How the devil had that come out? But he feigned anger. "I shall forget you ever said that," he said, and rose and left the room.

It took him only a few moments to realize that he was in no more danger from the police than he had ever been. No one could prove what he had done. The real danger he faced was that Edward would refuse to raise the two million pounds Papa needed. He had to win Edward's forgiveness. And to do that, he had to see him.

The next day he went to Nellie's at lunchtime, woke April, and persuaded her to send Edward a note promising him "something special" if he would come to the brothel that night.

Micky took April's best room and booked Edward's favorite, Henrietta, a slim girl with short dark hair. He had her dress in a man's evening clothes with a top hat, an outfit Edward found sexy.

By half past nine in the evening he was waiting for Edward. The room had a huge four-poster bed, two velvet sofas, and a big ornate fireplace. Micky reclined on one of the sofas, wearing nothing but a silk robe, sipping brandy, with Henrietta beside him.

An hour went by, and then another. Micky began to lose hope. Then, just before midnight, April put her head around the door and said, "He's arrived. He's having a drink first."

Micky posed Henrietta on the sofa with the hat low over her eyes. He turned the gaslights down, then sat on the bed, behind the door.

A few moments later Edward came in. In the dim light he did not notice Micky. Seeing Henrietta, he said, "Hullo. Who are you?"

She looked up and said, "Hello, Edward."

"Oh, it's you," he said. He shut the door and came inside. "Well, what's the something special April has been talking about? I've seen you in a tailcoat before."

"It's me," Micky said, and stood up.

Edward frowned. "I don't wish to see you," he said, and turned toward the door.

Micky stood in his way. "At least tell me why."

"I've found out the truth about Peter Middleton."

Micky nodded. "Will you give me a chance to explain?"

Edward hesitated.

Micky said, "Please."

Edward sat on the sofa. Henrietta moved close to him.

Micky sat on the opposite sofa. "I was wrong," he began. "But I was sixteen, and we've been best friends for most of our lives. Are you going to throw that away for a schoolboy peccadillo?"

"You could have told me the truth," Edward said indignantly.

Micky made his face sad. "It would have ruined our friendship."
"Not necessarily," Edward said.
"Well, it has now, hasn't it?"
"Yes," Edward said, but there was uncertainty in his voice.
Micky realized the time had come to go all out. He stood up and slipped off his robe. "Leave us, Henrietta," he said.
She looked startled, but she got up and went out.
Edward stared at Micky. "Why did you do that?" he said.
Micky put out a tentative hand and touched Edward's hair. "We're better off without her . . . aren't we?"
Edward swallowed hard. "Yes," he whispered. "Yes."

THE following week Micky spread out the plan for Santamaria harbor on the big table in the Partners' Room at Pilasters Bank. The drawing showed a new port on the Atlantic coast of Cordova, with ship-repair facilities and a rail link. None of it would ever be built, of course. The two million pounds would go straight into the Miranda war chest. But the survey was genuine, and if it had been an honest proposal, it might even have made money.
While Micky explained it to the partners, talking of building materials and labor costs, he struggled to appear calm. His entire future depended on the decision made in this room today.
All six partners were there. There would be a battle, but the odds were on Edward's side. Major Hartshorn and Sir Harry always did what their wives told them, and the wives got their orders from Augusta, so they would back Edward. Samuel would probably back Hugh. Young William was the only unpredictable one.
Edward was enthusiastic. He'd forgiven Micky—they were best friends again—and this was his first major project as Senior Partner.
As anticipated, the opposition came from Hugh. "I've been looking at what has happened to the last few South American issues we've handled," he said, and he handed round copies of a chart.
Micky studied it while Hugh continued. "The interest rate offered has gone up from year to year. Despite that, the number of bonds unsold has been higher each time."
Micky knew what that meant: investors were finding South American bonds less and less attractive.
Hugh went on. "Also, in each of the last three issues the bank has been obliged to buy Cordovan bonds in the open market to keep

the price up. We are gravely overexposed to that one sector."

For a few seconds no one spoke. Edward looked angry, but he was restraining himself, knowing it would appear better if one of the other partners contradicted Hugh. At last Sir Harry said, "Point taken, Hugh. But I think you may be overstating the case a little."

George Hartshorn concurred. "The plan itself is sound and the profits considerable. I think we should accept."

It was Samuel who spoke next. "I've been in the business twice as long as anyone else in this room, and Hugh is probably the most successful young banker in the world, and we both feel this project is more dangerous than it looks."

Everyone now looked at Young William. "South American bonds have always seemed risky," William began. "If we had allowed ourselves to be frightened of them, we would have missed out on a great deal of profitable business during the last few years. Cordova has gone from strength to strength under President Garcia. I believe we should be looking for more such business, not less."

Micky let his breath out in a long sigh of relief. He had won.

Edward said, "Four partners in favor, two against."

"Just a minute," said Hugh. "Are you confident that we can sell all or most of this issue?"

"Yes, if we price it right," Edward said.

"Then why don't we sell the bonds on a commission basis, rather than underwriting the issue."

Micky muffled a curse. That was not what he wanted. Normally when the bank launched, say, a million pounds' worth of bonds, it agreed to buy any unsold bonds itself, thereby guaranteeing that the borrower would receive the full million. In return for that guarantee, the bank took a fat percentage. The alternative method was to offer the bonds for sale with no guarantee. The bank took no risk and received a much lower percentage, but if only ten thousand pounds' worth of the bonds were sold, the borrower would get only ten thousand pounds. The risk remained with the borrower—and at this stage Micky did not want any risks.

William grunted. "Hmm. That's an idea."

Hugh had been cunning, Micky thought. If he had continued to oppose the scheme outright, he would have been overruled.

Sir Harry said, "If we do sell them all, we still make about sixty thousand pounds even at the reduced commission. And if we don't sell them all, we shall have avoided a considerable loss."

There was a general murmur of assent.

Micky began to roll up the map of the harbor. He had been defeated, but he was not ready to give up. That two million pounds was the key to the presidency of his country. He had to have it.

He would think of something.

EDWARD and Micky had arranged to have lunch together in the dining room of the Cowes Club. It was planned as a celebration of their triumph, but now they had nothing to celebrate.

By the time Edward arrived, Micky had decided what to do. His only chance was to persuade Edward to go against the decision of the partners and underwrite the bonds without telling them.

They ordered lunch, and when the waiter left, Edward said, "I've been thinking that I might get a place of my own."

"But why? You've got everything you need at your mother's."

"Everything but privacy," Edward said. "You might want to stay with me overnight, for example."

Micky saw how he could exploit this idea. He shook his head. "By the time you get the new house, I shall probably have left London."

Edward was devastated. "What the devil do you mean?"

"If I don't raise the money for the new harbor, I'll be recalled."

"The bonds will sell out, I'm sure," Edward said. He hit the table with his fist. "I wish Hugh had let me underwrite the issue."

"I suppose you have to abide by the decision of the partners."

"Of course. What else?"

"Well . . ." He hesitated. "You couldn't just have Oliver draw up an underwriting deal without telling anyone, could you? It might make the difference between my staying in London and my being recalled to Cordova."

The waiter brought their wine and poured them each a glass.

Edward said, "It would all come out eventually."

"By then it will be too late. And you can pass it off as a clerical error." Micky doubted if Edward would swallow it.

But Edward dropped his eyes. "If it means you'll stay, I'll speak to Simon this afternoon."

Micky picked up his wineglass. "To friendship," he said.

Edward clinked glasses. "To friendship."

2

THE issue of two million pounds' worth of Santamaria harbor bonds was a flop—much worse than Hugh had feared. By the deadline the bank had sold only four hundred thousand pounds' worth, and the next day the price fell. Hugh was glad he had forced Edward to sell the bonds on commission.

On the following Monday morning Jonas Mulberry brought the partners a summary of the previous week's business. Before the man left the room, Hugh noticed a discrepancy. "Just a minute, Mulberry," he said. "This can't be right." There was a huge fall in cash on deposit. "There hasn't been a big withdrawal, has there?"

"Not that I know of, Mr. Hugh," said Mulberry.

Hugh looked around the room. All the partners were there except Edward, who had not yet arrived. "Does anyone recall a big withdrawal last week?"

Nobody did.

Hugh stood up. "Let's check," he said to Mulberry.

The two of them went upstairs to the senior clerks' room. Hugh sat at a table, and Mulberry pulled a ledger from a shelf and set it in front of him. Another clerk, named Clemmow, piped up, "Is there anything I can do to assist, Mr. Hugh? I keep that ledger."

"What big withdrawals were there last week—a million pounds or more?" asked Hugh.

"Only one," the clerk said. "The Santamaria Harbor Company withdrew one million, eight hundred thousand—the amount of the bond issue less our percentage."

Hugh shot to his feet. "But they didn't have that much. They only raised four hundred thousand!"

Clemmow turned pale. "The issue was two million pounds—"

"But it wasn't underwritten. It was a commission sale!" Hugh shouted. All the clerks stared at him. "Show me the entries."

The clerk opened the ledger to a page marked "Santamaria Harbor Board." There were only three entries: a credit of two million pounds, a debit of two hundred thousand pounds' commission to the bank, and a transfer to another bank of the balance.

Hugh was livid. The money was gone. If it had simply been credited to the account in error, then the mistake could have been rectified. But the money had been withdrawn the next day. That suggested a carefully planned fraud. "By heaven, someone is going to jail for this," he said wrathfully. "Who wrote these entries?"

"I did, sir," said Clemmow. "On Mr. Oliver's instructions."

Simon Oliver was a Cordovan and the cousin of Micky Miranda. Hugh instantly suspected he was behind the fraud. "Find Oliver and bring him to me," Hugh said to Mulberry.

Hugh returned to the Partners' Room. "There's been a major fraud," he said grimly. "The Santamaria Harbor Company has been paid the full amount of the bond issue even though we only sold four hundred thousand."

They were all horrified. "How did it happen?" said William.

"I think it was done by Edward's clerk. I've sent for him, but my guess is the swine is already on a ship headed for Cordova."

Mulberry came in, and to Hugh's surprise he was accompanied by Simon Oliver. The man had a thick contract in his hand. He looked scared. No doubt Hugh's remark about someone going to jail had been repeated to him.

He held the document out to Hugh. "Mr. Edward told me to draw it up." He gave Hugh another sheet of paper. This was a contract brief—a short note of the terms of an agreement, given by a partner to the clerk who was to draw up the full contract. It was in Edward's handwriting, and it quite clearly said that the loan was to be underwritten.

That settled it. Edward was responsible. There had been no fraud, and there was no way the money could be got back. The whole transaction was perfectly legitimate. Hugh was enraged.

"All right, Oliver, you can go," he said.

Hugh looked at his partners. "Edward went against our collective decision," he said bitterly. "And it has cost us one million, four hundred thousand pounds."

Samuel sat down heavily. "How dreadful," he said.

Sir Harry and Major Hartshorn just looked bewildered.

William said, "Are we bankrupt?"

Hugh reflected for a moment. "Technically, no," he said. "But if something happens to cause a fall in South American bonds, we will be in deep trouble."

Jonas Mulberry interjected a question. "What about our liquidity, Mr. Hugh? We'll need a large deposit before the end of the week to meet routine withdrawals. We can't sell the harbor bonds. It would depress the price."

That was a thought. Hugh worried at the problem for a moment, then said, "I'll borrow a million from the Colonial Bank. Old Cunliffe will keep it quiet. That should tide us over."

William said, "What about Edward?"

"Edward must resign," Samuel said. "We cannot trust him."

Sir Harry said, "Then who will be Senior Partner?"

There was a moment of silence. Samuel broke it by saying, "Oh, for goodness' sake, can there be any question? Who uncovered Edward's deceit? Who have you all looked to for guidance? You *know* who the new Senior Partner must be."

Hugh was taken by surprise. His mind had been on the problems facing the bank, and he had not given a thought to his own position. Slowly it dawned on him that he was about to achieve his life's ambition: he was going to be Senior Partner of Pilasters Bank. He looked at William, Harry, and George. They all had a shamefaced air. They had brought about this disaster by allowing Edward to become Senior Partner. Now they knew Hugh had been right all along, and he could see in their faces that they wanted him to take over. "What do you think, William?"

He hesitated only for a second. "I think you should be Senior Partner, Hugh," he said.

"Major Hartshorn?"

"I agree."

"Sir Harry?"

"Certainly. And I hope you'll accept."

It was done. Hugh took a deep breath. "Thank you for your confidence. I hope I can bring us through this calamity with our reputation and our fortunes intact."

At that moment Edward came in. "This place is in turmoil," he said. "Clerks whispering in the corridors, hardly anyone doing any work. . . . What's going on?"

Nobody spoke.

Consternation spread over his face. "What's wrong?" he said, but his expression told Hugh that he could guess. "You'd better tell me," he persisted. "After all, I am the Senior Partner."

"No, you're not," said Hugh. "I am."

Chapter Three: November

1

MISS Dorothy Pilaster married Viscount Nicholas Ipswich at Kensington Methodist Hall on a cold, bright morning in November. Afterwards a lunch was served to three hundred guests in a vast heated tent in the garden of Hugh's house.

Hugh was very happy; his sister was radiantly beautiful, and her new husband was charming to everyone. But the happiest person there was Hugh's mother. Smiling beatifically, she sat beside the groom's father, the Duke of Norwich. For the first time in twenty-four years she was not wearing black; she had on a blue-gray cashmere outfit that set off her thick silver hair.

"I used to think I had been unlucky," she murmured to Hugh in between courses. "I was wrong." It made Hugh want to cry.

He took a sip of champagne. It was a lavish wedding, and Hugh was glad he could afford it. He had steered the bank through the immediate crisis. The balance sheet was still weak, but they now had enough cash to meet normal withdrawals. They were safe from everything except some unexpected catastrophe.

A footman came to Hugh's side and said quietly, "Mr. Mulberry from the bank is on the telephone, sir, asking for you."

Mulberry knew Hugh was in the middle of a wedding. He would not telephone unless something was wrong. Hugh stood up. "Please excuse me, Mother. Something I have to attend to."

He hurried into the house. The telephone was in his library. He picked it up. "What's happened, Mulberry?"

"A telegram from New York. Civil war has broken out in Cordova. The Miranda family has attacked the capital city, Palma."

Hugh's heart was racing. "Any indication of how strong they are?" If the rebellion could be crushed quickly, there was still hope.

"President Garcia has fled. There's another cable from our Cordova office, but it's still being decoded."

"Telephone me when it's ready." Hugh hung up, then cranked the machine, got the operator, and gave the name of the bank's stockbroker. He waited while the man was called to the telephone. "Danby, this is Hugh Pilaster. What's happening to Cordovan bonds?"

"We're offering them at half par and getting no takers."

Half price, Hugh thought. Pilasters was already bankrupt. Despair filled his heart. "What will they fall to?"

"Zero, I should think. No one pays interest on government bonds in the middle of a civil war. I say, your bank will be all right, won't it?"

Hugh hesitated. He hated to tell lies, but the truth would destroy the bank. "We've got other assets, Danby. And now I must get back to my guests." Hugh had no intention of going back to his guests, but he wanted to give an impression of calm.

Before he could ask for another number, Mulberry called again. "Mr. Cunliffe from the Colonial Bank is here, sir," he said. "He is asking for repayment of the loan."

"Damn," Hugh said fervently. He knew Cunliffe was only the first. Tomorrow morning depositors would be queuing outside the doors, wanting cash. And Hugh would not be able to pay them. "Tell Mr. Cunliffe that you were unable to get authorization for the check, because all the partners are at the wedding," he said.

"Very good, Mr. Hugh."

"And then . . ." Hugh paused. He hated to say the dreadful words. He shut his eyes. Better get it over with. "And then, Mulberry, you must close the doors of the bank."

Hugh put down the phone. Staring at the bookshelves of his library, he saw instead the grand façade of Pilasters Bank and imagined the closing of the ornate iron doors. Pilasters had crashed.

2

"We are all absolutely penniless," said Hugh.

They did not understand at first. He could tell by their faces.

They had gathered in the drawing room of his house. The guests had gone at last—Hugh had not told anyone the bad news until the party was over—but the family were still in their wedding finery. Augusta sat with Edward, both of them wearing scornful, disbelieving expressions. Samuel sat next to Hugh. The other partners—Young William, Major Hartshorn, and Sir Harry—stood behind a sofa on which sat their wives—Beatrice, Madeleine, and Clementine. Nora, flushed from lunch and champagne, sat in her usual chair beside the fire. Nick and Dotty held hands, looking frightened.

Hugh felt most sorry for the newlyweds. "Dotty's dowry is gone, Nick. I'm afraid all our plans have come to nothing."

Nora looked bewildered. "We can't be penniless," she said.

"But we are," said Hugh patiently. "All our money is in the bank, and the bank has failed."

Augusta stood up. "We must salvage what we can. There must be quite a lot of cash in the bank still—gold and banknotes. We must get it out and hide it before the creditors move in. Then—"

Hugh interrupted her. "We'll do no such thing," he said sharply. "Be quiet and sit down, Augusta, or I'll have you thrown out."

She was sufficiently surprised to shut up.

Hugh said, "There is cash at the bank, and as we have not officially been declared bankrupt, we can choose to pay some of our creditors. You'll all have to dismiss your servants. Send them to the bank with a note of how much they are owed. I will pay them off."

"It's not possible to live in this house with no servants," Nora said.

"That need not trouble you," said Hugh. "You won't be living in this house. I will have to sell it. We will all have to sell our houses and look for small cheap places to rent."

"This is absurd!" Augusta cried.

"It's the law," Hugh retorted. "Each partner is personally liable for all the debts of the business."

"I'm not a partner," Augusta said.

"But Edward is, on paper, and he owns your house."

"I have absolutely no intention of moving," said Augusta, "and I imagine the rest of the family feel the same."

"Quite right, Augusta," said Madeleine. "George and I will stay where we are. This is foolishness. We can't possibly be destitute."

Hugh despised them. Clinging to wealth that was no longer theirs would destroy the family's reputation as well as its fortune.

Augusta turned to her daughter. "Clementine, I'm sure you and Harry will take the same view as Madeleine and George."

Clementine said, "No, Mother."

Augusta gasped. Hugh was equally startled. It was not like his cousin Clementine to go against her mother. At least one family member had some common sense, he thought.

Clementine said, "It was listening to you that got us into this trouble. If we had made Hugh the Senior Partner instead of Edward, we would all still be as rich as Croesus. We had better let Hugh do all he can to guide us through this dreadful disaster."

William said, "Quite right, Clementine."

The battle lines were drawn. On Hugh's side were William and Samuel, and Clementine, who ruled her husband, Sir Harry. They would try to behave decently and honestly. Against him were Augusta and Edward, and Madeleine, who spoke for her husband, Major Hartshorn. They would try to snatch what they could and let the family's reputation go to hell.

Then Nora said, "You'll have to carry me out of this house."

There was a bitter taste in Hugh's mouth. His own wife was joining the enemy. "Don't you owe me any loyalty at all?" he asked.

She tossed her head. "I didn't marry you to live in poverty."

"All the same, you *will* leave this house," he said grimly.

WHEN they had gone, Hugh sat staring into the fire, racking his brains for some way to pay the bank's creditors. He was determined not to let Pilasters go into formal bankruptcy. As the afternoon faded into twilight, the outlines of a plan began to form in his mind.

At six p.m. he went to see Ben Greenbourne.

Greenbourne was past seventy but still fit, and he continued to run the business. He had a daughter, Kate, but Solly had been his only son, so when he retired, he would have to hand over the business to his nephews, and he seemed reluctant to do that.

Hugh called at the mansion in Piccadilly and was shown into the library. In this room he had first learned that Bertie was his son.

The old man appeared fifteen minutes later and apologized for keeping Hugh waiting. "A domestic problem detained me," he said, looking tired and worried. He did not say what the domestic problem was, and Hugh did not ask.

"You know that Cordovan bonds have crashed," Hugh said, "and that my bank has closed its doors as a result."

"Yes. I am very sorry."

"It's twenty-four years since an English bank failed."

"That was Overend and Gurney. I remember it well."

"So do I. My father went broke and hanged himself."

Greenbourne was embarrassed. "I am most terribly sorry, Pilaster. That dreadful fact had slipped my mind."

"A lot of firms went down in that crisis. But much worse will happen tomorrow." Hugh leaned forward and began his big pitch. "In the last quarter of a century the business done in the City has increased tenfold, and we are all more closely intertwined than ever. Some of the people whose money we have lost will be unable to pay their debts, so they will go bust, too. Next week dozens of banks will fail, hundreds of businesses will close, and thousands of people will find themselves destitute—unless we take action to prevent it."

"Action?" said Greenbourne. "Your only remedy is to pay your debts. You cannot do so; therefore, you are helpless."

"Alone, yes, I'm helpless. But suppose a syndicate of bankers was formed to take over Pilasters. The syndicate would guarantee to pay any creditor on demand. At the same time, it would begin to liquidate Pilasters' assets in an orderly fashion."

Suddenly Greenbourne was interested. "I see. If the members of the syndicate were sufficiently respected, their guarantee might be enough to reassure everyone, and creditors might not demand their cash immediately. With luck the flow of money coming in from the sale of assets might cover the payments to creditors."

"And a dreadful crisis would be averted."

Greenbourne shook his head. "In the end the syndicate would lose money, for Pilasters' liabilities are greater than its assets."

"Not necessarily. We have more than two million pounds' worth of Cordovan bonds, which are today valued at nothing. But they may not be worthless forever. The rebels may be defeated, or the new government may resume interest payments. If the bonds came up to just half their previous level, the syndicate would break even."

Greenbourne shook his head. "It might work but for those Santamaria harbor bonds. That Cordovan minister, Miranda, strikes me as an out-and-out thief, and his father is apparently the leader of the rebels. My guess is that the whole two million pounds has gone to pay for guns and ammunition. In which case, investors will never see a penny."

"I'm afraid you may be right," Hugh said. "All the same, there's a chance. But the plan depends on you. If you agree to head the syndicate, the City will follow your lead."

The old man was silent; then he said firmly, "No."

Hugh slumped in his chair. It was his last shot, and it had failed.

Greenbourne said, "All my life I have been cautious. Where other men see high profits, I see high risks, and I resist the temptation. Your uncle Joseph was not like me. He would take the risk—and he pocketed the profits. His son, Edward, was worse. If I spend money to rescue you, the foolish investor would be rewarded and the careful one will suffer."

Hugh had wondered before coming here whether to tell the old man that Micky Miranda had murdered Solly. Now he considered it again, but he came to the same conclusion: it would distress the old man, but it would not persuade him to rescue Pilasters.

He was casting about for a way to change Greenbourne's mind when the butler came in. "Pardon me, Mr. Greenbourne, but you asked to be called the moment the detective arrived."

Greenbourne stood up immediately, looking agitated. "I'm sorry, Pilaster, but I must leave you. My granddaughter, Rebecca, has disappeared, and we are all distraught."

"I'm so sorry to hear that," Hugh said. He knew Solly's sister, Kate, and he had a vague memory of her daughter—a pretty, dark-haired girl. "I hope you find her safe and well."

The old man went out, leaving Hugh amid the ruins of his hopes.

3

Maisie sometimes wondered if there was something infectious about going into labor. It often happened in a ward full of women nine months pregnant that days would go by without incident, but as soon as one started labor, the others would follow.

It had been like that today. It had started at four o'clock in the morning, and they had been delivering babies ever since. The midwives and nurses did most of the work, but when they were overstretched, Maisie and Rachel would pitch in.

By seven o'clock, however, it was all over, and they were enjoying a cup of tea in Maisie's office with Dan, when Hugh Pilaster came in. "I bring bad news, I'm afraid," he said.

Looking at his face, Maisie saw that he was grief-stricken, and she thought someone had died. "Hugh, what has happened?"

"You keep all the hospital's money in my bank, don't you?"

If it was only money, Maisie thought, the news could not be that bad. Rachel answered Hugh. "Yes. My father handles it."

"And he invested your money in Cordovan bonds."

Maisie said, "What's wrong, Hugh? For goodness' sake, tell us."

"The bank has failed," he said. "All your money is gone. You'll probably have to close the hospital. I can't tell you how sorry I am."

Rachel was white with shock. Dan put his arm around her, but she would not be consoled. "What is going to happen to the women who come here for help?"

"I would gladly give you the money out of my own pocket," Hugh said. "But I've lost everything, too."

"Surely something can be done," Rachel persisted.

"I did try. I asked Ben Greenbourne to rescue the bank, but he refused. He has troubles of his own. His granddaughter, Rebecca, is missing. Anyway, without his support nothing can be done."

Rachel stood up. "I think I'd better go and see my father."

"I must go to the House of Commons," Dan said.

They went out.

Maisie's heart was full. She was dismayed at the prospect of closing the hospital, but most of all she ached for Hugh. He had once said that he was going to be the cleverest, most conservative and richest banker in the world one day; instead he had suffered the same fate as his father. Their eyes met across the room. Maisie read a silent appeal in his look. Slowly she got up and went to him. He put his arm around her and hugged her to him hard. And then, at last, he began to cry.

WHEN Hugh had gone, Maisie made a tour of the wards. For eleven years she and Rachel had given comfort to hundreds of women. She had seen this as the first of dozens of female hospitals all over the country. Now it would not happen.

She spoke to each of the women who had given birth today. The only one she was worried about was Miss Nobody. She was a slight figure, and her baby had been very small. Maisie guessed she had been starving herself to conceal her pregnancy from her family.

She sat down on the edge of Miss Nobody's bed. The new mother was nursing her child, a girl. "Isn't she beautiful?" she said.

Maisie nodded. "She's got black hair like yours." She reached out and stroked the tiny head. Like all babies, this one looked like Solly. In fact— Maisie was jolted by a sudden revelation.

"Oh, good heavens," she said. "You're Ben Greenbourne's granddaughter, Rebecca, aren't you?"

The girl's eyes widened. "How did you know? You haven't seen me since I was seven years old!"

"But I knew your mother well. I was married to her brother, after all." Kate had not been as snobbish as the rest of the Greenbournes, and had been kind to Maisie. "And I remember when you were born. You had black hair, just like your daughter."

Rebecca was scared. "Promise you won't tell them."

"I promise I won't do anything without your consent. But you ought to send word to your family. Your grandfather is distraught."

"He's the one I'm frightened of."

"I can understand why. He's a hard-hearted old curmudgeon. But if you let me talk to him, I think I can make him see sense."

"Would you?" said Rebecca in a voice full of youthful optimism.

"Of course," Maisie said. "But I won't tell him where you are unless he promises to be kind."

BEN Greenbourne's face was wet with tears as he came out of the ward. "I've left her with Kate for a while," he said in a choked voice. He pulled a handkerchief from his pocket and dabbed at his cheeks. Maisie had never seen her father-in-law lose his self-possession. She led him to her office and told him to sit down.

"All those young women—" the old man said. "Are they all in the same position as Rebecca?"

"Not all. Some are widows. Some have been abandoned by their husbands or have run away from men who beat them. But most are like Rebecca—girls who have simply made a stupid mistake."

"I didn't think life had much more to teach me," he said. "Now I find I have been foolish and ignorant. If you weren't here, where would these poor girls go?"

"They would have their babies in ditches and alleyways," Maisie said. "Unfortunately, the hospital has to close."

"Why is that?"

She looked him in the eye. "All our money was in Pilasters Bank," she said. "Now we are penniless."

"Is that so?" he said, and he looked very thoughtful.

HUGH undressed for bed, but he felt far from sleepy. He went over and over the bank's situation in his mind, but he could think of no way to ameliorate it. At midnight he heard a loud knocking at the front door. He went downstairs to answer it. A liveried footman handed him an envelope. "I beg pardon for knocking so late, sir, but the message is urgent."

Hugh opened the envelope and saw the neat, old-fashioned writing of a fussy elderly man. The words made his heart leap with joy.

Dear Pilaster,
On further reflection I have decided to consent to your proposal.
Yours, etc.,
B. Greenbourne

Chapter Four: December

1

THE Pilaster crash was the society scandal of the year. The cheap newspapers reported every development breathlessly—the sale of the great Kensington mansions, the auctions of the paintings and antique furniture, the modest suburban houses where the Pilasters now peeled potatoes and washed their own undergarments.

Hugh and Nora rented a small house with a garden in Chingford, a village nine miles from London. They left their servants behind. Nora, who had not done housework for years, took it badly and shuffled about in a grubby apron, complaining constantly.

Each partner received a small monthly allowance. In theory they were not entitled to anything. But the syndicate members felt the family's cooperation was helpful in selling off the assets, and it was worth a small payment to retain their goodwill.

Hugh followed the civil war in Cordova anxiously. At first the Miranda faction seemed set to win the war. President Garcia had fled the capital and taken refuge in the fortified city of Campanario, in the south, his home region. Hugh was dispirited. If the Mirandas won, they would never pay interest on loans made to the previous regime, and Cordovan bonds would be worthless for the foreseeable future. But then Tonio's family, the Silvas, joined the president's side, and the forces were evenly balanced. So were the financial resources: the north had nitrate mines and the south had silver, but neither side could get its exports financed or insured. Both appealed to the British government for recognition, in the hope that it would help them get credit. But so far the prime minister, Lord Salisbury, refused to favor either side.

Then Tonio Silva arrived in London.

He turned up at Hugh's suburban home on the day before Christmas. Hugh was in the kitchen giving the boys breakfast. Nora was getting dressed; she was going in to London to do her Christmas shopping, although she would have very little money to spend. Hugh had agreed to stay at home and take care of the boys.

Tonio had grown a beard and mustache—no doubt to hide the scars of the beating he had been given by Micky's thugs eleven years earlier—but Hugh instantly recognized the carrot-colored hair and reckless grin. It was snowing, and there was a dusting of white on Tonio's hat and coat. Hugh took his old friend into the kitchen and gave him tea. "How did you find me?" he asked.

"It wasn't easy," Tonio replied. "There was no one at your old house, and the bank was closed, so I went to your aunt Augusta's. She didn't know your address, but she remembered Chingford. The way she said the name, it sounded like a prison camp."

Hugh nodded. "It's not so bad. The boys like it here."

"Augusta hasn't moved."

"No. She refuses to accept reality, but she'll find out that there are worse places than Chingford."

"Cordova, for instance," said Tonio. "The war has reached a stalemate. Everything depends on the British government now. The side that wins recognition will be able to get credit and resupply its army. That's why I'm here."

"Have you been sent by President Garcia?"

"Better than that. I am now officially the Cordovan minister in London. Miranda has been dismissed. I hope to persuade the prime minister to support our side."

Hugh looked at him skeptically. "Lord Salisbury is trying to keep the lid on a boiling cauldron in Ireland. He's got no time for a distant South American civil war." Hugh did not mean to sound negative, but an idea was forming in his mind.

Tonio said rather irritably, "Well, all right. You're English. What do you think would engage his attention?"

"You could promise to protect British investors from loss."

"How?"

Hugh shifted in his chair. It was odd to be deciding the future of a country here in his kitchen. "British investors put two million pounds into the Santamaria Harbor Company—Pilasters Bank being the biggest contributor. I have no doubt the entire two million went into the Miranda war chest. We need to get it back. If your side won the war, could President Garcia hand over the nitrate mines to the Harbor Company in compensation for the fraud?"

Tonio said firmly, "I have been told by the president that I can promise *anything* that will get the British on his side."

Hugh began to feel excited. Suddenly the prospect of paying off all the Pilasters' debts seemed closer. "We ought to lay the groundwork before you make your pitch. I believe I could persuade old Ben Greenbourne to put in a good word with Lord Salisbury."

"We should act fast," Tonio said.

"We'll go into town right away. I can telephone Greenbourne from the bank." Hugh stood up. "Let me tell Nora."

She was in the bedroom putting on an elaborate hat with fur trim. "I have to go in to town," Hugh said as he put on a tie.

"Who's going to look after the boys? I'm going shopping."

"I'm sorry, Nora, but you can't. I have to speak to Ben Greenbourne urgently."

"I'm sick of this," she screeched. "Sick of this boring village, sick of the children, and sick of you. My father lives better than we do." Nora's father had opened a pub with a loan from Pilasters Bank. "I ought to go live with him and work as a barmaid," she said. "Then I'd be paid for doing drudgery."

Hugh stared at her. Suddenly he knew there was nothing left of their marriage; she hated him, and he despised her. "Take your hat off, Nora," he said. "You're not going shopping." He put on his suit jacket and went out.

Tonio was waiting impatiently in the hall. Hugh kissed the boys, picked up his hat and coat, and opened the door. "There's a train in a few minutes," Hugh said.

Outside, it was snowing harder. They hurried along a gravel road toward the village. The train came into sight as they crossed a bridge over the tracks.

A man was leaning on the parapet, watching the approaching train. As they passed him, he turned. It was Micky Miranda—and he had a revolver in his hand.

After that everything happened very quickly.

Hugh cried out, but his shout was a whisper compared to the noise of the train. Micky pointed the gun at Tonio and fired at

point-blank range. Tonio staggered and fell. Micky turned the gun on Hugh, but as he did so, smoke from the engine billowed over the bridge in a dense cloud. Suddenly they were both blinded. Hugh threw himself to the snowy ground. He heard the gun again—twice—but he felt nothing. He rolled sideways and got to his knees, peering into the fog.

The smoke began to clear. Hugh glimpsed a figure in the mist and rushed at him. Micky saw him and turned, but too late; Hugh cannoned into him. Micky fell, and the gun flew from his hand and sailed in an arc over the parapet and down onto the railway line.

Hugh fell on top of Micky. They both struggled to their feet. Micky stooped to pick up his walking cane. Hugh rushed at him again and knocked him down. As Micky scrambled to his feet, Hugh lashed out at him but missed. Micky struck at him with the cane and hit Hugh's head. The blow hurt. Hugh roared with rage, rushed at Micky, and butted his face. They both staggered back, breathing hard.

Then there was a whistle from the station. The train was leaving, and panic showed on Micky's face. Hugh guessed that Micky had planned to escape by train, and could not afford to be stuck in Chingford so close to the scene of his crime. The guess was right. Micky turned and ran from the bridge and toward the station.

Hugh gave chase. Micky was no sprinter, and Hugh was not in much better shape. Micky ran into the station as the train was pulling out. Hugh followed him, blowing hard. When they charged onto the platform, a railwayman shouted, "Oy! Where's your tickets?"

By way of reply Hugh yelled, "Murder!"

Micky ran along the platform, trying to catch the receding rear end of the train. Hugh charged after him, doing his best to ignore the stabbing pain in his side. The railwayman joined in the chase. Micky caught up with the train, grabbed a handle, and jumped on a step. Hugh dived after him, caught him by the ankle, and lost his grip. The railwayman tripped over Hugh, and they both went flying. When Hugh got to his feet, the train was out of reach.

The railwayman got up, brushing snow off his clothes, and said, "What the 'ell was all that about?"

Breathing like a leaky bellows, Hugh blurted out, "A man has been shot." He led the railwayman to the bridge, where Tonio lay.

Hugh knelt by the body. "My God, what a mess," said the railwayman. Hugh forced himself to slide his hand under Tonio's coat and feel for a heartbeat. There was none. He felt a wave of grief that pushed him close to tears.

With anguished clarity he could see how Micky had planned this. Micky had friends in the Foreign Office; one of them must have told him that Tonio was in London. Tonio had lodged his letters of accreditation, so Micky knew his days were numbered. But if Tonio were to die, the situation would become muddled again. There would be no one in London to negotiate on behalf of President Garcia, and Micky would be the de facto minister.

But how had Micky known where to find Tonio? Perhaps he had people following Tonio—or maybe Augusta had told him that Tonio had been there asking where to find Hugh. Either way, he had followed Tonio to Chingford. Micky knew Tonio had to come back to the railway station sooner or later, so he had lurked there, waiting to kill him.

It was a fearfully risky scheme, but it had almost worked. If things had gone as he planned, no one would have recognized Micky. Chingford had neither telegraph nor telephone, so he would have been back in London before the crime could be reported.

But he had failed to kill Hugh. And, Hugh suddenly realized, technically Micky was no longer the Cordovan minister, so he had lost his diplomatic immunity. He could hang for this. Hugh stood up. "We must report the murder. When's the next train?"

The railwayman took a large watch from his waistcoat pocket. "Forty-seven minutes," he said.

"We should both get on it. You go to the police station in Walthamstow. I'll go on to town and report it to Scotland Yard."

They carried Tonio to a bench in the waiting room. Hugh paced up and down while the railwayman sat on the opposite bench and stared at the body in fearful fascination. After a while Hugh sat beside him. They stayed like that, silent and watchful, sharing the cold room with the dead man until the train came in.

2

MICKY Miranda was fleeing for his life. His luck was running out. He had committed four murders in the last twenty-four years and had got away with the first three—but this time he had stumbled. Hugh Pilaster had seen him shoot Tonio Silva in broad daylight, and there was no way to escape the hangman but by leaving England.

Back in London, Micky hurried through Liverpool Street Railway Station and dived into a hansom cab. He went straight to the office of the Gold Coast and Mexico Steamship Company. The place was crowded, mainly with Latins. But his expensive clothes and upper-class arrogance got the attention of a clerk, and Micky said, "I want to book passage to Cordova."

"There's a war on in Cordova," said the clerk.

Micky suppressed a sarcastic retort. "You haven't suspended all sailings, I take it."

"We're selling tickets to Lima, Peru. The ship will go on to Palma if political conditions permit."

That would do. "When is the next departure?"

"The *Aztec* is leaving Southampton tonight, if you're in a hurry."

Thank heavens! His luck had not quite run out. "Reserve me a stateroom—the best available."

"Very good, sir. May I have the name?"

"Andrews," he said. "M. R. Andrews." The police might check passenger lists, looking for the name Miranda. Now they would not find it. He was grateful for the insane liberalism of Britain's laws, which permitted people to enter and leave the country without passports. Then he realized he had another problem: Scotland Yard could circulate his description to all port towns by telegraph.

The clerk gave him his ticket, and he paid with banknotes. He pushed through the crowd and went out into the snow, still worrying. The police would be looking for a well-dressed man of forty traveling alone. One way to get past them would be to appear as an older man with a companion. In fact, he could pretend to be an invalid and be taken on board in a wheelchair. But for that he would need an accomplice. That meant Edward.

He hailed a hansom. "Drive to Hill Street," he told the cabbie.

Edward had moved to a small house in Mayfair. He answered the door in a stained silk dressing gown. The skin rash was all over his face now.

"I'm leaving the country," Micky said.

Edward said, "Oh, take me with you," and burst into tears.

"What the devil is the matter?" Micky said unsympathetically.

"I'm dying," Edward said.

"You're not dying, you fool. You've only got a skin disease."

"It's not a skin disease—it's syphilis."

Micky gasped in horror. He might have it too! The ship went via Lisbon. He could see a doctor there in a few days' time. That would have to do. But Edward was in no state to help smuggle him out of the country. There was only one candidate left: Augusta. She was his last chance. He turned to go.

"Don't leave me," Edward pleaded.

There was no time for sentiment. "I can't take a dying man with me," he snapped, and he went out without looking back.

AUGUSTA appeared her usual imperious self as she came into the drawing room in a purple silk dress with leg-of-mutton sleeves. Micky recalled the lust he had once felt for her, but there was none left. He would have to fake it.

She did not offer him her hand. "Why have you come here?" she said coldly. "You've brought ruin to me and my family."

"I didn't know that Cordovan bonds would become valueless because of the war," he said. "Did you?"

She hesitated. Obviously she had not. A crack had opened in her armor, and he tried to widen it. "I wouldn't have done it if I'd known. I would have cut my own throat before harming you." He could tell she wanted to believe this. "Anyway, it's irrelevant now. I'm leaving England today, and I will probably never come back."

She looked at him with sudden fear in her eyes. "Why?"

There was no time for beating about the bush. "I have just killed Tonio Silva, and the police are chasing me. I've booked passage on a steamer leaving Southampton tonight. I want you to come."

Her eyes widened. She took a step back.

He took her hand. "Having to leave quickly has made me realize something I should have admitted to myself a long time ago. I think you have always known it. I love you, Augusta."

As he acted his part, he watched her face, reading it the way a sailor reads the sea. She gave the hint of a smile, but he saw she was still undecided. He put his hand on her corseted waist and drew her gently toward him. When their faces were close, he said, "I can't live without you, dear Augusta."

He could feel her trembling beneath his touch. He spoke into her ear, brushing her face with his lips. "You're the most desirable woman I've ever met. Augusta . . ." He paused.

"What?" she said.

He almost had her, but not quite. He had to play his last card. "Now that I'm no longer minister, I can divorce Rachel."

"What are you saying?"

He whispered into her ear, "Will you marry me?"

"Yes," she said, and he kissed her.

3

April Tilsley burst into Maisie's office at the female hospital, dressed to the nines in scarlet silk and fox fur, carrying a newspaper and saying, "Have you heard what's happened? Micky Miranda shot Tonio Silva!"

Maisie knew who Micky was, but it took her a moment to remember that Tonio had been one of that crowd of boys around Solly and Hugh when they were young. He had been a gambler in those days, she recalled, and April had been sweet on him. "Micky *shot* him?" she said in amazement. "Is he dead?"

"Yes. It's in the afternoon paper. It also says . . ." April hesitated. "Police want to question him about other murders—those of Peter Middleton and Solomon Greenbourne."

Maisie sat down heavily. "Solly!" she said, and she felt faint. "Micky killed Solly?"

April handed her the newspaper, and Maisie read the story. It said the murder of Antonio Silva had taken place in Chingford. Her heart missed a beat. "Chingford! That's where Hugh lives!"

"Hugh Pilaster? Are you still carrying a torch for him?"

"He must have been involved, don't you see? It can't be a coincidence. Oh, dear Lord, I hope he's all right."

"I expect the paper would say if he had been hurt."

"It only happened a few hours ago. They may not know." She stood up. "I must find out," she said. "I'm going to his house."

4

Hugh was impressed by the way Scotland Yard responded to his report. The case was assigned to Detective Inspector Magridge—a sharp-faced man of about Hugh's age, meticulous and intelligent. Within an hour he had circulated a description of Micky Miranda.

He also sent a detective sergeant to interview Edward and another to see Augusta.

A police constable assigned to check London steamship offices reported that a man answering the description had booked passage on the *Aztec,* sailing from Southampton tonight. The police there were instructed to have men at the railway station and at dockside.

The detective sent to see Augusta came back to report there was no answer when he rang and knocked at the door of her house.

"I have a key," Hugh said.

Magridge said, "She's probably out, and I want the detective to go to the Cordovan ministry. Why don't you check the house?"

Glad of something to do, Hugh took a cab to Kensington Gore. He rang and knocked, but there was no answer. The last of the servants had left, obviously. He let himself in.

The house was cold. Hiding was not Augusta's style, but he decided to search the rooms anyway. The first floor was deserted. He went up to the second floor and checked her bedroom.

What he saw surprised him. The wardrobe doors were ajar, the drawers of the chest were open, and there were discarded clothes on the bed and chairs. At first he thought Augusta had been robbed. Then another thought struck him.

He ran up two flights of stairs to the servants' floor. When he had lived here, the suitcases and trunks had been kept in a big closet known as the box room. He found the door open. The room contained a few suitcases and no steamer trunk.

Augusta had run away.

He quickly checked all the other rooms. As he expected, he saw no one. The servants' rooms were already acquiring the musty air of disuse. But Uncle Joseph's bedroom looked exactly as it always had. He was about to leave when his eye fell on the lacquered display cabinet that held Joseph's valuable collection of snuffboxes.

The cabinet was empty.

Hugh frowned. He knew the snuffboxes had not been lodged with the auctioneers: Augusta had so far prevented the removal of any of her possessions. That meant she had taken them with her.

They were worth a hundred thousand pounds. She could live comfortably for the rest of her life on that money. But they did not belong to her; they belonged to the syndicate.

He decided to go after her.

He ran down the stairs and out into the street. There was a cabstand a few yards along the road. The drivers were chatting in a group, stamping their feet to keep warm. Hugh ran up to them, saying, "Did any of you drive Lady Whitehaven this afternoon?"

"Two of us did," said a cabbie. "One for her luggage."

Hugh's deduction was confirmed. "Where did you take her?"

"Waterloo Station for the one-o'clock boat train."

The boat train went to Southampton—where Micky was sailing from.

"But they missed the train," the cabbie added.

"They?" Hugh said. "There was someone with her?"

"An elderly chap in a wheelchair."

Not Micky evidently. Who, then? No one in the family was frail enough to use a wheelchair. "They missed the train, you say. Do you know when the next boat train leaves?"

"At three."

Hugh looked at his watch. It was two thirty. He could catch it. "Take me to Waterloo," he said, and jumped into the cab.

He reached the station just in time to get a ticket and board the boat train. As it pulled out of the station and picked up speed, he set out to look for Augusta.

He did not have to look far. She was in the next coach.

With a quick glance he hurried past her compartment so that she would not see him. Micky was not with her. He must have gone by an earlier train. The only other person in her compartment was an elderly man with a rug over his knees.

He went to the next coach and found a seat. There was not much point in confronting Augusta right away. She might not have the snuffboxes with her. They could be in one of her cases in the luggage car. To speak to her now would serve only to forewarn her. Better to wait until the train arrived.

It was still snowing when the train arrived in Southampton. Hugh leaned out of the carriage window. There were policemen everywhere. That indicated Micky had not yet been caught.

He jumped off while the train was still moving and got to the ticket barrier before anyone else. He spoke to a police inspector. "I'm the Senior Partner of Pilasters Bank," he said, giving the inspector his card. "I know you're looking for a murderer, but there's a woman on this train who is carrying stolen property belonging to the bank. I believe she is planning to leave the country on the *Aztec* tonight, taking it with her."

"What property would that be?" said the inspector.

"A collection of jeweled snuffboxes."

"And the name of the woman?"

"She's the dowager countess of Whitehaven."

The policeman raised his eyebrows. "I do read the newspapers, sir. I take it this is all to do with the failure of the bank."

Hugh nodded.

"Very well," said the inspector. "Stay here with me at the ticket barrier. We'll detain her as she passes through."

Hugh was tense as he watched the passengers stream off the train and out the barrier, where they had to turn in their tickets. He was fairly certain Micky was not on the train; nevertheless he scrutinized the face of every passenger.

Augusta was the last to leave. Three porters were carrying her luggage. When she saw Hugh at the ticket barrier, she turned pale.

The inspector was all politeness. "Pardon me, Lady Whitehaven. May I have a word?"

Hugh had never seen Augusta so frightened, but she had not lost her queenly manner. "I'm afraid I can't spare the time, Officer. I have to board a ship that is sailing tonight."

"I guarantee the *Aztec* won't leave without you, my lady," the inspector said smoothly. He glanced at the porters and said, "You can put those down for a minute, lads." He turned back to Augusta. "Mr. Pilaster here claims you have in your possession some very valuable snuffboxes that belong to him. Is that so?"

She began to look less alarmed, which puzzled Hugh. "I don't see why I should answer such impertinent questions," she said.

"If you don't, I shall have to look through your bags."

Augusta hesitated. "Very well, I do have the snuffboxes," she finally said. She pointed to a suitcase. "They're in there."

"The key, please," said the inspector.

Again she hesitated; again she gave in. She took out a small ring of luggage keys, selected one, and handed it over.

The inspector opened the case. It was full of shoe bags. Augusta pointed to one of the bags. The inspector opened it and drew out a cigar box. Inside were numerous small objects carefully wrapped in paper. Selecting one at random, he unwrapped it. It was a small gold box inlaid with diamond chips in the design of a lizard.

The inspector looked at Hugh. "Do you know how many there should be, sir?"

Everyone in the family did. "Sixty-five," said Hugh. "One for every year of Uncle Joseph's life." He counted them. They were all there. He began to feel the pleasure of victory.

"May I go now?" Augusta said.

The inspector bowed, and she went out, followed by her three heavily laden porters.

Suddenly Hugh realized he had seen no sign of the elderly man who had been with Augusta on the train. Was it Micky Miranda in disguise? And if so, where was he now?

5

A STEWARD led Augusta to a stateroom on the upper deck of the *Aztec.* She had spent all her cash on the best cabin available, thinking that with the snuffboxes in her suitcase she need not worry about money. Inside, there were flowers on the dresser and a bottle of champagne in a bucket of ice on a table.

She heard the traditional shout of "All ashore that's going ashore!" as the porters brought her luggage into the cabin. When they had gone, she stepped onto the deck and looked over the rail. As she watched, the gangways were withdrawn and the ropes cast off. A foghorn sounded, and slowly—almost imperceptibly—the huge ship began to move out to sea.

Augusta returned to her cabin and locked the door; then she opened her trunk and let Micky out.

He staggered across the stateroom and fell onto the bed. "Heaven help me, I thought I was going to die," he moaned.

"My poor darling, where does it hurt?"

"My legs." She massaged his calves with her fingertips, feeling the warmth of his skin through the cloth of his trousers. It was a long time since she had touched a man this way, and she felt a flush of heat rise at her throat.

She could wait no longer. She took his hand and drew it to her lips.

He looked at her curiously for a moment; then he pulled away from her. "You idiot," he sneered, getting off the bed. "You really thought I would marry you. You've got no money and no influence anymore, the bank is bust, and you even lost the snuffboxes. I heard the whole thing. What would I want with you?"

She felt a pain, like a knife in her heart. "You said you loved me."

"You're fifty-eight—my mother's age, for heaven's sake!"

She felt faint. Tears welled up in her eyes, and she turned away from him. She did not want him to see her shame and grief. "But when we get to Cordova—" she whispered.

"You're not going to Cordova. You can get off the ship at Lisbon and go back to England. I've no further use for you."

Every word was like a blow, and she backed away from him in horror. She bumped against the cabin door. Desperate to get away from him, she opened it and backed out.

The freezing night air cleared her head suddenly. She was behaving like a helpless girl, not a mature, capable woman. She had lost control of her life briefly, and it was time to seize it back again.

A man in evening dress walked past, but did not speak to her.

That gave her an idea.

She stepped back into the cabin and closed the door. Micky was straightening his tie in the mirror. "There's someone coming," she said urgently. "A policeman."

Micky's demeanor changed in a flash. The sneer was wiped off his face and replaced by a look of panic. "Oh, my God," he said.

Augusta was thinking quickly. "We're still within British waters. You can be arrested and sent back on a coast guard cutter."

"I'll have to hide." He climbed into the trunk. "Close the front, quickly."

She shut him in; then she flipped the latch to lock it.

"That's better," she said.

She sat on the bed staring at the trunk. In her mind she went over and over their conversation. She had made herself vulnerable and he had wounded her. He had caressed, then spurned her. As the minutes went by, her rage cooled and became a dark, vicious yearning for revenge.

Micky's voice, muffled, came from inside the trunk. "Augusta, what's happening?"

She made no reply.

He began to shout for help. She covered the trunk with blankets from the bed to deaden the sound. After a while he stopped.

Thoughtfully, Augusta removed the labels bearing her name from the trunk. She heard cabin doors slam; passengers were heading for the dining room. The ship began to pitch slightly in the swell as it steamed out into the English Channel.

The evening passed. Passengers trickled back in twos and threes between midnight and two o'clock. After that the ship was quiet but for the sounds of the engines and the sea.

Augusta stared obsessively at the trunk. It had been carried up here on the back of a muscular porter. She could not lift it, but she thought she could drag it. She took hold of the strap on top and pulled, tilting the trunk sideways. It tipped over and fell on its face. Micky began to shout again, and she covered the trunk with blankets once more. He stopped yelling.

She seized the strap again and pulled. It was very heavy, but she was able to move it a few inches at a time. After each tug she rested.

It took her ten minutes to drag the trunk to the cabin door; then she put on her fur coat and opened the door.

There was no one around. The passengers were now asleep, and if a crew member patrolled the decks, she did not see him. She dragged the trunk through the cabin door and rested again. After that it was easier, for the deck was slippery with snow.

She pulled the trunk up against the rail. The next part was more difficult. Taking hold of the strap, she lifted one end of the trunk and tried to bring it upright. On her first try she dropped it. The sound it made when it hit the deck seemed very loud, but no one came to investigate.

The second time, she made a more determined effort. She got down on one knee, seized the strap with both hands, and slowly heaved up. When she had the trunk tilted at a forty-five-degree angle, Micky moved inside, his weight shifting to the bottom end, and suddenly it became easy to push the whole thing upright.

She tilted it again so that it was leaning on the rail.

The last part was the hardest of all. She bent down and took hold of the lower strap. It took all her strength to lift the trunk an inch off the deck, and then her cold fingers slipped and it fell back.

But she could not give up. She had struggled so hard to bring the trunk this far. She bent down and seized the strap again.

Micky spoke again. "Augusta, what are you doing?"

"Remember how Peter Middleton died," she said. She paused.

There was no sound from inside the trunk. "You're going to die the same way," she said. "The water will be colder, and it will taste salty as it fills your lungs. But you'll know the terror he knew as death closes over your heart."

He began to shout. "Help! Help! Someone, save me!"

Augusta grabbed the strap and lifted with all her strength. The bottom of the trunk came up off the deck. Frantic scrabbling sounds came from inside as Micky tried hopelessly to get out. She closed her eyes, clenched her jaw, and pushed. As she strained with all her might, she felt something give way in her back, and she cried out with pain, but she kept lifting. The bottom of the trunk was now higher than the top, and it slid forward on the rail several inches; then it stopped. Augusta's back was in agony. She knew she could only lift one more time. She gathered her strength, closed her eyes, and heaved.

The trunk slid slowly forward on the rail, then fell into space. Micky screamed a long scream that died into the wind before the trunk hit the water with a mighty splash.

6

HUGH was desperately weary when at last his train pulled into Chingford. He hoped Nora would be asleep when he got home. He did not want to hear what a miserable day she had had, stuck in this remote village with no one to help her care for three rowdy boys. But there was a light on behind the curtains as he walked up the garden path. That meant she was still up. He let himself in.

He was surprised to see the boys in the front room, all in their pajamas, sitting in a row on the sofa. And he was astonished to see Maisie in the middle, reading to them.

All three boys jumped up and ran to him. He hugged and kissed them one by one—Sol, the youngest; then Samuel; then ten-year-old Toby. The younger two were simply overjoyed to see him, but there was something else in Toby's face. "What is it, old man?" Hugh asked him. "Where's your mama?"

"She went shopping," he said, and burst into tears.

"I got here around four o'clock," Maisie said. "There's a note." Maisie handed him an envelope.

He opened it and read a one-word message: "Good-bye."

Maisie said, "It wasn't sealed. Toby read it and showed it to me."

"It's hard to believe," Hugh said, but it wasn't. Nora had always put her own wishes above everything else. Now she had abandoned her children. The note implied that she was not coming back.

He did not know what to feel. His first duty was to the boys. It was important not to upset them further. "You boys are up very late," he said. "Time for bed. Let's go."

He ushered them up the stairs. Samuel and Sol shared a room, but Toby had his own bedroom. Hugh tucked the little ones in, then went in to the eldest. He bent over the bed to kiss him.

"Mrs. Greenbourne's a brick," Toby said.

"I know," Hugh said.

"She's pretty, too." He paused. "Is Mama coming back?"

Hugh sighed. "To tell you the truth, old man, I don't know."

"If she doesn't, will Mrs. Greenbourne look after us?"

Trust a child to go right to the heart of the matter, Hugh thought. "She runs a hospital," he said. "I don't suppose she has time to look after boys as well. Now, no more questions. Good night."

"Good night, Father."

Hugh blew out the candle and left the room, closing the door.

Maisie had made cocoa. "I'm sure you'd prefer a brandy, but there doesn't seem to be any in the house."

Hugh smiled. "We in the lower middle classes can't afford to drink spirits. Cocoa is fine."

Cups and a jug stood on a tray, but neither of them moved to it. They stood in the middle of the room looking at each other. Maisie said, "I read about the shooting in the paper and came here to see if you were all right. I found the children on their own and gave them supper." She smiled a resigned, accepting smile that said it was up to Hugh what happened next.

Suddenly he began to tremble. "It's been quite a day," he said shakily; then he threw his arms around her. "Hug me hard."

She squeezed his waist.

"I love you, Maisie," he said. "I've always loved you."

"I know," she said.

He looked into her eyes. They were full of tears, and as he watched, one tear trickled down her face. He kissed it away.

"After all these years," he said. "After all these years."

EPILOGUE

1892

DEATHS

On the 30th May, at his residence in Antibes, France, after a long illness, the Earl of Whitehaven, formerly Senior Partner of Pilasters Bank.

—*The Times*

"Edward's dead," Hugh said, looking up from the newspaper. Maisie sat beside him in the railway carriage, wearing a summer dress in deep yellow and a little hat with yellow taffeta ribbons. They were on their way to Windfield School for Speech Day.

"He was a rotten swine, but his mother will miss him," she said.

Augusta and Edward had been living together in the south of France for the past eighteen months. Despite what they had done, the syndicate paid them the same allowance as all the other Pilasters. Like Edward, Augusta was an invalid. She had injured her back and spent most of her time in a wheelchair.

The train chugged into Windfield station, and Maisie and Hugh got out. It was the end of Toby's first year and Bertie's last year at the school. The day was warm, and the sun was bright. Maisie opened her parasol, and they walked to the school.

It had changed a lot in the twenty-six years since Hugh had left. His old headmaster, Dr. Poleson, was long dead, and the new head less frequently wielded the notorious cane they had called the striper. The fourth-form dormitory was still in the old dairy by the chapel, but there was a new school hall that could seat all the boys.

Inside the hall, they were surprised to meet Ben Greenbourne, looking older and rather frail. Maisie, blunt as ever, said, "Hello. What are you doing here?"

"My grandson is head boy," he replied gruffly. "I've come to hear his speech."

Hugh was startled. Bertie was not Greenbourne's grandson, and the old man knew it. Was he softening in his old age?

"Sit down by me," Greenbourne commanded. Hugh looked at Maisie. She shrugged and sat down, and Hugh followed suit.

"I hear you two are married," Greenbourne said.

"Last month," Hugh said. "My first wife didn't contest the divorce." Nora was living with a whiskey salesman, and it had taken Hugh's hired detective less than a week to get proof of adultery.

"I don't approve of divorce," Greenbourne said crisply; then he sighed. "But I'm too old to tell people what to do. The century is almost over. The future belongs to you. I wish you the best."

Hugh took Maisie's hand and squeezed it.

"Will you send the boy to university?" Greenbourne asked.

"We can't afford it," Maisie said.

"I'd be glad to pay," Greenbourne said.

Maisie was surprised. "It's kind of you," she said.

"I should have been kinder years ago," he replied.

The schoolboys began to file into the hall.

Maisie said to Greenbourne, "Hugh has adopted Bertie legally."

The old man turned his sharp eyes on Hugh. "I suppose you're the real father," he said bluntly.

Hugh nodded.

"I should have guessed a long time ago. It doesn't matter. The boy thinks I'm his grandfather, and that gives me a responsibility." He coughed and changed the subject. "I hear the syndicate is going to pay a dividend."

"That's right," Hugh said. "All the members will get about five percent on their investment. The new government in Cordova handed over the assets of the Miranda family to the Santamaria Harbor Company, and that made the bonds worth something again."

"What happened to that chap Miranda? He was a bad lot."

"Micky? His body was found in a steamer trunk washed up on a beach. No one ever found out how it got there."

A schoolboy came around handing out inky handwritten copies of the school song to all the parents and relatives.

"And you?" Greenbourne said to Hugh. "What will you do when the syndicate is wound up?"

"I was planning to ask your advice about that," Hugh said. "I'd like to start a new bank by floating shares on the market. Pilasters Limited. What do you think?"

"It's a bold idea, but then you always were original." Greenbourne looked thoughtful for a moment. "The funny thing is, the failure of your bank has actually enhanced your reputation. After all, who could be more reliable than a banker who pays his creditors even after he's crashed?"

"So . . . do you think it would work?"

"I'm sure of it. I might even put money into it myself."

Everyone stood up as the headmaster came in, followed by the housemasters. Then Bertie, the head boy, came to the lectern and said in a ringing voice, "Let us sing the school song."

Hugh caught Maisie's eye, and she smiled proudly. The familiar notes sounded on the piano, and then they all began to sing.

An hour later Hugh left them having tea in Bertie's study and slipped out through the squash court into Bishop's Wood. It was hot, just like that day twenty-six years ago. He remembered the way to the swimming hole and found it without difficulty. He sat on the rim of the quarry and threw a stone into the pool. It broke the glassy stillness of the water and sent out ripples in perfect circles.

He was the only one left, except for Albert Cammel out in the Cape Colony. The others were all dead: Peter Middleton killed that day; Tonio shot by Micky two Christmases ago; Micky himself drowned in a steamer trunk; and now Edward, dead of syphilis. It was almost as if something evil had come up out of the deep water that day in 1866, bringing forth all the dark passions that had blighted their lives—hatred and greed and selfishness and cruelty—fomenting deceit, bankruptcy, disease, and murder. But it was over now. The debts were paid. If there had been an evil spirit, it had returned to the bottom of the pond. And Hugh had survived.

He stood up. It was time to return to his family. He walked away, then took a last look back.

The ripples from the stone had disappeared, and the surface of the water was immaculately still once again.

ABOUT THE AUTHOR

For Ken Follett the writing life is rarely dull. "Follett loves to play, and he loves to work," one of his publishing friends has said. "He'll travel halfway around the world to attend a party for people he likes. And he'll have fun with almost everyone there, from the bartender to the most distinguished guest." When Follett is writing, he will work for several months straight, with barely a weekend off, seeking occasional relief by jamming with a blues band.

Ken Follett

Follett confesses that he always wanted to be rich and famous. To realize that dream, he abandoned a career in journalism and joined a publishing company to "learn how books become best sellers." And learn he did. With the brinkmanship typical of his plots, he quit his publishing job *before* he'd sold his first best seller, *Eye of the Needle.* The success of this and his subsequent books has made him one of the world's best-known authors.

Follett really gets a kick out of being a popular writer. "What I enjoy," he says, "is writing a book and then having *millions* of people read it and love it."

A Dangerous Fortune, Follett's eighth best seller, was inspired by a news article about the collapse of a big investment bank in 1890. "What caught my imagination," he explains, "was the situation of three very wealthy Victorian patriarchs having to sell everything and live in poverty to pay off their debts." Follett's quest for accuracy is insatiable. To re-create Victorian England in his novel, he researched the era down to the last detail, from bond issues to society balls.

Living in London with his second wife, Barbara, and children from their previous marriages, Follett is hard at work on his next story, about British convicts transported to the American colonies during the eighteenth century.

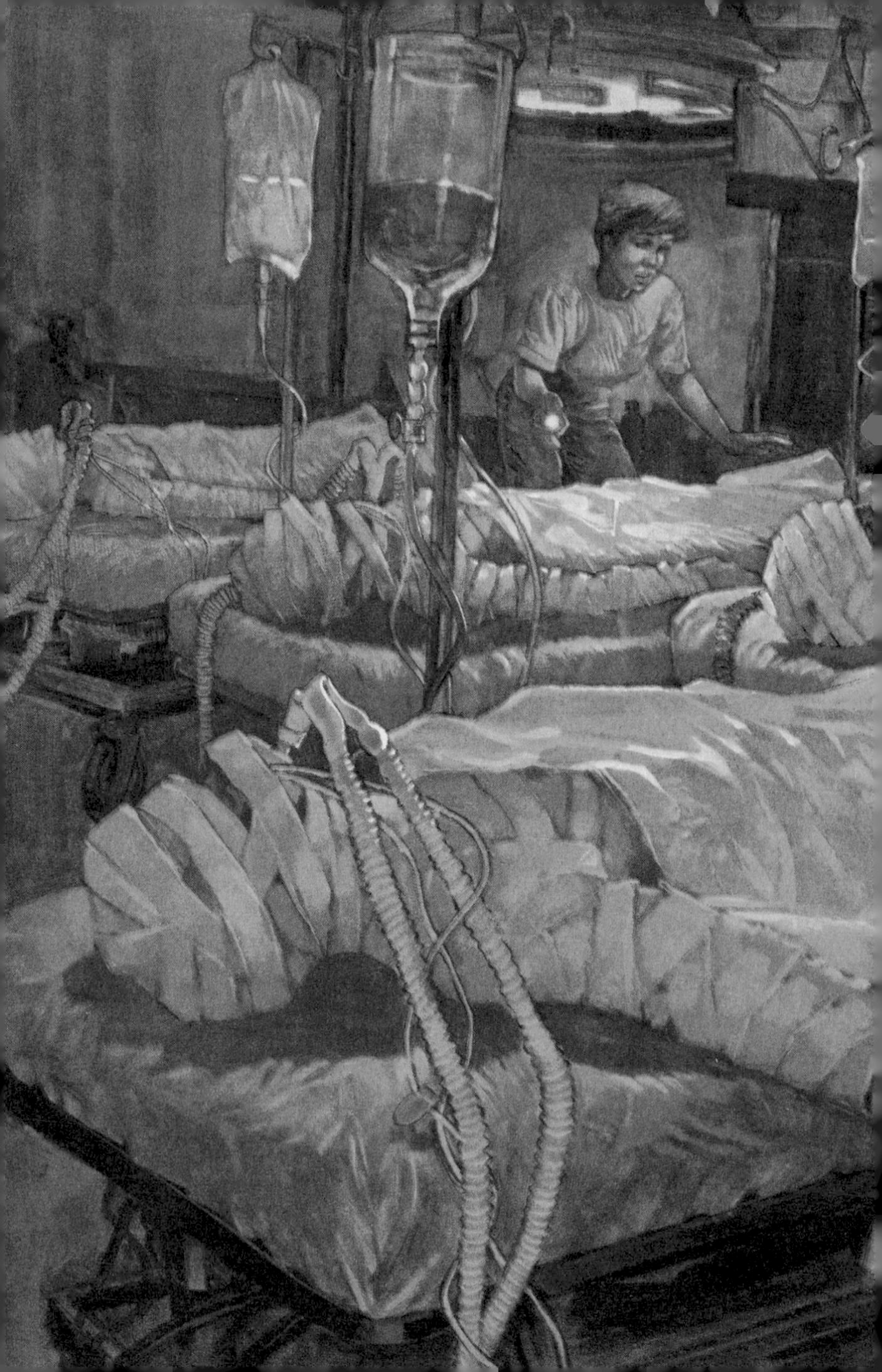

The Select

F. Paul Wilson

Ward C.

Silent.

A world sealed behind glass.

Seven patients lie there, each wrapped in gauze from head to toe, with only the eyes exposed. Burn victims whose last, best hope lies in the miracles performed at the famous Ingraham College of Medicine.

For first-year student Quinn Cleary, it is an honor to be asked to assist in the work of ward C. But there is that one patient who troubles her—one whose eyes seem haunted with more than pain. It's as if they are trying to tell her something. . . .

CHRISTMAS BREAK

The Ingraham College of Medicine
Laurel Hills, Maryland

Known as the 24-karat medical school, the Ingraham (pronounced ING-gram) College of Medicine has become one of the most respected and prestigious institutes in the nation. Nestled in the wooded hills of Frederick County, Maryland, less than an hour's drive from Baltimore and Washington, D.C., it has built its teaching staff by culling the great names from all the medical specialties. The Ingraham faculty is considered without peer.

The same can be said of its student body. Every December the nation's highest scorers on the MCAT are invited to the Ingraham, as it is known, to take a special entrance exam. It is a highly coveted invitation. The Ingraham is entirely subsidized by the Kleederman Foundation—its students pay no tuition, no book or lab fees, and receive free room and board. (A strict condition of acceptance is that you must live on the Ingraham campus the entire four years.) But academic excellence is only part of the Ingraham's requirements. The admissions office stresses that it is looking for "well-rounded individuals with something extra, who will be committed to the practice of medicine in a primary-care setting, especially in areas where it is needed most." Academic brilliance is, of course, an important requirement, but the Ingraham is not looking to turn out academic physicians who will spend their careers hunched over microscopes. The ideal candidates are students who were not only top in their class academically but also active in campus affairs.

The Ingraham alumni are considered the cream of the crop. Without exception its fifty annual graduates are offered the medical world's most highly regarded residencies. Yet an extraordinary number of alumni eschew the high-paying subspecialties for primary care and can be found practicing in the nation's poorer areas. They have earned the Ingraham an unequaled reputation for academic excellence and social commitment.

—*American Medical Schools in Perspective*
by Emmett Fenton (Bobbs-Merrill, 1993)

CHAPTER 1

"QUINN! Quinn, come on!"

Quinn Cleary heard the voice but continued to stare out over the cluster of buildings below her and at the surrounding hills beyond. From here on the hilltop, the high point on campus, she'd been told she could see three states: Maryland, of course; West Virginia to her right; and Virginia due south, straight ahead. And down the gentle slope sat the circle of beige brick-and-stone buildings—all clustered around the central pond—that made up the Ingraham.

A touch on her arm. She turned. Matt Crawford stood there—dark, curly hair, deeply tanned skin, dark eyes looking at her curiously. "Are you in a trance or something?"

"No. But isn't it beautiful?" She looked again at the manicured sloping lawns, sculpted out of the surrounding wooded acres. "Isn't it almost too good to be true?"

"Yeah. It's great." He gripped her elbow gently. "Come on. We don't want to get too far behind."

Reluctantly Quinn let herself be turned away from the grand view. Her long legs easily matched Matt's strides as they hurried to catch up with the other hopefuls following Mr. Verran on the campus tour. She was tall and slender—too slender, she thought, almost boyish-looking, with her short red-blond hair and her mostly straight-up-and-down body. She'd look at herself morosely and think that the only rounded things on her body were all above the shoulders: a round Irish face, full-lipped mouth, and big blue eyes. She'd especially disliked her lips, had always thought they were too fat. But now they were the in thing. Full lips were all the rage.

Who could figure out fashion? Which was why Quinn was rarely in fashion, favoring loose and comfortable slacks, blouses, and sweaters. A little behind the times perhaps, but good quality, bought on sale.

But Quinn knew neither looks nor fashion sense would make a difference when she sat for the entrance exam in the morning. What would count then was what was between the ears. And she was pretty sure she had good stuff between her ears. But was it the stuff the Ingraham College of Medicine wanted?

They've got to take me, Quinn thought. They've just got to.

The Ingraham was like a dream waiting to come true. Medicine was Quinn's dream—had been since she'd been old enough to dream—and the Ingraham was the only place that could make that dream come true, the only medical school she could afford.

Suddenly she heard running footsteps behind her.

"Hey, Matt, wait up," someone said.

She turned and saw a vaguely familiar looking guy trotting up the walk from the main campus.

"Timmy!" Matt said, grinning as he held out his hand. "I thought you weren't going to make it."

"Almost didn't," he said. "Got a late start from A.C."

"Atlantic City?" Matt said. "Oh, no. You didn't."

Now the newcomer was grinning. "Pass up some easy cash? How could I?"

Matt shook his head in wonder. "You're nuts, Timmy." He turned to Quinn. "You remember my roomie, Tim Brown, don't you, Quinn?"

Where Matt was average height, dark, and broad-shouldered, Tim was a fair, lanky six-footer, with sandy-brown hair and impenetrable wire-rimmed aviator-style dark glasses.

Quinn remembered meeting Tim, along with some of Matt's other friends, at Dartmouth the previous year. "I think so. Green Key Weekend, right?"

Tim lifted his shades and looked at her. His blue eyes were bloodshot. "If you guys say so. I don't remember much from that weekend." He extended his hand. "Nice to meet you again, Quinn. Is that your first name or your last?"

His hand was cool and dry as Quinn briefly clasped it. "My last name's Cleary."

"Quinn Cleary." Tim dropped the shades back over his eyes. "That has a nice sound to it."

Quinn felt the sudden warmth in her cheeks. She cursed her tendency to blush, even at a throwaway compliment like Tim's. She didn't want him to get the idea that she was attracted to him or anything like that. She might be unattached, but no way was she attracted. She didn't know him personally, but what she'd heard from Matt at Dartmouth was more than enough.

Timmy Brown: wild man.

But what was he doing here at the Ingraham? He couldn't have been invited to sit for the entrance exam. They took only the MCAT's top scorers. Hadn't Matt told her Tim was a business or economics major?

It was none of her business. Her business now was the tour, which so far had been a fantasy. The dorm was like a luxury hotel; the labs were state of the art; the lecture halls were equipped with the very latest audiovisual technology. And now they were about to tour the major medical-research facility right on campus.

But Matt and Tim were hanging back, laughing at a story Tim was telling about the casino he'd been thrown out of the night before. They'd last seen each other only days ago, yet they were acting like two old war buddies reunited after years of separation.

Quinn felt a twinge of jealousy. Matt was *her* friend, had been forever. Their mothers had gone to high school together. She and Matt had fumbled through an attempt at something more than friendship when they were sixteen, but once they put that behind them, they'd continued like brother and sister, with Matt coming from the rich wing of the family tree and Quinn from the poor.

"Listen," she told them, "I want to catch this end of the tour. I'll meet you later."

She caught up with the rest of the hopefuls. There were about fifty in the group—another fifty had taken the tour in the morning—all of them going for their interviews in the afternoon and sitting for the test the following day. And there were a number of groups taking the test during the week. Quinn had known there would be fierce competition for each seat in next year's class, but this was a bit daunting. The Ingraham took only fifty a year.

I'll make it, she told herself. I have to.

She joined the lead section, all following close behind the Ingraham's chief of security, Louis Verran.

Mr. Verran was a short, dark, balding, stubby man with a five o'clock shadow even though it was only early afternoon. He could have been some sort of middle manager at a bindery or the like.

Smoking was not allowed anywhere on the Ingraham campus, he'd told them at the outset, and one of his duties was the strict enforcement of that rule, yet that didn't stop him from carrying an unlit cigar everywhere and using it as a pointer.

Despite the chill December wind, Mr. Verran was dressed in a short-sleeved shirt and seemed perfectly comfortable. Maybe the extra pounds kept him insulated. "The campus security office is located in the science center, where the tour will be finishing up," he said as they passed the five-story building on their way to the hospital.

Quinn had noticed security cameras mounted on the walls of all the campus buildings. The science center was no exception.

"Is security a problem here?" someone asked.

"No, and it never will be. Not with me in charge," the security chief said, flashing a lopsided grin. "It's my job to make sure that anybody who's on this campus belongs here, and to keep out anyone who doesn't. It's my guarantee that as a student you'll be able to walk anywhere on this campus at any hour and not give a second thought to your personal safety. You'll have other things to worry about." Another grin here. "Like your grades."

Nervous laughter from the Ingraham hopefuls.

Quinn had noticed that the group was pretty ethnically balanced. The Ingraham seemed color-blind, but not sex-blind: there were very few women in the group.

Mr. Verran led them past a guardhouse that watched over a gate in the ten-foot-high Cyclone fence that ran around the campus. "It's all public access beyond this point," he said, gesturing to the eight-story Laurel Hills Medical Center and its multilevel parking lot, all gleaming white in contrast to the masses of beige brick behind them. "But not the campus. You need special I.D. to get on campus."

He led them on a quick tour of the first floor of the medical center, reeling off facts: five hundred and twenty beds, two hundred and ten physicians, representing every specialty, drawing patients from Washington, D.C.; Virginia; West Virginia; Pennsylvania; and, of course, Maryland. He whisked them past the labs—hematology, special chemistry, virology, parasitology, toxicology, cytology—past radiology, with its array of every imaging device known to man, and skirted the emergency room.

Quinn had learned from her premed courses at UConn that this medical center was on the cutting edge of technology. They've got to take me, she thought. I've got to go here.

Mr. Verran led them back to the campus. At the entrance to the science center, a motion detector opened double sliding-glass doors. "Everybody wait here while I make sure they're ready for us upstairs," he said once they were clustered in the lobby.

Quinn watched him walk to the security desk, centered in the lobby like an island in a stream, and speak to the two blue-uniformed security guards stationed there. She wondered why they needed this sort of security—the high fence, the guard posts at all the gates. She could see it in an inner city—downtown Baltimore or D.C. maybe—but out here in the woods?

Her musings were interrupted by Mr. Verran's return. "Okay," he said, clapping his hands, "they're ready for us. Take the elevators, and we'll reassemble on the third floor."

Quinn followed the rest of the tour in a state of rapture. The Ingraham's five-story hilltop science center was a temple to the art and science of medical research. The third floor was actually a miniature pharmaceutical plant, producing experimental compounds for trials in the treatment of lupus and cancer and AIDS.

The fourth floor housed the center's experimental animals. The pungent odor of its inhabitants filled the air. The stacked cages full of doomed rats and mice didn't bother her. As a farm girl, she'd learned early on not to get attached to the livestock, but she was glad to move up to the top floor.

"This is Dr. Alston," Mr. Verran said when they reached the fifth floor. He presented a tall, gaunt fiftyish man in a lab coat, with watery hazel eyes and slightly yellowed teeth. "He's not only director of medical education at the Ingraham but one of the country's foremost dermatological pathologists." He glanced at Dr. Alston. "Did I say that right?"

Dr. Alston smiled and nodded tolerantly.

"Looks like Uncle Creepy," a voice whispered near her ear.

Quinn glanced around and saw Tim Brown standing close behind her. He was still wearing his dark aviator glasses.

"I'm going to place you in his hands for the final leg of the tour," Mr. Verran was saying. "The research they're doing up here is so secret even I don't know what's going on."

Dr. Alston stepped forward. His smile toward the security chief was condescending. "Mr. Verran has a tendency to exaggerate. However, we do try to keep a lid on the data from the fifth floor. Our projects here have commercial applications, and we wish to protect the patents. Any profits from those applications will, of course, be plowed back into more research and to maintain funding of the school and the medical center. Follow me, please."

As they trooped after him down the hall, he continued speaking. "I can't show you much, I'm afraid. My project is in the human-trials stage, and we must respect the subjects' privacy. But I can tell you that I'm working with a semisynthetic rejection-proof skin graft, which, I hope, once perfected, will completely change the lives of burn victims all over the world. But perhaps— There he is now."

Down the hall ahead of them, someone in a lab coat had stepped into the hallway.

"Oh, Walter, just a moment, please."

The other man turned. He was older, shorter, plumper than Dr. Alston. He sported an unruly mane of white hair and bright blue eyes. He looked at Dr. Alston over the top of his reading glasses, then at the crowd of applicants, and smiled absently.

"This is Dr. Walter Emerson," Dr. Alston announced. "Very possibly the world's top expert in neuropharmacology. Walk us through your section, won't you, Walter?"

The shorter man shrugged. "Very well, Arthur."

Dr. Alston half turned and began moving his companion down the hall. The group followed.

"Dr. Emerson is too modest to tell you so himself, but the work he is doing with a new anesthetic compound is absolutely astounding. He hasn't named it yet, but it does have a code number: 9574. If we're successful, 9574 will revolutionize operative anesthesia."

The tile wall to Quinn's left became plate glass, and she stopped, staring at a room beyond the glass—a ward filled with hospital beds. And in those beds, pure white bodies. Quinn blinked. No, it wasn't pale skin; it was gauze. The bodies were wrapped from head to toe. They didn't move. Seven beds, seven bodies, and not a sign of life. They looked dead.

But they had to be alive. Nurses—gloved, gowned, masked—glided among them like wraiths. There were IVs and feeding tubes running into the bodies.

She felt someone bump against her back and knew it was Tim.

"My Lord," he said. His voice was hoarse.

What? No crack about mummies? She glanced at his face and saw his awed expression. He seemed genuinely moved.

Quinn stared again into the ward and was startled to see a body—patient—in a bed directly on the other side of the window. Only the bridge of the nose and a pair of dull blue eyes remained uncovered. Those eyes were staring at Quinn, searching her face. The patient looked vaguely male: the shoulders were broad; the chest was flat.

The entire tour had stopped and gravitated toward the window, crowding behind Quinn.

"Oh, dear." It was Dr. Emerson, squeezing toward the front. He looked flustered. "This is ward C—Dr. Alston's ward. The curtain should have been drawn on this window. Not that there's anything confidential going on, but for the sake of these patients."

"Wh-what happened to them?" Quinn said.

"Burns," Dr. Emerson replied, his voice soft. "Third-degree burns over eighty or ninety percent of their bodies. Not fresh burns. No, these are burn-center survivors. They're so covered with stiff, thick scar tissue that they can barely move. All of them are in constant misery." He sighed. "Arthur is their last hope."

Quinn could not take her eyes off the patient before her. His eyes seemed to be trying to tell her something.

"Their beds are rotated by the window," Dr. Emerson was saying. "They can't move. Very few of them can even speak. So they're moved around to let them watch the hustle and bustle of the hallway. The nurses have been trained to speak to them constantly. Even if they're not sure they are being heard or understood, they're communicating with these patients continually."

Communicating—that was what the blue eyes of the patient before Quinn seemed to be trying to do. They narrowed with the effort. Quinn sensed a silent desperation there.

The patient began to move, twisting ever so slightly.

"Dr. Emerson," Quinn said, pointing through the window, "is something wrong?"

"Oh, dear. He seems to be in pain." Dr. Emerson moved away and spoke through the door to a nurse in the ward. Then he returned to Quinn's side. "He'll get some relief now."

A nurse approached the bed with a syringe, poked the needle into the IV line, and depressed the plunger.

Dr. Emerson gently took Quinn's arm. "Come, my dear. These patients and their pain are not on display."

As Quinn allowed herself to be drawn away, she glanced back and thought she saw tears in the patient's eyes before the inner curtain was drawn across the window.

The remainder of the tour was a blur. All she saw was those pain-racked blue eyes calling to her from their gauze cocoon. She knew she had to get back to that patient. Someday, someway, she would. Easing pain, healing the unhealable—that was what it was all about. That was what the Ingraham was all about.

They've got to take me, Quinn thought for the hundredth time. They've just got to.

CHAPTER 2

MATT stared at the list on the bulletin board in the cafeteria: WHERE ARE THEY NOW?

"This place cranks out its share of dedicated docs, doesn't it?" Tim said over Matt's shoulder.

Matt read down the list. In any urban area across the country, Ingraham graduates manned inner-city clinics. And never too far away was a Kleederman-owned medical center or nursing home.

"So where are the real medical students?" Tim asked as they turned and joined Quinn at a small table in a corner of the cafeteria.

Matt looked around at the tables occupied by hopefuls, but no medical students. The cafeteria was a large, open two-story affair, with a curved stairway leading to the attached classroom building. The three outer walls were all glass, flanked with white curtains, offering a panoramic view of wooded hills. No expense had been spared in outfitting the Ingraham's facilities, even the cafeteria.

"Home for Christmas break," Matt said. "Like we should be."

"Right," Tim said, his eyes unreadable behind his shades. "But we want to go to the Ingraham so bad we give up part of our vacation to come and take their test. Are we all that desperate?"

Matt saw Quinn flinch. The Ingraham was her only chance. His family could send him to any med school that accepted him. Tim's family could help him out. But Quinn's family was just getting by.

Matt wished he knew some backdoor way to get Quinn in, but people said the Ingraham was influence-proof. Only the best and the brightest. Well, Quinn certainly qualified there. She was born to be a doctor. But she looked so scared. He wanted to tell her it would be okay, it would all work out.

Tim drained his Pepsi and looked around. "They ought to serve draft beer here. Might liven up the place."

Uh-oh, Matt thought. Tim's getting bored. And when he got bored, he got strange. Matt saw Quinn staring, and tried to change the subject. "How'd you do in A.C. last night?"

"About a thousand."

"Blackjack?"

"That's my game."

Quinn's eyes were wide. "A thousand dollars? In one night?"

Matt wondered how many weeks she'd slaved at her two waitressing jobs during the summer to earn a thousand.

Tim looked around again. "There's got to be some beer here."

"It's a medical school cafeteria," Quinn said with a hint of annoyance. "There's no beer here."

Tim smiled. "Ten bucks says I can get us some."

"Okay," she said. "Ten—"

Matt laid a hand on her arm. "Never bet against Tim. Trust me."

Quinn crossed her arms. She didn't have ten bucks to throw away, but this seemed like such a sure thing. And besides, she wanted to take the wind out of Mr. Cocksure's sails.

"Oh, well," Tim said, rising, "looks like I'll have to get it anyway. My integrity is at stake." He wandered away toward the kitchen.

Quinn turned to Matt, eyes blazing. "Do you actually live with him? I thought you told me your roomie was a business major or something. I can't believe he wants to be a doctor."

"He's an economics major, but he squeezed in the required science courses for med school last year to give him the option in case he wanted it. I guess he decided he wanted it."

"Great," she said, leaning back. "I spend three and a half years breaking my back as a premed bio major. He 'squeezes in' a few science courses and gets invited to sit for the Ingraham's exam. How does that happen?"

Matt grinned. "Tim's not like the rest of us mortals. He has an eidetic memory. Never forgets a thing. That's how he wins at blackjack—remembers every card that's been played."

"All fine and good, but that's not enough to—"

"Plus he has a keen analytical mind. You remember calculus—all the equations you had to memorize? Tim never bothered. He'd go into the test and *figure them out.*"

"You could hate a guy like that."

Matt sighed. "Sometimes I do. Not easy to be friends with a guy who can ace every test without breaking a sweat. If he weren't such a nice guy—"

"Nice guy?" Quinn said, her voice rising. "Matt, he's got to be one of the most irresponsible, self-centered, egotistical—"

"He's just testing you, Quinn," Matt said. "It's a game he plays, but only with people he likes."

Her cheeks reddened. "That kind of like I can do without."

"Once you get to know him, he's a lot of fun. And believe me, he—" Matt glanced up. "Speak of the devil, here he comes now."

Tim glided up and set three paper cups on the table. "Rolling Rock for the men and"—he pushed one of the cups toward Quinn—"a Coors Light for the pretty lady."

Quinn glanced down at the white foam. "How on earth—"

"Nothing to it, my dear. I used to work in a kitchen. The help always have their own private stock. These folks were happy to part with three cans for ten dollars." He lifted his cup. "Cheers."

"No, thanks," Quinn said. She pushed hers across toward Tim. "But do drink up. There's a lot of people vying for the Ingraham's fifty places. I need all the edge I can get." She rose. "Excuse me. I've got my interview."

Matt was startled—this wasn't the Quinn he knew—but as she turned to leave, she winked. Matt relaxed. So that was it. Tim had pushed Quinn, so Quinn was pushing right back. Good for her.

Tim turned to Matt and grinned. "I like her. Where'd you find her? Are there any more where she came from?"

"Known her since we were toddlers, and she's one of a kind. But not your kind."

Tim's eyebrows rose. "Oh, really? You staking out that territory for yourself? Because if you are, just say the word and I'll—"

"Nah. We're just good friends."

"Good," Tim said, watching her retreating figure. "Because I think I like being around her."

Matt wasn't sure how he felt about that, but Quinn was quite capable of taking care of herself. She wouldn't let anyone distract her from becoming a doctor. He silently wished her well on her interview. She'd need all the help she could get. The Ingraham was widely criticized for peopling its student body mostly with males. He hoped she got somebody with enough perception to recognize what a prize the Ingraham would have in Quinn Cleary.

DR. WALTER Emerson rubbed his eyes and waited for the next applicant to arrive. These interviews were tiring but a necessary evil. You had to meet these people face to face to decide whether they would make the kind of doctor worthy of the enormous investment in each one of them. But it pained him to know that so few of the hopeful, eager faces he'd seen this week were going to be asked to return to the Ingraham in September.

A soft knock. "Come in," he said.

He immediately recognized the slim strawberry blonde who entered as the girl he'd seen on fifth science earlier in the afternoon. He remembered her staring at ward C, her wide blue eyes filled with wonder and empathy. He glanced down at her file: Quinn Cleary, twenty-one, full scholarship to the University of Connecticut, premed biology major, president of the biology club, stringer for the school paper, high MCATs. A fine catch for any medical school. Too bad she was lacking a critical factor—a Y chromosome. Walter had gone around and around on this with the board for years. If the Ingraham was to remain a premier training center, the foundation's board would have to alter its antiquated sex preference.

Well, he'd see what he could do for her. For some reason Walter felt attached to her. Maybe he'd seen something of his old self in this youngster as she'd looked at those patients, something in her eyes, the desire to do something for them.

And then an epiphany—his daughter. This girl reminded him of Clarice. Clarice was twenty-five in Walter's mind. Would always be twenty-five. That was when a drunk had run a stop sign and brought her life and her mother's to a fiery end.

"So, Miss Quinn Cleary," he said after she'd seated herself across from him. He smiled to allay the tension he sensed in her. "Let me get the question I must ask out of the way: Why do you wish to become a doctor?"

"Because I . . ." Her voice trailed off. "I . . . I had a whole speech prepared, and now I can't remember it."

"Good. I've been listening to speeches all afternoon. Let's get down to the real you. Why a doctor?"

"Well, because I know I can do it and do it well."

"Competence *is* the bottom line, isn't it? But what about bettering the lot of your fellowman?" Walter had heard that ad nauseam, year after year.

Quinn Cleary shrugged. She seemed to be relaxing. "Well, benefitting mankind's great, but that's not what's driving me. I mean, you don't spend four years in premed, four years in medical school, then two, three, maybe five more years in a residency just to help people. Plenty of people need help this minute. If helping people is all you care about, why put it off for ten years? Join the Peace Corps or go feed the homeless."

How refreshing she was. Walter felt his afternoon lethargy slipping away. "You're not an altruist, then, I take it?"

"I care a lot about people, sometimes too much, I think. But there's got to be more to becoming a doctor than that."

"Oh, yes," Walter said, allowing a smile. "How could we forget. There's the status, the respect, the money."

The girl returned his smile. "Money—that would be a new experience. But at the risk of sounding holier-than-thou, it's doing the job and doing it right—that's what matters."

Walter made himself sound dubious. "Does it really, now?"

"Yes," she said, her cheeks coloring. "And if that sounds corny or phony, I'm sorry, but that's the way I feel."

Spunky too. Walter decided he was going to do his damnedest to get this young lady into the Ingraham. But everything depended on the test the next day. She'd have to correctly answer those special questions. He couldn't help her with those. Nobody could.

Louis Verran sat at the main console in the monitoring room in the basement of the science center and struck a match. Elliot and Kurt weren't due in for another thirty minutes, so he had the place to himself. He held the flame to his panatela and puffed. This was his domain, the only place on the whole damn campus where he made the rules, and he did not have one against smoking here.

He scanned the readouts, checking to make sure the pickups were tracking their target data. The dorm was hopping. The hopefuls had all been fed—nicely stuffed on chicken *française* and all the trimmings—and escorted to their rooms. Now time for them to settle in and go beddy-bye by lights-out at eleven p.m.

Everything was operative. One hundred and four sets of readouts, one for every room in the V-shaped dorm's two wings. Almost half of those rooms were occupied by hopefuls tonight. A pair in each. One hundred nervous, twitchy bodies in all.

He decided to run some random checks. He activated the audio in 241. A couple of girls in that one.

". . . think this could be some sort of test too?"

It was the third time Trish had asked that since dinner, which Quinn was still marveling at. Quinn glanced over at where her roommate for the night sat with an MCAT review-course manual open on her lap. Trish was pudgy, with long, frizzy hair and mild acne.

"I don't know what you mean," Quinn said.

Trish rolled her eyes and sighed. "This room. Spending the night in the med students' rooms. They could be testing us to see how well we respect their rules. What do you think?"

A handsome room—a two-room suite, actually. Cedar-paneled walls, a thick rug on the floor, and their own cheerfully tiled bathroom. The front half was a sitting room, with two desks, plus a neatly upholstered couch, a round table, and two comfy chairs. The inner room had the beds and a view of the woods. The elaborate built-in headboards had drawers and bookshelves and compartments of various sizes; two huge closets were also built in.

"Could be. They certainly have enough rules around here."

The Ingraham had a reputation of exerting an unusual amount of control over its students. That seemed to stretch to its applicants as well. All applicants had to attend the full orientation and spend the night in the Ingraham's dorm prior to the test.

"So, aren't you going to study?" Trish asked.

"I don't think this is the kind of test you can study for. But you go ahead. I think I'll take a little walk." Quinn strolled out into the hall and headed for Matt's room, down on the first floor.

Tim and Matt had somehow finagled a room together. Quinn begrudgingly admitted to herself that she had warmed to Tim over dinner. She'd actually laughed at his unsuccessful attempts to conjure up some white wine.

She found him stretched out on the couch reading a comic—and

still wearing his shades. Matt sat listening to his Walkman. He waved.
Tim said, "The Mighty Quinn. Welcome."
"How'd you two manage to get assigned to the same room?" she asked, dropping into a chair.
Tim said, "I traded with the guy who was originally here."
"You sure there isn't a rule against that?" Quinn said.
Tim put down his comic. "Hell of a lot of rules, don't you think? What's this deal with you've *got* to sleep in the dorm the night before the test? Why should they care?"
Quinn said, "Maybe they want us all to start off tomorrow morning on equal footing: same dinner, same amount of sleep on the same kind of mattress—that sort of thing."
Matt nodded. "Maybe."
"Well, I don't know about you guys," Tim said, "but this kind of thing makes me feel like some sort of a lab rat."
"Obviously, this place isn't for free spirits," Matt said.
"But the price is right," Quinn said.
Tim shrugged. "No arguing that."
"Makes you wonder what *they're* getting out of it," Matt said.
"TANSTAAFL," Tim said, and pointed to Quinn.
"There Ain't No Such Thing As A Free Lunch," she replied. "From *The Moon Is a Harsh Mistress* by Robert A. Heinlein."
"Hey, very good," Tim said, nodding and mock-applauding.
Surprised to find herself enjoying his approval, Quinn shook it off and said, "Who wouldn't want to go to medical school here?"
"Nobody," Matt said, "until you realize that you *must* spend all four years right within these walls."
"And if you quit, you pay," Tim said.
Quinn was startled. She hadn't heard about that. "Pay?"
"All your back tuition, room, board, book and lab fees."
"But if you get sick or hurt—"
"If you get sick or hurt or change careers," Tim said, "it's goodbye and good luck. But if you want to graduate from another med school, watch out."
"Speaking as the son of a high-priced lawyer," Matt said, "let me assure you, contracts can be broken."
"Not this one. Some parents took the Ingraham to court a few years ago. Their kid wanted to transfer to Cornell after two years here. They spent years battling it and lost. They had to pay."

"Well, if I get in," Quinn said, "I'm staying." And she meant it. But Tim's remark about no free lunch nagged at her.

Matt was staring at Tim. "Where'd you learn so much about the Ingraham contract?"

"*Time* had an article on it." Tim lifted his sunglasses and rubbed his right eye with his finger. "Let's see. It was the October fifteenth issue, page twelve, lower-right-hand corner."

Quinn stared in amazement, then glanced at Matt for his reaction. He was grinning at her. "Didn't I tell you?"

"Incredible," Quinn said. Matt hadn't exaggerated. Tim Brown's memory was phenomenal.

She looked at her watch. It was ten fifty. "I'd better be getting back."

"A curfew," Matt said. "Can you believe it? I haven't been here a full day yet, and already this place is getting on my nerves."

Tim pressed a finger to his lips. "Careful, my friend. The walls may have ears."

"You bet they have ears, wise guy," Louis Verran muttered as he switched to another set of pickups.

"Mattress sensors positive all over the place, boss," Kurt said from his console.

"All right," Verran said. "It's almost eleven. Nighty-night time. Let's get some slow waves going."

He flipped the power switch and gave the rheostat a clockwise turn on the slow-wave inducer. Getting them to sleep before midnight was always the trickiest part of the entrance-exam stay. Most of these kids were wired about the test tomorrow. Without a little help, too many would spend the night tossing and turning. Big no-no. They had to sleep. All of them. For at least five full hours.

So each suite was hardwired with, among other things, slow-wave–spindle inducers. A huge expense, considering that they were used only one night out of the year. The inducer created an electromagnetic field in the rooms, which connected with human brain waves, inducing sleep. Worked great: thirty to sixty seconds and the kids were in dreamland.

"Good evening, gentlemen," said a voice behind Verran.

Verran suppressed a growl of annoyance as he turned to face Dr. Alston. The ghoul was always meddling. Didn't know the first thing

about running security, but he always had two cents to contribute.
"Dr. Alston," Verran said, forcing a smile. "Back again for another evening of fun and games, I see."

"Hardly, Louis," Alston said grimly as he sniffed the air. His gaze came to rest on Verran's smoldering cigar. "Louis, is that another cigar?"

Louis held it up before him, appearing to scrutinize it. "Good Lord, Doc, I believe you're right."

Elliot leaned on his console and coughed to hide a laugh.

"We'll settle this some other time," Dr. Alston said. "Right now, how are we doing?"

Verran clamped the cigar between his teeth and leaned left so he could see Kurt behind Alston. "What's the status?"

"Getting there," Kurt said. "Twenty percent down already."

Verran glanced at the timer. "Right on schedule."

Dr. Alston pulled up a chair and sat down, fanning the air with a manila folder every time some smoke drifted his way.

Half an hour later Kurt said, "There goes the last of them. They're all down."

Verran nodded his approval.

"Excellent," Dr. Alston said. "Let the music begin."

Verran nodded to Elliot, who began to work the switches on his console. Soon the music, as Dr. Alston called it, began to filter through the occupied dorm rooms.

CHAPTER 3

"How can you guys eat?" Quinn said.

Tim looked up from his blueberry pancakes. "Are you kidding? I'm going for seconds."

Matt was already back on line, rejoining the bustle around the buffet area. The morning sun shone brightly through the tall cafeteria windows. All around them the Ingraham hopefuls clustered at scattered tables, creating pockets of nervous chatter.

Tim studied Quinn out of the corner of his eye. She looked good this morning, dressed in a navy sweater, which deepened the tint of her eyes, and white slacks. Her short strawberry-blond hair looked just right; she wore a hint of eye makeup. But watching her fidgety hands, he could see the stress she was putting on herself. This test was too important to her. Tim had an urge to hug her and tell her not to worry. But he didn't know her well enough for that. Yet.

"Didn't you sleep well?" he said.

"Like the dead. Which is weird, because I'm usually up and down all night before a big test. Maybe they put something in the food."

"Maybe," Tim said. He'd slept like the proverbial log himself, but he'd expected to. He'd had next to no sleep the night before.

Quinn was staring toward the far end of the cafeteria. "Say, isn't he somebody? I mean somebody famous."

Tim turned and spotted him—tall, lean, striding toward the curved stairway with Dr. Alston. Tim lifted his dark glasses for a better look—strong features, dark hair graying at the temples, distinguished-looking in a tailored gray suit.

Matt returned then, carrying a plate heaped with scrambled eggs and hash browns. He cocked his head toward the newcomer. "Isn't he—"

At that instant the name clicked. "Senator Jefferson Stephen Whitney," Tim said. "Or I guess I should say former Senator."

The image of an article from *The Wall Street Journal* flashed before Tim's eyes, with a photo. He saw the headline now: SEN. WHITNEY CANCELS CAMPAIGN; ACCEPTS NEW FOUNDATION POST.

"He was a hotshot Senator from Wisconsin in the '70s," Tim said. "Made lots of waves trying to revamp the FDA. Looked like he was going to be up there for a long time, but when it came time for reelection, he opted out and took a position with the Kleederman Foundation. He's been on its board ever since."

"That explains why he's here," Quinn said.

"Right. The Kleederman Foundation is paying for this breakfast we're eating and for all the rest of the Ingraham's bills."

Dr. Alston and the former Senator had mounted the stairway to the landing and stopped to face the cafeteria. Tim noticed that a microphone and stand had been rigged up.

"Good morning, everyone," Dr. Alston said. "I trust you all slept well and are enjoying the breakfast that the Ingraham's staff has prepared for you."

Polite scattered applause.

"We are privileged this morning to have a surprise visit from former United States Senator Jefferson Whitney, a director of the Kleederman Foundation. Senator?"

Tim noted that this round of applause was less scattered and more vigorous. Even he joined in. After all, this guy represented the deep pockets that supported this place.

"Good morning," Whitney said, flashing an easygoing smile. "I know you're anxious to get to the test, so I'll be brief." He paused, then, "You see today as an important day for your future."

Tim saw Quinn's head nod almost imperceptibly.

"But you should not lose sight of the fact that this is an important day for the Ingraham as well. You are the cream of the crop. Your college careers are testimonies to your desire for excellence. You are the people we want as Ingraham students. We'd love to take you all. Unfortunately, the Kleederman Foundation's funds are finite. But for those of you who are accepted, not only will you receive the gift of the finest medical education in the world, but you will have a chance to go out and shape the future of American medicine.

"So I wish you all well today. And please remember that no matter what happens, every one of you is already a winner. I know I speak for the Ingraham College of Medicine and the Kleederman Foundation when I say that we are proud of all of you."

More applause. Tim clapped mechanically. "Amazing," he said. "Platitudes trip off his tongue."

Quinn looked at him sharply. "Give him a break, will you? I think it was very nice of him to take the time and come speak to us."

Tim winced. He was not scoring points with Quinn.

Matt, ever the peacemaker, said, "Tim doesn't trust politicians."

"Senator Whitney isn't a politician. He heads a foundation."

"The fact that everybody still calls him Senator Whitney says something," Tim said. "Once a politician, always a politician." He raised his orange-juice glass in Whitney's direction. "But if he's going to foot the bill for med school for me, he's a prince."

Another cool look from Quinn. This was going nowhere. He took his empty plate and stood up. "Seconds anyone?"

TIM chewed his pencil as he considered question 200.

The test was a horror. A lot like the MCAT, only worse. The biology questions were off the wall. The chemistry questions were even tougher.

Tim glanced around. About twenty-five hopefuls had been seated in this classroom; the rest were scattered throughout the building. To his left, Quinn furrowed her brow in concentration as her foot beat a soft, nervous tattoo on the floor. To his right, Matt was hunched over his exam booklet, scribbling on his scratch sheets. All around Tim, nervous people were trying to score for their future.

Not that Tim was taking this lightly himself. It would take a lot of financial pressure off his family if he got accepted here, but it would also be a declaration of independence. No more checks for Dad to write for tuition. For the first time Tim would be self-sufficient.

But question 200 was strange. It asked for the first corollary of the Kleederman equation. No problem there. Tim knew the answer. Trouble was, he couldn't figure out how he knew it. Usually he could picture the book, page, and paragraph where he'd read about any given subject.

But what about now? Johann Kleederman—Tim could see before him an article from *U.S. News & World Report.* Born in 1935 in Switzerland, where he and his wealthy parents weathered World War II, Johann Kleederman took over the reins of the family pharmaceutical company after his father's death in 1960 and began a rapid extension into the U.S. market. He set up his foundation in 1968 and became a pioneer of managed health care during the '70s. He'd spent recent years buying up nursing homes and financially troubled hospitals, a move considered by many to be eccentric and risky. Still, these facilities controlled by Kleederman Medical Industries, a multinational conglomerate that included the innovative and extraordinarily profitable Kleederman Pharmaceuticals, were considered the best managed, most cost effective in the world. Tim could even see an old photo of the reclusive, balding Kleederman in the upper-left corner of the page. But the Kleederman equation? Nothing in the article about that. No picture came. Just the answer.

Tim gave a mental shrug and blackened the B box next to 200 on his answer sheet. Who cared? The grading computer was only going to note if the response was correct or incorrect.

The next two questions also referred to the Kleederman equation. These answers too popped unbidden into his mind. So be it. He marked them down and went on.

The questions then segued into general knowledge, such as who won last year's World Series. Tim smiled to himself. The Ingraham was trying to weed out the science nerds who spent their entire lives squinting into microscopes. They could be researchers, but never physicians. And the Ingraham wanted to graduate physicians.

After the general-knowledge section the questions got weird. Questions involving values and decision making—about being a general in battle and deciding who was expendable, about being a surgeon surrounded by wounded soldiers and having to decide who would be treated first. Triage. There didn't seem to be any one correct answer to these.

Maybe that was the point. Maybe the Ingraham wasn't looking so much for answers to the questions as it was looking for answers about the person taking the test.

The realization galvanized Tim. All he had to do was dive into these and cut loose. But not too loose.

FINISHED.

Tim glanced at his watch: ten minutes to spare. Everything done. All his four hundred multiple choices had an A, B, C, D, or E box blackened to the right of it.

He glanced over at Quinn. She was still working. He noticed two unanswered questions at the top of one of her columns. He checked his exam booklet. Those were two of the Kleederman questions. Maybe Quinn wasn't familiar with the equation. Since the Kleederman Foundation was the pocketbook for the Ingraham, they might dump on anyone missing those.

The proctor was standing by her desk arranging her papers. When her back was turned, Tim rose, leaned over Quinn's shoulder, and blackened the B and C boxes next to questions 201 and 202, then straightened and strode down the aisle. Over and done with before anyone saw him.

My good deed for the day.

QUINN stared at the two marks Tim had made on her answer sheet. He'd blackened in choices on two of the three questions that had completely stymied her. What on earth was the Kleederman equation? She'd never heard of it, but obviously Tim had. Instinctively she reversed her pencil and moved to erase the marks. She had always done her own work. But almost of its own accord, her pencil froze, the eraser poised above the paper. Her whole future was at stake here. This was real life. The Kleederman questions could mean the difference between acceptance and rejection.

But still, they weren't her answers. As she lowered the eraser to the paper, the proctor's voice cut through the silence. "Time's up. Pencils down. Any more marks and your test will be disqualified."

TIM stood with Matt at the central pond and waited for Quinn to come out of the class building. A chill wind had come up, scraping dead leaves along the concrete walks. Finally she showed up, walking slowly. Tim wondered at her grim expression.

"How'd you do?" Matt asked.

Quinn shrugged. "You ever hear of the Kleederman equation?"

"Sure," Tim said. "It's—"

"I know *you* did." The look she tossed him was anything but friendly. "I want to know about Matt."

That look unsettled Tim. He'd thought he'd be her knight in shining armor. What was eating her?

Matt scratched his head. "It has to do with distribution of medical services among an expanding population."

"You've heard of it too?" She shook her head in dismay. "Why haven't I? Three questions, and I couldn't even guess at an answer."

"Cheer up," Tim said. "You got two of them right, anyway."

Her head snapped up. Her expression was fierce. "No. *You* got two of them right, not me. I didn't have a clue. I don't hand in other people's work, Tim."

He groaned. "Oh, no. You didn't erase them, did you?"

There was pain in her eyes. "No, I didn't. And I'm not proud of myself for that." She turned and walked off toward the dorm.

"You marked a couple of answers on her sheet?" Matt said.

"Yeah. They were blank. Thought I was doing her a favor." He didn't want to show it—didn't even want to admit it—but he was hurt. "Boy, I just can't win with her."

"With nine hundred ninety-nine other people you'd be a hero. But Quinn's got her own set of rules. You tested her on her own standards, and she feels she failed. Didn't I tell you she's one of a kind?"

"You got that right. Kind of old-fashioned, though."

"Yeah," Matt said softly. "She's an old-fashioned girl."

"I didn't think there were any of those left." To his dismay, Tim realized he was becoming enthralled with Quinn Cleary.

SPRING BREAK

Adrix (adriazepam), the new nonhabituating benzodiazepine with strong antidepressant properties from Kleederman Pharmaceuticals, has quickly become the second most widely prescribed tranquilizer in the world.

—*Medical World News*

CHAPTER 4

In what had become a daily ritual, Quinn sat by her bedroom window and aimed the binoculars across the front yard toward the end of the driveway. And with each new day the suspense had grown.

The yard was pretty drab now, but soon spring would bring the forsythia into buttery bloom. Acres of farmland stretched out behind the old house. If this kind of acreage were situated along Long Island Sound, they'd be rich. Developers would be banging on their door. But not here in the hinterlands of northeast Connecticut.

"Is there no mail yet?"

Quinn turned at her mother's voice, which was still touched with the lilt of her native Ireland. She was standing in the doorway.

"Henry's late," Quinn said.

"He'll get here," Mom said.

"It's got to come today," Quinn said, raising the glasses again.

"Don't be forgetting the old saying," her mother said. " 'Be careful what you wish for—you may just get it.' "

Quinn suspected her mother was glad they couldn't afford medical school. Not through any malice. Mom had her own reasons for wanting Quinn home, and none of it made any sense to Quinn.

The phone rang. Quinn dashed down to the kitchen and grabbed the receiver off the wall. It was Matt. "Quinn! Did you hear yet?"

"No, Matt. No mail yet today."

"It'll be a yes. Has to be."

Matt had received his acceptance the previous Saturday. Here it was Friday, and she still hadn't. "Look, Matt, let's face it. All the acceptances went out, and I wasn't in there."

"I don't believe that, Quinn. And neither does Tim."

The memory of the exam in December, the answers Tim had marked on her sheet, and how she'd passed them in still rankled.

"Matt, did Tim . . . make it?"

"Yeah, Quinn. Tim made it too."

Quinn slumped into one of the ladder-back chairs at the rugged, porcelain-topped kitchen table. Tim had made it. That meant the two answers he'd given her had probably been correct. Then why haven't I made it? she thought.

"Call me back if you hear anything," Matt said.

"Okay. Sure." Quinn hung up and sat there, drumming her fingers on the tabletop. This waiting was driving her nuts.

And then a faint squeak—the mail truck's brakes.

She waited until it had rolled on, then, as casually as she could, strolled out to the road and withdrew the slim stack of letters from the mailbox. Electric bill . . . phone bill . . . bank statement . . . the Ingraham College of Medicine.

Quinn's heart stumbled over a beat. The envelope was light—no more than a single sheet of paper. It's got to be a rejection, she told herself. It only takes one page to tell you to go pound salt.

Her fingers trembled as she tore open the envelope:

> Dear Ms. Cleary:
>
> Every year, the Ingraham College of Medicine reviews hundreds of applications and entrance-exam scores. It is a most difficult task to select the fifty applicants who will attend the Ingraham. The admissions office regrets to inform you that, after careful consideration, your name was not among those selected for acceptance to next year's class. However, since your scores were ranked within the top one hundred, your name has been placed on the waiting list. This office will inform you immediately of any change in your status. If you do not wish your name placed on the waiting list, please inform the admissions office immediately.

Quinn's vision blurred. She blinked to clear it, and forced her wobbly legs to walk her back toward the house. Her whole *life* had been about becoming a doctor. And suddenly it was all gone in a few seconds—the time it took to tear open an envelope. Gone.

Get a grip, Cleary.

She'd turned twenty-two the previous month. She was supposed to be an adult. Okay, she told herself, an awful setback. But there were other ways. Loans and maybe work-study programs. Maybe even the military. Besides, the Ingraham hadn't slammed the door on her. She was on the waiting list. She'd call the admissions office and find out how many were ahead of her. She'd call them every month. No, every week. Everyone in that admissions office was going to know the name Quinn Cleary. And if any name was going to be moved off the waiting list into acceptance, it was going to be hers.

As she stepped onto the porch, she glanced up and saw her mother there, waiting for her. Her mother's eyes were moist; her lips were trembling. She held out her arms. "Oh, Quinn."

She knows, Quinn thought. Does it show that much?

Quinn held back. She was a woman now. But the sympathy she saw in her mother's eyes tore something loose in her. Everything she had dammed up—the agony of waiting, the crushing disappointment, the fear and uncertainty about what was to come—all broke free. She clung to her mother and began to sob.

"YOU'RE secretly glad I was turned down, aren't you?" Quinn said it without rancor. She'd pulled herself together, and was sitting at the kitchen table while Mom brewed some tea.

Mom looked at her. "I feel your hurt like my own, Quinn, dear. But, well, yes, deep down inside, some part of me is . . . relieved."

Mom set the teapot between them. "It's not that I don't want you to be a doctor. It's just—" She paused. "Oh, Quinn, I know you're going to be thinking this sounds crazy, but I'm worried about your going to medical school. It's just this . . . feeling I have."

Uh-oh. One of Mom's feelings. Quinn shook her head. No use in arguing. Mom sometimes had premonitions. Some turned out true, but most were just fears of what might go wrong. Quinn decided to play along. "What's it like—this bad feeling about med school?"

"Nothing specific. It's just that Ingraham place. I have this feeling you'll be in danger there."

"Well, you don't have to worry now." Saying those words triggered a pain in her chest. "I've got to call Matt." Quinn felt humiliated. But might as well grit her teeth and get it over with.

TIM sat in Matt's bedroom and watched his friend hang up the phone. Matt stared at it accusingly. After a moment he faced Tim. "They turned her down."

Tim had already gathered that. He felt a pang, almost like a soldier who'd just lost a comrade. He'd been looking forward to spending time with Quinn. "Doesn't seem right," he said. "I mean, she strikes me as someone who was born to be a doctor."

"Damn right," Matt said angrily. "Do they have any idea what they've just done to her life?" He stood and began to stalk the room. "I've had reservations about that place from the start, but this ices the cake. I'd like to turn them down, just for spite. I'm not kidding."

The seed of a scheme began to germinate in Tim's mind.

SUMMER

> Fenostatin (Hypolip—Kleederman Pharm.) has surpassed lovastatin as the number one selling lipid-lowering agent. It has consistently lowered LDL and triglycerides while raising HDL with a daily 10-mg dose, without the risk of rhabdomyolysis seen with other HMG-CoA reductase inhibitors.
>
> —*Medical Tribune*

CHAPTER 5

"INGRAHAM admissions. Marge speaking. How may I help you?"

"Hi, Marge. It's Quinn Cleary."

"Quinn! How are you, dear?"

"Still hanging in there. Any word?"

"No, honey. I'm sorry. Nobody's called. As I told you, it's very rare that someone turns down an acceptance here."

"I know. But I can still hope, can't I?"

"And we're hoping right along with you, sweetheart."

"That's nice, Marge. Thanks. Talk to you soon."

Quinn had called the admissions office so many times since spring break, she'd got to know the staff on a first-name basis. She shook her head. Too bad Marge didn't decide who got in.

August was boiling the fields outside and baking her here in the kitchen. Quinn yawned and rubbed her burning eyes. She was beat. She was working her usual two waitress jobs and spending all her free hours filling out student-loan applications and financial statements.

But money was tight. The bankers said with the economy the way it was, a lot of the government funds for student loans had dried up.

There was still the navy, but if they paid her way through med school, they'd want one year of service for every year of medical education they funded. A stiff price. She sighed. The Ingraham . . . She still got low when she thought about what she'd be missing.

"I'M NOT going to the Ingraham," Matt said.

Tim sat up and stared at him. They were lying on loungers beside Matt's Olympic-size pool out on the back lawn.

"I mean it," Matt said, keeping his eyes closed against the glare of the sun. "I told you there were things I didn't like about the place. But I sloughed them off. Then the other night my father sits me down and says he and Mom really wish I'd consider going to Yale. He went to Yale and Yale Law, my grandfather too, and I hadn't realized how much the place means to them."

Tim felt bad. He was so comfortable with Matt, and now the guy was dumping him, which he knew was not really the case. "What did the Ingraham folks say when you told them?"

"Haven't yet," Matt said. "Think I could demand that they substitute Quinn for me? She says she's eleventh on the waiting list."

"Yeah, right," Tim said. "They'll jump her over ten names on your say-so."

"You got a better idea?"

"I might. Give me a minute." The half-formed scenario from the previous spring came to mind. Tim lay back on the lounger. He'd spoken to Quinn twice this summer. During that last call she'd said something about how she'd become best friends with the admissions-office staff. He bolted upright. "I've got it!"

Matt opened his eyes, squinting up at him. "Yeah?"

"Hand me that phone. I have to call Ms. Quinn Cleary."

QUINN felt uncomfortable and scared about this off-the-wall scheme, yet she felt she had no choice but to accept Tim's offer to drive her down to Maryland. He raced along Route 95 in a gray Olds Ciera that he seemed to love. He even had a name for it.

"Why a griffin?" she said when he told her the name.

"Just Griffin. The gray 1985 Olds Ciera is the invisible car. GM sold a zillion of them, or Buicks or Pontis that look just like it.

Nobody wants to steal it or bother it. Nobody even sees it. So I named it Griffin, which, if you know your H. G. Wells, is the—"

"Name of the Invisible Man." She smiled.

At the Ingraham, after checking Tim's name on a list, the guard raised the gate and admitted him to the student lot. Quinn stared at the tight cluster of beige brick-and-stone buildings that made up the Ingraham. She hardly recognized the place. Now the oaks and maples were lush and green. She watched a couple of new students hurry up the slope to register.

"Here we are," Tim said as he pulled into a parking slot.

"Do you think this has even a slight chance to work?"

"Of course. It was designed by the Master Plotter. Registration's in the class building. That's where I'll be. You head for the admissions office and do your thing. I'll catch up with you there."

Quinn was terrified. "What if this doesn't work?"

"It will. But even if not, what have you lost? By tonight you'll either be registered here or right back where you were two weeks ago, when we cooked this thing up."

Quinn nodded. He was right.

As she stepped out of the car, Tim said, "Good luck, Quinn."

"Thanks. I'll need it." She walked up the slope to the administration building and followed the little black-and-white arrows planted in the grass to the admissions office. She paused in the empty hallway outside the door. Her heart began to pound. How on earth was she ever going to pull this off? She shook herself and stepped inside.

The admissions office turned out to be a small room with a long marble counter separating the staff from the public. A woman with graying hair sat at a cluttered desk just past the counter. A plastic nameplate on her desk read MARJORY LAKE.

Quinn cleared her throat. "Are you Marge?"

The woman looked up. "If you're looking for registration, it's—"

"I'm Quinn Cleary," she said.

Marge bolted out of her seat. "Quinn? Is that you, sweetheart? Claire! Evelyn! Look who's here. It's Quinn."

Two other women, both short, plump brunettes, crowded forward, welcoming her like a relative. Then Marge looked at her, puzzled. "But what are you doing here? We didn't . . . No one's—"

"I know," Quinn said. "I just decided I wanted to be here in case someone doesn't show up."

Quick poor-kid glances were exchanged; then Marge said, "Well, you're welcome to wait as long as you like. Want some coffee?"

"Sure. Coffee would be great."

TIM showed up an hour later. Quinn introduced him to the girls, as they called themselves. She told them she was going out to stretch her legs but would be back to see if there was any news.

She and Tim found a shady spot under an oak by the central pond and sat on a bench. The sun was in and out, and the air, heavy with moisture. Off to her left Quinn saw a parade of sweaty new arrivals lugging suitcases, boxes, and stereos into the dorm. She looked around and was struck by how planned the Ingraham looked. The dorm, the cafeteria, and the administration, class, and faculty buildings were all two stories, all of similar design and color. And off to her right, up the slope, rose the science building and, beyond that, the medical center, each set higher than the one before it, like steps to knowledge and experience.

She faced Tim. "What's in this for you? You don't know me. Why should you care if I get into the Ingraham?"

He hesitated, as if searching for the right words. "Places like the Ingraham—they're systems. A bunch of nerds get together and figure out a way to set up a place so they can call all the shots. They've got the bucks. That gives them power, and they think they can make everybody jump through their hoops. But they couldn't make Matt jump. With his family's kind of clout he can tell *them* to jump. People like you and me, though, Quinn—if we want to get into their system, when they say, 'Jump,' we've got to ask, 'How high?' "

"You can't change the way the world works, Tim."

"I'm not saying I can. But I make it a point to screw them up every chance I get."

"Oh," Quinn said. "And I suppose helping me get into the Ingraham is screwing them up."

Tim slumped forward and rested his forehead on his arms. He spoke to the grass. "This conversation is heading for the tubes."

"No," Quinn said softly. "You're going out of your way to do me a favor. Can you blame me for being curious as to why? TANSTAAFL. Remember?"

Tim lifted his head. "Okay, I like you. I like you a lot."

Quinn felt herself flushing.

"And I don't know of anyone," he continued, "who wants to be a doctor more than you. I mean, it shines from you."

"Really, Tim—"

"No, I mean it. And show me a system like this one that's messing up somebody I know, and it's like waving a red flag in front of a bull. I want to beat that system. And Matt is the wild card here. I'll bet they've got no contingency plan for what Matt's going to do." He checked his watch. "Registration's pretty well closed. Any minute they ought to be realizing they're shy one body."

They headed back to the admissions office.

Quinn sensed the change as soon as she walked through the door. The air was charged. Marge's eyes went wide when she saw her. "Quinn, we've just heard from registration. Somebody hasn't shown up. I can't believe it."

Quinn felt Tim's elbow bump her ribs. She ignored him. "Maybe that's my chance," she said to Marge. "What's his name?"

"Crawford. Matthew Crawford."

"Are you going to call him? Maybe he's just had car trouble or something."

"Whatever the cause, I'll have to check with Dr. Alston first. Then we'll call." Marge picked up her phone and smiled at Quinn. "This could be your lucky day, hon."

Quinn stepped back so as not to appear to be listening, crossed her fingers, and waited. Marge's conversation was garbled, but Quinn heard her hang up and dial another number. Then she heard Marge slam her receiver into its cradle. "He's not coming."

Cheers from Claire and Evelyn. Quinn grabbed Tim's hand and squeezed, then realized what she was doing and let go.

"It's okay," Tim said. "I wash them regularly."

Marge was up at the counter, motioning Quinn closer. "He's not coming," she said. "He decided to go to Yale Med instead. I spoke to his mother, and she said as far as she knows, he sent us a letter last month. She couldn't imagine why we never received it."

She returned to her desk and tapped a number into her phone. "Dr. Alston? It's Marge. . . . Yes, we called him. Apparently, he's decided to go to Yale instead. . . . Yes, sir, I can do that, but I think you should know, one of the wait-list students is here. Her name is . . . Let me see." Marge winked at Quinn as she made a noisy show of shuffling through the papers on her desk. "Here it is:

Cleary. Quinn Cleary. . . . Yes, I'll do that, sir. Do you want me to start making those calls now? . . . Okay, I'll wait. . . . Right, sir."

She hung up and approached Quinn, her air conspiratorial. "Well, Quinn, honey, you've sure thrown Dr. Alston a curve. When I told him you were here, he was actually speechless. And if you knew Dr. Alston, you'd know that he's never speechless. He's going to check your application and talk to the committee."

Quinn felt light-headed. "Then I have a chance?"

"You sure do. Between us, if I get the word to start calling the waiting list, there's a good chance that most of them will already be committed to other schools, and those that aren't"—her voice sank to a whisper—"they may not be home, if you know what I mean."

"I SMELL a rat."

Dr. Walter Emerson was startled by Arthur's vehemence.

"Do you, Arthur? I do most of the rat studies here, so if anyone should recognize that smell, it's me. And I don't."

"Really, Walter," Alston sniffed. "This is serious business."

Walter glanced around. Six of the Ingraham's admissions commitee sat around the polished table in the oak-paneled conference room. Senator Whitney, who represented the Kleederman Foundation and had veto power, would be flying in later for his annual welcoming address to the first-year students.

"I'm not taking it lightly, Arthur," Walter said. "But I see no point in viewing this as some sort of conspiracy."

"You've got to admit it looks suspicious," Arthur said, tapping the tabletop with a pencil. "Both students are from Connecticut. I find it a little hard to swallow that as mere coincidence."

So did Walter, but he wasn't going to admit it. He'd been oddly thrilled when he'd learned that the unorthodox student sitting on their doorstep was Quinn Cleary—that bright young woman he'd interviewed. He'd recommended her highly and had been disappointed when she'd been wait-listed. "But they went to different schools. It's certainly not an obvious connection."

"Exactly. That's why I said I *smell* a rat. I haven't found one yet." He looked around the table. "Does anyone have anything to add?"

The others seemed largely indifferent. And why not? None of them had ever met Quinn Cleary. But Walter had. "Hear me out," he said, rising and walking slowly around the table. "Last winter we made out a list that we put on hold for possible admission to the Ingraham. All but Miss Cleary took that lying down. She took the initiative of coming down here on registration day in the hope of being admitted. That takes determination. That takes desire."

"But—" Arthur began.

"Plus she's female," Walter said, pressing on. He had the other committee members' attention, could see the growing interest in their eyes. "The Ingraham is constantly criticized for not taking enough women. Here's a chance to accept a woman who has great potential. I say we accept Quinn Cleary now."

"But the Kleederman equation questions," Arthur said. "She missed one."

"She may have answered only two of the three, but she got them both right," Walter said. "And if she'd got all three, she would have been one of our first choices for acceptance, am I correct?"

"Yes." Arthur's tone was reluctant. "But—"

"But nothing." Walter faced the others. "What do you say? Do we take her in, or do we tell her that initiative, tenacity, and determination have no place at the Ingraham? Which will it be?"

One committee member said, "I'm for taking her," and one by one, the others agreed.

"Then it's done," Walter said.

Arthur cleared his throat. "Not quite. The Senator should be arriving within the hour. I'll have to show him Cleary's record and convey to him the sentiments of the committee."

"And what are your sentiments, Arthur?"

"I don't like prospective students to try and pull a fast one, but since I have no hard proof, if she meets with the approval of all of you and the Senator, I shall go along."

Good, Walter thought. Only one more hurdle.

THE wait didn't just *seem* endless; it *was* endless.

Hours on those hard, narrow chairs in the admissions office. Quitting time had come and gone for Marge and Claire and Evelyn, but all three had stayed on, encouraging Quinn, as had Tim.

And then someone was walking down the administration building's deserted main corridor, coming their way. Quinn could barely breathe. A white head poked through the doorway. "Miss Cleary?"

"Yes?" Quinn said, rising, trembling.

He smiled. "Do you remember me?"

"Of course. You're Dr. Emerson. You interviewed me."

"Right. And recommended you very highly."

"Thank you."

"The committee has voted to let you take the place of the no-show." He thrust out a gnarled hand. "Welcome to the Ingraham."

Marge cried, "Yes!" and Evelyn cheered and Claire said, "Praise the Lord!" over and over as Quinn stepped forward on wobbly knees and shook Dr. Emerson's hand.

"Looks like you've gathered quite a cheering section here," he said, his eyes twinkling. "People seem to warm to you very quickly. That's a valuable asset for a doctor. Don't lose it."

Then he was gone, walking back down the hall. Quinn stood in a daze. She'd made it.

I'm in! I'm going to be a doctor!

She felt tears spring into her eyes as she glanced at Tim. He smiled and gave her a thumbs-up. Matt and Tim—such good friends. They'd saved her life. How could she ever repay them? She thanked the admissions-office ladies with all her heart, then leaned over and kissed Tim on the forehead. "Thank you," she whispered.

He seemed embarrassed. "Nothing to it."

Louis Verran sat amid his blinking indicator lights and flashing readouts. He'd spent most of August tuning up the electronics. Everything was working perfectly now, and all the controls were at his fingertips. Monitoring was where he felt truly alive.

He was reaching for a fresh cigar when Alston walked in with Senator Whitney. Verran shoved the cylinder out of sight.

"There's been a change in the roster," Alston said. "Room two five two in the dorm won't be empty, as originally planned. We're sticking a female in there. Her name is Cleary, Quinn."

Verran nodded. "No problem. It's all tuned up and ready to go."

"Good." Senator Whitney smoothed the streaks of gray at his temples. "I want you to keep a close eye on that girl. Her advent is a bit unusual, so we just want her under scrutiny for a while."

"You got it." The Senator represented the folks who wrote Verran's check, so Louis would get it done. Pronto. After they left, Verran tracked her down to one of the pay phones in the administration building. He had taps on every phone in the complex.

Her first call was nothing special—a call to her mother, burbling and sobbing over how happy she was about getting in at last. The second call was more interesting—to a guy named Matt Crawford. The name sounded familiar, and Louis had to smile when he checked it against the name of the kid who hadn't showed today. Wouldn't Alston like to know about this. The girl had pulled a fast one, but no harm done. In fact, Verran kind of admired her pluck.

All the more reason to keep an eye on her. Kids with pluck were unpredictable. Louis Verran didn't like unpredictability.

She finished her call to Crawford and left the hall phone.

You've had your fun, Quinn Cleary, he thought as he removed his headphones. Now be a good little med student and keep your nose clean for the next four years, and we'll all love you. But if you don't, I'll know. And I'll land on you like a ton of bricks.

FIRST SEMESTER

> Second-quarter sales reports place Kleederman Pharmaceuticals firmly in the top spot as the highest-grossing and most profitable pharmaceutical company in the world.
>
> —*The New York Times*

CHAPTER 6

"I DON'T think I can go in there." Quinn stood with her back pressed against the tiled wall of the hallway. She was afraid she'd tip over and fall if she moved.

"Sure you can," Tim said. "There's nothing to it."

"There are dead bodies in there," she said through her tightly clenched teeth. "Twenty-five of them."

"Right. That's why they call it the anatomy lab."

Quinn's euphoria at becoming an Ingraham student had been short lived. It had floated her through the first night. All sixteen women enrolled in the Ingraham—seventeen now, with Quinn—were housed in what they called Women's Country, a cluster of rooms at the end of the south wing's second floor. Since the four women originally in the new class had already been paired off,

Quinn wound up with a room to herself, which she did not mind.

Her high lasted through most of the following day's orientation lectures, but it began to thin when she checked in at the student bookstore and received her microscope, her dissection kit, and a three-foot stack of textbooks and laboratory workbooks.

The last wisps were shredded by her first anatomy lecture. The Ingraham professors weren't about to coddle anyone. Quinn's concentration was taxed to the limit that first morning. She would not be sailing through these courses, as she had at UConn.

But she'd handle it. She'd take anything they put to her.

Except perhaps a dead human being. This was different. Starting today, she'd be dissecting something that once had been *somebody*. Intellectually, she'd been able to handle that, at least until she'd approached the doorway to the anatomy lab, felt the sting of the dank, formaldehyde-laden air in her nostrils, and caught a glimpse of those rows of large, sheet-covered forms.

"Come on, Quinn," Tim said, taking her elbow. She took a deep breath. As they pushed through the double doors, he said, "I checked the list. Our table's number four."

"*Our* table?"

"Not my doing, I swear. 'Brown' is the last of the B's, and 'Cleary' comes before 'Coye.' Now come on. Let's go meet Mr. Cadaver."

Table four was in the far-left corner. As they made their way past the rows of tables, Quinn studied the faces of her fellow students—some green, some as gray as their lab coats, all a bit anxious. She took heart. Maybe she wasn't such a wimp.

"Here we are," Tim said. "Table four." He moved to the far side of the sheeted form. "And here's Mr. Cadaver." He lifted the edge of the sheet and peeked beneath. "Oops. Sorry. *Mrs.* Cadaver."

"Tim," she whispered, "knock it off. Aren't you the least bit . . ." Words failed her.

Tim lowered his dark glasses and looked over the rims with his blue eyes. "The truth is, I'm terrified," he said softly. Then he snapped the glasses back up.

Quinn jumped as the overhead speakers came to life. She looked around and saw their anatomy professor, Dr. Titus Kogan, standing in the lecture area holding a microphone.

"All right, gentlemen and ladies. We're about to start the first dissection. But before we begin, I want each of you to listen carefully. For the next nine months you will be dissecting the cadavers at your assigned tables. Never forget that you are dismantling the body of a human being. This is a rare and precious privilege. All of these people are anonymous, but that doesn't mean they didn't have names, didn't have friends and family. They all deserve our respect. Now roll your cover sheets down. It is time to begin."

Quinn looked at Tim across the table. He raised his eyebrows. "Ready, partner?"

"Sure," she said, steeling herself. "Now or never."

They each grabbed a corner of the green plastic sheet and drew it swiftly toward the end of the table. A thin old woman lay face down. Quinn wanted to edge the sheet up, at least to cover her buttocks, but she left it where it was. As she tucked the plastic sheet under the cadaver's feet, she noticed a tag tied to her left great toe. She turned it over and read the print:

FREDERICKSON FUNERAL HOME
TOWSON, MD.
DOROTHY HAVERS

Dorothy Havers. They weren't supposed to know their cadaver's name.

Quinn pulled her dissection kit from her lab-coat pocket, removed the scissors, and snipped the string.

"What are you doing?" Tim asked, leaning over from his side.

"Nothing." She stuffed the tag into her pocket.

"Good afternoon, Miss Cleary."

Quinn turned and recognized the white-haired figure standing by their table. "Dr. Emerson, I didn't expect to see you here."

"Oh, you'll see a lot of me around here," he said, smiling. "Neuropharmacology is my field and my love, but it does me good to get back to the basics of gross anatomy."

Quinn liked Dr. Emerson. She had a feeling he'd played an important part in her acceptance, but she would have liked him anyway. He radiated a certain warmth that invited trust.

Quinn then asked the question that had been plaguing her since they'd removed the plastic sheet. "Why is she face down?"

"Because you'll be looking for the greater occipital nerve at the back of the neck. Dr. Kogan will be starting you off momentarily."

"Okay," Quinn said. "But first—" She freed the plastic sheet from under Dorothy's feet and drew it up to the middle of her back.

Dr. Emerson was looking at her curiously. "Are you afraid your cadaver's going to catch a chill?"

She's not just a cadaver, Quinn thought; she's Dorothy. Quinn shrugged. "We'll only be working on the neck, so I just thought—" She ran out of words.

Apparently, she didn't need any more. Dr. Emerson was nodding slowly, his eyes bright. "I understand perfectly, Miss Cleary."

TIM's head was killing him as he pulled into the student parking lot. Too much sour mash. He leaned forward and gently rested his forehead on the steering wheel, then shook himself and straightened. He'd made it from Baltimore in forty minutes. He glanced at his watch: two minutes to get to Alston's lecture. He jumped out of the car and hurried toward the class complex. He eyed the security cameras, wondering if they were eyeing him.

As the days had stretched into weeks, Tim had found himself falling into the rhythm of the Ingraham's class and lab schedule. The basic first-year courses were mostly memory and regurgitated facts. And regurgitating facts was Tim's specialty.

Sure, there was the roving bull session in the dorm, but he could take only so much of speculating and arguing about the future of medicine. And with everybody's head but his own buried in a book most of the time, he'd found himself getting bored. The only answer was to get off campus.

He was passing the pond when he heard a familiar voice say, "You look awful. Where have you been?"

He stopped and saw Quinn hurrying up the walk behind him.

"Baltimore."

"Did you get mugged or something?"

He'd stayed up all night playing five-card stud. "No. Just not enough sleep."

"Well, come on. We're late."

Dr. Alston's medical ethics—the semester's only nonregurgitant course. It was scheduled for seven on Wednesday mornings. Tim had never missed it; the class was actually stimulating. Dr. Alston seemed to take delight in being controversial. His manner was brusque, witty, acerbic, and coolly intellectual.

Tim vividly remembered the first lecture, a couple of weeks

before. "Most medical schools don't offer this course," Dr. Alston had said. "A few schools may offer something *called* medical ethics, but I assure you it's nothing like my course. Their courses are dull."

Amid polite laughter he'd stepped off the dais and pointed at one of the students. "Mr. Kahl, consider, if you will, you have a donor kidney and four potential recipients with perfect matches: a nine-year-old girl, a thirty-five-year-old ironworker with a family, a forty-seven-year-old homeless woman, and a wealthy sixty-two-year-old C.E.O. Who would you give the kidney to?"

Kahl swallowed hard. "The little girl."

"She has no money, you know."

"Money shouldn't matter."

He turned to another student. "How about you, Mr. Greely?"

Tim was impressed. This was Dr. Alston's first lecture to the class, and already he seemed to know every student by name.

"I believe I'd also give it to the little girl," Greely said.

"Really? Why?"

"Because she's got the most years ahead of her."

"Years to do what? You don't know what she'll do with her life. Who would you choose, Miss Cleary?"

"The ironworker," Quinn said. "He's got a family to support and a lot of productive years ahead of him."

"What about the C.E.O.? He's very productive."

She paused, then, "Yes, but maybe he'll get twenty years out of the kidney. The ironworker might get twice that."

"Perhaps, perhaps not. But the C.E.O.'s in charge of thousands of workers. Without him his corporation could go under."

"Should doctors be playing God like this?" Tim called out.

Dr. Alston looked up and pointed at him. "An excellent question, Mr. Brown. But 'playing God' implies an endless bounty doled out to some and not others. That is not the case here. There are barely enough donor organs available at any one time to fulfill the needs of one tenth of the registered recipients. No, Mr. Brown, we are hardly playing God. It seems more like we are sweeping up after Him."

He surveyed the class. "In an ideal world," he said, "there would be a donated organ for every person who needed one. The grim truth is that there isn't. And there never will be. And what is even grimmer is the increasing gap between the demand for high-ticket state-of-the-art procedures and society's ability to supply them.

"Consider, there are now around thirty million people over age sixty-five on Medicare. By the year 2030 the baby boomers will swell the Medicare ranks to sixty-five million. Who is going to supply their enormous demand for medical care? The national debt is now approaching five trillion dollars. Who is going to pay for all that medical care? Choices will have to be made. Some will get their transplant, their chance to resume a normal life. Others will not. Who will decide? The guidelines will be drawn up by politicians and administered by bureaucrats."

Groans arose from the students. Dr. Alston raised his arms to quiet them. "But ultimately, you will have a say, often the final say. Look at the tacit decision you all made this morning. How many of you considered the homeless woman for the transplant?"

Tim scanned the hall. Not a hand went up.

Dr. Alston nodded slowly. "Why not, Mr. Jessup?"

"Uh, I . . . Because it seemed the other candidates could put the transplant to better use."

"Exactly! Societal worth is a factor here. There are individuals who contribute nothing to the community. In the rationing of medical resources what tier should they occupy?"

"No one's completely useless," said a female voice. Tim recognized it as Quinn's.

Dr. Alston's eyes gleamed. "How right you are, Miss Cleary. And someday it might fall to you to help these people become useful. But more on that another time. The purpose of this course is to give you the tools, the perspectives to make the monumental moral and ethical choices that will become an everyday part of medical practice in the future."

So saying, Dr. Alston had ended his introductory class in medical ethics. Tim vowed then never to miss one of these classes. He was remaining true to that vow this morning, hangover and all.

"Not tonight," Quinn told Tim as he tried to get her to sit in on the bull session when it moved to his room. "I've got to crunch pathology."

"Lighten up, or you'll wind up like Metzger," said a second-year student. "He studied so hard he went completely batty."

"Or how about that guy who went over the wall two years ago?" said another student. "What was his name?"

"Prosser," said the first. "Yeah. Work too hard and you might pull a Prosser."

"What does that mean?" Quinn said.

"One night he upped and left. Vanished without a trace. No one's heard from him since."

"Okay," Quinn said, "I'll stay. But not too long."

No one knew how it got started, but it had been going as long as anyone could remember—the floating bull session, wandering from room to room, changing personnel from night to night, hibernating during class hours, but reawakening every night after dinner to pick up where it had left off.

Quinn rarely got involved in the sessions, but when she did sit in, the topic almost always gravitated toward Dr. Alston's lectures. Like tonight.

"If rationing of medical services is inevitable, maybe the elderly should be put at the end of the waiting lists," said Judy Trachtenberg, who occupied the room next to Quinn's.

"Sure," Tim said. "I can just see you telling your grandmother she can't have that hip operation, because she's over seventy-five."

"So I'd find a way to squeeze her in," Judy said with a shrug.

Her casual attitude offended Quinn. "You can't say these are the rules except for my friends and family."

"Well, we need some kind of system," Judy said.

"Do it on a need basis," Tim said. "The guy whose heart is just about to quit gets first spot on the list, and so on."

"In other words, under your system, people will have to get sicker before they can get well?" Quinn said.

Tim scratched his head, his expression troubled. "You know, I never looked at it like that."

"Okay, Quinn," Judy said, "what's your solution to the mess?"

Quinn sighed. She had a sudden vision of the future: an elderly woman with a failing heart, gallstones, and arthritis being told repeatedly that none of her conditions met the established criteria that would allow immediate medical intervention. True enough according to the numbers the medical facilities had used to encode her diagnoses for the government computers. True enough when each condition was considered one at a time. But all three?

Was that what it was going to be like? Number-coded doctors treating number-coded diseases afflicting number-coded patients?

Why wasn't there a code for the quality of life? There had to be another way. "No solution," she said. "Sooner or later the politicians and bureaucrats are going to take over. They can control the funds and the distribution of their so-called resources, but they can't control the delivery of compassion, can they?"

Judy groaned, but Tim cut her off with a wave of his hand. He nodded at Quinn. "You said it. The empty suits can't get a piece of that special chemistry that happens between a doctor and a patient unless we let them. And part of that chemistry is compassion."

"The floor's getting gooey with idealism," Judy said. "How about a little realism here?"

"We're still students," Tim said. "We're not supposed to be realists. That comes later. For the moment let's believe in the healing power of compassion."

Quinn saw the fire in his eyes and knew she'd found a kindred spirit.

I like you, Tim Brown. I like you a lot.

"Compassion," she said. "Let 'em find a procedure code for that."

"I BELIEVE it's time to start the night music," Alston said.

Louis Verran concealed his annoyance as Alston leaned forward over his shoulder, studying the main console.

"You're the boss," Verran said, not meaning a word of it.

Alston pointed to one of the readouts. "My goodness, what's going on in room one oh seven?"

Verran glanced up. The mattress-weight sensor for bed B had risen into the red. "Looks like some extra bodies on the bed. I'd guesstimate about four. Probably an orgy," he added, keeping his face deadpan. He activated the audio. All of the rooms had been wired with electret microphones. The sounds of male voices quizzing each other on hepatic histology swelled through the speakers.

"Orgy indeed!" Alston said.

Verran took a deep puff on his cigar.

Alston backed away. "Must you, Louis?"

"If you can't stand the smoke," Verran muttered, "stay away from the console." He glanced at Alston and was startled by the fury that flashed for an instant across his features. Verran realized his remark had caused the mask to slip and allowed a darker side of Dr. Arthur Alston to peek through.

Verran glanced at Kurt and Elliot. His assistants gave no indication that they had heard or seen anything. Verran had known them both when he'd been with the CIA. He'd hired them away from the Company when he'd landed this job.

Elliot, tall, slim, and dark, was careful, meticulous. One of the best electronic-surveillance jockeys in the business, he could bug a room six ways from Sunday with no one the wiser. But he'd been stopped on the street in Costa Rica one night and couldn't explain all the electronic junk in his trunk. Spent one very rough week in an Alajuela jail before the Company could extricate him. After the Costa Rica incident he refused all foreign assignments, which meant his career was dead in the water. Kurt, good-looking, with shaggy blond hair, was fast on his feet but a little flaky. He had gained a reputation around the Company as something of a loose cannon and had been passed over a number of times for promotion. Neither had hesitated when Verran offered them jobs at the Ingraham. He'd never regretted it, and neither had they.

But he did regret having to deal with Alston. After seeing Alston's ferocious reaction to his crack, Verran was suddenly glad he didn't have to answer to him. They both answered to the foundation, however. And the foundation answered to Mr. Kleederman.

"I assure you, Louis," Alston said levelly, "I wouldn't be here if I didn't have to be."

Verran put his cigar in the ashtray as a peacemaking gesture. The creep was a long-term irritation, as his ulcer was, but he'd have to learn to live with him, or both their heads could wind up on the chopping block. "I've got nothing against you, Doc. It's just that we're dealing with delicate equipment here. I get nervous when anybody but me or Kurt or Elliot gets near it."

Alston accepted the truce with a slight nod of his head. "So," he said, clearing his throat, "it seems to me that we've given them enough time to acclimate to their new surroundings. All the equipment is in a state of readiness, I assume?"

"Every SLI unit is ready and working like a dream."

"Excellent. Are our new charges all behaving themselves?"

"All but one: the Brown kid."

"Timothy Brown? The high-IQ boy from New Hampshire? What's he been up to?"

"All-nighters," Verran said. "Off campus."

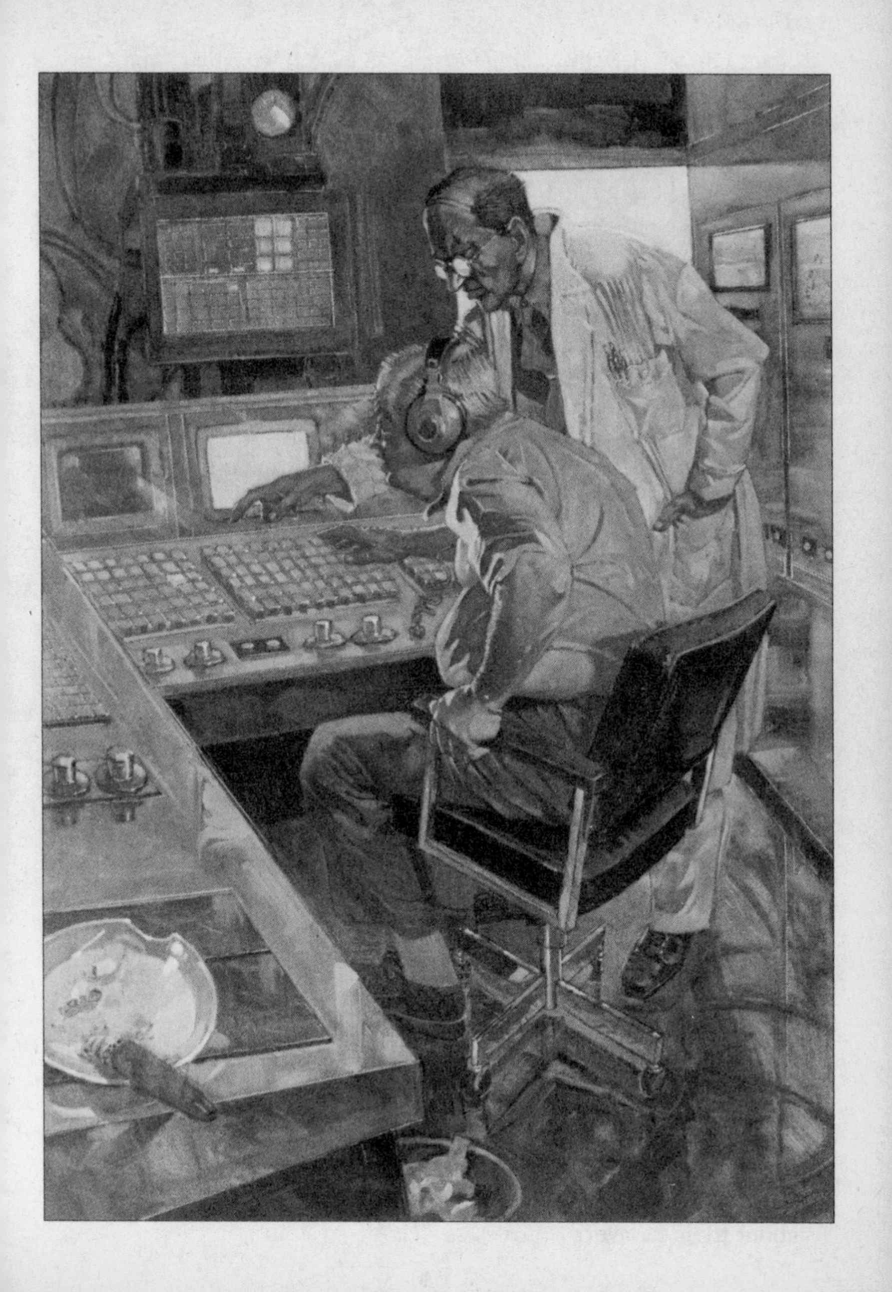

"Really?" Alston frowned. "That's not good. Weekday nights?"

"Let me check." Verran swiveled to his computer and punched in Brown's room number. His data file scrolled down the screen. "One Tuesday into Wednesday, and one Saturday into Sunday."

"Hmm. I don't like that midweek absence. Let's hope he doesn't make a habit of it. I don't particularly care about the weekends. Night music on weekends is a lagniappe, anyway. We'll let it go for now. But do keep a close watch on young Mr. Brown. I do not want another fiasco like two years ago."

Neither did Verran. His stomach burned at the memory. One of those was enough for a lifetime. "Will do," he said. "You're the boss."

Alston smiled, and it looked almost genuine. "Yes. The maestro, as it were. Very well, let the Ingraham's nocturnal concert begin."

OCTOBER

> Carbenamycin (Carbocin—Kleederman Pharm.), the new macrolide released just two years ago, has become the most prescribed antibiotic in the United States.
>
> —*P.M.A. News*

CHAPTER 7

A WARM day for October, with a high, bright sun cooking the asphalt of the parking lot. Good driving weather.

"Are you sure you don't want some company?" Tim said, leaning against his car and speaking through the open window.

"Any other time and I'd say yes," Quinn said as she adjusted the seat belt. "But this is personal."

"Take good care of Griffin for me, drive carefully, and wear shorts more often—you've got dynamite legs."

She felt her cheeks go crimson; they didn't cool until she reached the highway. Then she smiled and shook her head. He was a clown.

She found Route 70 and followed it east. Company would have been nice, but how could she explain to Tim this need to learn about their cadaver?

She took the inner loop on 695 to York Road in Towson and followed that south to the Towson Library. Inside, the librarians gave her a stack of back issues of the Towson *Times*, the local weekly, and she began to search through the obits. Quinn finally spotted the heading:

DOROTHY HAVERS, LONGTIME TOWSON RESIDENT, AGE 82

Dorothy O'Boyle Havers, the only daughter of Francis and Catherine O'Boyle, both Irish immigrants, died on July 12 of natural causes at the Laurel Hills Medical Center. She had been a resident of the Towson Nursing Center for seven years. Mrs. Havers was predeceased by her husband, Earl, and two daughters, Catherine and Francine. No plans for viewing or burial were announced.

Ireland. Dorothy's family came over from Ireland, just like Quinn's mother's. Quinn reread the obit and was swept by a wave of sadness. No one caring if she lived or died. Nobody to view her remains. Nobody left to mourn. So she'd willed her body to the Ingraham. And had died right next door to it. Poor woman.

But what had she died of? That might be interesting to know during the dissection. She wondered if they'd know at the Towson Nursing Center.

"DOROTHY Havers?" said Virginia Bennett, R.N., head nurse. "I remember that name. You say you're related to her?"

"Her great-niece," Quinn said.

"Well, I'll be." Nurse Bennett seemed pleasant enough. "We searched high and low for a next of kin last year when we were transferring her to the medical center, and couldn't find anyone."

"We have a common relative in Ireland," Quinn said, amazed at how easily the lie tripped off her tongue. She'd figured no one would tell her about Dorothy unless they thought she was related. "I came across her name while I was researching the family's medical history—an aunt has ovarian cancer. Was she very sick?"

"Just a little heart failure if I remember. But Dr. Clifton—he's one of our doctors—is very conservative. He refers patients to the medical center at the first sign of trouble. But he's top-notch. A graduate of the Ingraham." Nurse Bennett glanced past Quinn. "Wait. There he is now. Maybe he can help you. Dr. Clifton?"

Quinn turned and saw a young dark-haired doctor approach, dressed in a sport coat and carrying a black bag.

"Dr. Clifton, this is Dorothy Havers' great-niece."

He blinked twice, then smiled. "I didn't know Dotty had a great-niece or any kind of relative."

Quinn repeated her story.

"No," Dr. Clifton said. "Dotty had no history of cancer. Her main problem was arteriosclerosis—coronary and cerebral. We were sorry to lose her this summer. She was a nice lady."

"I wish I'd known her," Quinn said truthfully. "Was she in bad heart failure when you transferred her to the medical center?"

"Bad enough in my clinical opinion to need more intense care than a nursing home could provide," he said stiffly. "Is there a point to these questions, Miss . . ."

"Sheedy," Quinn said, barely missing a beat. "No. Just curious."

"Well, Miss Sheedy, I have rounds to make. Excuse me."

"Not much of a bedside manner," Quinn said after he'd hurried off.

"Must have had a bad day," Nurse Bennett said. "Usually he's very easygoing."

As Quinn left the Towson Nursing Center, she noticed the small print on the entry plaque: OWNED AND OPERATED BY KLEEDERMAN MEDICAL INDUSTRIES. KMI is everywhere, she thought. I guess I'll be pretty well connected after I graduate.

She wondered why she took no comfort in that.

QUINN looked up from her dissection of the accessory nerve to see Tim opening his kit on the other side of their cadaver. He'd just arrived—late as usual.

"I've been thinking. I want to name our cadaver," Quinn said.

Tim glanced up at her. "Any particular name in mind?"

"Dorothy."

"Dorothy—like Dorothy of the Oz variety?"

"Exactly."

"Should we scare up a little dead dog and name it Toto?"

"I don't know why I even bothered."

Tim must have tuned in to her tone. "Okay, Dorothy it is. Why is this suddenly so important?"

"I've got my reasons," Quinn said.

Tim stared at her. "Dorothy's her real name, isn't it?"

She hesitated, but then she told him everything, from finding the toe tag to Dr. Clifton's cool response to her questions.

Tim grinned. "Probably afraid you were some money-hungry relative fishing for a hint of malpractice."

Harrison, the teaching assistant, walked up to Quinn. "Dr. Emerson asked me to tell you to stop by his office in the faculty building after class. Something about a job." He strolled away toward another table.

"What do you think Emerson wants with you?" Tim asked.

"I haven't the faintest."

"Got to watch out for these old guys." Tim winked.

Quinn almost threw her scalpel at him.

WALTER Emerson sat poring over the latest printouts on 9574. The new data were good—better than he'd hoped for.

"You wanted to see me, Dr. Emerson?"

He glanced up and saw the slim strawberry blonde standing in his doorway, exactly as she had last December, when she'd arrived for her interview. A sight for sore eyes, he thought.

"Miss Cleary. Yes, I did. Come in. Have a seat."

"Harrison mentioned something about a job," she said as she seated herself.

"Yes. I need a research assistant. It's a part-time job. Actually, 'research assistant' is a euphemism for dishwasher and all-purpose gofer. But you'd be working on the sacrosanct fifth floor of the science center and get a firsthand look at neuropharmacological research that would prove useful later on in your schooling here. And we can arrange your hours around your schedule."

Walter watched her chew her lower lip, weighing the pros and cons. "The pay is ten dollars an hour," he added.

"Can I give it a trial run?" she said. "I'd really like to do it, but I don't want to commit to the job and then find out it's eating into my study time too much."

"Fine," Walter said. "We'll give you three or four weeks—till the first of November, say."

She smiled. The room brightened. "Okay. Great."

"Wonderful. Come up to fifth science tomorrow afternoon, and I'll officially show you around."

"I'll be there," she said, rising. She turned at the door, her expression troubled, hesitant. "But . . . why me?"

How could he put this? He knew she could use the income, but that wasn't the prime criterion. Walter had watched her in the anatomy lab, and he'd come to realize that his first impression had been correct: Quinn Cleary was one of the good ones. Once she got into the real world, she was going to buff the shine on the Ingraham's already bright name. And of course, it didn't hurt that she reminded him so much of his daughter, Clarice.

"Because I think that not only can you do the job but perhaps you can make a contribution as well."

That smile again. "Okay. I'll sure try."

And then she was gone, and Walter Emerson's office descended into relative gloom.

"So IT's legit?" Tim said. "He's not just some dirty old man?"

He had stopped by Quinn's room to see what Dr. Emerson had wanted, and was stretched out on the extra bed, hands behind his head.

"Actually, he's a rather clean old man," Quinn said. She swiveled in her desk chair and pointed to him. "Source?"

"Easy: the Beatles, *A Hard Day's Night*."

Quinn shrugged resignedly. She should have known. With Tim's phenomenal memory a Beatles movie would be easy pickings.

Tim sat up and worked a folded envelope out of the back pocket of his jeans. "And now *my* news. My folks sent down a bunch of my mail from home, and guess what? The Taj Mahal—that's Donald Trump's big casino in A.C.—has offered me a free room any night I want between November first and February twenty-eighth."

"Why would they want to do that?"

"I used to be a regular winner there last winter and spring. But I haven't been there for some time, and they want me back."

"Why would they want you back if you won money from them?"

"Because the odds are in their favor. They figure if I play there long enough, they'll get their money back."

"Are you going?"

"Of course. And you're invited."

Quinn laughed. "To spend the night with you in an Atlantic City hotel room? *Now* who's the dirty old man?"

"The room'll have two double beds. You could have your own. Of course, if you got lonely—"

"Dream on, Brown."

"Okay, but seriously, I'd like to show you how I work these places. It'll be fun."

She looked at his eager face. She'd turn down flat a similar proposition from anyone else, but Tim . . . Somehow she trusted Tim. "I'll give you a definite maybe. Let's think about it."

"Great. I was looking at the second weekend in November, right after the big anatomy midterm. We'll need a break then." He waved and headed for the door.

Quinn couldn't help smiling as she swiveled back and forth in her desk chair. A weekend in Atlantic City with Tim—that could be fun. She'd never been to a casino in her life.

But sharing a room . . .

What am I afraid of? Tim?

No. She liked Tim—found herself liking him more so with each passing day. Maybe it was involvement she was afraid of. She'd dated plenty in college—sweet guys, determined gropers, and the whole spectrum between—but she'd always kept her emotional distance. No entanglements.

She turned back to her desk, cleared her thoughts of men and November, and concentrated on her pathology notes. Tomorrow was the immediate concern.

LOUIS Verran cursed as he adjusted the volume from room 252. It didn't help—just made the static louder. He'd heard Atlantic City mentioned, and that was about it.

Alston wanted a close watch on those two first-year kids, Brown and Cleary. And now the pickup in 252 was full of static. Electret mikes weren't supposed to go bad early in the first semester.

Damn. He resisted the impulse to bang on the control panel. The problem wasn't here; it was in the dorm. He turned to Kurt. "When was the last time the audio from two five two was replaced?"

"I'll check." He tapped his keyboard a few times, then looked up at Verran. "Two years come December. What's up?"

"It's dying."

"I'll put it down for replacement over Thanksgiving break."

"Can't wait," Verran said. "I'll do it myself tomorrow."

CHAPTER 8

THE beige brick science center loomed over Quinn as she hurried up the slope. The glass doors slid open at her approach. She hurried through the high-ceilinged, marble-floored lobby toward the elevators. She was excited. Today she started her new job.

"Can I help you, miss?" said a woman's voice.

Quinn turned and saw a heavyset black woman behind the security desk. Her badge read CHARLENE TURNER.

The woman wore a smile, but her eyes and manner were all business. "What's your name?"

"Cleary. I'm going to be working for Dr. Emerson."

The woman tapped something into her keyboard. "Ah, I got you. Cleary, Quinn—student assistant to Dr. Emerson." She opened a file drawer and withdrew a manila envelope. From it she produced an I.D. badge and something that looked like a credit card. She compared the photo on the badge to Quinn.

"Yeah, that's you all right." She handed both to Quinn. "The badge goes on your coat or some other visible place as soon as you enter this building, and it stays there as long as you're in here. The other goes in your wallet. Don't lose it. Big trouble if you do."

Quinn immediately clipped the I.D. to the belt on her slacks. But the card . . . "What is this?"

"Your security key," Charlene Turner said. "You can't get to the fifth floor without it. It's got a magnetic code in that little strip at the end. Just stick it face up into the slot in the elevator."

"Okay. Thanks." They do go a little overboard in their security here, Quinn thought as she headed for the elevators.

One of the pair was standing open when she got there. On the control panel were six buttons—for floors 1 through 5, plus the basement. Next to the 5 and B were pairs of little indicator lights. The red one was glowing next to each. Quinn inserted her card into the slot above the row of buttons and pressed 5. With a soft click the red light next to 5 went off, and its companion lit up green. The elevator doors closed, and the car started up.

"All right," Quinn said, smiling as she removed the key card and slipped it into her pocket.

Stepping out on the fifth floor, she was lost for a moment. Then she saw the window onto ward C. She'd forgotten completely about ward C. Now she remembered peering through that window and meeting that pair of blue eyes from within their gauze frame, remembered the tears as she'd moved away.

As if in the grip of some invisible hand, Quinn gravitated to the window. She couldn't resist. She stopped and gazed within.

It was the same—the still, white shapes under their sheets, the nurses gliding among them like benevolent phantoms. Not a whisper of sound penetrated the glass . . . like watching a silent movie.

Quinn forced herself to look down at the bed directly before the window, wondering if the person with the blue eyes was still here.

The form on the bed by the window was sleeping. Yet even though the eyes were closed, Quinn knew it wasn't the same patient. This one seemed female.

"Miss Cleary?"

Quinn spun around.

Dr. Emerson was standing behind her. "I didn't mean to startle you, but they called from downstairs to let me know you were on your way up."

"I wasn't sure where to go."

He smiled. "My fault." He glanced at the burn-ward window. "This is where we first crossed paths, I believe."

"Yes. It's these patients. They're—"

"The other patients, in the medical center next door, come and go," he said. "But these are our orphans, the ones nobody wants. They need more care than a nursing home can provide, yet no hospital can afford to keep them. So they wind up here, where they allow us to try experimental cures for their damaged skin."

Quinn swallowed. "Experimental?"

He laughed. "You say that as if we're mad scientists, Miss Cleary. Every new drug and therapeutic advance, such as Dr. Alston's skin grafts, goes through exhaustive testing on animals. And once all that testing has been reviewed by the FDA and found suitably safe, then it's tested in human volunteers. Very carefully tested."

Quinn glanced through the window. "But these—"

"Are all volunteers. Or have been given over to our care by their families." His voice softened. "The Ingraham is their last, best hope. Dr. Alston takes samples of a patient's healthy skin and grows sheets of new cells in cultures. Then he coats this synthesized micromesh with the patient's own DNA, so there's no rejection of the mesh. The skin cells in the mesh begin to multiply, and soon you've got a patch of healthy skin. It's worked wonders in the animal studies. He's maybe two years away from FDA approval."

Quinn almost wished she were working for Dr. Alston. Dr. Emerson seemed to be reading her mind. "I never told you, but your duties in my department will have an impact on the burn patients." He gestured down the hall. "Let me show you my lab, and things will be clearer."

The prospect of dealing with real patients pumped up Quinn's excitement as she followed Dr. Emerson down the hall, past the nurses' station, and through a narrow doorway.

"Not very glamorous, I'm afraid," he said. "But here's the front section of my little domain."

It was a small room, its walls lined with desks and computer terminals. A middle-aged woman with gray-streaked hair was hunched over a keyboard, typing madly.

"Alice," Dr. Emerson said, touching her on the shoulder, "this is Quinn Cleary, the student assistant I told you about."

Alice turned and extended her hand to Quinn. Her smile was warm and welcoming. "Am I glad to see *you*. We're so backed up on data entry, you wouldn't believe. Take a seat and I'll—"

"I think I'll give her the tour first, Alice," Dr. Emerson said with a tolerant smile.

He led Quinn through a door at the rear of the office. "This used to be the vivarium, but we moved the little fellows back down to the fourth floor. Not many rats left. We're long since past that stage." He gestured to the workstations, where two technicians were measuring minute amounts of clear fluid into pipettes and inserting them into a wide assortment of autoanalytical machines. "Now we've converted this area to analysis of the sera we draw from the ward C patients."

Quinn's face must have reflected confusion, because Dr. Emerson nodded and motioned her back the way they had come. "Follow me."

Quinn followed him out into the hall to the nurses' station.

"Marguerite," he said to the slim middle-aged mocha-skinned nurse at the counter, "one of the 9574 vials, please."

The nurse reached behind her and plucked a two-ounce bottle

from a pocket in the top of the medication cart. She handed it to Dr. Emerson, who in turn handed it to Quinn.

"This," he said, "is the reason Dr. Alston and I have our labs on the same floor. It's the new anesthetic I'm developing. We have no name for it yet, so we refer to it by its entry number in the log when we isolated it. This is the nine thousand five hundred and seventy-fourth compound we've registered at the Ingraham."

Quinn stared at the bottle of clear fluid. "It's good?"

"Good?" His entire forehead lifted with his eyebrows. "It's wonderful. It's a naturally occurring neuroamine, secreted in minute amounts in the brain stem during REM sleep."

"Really?" Quinn placed the bottle on the counter. She couldn't help but smile. His enthusiasm was catching.

"Yes. You're paralyzed during dream sleep, you know. Otherwise you'd be talking, laughing, generally thrashing about in your dreams. Yet your eyes move, and your chest wall moves, allowing your lungs to breathe. So what you've got is a selective paralysis."

Quinn said, "I thought you said it was an anesthetic."

"It is. At higher doses it produces total anesthesia. I'm working on the mechanism for that now." The years seemed to drop away from him as his enthusiasm grew. "What we've got here is a general anesthetic that causes complete paralysis but allows the patient to continue breathing on his own. The anesthesiologist won't have to intubate and ventilate the patient. It can be used in every kind of surgery except chest procedures. There's zero chance of allergic reaction, because 9574 is a human neurohormone—everybody's got their own. And there's no postanesthesia side effects. You come to in the recovery room like someone awakening from a nap."

"It sounds almost too good to be true."

"It does, doesn't it?" He began gesturing excitedly with his hands. "But that's not the whole of it. It would be almost perfect with just those features, but it's also completely nontoxic. Its LD_{50}—"

"LD?"

"LD_{50}," Dr. Emerson said, "stands for the lethal dose of a given compound for fifty percent of the experimental animals. Every drug meant for human use must register one. The wonderful thing about 9574 is, as I said, that it's nontoxic. We haven't found a lethal dose yet."

Triumphant, he threw out his arms and struck the bottle of 9574, sending it skittering toward the end of the counter. The nurse, Marguerite, lunged for the bottle. She caught it just as it dropped toward the floor. Then, panting and shaking her head, she carefully replaced the vial in its slot.

"Thank goodness you caught that," Dr. Emerson said. He seemed quite upset.

"Dr. Emerson," she said, "that was too close."

"Amen," he said, then turned to Quinn. "We have precious little of 9574 available. Consequently, we treat it like gold."

"But who are you using it on?"

"Why, the ward C patients, of course.

"But why would you want to paralyze them?"

"It's not so much the paralysis we want for them," he said. "It's the anesthesia. Most of the ward C patients have horrific scarring, stiff tissue that resists movement. We use 9574 on them during their physical-therapy sessions. It allows the therapists to stretch their limbs and exercise their joints. If left alone, most of them would end up curled into a fetal position. Without 9574 the pain of physical therapy would be unendurable."

"But didn't you say the lower dose paralyzes and the higher dose anesthetizes? Wouldn't that mean they're completely paralyzed during therapy?" Quinn was starting to feel uncomfortable.

Dr. Emerson looked at her closely. "You've been listening. The paralysis with 9574 is a harmless side effect for some of the ward C patients. But for four of them the therapists need the paralysis that 9574 offers. Those four are brain damaged from anoxia—either from the smoke and heat of the fire or from shock. They are disoriented and confused. Two are frankly psychotic. The therapists would have to fight them all the way without 9574."

Quinn's heart went out to the patients in ward C. "Those poor, poor people."

Dr. Emerson put a hand gently on her elbow. "It's time to introduce you to the nitty-gritty of medical research."

THAT'S the trouble with Women's Country, Louis Verran thought as he waited outside the dorm and watched the windows of the south wing's second floor. Too much of a class mix.

It had been Alston's bright idea—not a bad one, really—to room each class as a unit, generally one class per floor per wing. One quick look at the class schedule told you when a certain wing would be deserted.

But Women's Country was different. The broads had formed an enclave of first-, second-, third-, and fourth-year students, which made it almost impossible to find a time when everybody was out. Except dinnertime. Hardly anybody on campus missed dinner.

He had his walkie-talkie on his hip and Kurt watching the elevators over at science, ready to let him know as soon as the Cleary girl left the building. She'd probably go straight to the cafeteria, but Verran was not taking any chances.

Watching the dorm door, Verran saw a couple of more girls leave, and decided to make his move.

The hallway looked deserted. No word from Kurt, so that meant Cleary was still up on fifth. He checked up and down the hall, then used the master key to let himself into 252.

QUINN looked up from the computer screen at her new workstation and glanced at the clock. Dinnertime already. She rubbed her eyes. Dr. Emerson hadn't exaggerated about the nitty-gritty—nothing more than keyboard pounding. He had left a little while before. Alice was on her way out, while Quinn straightened up her work area. When everything was neat, she headed for the elevator. She was glad the curtains were drawn across ward C.

When she got to the elevators, she saw that the floor indicator showed both cars on the lobby level. She slipped her card into the slot next to the call button and pressed the button, but neither light moved. She noticed the EXIT sign over the stairway door down the hall. Why not? Her legs could use a good stretch.

At the door, she found a little red light and a card slot in the lock assembly. She plugged in the card, the light turned green, and the door opened. Seemed you couldn't get on or off the fifth floor unless you had a card.

On the first floor, she opened the stair door into a hall around the corner from the lobby. She noticed the red steel door of a side exit. Going out this end, she realized, would save her a lot of steps. But as she approached it, she saw the standard warnings: THIS IS NOT AN EXIT. ALARM WILL SOUND IF OPENED. But she also noticed a slot identical to the one on the fifth-floor door. Quinn slipped her security card into the slot. The lock clicked, and the light turned green.

She grinned. "Yes!" She let herself out and saw another slot on the outside. She could enter here as well as exit. Her little key card was going to come in very handy, especially in bad weather.

Outside, she paused for a moment in the mild October air to take in the orange glow of the sunset. Beautiful. She was hungry, but she felt grubby. She decided to make a quick trip back to the room to freshen up before dinner.

VERRAN palmed the defective electret mike, withdrew the new one from his coat pocket, and stuck it into the hole. "Piece of cake," he said softly.

Then he heard a rustle in the hall on the far side of the door. He froze. He heard a key slipping into the lock. He dived for the floor on the side of the bed near the window and lay there, holding his breath, sweating. The door opened, and the light came on in the front room, then the overhead in the bedroom.

Damn! He was going to get caught. Why hadn't Kurt called? Even if he came up with a remotely plausible story, it still would be all over campus before morning: Chief Verran found huddling on the floor of a female student's room. He'd never live it down.

A door closed. Water started running in the bathroom.

Verran risked popping his head up and checking the room. Empty. She was in the john. He didn't hesitate. Panting, sweating, his heart pounding, he slipped out into the hall and very carefully closed the door behind him.

"SHE didn't come by me, Lou. I was watching the whole time, and I swear she never stepped out of those elevators."

Verran stared at Kurt. They were facing off in the center of the control room. Elliot was at his console, trying to make like a chameleon and blend in with the background.

"Then who came into Cleary's room? Little Red Riding Hood?"

"Wait, Lou. I'll prove it to you." Kurt fairly leaped to his console and began typing furiously. "We issued her a key card, right?"

Verran stood over Kurt's shoulder and peered at his screen. The electronic locks in science were linked to this control room, not merely for security but for monitoring as well. The system kept a record of each time a lock was opened and whose key was used.

Kurt called up a list of current key holders, highlighted Cleary's number, then plugged it into an activity search with today's date. "There! What'd I tell you?"

Verran stared at the screen. It listed three locations where Cleary had used her key that day. The first was the fifth-floor access slot in the elevator at three twelve p.m.; the second, the fifth-floor west stairwell door; the third, the fire door on science's west flank at five sixteen.

"My apologies, Kurt," he said. "She fooled us both."

"Yeah, okay, Lou," Kurt said.

Elliot finally must have thought it was safe to open his yap. "You able to get the bad bug, Chief?"

Verran reached into his coat pocket. "It's right—" The pocket was empty. He tried the other side. Empty too.

"You lose it?" Elliot said.

Verran pawed through his pockets again. He prayed he hadn't lost it; there'd be hell to pay if the wrong person found it.

Kurt rummaged in the cabinet under his console, came up with a metal detector, and approached Verran. "Here. I'll give you the once-over. If it's on you, we'll find it."

Kurt began waving the business end of the detector over Verran's clothing. The indicator needle lay dormant. "It's not on you, Lou," Kurt said. "You must have dropped it somewhere."

"All right, all right," Verran snapped. "Let me think."

Kurt and Elliot stayed mum while Verran retraced all his moves since switching the bugs. "It must have come out of my pocket when I hit the floor."

Kurt held up the metal detector. "Want me to go back to the room and see if I can find it?"

"No," Verran said, glancing at the clock. "They'll all be wandering back from dinner now."

"You can't just leave it there."

No, they couldn't just leave it there. The discovery of an electret mike in a dorm room might tip the first domino. The whole scenario played out in Verran's head: questions asked, jokes made, talk about the place being bugged, people starting to search their rooms. That one little mike could bring down the whole operation. "It's small. If it's in the room, it's over by the window. Nobody's going to see it there. We'll pick it up tomorrow. No sweat."

No sweat? he thought. Then why am I shaking inside?

QUINN PINNED HER I.D. BADGE onto her new white lab coat and turned to Tim. "How do I look?"

Tim glanced up from the spare bed in her room, where he was reading the Baltimore *Sun*. "Very scientificky."

"You going to stay here while I'm out toiling to push back the frontiers of medical science?"

"Yeah. Just for a little while, if you don't mind. My roommate, Kevin, is sacked out, and I figured I'd let him sleep."

Quinn didn't mind at all. And not just because she liked having him around; it had been kind of creepy coming back to the room during the dinner hour the day before. She'd had the weirdest feeling that someone was lurking about. "Why not hang out till I get back, and I'll buy you dinner," she said.

"Deal," Tim said, and stuck his head back into the newspaper.

TIM had been dozing on Quinn's extra bed. The sound of the key in the lock roused him. He quickly leaped up and tiptoed in his stocking feet to the door, where he flattened himself against the wall next to the hinges. As the door began to swing inward, he grabbed the knob and yanked it. "Booga-booga!"

Only it wasn't Quinn staring at him with a shocked expression. It was some fat fiftyish guy. "Who the hell are you?" Tim said.

"That's my question, buddy," the guy said. He looked rattled. He carried a flashlight in one hand and some sort of electronic baton in the other.

Tim gave him a closer look and recognized him. "You're Mr. Verran, the security guy."

"Chief of security. And you still haven't answered."

"Oh. Yeah. I'm Tim Brown, first-year student here. I'm waiting for Quinn Cleary. This is her room."

"I know that. Let's see some I.D."

Tim fished his photo I.D. card out of his wallet and gave it to Verran. He noticed a tremor in the older man's hand.

Verran handed back Tim's card. "There's . . . there was a report of some guy hiding out in one of the girls' rooms. I came by to check up on it. Where's the assigned occupant?"

"She's over in science, working for Dr. Emerson."

"She know you're here?"

"Of course. We're going to dinner together when she gets back."

The walkie-talkie on Verran's hip squawked. He unclipped it from his belt and turned his back to Tim. "Yeah?"

"She's on her way, Lou," said a tinny voice.

"Right." Verran turned back to Tim. "I've got to go. But I'll check up on you, buddy."

Tim watched him hurry down the hall, then looked around. Women's Country was empty. Who would have called security? Tim closed the door and wandered back toward the spare bed.

And why a flashlight and that other, weird-looking gadget? Not exactly equipment for confronting a prowler.

Tim stepped over to the window. "Damn." Sudden pain in the sole of his right foot. Something had jabbed into it. Something sharp.

He dropped back onto the bed and pulled his foot up where he could see it. Some sort of pin had pierced his sock and was stuck in his sole. He pulled it out and held it up to the light—a little black thing, a flat, circular, hockey-pucklike knob, maybe a quarter-inch across, stuck on a straight pin. What was it? A tie tack?

Then he heard the key in the door. He hoped this time it was Quinn, not just because he didn't want to deal with Verran's homely puss again but because he was hungry for the sight of her. Images of her face—talking, bending over books, wielding her scalpel—had been popping into his head at all hours.

As she stepped into the room, the sight of her sent a smile to his face and a wave of warmth through him. What have you done to me, Quinn Cleary? he thought.

He said, "How were things at the office today, dear?"

She smiled.

He held out the weird black stickpin he'd found. "By the way, is this yours?"

She looked at it. "Never seen it before. What is it?"

"Beats me. I found it on your floor, over there by the window." Tim shrugged into his sport coat and stuck the pin into the lapel; then he struck a pose. "May I present the very latest in men's accessories. Think it'll catch on?"

Quinn squinted at his lapel. "I can hardly see it."

Tim glanced down. The tiny black hockey puck was almost lost in the herringbone pattern. "Oh, well. Let's go eat."

He followed Quinn out the door.

About time, Verran thought as he watched Brown and Cleary leave and head for the cafeteria. He waited in the bushes until they disappeared. Then he slipped back into the dorm and hurried up to Women's Country.

No one about. Quickly he unlocked 252 and closed the door behind him. He turned on the metal detector and went immediately to the space near the window where he'd hit the floor when Cleary had surprised him. Slowly he waved the detector over the thick carpet, keeping a close eye on the needle in the illuminated gauge in the handle. It didn't budge.

He carefully swept the detector over the carpet all the way to the door. The only flicker from the needle turned out to be a dime.

Great. Just great. The detector was working fine, but no bug. Where was it, then?

NOVEMBER

> Claropril (ACE-1), the new ultrapotent ACE inhibitor from Kleederman Pharmaceuticals, has captured a twenty percent share of the antihypertensive market a mere six months after approval.
>
> —*Modern Medicine*

CHAPTER 9

Tonight the bull session had wound up in the teaching assistant Harrison's room. Quinn had been in the middle of updating her histology notes when Tim had popped in and dragged her away to it. "Come on, Quinn," he'd said. His sharp blue eyes were bright. He wasn't wearing his dark glasses as much as he used to. "You want to crack like that guy Prosser, who disappeared a couple of years ago? There's more to medicine than histology, you know."

She did need a break. Between classes, labs, studying, and working with Dr. Emerson, she was beginning to feel a bit frazzled.

Quinn and Tim made it ten people in Harrison's room. "You're just in time," Judy Trachtenberg said. "Harrison is going radical on us. He thinks chiropractors ought to be included in the tiers."

"Tiers?" Quinn said.

They quieted and looked at her.

"Tiers of eligibility," Tim told her. "You know."

"Oh, right," Quinn said. The previous week Dr. Alston had directed them to create two sets of tiers: the first set listing levels of care in descending order of sophistication, the second set dividing the population into groups in descending order of their value to society. Quinn had found it a chilling exercise, but she'd considered it no more than that—an exercise in ethics. The bull session seemed to be taking it seriously.

"What do you think?" Harrison said. Quinn wondered if anyone knew his first name. "Yes or no on the back crackers?"

"Definitely yes," Tim said. "Acupuncturists too. We've got to find a tier for every therapy if this is going to work."

Quinn watched and listened in shock. "I thought you were against any kind of rationing, Tim."

"I was," Tim said.

"Well, what happened?"

"That was before I realized the scope of the problem. The day is coming when there won't be enough care to go around. And that means some people will have to make do with lower levels of care. Tiering is the only way to decide who gets what. The only way."

She saw heads nodding in agreement all around the room. "But who's going to decide who gets stuck in which tier? Who's going to arbitrate human value?"

"You can bet we'll have a say in it," Tim said. "Especially those of us who go into primary care. We'll be deciding who gets referred and who doesn't."

"But this tiering idea—this dividing people up and stacking them in order of how useful they are—is so . . . cold," she said. "Tim, remember how we talked about finding a code for compassion?"

"Yeah," Tim said softly, his eyes suddenly distraught. "I remember. Trouble is, I don't know how I forgot."

Something in Tim's eyes unsettled her.

QUINN wandered across the lab to where Dr. Emerson was reading a journal article. He looked up at her approach and smiled.

"Uh, Dr. Emerson," she said, not sure of how to broach this, "can I ask you a strange question?"

"Sure," he said, still reading. "I've always liked strange questions."

"What's going on here?"

He looked up at her over the top of his reading glasses. "I'd think you'd know the answer to that by now. We're putting 9574—"

"No, not here in your lab. I mean in the Ingraham."

Dr. Emerson put the journal down and removed his glasses. He stared at her. "I'm not quite sure I'm following you, Quinn."

She dropped into the seat opposite him. "It's just that everybody here seems to think alike, seems to have the same point of view."

"That's not so unusual," Dr. Emerson said. "It happens at many academic institutions. Certain points of view gain favor within a department."

"But I'm not talking about a department. I'm talking about a whole institution—students and faculty alike." Quinn took a deep breath. "Everyone's starting to sound like Dr. Alston."

Dr. Emerson laughed. "Oh, I hope not." He waved someone in from the hall. "Arthur! Come in. I want you to hear this."

Quinn turned and started at the sight of Dr. Alston.

"Miss Cleary here just paid you a compliment," Dr. Emerson said.

Dr. Alston smiled thinly. "Did she now?"

"She says the whole student body is beginning to sound like you."

Dr. Alston's gaze became penetrating. "May I infer that you have somehow managed to remain immune to my rhetoric?"

Quinn swallowed. This wasn't going well. "I find it difficult to accept the concept of rationing medical care on the basis of social and economic worth."

"Given the inevitability of such rationing," he said, his manner cooling quickly, "what criteria do you propose?"

"I don't know," Quinn said. "But I'm sure there are plenty of other 'inevitabilities' that have never become reality."

"I'm sure there are too, Miss Quinn," Dr. Alston said, nodding slowly as he stared at her. His gaze made her uncomfortable. "You've given me something to ponder."

He nodded good-bye to her and Dr. Emerson, then left.

Quinn shook off a chill and turned back to Dr. Emerson. "Why do I seem to be the only one in the Ingraham who isn't falling into line behind Dr. Alston's bleak outlook?"

"Knowing Arthur," Dr. Emerson said, "I'm sure he's wondering the very same thing."

As Louis Verran knocked on Alston's office door, he wondered what Alston wanted. Verran just hoped he hadn't somehow heard about the lost bug.

"Come in," came the reply from the other side.

Verran stepped into the office of the director of medicine—the largest in the faculty building—and saw him behind his desk, leaning back in his chair, his fingers steepled before his mouth.

Verran took one of the chairs. "What's up, Doc?"

"One of the dorm SLI units is malfunctioning. I don't know the number, but I know the student's name. The truth is, I'm disturbed by the fact that if I hadn't learned of this by sheer happenstance, she might have gone all semester without hearing the night music."

A malfunctioning SLI unit undercut the Ingraham's very purpose. "What makes you think it's not working?" asked Verran. "All our SLI indicators are green. No signs of trouble anywhere."

"She told me she saw all her fellow students swinging their points of view toward mine." Alston leaned forward. "Her viewpoints are not changing. Ergo, she's not hearing the music. Conclusion: her SLI is malfunctioning. I want you to check into it immediately."

Verran gritted his teeth. He didn't need Dr. Scientist to tell him that. "Right. Who's the kid?"

"You're supposed to be watching her already—Quinn Cleary."

"Oh, no," Verran said. "Not two five two again."

Alston straightened. "Again? You've had trouble with her before?"

Verran had to be careful. He couldn't spill about almost getting caught or about the missing bug. "Just her room. Her audio pickup went on the fritz last month, and I had to replace it."

"Did you, now?" Alston paused and leaned back. "Strange that two electronic devices should malfunction in the same room within a matter of weeks. I wonder. Is something going on here?"

"Well," Verran said, rising, "so far as I know, room two five two's SLI is working perfectly."

"It had better not be, Louis," Alston said. "Or otherwise we've got ourselves a big problem. I do not want another problem. I had enough problems two years ago to last me a lifetime."

Verran nodded. This was one point on which he and Alston were in complete agreement. That had been a nightmare. "Amen, Doc." He turned toward the door. "I'll let you know as soon as I check it out. I'll use the old exterminator ploy."

Alston nodded. "Odd, but lately every time there's trouble, this Cleary girl is involved. Am I going to regret letting her in?"

Verran hoped Alston wouldn't regret it. Because if Alston regretted letting Cleary in, then inevitably Verran would.

Of course, the one who'd wind up regretting it most would be the Cleary girl.

"DON'T lock your door, Quinn," Tim said as he heard the clink of her key chain. "They're spraying today."

"Oh, that's right."

Tim watched her tuck the keys back in her pocket. She looked great in her slacks and sweater. He sighed. Today was going to be an especially long day, for tonight they were taking off for A.C.

He stepped across the hall and took another look at the sign pinned to the bulletin board:

> NOTICE
>
> The exterminators will be performing their periodic spraying of the dorm. The second floor is scheduled first, on Friday morning, November 18. All rooms must be vacated between 8 a.m. and noon. Please leave your room unlocked.
>
> Louis Verran, chief of campus security

Something about the notice bothered Tim, but he couldn't nail it down. "Seen any bugs around your room, Quinn?"

"Not a one," she said. "Sounds like preventive medicine to me."

"Seems strange to start spraying on the second floor."

She tugged on his sleeve. "Come on. We'll be late for pathology."

Maybe it was Louis Verran's name on the bottom of the notice that bothered him. He hadn't told Quinn about his little run-in with Verran in her room. But something about Verran's demeanor that night had lingered like a bad aftertaste. He'd looked guilty. And then this notice. The second floor was going to be empty, all the doors unlocked, with Louis Verran in charge.

LOUIS Verran watched Elliot checking the SLI units in the headboards of room 252. All the works were exposed, and he was pulling and probing the tangled wires and circuit boards.

"How's it look?" Verran said.

"Perfect so far, Chief."

If the problem wasn't the unit, then it had to be Cleary. A malfunctioning unit was one thing, but a malfunctioning student . . . They'd had one of those two years before. Please, never again.

TIM sensed rather than saw Quinn lean over his shoulder.

"I've got to get back to the dorm," she whispered.

"Now?"

The clock on the auditorium wall said nine thirty. Still ten minutes to go in Dr. Hager's pathology lecture on inflammation.

"I forgot my histo notes. I want to have them for the review."

She edged out of the row and started up the steps to the exit. Tim hesitated, then got up and trailed after her.

"Wait up," he said in the hallway.

She turned, surprised. "You forget something too?"

"No. I just . . ." He didn't want to tell her of his misgivings about Louis Verran. "I don't think you should go alone."

She stared at him. "What? You've got to be kidding."

"They've got a bunch of outsiders wandering the halls."

"My hero," she said. Then she touched his arm. "Thanks for the thought, but I—"

"No arguments," he said. "I'm going with you, and we haven't got much time. Besides, I'm not letting some creep who's been sniffing too much bug spray ruin *my* weekend in A.C."

"Some hero," she said, and laughed.

Tim loved the sound.

It took them less than five minutes to make it back to Women's Country. Quinn pointed down the hall. "See? Nothing to worry about. There's the chief of security himself at my door."

Verran bustled toward them, an anxious look straining his features. "What are you two doing here? Didn't you read the notice?"

"I'll only be a second," Quinn said, starting forward.

"You can't go in there right now. He's spraying."

"Yeah, right," Tim said. He stepped around Verran and headed for Quinn's door. He'd had enough. Too many screwy coincidences here: fifty-two rooms on the floor, and they just happen to be spraying 252 when he and Quinn arrive unannounced.

Tim heard Verran hurrying after him, but didn't slow. But as he was reaching for the knob, the door opened.

A tall dark-haired man in his early thirties stood there. He wore gray coveralls with an oval patch on the left breast that said A-JACKS EXTERMINATING. He carried a toolbox in one hand and a two-gallon spray canister in the other. He smiled at Tim. "Hey, how's it going?" then looked past him. "All set, Mr. Verran. Where to next?"

Verran hauled up next to Tim, puffing. "What? Oh, yeah. We'll go to two fifty-one next." He glared at Tim.

Tim saw Quinn behind Verran. She was giving him a funny look. What could he say? Something wasn't right, but he hadn't the vaguest idea what. He turned back to the exterminator and saw that he too was staring at him. Not at him exactly—at his lapel.

"That's a neat-looking pin you got there," the bug man said. "Where'd you get it?"

"Found it," Tim said.

"Take a look at this, Mr. Verran," the bug man said, pointing to Tim's lapel. "You ever seen anything like that?"

Verran came around and looked. He stiffened.

Tim was irritated. "Is it okay if she gets her notes now?"

The bug man seemed surprised. "Oh, uh, yeah. Sure."

Tim waved Quinn into the room, followed her in, then closed the door behind them. "How's the room look?" he said.

Quinn glanced around. "Fine." She looked at him closely. "Tim, are you all right?"

"Yeah. Let's get out of here." Before he closed the door, he took one last look. Something had been done to this room, something more than bug spraying. But damned if he could figure what.

KURT was laughing.

"What's so funny?" Verran said.

"We spend weeks combing the whole campus for this bug you lost and all the time this jerk's been wearing it like a stickpin on his coat." Kurt dissolved into helpless laughter again.

Elliot too was grinning like an idiot.

Verran ground his teeth. "Better get a grip on yourself," he told Kurt, "because it's going to be your job to get it back."

Kurt stopped laughing.

"Brown and Cleary are taking off for Atlantic City tonight, Chief," Elliot said. "I heard them talking."

"Maybe our luck is starting to change," Verran said. "We can grab the bug back while he's out of town."

"What if he's got it with him when he leaves?" Elliot said.

Maybe that could be worked to their advantage, Verran thought. What was the old saying? When somebody hands you a lemon . . .

"Here's what we'll do," he said. "We'll watch him leave. If he's wearing the same jacket as he had on this morning, we'll assume he's got the bug on him. You two will tail him to Atlantic City and look for a chance to rough him up a little. Make it look like a mugging."

Kurt ground a fist into his palm. "Awright!"

"I don't know about this, Chief," Elliot said.

Verran knew how twitchy Elliot got at the thought of winding up in jail again. "It'll be all right, Elliot," Verran said. "I promise."

Verran swung on Kurt. "And no permanent damage."

CHAPTER 10

"I HOPE I'm not making a mistake," Quinn said as she dropped her overnight bag into Griffin's trunk.

Tim settled his bag next to hers and slammed down the trunk. "What do you mean?"

"I mean that we're traveling as friends, and there isn't going to be any hanky-panky."

He laughed. "Hanky-panky?"

She reddened. "One of my mother's expressions. But you know what I mean. I just don't want any . . . misunderstandings."

"You mean we're not going to have the night of wild Dionysian sexual abandon that will finally give meaning to my miserable life?" He grinned. "Only kidding."

"You'd better be. Otherwise you're going to be one very disappointed medical student."

As Quinn moved toward the passenger door, a black Celica pulled into the spot on her side. With all the empty slots, she wondered why it had to park so close to them. A big blond fellow got out and gave them a friendly nod. Quinn recognized him as someone she'd seen at the security desk in the science center. She noticed him looking past her directly at Tim, almost staring. Then he slammed his door and strode up the incline toward the administration building.

Quinn settled into the front seat and looked at Tim as he started the engine. She liked Tim, liked him a lot. But this was not the right time for a serious relationship. There would be plenty of time later. For now, she had to keep focused on the future.

"MMMMMM," Tim said as they turned onto New Jersey Route 40. "The road to Atlantic City. I can smell the money already. Now's as good a time as any to plan our strategy."

"Strategy?"

"Sure. We're both going to play."

"But I don't know anything about gambling. And I can't afford—"

"You'll be playing with my money. Here's how it works. In the casinos blackjack is dealt—"

"Blackjack? I've never played blackjack."

"Sure you have. It's twenty-one. The guy who gets closest to a twenty-one value in the cards he's dealt, without going over, wins. Number cards are face value, picture cards are worth ten, and the ace can be worth one or eleven—your choice. You get dealt an ace and a picture card, that's blackjack, and you win automatically. We play the casino—the house—represented by dealers. If the cards they've dealt themselves total sixteen or less, they deal themselves another card. When the cards total more than sixteen, they take no more. The casinos have calculated that this gives them the best odds."

The whole concept baffled Quinn. "Well, if you know the house is going to win, why bother gambling at all? You should simply walk in, hand your money to the dealer, and walk out again."

Tim stared at her. "Sometimes you win. And it's not the winning or losing but the process itself that matters. It's a chance to beat the system. And everybody likes to beat the system. Especially me."

"I think we've had this conversation before."

"Right. While we were waiting to hear if the Ingraham was going to accept you. You see, the casinos have got their own system. But no casino's system is set up to handle a wild card like me. After a few decks have been played, I have a pretty good idea what's left in the shoe."

"Now I'm completely lost. The shoe?"

"Casinos don't deal blackjack from a single deck anymore, since a bunch of people worked out a counting system that gave them a decent edge over the house. So the casinos started shuffling up to eight decks at a time and loading them all into this hopper called a shoe and dealing from that. Most folks can keep track of a fifty- or hundred-card deck, but not four hundred cards. But I can."

"Your photographic memory," Quinn said.

"Yep. I don't need to know the order. All I need to know is if there's a predominance of high cards or low cards. That's when I beat their system. And you're going to help."

"What do you mean?"

"Know what this is?" He held up his right hand. His thumb and pinkie were extended, the three middle fingers folded down. He wiggled it back and forth. "It's the Hawaiian hang-loose sign."

"I still don't get it."

Tim patted her knee. "You will, Quinn. By the time we get to A.C., all will be clear. Then we'll both beat the system."

ATLANTIC City wasn't at all like Quinn had pictured it. The post-cards and photos she'd seen over the years had shown sunny beaches; tall, new, clean buildings; and a wide boardwalk filled with smiling, happy people. The city she saw as they came in from the marshy salt flats was old, worn, battered, and beaten.

"This looks like Beirut," Quinn said.

"Yeah, but it's a Beirut laid out by the Parker Brothers."

Despite the desolation, Quinn had to smile as they passed the avenues: Atlantic, Illinois, New York, Pennsylvania . . .

"Right. Monopoly."

They turned onto Virginia, and moments later they were entering an Arabian nights neverland. Stone elephants lined a long, walled entry to a Hollywoodized vision of a maharajah's palace, with faux Arabic script spelling out "Donald J. Trump presents the Taj Mahal." Tim stopped under the canopy, where turbaned attendants unloaded their baggage and whisked the car away.

"Sort of like stepping out of Kansas into Oz, isn't it?" Tim said as they followed their bags toward the registration desk.

QUINN was taken aback by the casino's gaming floor. She'd expected the flashing lights, the bells, the clatter of the slots, but she wasn't prepared for the ceaseless swirl of people and the layer of smoke that undulated over the tables like a muslin canopy. It was fascinating. She had always been a people watcher, and this was a people watcher's paradise.

Tim led her into the maelstrom. "Let's relieve Mr. Trump of some of his money," he said.

She followed him to the blackjack section—rows of curved tables, some full, some empty. They wandered up and down the aisles, Tim's eyes flickering from table to table. "I'm looking for the right table," Tim said. "It's got to be nearly full, and the dealer is just starting a new shoe." He stopped. "I think I just found it." He led her to the right.

"But it's only got one seat," Quinn said.

"That's for you. I'll be standing right behind you, teaching you the game, waiting for another seat to open up."

As Tim held the seat out for Quinn, he scanned the cards already on the table. Once the cards already played were filed in his memory, he squared Quinn at the table and dropped twenty hundred-dollar bills on the table.

"Hundreds," he said, and waited for Quinn's reaction.

As the dealer called out, "Two thousand in hundreds," Quinn nearly gave herself a whiplash as she snapped her head around to look at him. Tim winked, pushed the chips in front of her, then moved behind her. The other players were three middle-aged men with drinks in front of them, and a chain-smoking woman.

"What do I do now?" Quinn said.

"Bet a hundred. Put out one chip."

"That's a hundred dollars!"

Tim winked at the dealer, a pretty blonde wearing a ton of eye shadow. "She's a beginner."

Quinn slid the chip forward and was dealt an eight and a ten. The dealer had a king showing.

"What do I do now?"

"Stick."

The dealer turned over a nine and raked in Quinn's chip.

"What happened?" Quinn asked.

"We lost."

"We lost a hundred dollars? Just like that?"

"Put out another chip."

"How about half a one?"

"Quinn—"

"Sorry." She placed the chip and got a four and a five in return. The dealer had a seven showing. "What do I do now?"

"The very best she can do is eighteen. Since that's over sixteen, she has to stick. You're a sure loser with what you've got, so take another card."

"I'll take another card, please," Quinn said to the dealer.

Tim said, "Real gamblers say, 'Hit me,' or just tap their cards."

Quinn tapped her cards. "Hit me. Please."

A ten of clubs landed in front of her. The dealer turned over a queen. She placed a chip next to Quinn's.

"I won?" she said.

"You won."

Quinn reached for one of the two chips in front of her.

"Let them ride," Tim said.

"Two hundred dollars all at once?"

Quinn was dealt a jack. Then came an ace.

"Blackjack!" Tim said, and Quinn screeched excitedly.

"I like this game," she said.

The other players were smiling. They loved her. Of course they did, thought Tim. How could they help it?

Quinn was feeling more comfortable now. She'd caught the rhythm of the play, but after a while her pile of chips had shrunk. She had a moment of uncertainty when one of the men quit his seat and Tim claimed it, taking half of Quinn's chips with him. The curve of the table gave her a clear view of him. It would make it easy to see the hand signals Tim had set up between them.

Quinn held her own through the next few hands; then she glanced his way and noticed his left hand was splayed in the Hawaiian hang-loose configuration he'd shown her. That was the signal to push her bets to the limit.

She glanced at the plastic sign before her on the table. It said the table limit was five hundred dollars. With an extreme effort she ignored the sick feeling in her stomach and pushed five hundred-dollar chips into the play area.

A queen and a two landed in front of her. What did Tim want her to do with that? The dealer had a five showing.

She repressed a gasp as she saw that Tim had bet five hundred dollars too. Then she saw his left hand balled into a fist. She took a deep breath and waved the dealer off. "I'll stick," she said hoarsely.

The dealer flipped her own down card—a jack. Fifteen. She had to draw. Quinn held her breath . . . and watched the dealer pull a king. Quinn felt too weak to cheer. She'd just made five hundred dollars in thirty seconds.

She stopped and turned around. She had a feeling of being watched. But no one seemed to be paying any attention to her. A yellow card popped out of the shoe, and the play paused. Tim stood up and stretched. "Maybe we should have had dinner, hon," he said. "I'm starved. Want to get something to eat?"

"Uh, sure, *hon.* I could sure go for a steak now myself, *hon.*"

Tim laughed out loud. He pocketed their chips and guided Quinn away from the table. "You were great," he whispered.

"How much *did* we make?"

"I figure we're almost two thousand ahead."

Quinn sagged against him. "I don't know how much of this I can take."

"Hang in there, kid. It's just a start."

"Let's go outside," Quinn said. "I could use some fresh air."

"Sure. This way."

QUINN breathed deeply as she ran up to the railing of the Boardwalk and threw her arms wide to catch the cool breeze from the Atlantic. Tim leaned on the rail beside her, and they listened to the ocean rumbling beyond the darkened beach. Quinn noticed a stairway to their left. "Let's go down on the beach for a minute." She kicked off her shoes. "I want to get some sand between my toes."

Tim followed her, grumbling, "I hate getting sand in my shoes."

At the bottom of the steps Quinn felt a prickle at the back of her neck—again that feeling of being watched. She turned and saw two dark figures moving along the Boardwalk above them, hugging the rail, watching her and Tim. Something furtive about them.

She tapped Tim on the arm. "Maybe we should go back up."

"We just got here."

Quinn glanced up again. The two figures were at the top of the steps now, staring down at them, both definitely male, wearing knit watch caps. As she watched, they pulled their caps down over their heads—ski masks!—and began sprinting down the steps.

"Tim," she cried.

She saw him turn at the sound of their pounding feet, but he had no time to react before they were upon him. They knocked him onto his back in the sand, punched his face, then began tearing at his coat pockets, ripping them open. For a few heartbeats Quinn stood paralyzed with shock and terror; then she began screaming for help and beating on the backs of the assailants.

One of them turned and shoved her back. The blow was almost casual, but she went down. In the cold moonlight she saw chips scattering on the sand. The smaller of the attackers began to scoop them up, while the bigger one kept battering Tim and tearing at his coat. Finally the bigger one got to his feet at about the same time Quinn regained hers. He lunged toward her, but she leaped for the stairs, shouting for help. She was halfway up when he caught her.

Suddenly Tim loomed up beside them—bloody nose, bloody mouth. He yanked the big one around and slammed his fist into the nose behind the mask. Quinn heard a crunch, heard a cry of pain, and then the smaller one was pulling his partner away.

Quinn kept up her shouting. She craned her neck up and saw security guards rushing toward them from the casino entrance. When she turned back, the two muggers were already disappearing into the darkness under the Boardwalk. Then she saw Tim slump against the handrail, gasping, retching. Quinn darted to his side. All she wanted to do was throw her arms around him and cry.

So that was what she did.

"AT LEAST I didn't lose any teeth." Tim sat on the bed in the hotel room with an ice pack against his right cheek.

Quinn knelt beside him. She felt cold all over. "You could have lost your life."

They'd been to the hotel infirmary, in and out of the hotel security office, and to the Atlantic City Police Department and back.

The consensus was that it had been a random mugging, but Quinn remembered that feeling of being watched. She suspected the two attackers had watched them win heavily, seen them go outside to the deserted Boardwalk, and made their move.

Tim fingered the tears in his sport coat with his free hand. "Look at this. Torn to shreds." He looked at her, reached out, and rubbed her arm. His warm touch felt good. "You okay?"

She nodded, then put her hand over his. "You were very brave."

He snorted. "Brave? They were punching my lights out."

"No. I mean after, when the big guy was attacking me. I know they hurt you, but still you got up and came to help."

"I couldn't very well let him maul you, could I?"

Quinn slid closer and leaned against him, resting her head on his shoulder. "Does this hurt?"

"I'd say that's just what the doctor ordered."

Quinn felt oddly warm. Short of breath too. All the good feelings she had for Tim crowded close around her, and all the doubts and reservations she'd had, all the irritations he'd caused, were gone, blown away. Tonight they'd walked together through a fire.

She lifted her head and kissed him on the lips, gently. "Sorry," she said. "I don't know why I did that."

"Do it again," he said softly. "But easy on the lower lip. It's killing me."

And what followed came very naturally, very slowly, with their clothes being shed bit by bit.

QUINN lay face down on the sheets and shivered in the dark as Tim's fingers traveled lightly up and down her spine. She lay quiet, her thoughts in turmoil.

"What have we done, Tim?" she said finally.

"You mean, have we ruined a beautiful friendship?"

"Exactly."

He moved closer. His lips brushed her ear. "I desperately hope not. But we can't pretend this didn't happen."

"I know."

"Do you want to stop and never do this again?"

"No. Oh, no. But every time you stop by the room, are you going to want to be like this? Am I? I didn't want to be involved, Tim. I really didn't."

"Are you involved?"

Quinn turned toward him. She couldn't remember feeling this way about anyone else. Ever. This had to be love. "Yes. Yes, yes, yes. Are you?"

"Have been since I first saw you last December." He nuzzled her throat. "But I have an idea. A compromise. We'll make it a rule between us that we don't make love on campus. When we can, we'll sneak away to the No-Tell Motel or something, but at the Ingraham we stay strictly platonic."

Quinn tried to see his face in the dark. Was this one of his put-ons? She wished she knew, because it sounded perfect to her.

"WHAT THE HELL HAPPENED TO you?" Verran was staring at Kurt's swollen, purpling nose as he and Elliot arrived in the control room.

"The kid got in a lucky one when I wasn't looking."

Verran held out his hand. "Where's the bug?"

Elliot leaned forward and dropped it into Verran's palm. Verran bent and placed the errant bug on the concrete floor, straightened, then ground it flat under his heel.

Elliot grinned and headed for his console, while Kurt went to find some ice for his nose. Verran surveyed his little domain with quiet satisfaction. Only one problem remained to mar his serenity: the Cleary girl.

Elliot had run an exhaustive check on her SLI unit the day before and had found everything in perfect working order. No, the problem definitely wasn't with the unit; it was with the girl.

DECEMBER

MOST ACTIVE ISSUES—After a year of unprecedented growth, during which the company introduced three new successful products, Kleederman Pharmaceutical stock hit 150 at the opening bell today and split three for one. It then surged another three points per share, closing the day at 53⅛.

—*The Wall Street Journal*

CHAPTER 11

TIM had dragged Quinn to another bull session in Harrison's room. He had told her the usual: she was working too hard lately and needed a break. But that wasn't the main reason. He simply needed to be with her a little more.

During the weeks since Atlantic City, Tim had had an awful time keeping his hands off her, but he had stayed true to his word. For him the substance of their relationship was simply being with her, sharing her presence. But between the hours spent in classes and labs, plus Quinn's job, there wasn't any time for them simply to be together. Tim hungered for her presence. And that baffled him. He'd always been so self-sufficient.

He looked at her face now, at the troubled expressions playing across it as Harrison elaborated on his ideas for a central government authority to oversee the equitable redistribution of all medical resources. Tim couldn't understand her reaction. Harrison's plan made perfect sense to him.

"What about the patients?" Quinn said, and eight uncomprehending faces stared at her.

"Well," Harrison said slowly, "it's *for* the patients that tiering is necessary. They can't all receive top-level care. And someone has to decide who deserves what level of care. No one's happy with that, but it's a reality that has to be faced."

"As physicians, we should be treating illness wherever we find it, not just in a select population. That's a God game I don't want to play," Quinn said.

"But it's going to be the only game in town," Harrison said. "That's why it's so important that graduates of the Ingraham go into primary care. That's where the front lines are. That's where we can make a difference."

Tim had the oddest feeling while listening to the conversation, a deep part of him completely agreeing with Quinn and yet another part tugging him the other way. But what had rocked Tim back on his heels was Harrison's last statement: "That's why it's so important that graduates of the Ingraham go into primary care. That's where the front lines are. That's where we can make a difference."

It had been a typical Harrison statement. That wasn't the problem. The problem was that the same statement, *word for word,* had gone through Tim's mind in response to Quinn's question. Almost as if he'd been coached.

Suddenly he wanted out of the session. Not to walk out. To run.

"GUESS who's on his way down?" Elliot said.

Verran groaned. "All right, pull that last bull-session tape. Maybe it'll get him off our backs."

Alston had developed this thing for the Cleary girl. He'd been dropping by the control room regularly since Thanksgiving, looking for anything Verran could get on her.

"Good evening, gentlemen," Alston said, breezing through the door. "Any new elucidating snippets of tape for me, Louis?"

"As a matter of fact, yes," Verran said. "Let her roll, Elliot."

Alston took a seat and cocked his ear toward the speaker.

Verran didn't record everything that went on in the dorm. He couldn't. So he sampled here and there. He'd rotate from pickup to pickup, eavesdropping from within the rooms or along the telephone lines, listening for anyone who might be talking about the Ingraham. But when Verran had heard Cleary sounding off in last night's bull session, he'd recorded the whole thing.

Verran tracked the growing concern on Alston's face as he listened, even after Cleary had quit the session. He knew exactly what Alston was thinking: Who can I blame this on?

"What do I have to do, Louis, to induce you to repair that young woman's defective SLI unit?"

"There's nothing to repair."

"It's quite obvious that you're not getting the job done."

Verran had suddenly had enough. "Here's the story, Doc. Her unit checks out. You hear that—it's in A-one shape. So tell me what you're going to do about it."

Alston was silent for a moment. His voice sounded tired when he finally spoke. "What else can I do? She'll have to flunk out."

TIM was feeling restless, edgy. He couldn't handle studying tonight. He wanted to be with Quinn, but she was booking it for the anatomy practical the next day. So he wandered.

He wound up in the north wing's first-floor lounge. A student named Joe Nappo was stretched out on a couch watching some cop movie. Tim dropped into one of the seats. He didn't recognize the movie, but he did recognize Peter Weller's face from the *Robocop* flicks. On the screen, Weller was tearing his apartment apart, looking for something. Tim stared at the screen without really following the action. He had other things on his mind.

The last bull session still bothered him. It baffled him how he could believe one way and think another. The shrinks had a term for it: cognitive dissociation.

On the screen, Peter Weller pulled his telephones apart, then began unscrewing the plates over the electrical outlets.

Tim had always prided himself on not thinking like everybody else. Yet he could sense himself becoming an intellectual clone of Dr. Alston. He sounded like an echo of everybody else at the bull sessions. *Everybody else.*

On the screen, Peter Weller was holding up something he had found—a small dark object. The camera moved in for a close-up.

Tim bolted upright in his chair. The object in Peter Weller's hand looked startlingly familiar, like a tiny hockey puck on a pin. "Hey, Joe," Tim said, "what's going on? What's he up to?"

Nappo spoke without turning around. "He just found out his apartment's bugged."

Tim stared at the screen in shock, then got up and hurried for the door. His thoughts swirled in a chaotic jumble as he trotted down the hall and burst into the chill December night outside.

A bug. He'd never expected to see one in real life. Certainly not at the Ingraham. The very idea seemed ludicrous. Why would anyone want to monitor the blatherings of a bunch of medical students?

Tim shook his head. If room 252 is bugged and if campus security is in charge of the bugging and if Louis Verran is in charge of security, then one would expect Louis Verran to display an inordinate interest in room 252. Which he had. This was getting scary.

Tim stopped short and watched his breath fume in the cold air. Louis Verran saw the bug in my lapel last month, he thought, and twelve hours later I got rolled in A.C. My little stickpin just happened to be missing along with my chips.

He swung around and headed back toward the dorm. Normally, the glow of the lights in the rooms would have seemed warm beacons beckoning him in from the cold. Tonight they looked like a multifaceted cluster of eyes watching him.

If Quinn's room was bugged, there was a good chance his was too. Tim could think of only one way to find out: tear it apart.

He headed for his room.

It took a fair bit of doing, but Tim convinced his roommate, Kevin, to bunk down the hall for the night. He told Kevin that he and Quinn needed some time alone and that the inhabitants of Women's Country were too nosy. Pretty thin, but it was the best Tim could come up with on short notice.

As soon as Kevin was gone, Tim locked the door and stood looking around. Where to begin? He decided to try the bedroom first. Flashlight in hand, he crawled around the room, peering into every nook, cranny, and crevice. He emptied the closets, pulled out the drawers, cleaned out the bookshelves.

Nothing.

Then he remembered what he'd seen in the movie. He dismantled the telephone. Then he removed the wall plates from all the electrical sockets and light switches. He dissected the desk lamp.

Nothing.

Tim stopped and surveyed the carnage around him. There was something here. There had to be. His gaze drifted past the light fixture in the ceiling, then darted back to it. Of course! A sensitive bug positioned up here would pick up every word said in the room.

He pulled a desk chair over, and he was there. He loosened the central screw, and when the frosted glass diffuser came free, he set it on the bed, then squinted at the two sixty-watt standard bulbs. He couldn't see much in the glare, plus they'd been on for hours and were hot. He craned his neck this way and that, but saw nothing.

Damn, he thought. Not only was it the perfect place but it was the last place. He gave up and was fitting the diffuser back when he spotted something in the tangle of wires behind the bulbs—a tiny thing, like the one he'd found in Quinn's room, its pin inserted into a wire above the bulb sockets. Completely unnoticeable.

An uneasy chill rippled through him. He realized that deep within he hadn't expected to find anything. He'd been suspicious, there were unanswered questions, but this whole exercise had been something of a game. Now it was no longer a game. Hard evidence was half a dozen inches from his nose.

Now what? Report it? To whom? Certainly not Louis Verran.

This opened the door to another question: Why did the administration insist that all the students live here the entire four years? It didn't make sense. Unless there was something else going on.

He'd been puzzled by the seemingly alien thoughts taking hold in his mind. What if they'd been planted there?

Tim shook his head. This was getting wilder and wilder.

Nah. How could they possibly put ideas into your head? Where could they hide the equipment? His gaze drifted to the only piece of furniture in the room he hadn't disassembled: the headboard unit.

Before attacking that, he replaced the diffuser without touching the bug—better not to tip off the listeners. Then, screwdriver in hand, he approached the headboard.

"Yo, Chief."

Louis Verran looked up from his copy of *Shotgun News* and saw Elliot motioning him to his console. He rose and waddled over. "What's up?" he said, scanning Elliot's readouts.

"I've been picking up strange noises in room one two five."

"Yeah? Like what?"

"Sounds like furniture being moved. And I'm almost sure he was fooling with the ceiling fixture."

Great, Verran thought. Just what we need. "The pickup still working?"

"Yeah. Perfectly."

Verran let out a deep breath. "So even if he was fooling around with the fixture for whatever reason, he didn't find anything."

"I can't say that for sure," Elliot said. "All I can say is, he didn't touch the pickup. But I wish I could say the same for his SLI. It went dead five minutes ago."

"What do you think's wrong with it?" Verran said. He felt a sheen of cold sweat break out between his shoulder blades.

Elliot glanced at Verran. "I think it's being tampered with."

"You mean he's into the headboard?"

Elliot nodded. "Not only into it, I think he unplugged the unit."

"Who?" Verran said. "Who is it?"

"Brown."

Verran rubbed a trembling hand over his eyes. It was happening again, just like two years before. "Call Kurt. Get him down here right away."

"Take it easy, Chief. This could all be a false alarm."

"Like hell! That Brown kid has been trouble since the day he stepped onto this campus. We've got to do something about him."

As Elliot made the call, Verran pressed a hand against the right side of his abdomen. His ulcer was kicking up again.

Trouble. Nothing but trouble.

CHAPTER 12

All right, Tim thought as he stared at the maze of wires. I've found it. But what have I found?

It hadn't been easy getting into the base of the headboard. Finally, after an hour, he'd managed to loosen the steel-bolted panel and expose the innards. He'd never seen anything like this—wires and circuit boards, and a big black shiny disk facing the bed.

Whatever it was, he knew something big was going down. The same rig was probably inside every headboard in the whole dorm.

What if there was a trip switch in there that set off an alarm somewhere when the headboard was tampered with? Maybe he should get out of here. Tim was scared now. He wished he'd never begun this search, wished he'd left well enough alone.

But damn it, things hadn't been well at all. Somebody had been tampering with his mind, skewing his values. How could he have let that go on? Funny thing, though. Quinn seemed unaffected, which might explain why Verran kept returning to her room. Maybe the thing in her headboard wasn't working.

He had to tell her. He snatched Quinn's room key off his dresser and shoved it into his pocket. They'd traded keys a while back—he'd given her a set to his car, and she'd given him one to her room.

But he couldn't talk to her there or anywhere else in the dorm. Where? He grabbed a scratch pad and a pen as he left.

ABRUPTLY Quinn was awake, and she didn't know why.

She heard the hall door click closed, and sat up. "Who's there? Tim, is that you?"

"Just me, Quinn." His voice sounded strange—strained.

He flicked on the light. "Sorry it's so late. I couldn't sleep."

She stared at him and gasped. He looked pale, haggard, and frightened.

"Tim, what's wrong?"

"Nothing. I just had to see you." He held his index finger to his lips and thrust a notepad toward her.

Quinn stared at the block printing: THE ROOM IS BUGGED!!

She looked at him, completely bewildered. Was this one of his gags, or had he gone off the deep end?

He took the pad and scribbled lengthwise on the next sheet: MAKE SMALL TALK!

Quinn fumbled for something to say. "Uh, you ready for the anatomy practical?"

He was writing as he spoke. "You know me. I'm a quick study." He held up the new note: MEET ME IN MY CAR. I'LL EXPLAIN EVERYTHING.

"Yeah. I wish I had a memory like yours," Quinn said as she

grabbed the pen and pad from him and jotted her own note: ARE YOU FOR REAL??

His slow, grim nod gave her a chill. He yawned loudly as he retrieved the pad and scribbled. "Well, I'll leave you alone and see if I can get some sleep." He handed the pad back to her: I'LL WARM UP THE CAR.

She nodded. "Good idea. See you soon."

Tim waved and left her there, wondering what on earth had come over him. Then she jumped out of bed and began to dress.

"CAN you hear me, Chief?"

It was Elliot's voice, transmitting from room 125. Louis Verran stood in the control room with his face all but pressed against the fabric of the speaker.

"Listen, we're in the bedroom of one two five. We came inside when he left. I was right, Chief. He's got the whole place torn apart, including the headboard. We're going to go looking for him. Out."

"Yeah," Verran muttered. "Out."

This was bad. Very bad. And Louis Verran would have to call Dr. Alston and tell him that the nightmare scenario from two years before was starting a rerun.

TIM checked his pockets as he galloped down the stairs, and realized he didn't have his car keys. He'd have to stop off at his room.

When he opened his door, the room was dark. As he reached for the switch, someone grabbed his arm and yanked him inside. He started to yell, but a fist rammed into one of his kidneys, and all that escaped him was an agonized groan. The pain drove him to his knees, gasping, retching.

Something—a rag of some sort—was forced into his mouth. He heard the *scritch* of tape being pulled from a roll, and then a piece was pressed over his mouth. He fought panic as another piece of tape went across his eyes. Metal bands tightened around his wrists.

QUINN knew something was wrong before she reached the parking lot. As she hurried down the slope, she spotted Tim's car in its usual spot, but the motor wasn't running. She approached Griffin cautiously and peered within.

Empty. What's going on, Tim? What are you up to?

She shivered in the chill breeze. She'd thrown on a sweat suit and a jacket, but still she was cold.

"Meet me in my car"—that was what the note had said.

Quinn pulled out her key ring and picked out Tim's car keys. She opened the door, got inside, and started the engine. If Tim wasn't going to heat up the car for her, she'd heat it up for him. But she wished he'd hurry. It was creepy out here.

Tim tried to keep the encroaching panic at bay by cataloguing what he knew. First off, he was still alive. That was a good start. Second, he was unharmed—relatively. Third, he was still on campus—where, he wasn't sure. After binding and gagging him, they'd dumped him into a laundry hamper and wheeled him out of the dorm. He'd bumped along a fairly level series of concrete walks. Then he'd been pushed uphill a short distance, into a building, into an elevator for a short trip down, along a hallway, and into this room, where he'd been strapped into a padded armchair.

His best guess: he was in the basement of the science center.

Suddenly the tape was ripped away from his mouth. Tim spit out the gag and gulped air. He grimaced with pain as the tape was ripped from across his eyes. He squinted in the unaccustomed glare, but gradually the light and shadows began to form.

"Mr. Brown, Mr. Brown," said a tired voice he recognized instantly. "Whatever are we going to do with you, Mr. Brown?"

Tim blinked to bring the figure standing before him into focus. "Dr. Alston! You're in on this?"

"On what, Mr. Brown? What do you think is going on here?"

Tim glanced around. He could have been in an electronics hobbyist's heaven—monitors; speakers; computers; white, red, and green blinking lights. Louis Verran was off to the right, watching a monitor. Tim found a certain grim satisfaction—if no comfort—in realizing that his suspicions were correct.

He tried to pull his arms free, but they were bound to the chair. He noticed wires connected by clamps to his fingertips. Were they going to shock him? He looked at Alston, who smiled.

"No, Mr. Brown. We have no intention of torturing you. But we do want to make sure you stay put until we are through."

No question about staying put. He was trapped like a lab animal.

But Dr. Alston was a sane, respected physician, researcher, and academician. Wasn't he?

Alston said, "Again, what do you think is going on?"

Tim saw no use in lying. "I think you're brainwashing us." He saw Dr. Alston stiffen.

Bingo.

"What on earth could lead you to such a far-fetched conclusion?"

Briefly Tim ran down the suspicions he'd developed about the stickpin bug, the change he'd perceived in his own attitudes, his search of his room, and what he'd discovered.

Dr. Alston listened with visibly growing agitation, glancing frequently at Verran. "So am I to understand it that if you hadn't stepped on that misplaced bug, you would still be a model student?"

"Not quite," he said. "Another student's unchanged opinions made me aware of the change in mine."

Verran said, "He means Cleary, the girl in two five two."

Tim said, "If anything happens to her—"

Dr. Alston turned to him. "You'll do what? I'll tell you what you'll do, young man. You'll sit here and listen. And once you've heard the whole story, I'm sure you'll feel quite differently about it."

Alston began to pace. "When Mr. Kleederman set up his foundation, he peopled its board with an international array of high government officials and other influential men who shared his vision. Kleederman Pharmaceuticals was already well established in the U.S., but even then he saw the writing on the wall: the new drug-approval process was going to thicken into a stagnant quagmire unless intelligent changes were made. So he embarked upon a course to find a better way to bring new pharmaceuticals to the sick of the world."

"And perhaps in the process," Tim said, "make Johann Kleederman a multibillionaire?"

"I don't believe he is driven by money. No, he truly has a vision. Disease is a scourge upon mankind. Yet petty bureaucrats entangle new compounds in endless miles of red tape, delaying their use for years. Mr. Kleederman finds that unconscionable, and so do I."

"Everybody complains about the FDA, but what's that got to—"

"The bedrock of Mr. Kleederman's vision is Kleederman Pharmaceuticals. From there he branched out into medical centers that provide top-quality care to everyone, regardless of ability to pay. He gathered the medical centers, the nursing homes, and the pharmaceutical company under the umbrella of Kleederman Medical Industries. KMI funds the Kleederman Foundation, which in turn funds the Ingraham College of Medicine."

"Fine," Tim said. "But none of that explains the bugs."

"Tell me, Mr. Brown, do you have any idea what it currently costs to bring a new drug to market in the United States?"

Tim picked a number out of the air. "Fifty million."

"Oh, if only that were so," Alston said, laughing. "Two hundred thirty-one million dollars, to be exact."

Tim blinked at the staggering figure. "But you've got seventeen years under patent to get your money back."

"The seventeen-year patent clock begins running as soon as the compound is registered, and it often takes a full seven years from registration to final FDA approval. That leaves you only ten years with exclusive rights to sell a product you developed from scratch."

"I haven't seen the pharmaceutical companies standing in line to file for bankruptcy."

"But profits aren't the point. At least not the whole point. I'm also speaking of a tremendous human cost as beneficial drugs sit on the shelf while their paperwork drags through the approval process. For every ten thousand investigational compounds, only ten—ten!—make it past rodent and primate studies. Of the ten surviving compounds, only one makes it through human studies and gets to market. A one-in-ten-thousand success rate, Mr. Brown. And that lone surviving compound has only ten years to make up all the negative costs of the nine thousand nine hundred ninety-nine compounds that didn't make it. Any suggestions?"

Tim thought a moment. "Find a way of weeding out the useless compounds earlier in the process."

Alston grinned and clapped his hands. "Exactly Kleederman's solution. Running an investigational compound through the endless mandatory animal studies only to learn that it's worthless in humans is a sinful waste of time and money."

"So what are you talking about? Trying it on humans first?"

"Of course not. We run it through some rodents and primates to make sure it's not toxic. Then we try it on humans."

Tim stared at him, not wanting to believe this.

"The problem, of course," Alston went on, "is the supply of

human subjects—sick human subjects—to evaluate a drug's efficacy. That's where the Ingraham's graduates come in."

Tim saw a mental image of the WHERE ARE THEY NOW? board. "All those inner-city clinics, the nursing homes—"

"Precisely. The inner cities especially are loaded with disconnected people rife with diseases. We needed a way to funnel those patients to the Kleederman medical centers, where investigational compounds could be tested. Since we could not count on run-of-the-mill physicians, the foundation decided to produce a custom-designed physician to serve its needs. And the only way to do that was start their own medical school. Voilà, the Ingraham."

"So you admit it then. You *have* been brainwashing us."

"No. Attitude adjustment. We don't change who you are. We simply mold your attitudes concerning the appropriateness of certain sickly individuals' reimbursing a society they've never contributed to, or of allowing individuals with but a few useless years left to help make this world a better place. And when you find such individuals, you feel a compulsion to refer them to the nearest KMI center."

Tim thought of Dorothy, the cadaver he shared with Quinn. Her doctor had been an Ingraham graduate who referred her to the medical center next door. Had she been a human guinea pig?

He swallowed his loathing. "So all this talk about rationed medical care has been a smoke screen."

"Not completely. Rationed care is on the way. But that was merely a vehicle to introduce the concept of social tiering to your conscious minds while the subliminal learning and indoctrination units were whispering it to your unconscious."

"How? I've never heard of a subliminal method that's a hundred percent effective."

"None is. But the Ingraham system works, not by chance, but by careful selection of its students."

Dr. Alston pulled a chair closer and sat a few feet before Tim, leaning forward. He was really into his story now. "The special entrance exam is the key. All the best premed students in the country apply here. From those applications we choose the brightest and the most outgoing, and we insist they spend the day and night here before the entrance exam. While they're asleep that night, we introduce them to the SLI unit by implanting information about a nonexistent formula called the Kleederman equation. Then in the exam we ask them three questions about it. Those who answer them correctly reveal themselves as being susceptible to the SLI's influence. We choose our students exclusively from that." He barked a laugh. "Isn't it brilliant?"

"Not so brilliant," Verran spoke up. "What about Cleary?"

Alston seemed uncomfortable. "Miss Cleary answered two of the three Kleederman questions on her test and got them both right. She couldn't have done that unless she was susceptible to the SLI. There's a variable here that I haven't been able to identify."

Tim repressed a smile as he realized he was the variable. But the inner smile died as it dawned on him how he'd been duped and manipulated, how they'd all been duped and manipulated. How far did this conspiracy go? The Ingraham wasn't a complete front. There was a real medical center, and genuinely important research, like Dr. Emerson's, was going on here.

"Is everybody on staff part of this?"

"Heavens, no. Only key personnel. The rest have no idea."

"How do you people do that to us and live with yourselves?"

"Quid pro quo, Mr. Brown. You get the world's finest education at no cost, and—"

"No cost? What about our souls?"

"Don't be so dramatic. All we get in return are a few referrals."

"Right. Referrals to an early grave. How many deaths on your hands, Alston?"

He shook his head with annoyance. "Look, Brown, I'm not some megalomaniacal comic-book villain. There's nothing haphazard or whimsical here. It's all been carefully thought out."

"How'd they get you?"

"They read some of my articles critical of FDA policies and protocols and recruited me. I joined them enthusiastically. We're bringing amazing new therapies to medicine, to the world. This is the most important thing I will ever do with my life."

Am I being recruited? Tim wondered. He decided that it might be best to feign a growing sympathy with Alston's point of view. "But I don't see how this can work."

Alston smiled. "Oh, it's already working, Mr. Brown. Consider the lives saved by adriazepam and fenostatin and carbenamycin—compounds that would still be lost in the investigational jungle if not for our program."

"I never looked at it that way," Tim said, hoping he sounded convincing. "Maybe you're not as crazy as you sound."

Alston frowned. "I see nothing crazy about trying to remain on the leading edge of technology and therapeutics. But we must be willing to take risks."

Risks, Tim thought. Right. But with whose lives?

"It's a glorious challenge. But if you're not with us, you're against us. So what do you say, Mr. Brown? Do you want to be part of this?"

Suddenly Tim was afraid again. He knew too much. He could blow the lid off the Ingraham. They had to get rid of him, unless he convinced Alston that he'd play along. Alston was offering him a chance. Tim saw no choice but to take it. He'd be a model student until he saw an opening. Then he'd blow the whistle loud and clear.

"Count me in," Tim said.

Alston stepped over to Verran's console. "Well, Louis, what do you say? Can we take Mr. Brown at his word?"

Verran shook his head. "He's lying."

Tim's stomach plummeted at the words. "I'm not!" he said.

"The chair's a lie detector, kid," Verran said.

"Damn you!" Alston said. His face was contorted with anger as he leaned close to Tim. "We must now take extreme measures to protect ourselves." He pulled a syringe and a vial of clear fluid from his pocket.

Panic raked the lining of Tim's gut. "What's that? What're you going to do?"

Alston said nothing as he filled the syringe and approached him. Tim made a desperate, futile attempt to squirm away from the needle as Alston plunged it into his deltoid without bothering to roll up the shirtsleeve. Tim passed out.

CHAPTER 13

Quinn checked the dashboard clock: 5:32 a.m. Still no Tim. Where had he been all this time? Her concern was mounting with every passing minute. He had looked so strange, so frightened. He'd said to meet him here. She wished she'd brought those notes with her.

She stepped out of the car into the cold predawn air and trotted up the slope to the dorm. Inside, she hurried down the lighted hall and went upstairs to her room. She searched through her rumpled bedsheets for the notes. Where were they? She was sure she'd left them right here. She tore the bed apart.

Gone.

She sat on the bed, dumbfounded. Where on earth— Unless Tim had come back and taken them.

Quinn ran back downstairs and began knocking on Tim's door, calling his name.

"Hey, Quinn, what's up?" Kevin was coming down the hall, dressed in a T-shirt and boxer shorts, his pillow slung over his shoulder. "You two have a fight?"

"Where's Tim?"

He grinned. "Hey, you spent the night with him, not me."

"What are you talking about? I just got here."

His grin vanished. "You kidding?"

"Open up, will you? He was acting strange last night."

Kevin unlocked the door, and Quinn pushed ahead, rushing through the front room to the bedroom.

Neither bed had been slept in. The room looked just like all the bedrooms looked after the maids were finished. Quinn ran to the closet. It wasn't empty, but there were a lot of unused hangers.

With her heart pounding, Quinn pushed past Kevin and ran full tilt for the parking lot. She slid to a halt on the frosty grass at the top of the rise. Even from up here she could see that Griffin was gone.

"Tim," she called to the dawn, knowing there would be no reply, but compelled to cry out for an answer. "Tim!"

QUINN stumbled through the day in a daze. Her mind was on Tim and where he could be, and how he was, and why he hadn't made any of his classes and missed the practical.

She'd stopped by the security office to see if they had any idea where Tim might be, but Mr. Verran didn't seem concerned. "So? He's skipped a few classes and took off on a long weekend."

Quinn knew he was wrong. Tim might have a cavalier attitude about studying, but he didn't miss tests.

Verran wouldn't hear of reporting Tim as a missing person. There was a twenty-four-hour minimum before anyone would start looking for him. Quinn left the security office angry and frustrated.

After a halfhearted attempt at dinner, she returned to her room and called Matt at Yale, praying he'd heard from Tim. But Matt hadn't heard a word and was dumbfounded. She made him promise to call her the minute he heard anything.

The next call had been the toughest: Tim's folks. Mrs. Brown answered and quickly passed the phone to her husband. Mr. Brown listened and asked questions, then took Quinn's number and said he would call her if he heard from his son.

After that, she'd sat on her bed for a while in her darkening room. She felt alone in the universe. Then she locked her door and angled the back of a chair under the knob. Without undressing, she crawled into bed, pulled the covers over her head, and cried. Eventually she slept.

AN INSISTENT pounding on her door yanked Quinn from sleep. The room was bright. She glanced at her clock: after nine. She stumbled to the door, moved the chair away, and opened it.

"Quinn Cleary?"

She recognized the voice. "You must be Mr. Brown."

On a good day Tim's father might have passed for Tim's older brother. But this obviously was not a good day. He looked haggard and worn. Mr. Verran stood behind him in the hall.

"Yes," Mr. Brown said, extending his hand. "Have you heard anything from—"

"No. Nothing." His palm was moist against hers.

"Mr. Verran has agreed to drive me to the sheriff's office to make out a missing person's report on Tim. Since you were the last one to see him, I was hoping—"

"Of course. Just let me grab my purse."

DEPUTY Ted Southworth of the Frederick County Sheriff's Department sat before the three of them, filling out forms. He was professional and sympathetic as he quizzed Mr. Brown about Tim: physical characteristics, credit-card numbers, hobbies, close friends, on and on. Mr. Brown had a wallet-size graduation photo.

Next the deputy asked Mr. Verran if he could add anything. Quinn sensed a strained atmosphere between the two. The Ingraham security chief shrugged. "Not much. He does stay out all night rather frequently though. More than any other student."

Quinn flushed. She wondered how Mr. Verran managed to keep such close tabs on Tim's comings and goings.

His father apparently wondered the same thing. "Really?" he said. "That's news to me. How do you know?"

"The gate in and out of the student parking lot. Every kid with a car gets a coded card to work it. The gate records the date and time and card owner every time it opens."

"We haven't heard from you yet, Miss Cleary," the deputy said.

Quinn had been dreading this moment since Mr. Brown had asked her to accompany him here. How much should she tell them? Certainly not about their relationship, their intimacy. That was none of their business. But what about that bizarre scene when they'd sat writing things on the notepad because Tim thought the room was bugged? It might offer some clue to Tim's state of mind at the time, and that might lead them to where he'd gone.

Quinn told them all about it—the scribbled notes, waiting in the car, everything. The office was tomb-silent when she finished.

"Bugged?" Mr. Brown said finally. "He told you he thought the room was bugged?"

"He wrote it," she said. "On the notepad."

"Do you still have those notes?" the deputy asked.

She shook her head. "That's the weird thing. I couldn't find them. I was sure I'd left them on my bed."

"Bugged?" Mr. Brown said again. He turned to Mr. Verran. "Where on earth would he get an idea like that?"

Verran shrugged. "They're under a lot of pressure at the Ingraham. Every once in a while one of the kids cracks."

"This isn't the first time this has happened," the deputy said.

"It isn't?" Mr. Brown turned to the security chief. "You mean other students have disappeared without a trace?"

Mr. Verran looked acutely uncomfortable. "Two years ago we had a second-year student run off before finals."

"Proctor, wasn't it?" Deputy Southworth said.

"Prosser. Anthony Prosser."

"Did he ever turn up?"

"I'd heard that he did," Mr. Verran said.

"Listen to me, both of you," Mr. Brown said. Quinn saw angry fire flashing in his eyes. "We just had Tim home a few weeks ago, at Thanksgiving. He was as sane and relaxed as could be. One thing that young man never felt is academic pressure. And if he said a room was bugged, you can bet he had good reason to think so."

"I'm sure you're right," Deputy Southworth said. He rose and extended his hand across the desk. "Mr. Brown, I'm going to get this missing person's report out immediately. We'll put out an APB on his car and run a check on his credit card. I have the number of your hotel, and I'll be in touch as soon as I hear anything."

Mr. Verran rose from his own chair, speaking sorrowfully. "We've done what we can here. I'll drive you both back."

Mr. Brown didn't move. He stood by the desk like a statue, his eyes blinking back tears.

Quinn touched his elbow. "Let's go, Mr. Brown. You never know. Maybe Tim's waiting for us back at the dorm."

He gave her a weak, grateful smile. "Yeah, maybe he is."

Neither of them believed it.

QUINN was sitting, staring out the window but seeing nothing, when someone knocked on her door. It was Mr. Brown. With him were Mr. Verran and a man she'd never seen before.

"Quinn," Mr. Brown said, "could I trouble you to let this man check your room for bugs?"

She stifled a gasp. Tim had said the room was bugged, and now here was his father actually looking to prove it. In the hall behind him, Mr. Verran did not look too happy.

"Sure," she said. "I guess so."

"All right, Don," Mr. Brown said to the stranger. "Do it."

The man stepped past Quinn, produced a wand of some sort, and began waving it all around the room.

"What's he doing?" she asked.

"Looking for electronic pulsations, microwave transmissions."

The feeling of unreality swept over Quinn again as she watched.

"Not a blip," the man said to Mr. Brown when he was finished. "The place is clean, just like your son's."

Tim's father nodded. He turned to Mr. Verran, who was still outside in the hall, hovering, watching. "I had to know for sure. You understand that, don't you?"

"Of course," Mr. Verran said. "I'd've done the same thing."

Mr. Brown turned back to Quinn. "Thank you. I'll let you know if I hear anything." He touched her arm and managed a smile that was heartbreakingly close to Tim's.

As soon as the door closed, she broke down and cried.

QUINN WAS ALREADY UP AND showered when someone knocked on her door Sunday morning. She ran to it, hoping, praying.

It was Mr. Brown. He wasn't smiling. "I think we've found him."

Quinn's knees were suddenly weak. "He's . . . all right?" She reached behind her, found a chair, and sat down.

"We don't know. They found his car at the airport south of Baltimore. They checked with the airlines and learned that he purchased a one-way ticket to Las Vegas Friday morning."

"Vegas," Quinn said softly, trying to comprehend.

"And a further check of his credit card shows he arrived and rented a car from Avis. Signed for a week's rental. I don't understand any of it, but I'm so relieved to know he's alive. I've had these visions of Tim lying in a ditch somewhere."

Quinn said nothing. She was too numb with relief to speak.

Mr. Brown shook her hand good-bye. "I'm going to Las Vegas to look for him."

"You'll call me as soon as you find him?"

He nodded and let himself out.

Quinn remained in the chair, staring at her trembling hands. Las Vegas . . . What on earth? At least she knew he was still alive. Why didn't she feel better? She stood and shook off the torpor.

A walk—that was what she needed. Fresh air to clear her head.

Outside, Quinn followed the walk around the pond and found herself nearing the science center. She checked the pocket of her coat for her wallet. Her security card was in it. She thought, Why not? Setting up the data on 9574 for analysis might distract her.

Up on the fifth floor, she passed ward C with her usual quick glance through the window. She stopped. Something had changed. There were eight patients today. A new burn victim had arrived.

Quinn continued down the hall toward the lab, wondering what catastrophe had befallen that poor soul.

"I WISH I knew what they talked about," Louis Verran said as he watched Tim Brown's father leave the dorm on the video monitor.

"Well," Kurt said, stretching languidly after his flight back from Vegas, "you're the one who wanted the bugs pulled."

"And a good thing I did. You two guys have any idea how I felt when Brown's old man showed up with that industrial-espionage consultant?"

"Well, the rooms are clean now," Elliot said. "And don't forget whose idea it was to check out the girl's room."

"Okay, okay." Verran rubbed a hand across his queasy stomach. If Elliot hadn't checked Cleary's room, they wouldn't have found the notes. It seemed like they'd managed to keep the lid on everything. The only ongoing risk would be Deputy Southworth. He had asked an awful lot of questions about Prosser two years before, and he'd made it clear he wasn't satisfied with the answers.

Verran turned to Kurt. "You ditch the rental good in Vegas?"

"Just like you said: wiped clean as a whistle and sitting smack-dab in the middle of the MGM Grand parking lot."

Verran nodded. Hide in plain sight—that was the best way.

FLOATING. In darkness. With no sense of movement or direction, without so much as the sensation of air passing over his skin.

I'm alive.

Tim didn't know where he was or how he got there. He seemed to be awake. He was becoming aware of faint noises around him, of movement, of an antiseptic odor. He tried to open his eyes, but they wouldn't budge. And then he remembered—he had passed out after being stuck with a needle early Friday morning. Suddenly he wanted to shout his rage, but he couldn't even open his mouth.

The eyes. He concentrated on the lids, forcing them to move. Light began to filter through. Shapes took form. White shapes.

And then he saw himself, or at least his torso, lying in bed on his right side, under a sheet. He tried to roll over, but his body wouldn't respond. His left arm, lying along his left flank, was wrapped in white. Some sort of cloth. Gauze.

Maybe he was still dreaming. That had to be it. Because he couldn't feel *anything*. Almost like having no body at all.

Then he saw the tube running into the gauze from an IVAC 560 on a pole beside the bed. He was on IVs! Had he had an accident?

He wasn't alone. There was another bed next to him, half a dozen feet away. And a white-swathed body under the sheet. And beyond that, another. And another. All mummy-wrapped, with tubes running in and out of them. And beyond them all, a picture window, looking out into a hallway.

Tim realized he'd seen this place before. But he'd seen it from another perspective—from the other side of that window.

I'm in ward C!

Tim battled the panic. He was a prisoner in Alston's private preserve. Another faceless ward C patient. And something else—snaking up past his right eye, a white tube. A feeding tube, through a nostril, down the back of his throat, and into his stomach.

Quinn had told him about the anesthetic Dr. Emerson was developing and how it was being used on the patients in ward C. She'd called it 9574, and it supposedly paralyzed all the voluntary muscles while it let the diaphragm go on moving, as in sleep. Obviously, he'd been dosed with it as well, but it didn't have complete control of him. He'd managed to open his eyes, hadn't he? He could move his eyeballs, couldn't he?

He had to get control of his body. He could move his eyes, but he needed his hands. He looked at himself. He searched out his right hand where it lay flopped out before him on the mattress, palm up. If he could just move it. Maybe start small. Just a finger. He picked his little finger, his pinkie. He imagined himself inside it, pulling the tendon, pulling for all he was worth.

And then it moved. It moved!

He tried it again. Yes, the tip was in motion, flexing and extending, back and forth. And he could actually feel a faint tingle. He was regaining control. He was going to get out of here. And then he was going to bring the walls down.

"Good morning, Number Eight. About time you woke up."

A nurse—dark skin, brown eyes, her nose and face behind a surgical mask, her hair tucked into a surgical cap—was looking down at him. She held up a syringe filled with clear fluid. "Time for your two-o'clock dose."

She poked the needle into the rubber tip of the Y adapter on the intravenous line and emptied the syringe into the flow. She patted his shoulder. "I'll be back in a sec to turn you."

Tim watched her go, then tried to move his finger again, but this time it wouldn't budge. The nurse's syringe had been loaded with 9574. The fresh dose had turned him into dead meat again.

Movement at the window into the hall. Someone standing there, looking in. His eyes focused so slowly.

Quinn! It was Quinn, looking right at him. Didn't she recognize him? But no, how could she? He was swathed from head to toe in gauze. He tried to shout, begged his hands to move, but his voice remained silent, his limbs remained inert. Fear, frustration, terror, and rage swam around him. Helpless. He was utterly helpless.

And then Quinn turned and walked on.

Tim's vision blurred. He knew a tear was running down his cheek, but he couldn't feel it.

MATT Crawford crossed the living room of his New Haven apartment. He'd been putting it off all day. By nine o'clock he could hold out no longer. He picked up the phone and called Quinn.

What a nightmare wild man Brown had started by running off to Las Vegas. Both his parents were ready for rubber rooms. Matt had spoken to Tim's mother just the day before, and all she'd done was cry. She'd heard from Tim's father in Vegas, but his search for Tim was getting nowhere. Apparently, Tim hadn't used his credit card again after renting the car at the airport. Matt knew how Tim liked to keep you off balance, be unpredictable, but this wasn't like him. This smelled bad.

Quinn picked up the phone on the third ring. When Matt said hello, her words frantically spilled out. "Matt! Is it about Tim? Have you heard from him? Did they find him?"

"No, Quinn. I just called to see how you're doing."

Matt heard soft sobbing on the other end. "I'm afraid, Matt. I've got this horrible feeling I'm never going to see him again."

"You'll see him. I guarantee it. When are you getting in?"

Christmas break was a few days away.

"For Christmas? I won't be leaving until next Friday."

"The twenty-third? Our break starts the sixteenth. Why so late?"

"Well, I'm working on this project. I can get overtime if I stay, and I thought if Tim comes back, I ought to be here."

Matt hated the thought of her being alone in a deserted dorm. "How about I come visit you down there?" he found himself asking.

"That's nice of you, but really, I'll be busy in the lab. I'll be fine. And I promise to call you as soon as I get back home."

After Matt hung up, he sat there, wondering, feeling uneasy. He decided then to leave for Maryland Friday afternoon without telling Quinn. He'd catch her by surprise and work on her all weekend. By Sunday he'd have her packed up and ready to go. But what about Tim?

Tim, old buddy, where the hell are you?

Tim existed in a timeless space of boredom, rage, and terror, dwelling in a nightmare in which he had no body.

The staff took good care of that body. Three times a day his limbs were moved to keep the joints limber. He was turned every few hours to prevent pressure ulcers in his skin. And all the nurses spoke to him constantly, like girls talking to their dolls.

Despite all the care, he was afraid for his body. He felt nothing. What had they done to it? Had they scorched his skin? Was he now a burn victim, like the others? Tim had also begun to fear for his mind. Imprisonment in an inert body was affecting it. Every so often he would catch his thoughts veering off wildly, and he knew one day those thoughts could slip their bonds and never come back.

The only thing that kept his mind in line was focusing on movement—brief, tiny increments of victory over the drug that crippled his nervous system. He'd learned to recognize the signs that his previous dose of 9574 was wearing off. Mostly it was a tingling. When the sensation came, he focused his will on his fingers, making them the center of his world, demanding they obey him.

Tim couldn't be sure, but it seemed to him that the episodes of tingling were lasting longer, starting a little sooner before each new injection. Was he building up a tolerance to the drug?

He clung to that thought. There was another sensation today: a dull pain on the outer aspect of his left thigh. He ignored that. It was his hands that concerned him. He concentrated his will.

"Is Number Eight awake?"

"Yes, Doctor."

Alston. Dr. Arthur Alston. Tim wanted to spring up and hurl himself at his throat, but all he could do was lie there.

Suddenly Dr. Alston's masked face loomed over him. "Hello, Brown. I'm sorry it had to come to this, but you gave me no choice. Don't look for rescue from the ward C nurses. They know you're here because you're a threat to the foundation."

Dr. Alston's face was replaced by the mocha-skinned nurse's.

"All right, Marguerite," Alston said. "Turn him on his side."

Hands Tim could not feel rolled him onto his right side.

"Perfect," Alston said to Marguerite. "Now the tray, please."

Tim heard the soft clank of a metal tray. His mind screamed out to know what Alston was doing. Alston must have sensed Tim's thoughts. "You're earning your keep, Number Eight. What we've needed for a while is another test subject whose skin grafts can be cultured and then tested on fresh burns."

Another test subject? Tim thought.

"You do realize, don't you, that you're not the first student to learn too much. We've had a few unfortunate incidents in the past, when the SLI has triggered psychosis, but until now, only one other student has learned as much as you. That was Anthony Prosser."

Tim remembered the phrase he'd heard: "to pull a Prosser." It meant to go over the wall and never be heard from again.

"Anthony has been known as Number Five for two years now. During that period he has made an enormous contribution to our graft research. But now"—Tim heard Alston sigh—"now he's given all he has to give. He just lies there, completely mad. But we're not abandoning him. We'll take care of him as long as he lives."

Give? What did Prosser give?

"So, as unfortunate as it was that you had to stumble on our little secrets, in a way it proves rather timely. Number Five has run out of undamaged skin. You can take over where he left off."

Tim's brain was screaming: They're going to burn me!

"We've been culturing your skin cells since you arrived. Yesterday we added a sedative to your afternoon dose of 9574. While you were unconscious, I inflicted a thirty-six-square-inch third-degree burn on the lateral aspect of your left thigh."

They'd already burned him!

"We're not murderers, Number Eight. So we chose this method of neutralizing your threat to the foundation and the Ingraham. In a very important way you're still contributing to the medical well-being of your fellowman. Which was one of the reasons you came to the Ingraham in the first place, isn't it, Number Eight?"

But you did kill me, Tim thought. Because this is worse than death. This is hell.

CHAPTER 14

SNOW.

As she hurried toward science, Quinn brushed at a flake that had caught in her eyelashes. The Baltimore radio stations were all talking about the big snowstorm. Pennsylvania and New Jersey were slated to take the brunt, with Maryland collecting a few inches.

Normally, she'd be excited. Quinn loved snow, loved to ski. But now she felt no interest. Not much seemed to matter anymore.

Since this was the last day before Christmas break, December 16, the administration let the students get a head start on the storm. Everyone who was going home, that is. For Quinn it meant an early start in Dr. Emerson's lab. She'd had lunch, helped a couple of friends load up their cars, and waved them off.

Merry Christmas. . . . But Quinn wasn't feeling very Christmasy. She bit back a sob. Why did you leave me, Tim? Why did you make me care about you and then run off like that? Why?

She groaned as she entered science. The lobby was festooned with Christmas ornaments. There wasn't going to be any getting away from the Season to Be Jolly.

Fifth was no better. Santa faces, fake holly, and tinsel garland hung all over the place. Quinn stopped at the ward C window as a thought struck her: Here I am in the dumps about my Christmas. What about theirs? Her gaze roamed the ward and came to rest on the patient against the far wall. He appeared to be male, and his body was long and slim. Like Tim's, Quinn thought with a pang.

QUINN!

It was Quinn. And she was staring directly at him. If only he could reach up and yank the gauze off his face or screech her name or just wave. If only he knew sign language.

And then Tim realized that he did know a sign language of sorts.

QUINN stared at the bandage-covered face. She had a feeling he was staring back at her, trying to tell her something.

Movement caught her eye. His left hand was twitching. The fingers were curling into a fist. No, not all of them. Just the middle three. The thumb and pinkie finger remained extended. And then, ever so slightly, the hand wagged back and forth.

Why, it almost looked like—

As she cried out, her knees buckled, and she fell against the window with a dull thunk that echoed down the hall.

Tim's Hawaiian hang-loose sign. The patient was doing a crude version of the signal Tim had used in the casino.

"Are you all right? You're as white as a ghost." Quinn looked up and saw a nurse holding her arm. I've just *seen* a ghost, she thought.

"What's wrong?" the nurse was saying, looking at her closely. "Are you a diabetic or hypoglycemic?"

It couldn't be Tim, not in ward C. Quinn started to say something, then bit back her words. If she said anything about it, they'd think she was losing it. They'd send her home. For good. "My period," she improvised. "I always get bad cramps."

The nurse's face relaxed. "Come on over here."

Keeping one hand on the wall to steady herself, Quinn followed her to the nurses' station, where she choked down two tablets. Thanking the nurse, she made it down the hall to the lab and told Alice she didn't feel well.

Alice shooed her out, and Quinn stood outside the lab looking down the hallway. Taking a deep, tremulous breath, she marched back down the hall. She had to stop at ward C.

Both nurses were in there now, standing around the patient who'd signaled her. Marguerite was just removing a syringe from his IV line. Quinn pressed closer to the glass. She could make out the patient's left hand. It now hung limp and lifeless.

The nurse who had helped Quinn a few moments before looked up and smiled at her. Quinn gave her a friendly wave, then forced herself to walk on.

What had just happened here? What was real? What was not? She had to get out of here, back to the dorm to think.

When she got outside, the snow was falling heavily.

QUINN sat cross-legged on the bed in her darkened room and watched the snowflakes tumble through the bright cones from the dorm's exterior floodlights. As crazy as it sounded, that patient had to be Tim. The more she thought about it, the more convinced she became.

Her first impulse had been to call Deputy Southworth and demand that he charge into ward C and save Tim. But what if she did manage to convince Deputy Southworth to do that and they found out the new ward C patient was a farm boy who'd been riding a tractor when the fuel tank exploded under him? She had to be able to say she had looked into the patient's face and it was Timothy Brown.

And that was just what she was going to do. Tonight.

It was the only way.

MATT RUBBED HIS BURNING EYES. His arms were leaden, his fingers cramped from gripping the steering wheel. He'd finally made it to the Pennsylvania Turnpike. He had been crawling for miles, with hours more to go most likely. Snow was not exactly falling—racing horizontally was more like it. The passenger-side windows of Matt's Cherokee were caked with an inch of white.

This is crazy, he thought. The best thing to do would be to find a motel and spend the night. The roads would be clearer in the morning.

He picked up the cellular phone and punched in Quinn's number. If he wasn't getting there till tomorrow, he wanted to make sure she didn't zip off to Baltimore or the like for the day.

The signal was shaky, but he recognized her hello.

"Hey, Quinn, it's Matt."

"Oh, Matt. Thank God you called. It's Tim. I think he's here."

"What? He came back?"

"No. I don . . . ink he ever went away . . ."

The signal was breaking up. Through the static Matt thought he'd heard her say something about Tim not going away. "Come again, Quinn? I didn't catch that."

"I th . . . s here at . . . ngraham . . . ink they're hiding him."

"Quinn—"

". . . 'm going . . . ind out . . . sure . . . night . . . sheriff's . . . Southworth . . ." And then he lost the signal completely.

Something about somebody hiding Tim at the Ingraham? What was happening? And Quinn sounded strange. Frightened.

To hell with knocking off, he thought. He'd push through to the Ingraham tonight.

QUINN waited for Matt to call back. He'd sounded as if he'd been calling from a car phone. Why would he do that from Connecticut?

She waited awhile, and when he didn't call again, she decided it was time. Enough waiting. Time to *do.* She had everything ready: her sneakers, her security key card, and her penlight. All she had to do was put on her coat and slip into her boots.

She had to do this. She couldn't last another night wondering if that had been Tim in ward C. If that was him, at least she'd know he was alive and where he was. But that would mean there was something hideous about the Ingraham.

I have to know, she thought as she slipped into her overcoat. With her sneakers jammed into the pockets, Quinn exited the dorm, ducking past the camera in the lighted doorway and dashing outside, where the snow was gusting through the frigid air. The flakes seemed smaller now, and there were fewer of them falling.

She had decided against the direct route to science through the central campus. That would mean running the gauntlet of cameras on all the flanking buildings. She opted instead for the rougher, woodsier route that approached the building from the rear.

When she reached science, Quinn paused in the darkness outside the cone of light in front of the emergency exit door on the west side and looked around. No one about; nothing moving.

She took a deep breath, then marched up to the door, slipped her card into the slot, and entered. She eased the door shut behind her. Then with nervous glances down the hall, she changed from boots to sneakers. She didn't dare leave a trail of wet footprints in the hall.

In case anyone in security came to check, Quinn had a story ready: she couldn't sleep, so she'd come over to see if Dr. Emerson was around and if she could put her insomnia to good use.

But no one came, so she carried her boots over to the stairwell door, unlocked it with her card, and ducked inside. She left the boots in a corner and started up the steps.

On fifth, Quinn carded herself out of the stairwell, blocked the door open with her coat, then checked the hall. Most of the overheads were out. The radio at the nurses' station was playing softly.

Quinn glanced into ward C as she passed the window, but it was dark in there. She stayed close to the wall as she edged toward the lit nurses' station. She knew there were two nurses on the late shift—she heard the muffled sound of their voices. She peeked around the corner at the station.

Empty.

The music and the voices were coming from the little lounge room behind the med cabinet.

This was her chance. She had to act now. Without giving herself time to lose her nerve, she dropped into a crouch, scurried around the corner, and ducked through the door into ward C.

Now you're over the line, she thought as she eased the door closed and felt her terrified heart beating a mad tattoo. Now you've got big trouble if you're caught.

For a few seconds Louis Verran didn't know where he was. He jerked forward in his chair and looked around. He was in the control room. He'd dozed off.

Verran got up and stretched. His gut burned. He needed a break. He was still feeling the stress of the previous week. Hauling in the Brown kid, putting him in storage—none of it was his cup of tea. He hadn't figured on any rough stuff when he took this job. At least they used to get off the first weekend of Christmas break. Not this year. Because Cleary was staying and because Alston wanted close tabs on her, only one of them was off tonight. Elliot had drawn the high card. Kurt was sacked out next door in the on-call room.

As he grabbed for his bottle of Mylanta, Verran saw the red light blinking on the recorder. Cleary'd been on the phone. When had that happened? He hit the REWIND button.

An incoming call from her friend Matt. Lots of static. Then he heard Cleary say, "It's Tim. I think he's here."

Acid surged anew into Verran's stomach.

"I don't think he ever went away. I think he's here at the Ingraham. I think they're hiding him. I'm going to find out for sure tonight. If something happens to me, call the county sheriff's office. Ask for Deputy Southworth."

Verran tore off the headphones. When had her friend called? The recorder had no timer. Cleary could be up in ward C right now.

He dialed the ward C nurses' station. Doris, the shift's head nurse, answered.

"This is Verran. Anybody strange wandering around up there?"

"Strange?" Doris laughed. "There's nobody wandering around up here but us chickens."

"Check ward C *now.* We may have a trespasser." He could hear her swallow.

"Yes, sir."

He hung up and began shouting for Kurt.

The penlight trembled in Quinn's hand as she weaved her way toward the rear of ward C to where she'd seen the patient who'd signaled her. As she approached the bed, she heard a phone ring at the nurses' station. She flashed the light on the patient's bandaged face. Holding her breath, Quinn hooked a finger under the facial bandages and pulled down.

It wasn't Tim. She rearranged the bandages into their original position. How could she have been so wrong? She'd been so sure.

Wait. She flashed her light along the body. This patient was short and heavy. The one who'd signaled her had been long and lean, like Tim.

As she turned to survey the darkened ward, she saw a shadow appear at the window in the door. Quinn dropped to the floor. A heartbeat later the door swung open, and the lights went on.

WHEN Tim saw a familiar strawberry-blond head bob past the hall window, he thought he was dreaming. But when he saw her slip through the door and begin flashing a penlight, he prayed it was real. It had to be real. He wanted to laugh, to cry, to shout with joy. Quinn was here! She'd seen! She believed!

Then he wanted to scream at her when she approached the wrong bed.

Over here! Over here! They moved me over here.

He was bewildered when she suddenly dropped into a crouch. Then the lights came on, and he understood.

Tim watched the heavy blond nurse called Doris step inside the door. She appeared wary as she stood surveying the ward. Had she heard something? Was she looking for Quinn?

He could see Quinn crouched beside Number Four's bed, statue-still. Apparently satisfied, Doris turned off the lights and closed the door behind her. Quinn's shadow popped up immediately, and she began to flash her penlight at the patients around her.

Over here, damn it!

Maybe she caught the thought. Whatever the reason, she came directly toward him and shone the light in his face.

She didn't have to pull at his bandages. She seemed to know as soon as she saw his eyes. "Oh, Tim." It was a whisper encased in a moan. She bent and buried her face against his neck, sobbing, "I knew you'd never leave me like that."

He felt his own sobs welling up in his chest, with nowhere to go, searching for a voice, an exit. If only he could speak. Because as wonderful as this was, she had to go now.

Get out of here. Get somewhere safe and call the cops, the FBI, the CIA, the Pentagon. Just make sure you're safe first.

And then, over Quinn's shoulder, he saw the other nurse, a thin brunette called Ellie, walking past the window in the hallway. She stopped abruptly and stared into the ward. Then she darted back the way she had come.

Quinn hadn't seen a thing. She had to get out of here! Tim tried his voice again, knowing he couldn't make a sound. Yet he had to try. "Go."

The word shocked him. His voice sounded like a tree limb scraping against a stucco wall, but it *was* his voice.

Quinn straightened, staring at him. "Tim! Can you speak?"

He tried to tell her that a nurse had seen her, but his lips and tongue wouldn't cooperate. He had to keep it simple. "Go!"

"Not without you. I'm never—"

Then the overhead lights came on.

QUINN saw two nurses standing inside the door, gaping at her.

"Who are you?" said the heavy one. "What are you doing?"

Quinn was tongue-tied for an instant. Then she realized that they didn't know who she was. The only times she'd been there were in the afternoon. So she blurted the first thing that came to mind. "I thought they might be lonely," she said as lamely as she could. She tried to look dazed as she shuffled toward the door. "But no one will talk to me."

The nurses glanced at each other; then the heavy one spoke again. "You could have brought an infection in here."

"Oh, no," Quinn said with intense sincerity as she continued her approach. "I wash my hands every day. But they still wouldn't talk to me. Will you talk to me?"

Another glance between the nurses; then the thin one said, "Come on out. We've got coffee and doughnuts, and we'll talk."

Quinn gave a sleepy smile as she walked between them out the door . . . and kept walking. She turned right toward the hallway. The heavy nurse grabbed her shoulder. "Not that way."

Quinn pulled away and began running down the hall, ignoring the shouts behind her. She could see that the door to the exit stairs was still propped open by her coat. She was scared, but her adrenaline was flowing now. She knew she could outdistance either of the nurses. Once back in her room, she'd barricade the door and call the sheriff's. She'd blow the lid off ward C, and Tim would be free.

She was halfway there when the door opened the rest of the way and a blond man stepped over her coat and into the hall. Quinn recognized him immediately—the campus security man she and Tim had seen in the parking lot before leaving for Atlantic City. His sudden grin had a nasty twist to it.

Quinn skidded into a turn and ran the other way. The heavyset nurse had been close behind her, but Quinn's sudden change in direction took the nurse by surprise. Quinn dodged around her and kept going, with the blond man in pursuit.

The thin dark-haired nurse was at the nurses' station, on the phone, undoubtedly to security. When she saw Quinn coming, she dropped the receiver and moved to intercept her. Quinn barreled right into her, sending her flying backward into the meds cart, knocking it over. She had a brief glimpse of the bottles and syringes flying off, smashing on the floor.

As Quinn darted around the nurses' station counter, the blond man, close behind, stumbled. She heard a crash, then groans and angry curses. She dashed back toward the hall, but the two nurses were there, blocking the way. They clutched at her arms. As she shook them off, her sneakers slipped on the wet floor.

Grabbing the counter to prevent a fall, Quinn noticed three multidose bottles of a clear liquid near her right hand. She grabbed one and flung it at the big nurse. It struck her, bounced off, and smashed. Quinn took another and winged it at the thin nurse, who deflected it with her hands. That too smashed. Quinn threw the last at the heavy nurse, who ducked. It sailed over her head and shattered against the far wall. Before the nurse could straighten, Quinn was past her and again sprinting down the hall.

This time she made it to the stairwell. She grabbed her coat as she passed, pulled it on, and fumbled her key card from the pocket as she bounded down the steps. She burst from the stairwell onto the first floor, jammed the card into the emergency-door slot, and ran out into the icy air. She ran down the hill toward the campus buildings. Then she heard the exit alarm sound from the science building—someone had come through without using a card. She turned and saw the big blond guy from security following her. She heard a whimper of fear and realized it had come from her.

One of the faculty-office windows was lighted. Dr. Emerson's?

"Oh, please," she said softly, pushing her speed.

She ran inside the building, locked the door behind her, then

kicked off her sneakers—wet footprints were easy to follow. She padded down the hall in her socks toward Dr. Emerson's door. She burst into his office and slammed the door behind her.

Dr. Emerson jumped in his seat. "Quinn, what's wrong?"

"You've got to hide me! Security's after me! You've got to call the sheriff's department!"

"What are you talking about?"

"Tim Brown! I just came from ward C, and Tim Brown is *there.* And Dr. Alston's using your compound to keep him there, and we've got to get him out. So please, please call the sheriff."

Dr. Emerson closed his eyes and shook his head. "This is terrible," he muttered, looking heartbroken.

"What's wrong?"

"This just confirms my worst fears." He rubbed a hand over his eyes, then straightened in his chair. "Very well. Hide in that closet over there. I'll try to get the sheriff's office."

"Oh, thank you."

Quinn hurried over to the closet, stepped inside, and closed the door behind her. On the far side of the door she heard Dr. Emerson pick up the phone and dial. She listened as he spoke. "Sheriff's office? . . . Yes, this is Dr. Emerson at the Ingraham. I have a very frightened young woman in my office who feels she is in some danger. Could you send a car over immediately? . . . Yes, I'm in room one oh seven in the faculty building. Thank you." He hung up and said, "They'll be here shortly."

Quinn breathed a deep sigh of relief and slid to a sitting position on the floor of the closet. She hadn't been sure she could trust anyone connected with the Ingraham, including Dr. Emerson. Now she chided herself for doubting him.

Outside, in the office, a door opened. "Where is she?" a voice said.

Dr. Emerson, sounding very tired, replied, "In the closet."

Quinn was rising when the closet door was flung open. She screamed when she saw the blond guard standing there, smiling.

No, it can't be!

She tried to dart past, but he grabbed her arm. Quinn winced.

"Don't hurt her," Dr. Emerson said.

"Are you kidding?" the guard said. "After all she's put me through?"

As she was dragged past his desk toward the hall, Quinn stared at Dr. Emerson in shock and disbelief. "You? You too?"

He wouldn't meet her gaze, staring instead at his desktop.

"How could you? I thought you were my *friend.*"

Finally he looked up at her. His face was stricken, filled with grief. There were tears in his eyes. "So did I. But there are some processes that cannot be stopped once they are set in motion."

Quinn's hurt suddenly turned to fury. She shoved the security man, wrenching her arm away from his grasp with a sudden burst of strength that took her as much by surprise as it did him. She was free and running again, but with nowhere to go.

Quinn glanced over her shoulder and saw the guard racing after her, his face a mask of rage. She stretched her legs to their limit, but her socks gave her little traction on the polished floor. He gained quickly this time and tackled her just as she was banking into a turn in the hall. His weight slammed her to the floor. He lurched to his knees and hovered over her, murder ablaze in his eyes.

He grabbed her hair. "I've had enough from you," he said, and slammed her head down against the floor. Jagged bolts of white light arced from the back of her skull and met in the space behind her eyes, then plunged into darkness, dragging Quinn with them.

CHAPTER 15

FINALLY!

Matt felt the crushing fatigue begin to lift as he turned up the drive toward the Ingraham's gates. It had stopped snowing, and the going had become much faster once he'd crossed into Maryland.

The guard in the gatehouse looked at him suspiciously as Matt pulled up to the brightly lighted entrance. The guard seemed reluctant to open the window to his heated cocoon. "Help you?"

"Yeah. I'm here to visit a first-year student named Cleary."

"They've all gone home for Christmas break."

"She's still here. She's expecting me. I've been stuck in the storm. Please give her room a call. Two fifty-two."

The guard shrugged and dialed his phone. And waited. Finally he shook his head and hung up. "No answer. Like I told you, they've all gone home."

An uneasy feeling began to worm through Matt. Quinn had

sounded frightened. "I know she's here. I spoke to her a couple of hours ago. Maybe something's happened to her. Maybe—"

"The only thing that's happened is she's gone home."

"She could be hurt. Let me go up and check on her."

The guard shook his head. "Nobody goes wandering around this campus at this hour without an escort. I suggest you turn around and take the road two miles west to the Quality Inn and spend what's left of the night there. Come back after eight."

"But—"

The guard shut his window.

Matt picked up the car phone and dialed Quinn's number. He let it go on ringing until he couldn't stand the sound any longer, then hung up. Quinn's words echoed through Matt's brain: "It's Tim. I think they're hiding him here."

Matt rubbed his eyes. He was too exhausted to think straight right now. But he'd be back at eight to find Quinn.

Tim lay on his right side in an agony of suspense. He'd seen Quinn flash past the hall window being chased by the blond bastard who'd punched him in the face.

She got away. She had to have got away.

But just in case Quinn had been caught, Tim was doing his damnedest to get his arms and legs working. His two a.m. dose of 9574 was late. How else to explain this gnawing pain in his left thigh and the sudden ability to flex his elbows, bend his knees?

But he had to be careful. They'd left the lights on, so any movement could be seen. He saw some of the other patients moving, twitching, jerking, like B-movie mummies in the earliest stages of reanimation. Quinn's escape must have upset the dosage schedule.

Then the door opened, and Doris strode directly to Tim's bed. She frowned as she looked down at him. "Is that graft on your leg hurting you? It's all your girlfriend's fault. She went crazy out there. Broke near every vial of injectable we have. Threw them at us. But not to worry. There'll be more along as soon as Dr. Alston opens up the third floor for us." She smiled sourly. "And who knows. Maybe your girlfriend will be up here by then, getting her own dose. Kurt caught her."

Oh, no. Not Quinn. Not here.

Doris turned and walked among the other patients, reassuring them, checking their dressings. Suddenly the room began to vibrate. It took Tim a moment to recognize the sound: a helicopter. Who'd be coming at this hour? Doris must have wondered too. She bustled out, turning off the lights.

Tim burst into furious activity, moving his limbs, rubbing his hands, massaging his muscles. How long did he have before Doris returned with a fresh supply of 9574? An hour? A few minutes? Whatever the answer, he had to be ready for her.

"Do I have to tell you how upset Mr. Kleederman is, Arthur?"

Quinn heard the distantly familiar voice through the pain that hammered against the inner wall of her skull. She was on her back, on what felt like a couch. The air smelled like old cigar smoke.

"No. Your very presence here at this hour is testimony to that."

A new voice—Dr. Alston. No surprise there. She'd guessed he was in on this. She forced her eyes to open a slit. She saw Dr. Alston half turned away from her. The man he was speaking to was tall, sleek, well dressed—former Senator Whitney.

"We need a major overhaul of the screening process, Arthur."

"The screening process works extremely well," Dr. Alston said. "But no system dealing with human variables can be perfect."

Through her lid slits Quinn saw the Senator point her way. "This will be the third student to disappear in two years. Sooner or later someone is going to become suspicious and demand an investigation. Tell me, Arthur, how do we explain two students disappearing this year? And she does have to disappear."

"I—" Dr. Alston didn't seem to have an answer.

"I don't like this, Arthur, but you and I know she's got to go."

Quinn knew she had to be hallucinating. A former U.S. Senator and a respected professor were discussing the necessity of making her disappear. This couldn't be true.

Then came a third voice: "I think I've got the answer." Security chief Verran was speaking. "We put the two disappearances together. Link them. Make them one disappearance."

"We're listening," Whitney said.

"I've sent Elliot to Baltimore—to the airport—to get the Brown kid's car out of the long-term lot and drive it back here. My plan is to say Brown came back, picked up his girlfriend Cleary, and the two of them drove off together. We haven't seen them since."

"I see," Whitney said. "I like it. Excellent thinking, Louis."
"But we've still got a car to get rid of," Dr. Alston said.
"Destroy it tonight." A new speaker, a fourth voice.
Verran's voice said, "What do you mean, Kurt?"
The blond man who had chased her and knocked her out stepped into Quinn's field of vision. "Crash and burn. We inject a little booze into the guy's bloodstream, pour a little down his throat. The two lovebirds go racing down the icy road, skid into a tree, the gas tank explodes—boom. Case closed."
Quinn watched Dr. Alston and the former Senator look at each other. Her heart began to pound.
Why aren't they saying anything? The man's talking about a double murder. Why isn't anybody telling him to shut up?
Suddenly Whitney said, "You could . . . handle this?"
"Sure," Kurt said. "No problem."
The following silence was shattered by the ringing of the phone. Verran spoke monosyllables into the receiver, then hung up. "It's Doris up on fifth, Doc," he said. "She's howling for that fresh supply of juice you promised her."
"First we settle this," Whitney said. "I think the car crash sounds like the answer."
"But we're talking murder here," Dr. Alston said.
Whitney spun on him. "I don't like it any more than you do, but extreme problems sometimes call for extreme solutions."
Dr. Alston shook his head glumly and shrugged.
Ice crystallized in Quinn's veins as former Senator Jefferson Whitney pronounced sentence. "All right, then. We'll wait for the car to arrive. Then we'll leave the matter in Kurt's hands."

As TIM's reflexes began to return, the feeding tube began to trigger his gag reflex. He had to get it out. He wrapped his fingers around the glossy plastic tubing and began pulling until he felt its soft, blunt end scrape against the back of his throat. Finally it dropped free onto the mattress.
Now the IV. His fingers pushed aside the overlying gauze on his forearm and fumbled with the tape over the IV site. His nervous system didn't seem ready for fine manipulation yet. No matter. One way or another, that IV was coming out.
Tim guided his twitching fingers around the tape and hub of the

IV needle, grasping them as one, and yanked back. The needle pulled free. A droplet of blood welled in the puncture site. He jabbed the IV needle into his mattress, then pushed the tape and gauze back into place.

Okay, he was ready.

As EXHAUSTED as Matt was, sleep would not come. He lay among the mute shadows of the motel room and listened to a snowplow scrape by on the road outside. The more he lay here and thought about it, the surer he was that Quinn was in trouble. Big trouble. He'd replayed their fragmented conversation countless times in his mind, looking for an answer. The last two words he'd heard kept nudging him: "Sheriff . . . Southworth."

Matt threw off the covers and sat on the edge of the bed. He pulled out the slim Frederick County phone book, looked up the number of the sheriff's office, and dialed. A man announced himself as Deputy Harris, and Matt asked for Sheriff Southworth.

Harris said, "There's a Deputy Southworth. But he won't be in till eight. Can I help you?"

Matt hesitated, then told Harris about Tim's disappearance—Harris was familiar with that—and Matt's phone call to Quinn. "And now Quinn's gone too."

"We don't know that yet," Harris said.

"But she did mention the name Southworth. Couldn't you give him a call?"

"I guess I could. Ted's been following the Brown case."

Matt gave Harris his room number at the motel, then hung up. The phone rang three minutes later.

"Did you just call the sheriff's office?" said a deep voice.

"Yes. Deputy Southworth?"

"That's me. Start talking."

TIM froze as the door opened and the lights came on. Ellie entered, pushing a wheeled tray. She was alone. He was relieved to see her instead of Doris. He didn't know if his plan would work on the bigger woman. He kept his face slack and expressionless.

"Well, Number Eight, looks like you've been busy."

Ellie wheeled the tray toward Tim. He noticed eight syringes lined up on the tray. She stopped beside the bed and gazed at the feeding tube on the floor. "Now how did you manage that?"

Tim's right arm and the IV line were under the sheet. His left arm lay on top. He moved his left index finger.

"I see. Getting a teeny bit of movement back are we? So are the others. Well, we'll fix that. The new supply arrived just in time."

Tim watched her empty a syringe from the tray into the IV line. He pulled the IV needle out of the mattress with his right hand. Then he reached up with his left hand, grabbed a fistful of the starched white uniform, and yanked Ellie toward him. Her eyes widened with shock, which changed to pain and fear when Tim rammed the IV needle through her uniform into her abdomen.

She started shouting, struggling, but Tim pulled her farther over the bed, pressing her face against his chest, muffling her cries. Suddenly she went limp—the 9574 had gone to work.

He released the nurse and let her slip to the floor like a stuffed toy. He sat up and grabbed one of the syringes from Ellie's tray, then lay back and began waiting again. He hoped it didn't take Doris too long to come looking for her co-worker.

"ELLIOT," Verran said to the slim dark man who had just arrived, "did you bring the car?"

Still feigning unconsciousness, Quinn watched them through her barely parted lids. She recognized the newcomer as the exterminator who had been in her room with Verran. "Left it in one of the public lots by the hospital."

"Good," Whitney said. "I'll return to Washington now. I'll expect a call when this matter has been satisfactorily disposed of." Then he brushed past Kurt and Dr. Alston and strode through the door.

"A rat deserting a sinking ship," Verran said. "He wants to be out of state when the sinking ship goes down."

"When what goes down?" Elliot said.

Verran jerked his thumb at Quinn. "Her and the Brown kid are going to have an accident in that car you just brought in."

Elliot was visibly upset. "I didn't sign on for anything like this."

"We've no other choice," Dr. Alston said.

Quinn listened in horror. She looked for a way out, but there were four men between her and the exit.

"All right," Verran said. He sounded tired and unhappy. "Let's get it over with. Elliot, get up to five and wheel Brown down here."

"ELLIE?"

Tim closed his eyes as he saw Doris stick her head through the door and scan the ward. He heard her step inside.

"Ellie, where are you?"

He heard Doris' footsteps turn, stop abruptly, then, "Oh, no! Ellie! Ellie, what's wrong?"

He opened his eyes then and saw Doris bending over the unconscious nurse. Holding the syringe like a dagger, Tim poised the needle over Doris' back. He plunged it into her, just above her bra strap, and rammed the plunger home.

Doris reared up, clutching frantically at her back. When she turned and saw Tim up on his elbow, her eyes bulged. "You!" She began to gasp for air. And then she saw the tray of syringes next to the bed. She coughed. "Oh, no. No!"

Tim grabbed for her, but she lurched away from the bed, toward the door, her hands still clawing at her back. She pulled the door open and stumbled through the opening out to the nurses' station.

"Damn," Tim croaked. If she got to a phone . . .

Tim slowly pushed himself up to a sitting position. The room spun for half a minute. When his equilibrium returned, he slowly slid his legs down to the floor. His knees wobbled, but held as they accepted the burden of his weight.

Still holding on to the bed for support, he took a tentative step toward the door. He took a second step.

Suddenly he spotted a security key card like Quinn's protruding from the pocket of Ellie's uniform. He stretched over and got it, then grabbed the remaining syringes from Ellie's tray. With those in one hand and the key in the other, he weaved his way across the ward. He pushed on the door and found Doris on the floor, the syringe still protruding from her back, the phone still in its cradle.

From outside in the night, he heard the thrum of a helicopter again. Whoever had flown in was flying out.

No time to lose. Tim shuffled to the elevator and shoved Ellie's card into the slot. When the car arrived, he stepped in, inserted the card, and pressed the basement button. If they were holding Quinn in the science center, she'd be in the basement.

As his car started down, Tim was startled by his reflection in the metal doors. He was one hell of a sight. His left thigh was apparently bleeding, and he looked like Kharis the mummy after a run-in with a mob of angry villagers. He pawed the gauze from his face but left the rest in place. It was the only clothing he had.

As the car slowed to a halt, Tim glanced up at the floor indicator; 1 was lit. "Oh, no," he cried softly. "No."

When the doors opened onto the lobby, he'd be in plain view of the security desk.

LOUIS Verran's stomach shot him another stab of pain. He glanced over at the girl, Cleary. She hadn't stirred. Kurt must have clocked her good. When he'd carried her in, Verran thought she was dead. Wasted worry, it turned out. But now, thanks to Kurt and the Senator, she was going to be truly dead, and soon.

Verran used to think of himself as one of the good guys. But he certainly hadn't been hanging out with the good guys. And now Cleary had to be silenced. She could put all their heads in a noose. He sighed. You do what you have to do, and then you try to forget about it and hope you never have to do it again.

The phone rang. It was Elliot. "We got trouble, Chief."

"Aw, no," Verran groaned. "What now?"

"I'm on five, and we've got two doped-out nurses on the floor and ward C is shy one patient—Brown."

Alston rose to his feet. "What is it, Louis? What's happened?"

Verran waved at Alston to shut up. "Find him, damn it," Verran said into the phone. "Start looking. We'll start on one and work our way up. Get moving." As he hung up, he pointed to Alston. "You messed up again, Doc. Brown is on the loose."

"Impossible. He was dosed with . . ." Alston's voice trailed off.

"But they ran out of the stuff, didn't they?"

"Good Lord!"

"We'll seal the building until we find him," Verran said.

The phone rang again. It was Bernie from the lobby security desk. Since Bernie wasn't part of the big picture at the Ingraham, Verran immediately began inventing explanations in case he'd found Brown wandering around. But that wasn't the problem.

"Mr. Verran, there's a couple of men here to see you."

Verran's mouth went dry. "Who?"

"I only got the name of one. He says he's Deputy Southworth from the Frederick County Sheriff's Office, and he wants to talk to you about the disappearance of one of the students."

"At this hour? He wants to talk about Timothy Brown *now?*"

"No, sir. Someone named Quinn Cleary."

Verran almost dropped the phone. For a few heartbeats his voice failed him. "Tell him I'll be right there." He hung up and turned to the others. Suddenly he was exhausted. "A couple of guys from the sheriff's department are upstairs asking about a missing student named Cleary."

"Cleary?" Alston said. "How would anyone know she's gone?"

"We are about to go up and find out. Kurt, keep an eye on her."

"You let me do the talking," Alston said as they hurried toward the stairs to the lobby. "I'll handle this yokel."

"You do that, Doc," Verran told him.

When they stepped into the lobby, Verran spotted Southworth, but the guy with him wasn't another deputy. Verran told Bernie to take a break. He introduced Alston to Southworth, who in turn introduced the kid as Matt Crawford, a friend of Cleary's.

Yeah, the guy who'd called her from Connecticut. But how had he got here so fast?

Verran heard the elevator bell sound behind him. Everyone turned to look. He sighed quietly when he saw the empty car.

As THE elevator doors closed, Tim released the breath he'd been holding. He'd flattened himself against the side wall by the control panel. He hadn't been able to see the security desk, but he'd heard voices out there and knew he'd acted not a second too soon.

The elevator continued its descent to the basement. As the doors opened, he heard a muffled shout of pain. But it wasn't Quinn's voice. It was a man's.

QUINN'S hopes had risen when she'd heard that Tim had escaped. They leaped higher when Verran said there were a couple of deputy sheriffs up in the lobby. Now they soared as Verran and Alston walked out. That left only one man to get past. But big blond Kurt was the most formidable.

She spied on him through her lashes. For a moment he stood at the door to the hall watching Alston and Verran; then he closed it and approached her. Quinn closed her eyes.

"C'mon, baby," he said, his voice close as he shook her shoulder. "Wake up and play."

Quinn repressed a shudder and willed her body to remain limp.

"You're too fine to waste without a little taste." As he leaned over her and began nuzzling her neck, Quinn came unglued. She opened her eyes and saw his ear an inch away from her lips. In a panic she bit it.

She more than bit it. She locked her teeth onto the earlobe and ground down with her jaws. She grabbed his shirt and held on as he reared up, howling in pain. Finally, with a violent shove, he broke her grasp and sent her sprawling. He leaned against the wall, groaning, blood running down his neck from under the hand he had clasped to his head.

Quinn tried to dart past Kurt, but his hand caught her arm and flung her back onto the couch. He came toward her with his fist balled. "You just made the biggest mistake of your life."

Quinn screamed and raised her arms to protect herself, then gasped in shock as a familiar face appeared over Kurt's shoulder.

TIM was pushing his legs as fast as he thought they'd safely carry him, but when he heard a faint scream that sounded like Quinn's voice, he ditched all caution and broke into a tottering jog.

He reached a door marked ELECTRONICS, threw it open, and saw Kurt leaning over a woman on the couch. Her mouth was all bloody, and she was screaming.

Quinn!

Tim would have leaped on Kurt's back and flailed away at him, but he knew he hadn't the strength to do more than annoy him. Restraining himself, he uncapped one of the syringes in his hand, crept up behind Kurt, and raised it over the exposed back. With a grunt of effort he drove it into Kurt and pressed the plunger.

But the needle struck a rib and bent, jamming the plunger. Kurt let out a howl and straightened up. He whipped his right arm around as he turned. Tim tried to duck, but the flying elbow caught him on the side of the head, sending him sprawling against one of the consoles. The remaining syringes slipped from his grasp as the room dimmed and wobbled.

"Well, I'll be damned," Kurt said. "Look who it is."

With the whiteness of his rage-contorted face accentuated by the glistening crimson smear painting his left ear and side of his neck, he was a fearsome sight as he closed in on Tim. Kurt's right fist caught him with a solid uppercut to the face that knocked him to the floor. Tim's vision swam, and he lost sight of everything but the berserk monster looming over him.

For a few heartbeats Quinn couldn't move. One moment she'd been cowering on the couch, waiting to be bludgeoned by Kurt's fists; the next, Kurt was turning away from her and battering Tim.

Tim! He was down now, huddled against the wall, virtually defenseless as Kurt began kicking him. She had to do something.

As she rose from the couch, she noticed a syringe dangling from the back of Kurt's shirt. As she watched, it slipped from the fabric and fell to the floor. She spotted a number of other syringes scattered on the floor, and her mind began to race. Obviously, Tim had brought them. He'd tried to inject Kurt with one. What was in them? A sedative? A poison? Or . . . 9574? Of course!

She snatched a pair off the floor, uncapped both, and sneaked up behind Kurt where he was viciously driving those big boots into Tim's slumped, defenseless body.

"Stop it," she screamed, plunging one of the needles to the hub into the back of Kurt's thigh and emptying it. It wasn't an intravenous injection, but if nothing else, it would stop him from kicking Tim. Kurt lurched around. Quinn tried to jab him with the other needle, but he took a swing at her, and she had to duck away.

And then she saw that the door was wide open. She ran, shouting, "I'm going for help, Tim."

Tim lay slumped on the floor—a still, bloodied form. A sick, cold anger added its own power to the terror already fueling her feet. Kurt had hurt Tim. She'd get him for that. But footsteps pounding behind her shattered her little fantasy. The elevator was out of the question.

The stairs! Where were the stairs?

And then she saw the EXIT sign. She lost ground pulling open the door. Kurt grabbed her as she reached the first landing, snagging her ankle. Quinn clung to the railing with her free hand and twisted around to look down at him. He had her now.

"No," Quinn shouted. Blindly she stabbed at his face with the second syringe, squeezing the plunger as she struck.

Kurt released her ankle. His expression was a mixture of shock and dismay. Then his body stiffened. He teetered backward and landed headfirst on the steps below him. With a sickening snap his head bent on his shoulders. His body shuddered once, then lay still.

Quinn stood trembling on the landing. She just hoped the deputies were still in the lobby.

Louis Verran was actually allowing himself to relax.

Cleary's friend Crawford didn't really know that much. He'd only heard snatches of Cleary's end of the conversation on his car phone. And Verran had to hand it to Doc Alston—he handled Southworth beautifully.

A bad moment came when Dr. Emerson walked through the front doors. He looked dazed, like a guy in shock.

"Walter," Alston said, "what on earth are you doing here?"

But Emerson said nothing. He walked past them like a zombie, stepped into the elevator, and went up to fifth.

"You see?" Alston said to Southworth. "I'm not the only faculty member here at this hour."

"Fine," Southworth said. "But let me get this straight. Mr. Verran called you in because Timothy Brown had reappeared?"

"Louis called to inform me that Mr. Brown had returned," Alston said with exaggerated patience. "As director of medical education, I thought it my duty to question him. Brown wanted none of it. All he wanted was to collect Ms. Cleary and take her skiing."

"I don't believe any of this," Crawford said.

Alston shrugged dramatically. "I don't know what else I can tell you, young man. The two of them drove off together."

"Just when did Brown show up?" Southworth asked.

"Just before midnight," Verran said, jumping in.

"And that would explain that fragment you heard from your friend," Alston told Crawford. "About Tim being here. That was what she meant—he had returned."

"No," Crawford said, shaking his head. "Quinn said—"

Alston raised his hand. "You were tired. She was tired and overwhelmed by her friend's return. I suggest we all get a good night's sleep and discuss this further in the morning."

Southworth looked at Crawford. "Dr. Alston's got a point. I'll put out a bulletin on Brown's car, and we'll see if they're picked up."

Matt gave a reluctant shrug. "All right. None of this makes sense, but if they're not here, I guess they're not here."

Alston put a hand on Crawford's shoulder, guiding him toward the doors. "Don't worry. We'll find them. The Frederick County Sheriff's Department is second to none in its dedication."

That's it, Doc, Verran thought. Lay it on thick.

Then, behind him, through the door to the basement stairs, Louis Verran thought he heard a female voice shout "No!" But it was so faint, he couldn't be sure. No matter. Southworth and Crawford hadn't heard it. They were almost to the doors.

Keep going. Keep going.

A door opening behind him. Verran turned and thought his heart was going to stop as his worst nightmare became real: the Cleary broad, blood smeared around her mouth, was sprinting across the lobby floor, screaming, "Matt! Oh, Matt! Matt, Matt, Maaaaaaatt!"

She leaped into Crawford's arms, and they hugged like a long-lost sister and brother while she babbled a mile a minute.

Suddenly Southworth grabbed Alston by the shoulder and shoved him back toward the security desk. Verran felt his stomach acid explode.

"Seems we've got a little bit of a discrepancy here, Verran," Southworth said as he and the others reached the desk. He stood two feet back from the counter, with his hand resting on the grip of his pistol. "This young lady says she's Quinn Cleary—and Crawford here confirms that—and she says Tim Brown is being held downstairs as a prisoner. What the hell do you have to say about that?"

"Call an ambulance," Cleary was saying. "Tim's hurt."

"Show me where," Crawford was saying. "Maybe we can—"

"Everybody stay put," Southworth said. "I want some answers."

Southworth was reaching for his radio remote when Verran heard the stairway door opening again. It was Elliot. And he had a gun. He raised it in a professional two-handed grip and aimed the wavering barrel at the deputy. Elliot was on the edge of panic. "Your gun, Southworth," Elliot said. "Take it out and put it on the counter."

Southworth remained cool, didn't move.

"Do it!" Elliot's voice cracked on the first word.

Southworth removed his revolver from the holster and placed it on the counter.

"Take it, Chief," Elliot said; then he glanced at Alston. "And now I want to know what's gone down. I come back from fifth and Brown's dead in the control room"—Cleary moaned—"and I find

Kurt on the stairs with a broken neck." He glanced back at Verran again. "Go ahead, Chief. Take the gun."

"I don't want it," Verran said. "It's over, Elliot."

Alston reached around Verran and picked up Southworth's gun. "Louis is right, Elliot," he said. "The dominoes have begun to fall." He turned to Southworth. "I'm going to borrow this, Deputy. You may have it back in a few minutes." Alston strolled to the stairway door and made his exit.

Fright and confusion swirled across Elliot's face. "What's he—"

Verran jumped as the single gunshot from the other side of the stairway door answered his question.

And then Elliot was running for the front doors. Before he was through them, Southworth had his radio in hand and was calling for emergency medical assistance and putting out an APB on Elliot. Then he jabbed an index finger at Verran. "Stay put."

Verran could only nod. His whole world was falling apart.

WITH Matt at her side, Quinn crowded close behind Southworth as he headed for the elevator. "We've got to get to Tim. He couldn't be dead." She didn't care what Elliot had said. Tim was alive.

Quinn clung to Matt as the deputy used her security key card to take them down to the basement. The car stopped, and the doors slid open. Quinn ran to the room where she'd been a prisoner and skidded to a halt at the door. Tim lay huddled against the wall, one arm splayed out at an unnatural angle. He was perfectly still.

She screamed, "Tim."

The body jerked; the limp arm stiffened; the thumb and pinkie finger straightened and waggled back and forth.

Quinn didn't know whether to laugh or to cry as she knelt beside him and slipped her arms around him. "Oh, Tim."

"JUST a couple more questions," Deputy Southworth said as Quinn fidgeted in her seat behind the counter. The police had taken over the security desk as a command center. She was anxious to get to the hospital and see Tim.

The medics had wheeled him out of the basement on a gurney. He'd looked awful. Matt had gone along, and after they were on their way, the people from the morgue had removed the two bodies from the stairwell. The state police led Louis Verran away in handcuffs. New nurses were brought in to care for the patients in ward C. Things were settling down.

"Now, is there anyone else you can think of who might be directly involved in this?"

"Only one." Quinn's throat constricted. "Dr. Emerson. He's over in the faculty building. Or at least he was." She told Deputy Southworth what had happened in Emerson's office.

"Dr. Emerson, first name Walter? Old guy?"

"That's him. Why?"

"He came through here shortly after we arrived. Took the elevator. Does he have an office upstairs?"

"A lab. On fifth. He's probably locked himself in." Quinn fished in a pocket for her key ring, then held it up. "But I have a key."

She rose from her seat and started for the elevators.

"Wait a minute," Deputy Southworth said. "I'll take those."

"All right," she said. "But I'm going with you. I want to be there when you arrest him."

"You've really got it in for him, don't you?"

Quinn nodded grimly. She had put her life in Dr. Emerson's hands, and he'd handed her over to her executioners.

On fifth, she led the deputy to Dr. Emerson's lab. She stood close by Southworth as he unlocked the door, and edged in behind him as he stepped through. "There he is," she said as she approached the familiar figure sitting at one of the computers.

Dr. Emerson didn't look up.

"It's all over, Dr. Emerson," she said, fighting tears. She was supposed to be angry, vindictive. Why did she feel so sad?

He didn't move—simply sat and stared at the screen.

Then Quinn noticed the bag of clear fluid suspended from a chrome pole. And the tube running down into his arm. She shook him gently, and his body started to topple.

"Holy—" Southworth said. He lunged forward and caught Dr. Emerson's body before it fell.

Quinn stood frozen, staring at the computer screen and the words that had been entered there. TO WHOM IT MAY CONCERN: IF MY CALCULATIONS ARE CORRECT, THIS SHOULD ESTABLISH THAT 9574 DOES INDEED HAVE AN LD.

"LD?" Southworth said, easing Dr. Emerson to the floor.

"Lethal dose."

EPILOGUE

"ANY news?" Quinn said as Matt stepped through the door to Tim's hospital room.

Late morning sunlight glared off the white of the bedsheets and the polished floor. She sat on the edge of the bed holding Tim's hand, not simply because she was so glad to have him back, but because it was one way of keeping him in bed.

Tim was a lousy patient. He had six broken ribs, a cerebral concussion, and a large third-degree burn on his left thigh, but he wanted out of the hospital. Now. Only Quinn's restraining presence and his atrophied muscles kept him in place.

He'd spent much of the morning explaining to the state police and the FBI all he knew. Quinn had been at his side, listening in awe to his incredible tale of mind control at the Ingraham and human experimentation on a national scale.

At first the various law-enforcement agents had seemed uniformly skeptical. But after investigating Verran's control room and dismantling a few of the headboards in the dorm, they were believers.

Matt waved a copy of the Baltimore *Sun* as he dropped into a chair. "KMI and the foundation are stonewalling. They say the charges are preposterous, and even if they should prove to be true, Kleederman and the directors know nothing."

Anger tightened in Quinn's chest. "You mean they're going to get away with it?"

Matt shrugged. "I called my father and talked it over with him. He says unless some pivotal conspirator spills his guts, it's going to be rough getting convictions on the higher-ups."

Tim said, "I don't see Verran making a deal, do you? They haven't caught that Elliot guy yet, and Alston and Emerson removed themselves. Without written records, where does that leave us?"

"Probably with a lot of lower-echelon indictments," Matt said. "But once they start asking questions at the KMI medical centers, someone's bound to crack, and the whole network will collapse."

A thought struck Quinn. "What about the graduates?"

"Right," Tim said softly. "All the 'Where Are They Now?' docs. They're the real victims. Their reputations will be ruined."

"Don't count on it," Matt said. "They won't believe they've been brainwashed, and frankly, I doubt there's any way to prove it. They'll say they were never affected by any science-fiction machine, or they'll say none of those contraptions were in *their* headboards when they were students at the Ingraham. And unless somebody turns up some written records, who's to say those SLI units weren't installed last summer?"

"So they'll go on as they are?" Quinn said.

"They're still well-trained physicians. They'll go on giving the inner cities excellent medical care—even better care now that the patients they're subconsciously compelled to refer to the medical centers will no longer be pharmaceutical guinea pigs."

"So it's over?" Quinn said, finally letting the relief seep through her. "Really over?"

"For all intents and purposes, yes," Matt said. "You two pushed over the first domino. Just a matter of time now before they all go down. It's over."

NEW MEDICAL SCHOOL OPENS

BUDAPEST—A new international charitable organization, the Eastern Europe Medical Care Foundation, has announced the opening of a tuition-free medical school in Budapest and a string of medical centers located in Hungary, Romania, Czechoslovakia, and Poland to bring the benefits of modern medical care to the poor, the disadvantaged, and the disconnected of Eastern Europe.

—The Frankfurt *Allgemeine Zeitung*

ABOUT THE AUTHOR

F. Paul Wilson does not regret a youth misspent watching horror movies and reading science fiction. For him, this childhood obsession was anything but wasted time. In his first year of medical school Wilson started selling his own science-fiction stories. He has succeeded in juggling the dual careers of writing and medicine ever since. "One keeps me fresh for the other," he says.

F. Paul Wilson

Being part of a family-practice group allows the doctor time to pursue what he calls a "compulsive disorder" to write. "I'm itching to get at it," he says. "I write every day, whenever I get the chance." Over the past twenty-odd years his literary output has been prodigious: more than fourteen books, including science-fiction novels and horror thrillers. Two thrillers, *The Keep* and *The Tomb*, were best sellers, and an astonishing four million copies of his books are in print in the United States. In *The Select,* his first medical thriller, Wilson has finally combined his two callings.

While this thoughtful doctor's first priority is a good story, *The Select* also reflects his serious concerns about the American medical profession. "Our strange blend of altruism and entrepreneurship has produced some of the best care in the world," he says. But, he adds, the system is being strained by increasing demands for highly technical—and highly expensive—treatments. When asked what makes a good doctor, he replies, "Intellect, heart, and empathy. That combination makes a healer. Quinn is my idea of a healer."

Wilson hasn't finished with the darker side of medicine. At his home in his native New Jersey, he is already outlining his next medical thriller. For this doctor, there seems to be no cure for writer's itch.

RIVERS OF GOLD

Janet Edmonds

The newspaper advertisement was startling:

> BRIDES WANTED: Decent, hardworking women wanted by honest, respectable farmers in Canada and the U.S.A. Marriage (by proxy) guaranteed before departure. Fares and expenses paid. Write fully and in complete confidence.

For Amity Jones, an English housemaid, the offer sounded too good to be true. She had always dreamed of a new life. Now here was her chance. Did she dare take it? Amity thought for a moment, then picked up her pen. There was no time like the present.

Chapter One

THE three other mourners drew back from the sodden graveside, not wishing to make too precipitate a departure, but nonetheless anxious to seek shelter from the driving rain. The vicar, too, saw no reason to linger. All the Joneses were buried in pauper's graves, and doubtless when Amity followed the rest of her family to a consumptive end, there would be even fewer pennies to make his efforts worthwhile. The sooner the gravediggers could fill in the hole, the sooner the parish could pay them and the grass begin to cover yet another unmarked mound in this, the least noticeable corner of the churchyard.

He glanced at the sole surviving Jones and hesitated. She seemed not to be aware that the brief ceremony was over and that her presence was keeping the gravediggers waiting. He wondered if he should say something—a few words of comfort perhaps—but thought better of it. Amity Jones was a quiet, respectful young woman, but she gave the impression that she would see right through his platitudes. Instead, he nodded his permission to the gravediggers to complete their work, and hurried back to his cozy vicarage.

Amity barely noticed his departure, any more than she had noticed that of the other mourners. She stood at the edge of the grave looking down, a small posy clasped between her hands. Then, as if aware of the gravediggers' attention concentrated on her, Amity looked up and stepped back from the edge of the grave. "I'm sorry," she said. "I'll not keep you. A dog shouldn't be out in this weather." She raised the posy of herbs and a couple of pansies, and sniffed it. It must have looked odd, but it seemed right somehow.

It had been her mother—that poor, dragged-down skivvy who had buried successive children and her husband as well—who had drummed into her one surviving daughter the message that education was the way out of the pit. Amity had taken such steps as were within her power to increase her knowledge beyond the restricted level at school. She had tackled Shakespeare, and she remembered some of Ophelia's words: *Rosemary, that's for remembrance . . . pansies, that's for thoughts,* and the reference to rue. All three plants had seemed fitting in the circumstances. All three were grown in her employer Mrs. Kilvrough's garden, and Amity had helped herself to them. Mrs. Kilvrough would not miss them.

She tossed the posy into the grave. "You can get on now," she told the gravediggers. "Don't mind about me."

She stayed until the coffin was hidden by earth, then left the churchyard. Her mother was dead, like the rest of her family before her, and now there was nothing to keep Amity in Long Westing.

When Amity returned to Westing Lodge, she ran upstairs to the small attic bedroom she shared with Eliza, the kitchenmaid. Amity removed her bonnet and shook it. If she was careful, the damage caused by the downpour could be kept to a minimum. She stepped out of her one good dress and hung it over a chair to dry.

She must remember to thank her mother's old friends who had made the effort to come today. It was embarrassing that she could not offer them the customary hospitality after the service.

She put on her housemaid's sober dress and the day's crisply starched apron and cap, and checked her appearance in the mirror. She looked neat and tidy, and that was about all. Her face was pale and drawn, and her brown eyes seemed too large. She looked tired and older than a nineteen-year-old had any right to look.

Mrs. Kilvrough had given her time off to attend the funeral, but she had made it very clear she expected Amity back at work before lunch. Amity felt no resentment about this—it was standard practice in smaller households—but a few more minutes would not matter.

She opened her cupboard and took down from the shelf a newspaper which she had tucked away a fortnight earlier. It had been left on the pile for lighting fires, but one advertisement had caught her eye, and she had whisked it away to be read at leisure. Now that she was alone, she could read it without provoking questions from Eliza.

The headline was startling enough. It read BRIDES WANTED. The rest of the advertisement was rather more restrained:

> Decent, hardworking women wanted by honest, respectable farmers in Canada and the U.S.A. Marriage (by proxy) guaranteed before departure. Fares and expenses paid. Write fully and in complete confidence.

There followed the name and address of an agency in Liverpool.

Amity had thought many times about emigrating. America had seemed like the pot of gold at the rainbow's end—and as unattainable. There had always been two insuperable barriers: she couldn't have abandoned her family, who depended on her meager earnings, and she couldn't have raised the fare. Now, in a few days, fate had removed the former and this advertisement the latter.

Amity was not a great believer in fate, but this did seem to be a most convenient coincidence. Every girl wanted to be married, and if Mrs. Kilvrough had maintained a larger household, her housemaid might have found a husband among its male members. But Mrs. Kilvrough lived the secluded life of an elderly widow, and the opportunities in this small Wiltshire village for meeting potential husbands were very limited. At least the advertisement guaranteed a marriage.

Amity took her writing things out of her cupboard. There was, her mother always used to say, no time like the present.

Chapter Two

MRS. Kilvrough heard that her housemaid had run after the postman with a letter the day after her mother's funeral. She tutted to herself. Jones was a good worker, but every so often she did something that was not quite what one expected of domestics. Jones was a minor as well as an orphan, and Mrs. Kilvrough was therefore in some sort responsible for her. She should at least have been informed of the gist of the letter.

Mrs. Kilvrough was rather more surprised to learn, however, some two weeks after the funeral, that the village butcher, Mr. Grogport, would like to speak to her. He was a prosperous tradesman but ill at ease in the drawing rooms of the gentry, and his hostess did nothing to make him feel more comfortable. She observed that his Sunday-best waistcoat was adorned with a heavy gold albert and that the cuff links were gold horseshoes. Add to this the figure of a man who lived well, and Mrs. Kilvrough realized that butchery was a trade which served its practitioners well.

Her smile was polite. "You wanted to see me?"

The butcher shifted his considerable bulk from one foot to the other. "Yes, madam, and very grateful I am for your time. It's about your housemaid, Amity Jones . . ." he began. His voice trailed off.

"What about her?" Mrs. Kilvrough's tone was guarded.

"She must be all alone now that her mother's dead."

Mrs. Kilvrough inclined her head. "Yes. But she has a home here for as long as she wishes to continue in my employment."

"The thing is, she must be eighteen or nineteen, and you must be what they call *in loco parentis* for a year or so. Isn't that right?"

"You have the expression correctly," Mrs. Kilvrough conceded. "The point, Mr. Grogport?"

"The point is, she is a decent, respectable, hardworking girl, with nothing much to look forward to, begging your pardon, but a lifetime in service. Now, I'm twice widowed, and it's more than time I took another wife. I've had my eye on young Amity, and I'd like your permission to pay my respects to her." His last words tumbled out in a rush, as if he were relieved to have them in the open.

Mrs. Kilvrough was taken aback by the butcher's suggestion. There was no denying it would be a good thing for Jones. Grogport was a prominent member of the parish council, and she would find herself mistress of a comfortable house. She would acquire a ready-made family, Mr. Grogport having had children by both his previous wives, but her husband's wealth would allow her to have as much help as she needed. Mrs. Kilvrough would have to find a replacement, but she was sufficiently fair-minded to acknowledge that Jones was unlikely ever to get another chance like this.

"Your offer is both generous and timely. Jones is a lucky girl to have such an opportunity. Pay your respects to her by all means, Mr. Grogport, and you may rest assured that I shall place my own encouragement firmly behind yours when she asks my opinion."

The butcher beamed. "Thank you, madam. I hoped you'd see it that way. Let's hope young Amity does, too." He lowered his voice. "I've a nice bit of beef that would suit you down to the ground."

Mrs. Kilvrough's smile had all the warmth her welcome had

lacked. "Do you know, Mr. Grogport, I was only saying to Cook the other day that it was time we had a nice piece of beef."

It was probably pure chance that when Mr. Grogport drove up in his smart trap the following Saturday to deliver an exceptionally good sirloin, Amity should be in the kitchen. It was certainly not pure chance that made Cook invite him to join them in a cup of tea and a slice of the cherry cake just out of the oven. A butcher who let the household have the sort of cuts Mr. Grogport had been supplying recently was a treasure to be cherished. But it didn't take Cook long to realize that his affability seemed to be directed towards young Amity. Well, Cook thought, the girl could do a lot worse.

Amity was unaware of any special effort being made. She knew Mr. Grogport, of course, but she saw nothing more than politeness in the questions he directed to her, and answered them simply but briefly. She thanked him for his condolences on the loss of her mother. Yes, doubtless the grief would wear off in time, and yes, she was indeed fortunate in her present position.

"You've no thoughts of bettering yourself yet?" he asked.

Amity remembered her letter, which must by now be sitting on some desk in Liverpool. Would that be judged an attempt at self-betterment or a last desperate ploy? "Not just yet," she said. "When I'm older perhaps."

"Sensible girl," he commented. "All the same, who knows what the future holds."

"Who indeed," Amity replied.

Mr. Grogport delivered the next weekend's roast himself, explaining that his boy was run off his feet and, besides, it was a nice little drive out to Westing Lodge. Would Miss Jones like to see the new cob he'd bought? "I'd like a woman's opinion."

Amity was surprised and made no attempt to hide it. "Yes, if you like," she said, "though I don't know anything about horses."

Amity followed him out into the yard and studied the cob from all available angles. It gleamed with good health and good grooming.

"You like him?" Mr. Grogport asked encouragingly.

"As far as I can tell, yes. You don't have to be an expert to see that it's in very good condition. It's a pretty color, too."

"I bought him as being suitable for a lady to drive. I thought I'd give him to the new Mrs. Grogport as a wedding present."

Amity smiled warmly. "Are you remarrying, Mr. Grogport? My

congratulations. Your wife will be a lucky woman indeed to have a wedding present like this. I hope you will both be very happy."

The butcher drew strength from the obvious sincerity of her good wishes. "I'll not deny I'm a good catch, though I shouldn't say it myself. The next Mrs. Grogport need want for nothing, and that's a fact. The thing is, Miss Jones, how do you fancy being her?"

Amity was quite sure she had misheard. "I beg your pardon, Mr. Grogport?"

He flushed. A proposal was always an awkward thing, and he hadn't bargained for having to repeat it. "I asked how you fancied being the third Mrs. Grogport," he said.

"Me? Why me?"

Mr. Grogport had prepared himself for a coy reluctance, but not such incredulity. Nor had he anticipated being asked for the reasons behind his choice. Consequently, his answer had the merit of sounding truthful even if it was not entirely flattering. "You're hardworking and respectable, and I don't think you're anybody's fool. With a bit of money spent on you, you'd be quite a taking little thing."

"Thank you for an honest answer," Amity told him. "But your proposal comes as a great surprise. I don't know what answer to give. May I think about it? You wouldn't want me to make a hasty decision we might later regret."

"No, no, of course not." Her request was a reasonable one, although he had hoped to get the matter settled today. "You could have a word with Mrs. Kilvrough," he volunteered. "I naturally sought her permission to pay my respects to you. And she thought it would be a very good thing for you."

Amity fixed on him a disconcertingly shrewd stare. "Then I needn't consult her, need I? Do you think you could wait another week while I consider the ins and outs?"

"It doesn't look as if I've much choice," he said ruefully.

Amity spent most of the night tossing and turning. She didn't need Mrs. Kilvrough to tell her that the offer she had received was better by far than anything else she might have expected. Why, then, did she find it necessary even to consider the matter?

She had no need to look far for the answer. Mr. Grogport was quite simply not the fulfillment of any girl's dream. She imagined lying next to that well-fed belly. She imagined those thick fingers fumbling under her nightgown, and she shuddered. The marriage bed held few secrets for a girl who had grown up in a hovel where the entire family slept in one room, but her mother had never seemed reluctant to accept her conjugal duties, and indeed, there had been a great bond of affection between her parents. With Mr. Grogport, Amity had a nasty suspicion that her feelings would develop into loathing.

Yet what other choice did she have? To remain in service and die an old maid? Or to be married by proxy to a farmer halfway across the world? Was there not a place in one's life for the bold gesture with unforeseeable consequences? Might not her deeper emotions be awakened by the sort of man who had boldly set himself up in a wild land with sufficient success to pay for a wife to go out and join him? Then she chuckled to herself. There was unlikely to be an answer to her letter. No, her decision must be made entirely on the situation as it now stood.

If Amity was distracted the next morning, no one noticed. Anyone who had so recently lost a last surviving relative was entitled to a degree of melancholia.

Two days after Mr. Grogport's proposal Mrs. Kilvrough sent for her housemaid. "I believe you have a follower, Jones," she said.

Amity tensed imperceptibly. "Mr. Grogport has paid his respects, madam. He assured me he had your permission to do so."

"I'm glad you ascertained that before encouraging him."

"With respect, madam, I'm not at all sure I've been very encouraging," Amity said apologetically.

"What do you mean? How explicit has been his interest in you?"

"He's asked me to marry him."

Mrs. Kilvrough smiled. "Good. When do you plan the wedding? You will want to wait a little, since your mother's death was so recent."

"I haven't actually accepted him yet. I asked him to give me till the end of the week, and he agreed."

"The end of the week! That was very generous of him. But if you take my advice, you'll accept before he has time to get restless."

"I'll bear that advice in mind, madam," Amity assured her.

Mrs. Kilvrough's assumption that acceptance was Amity's only possible course of action resulted in another restless night.

The next morning Mrs. Kilvrough sent for her again. "A letter has come for you, Jones," she said, tapping it against the fingers of her other hand. "The postmark is Liverpool."

"Liverpool!" Amity exclaimed, reaching forward and unceremoniously removing it from her employer's hands.

"Who in Liverpool would be writing to you?"

Amity bobbed a curtsy. "If I might have permission to go away and read the letter, I might find out," she suggested.

Mrs. Kilvrough could do nothing except permit her demeanor to register disapproval. "Very well," she said grudgingly.

Amity thanked her, and once she reached the back stairs, she raced up them two at a time and locked herself in her room. Sitting on her bed, she opened the envelope with shaking fingers.

It contained two sheets of paper. One was a leaflet explaining how the agency operated. The other was a letter from the director, saying that he was able to offer Amity a choice between a man with a small but prosperous tobacco plantation in Virginia and a somewhat older gentleman, Mr. York, forty-three, with an estate of nearly three hundred and fifty square *miles* in western Canada. The Virginian was a widower with five small children; Mr. York had described himself as having "no encumbrances." Both gentlemen had lodged sufficient money with the agency to cover all the expenses of a bride's journey, but neither had supplied a photograph. A quick decision on Miss Jones' part was requested because a ship would be leaving within the month.

Amity sat back against the pillow. Now what? Five minutes ago she had a relatively simply choice—to accept Mr. Grogport's offer or not. Suddenly her choices had widened. There was the tobacco farmer in Virginia and the rancher—at least she supposed that was what one called a man with so much land—in western Canada. The tobacco farmer sounded much like an English smallholder, with a brood of children to be fed and clothed. "Prosperous" was the word used to describe him, but that had probably been his choice rather than the agency's. Mr. York had the disadvantage of being older—almost as old as Mr. Grogport—but he also had the advantage of not presenting her with a ready-made family. Amity considered that he might very well have exaggerated his landholdings, or perhaps the agency had misread it. Still, the more she thought about it, the more she was inclined to favor Mr. York.

Amity was not, however, going to make a rash decision. On her half-day, the next day, Amity made her way to the village green and sat on a bench. She glanced around her. Were there greens like this in Virginia? Perhaps. After all, wasn't that where the first English colonists had settled? She was less sure about western Canada. Perhaps it was best, if she had decided to start again in a new land, to choose the one least likely to resemble what she knew, and since the balance was already tipped in favor of Mr. York, let it be he.

MR. GROGPORT was not happy when Amity declined his offer.

"I know everyone will say I'm foolish to turn you down," she told him, "and quite possibly they'll be right. But I've given it a lot of thought, and I am quite determined. Far better that you find another young woman to mother your children and run your household. Someone with more common sense than I seem to have."

Mr. Grogport, who thought she had hit the nail on the head in those last words, sadly took his leave.

Mrs. Kilvrough was not very happy, either, and not entirely because she saw the prospect of years of specially selected joints fading away. "You don't imagine you'll ever get a comparable offer?"

"No, madam," Amity said meekly.

"Well, at least I shan't have the bother of finding another housemaid and training her up."

Amity colored with the embarrassment of indecision. She had not intended to tell Mrs. Kilvrough about Canada until she gave her notice, but she knew that now she should, in all fairness, tell her employer something. "It's not *quite* as straightforward as that, madam," she began. "You see, I have made plans of a sort."

"Indeed? You'd better explain."

Amity judged that this was one of those times when absolute truth was not necessarily a good idea. "Mother and I both knew she was dying," she began. "We'd discussed the future, and it seemed a good idea to consider starting over again somewhere else."

"And where had you in mind?" Mrs. Kilvrough asked frostily.

"Canada, madam. There seem to be far more opportunities for advancement in the New World."

Mrs. Kilvrough's frown cleared, as if everything were now explained. "I see. You hope to persuade me to advance you to the position of parlormaid, with some small increase."

"No, madam. You are most generous, but I was not angling for such an offer. I meant what I said. Now that there is no family to keep me here, I shall try my luck elsewhere."

"And how do you propose to find the fare?"

Amity extended her original lie. "Once there was only mother and me, she insisted I keep more of my wages. I hope I have enough put by. I'm waiting to hear from the agency that arranges these things."

"Your correspondent in Liverpool, I assume?"

"Yes, madam." Amity hesitated. "I could give you my notice now, if you wish," she said reluctantly.

"I don't like the way you've behaved, Jones. There has been a degree of underhandedness, which disappoints me. However, you've been a good girl, who has tried hard to overcome the disadvantages of her upbringing. You may remain in my service until I find a replacement, and you may train her until you leave. Alternatively, you may go now with a week's wages in lieu of notice."

Amity thought quickly. Mrs. Kilvrough would have little difficulty finding a new housemaid, but free board and lodging for an indefinite period was far more valuable than a week's wages. She bobbed a curtsy. "I'll be happy to train my replacement," she said.

Mrs. Kilvrough looked at her shrewdly. "Yes, you never were a stupid girl. I suspect that Canada may be just the thing for you."

"Thank you, madam. I intend to make it so."

Chapter Three

AMITY York stood at the bow of the *Skagit Chief* surveying the scene before her with a sinking heart. So this was Dyea, the Alaskan port which Samuel York had assured the agency was most conveniently situated for his land. Amity could conceive of nothing convenient about it at all. The boat was even obliged to anchor well offshore because the water was so shallow.

The little town spread across a narrow valley between a succession of snow-covered mountains. Samuel had arranged for his bride to stay at Healy and Wilson's store. She was to hire a guide to bring her the rest of the way, and Healy and Wilson would put together the supplies she and Samuel would need to see them through the winter. Mrs. York would accompany these to the Throndiuck, which appeared to be the name of Samuel's ranch. She had been a little puzzled by the reference to supplies for the winter. Surely anyone who farmed as much as three hundred and fifty miles, or even three hundred and fifty acres, was entirely self-supporting?

Thus had she reasoned in the secure recollection of England's lush green fields, and there had been nothing at first to disabuse her of this assumption as the train had chugged across the vast Canadian plain. Talk of square miles began to make sense. Life here might well be lonely, she thought, but at least it wouldn't be impoverished.

Then the landscape had changed, becoming higher and more rugged until the last vestige of farmland was gone. The land now was magnificent and more than a little frightening in its scale and the absence of settlements. She had greeted with relief the train's descent into the lusher valleys that prefaced Vancouver, where she stayed until she could find a ship going north.

The *Skagit Chief* had been the only vessel sailing up the fretwork of channels and straits between the islands that lined the coast northwards. Even to Amity's untrained eye, the old stern-wheeler had seemed an inadequate vessel for the long, tortuous journey up the Pacific coast to Alaska. There had been many occasions when Amity had wondered whether it would ever make the next port of call.

Meantime, the farther north they went, the farther receded her vision of a rich and comfortable farm. The adventure Amity had welcomed in England began indeed to seem foolhardy.

She looked at Dyea and sighed. It was done. She became aware of the *Skagit Chief*'s captain at her shoulder.

"Admiring your new home, Mrs. York?" he asked. There was no irony in his voice.

"Studying it certainly. Will they send a boat out?"

"We'll get you into the scow. Your trunk as well." So saying, he led her round to the larboard side and helped her down the ladder into a scow that looked even less seaworthy than its host ship. He climbed down beside her.

A crewman rowed them in as far as the scow had draft, and then the captain carried Amity through shallow water to the gray tidal beach, while the crewman carried her trunk ashore.

Healy and Wilson's store was the only two-story building in the town, the upper floor providing accommodations for the Healys and the Wilsons and also for the occasional traveler. It was the only building inhabited by whites, the rest of the two hundred and fifty–odd inhabitants being Chilkat Indians.

Mrs. Healy, a brusque but kindhearted woman, told Amity she was lucky. "You've got a room to yourself, and that doesn't often happen, I can tell you. Not that we get many women here, of course."

Amity was privately amazed that so many people would want to stay in Dyea as to make accommodation a problem.

There were four other guests, all of them men, and at supper they looked at Amity with particular interest. One was Vladimir Kislov, an elderly Russian prospector who had chosen to stay in Alaska when the territory's ownership had changed from Russian to American, twenty-one years before, in 1867. In a heavy accent he told her that if she hadn't already been married, he'd have been tempted to change the habits of a lifetime and marry her himself.

Amity smiled at him. "And if I weren't already married, Mr. Kislov, I'd jump at the offer, and that's a fact."

He laughed uproariously at this sally and vowed he would visit her if ever his prospecting took him into Canada, because there was nothing he liked better than a pretty woman who made him laugh.

Amity, who had never been told by anybody that she was pretty, blushed, but wisely did not attempt a riposte.

Mrs. Wilson put a huge, fragrantly steaming bowl of moose stew on the table. Amity helped herself sparingly, unsure whether she would like moose, and Mrs. Healy looked at her plate disapprovingly. "You needs to build your strength up, Mrs. York. You want to get all the good food you can find, for, come winter, there'll be days when all the food you've got is the blubber you've put on before the freeze."

"I am very hungry," Amity admitted, "but the truth is, I've never had moose before, and I'm half afraid I shan't like it."

Another man entered the conversation. "If you like venison, you'll like moose. It's a staple up here, so you may as well get used to it."

Encouraged, Amity took some more and found it was everything he said it would be. As she ate, she cast surreptitious glances at her fellow diners, principally at the man who had just spoken. He was tall, with straight, dark hair that was not quite as black as that of the Chilkats. Like them, he had broad shoulders, but where they were squat and sturdy, he was long-limbed and rangy. Amity did not, on balance, think he could be described as handsome, but his face was certainly arresting, with its unusually high cheekbones, aquiline nose, and dark eyebrows. He wore the thick, drooping mustache favored by most men up here.

His features had been harshly etched by climate, and his eyes were gray. His voice was pleasantly deep. His accent had the softness of the Canadians' accent, but was overlaid with other indications, which Amity was unable to identify. She estimated his age in excess of thirty. Since she rather thought he might prove to be interesting to talk to, she found it a little galling that he exhibited no interest in her at all. Yet loath as she was to admit it, she found her eyes drawn to him repeatedly across the table. If Samuel York proved to be only half as magnetic as this man, she would be well pleased.

Sleeping for the first time for many weeks in a bed that stood still was unnerving, and the next morning Amity went down for breakfast feeling no more refreshed than when she had landed. The men were already seated at the table, including Mr. Kislov and the tall man who had advised her to get used to moose.

Mr. Kislov noted her heavy eyes and laughed, but not unkindly. "Not much sleep last night, I guess. Pining for that husband of yours? Lucky man. I wish I had a beautiful woman pining for me."

Mrs. Healy came in with a dish of bacon and flapjacks. "Then she'd pine to death, wouldn't she? You'd run a thousand miles away if you thought there was a woman waiting to pin you down," she said, and everyone, including the old Russian, laughed.

When Amity had blunted the edge of her hunger, she turned to the Russian once more. "You said last night that you were a prospector. What exactly do you prospect for?"

Everyone stopped eating and stared at her in amazement.

"I'm sorry. Have I said something I shouldn't?"

Mr. Wilson shook his head. "No, ma'am. It's just that there's only one thing worth prospecting for here—gold."

"Gold! Do you find any?"

Kislov turned to Amity. "I find enough to keep body and soul together, but don't be imagining you're looking at a rich old man."

"So there isn't really all that much gold here?" Amity asked.

He shrugged. "Who knows. It's a vast place. It's my belief that somewhere in that wilderness there's gold beyond the dreams of men. It's the dream of finding more than a few specks at the bottom of a river that keeps people like me searching. Treviscoe here—he's the same." And he indicated the tall man.

Treviscoe, Amity thought. That's a Cornish name. That explained at least a part of his accent. "You're a prospector, too?"

"Sometimes. I don't reckon to make a living at it, like Kislov," he said curtly, his tone discouraging further inquiry.

Amity turned back to Kislov. "I hope your dream comes true," she told him warmly. "I daresay you'll be too grand to visit a farmer and his wife, but if you're not, I'd love to hear all about it."

She was aware that Treviscoe shot her a surprised glance, and her words were greeted with a noticeable silence before the Russian laughed comfortably. "I reckon any strike will be a long way from farming country. Where did you say this farm was?"

Amity frowned. "I don't think I did. To be honest, I'm not sure I know. He calls it the Throndiuck, and I'm to hire a guide to take me there from Dyea, so it can't be too far." She became aware that embarrassed silence had fallen upon her companions.

It was eventually broken by Treviscoe. "The Throndiuck is a river, Mrs. York. It's an Indian word. I'm afraid you haven't quite grasped the scale of this country. I don't rightly know exactly how far it is from here, but it can't be less than five hundred miles. And it won't resemble any farm you've ever seen in England."*

Amity's worried expression cleared. "Oh, I'd already realized it must be very different from Wiltshire. To be sure, five hundred miles is a daunting prospect, but it's all part of the adventure."

"Hang on there," said one of the other men. "The Throndiuck, Mrs. York? Would you be Samuel York's wife?"

Amity colored self-consciously. "Yes. Samuel York's my husband." It was the first time she had used the words "my husband," and they seemed very strange to her.

"But I thought—" the man began, and was cut off by Treviscoe.

"You never thought in your life," he snapped. "All you do is open your mouth unnecessarily."

"That's true," Kislov agreed. "Why, I remember when that fool there . . ." And he launched into a funny story. Amity could scarcely follow it and noted only that the man didn't object to being the butt of their laughter. She had the uncomfortable feeling that some light onto the mystery of the man she had married was eluding her.

Once the meal was over, Mr. Healy took Amity into the little office at the back of the store and handed her Samuel York's list of supplies. "That's what your husband wants, Mrs. York," he told her,

---

*Before the gold rush, the river we now call the Klondike was usually called the Throndiuck, after the Indian name. At different times in the novel it has therefore been appropriate to use one or the other of these names. —Author Note

"but if there's anything else you think you'd better have, I'm to let you buy it and to advise you how much you'll need if it's the sort of thing that'll have to last till spring."

Amity studied the list. She wasn't surprised to see sugar and tins of marmalade there. But flour? What sort of farmer bought flour? The list was long, and the quantities were great. It would take quite a large cart to carry all this. She looked up and smiled shyly. "I really don't know how well equipped my husband's kitchen is. Have you any idea what else I might need?"

The storekeeper pursed his lips. "You'll not want much else in the way of food, and he's covered the things like nails and traps. As for kitchen equipment, I'd say you'd better assume he has none. After all, he—um—presumably lives alone. Most men living alone in the wilderness make do with a knife, a spoon and a stewpan."

Amity was more puzzled than ever. Samuel York's farm must need more than one person to work it, and she would have thought that one of the hands would have a wife who would cook.

"No need to be surprised, Mrs. York," the storekeeper said kindly. "When men are on their own up here, they tend to drop the little refinements. I don't know what your husband's got, but I'm sure he'll be so pleased to have you with him again that he won't object to a little duplication."

"I'm sure your advice is sound," she said, disguising her astonishment. It had not occurred to her that he had assumed she was a wife of some years who was rejoining her husband after he had gone on ahead. She wondered how long Samuel York had had his farm. After all, she was not old enough to have been married to anyone for very long. She could hardly ask without revealing the recent date—to say nothing of the proxy nature—of their marriage, and that was something she had no desire to broadcast. "I'll choose what I want, and if it turns out that he already has it, I shall cheerfully blame you."

The storekeeper grinned. "Feel free to do so, Mrs. York." They both laughed, and Amity spent an enjoyable hour selecting equipment. Healy told her that Jake Treviscoe was looking for a guide for her. "He's as good a judge of an Indian as anyone, and you need someone you can depend upon, not just to guide you but to keep control of your porters."

"Porters?" Amity queried.

"Someone's got to carry the stores," Mr. Healy said.

"I assumed . . . I thought there would be a cart or something."

"A cart! What use would that be? Come with me." He led her to the muddy street. He faced her away from the shore toward a distant cleft in the mountains.

"See that V on the horizon?" he asked. Amity nodded. "That's where you're going. The first stage of your journey is over that pass and into Canada. The pass's called the Chilkoot, and it's over three thousand feet high. You could get a mule up there in summer, but not a cart. In winter you'd have difficulty even getting a dog team up. No, Mrs. York. If you want to get over the Chilkoot, you walk, and so do your stores. Someone has to tote them as far as Lake Lindeman. You can get the rest of the way by river."

Amity relaxed. "That sounds rather pleasant," she said.

He looked at her rather oddly. "Yes, I suppose it does," he said.

Chapter Four

DURING the afternoon Jake Treviscoe sought her out. He was accompanied by a short, sturdy Chilkat.

"This is Ned Attla," Treviscoe said. "He's one of the best guides in the territory. His English isn't bad, and he says he reckons he knows where your husband's cabin is to within a mile or so. He's hired the porters, and Wilson will pay them half when they leave here. Your husband will give Attla the balance when you arrive safely. It's a great discouragement to desertion."

"I can imagine," Amity said dryly.

"I've had him hire a few women, too. I figured you'd feel more comfortable with some women along even if you can't talk to them."

"That was very thoughtful of you," Amity said. "And anyway, we can smile and nod and make signs. After all, it won't be for very long, will it?"

He shrugged. "A month if you're lucky. Probably two."

"Two months?" She stared at him, horrified. "Two months in a wilderness with no company but heathens?"

"Don't be a fool. In this wilderness they're the best people to be with. And as for being heathen, they're strict Presbyterians, and you'll not get them to work on a Sunday." He turned to the Chilkat. "Ned, this is Mrs. York, the lady you look after till you hand her over to her husband."

Ned Attla's inscrutable expression did not change. He bobbed his head briefly. "Nice to meet you," he said.

Amity smiled nervously. "And I'm delighted to meet you," she told him. "I'm sure we shall become great friends."

Treviscoe snorted, and the Indian's expression remained unfathomable. He made no reply, and Amity did not get the impression he was overwhelmed at the prospect.

"Ned will be here in the morning," Treviscoe said after dismissing the Chilkat. "Now, Mrs. York, what have you got on your feet?"

Amity stared at him. "My feet? Why, shoes of course."

"No use at all," he said. "Get yourself some boots for the walk in front of you. Two pairs—you'll need the second one if the first get soaked." With these words he turned away and strode off through the mud in the heavy, calf-length laced boots worn by most of the men Amity had seen here.

She followed his advice, and was horrified to be offered a smaller version of the same boots. The storekeeper laughed at her dismay. "Not very beautiful, are they? Never mind. They're what you need. They won't do for deep winter, of course, but your husband's better placed than me to provide you with good mukluks."

That night Amity snuggled down under the blankets, peering at her new boots, which sat against the wall, and at a large fur-lined jacket she had also bought for the journey and which now hung on a peg above. It was impossible not to contrast them with the sort of wardrobe she might have expected had she married the butcher. Now, for the first time, she began to have serious doubts about the wisdom of what she had done. It had nothing to do with the fact that she would have preferred prettier clothes and very little to do with the prospect of the long, arduous journey ahead. It had a lot to do with sudden, unexplained silences, with sentences not completed, with her own lack of knowledge about Samuel York and, above all, with the fact that no one tried to dispel her misconceptions. She was becoming increasingly unsure, as she slid into sleep, what to expect.

The next morning, when Amity stepped out of the store, she saw that Ned Attla had assembled nine men and four women, each standing by the backpack that he or she would carry over the pass. Amity blanched at the size of the packs the women would be carrying. She assumed she would be expected to carry one herself but doubted her ability to stagger even to the end of Dyea with such a load.

Jake Treviscoe had followed her out and caught her expression. "Don't worry," he said. "Ned decided that you looked too frail to carry anything. All you've got to do is keep up with them."

"Do they travel fast?" Amity asked.

"No. But they keep it up hour after hour. I mean no disrespect, Mrs. York, if I say you'll be hard put to maintain the same rate."

While the Chilkats loaded their packs onto their backs, Amity took her leave of the Wilsons, the Healys and her fellow guests, saying good-bye with particular regret to the old Russian. There was a genuine warmth about the old prospector that she would miss despite the brevity of their acquaintance.

THE first day's journey covered thirteen miles, the first five of which were, as Amity realized in retrospect, relatively easygoing. That night they camped beside the Dyea River, a furiously rushing current of ice-cold water. As they sat by the fire, eating bacon and beans, Ned Attla said to Amity, "From here on, the climb gets tough, and the last half mile's the worst. You'll have to watch your footing. It's just loose rock, and there ain't nothing easier than to slip and fall—and it's a long way to the bottom."

The next day, Amity saw his point. The view of the pass ahead was breathtaking. The walk looked hellish. Because of the importance of maintaining a steady speed while carrying heavy loads, Ned told Amity to bring up the rear. If she faltered, she would throw all the people behind her out of rhythm.

"But what if I slip?" she objected.

"Scream," he advised bluntly. "I'll stop and do what I can."

Amity found little comfort in his promise. "How far is it to the summit?" she asked.

"Four miles. Three of them bad, one of them worse," he told her tersely. "You can't do it in them clothes, though. The skirt'll get in the way. Hitch the bottom of your skirt up through your belt. It might make the next bit easier."

Amity hitched up her skirt and said, "I'm ready. Let's go."

Her companions, bent almost double under their huge loads, seemed unperturbed by the scree that their feet sent rattling down the slope. But their progress now was measured by the inch.

Amity had no idea how long it took them to reach the summit, but it must have been hours. The icy wind had whipped away the clouds, and she found herself looking out over a landscape of a grandeur and beauty of which she had never dreamed. Lakes peered out from behind tree-covered slopes, and here and there the thin ribbon of a river, black or silver according to the vagaries of the light, twisted between them. Amity had no idea of the scale of what she was seeing, only that in all that vast panorama, she could see no sign whatever of human habitation.

Ned took her arm. "Stand here," he commanded. "Put one foot here," and he pointed his boot at one spot. "The other one here," he went on. Amity did as she was told. "Now you have that foot in Canada and the other one in Alaska. How does it feel?"

Amity chuckled. "Uncomfortable," she said. "They ought to make it narrower."

It wasn't the answer he was expecting, and he bent double with laughter. His companions looked up, and he fired a volley of staccato sounds at them, which Amity took to be the retelling of her comment. The Chilkats roared with laughter. From then on, Amity felt she was a part of the group. It was comforting, and the wilderness seemed less threatening.

After the exhausting climb to the top of the Chilkoot, the downhill run to the crystal waters of Crater Lake, where they were to camp for the night, was almost a joy. The next morning they set off round the lake, camping at the far end. The next day's march brought them to the goal that marked the end of the first stage of their journey—Lake Lindeman.

The following day being Sunday, the Chilkats made no attempt to go anywhere, though their day of rest did not preclude catching the day's food. They selected a spot on the bank and crouched over it, spears in hand, waiting for fish. When a spear was finally plunged into the water, it was rare for it to fail to reach its target.

That night, as they sat round the campfire to eat the delicious fish, it occurred to Amity that if she was going to be living in this wild and empty land, she ought to learn as many skills as she could. She turned to her guide. "Could I be taught spearfishing?"

"Sure," Ned said, "we'll teach you. But the only fish you get to eat are what you catch—hunger is the best master."

The next day, the Chilkats set about felling some of the narrowtrunked spruces around the camp. "What's happening?" she asked.

"Most of my people go back to Dyea from here. We'll travel the rest of the way by river, but for that we need to make boats. Two is enough."

Shortly after that exchange, the women took Amity by the arm and led her along the shores of the lake before handing her a spear. With immense ingenuity of signs, gestures and facial expressions, they showed her how to select a good fishing place and how to crouch so that her shadow could not be detected by her prey. Her main problem was learning to adjust her aim to allow for the distortion caused by the water. The other women had caught all the fish they needed some time before Amity caught even one, but when that goal had been achieved, their faces were wreathed in smiles, and they stamped their feet on the ground in tribute. Back at the camp, they made sure that Amity had the one she caught, not because it was her ration, but by way of celebration. In the ensuing days Amity's skill improved so much that by the time the boats were finished, she was regularly catching almost half as much as the Chilkat women.

Ned Attla nodded approvingly. "Not bad," he said. "If you can feed yourself in this territory, you live."

There would be only one more night at Lake Lindeman before the two groups parted company and the boat party set off for the next lake in the chain, Lake Bennett.

Night was almost upon them when suddenly the Indians fell silent. Two of the men picked up their rifles and slipped into the shadows of the trees. It wasn't very long before a tall, familiar figure stepped into the circle of firelight. "Good evening, Mrs. York," said Jake Treviscoe's deep voice. It was the sound Amity least expected, and she attributed to surprise the fact that she was suddenly conscious of the beating of her heart. "Ned not around?" he continued.

"He was here a minute ago." She was glad her voice sounded normal. "What brings you here?"

"The Chilkoot Trail, same as you," he replied.

He set his pack down and joined the small circle, taking his seat among them just as Ned and his companion returned, their rifles held loosely at their sides now that they knew there was no danger.

"They must have heard you coming," Amity said.

"I'd have been surprised if they hadn't. How are you doing?"

"You'd better ask them," Amity told him. "At least I've kept up, and I've learned to spearfish, although I'm not as good as them, of course. Ned has a foolproof method—no fish, no meal."

He nodded. "Coupled with some expert instruction, that would about do the trick. Can you use a gun?"

"Good gracious, no. I was a housemaid, not a poacher!" As soon as the words were out, Amity realized she had given the first hint of her circumstances—female domestics were rarely married.

Jake Treviscoe seemed not to notice. "That's the next skill you need, then. Up here it's essential. Ned can teach you. I'll have a word with him."

Amity was aware of a twinge of disappointment. "Does that mean you're not joining us for the next part of our journey?"

"No. I'm off in the other direction. Maybe, come the spring thaw, I'll make my way to the Throndiuck and see how you're doing—that is, if you don't think your husband will mind."

"I'm sure he won't," Amity said warmly. "I should think he'd be quite glad to have a visitor." And so will I, she thought. It will be something to look forward to during the long, hard winter.

"If he is, it'll be due to your influence. He doesn't welcome them now," he told her.

"I expect that's because he's got into the habit of being on his own," Amity suggested, realizing that Treviscoe knew more about Samuel York than he had previously suggested.

"I expect that accounts for it," he said politely.

There was no further reference to Samuel that evening, but in the morning, when those Chilkats returning to Dyea had gone and Jake Treviscoe was also ready to leave, he took Amity a little to one side. His gray eyes were serious, and Amity wondered why her legs seemed suddenly weak. "Mrs. York," he began, "there's something I think perhaps you had better be . . . prepared for."

"What is that?" she asked, unconsciously taking a deep breath.

"Men come up here for all sorts of reasons, but no matter why they come, life here is isolated and lonely. Those that stay, like Samuel York, always change. Just thought you ought to know," he added almost apologetically.

Amity let out her breath. "Is that all?" she said. "Don't worry about me, Mr. Treviscoe. I can cope, and if I hear you've been in the region of our farm and not visited, I shall be deeply offended."

He took her hand and, in a totally incongruous gesture, raised it to his lips. "Do you know, Mrs. York, I begin to think I'm worrying about you unnecessarily," he said, and led her back to the lakeside.

A stiff, cold wind blew across the lake, and what with trying to keep warm and becoming accustomed to this form of travel, Amity had no time to think about the Cornishman's words. Nor was there time for contemplation once they left the relative calm of Lake Lindeman and were hurtling down the white-water torrent that led to Lake Bennett.

Amity sat amidships, among the stores, and clung to the sides as the boat dipped and rose in the swirling, rushing water. The Chilkats were skilled navigators, but it was still a nerve-racking ride, and Amity could only be relieved when they finally emerged into the wide expanse of Lake Bennett and beached the boats on its broad shores.

Fortunately, the weather held. It rained frequently, but the rain did not turn into snow, though Ned Attla was often to be seen anxiously studying the skies. In the following days Amity shot rapids that made the white water between the lakes seem quite tame. She also learned to use a rifle. Ned Attla's incentive was the same as the one that taught her to spearfish—no kill, no food. This time, however, it was a much bigger incentive. One elk or one bear provided more than enough food for the whole party, so when it was Amity's turn to shoot, no one ate if she missed, and time would have to be spent the next day on an additional hunt.

By the time they were within reach of her new home, Amity York had acquired skills undreamed of in Long Westing and had become stronger both in mind and body.

In all the weeks of traveling, the group passed only one sizable settlement—Fort Selkirk, with its wooden palisades. The Chilkats didn't stop there. They were Indians, Ned told her, and Alaskan ones at that. Without furs to trade, they were unwelcome in Fort Selkirk. So the boats sculled on past, making full use of the rushing torrent.

Chapter Five

It was with trepidation that Amity approached her new home, or rather where Ned Attla thought her new home would be. For nearly two weeks they had been running northwards down the Yukon River, but when they reached its confluence with the Throndiuck, they were obliged to row against the flow, making the last part of her journey slow and nerve-racking. After two more hard days' rowing, they beached the boats, and Amity clambered ashore. The cabin was so well sited among the trees that Amity didn't notice it at first. Ned had to nudge her and point before Amity realized her journey had ended.

There was no sign of life as she walked across the clearing to where the cabin stood. Amity's long journey through this wilderness had killed her dream of a prosperous farm, but she was not prepared for quite the privation she saw before her. The cabin was small but solidly built from whole logs, and its gabled roof was made of split logs covered with a thatch of spruce branches. There was a door and a shuttered window, both closed. Amity's heart sank.

Ned, who had followed her up from the river, nodded approvingly. "He has done well, your husband. Very well," he said.

Amity shot him a glance. "What do you mean?"

"This house will be warm and snug," he told her. "Look at the roof, the timbers. And the chimney," he added, walking round to one end of the house where the wall was made of mortared rocks and stones. "With a chimney like this, you have no need to fear fire," he said. He pulled the rope that lifted the inner latch and pushed open the door. Amity followed him in apprehensively.

The cabin consisted of one room. At one end was a substantial stone hearth and at the other a large rough-hewn bed. The space between the two was occupied by a square table and two simple upright chairs. A more ambitious bentwood rocking chair stood by the hearth. A blanket divided the sleeping area from the rest of the cabin. It was not in the remotest degree the sort of house Amity had expected as the home of a prosperous farmer. It was smaller than the two-room hovel in which she had grown up, though, to be fair, this seemed to have the sounder roof.

"Where is he?" she asked.

"Who knows. Off hunting most likely. His dogs are gone, so he'll probably be away for a few days, I reckon. Maybe a week or two."

"A week or two! When he knew I was on my way?"

The Chilkat gave one of his rare grins. "You know how long it took you to get here. D'you expect him to have been sitting around, waiting for you to come? He'll have reckoned it out close enough and added three or four weeks for bad weather, which we haven't really had." He paused and looked around him. "I tell you this, Mis' York—there's not many men up here that keeps their cabins as neat

as this one. It's likely Samuel York's way of getting the place ready for you so's you don't turn right round and go home again."

Amity decided that if the Indian's guess was correct, it showed her new husband in an unexpectedly touching light. "So we camp outside until he returns?"

"No, Mis' York. We use the cabin, if you don't object, of course. Up here a man uses any shelter he finds."

Like so many of the unwritten rules in this extraordinary place, this one made sense. Survival was what mattered here above all.

Outside, against the back of the cabin, was an enclosed stone shed. The solid timber door was barred with a substantial wooden crossbar. Ned lifted this and opened the door for Amity. "Your larder," he explained.

From the ceiling beams hung dried and smoked salmon and meat, among which Ned pointed out moose, bear and sheep. On raised boards were the remains of the last supplies of flour and sugar, beans and coffee. The whole larder was very orderly, and Amity decided that perhaps the neatness of the cabin itself reflected as much of Samuel's normal character as of concern for her first impression.

"It's good," Ned said. "No wolves or bears will get in here."

Amity looked at him, dismayed. "But surely such things won't come this close to human habitation?" she said.

"They go where there's food, just like us. You'll soon learn to keep a gun handy, but the easiest way of getting rid of them is to make the store inaccessible."

The Indians set about moving the supplies into the storeroom. Only then did they consider their own comfort.

DAY succeeded day, and it was ten days before the Chilkats told her she had a visitor. Amity took off her apron and hung it over the back of one of the chairs before going outside to welcome whoever it might be.

A heavy winter mist hung among the trees, which rose like hazy phantoms through the icy harbinger of the coming freeze. It deadened sound, so that the man who emerged from it had a disconcertingly wraithlike quality. Beside and behind him walked a succession of dogs. The first three carried packs; the others were harnessed one behind the other to a heavily laden travois—a hauling rig made of two parallel poles. One end of each pole was fastened to the harness of the rear dog, while the other end dragged on the ground. The space between them was bridged by the hide of some animal, and upon this was loaded the carcass of a bear.

Amity stepped forward. "Samuel?" she said.

"Amity?" He stopped to lower his backpack to the ground and came forward, taking her hand and shaking it awkwardly before pecking her dutifully on the cheek. "Have you been here long?"

"About ten days," she told him, wondering what the Indians made of so restrained a greeting between two people who supposedly had not seen each other for years.

"You made good time." He turned to Ned Attla. "My thanks. You've taken good care of her. I'll settle with you, and you can be on your way in the morning."

"Your wife's a useful woman," the Indian told him. "She's new to the country, but she learns fast. We'll not wait till morning. We'd rather be as far on our way as we can before winter closes in."

Samuel nodded. "Just give me time to stake the dogs." When that was done, he disappeared into the trees.

When he returned, he was carrying a selection of board-stiff pelts. Ned Attla and his companions went over them with the eyes and hands of experts, and there was some bargaining before the bulk of the pelts was loaded into one of the boats, and the Chilkats, after a brief farewell, launched it back into the river towards the Yukon.

While the bargaining had been going on, Amity had been able to steal a not-too-surreptitious look at the man she had married. He was somewhat above medium height and thickset without being stocky. He wore a full beard, which made it difficult to judge his features, and both his beard and his hair were now grizzled rather more for his age than Amity had expected. Like Amity's, his eyes were brown.

Once the Indians were on their way, he turned awkwardly back to Amity and the cabin, and she realized he had felt far more at ease with her former companions than he did with her. She felt hardly less awkward herself. She followed him inside and picked up the kettle. "I'll make us some tea," she suggested, and then, remembering there had been far more coffee than tea in the larder, she added, "Or would you prefer coffee?"

"Tea will be just fine," he said, and pulled up one of the upright chairs. They both watched the kettle come to a boil before Samuel broke the silence. "You had a good journey?"

"Interesting," Amity said. "A bit tedious in places, of course."

"The sea crossing was all right?"

"Not too bad. It took some getting used to, but the crew told us it had been an easy crossing."

"You were lucky, then. Mine wasn't."

"How long ago was that?"

He shrugged. "Twelve, fifteen years. You lose count."

Amity wished he would volunteer some more information. She wanted to find out as much about him as she could, but it felt impertinent to press. "Have you been in this valley for long?"

He thought about it. "Four winters."

"So what did you do before coming here?"

"This and that. I got taken on as a stevedore when I landed. That earned me a grubstake. Then I worked my way westwards and northwards. Bit of laboring, bit of lumbering—nothing for long. Just enough to get me another stage along the trail. What about you?"

Amity made the tea before she answered. "Much less interesting. I was a kitchenmaid from leaving school and got to be housemaid. If I'd stayed, I'd have been put up to parlormaid," she added.

"And you turned it down to marry me? I'm flattered." There was no irony in his voice.

Amity hesitated. "To be truthful, it isn't quite what I was expecting. The agency told me you were a prosperous farmer with three hundred and fifty square miles of land."

"This isn't farming land. They didn't ought to have told you that."

Amity tried to remember exactly what had been said. "To be fair, I may have assumed it was farmland. But if it's not, what is it?"

"Far more profitable," he said. "It's a trapline. I have a registered claim. It means no other white man can trap over this area. Indians aren't meant to, either, but they don't understand that sort of law, and there's room for them and me."

Amity nodded and another awkward silence fell.

Amity broke it. "Look, this is difficult for both of us. Now, you had a bear when you came back this morning, to say nothing of whatever was in the packs. Why don't you get on with whatever needs doing with all that, and I'll get a meal started. I'm generally held to be a passable cook."

Samuel seemed relieved at so practical a suggestion for easing the situation. "Call when it's ready," he said.

Amity had not wasted the days prior to Samuel's arrival. She and the Chilkat women had roamed the forests, gathering herbs and roots that would substitute for vegetables. The stew of dried caribou meat and huge wild mushrooms was accompanied by bannocks cooked over the fire in a frying pan, and to finish, Amity mixed the last blueberries of the season with some of the precious sugar she had brought from Dyea. The meal was a feast by any standard and Amity was justly proud.

Samuel ate without comment, but since his appetite was enormous, Amity took comfort from the fact that his plate was refilled three times. When he finished, he said, "You're right. You're a passable cook."

It was not effusive, but Amity guessed that when coupled with the amount he had eaten, it rated as pretty strong praise.

She cleared the table and took the dishes to the river to wash them. When she came back in, she was surprised to see Samuel still sitting on one of the upright chairs. "Wouldn't you be more comfortable in the rocking chair?" she asked a shade diffidently.

"Probably. This'll do, however."

Amity frowned. "But that's silly, Samuel." His name sounded odd, as "my husband" had sounded odd back in Dyea. "You've been away for days. Surely you deserve to be comfortable now you're home."

"Maybe," he said, not looking at her. "Thing is, I bought that chair for you. It's a sort of wedding present. Do you like it?"

"Of course I do. I've been enjoying it every evening. Perhaps we should share it."

"No. It's yours. If I need one, we'll send for another sometime."

Amity was touched. "I don't think my present to you can compare. Not yet, at any rate." She opened her trunk and brought out several skeins of dark gray wool. "I wanted to make you a sweater, but I had no idea what size it should be. Now that you're here, I'll begin work on it. You won't mind having to wait?"

"It'll beat having one that doesn't fit," he told her. "Make it on the big side. Up here it's several layers that keeps you warm."

Amity busied herself about the cabin for a while before settling down in her chair, determined to start on the sweater and glad to have an opportunity to watch him so that she might attempt to clarify her feelings now that she and her husband had actually met. He began honing his skinning knife on a whetstone at the table.

She recalled Jake Treviscoe's warning and was puzzled by it. It had led her to expect a truculent man who resented any intrusion. His praise of her meal was understated, but that was preferable to its being taken for granted. And then there was the rocking chair. In a house with no comfortable furniture except the bed, it was a particularly thoughtful gesture.

The bed. She glanced across to where its foot protruded beyond the partitioning blanket. She thought of the unappealing Mr. Grogport and pushed the more welcome image of Jake Treviscoe aside. Then she looked at her husband again. She felt no attraction for Samuel. Perhaps it might come with time and familiarity. But at least she found nothing about him to repel her.

All the same, as the short northern day drew to a close, she felt more than a little trepidation at the prospect of transforming this into a marriage in fact, as well as in law. "Shall I light the lamp?"

"I'll do it." Samuel took the lamp down from its hook in the rafters, trimmed the wick and saw it well alight before replacing the glass chimney. He put it on the table between them. "I reckon to save as much as I can on kerosene," he told her. "It's heavy stuff to bring in all this way."

"That makes sense," Amity agreed. "It was like that when I was a child at home. We couldn't afford oil or candles, so we all went to bed with the sun."

"I aim to do the same, except when the dark's too long to sleep it away."

Amity wound up her wool and speared the ball with her needles. "Shall I make us some tea . . . or something?" she asked hesitantly.

"Tea? Not a bad idea. I'll lace it—make us both loosen up a bit."

He poured a generous dash of whisky into both mugs of tea, and Amity found its warmth gave her courage. When she had nearly finished it, she said, "I'll go to bed now. I won't be long."

"Yes, maybe that's best." He caught her arm and turned her. "There's something I should say. I've waited a long time to have a woman again and a long time for you. I took a gamble on what I was getting, but I want you to know you're a far better looking woman than I'd hoped for, and you're a good cook. Let's hope we can make a go of it."

"Yes, indeed," Amity agreed. She looked at him a little shyly. "It was a gamble for me, too, you know."

"I hope you won't be disappointed."

"I'm sure I won't," she replied with the warmth she felt he deserved.

He really was a good man, she told herself as she undressed and put on the warm flannel nightgown she had made for this occasion. It was trimmed with cotton lace at the neck and wrists and embroidered on the yoke with lilies of the valley. Then she let down her hair and brushed it before shaking it back so that it fell in a dark curtain behind her.

Samuel joined her as she was finishing. "You look nice," he said with the awkwardness of one unaccustomed to paying compliments.

Amity smiled. "Thank you," she said, then got into bed. She averted her eyes while he undressed and climbed in beside her.

Amity recalled the preliminary cuddling and kissing—muffled in order not to wake the children—that had characterized her parents' marital affection, and expected something similar. She was therefore unprepared for the suddenness with which he sealed their contract, and was aware only of his weight and strength. When he was done, he turned over and was soon asleep.

Amity lay where he had left her, staring up at the roof timbers, bewildered and unhappy. Was that all there was? Surely not. She was conscious of the greatest feeling of disappointment she had ever had. She felt flat and unfulfilled, and something within her cried out that it should not be so. It was a long, long time before she fell into an uneasy sleep.

IT TOOK Amity some time to realize that what she had assumed to be an initial reticence had in fact been unusual loquacity on Samuel's part. He rarely spoke and confined himself to monosyllables when he did. He was not unappreciative of her efforts to improve the cabin. When she completed and hung a patchwork quilt to replace the drab woolen blanket screening the bed, he went to it immediately and ran his fingers over it. "Nice," he said, and made no further reference.

Nor did he ever comment upon her cooking, except on those occasions when she tried something new. She soon learned that "passable" meant he liked it, "interesting" or "different" that he didn't. He saw to it that they were never short of meat, and almost as soon as she arrived, he spent part of the lengthening evenings making her winter clothes from his cache of pelts in the forest: mukluks of caribou skin, with moss inside for added comfort and insulation; a parka of the same fur, with a hood edged with wolverine, which, he told her, would not freeze no matter how low the temperature fell. There were roomy caribou-skin trousers. Amity had never worn trousers, but as the temperature dropped and snow began to fall, she conceded that they would be more sensible out of doors than a long skirt.

He was surprised and impressed by her skill at fishing and hunting. When she succeeded in getting close enough to shoot her first buck without the need for advice or caution from him, he smiled one of his rare smiles. "I don't reckon to die yet a while," he said. "But it's good to know you'll be able to cope if I do."

He also taught her the tricky art of handling a dog team. "Come next spring's pups, we'll grow you a team of your own," he told her as she grappled with keeping the dogs on the trail.

As the snow deepened, Amity was forced to learn new skills, new cautions. Her first whiteout lasted a week, and the simple task of walking round to the larder to fetch a pail of flour suddenly became an expedition fraught with danger.

"I'm not going for you," Samuel told her shortly. "You've got to learn what it's like. Just remember, you can get lost and die between here and there."

"Don't be ridiculous," Amity told him scornfully as she closed the cabin door.

As soon as the full force of the blizzard hit her, Amity rocked on her mukluks, almost losing contact with the cabin wall within one step of leaving it. She succeeded in getting the flour, but as she inched her way back, there was a nasty moment when she lost her bearings. She felt the panic rising, but she had the good sense to stand still and make herself think. She had not moved since losing touch with the cabin. Therefore the wall must be within reach to her left. She took a deep breath and put out her mitten. Yes, there it was, hard and comforting.

That little episode taught her that the snow deceived not only the eye but the mind. It was just as well she learned this lesson early in the winter, for as the temperature dropped, Samuel's work began in earnest. He was rarely at home, being absent for as much as two weeks at a time, inspecting his traps and bringing home at the end of each tour a sled laden with lynx and mink, fox and marten, wolf and wolverine. These skins he taught her to scrape and salt before storing them, frozen into stiff boards, until the spring thaw would enable him to take them to Dyea.

One effect, both of Samuel's taciturnity and his frequent and prolonged absences, was to turn Amity in on herself. There were a few books in the cabin, and Amity read them all. However, they hardly occupied her mind to the full, and after a few weeks she found she had begun to talk to herself.

"The first sign of madness," they used to say in Long Westing of anyone caught moving their lips without the excuse of a listening companion. Amity now agonized over it. But when she asked Samuel about it, he seemed neither surprised nor concerned. "Doesn't everyone?" he asked.

His decisive, unemotional answer was distinctly comforting.

Her anxieties were finally laid to rest with the realization of a potentially far greater one—pregnancy. She worried over Samuel's reaction to the news. In the months she had been here the question of children had never once been raised. She watched him one evening, lashing the body of her new sled with strips of rawhide. "I think you'd be better occupied on something else," she told him.

"What?"

"A cradle. Samuel, I think I'm expecting."

"Have been for weeks. Plenty of time to make a cradle come summer."

"You knew?"

"Guessed. I wondered when you'd get around to telling me."

"Are you happy about it?"

He shrugged. "What if I wasn't? September, by my reckoning. Bad time. Still, can't be helped. Daresay we'll cope."

"Why is it a bad time?"

"It's easier to raise kids through the spring and summer. We'll make do." He made no further reference to her condition.

When the spring spate caused by the thaw had abated, he loaded most of the winter's catch into a canoe and prepared to set off down the Throndiuck. It would be the first time Amity would be left on her own for more than two weeks.

"You'll be fine," he told her. "I'll be straight back. But don't look for me this side of three months. I'll be back before you need me."
"And what if you're not? What if something happens to you?"
"Sooner or later someone will drop by. Someone always does."

SOMEONE did. Samuel had been gone nearly two months, and Amity was feeling quite proud of the way she was coping, when Jake Treviscoe stepped ashore from a canoe.

"How're you doing?" he said. He looked her up and down. "Blooming, I'd say."

The unexpectedness of his arrival flustered Amity to a degree she would not have believed possible. She tried simultaneously to smooth her skirts and to tidy her hair.

"So you came," she said. "I thought, from the way you spoke, you'd intended to visit during the winter."

"Missed me, did you?" He grinned.

"To be perfectly honest, I've not given you a second thought," she said cheerfully, and it was true. She had completely forgotten his undertaking to drop in. She thought he frowned, but it was probably just a trick of those eyebrows. "Coffee?" she went on. "Or tea? I've still got some left."

"Coffee will be fine." He looked about. "Samuel around?"

She led the way to the cabin. "No. He went off to Dyea with the winter's furs a couple of months ago."

"He must be sure you can cope."

"I can—in summer, at any rate."

"Marriage seems to be suiting you," he said. "When's it due?"

Amity found his bluntness embarrassing. "September," she said.

"Hmm. Spring would be better. Reckon I'll hang around a bit. Unless you think he'll have an objection," he added.

"I don't see why he should, but there's really no need for you to put yourself out. I'm perfectly well able to manage."

"Obviously, but the less time you're left alone in your condition, the better. Don't worry. I'll pitch a tent back in the trees. We don't want the neighbors gossiping, do we?"

Amity looked bewildered. "Neighbors? What neighbors?"

He laughed. "A joke. I was pulling your leg."

Amity had become so used to being either on her own or dependent upon the taciturn company of her husband that she found it difficult at first to sustain a conversation. Then she caught herself chattering away like a pet parrot. "I'm sorry," she said one day. "I must sound like old Mr. Kislov, going on and on like this."

"Doesn't bother me. Talk away. The north gets people like that sometimes." He paused. "Does your husband talk much?"

"He doesn't waste words," Amity replied.

"I don't think many people would argue with that," he said dryly. "Is he much changed?"

"From what?" Amity asked, forgetting that it had always been assumed that she was joining a husband who had gone on ahead.

Treviscoe looked at her levelly. "From before he came here."

She colored as recollection flooded back. "Oh, that," she said, and then thought quickly. The way things had worked out, there was nothing to be ashamed of. She took a deep breath. "I don't know what he was like before he came here," she said. "I married him—by proxy—in England. We'd never met before I arrived here. Everyone just assumed we'd just been parted while Samuel came out here, and I did nothing to disabuse them."

He nodded. "I can understand why. What I don't understand is why you needed to go to those lengths to find a husband."

"Oh, I had had an offer," Amity assured him. "The local butcher. A parish councillor to boot."

"I'm impressed," he said, but his eyes were laughing at her.

"You may laugh, but it's true," she told him indignantly. "He just didn't appeal. I suppose I didn't think Samuel could have been any *less* appealing."

"Now that really was a gamble."

Amity chuckled. "Yes, I suppose it was." Again she had a nebulous impression that there was something of which he was aware and she was not.

Amity enjoyed Jake Treviscoe's company, but she resolutely pushed from her mind the deeper interest in him that she knew lurked there. They settled into a comforting routine. The visitor took charge of hunting and fishing, of feeding the dogs and replenishing the woodpile. He even built a smokehouse for preserving the salmon that now came up the river. This left Amity free to catch up on her preparations for the baby.

In return for his work, Amity made sure that Jake ate well. He was more openly appreciative than Samuel. "I'll tell you this, Mrs.

York," he said one day as he pushed over his plate for a second helping of rabbit stew with dumplings, "if ever you're unsure what to do for a living, you could do a lot worse than open a lodging house."

"Up here?" Amity laughed. "I'd soon starve if I was dependent on the passing trade in this neck of the woods."

He laughed, too. "True, but if you ever move to a town, it's something to bear in mind."

"Do you spend much time in towns?"

"No more than I must. And then only in Alaska."

"Why the preference for Alaska?" she asked.

"No police," he said, and returned to his stew.

Amity thought about that, unsure how seriously he meant it. "You're in Canada now," she pointed out.

"But not a town. Besides, I had an incentive."

Amity looked at him sharply. His last remark could have been mistaken for a compliment had she not been aware that there was nothing worthy of a compliment in her thickened body and her working clothes. She was tempted to ask what the incentive was, but then she thought better of it. Like Samuel, Treviscoe said nothing of his past and little of his future, and she knew that if either of them wanted her to know something, she would be told.

Chapter Six

WHEN Samuel returned home and found a strange canoe beached there, he was definitely not pleased. As Amity went forward to greet him, she felt guilty. She knew she was not as overjoyed to see him as she should have been.

"Whose is that?" he asked, before giving Amity a perfunctory kiss.

"Jake Treviscoe's. You know him, I think."

"We've met. What does he want?"

"He was passing through and thought he'd see how I was doing."

"You know him?"

"He was in Dyea when I came through."

Samuel looked about him. "Where is he now?"

"Off getting meat for the dogs. He's been very helpful."

"Has he now? How long has he been here?"

"I'm not sure. About three weeks."

Samuel made no comment, but strode towards the cabin. He paused when he saw the smokehouse.

When Amity told him about it, he replied, "Mighty generous."

His eye took in the tent pitched in the trees. "What's that?"

"Mr. Treviscoe's. He said it would stop the neighbors' talking."

Samuel permitted himself a hint of a grin. "Thoughtful," he said. "What's he been doing with himself all day for three weeks?"

"Hunted and fished. And built the smokehouse, of course. I've already smoked far more salmon than we had last winter."

He nodded. "It'll be useful. What reason did he give for staying?"

"My condition. He thought it was better for there to be someone here until you got back, just in case."

"Fair enough," he said reasonably, but nevertheless Amity had the impression he was still not happy about their visitor.

It was late afternoon before Treviscoe returned with half a dozen spruce hens. His greeting was laconic. "Glad you're back. I'll be on my way in the morning."

"Thanks for your help," Samuel said.

"No thanks needed."

He ate with them that night, and although Amity was up at her usual early hour, when she went outside, she found his canoe was gone. She was conscious of a sense of disappointment. He had not said good-bye. There was no reason why that should hurt, but it did.

Samuel slept until the smell of bacon woke him up. He rarely outslept his wife, and Amity guessed he had been traveling from dawn to dusk for several weeks in order to be back home well before her confinement. He ate his breakfast without speaking. When she refilled his mug with coffee, he said, "Treviscoe gone?"

"There was no sign of him when I went out for water."

Samuel spent the day checking out the storeroom and the forest cache of pelts. "I'll make a start on your bread oven in a day or two," he told her when he came in. "That and a cradle—those are my priorities." He paused. "He did a good job on the smokehouse. You didn't notice him rooting around?"

Amity frowned. "No, nothing like that. Why should he?"

Samuel shrugged, but made no further comment.

That evening Samuel sat by the fire gazing into the flames, lost in thought. Amity rocked in her chair, apparently immersed in her sewing but glancing at him from time to time.

"I love this land," Samuel said suddenly.

Amity smiled. "That's just as well, since this is where you live."

"No, you don't understand. I've walked all over Canada, and it was just a place to earn a living. But when I got here, to Yukon territory, I knew this was where I belonged. So I found the perfect place, filed claim to a trapline and here I am, and I aim to stay." He spoke with a vehemence Amity had never heard before. "I'd hoped you'd feel the same way, but I don't think you do."

"I don't think I do, either," she admitted. "Perhaps that's because it's all so strange to me. In time maybe I'll love it, too."

"I want our son to love it. I want him to share my feeling for it."

Amity forbore to point out that she might be carrying a daughter.

"One false step and all this beauty would be lost," he continued.

Amity considered the immensity of the land outside. "I think you exaggerate," she said.

"On the contrary." Samuel sighed and rose from his seat. "I suppose you ought to know. If anything happens to me, you'll not want to be chained here. Move your chair away from the hearth."

Amity did so and watched while he slipped his skinning knife into a hairline crack in the mortar of the hearth. He levered up the stone and removed it. Reaching into a small cavity, he brought out a leather pouch, its drawstring wound tightly round its neck. He untied the thongs and tipped the contents onto the table.

Small nuggets of gold gleamed dully in the combined light of the fire and the lamp. Amity picked one up and held it close to the light, turning it in her fingers. "Is this what I think it is?" she asked.

"Very likely. It's gold."

"But there must be a small fortune here! How long did it take you to find as much as this?"

"Three or four years. Sounds a long time, but I found it by accident. I knew people were always hunting for gold in the territory, of course, and sometimes finding it. After I found the first little nugget, I sort of kept my eyes open. I kept finding bits in one particular spot. I did a bit of panning and found about an ounce in no time at all. I got frightened then. I hid it away and took a long time to go over all the implications. In the end, I took it into Alaska, where I figured they'd believe my story that it was the result of several months' work."

"Why didn't you sell it in Canada?" Amity asked.

"My trapping claim is registered at Fort Selkirk. They'd realize that my own claim was the most likely source. How long do you think it would have been before word got out?"

"But surely there's enough gold to share with a few others?"

"Sure, only it wouldn't be a few others. The gold would be a magnet for every no-hoper on the continent. Within two years—three at the most—this place would be pillaged to the bare earth and beyond. This clearing would be a shantytown in a sea of mud. I told you, I love this land. I don't like the thought of what could happen to it if there was a rush."

Even if Samuel was only half right, the picture he painted was not a pretty one. Amity put the nuggets back into the pouch. "Does all this mean that you no longer look for gold?" she asked.

"I don't pan for it, but if I come across a piece, I pick it up." He gave a rueful half smile. "I can't deny my own share of greed."

Amity held up the pouch. "Is this what you were afraid Jake Treviscoe would find?" she asked.

"I was more worried that he'd find his own deposits. Did he?"

"He said nothing to me, but then I don't imagine he would."

"Hmm." Samuel managed to inject a wealth of doubt and anxiety into the simple sound. He put the pouch back in its sanctuary. Then he replaced the stone and filled in the crack in the mortar with dry earth from the floor. It was a remarkably effective hiding place.

Amity tried to put Samuel's revelation out of her mind, and most of the time she succeeded. She had plenty to do, preparing for the coming winter as well as the coming baby, and it was only when she used her new bread oven that it sometimes occurred to her that she walked on a fortune.

The baby, David, arrived in early September. Amity, who had sat with her mother through many difficult confinements, was both amazed and grateful that hers was over very quickly. Samuel was beside her all the time. "Just remember you're not the first," he said.

He washed the baby, wrapped it warmly in the shawl Amity had knitted, and placed the child in her arms. Then he cleaned up the bed and changed the sheets. He opened a tin of milk, warmed it, then stirred in sugar. "This'll give you strength," he said.

Amity drank it obediently. When Samuel left her, she sank into a drowsy half sleep. A strange man, she thought. Will I ever really know him? She was asleep before she answered herself.

DAVID THRIVED AND BECAME the center of his parents' universe, uniting them as perhaps nothing else could. Everything except the need to survive was subordinated to his best interests. David was carried Indian fashion, on his mother's back. He slept as much as any parent could hope for.

Samuel's love for his son was greater than Amity had expected, and she tried not to feel neglected in the face of such absorption. She reminded herself that Samuel had never professed to love her, any more than she had claimed to love him. All the same, a little dissembling would not have come amiss.

During the long, dark months of winter Samuel's absences to visit his traplines left her with the undivided care of her son. She was as happy as she had ever been. The gold under the hearth was almost forgotten, and when she did think of it, it was as something held in trust for David. She and Samuel would have to provide his early schooling, but if he proved to be a clever boy, the gold could send him to school.

But nothing runs smoothly forever, not even soundly sleeping children, as Amity discovered when David began to teethe. Then one of their dogs broke its leg, and Samuel had to shoot it. Then a wolverine found its way into the new fur store and mangled half a dozen pelts, which meant the list of provisions from Dyea had to be pruned. Once again Amity thought of the gold. Surely one small nugget was all it would take to redress the balance? Samuel didn't see it in the same light. "Don't be stupid, woman," he said. "Too many people in Dyea are capable of putting two and two together."

During Samuel's absence that spring, she found time to paddle up and down in the ice-cold river looking for gold. Samuel had described nuggets that could be seen in the water, and she found where a little runnel trickled in, depositing the occasional piece of glinting ore.

She found something most days, and as the pouch filled, she became almost blasé about her finds. Eventually she could squeeze no more into the pouch, so she stopped until Samuel should return. The construction of another hiding place was best left to him.

He was far from pleased when he learned what she had done, and listened with unconcealed impatience to her reason. "To pay for his education? Are you mad? We can teach him all he needs."

"We cannot, Samuel. Oh, we can teach him to read and write, I suppose, but what more can he learn from us? Why, we don't even have basic readers for him."

"I'll get some readers next spring," he promised. "Some other books, too, if I've room. But don't you see? That's all the school learning he needs. It's far more important that he can track and kill, skin and cure, light a fire and build a cabin, train a team and work a trapline. Those things we can teach him. Those are the necessities."

Amity threw up her hands in exasperation. "David's my son, too, Samuel. My mother taught me that education was the ladder out of the pit, and she was right."

"And look where it got you—a mail-order bride to a man that you don't love. Is that your idea of getting out of the pit?"

"Of course it's not. That's exactly what I mean—with the money he could have behind him, David can be taken above all this."

Samuel studied her in silence for a few moments. "Thank you," he said with cold politeness. "That tells me clearly what you think of your home and your husband."

Amity was aghast. "Samuel, that wasn't what I meant. You've been a good husband to me, and I've been very happy. I just don't believe that what's all right for you and me may suit David at all. An education will equip him to make the choice, and gold can provide it."

Samuel shook his head. "Not while I'm alive. The gold stays hid."

There was a finality to his tone which Amity knew well enough not to argue with. She reminded herself that David was still young. She had sown the seed. There was time to nourish it. But over the ensuing months and years, whenever she referred to David's education, Samuel either ignored her or said, "Drop it." Once, when Amity tried to pursue the matter, he left the cabin and was gone for four days.

Gradually, what began as a small niggle of resentment turned into a corrosive sense of grievance in Amity. David was getting older. He was three already, and she recognized that he was a bright child. The important thing now was to provide for his future.

Samuel, true to his promise, had bought some readers, and David enjoyed looking at the pictures and hearing the stories. That winter Amity started teaching David his letters.

Samuel was proud of his son's new skill but wary. "He's too young," he said. "Don't push him."

"He's my son, too, remember? I'm the one who's with him all the time. I'll be the better judge of when he's ready."

"David is my responsibility until he comes of age. You can suggest, but the decisions are mine. He's *my* son, this is *my* house and you're *my* wife, and things will be done the way *I* want them."

Never before had he expressed so bluntly his view of their marriage. Amity made no reply. Instead, she put on her winter trousers, her mukluks and her parka. She picked up a knife and took one of the rifles from the rack over the fireplace.

"Where are you going?" Samuel asked.

"Out," she said, packing a backpack with some gear and a supply of food. She was aware of Samuel's half-amused observation, and it irked her. She paused with her hand on the latch.

"So David's your responsibility, and all I can do is suggest," she said. "Fine. Then there's not much point in suggesting anything to a man who's inflexible. Since David's your responsibility, you can look after him."

She opened the door and slammed it so hard that a small avalanche fell from the roof. By the time she had harnessed her own team of six malamutes, she was aware that Samuel had come out and was watching her, his amusement replaced by perplexity. "Where d'you aim to go?" he asked.

"Away from here. That's all you need to know."

"That's as may be, woman. But you're a damn fool if you don't have a destination in mind. You'll wander aimlessly out there until you're lost. I'll give you three days, and you'll be hammering on the door. Better pray the weather doesn't change."

He turned back to the cabin, leaving Amity with a feeling of angry impotence. Although she climbed onto her sled and whipped her team up with a fine show of bravado, she knew he was right. She needed a clear destination. She knew the area well for some twenty miles in any direction and decided that she would head west, roughly parallel with the Throndiuck until it joined the Yukon. Then she would follow the bigger river northwestwards to Alaska, where there were more settlements than in Canada.

The weather held for the rest of that day, and she set up camp in a place she knew from her earliest expeditions with a dog team. Before long, she had a cheerful fire going. Tomorrow she would hunt.

She sat by the fire for a long time after she had eaten, absorbing the enveloping silence that was like a tangible presence. She felt she was being touched by the magic of the north. Perhaps one needs to be alone to feel it. For the first time she had an inkling as to how Samuel felt about this land.

Amity crawled into her shelter, and once she was snug in her fur rugs, she found her thoughts turning to the drastic step she had just taken. To leave a cozy cabin in midwinter for no reason beyond a fit of pique seemed now to be close to insanity. The sensible thing would be to go back home in the morning. She knew Samuel well enough to guess that he would make no comment.

And if she did? Samuel would have won the right to dictate the way their lives should go from that time on. It wouldn't be a bad life, but it would be a hard one—unnecessarily hard, she thought bitterly, thinking of all the gold sitting in the river for the taking.

Amity sighed beneath her rug. All her life she had been poor. Now sheer good luck—Samuel's good luck—had placed within her grasp the power to change her destiny, and he would not allow her to make use of it. That was what she faced if she returned.

What if she went on? Uncertainty. She hadn't even taken the sensible precaution of putting a handful of nuggets in her pocket so that she could buy her passage back to England, or anywhere else. All the same, she was free. It might be only temporary, but for a while she was released from all responsibilities. The feeling was a novel one, and she liked it. She would carry on into Alaska until she found a settlement. After that, she would play it by ear.

The weather held the next day, and the dogs made good time despite the fact that they were breaking a fresh trail. Her hunting skill provided sufficient food for the dogs and for herself. By the following day, she had joined the Yukon. She was tempted by its relatively flat surface to take the sled on the faster terrain it offered, but she recalled Samuel's warning during her first winter that frozen rivers were unpredictable unless you knew them. Although it looked solid enough, the risk was too great, so she kept to the bank.

Still the weather held, but now she began to worry. Not only had she seen no hint of habitation yet but the novelty of freedom had worn off, and she was missing David. When she had stormed out, that was something she hadn't anticipated. If she could be sure of getting back before a change in conditions, she would swallow her pride and go, but she was beginning to think it wiser to continue—there must surely be something soon.

Midway through the next afternoon the expected change of

weather came. It began softly, a few gentle flakes, but Amity had been in the north long enough to know that the only good thing about that was that it gave her a warning. If she was lucky, it would enable her to dig herself in until the blizzard had blown itself out. She knew the theory of survival in such conditions: shelter first, then fire.

She staked the team across the trail she had been using. The snow would settle on the dogs and keep them warm. Then she constructed a shelter from the sled, its tarpaulin, and branches of spruce and jack pine. As the full force of the blizzard struck, Amity had time only to crawl under the tarpaulin and cover herself with her rugs. She also prayed.

She recalled Samuel's advice that in circumstances like this it was essential not to fall asleep, that the temptation to do so was overwhelming—and invariably fatal. The snow piled up against her bivouac, insulating her deceptively against the cold outside. Twice she dozed off, to wake again with a little start.

She sat up. It wasn't easy, because she had little headroom. The snow had drifted across the entrance, and its weight was pressing down on the tarpaulin roof, decreasing still further the space inside. She sang songs—ones she had sung at school and then all the hymns she knew. She made up stories to tell David at some future date.

Amity had no idea how long she spent beneath the snow. She knew only that it became increasingly difficult to resist the lure of sleep. Once, when it seemed the wind had stopped beating against her wall of spruce, she forced a hole and found the blizzard raging as strongly as ever. The sight was so depressing that she delayed trying again. At last, when she knew she must look, she pushed at the mound obscuring the opening, and ice-cold air flooded in. She enlarged the hole until she could peer through. A silent, dead world met her exhausted eyes. But no snow fell. Instead, the white globe of a full moon gleamed down from a clear, crisp sky. The storm was over. Now she could sleep.

SHE was shaken out of her slumber. Someone was bending over her, shaking her hard. She opened her heavy eyes, and a blue sky beamed down. Someone pulled her hood back from her face. "So it is you," said a familiar voice, and she found herself looking up into Jake Treviscoe's gray eyes. "Take it easy," he went on. "We'll get something warm into you. How long have you been here?"

"I've no idea," Amity told him. "I camped when the storm started." She tried to sit up, but her muscles wouldn't obey.

"Don't try to move until I can keep you warm," he warned. Soon he had a billycan of snow melting over a fire. When the coffee was made, he propped her up and fed her spoonfuls at a time.

"The dogs?" she whispered.

"Fine. Just hungry, but that's to be expected after five days."

Amity felt her strength returning as the warmth percolated down. When she had taken as much as he judged wise, Amity lay back and watched Treviscoe roast a jackrabbit. He removed her mittens and her mukluks and examined her fingers and toes.

He whistled. "By some miracle you've escaped frostbite. Let's get the blood moving before your luck gives out."

In between massaging her hands and feet and feeding her small quantities of jackrabbit, he erected the night's bivouac—a small tent of the type Samuel used. With Jake's help she crawled weakly into the tent. Jake followed, fastening the flap behind him, and arranged both his rugs and hers over the two of them. Then he drew her close to him.

Amity snuggled into the curve of his shoulder. This was an intimacy of which she had dreamed. She realized he offered it only for warmth, and she experienced a small pang of disappointment. Never mind, she told herself. This is more than you ever expected. Be content.

"Whatever would the neighbors say?" she said shyly.

He chuckled. "I'll not mention it if you don't."

Amity snuggled closer. "It's a bargain," she said.

There was a long, comfortable silence, which Jake eventually broke. "What on earth were you doing out here?" he asked.

"Samuel and I had a disagreement."

"It must have been mighty important to make you leave in the middle of winter."

"It seemed so at the time," she admitted reluctantly.

"I'll not ask what it was about, much as I'm curious to know, but what was York thinking of? Didn't he try to stop you?"

"He was just as angry as I was, though he did say I'd be back within three days."

"Then by now he's a worried man. How long had you been traveling before the storm hit?"

Amity considered. "I'm not really sure. Four days, maybe five."

"So you've been gone ten days already. If that blizzard reached your cabin, he'll have given you up for dead. We have to decide what to do. It will take more than a week to reach the next Eskimo settlement, maybe less to get home. Which is it to be?"

Amity hesitated. "There is another choice," she suggested tentatively. "I could come with you."

Jake was silent. He heard the wistfulness in her tone which told of a longing far greater than any married woman had a right to express, and he knew it met an answering chord in him. When he finally spoke, his voice was harsh. "Do you hate me, then?"

"Hate you? Why should you think such a thing?"

"Because if you came with me, it wouldn't be long before word got back to Samuel, and he'd load up his gun and come after us. A wife who leaves her husband because she can't stand the country is one thing. It doesn't make him a laughingstock. A wife who runs off with a wandering prospector is another matter."

"Are you afraid of him?"

"Of course I'm afraid of him. Samuel York's a damn good shot! Mrs. York, it's not as if we've fallen head over heels in love with one another. Then the game might be worth the candle, though I doubt it." He glanced down at her as he spoke and knew he had deliberately shattered a briefly held dream. He longed to hold her in his arms and kiss away the hurt in her eyes, but to do so would be to demolish his pretense of unconcern.

Amity was downcast. "Samuel called me a fool. I suppose he was right. I don't know whether he'll want me back, but I'll go."

"I don't think you need worry. If you've left him in the middle of winter with a child to cope with as well as a trapline, I should think he'll be overjoyed, even if he disguises it well."

The next day, Jake decided that they would wait until the following morning before they attempted the journey back to the York cabin, to let both Amity and the dog team recuperate fully. Amity learned that day that she owed her discovery to the fact that she had staked her team across the trail. The sound of a team traveling towards them had woken Amity's dogs. Jake had realized that the driver could not be far away. But it was only by chance that he found the small open hole by which air continued to enter Amity's little shelter.

Jake broke the trail back to Throndiuck, with Amity close behind. It wasn't until late afternoon four days later that they arrived back at the cabin. Samuel stood with a rifle cradled in his arms as the two teams approached. As soon as he recognized his own dogs, he put the gun down. "Took your time," he said to his wife.

She matched his taciturnity. "There was a bit of bad weather."

He nodded. Only then did he acknowledge her escort. "My thanks," he said. "You'll eat with us?"

"My pleasure," Jake replied.

"And David—how is he?" Amity asked anxiously.

"Bit late to start worrying, I'd have thought," Samuel said. "He's fine. Been asking for you."

Amity clambered off the sled and ran over to the cabin, leaving the two men to attend to the dogs.

"She coped well," Jake told his host.

"But she needed you to bring her back," Samuel said shrewdly.

Neither man referred to the matter again. Amity was too wrapped up in her son to notice the omission.

Jake Treviscoe slept on the floor by the fire. Amity listened to his breathing and recalled the one night when she had slept in his arms. That was how husbands and wives should sleep, she thought, though there had been a purely practical reason for it, and the feeling of being protected and cherished was certainly illusory. All the same, she missed it and longed for it again.

Their visitor breakfasted with them this time but refused Amity's invitation to stay. "I'll get back across the border," he said. "I feel easier in Alaska. Besides, I've my own trapline to see to."

When he had gone, Amity half expected Samuel to demand explanations, but he didn't refer to her adventure at all, except obliquely when he announced that now that she was back, he'd inspect his own traplines.

"It'll be a week or so," he said. "Can't say for sure."

Amity nodded, bewildered. It was as if nothing had happened. Surely he had some interest in what had gone on while she was away? Apparently not. All that mattered was that there was someone to look after David and thus free him to inspect his traps.

He was gone by noon, and Amity quickly slipped back into her routine, finding comfort in doing repetitive chores. Only at night, as she lay alone, did she indulge in waking dreams, in which, deplorably, her husband played no part.

It was three days after Samuel returned, when David was asleep and Amity was sewing by the fire, that Samuel asked suddenly, "Did you come back of your own accord?"

The question took her off guard. "Yes."

"My guess is you got into difficulties and needed Treviscoe's help. I'd not be surprised if he insisted you came back."

"You'd be wrong. He gave me the choice between going on to an Eskimo settlement in Alaska or coming back here. I chose to come back, because I hadn't the slightest idea what I wanted to do after I got to Alaska. Besides, I was missing David."

"I can never pretend you're not truthful," Samuel commented. "It sounds like a case of the devil, you know."

Amity put her sewing to one side and considered the matter. "That's part of it," she said. "It's not all of it. I discovered something. I discovered in myself a tiny part of the love you have for the land. I began to catch a glimpse of what it means to you."

"Then maybe the whole business was worthwhile. You took a gamble coming here. I hope you'll never regret it."

She turned to face him. "Samuel, I don't."

"Not now. Later."

"Why should I regret it later if I don't now?"

He shrugged. "I don't know. Maybe you never will. I'd like to think that."

That exchange subtly changed the atmosphere between them, and when they went to bed, their coming together was by mutual agreement if not by any overwhelming passion. Amity fell asleep that night more content than she had been for a long time.

Chapter Seven

As THE months and the years passed, Amity became increasingly content with the life she had chosen. She did not become as wholehearted in her love of the land as Samuel, but she understood the hold it exercised over him.

Then, shortly before his fifth birthday, David discovered the Throndiuck's secret. He had been fishing upstream of the cabin. A fish broke the surface of the water, and as it dropped back, the briefly ruffled surface caught and refracted the sunlight. David saw something gleam on the streambed. He was quickly barefoot and in the cold water. It took a few minutes' searching before he found it—a small stone about the size of a large pea. It gleamed less out of the water, but it was still attractive, so he took it back to the cabin.

"Look what I've found," he announced to Amity, who was hoeing the small vegetable patch. "A funny stone. It was in the river, near where the fish were rising."

Amity's hoe stopped moving while she thought rapidly. She knew of only one kind of stone "funny" enough to attract the attention of a child who had grown up playing with stones of infinite variety. If he had found gold, it would be best not to make too much of it. The hoe moved again. "In a minute, Davy. Let me finish this row."

When she had finished, she turned to her son. "Now then, what's this you've found?"

He placed his find in her upturned palm. "What is it, Mummy?"

Amity turned it over. No wonder it had caught the child's attention. It must be one of the largest nuggets she had seen. "I don't know," she lied. "It's certainly unusual. Maybe your father will know what it is. Why don't you put it indoors so you don't lose it?" She returned to her hoeing.

When Samuel came back from fetching wood, she made sure to warn him of David's discovery. As soon as David saw him, he came running out of the cabin shouting, "Look what I've found!"

Samuel studied the nugget, turning it over in his fingers. He nodded. "It's not bad as these things go."

"What is it? Mummy said she didn't know."

"She's probably not seen any before. It's called iron pyrites. People call it fool's gold. That's because some people who find it are foolish enough to think it really is gold."

"How d'you know it's not?" David asked, fascinated.

"Because I've seen the real thing. Most people haven't." He handed the nugget back to the boy and turned to Amity with a question about supper, all interest in David's find apparently gone.

David played with his stone for a day or two. Finally, when it had been forgotten, Amity quietly slipped it into a little pouch, which she tucked under one of the pallets in the fur store on which the pelts were stacked.

He did notice its absence eventually. "Where's that fool's stone?" he asked suddenly.

"Oh, you probably dropped it somewhere."

Eventually he came across another, smaller one, which Amity

wisely left around for a lot longer before it, too, disappeared. From time to time there were others, but both Amity and Samuel were confident that when the winter made the search for them impossible, David would forget about them.

"I'll whip them out of sight if he's got any when someone comes by," she promised Samuel. It didn't happen very often. Old Kislov had visited once, and two or three times a year some Indians stopped by. From time to time drifters spent the night, before going off in search of furs or gold or "excitement." The general opinion seemed to be that all three commodities were more easily come by in Alaska, but Samuel told her that was because there were no police there. The police from Fort Selkirk were supposed to patrol this part of the territory, but none had visited since Amity's arrival.

When spring came, they learned that David's interest had not died with the snow. Once the Throndiuck had settled down to its summer speed, hunting for fool's stones occupied him more frequently than his parents wished. They went to some pains to employ him elsewhere. There were his lessons with Amity and fishing and trapping trips with his father. Samuel was also teaching him about guns. None of these ruses succeeded entirely, and the pouch under the furs gradually filled.

AMITY stood the flatiron on the hearthstone to cool and glanced out the window at the sky. David should have come in by now for the afternoon's lessons. She went to the door and caught sight of his light brown hair down by the river. She saw something else, too.

Standing well back in the shadow of the trees on the other side of the Throndiuck were three men, who were watching David.

Amity slipped quickly back into the room, out of sight from the door. She had no doubt they had seen David discover something. Why else should they watch him from the semiconcealment of the trees? What should she do? If only there were a rear entrance, she could slip out and find Samuel. She could only hope that he'd return early. If she herself went out there with a gun and ordered David in, the men would know she knew there was gold. Instead, she decided she had to behave entirely normally and go out there, apparently angry with David for missing lessons, and drag him back in. If she acted well enough, she could have David in the cabin, the door barricaded and a gun loaded against their arrival. It was worth

a try. She pulled on her worsted jacket and slipped a sharp kitchen knife into the pocket.

She appeared at the door. "David! David, where are you?"

The light brown head bobbed up, startled by the unaccustomed sharpness of the call.

"There you are! What on earth do you think you're doing?" Amity was halfway to the river by now. "You know you were told not to wander off, and it's time for your arithmetic lesson." She grabbed his arm and hauled him away from the creek.

At that time of year the creek was shallow enough for a man to cross it on foot. When Amity thought she heard behind her a change in the sound of the river, she increased her pace, which

poor David protested loudly, twisting and turning in an attempt to free himself from his mother's grasp. They had not quite reached the cabin when the strangers caught up with them.

"That ain't no way to treat the boy," said the first man, a tall, bearded man with a thin, sallow face and lank, graying hair beneath his broad-brimmed hat. He caught Amity's wrist in so tight a grasp that she was obliged to let go of David.

"Well now, sonny," said the smallest of the three, a weaselly little man with a straggly beard. Amity noticed that his eyes were disconcertingly prominent and so pale a blue as to be almost colorless. "What was that you was playing with?" he coaxed. David was flattered by the interest. He held out his hand, and the man took the small piece of golden ore. "Hmm," the man said. "This all you found?"

David put his hand in his pocket and brought out two more.

The third stranger, a huge bear of a man with a lumbering gait, whistled. "You know what this is, boy?" he asked.

"Oh yes. Daddy told me. It's called fool's gold."

"Give it here." The first man's tone carried the authority of leadership, and he was obeyed accordingly. He examined the nugget carefully but without easing his grip on Amity's wrist. "If your daddy believes this is fool's gold, then he's the fool. This is the real thing. Boy, if you've got more of this, you could be richer than a king."

"There's lots more of it," David told him.

"Where?" The question was snapped.

"In the creek," David said.

"What do you do with it?" the weaselly man asked.

"Sometimes I put it back. Sometimes I bring it home. I usually lose it, though."

"Lose it, my eye," the first man said. He glanced at Amity. "What have you done with it?"

"Nothing. Like David says, we thought it was fool's gold. I suppose he dropped the pieces in the grass and just couldn't find them."

He twisted her arm behind her back until she cried out. "Don't take me for a fool. You knew what it was, and you hid it somewhere."

"It'll be inside," the big man suggested.

The leader nodded. "Bring the boy in." He shoved Amity forward, still holding her arm behind her back. The others followed, closing and barring the door once they were all inside.

As the leader pushed her across the threshold, the knife in her pocket banged against his leg, and as soon as they were inside, he investigated further.

He held up the knife. "Well now, d'you always take a knife with you to fetch in your son? Or could it be that you'd seen us watching him and guessed what we was seeing? Gold—that warrants a knife." He pulled her towards him, so that the tip of the knife nestled under her jaw. "Where is it, lady?"

"There isn't any," Amity insisted. "Yes, I saw you, but I didn't know who you were." She looked towards the door. "Why don't you go while you can? My husband will be back soon."

"Then we'll be waiting for him, won't we?" He turned to his companions. "How long since either of you had a woman?"

They considered, and concluded it amounted to months.

"Me, too," the leader said. He pressed the knife harder against her throat. "Lady, you're going to tell us where the gold's hid, and until you do, we're going to have you, one after the other, over and over again—and the boy's going to watch. D'you understand?"

Amity nodded as well as she could. Her mind was numb. "There is no gold," Amity whispered.

He removed the knife from her throat only as long as it took to slice it down her dress, scoring the skin of her belly on its way down.

David saw the blood and screamed, wriggling to free himself from the hold of the bearlike man. "Shut him up," the leader roared, and pushed her back onto the kitchen table.

Amity refused to cry out against the pain of his assault. She did not want to upset David any more than he was already. Let it be over soon, she prayed. Oh, God, let it be over soon. Her resolve crumbled when it was the big man's turn, and scream after scream was torn from her.

Those were the screams that Samuel heard on his way home through the forest. He ran, loading his gun, to the edge of the clearing. The door was shut—unusual in the summer—and Amity's dogs were restless on their stake line. The window was unshuttered, and through this Samuel could hear sounds—not screams now, but groans of misery. He cocked his rifle and, crouching, ran to the cabin.

One glance through the window was enough to tell him the worst, but it was some moments before he could get a clear line to one of the men without any risk of hitting his wife or son. In that brief interval David caught sight of his father and shouted, "Daddy!"

The leader glanced up. He fired his own revolver at the same time as Samuel squeezed the trigger. Samuel's aim, distracted by David's shout, grazed the man's arm.

The other bullet found its target, and Samuel slumped across the window frame, dead.

"Daddy!" David shrieked.

The butt of the pistol lashed out and hit the child on the side of the head. David slid in a crumpled heap on the floor. The leader savagely pulled Amity upright. "There's your husband, and there's your son," he said. "Now where's the gold?"

Amity shook her head to clear her thoughts from her agony. Her life depended upon it, though deep down in a sickening despair she knew the man dared not leave her alive, and with the death of David she had no wish to live. Very well. If die she must, she could at least do so with the satisfaction of denying them the gold.

"There is no gold," she whispered again.

The man caught her hair in an agonizingly tight grip and forced her head backwards till she thought her neck would crack. "Then I'll tell you what we're going to do, lady. We're going to go on until we've finished, and then we're going to kill you like we've killed them." He let go, so that her head flopped to one side.

Long before they had tired, she was barely conscious. Dimly she heard someone say, "Don't waste a bullet. She's half dead now."

"Best make sure."

"We will. We'll fire the place and scoot. Give it a day or two, and we stumble on the remains. Do a bit of prospecting and file our claim."

Little of this exchange penetrated Amity's semiconsciousness, but the word fire registered and was remembered sometime later, when an acrid burning scent reached her nostrils. It stung her eyes and made her gasp for breath. She tried to sit up but tumbled sideways off the table and lay in the clearer air of the floor beneath. She was lying beside the body of her son and put out a tentative hand to stroke for the last time the face she had held so dear.

He stirred under her touch, and she stared at him disbelievingly. But when he began to gasp for breath, the certainty that he was alive spurred her to action. She glanced round her and saw an orange flame run along the bottom of the screening blanket. Fire!

She half pulled, half pushed the boy towards the only opening she could see. The curtains were blazing, and there was someone lying over the frame—Samuel.

She had only the haziest memory of how or why he was there. It looked as if he needed help, too, but David came first. She dragged the boy onto his father's body and pushed David through the window. "The woods," she croaked. "Make for the woods."

She made no attempt to see whether he followed her order, but knelt down beside her husband. "Wake up, Samuel. Wake up. We've got to get out." She shook him, and when that had no effect, she pulled his head back and slapped his face. Her hand came away sticky. She stared at it, confused—blood. She looked at Samuel, shock clearing her perceptions. She remembered the firing of guns. Two guns, she thought, and looked down at Samuel again and was sickened. She had slapped the side of his face that was still there.

She might have knelt there, numbed and shaken, had not the primitive instinct of survival taken over. She scrambled through the now blazing window and tumbled onto the earth beneath. Picking herself up, she ran for the woods. Once there, she paused to vomit. Then she found David, and together they crouched among the trees and watched their home burn to the ground.

Some things didn't burn. The roof collapsed, smothering the remaining flames before they gained a hold on the fur store and the larder. The stone chimney, intact, poked its finger at the sky.

Once the fire was out, Amity's head cleared fast, and she recalled that final exchange, of which she had been barely aware at the time. "Give it a day or two," they had said. That wasn't long, she thought with panic. She and David must be gone before they came back. But where could they possibly go and feel safe from pursuit? Dyea? It was the only town she knew, but it was impossibly far away.

No. Not Dyea. Fort Selkirk. It was half the distance. Samuel had always avoided the place, but it was in Canada, and therefore the police would be there. They must be told Samuel had been murdered. Amity shuddered. She had no wish to describe any part of what had happened. Even thinking about it made her feel sick. But it was the only hope of bringing his murderers to justice. Once at Fort Selkirk, she would file her own claim to the gold. As soon as those men returned to assay what they took, they would find the claim already filed, and identify themselves as Samuel's killers.

She forced herself to think calmly. Time was of the essence. The pouch under the pallet in the fur store was charred and crumbling away when she tried to move it, but there was nothing wrong with the gold it contained. The larger stock, beneath the hearth, would be more difficult to reach because of the collapsed roof. And there was the awful awareness that Samuel lay buried beneath. Clothes were a problem, too. All she had was her ruined dress.

She sent David into the forest to fetch the cache of furs Samuel had hidden there. They were something else to trade in Fort Selkirk, but more important, some of them could be turned into a rough-and-ready skirt and waistcoat.

While the boy was gone, she estimated where the window had been, and made two sticks into a cross and hammered them into the ground with a stone. Then for a few minutes she stood in prayer.

It was easy to locate the loose hearthstone, but it was hard to get at it. Her bruised body cried out to her to be left alone, and she longed to give in. Her head told her otherwise, however, and she drove herself to clear the debris. This was one thing of which she could be sure: if the gold was there, she and David could go far, far away. At last she held the bulging pouch in her hands.

When she clambered back over the rubble, she found David sitting quietly on the pile of furs.

"There's a good boy," she said gently. "Now we're going to take the canoe down to Fort Selkirk and tell them what happened to Daddy, so they can catch the men and punish them. I want you to put these furs in the canoe—except these," she added, extracting three from the pile. Two would make a skirt, the third a waistcoat. "Then take food from the larder and stow it in the canoe, too. A lot of dried meat, some flour, beans, coffee. Will you do that?"

David made no answer, but he immediately set about doing as he was told. Amity looked after him, puzzled. Now she came to think about it, she hadn't had a word out of him since she found him—no words at all, and no tears. She shrugged. There would be time enough to worry about him when they were safely away from here.

She used a meat-hook from the larder to force holes in the caribou skin, and then she unlashed the rawhide from the sled to lace the various pieces of leather together. The sled would have to be left here and the dogs turned loose. When the men returned, she thought there was a good chance they'd assume the dogs had been stolen by Indians.

When everything was ready, she collected the dogs' harnesses. They were valuable, and there was no need to leave them behind. She took David's hand. "Come on. Let's say good-bye to Daddy."

She started to repeat the all-too-familiar words of the burial service, but tears began to choke her voice, and she dared not go on. Once she gave way, they would be finished. She took a deep breath. "That'll do," she told David. "We'll go now."

She unclipped the dogs and watched them bound uncertainly into the trees. They'd soon find their feet. The Indians often turned their dogs loose to scavenge for themselves. Usually they survived.

She pushed the canoe down the muddy ramp of the bank. As she did so, a thought struck her, and she looked back over her shoulder.

"Wait here," she said, and ran back to the cabin. She tore the cross out of the ground. Indians might steal dogs and root around in the debris for anything worth salvaging, but they wouldn't plant a cross for a man they didn't know was there. She carried the cross back to the canoe.

"We'll take it," she said. "It will help us remember Daddy."

Chapter Eight

AMITY secured the canoe to the little wooden landing stage at Fort Selkirk and helped David out. Hand in hand, they walked through the open gates in the palisade, a relic of the days when every settler lived in terror of Indian attack. There was a small church and a police post, and apart from that, she could see little to suggest it had more to offer than Dyea. The solitary store seemed no larger than Healy and Wilson's, though a shingle on the door announced that gold was assayed there. Amity made her way to the police post.

The North-West Mounted Police was a body of men whose legendary, though somewhat exaggerated, reputation for always bringing malefactors to justice brought comfort to the law abiding and encouraged the other sort to settle in Alaska.

Amity paused at the foot of the short flight of steps that raised the post above the mud of the main street. She steeled herself to be less than entirely truthful. She was going to tell them the sequence of events that resulted in Samuel's murder, but not her own ordeal. Murder was the more serious offense in the eyes of the law, and she hoped to see all three men hang for Samuel's. Rape was almost unmentionable, and as she knew from widespread exchanges heard in her youth, most people believed it to be impossible—maintaining that whatever the woman got, she had "asked for." She doubted whether the citizens of Fort Selkirk were any different from those of Wiltshire, and could face neither the pity of those who did believe her nor the disbelief of the others. She gripped David's hand and climbed the steps.

Sergeant Robert Woolacombe was a shrewd judge of character, an attribute honed by a quarter of a century of dealing with the highly individualistic characters who chose to scrape a living far from civilization. Amity's was a new face, though there was something familiar about the boy. He smiled and asked, "What can I do for you?"

Amity glanced up at the wall behind his head. A picture of the queen reassured her. "I have come to report a murder," she said.

Sergeant Woolacombe reached for some paper and a pencil. "Right," he said, keeping his voice matter-of-fact. "First of all, who are you?"

"Amity York."

He wrote it down and glanced at her curiously. "Would you be anything to do with Samuel York, up on the Throndiuck?"

"His wife—widow, I should say."

His interest sharpened. "Who's this?" he indicated David.

"Our son, David," she said.

He nodded. He would check, but he was fairly sure York had never come in to register the birth. Still, the likeness was indisputable.

"Widow, you said? So Samuel York's dead?"

"Murdered. That's why we're here." Amity shuddered. "He was shot in the face at point-blank range."

"I don't suppose you'd care to hazard a guess who might have done it?"

"I don't know their names, but there were three of them, and I can describe them quite well."

"You saw them?"

"I was there when they shot him. So was David."

The sergeant picked his words with care. "Mrs. . . . York, I don't wish to seem heartless, but how come they let you live?"

"They didn't. At least, they didn't think they had. They hit David with a pistol, knocking him unconscious, and then . . . they hit me with something and set fire to the cabin. I came to and got us out. I tried to get Samuel out. That's when I discovered he was dead."

From long experience, Sergeant Woolacombe knew instinctively at what point Amity's story deviated from the facts, but he chose not to comment. "Let me pull up a chair for you. Now, Mrs. York, I think you'd better tell me what happened, right from the beginning."

Amity recounted the events with scrupulous accuracy except for the rape. This became a beating to make her reveal the hiding place of whose existence the three men were so convinced. The sergeant noted a very ugly contusion on the side of the boy's head, but nothing on his mother's. He drew his own conclusions, which were not far from the truth, but all he said was, "You do realize you'll have to repeat all this in court, under oath, if we catch them?"

Amity hesitated, and agreed.

"I have to ask you a question you would probably rather I didn't. Was it really fool's gold, or was it the real thing?"

"It was real," she said. If she was going to file a claim, the fool's gold version would soon be seen to be a lie and would, in turn, cast doubt on the rest of her story.

"And was there a cache elsewhere?"

"Yes."

"And it's still there for them to hunt for when they come back?"

"I brought it with me."

"You haven't left it in the canoe, I hope?" he asked.

Amity forced a tight smile. "I'm not that foolish. It's here." The pouches were tied round her waist by means of a leather thong, and now she pulled them out and handed them to the sergeant.

He loosened the neck of each and peered inside before taking out two or three nuggets and looking at them carefully. "Oh, Mrs. York! What have you done?"

Amity was bewildered. "What do you mean what have I done?"

He didn't answer the question immediately. Instead, he asked another. "What do you intend to do with this?"

"I'm not really sure," she told him truthfully. "Go Outside or build a new life here. I don't know if Samuel's trapline gives him legal claim on the river, but if not, I want to file a claim in my name and one in David's."

"I think Samuel York has already done that," the sergeant told her. He went over to a shelf of files and ledgers and took one of them down. He leafed through it for several minutes. "Yes, here we are. I thought he had. Seven years ago."

"Seven!" Amity exclaimed. "Why, that was before I—" Best not go into that, she thought. "He never so much as hinted at it. Well," she went on, "if Samuel has already filed a claim, those men won't be able to do so. I suppose David or I will inherit it. Can you inherit a claim?"

"It can be done," the policeman told her cautiously. "You want to go back there and work it after all that's happened?"

Amity shuddered. "No. I intend to sell it. With this to demonstrate what's there, I shouldn't have much difficulty, should I?"

"None at all. When people see that, they'll be falling over themselves to get their own share. I fear that once you show the contents of those pouches outside these walls, you will open Pandora's box."

She nodded. "That was why Samuel would never use them." She looked up at him, her exhausted face suddenly gray and haggard. "But what good did his high-minded fancies do us? We'd have done better to collect as much as we could and get out and enjoy it. Now Samuel's dead. The very least I want out of this is to see the men who did it hang, but I want a decent life for my son, too. The gold will provide it, and selling the claim will provide some more."

"I'm afraid that's where you're wrong. Unfortunately, neither you nor your son can inherit it."

Amity sat very still. "Why not?"

"I'm afraid neither of you is a legitimate heir to Samuel York."

She looked at him in disbelief. "Is this some cruel joke?"

He shook his head, guessing that what he was going to have to tell her would come as an even greater cruelty. "Mrs. York, what were the circumstances of your . . . marriage . . . to Samuel York?"

Briefly, defiantly, Amity explained.

"Then I'm afraid I have to tell you that your . . . that Samuel was already married to someone else. They were married in the church here about nine years ago. She left him, I think not long afterwards. So far as I know, there was never a divorce. Yours was almost certainly a bigamous marriage, and that means the boy is . . ." His voice trailed off, unwilling to hurt more than it had to.

"Don't mince words, Sergeant," Amity said bitterly. "The boy's a bastard. That's what you were going to say." She paused and then, clutching at straws, said, "You don't think she could be dead?"

"Edda York? I doubt it. She was one of this world's survivors. I don't think Samuel thought so, either. He would have attempted to register the boy's birth with us if he had been legitimate."

Amity nodded. Now she knew why Dyea was so much more attractive to Samuel as a trading post. No one there knew about— What had he called her? Edda. Or did they? She cast her mind back to some of the half-finished sentences that had so puzzled her. She became dimly aware that the sergeant was speaking again.

"Mrs. . . . um . . . York," he began awkwardly, "there is one other matter. The gold. Who found it?"

"Each of us. Samuel had put together a little before I came, but it was a tiny proportion of what David and I found."

"Did Samuel know about the gold you and David collected?"
"Oh yes. He didn't approve, but he knew."
"Good. Then I'll assume he meant you to have it. You see, if he didn't know about it, you've no right to it—it goes to the real Mrs. York. As it is, I think we can safely assume it was his way of seeing you were looked after in case anything happened to him. Anyway, there's not much chance of Edda York reappearing, and even if she does, I'll stick to my opinion. I don't think you need worry."
"Just as well, since you've given me more than enough to worry about already," Amity told him. "Now I've a double reason for wanting those murderers brought to justice. They've not only killed a good man, they've left my son without a name. Oh, I know that was the position all along, but now it's known."
"I'm going to send someone up there right away—Trooper Jim Hillswick. He'll verify your story and see whether there's any sign of the men. I'd like you to stick around at least until he gets back. Why don't you go to the minister, tell him I sent you, and ask him to take you in for the time being?" He noted her cobbled together caribou skins. "They'll find you some decent clothes, at any rate."
Amity stiffened. "We don't need charity, Sergeant. We're more than capable of paying our way."
"That's right, but start waving those pouches around and you'll be lucky if robbed is the worst thing that happens to you. Your best protection for now is the church." He reached for his wide-brimmed hat. "I'll take you along there."
Amity hesitated. "I'd rather stand on my own feet, if you don't mind, but I'll be glad to be able to say you sent me."
"Suits me. Straight up the street, next to the church."
She walked out with her head held high, betokening a confidence she was far from feeling. How could life be so brutal? What had she, Amity York—no, Amity Jones, she thought bitterly—ever done to deserve a punishment as intense as this? Oh, Samuel, her heart cried out, how could you have done this to us?
By the time she defiantly introduced herself as Amity Jones to the minister and his wife, Mr. and Mrs. Pedmore, word had already spread through the handful of white settlers that the rarely seen Samuel York had been killed and his woman and her son had reported his murder to the police. Before long there was some speculation about her story. Amity was aware of curious glances

cast in her direction and that she must be a suspect in Samuel's death. It required an effort of will to go out.

Mr. Mauldon, the storekeeper, gave her a very fair price on her caribou skins and an even better one on the harnesses, which were particularly well made. This meant that Amity was solvent, provided she managed her resources thriftily.

David was her main source of anxiety. He had still not spoken since that fateful day, nor had he cried. Instead, he followed Amity like a little shadow, clinging to her, and at night awoke screaming from nightmares.

She guessed that the cause of his withdrawal was shock and that if only he could cry, the situation might be eased. She, too, had not yet grieved for Samuel, and she began to feel guilty because she had not done so. She knew it was not lack of feeling. She had not married Samuel out of love. But as the years had passed, she had come to feel something very close to it.

Amity had no idea what Trooper Hillswick would find at the cabin that would absolve her from any suggestion of guilt. She also had little faith in the prospect of his finding the murderers.

By the time Trooper Hillswick returned from the Throndiuck, the weather had begun to worsen. Amity was resigned to the fact that she and David would have to stay in Fort Selkirk until the thaw.

After hearing the younger man's report, Sergeant Woolacombe asked Amity to drop in for a chat.

Both men were at the police post when she got there. "Sit down, ma'am," the sergeant said. "Fetch Mrs. Jones some coffee, and give the boy there one of those lollipops."

Amity noted the use of the courtesy title with some amusement. She took the seat and drew David within the circle of her arm.

"You've had a long wait, Mrs. Jones. Young Jim here has mixed news for you. You'll be pleased to know what he found at your cabin does seem to support your story. He found the ruins, of course, and he found Samuel's body. He took the liberty of burying it in a more fitting manner just inside the trees. He also tells me someone had removed a hearthstone."

Amity threw him a startled look. "But Sergeant, I told you—"

"Yes, I know, but I didn't tell Jim. I wanted to know what he found for himself. There were a lot of bootmarks about, and they weren't all the same. There was the remains of a campfire that had been kept going for several days, so it looks as if there were some people around. Whether or not they were the three you mentioned, we don't know, of course. However, they had been panning—there were some small piles of spoil near the river. It's likely they took out what they could get and are hoping to register their own claim. Trouble is, Jim trailed them for quite a way. They kept on along the Throndiuck valley to the Yukon and then headed downstream for Alaska. No point in following them there, so he came home to report."

"Might they not double back?"

"They might, but I'd be surprised. My guess is, they've got what they came for—a good grubstake—and come spring, they'll just happen by your cabin, where they'll have the good fortune to discover gold, and one of them will try to file a claim then."

Amity nodded. "Another good reason to stay here till the thaw." She stood up. "I am grateful you no longer think I invented a story to cover my guilt. I am glad your trooper found traces of the three men."

"That wasn't what convinced me," Sergeant Woolacombe said. "It was Jim's finding the hole where you'd hammered in the cross. I don't reckon you're cold-blooded, and I don't reckon you're a hypocrite. It's my belief you'd have to be both to murder your husband, burn the house down and then wait around to put in a cross. Now, you might have made the cross on the way here—a sort of sentimental finishing touch to the story—but there wouldn't have been a small hole in the ground in the right spot."

Amity laughed nervously. "Then I'm luckier than I imagined." She sighed. "No need to keep the other secret now, is there?"

"I should, for now. You'll have to dip into the gold, of course, but do it gradually. Everybody finds the odd bit here and there."

"Holding back the flood as long as possible, Sergeant?"

"Something like that," he said wryly.

ONCE it became clear that the return of Trooper Hillswick would not lead to the arrest of Amity Jones, attitudes towards her changed significantly. The minister's quiet suggestion that she was more sinned against than sinning was held to have some merit.

To the other citizens of Fort Selkirk, Amity seemed a remarkably self-possessed woman. A hard woman, but up here and on her own, such hardness would serve her well.

Amity had still not grieved for Samuel, nor had she found any outlet for the anger gnawing away inside her—anger at the injustices life had thrown at her. She knew that somewhere deep inside her was a core of molten emotion that she wished could somehow come to the surface, erupt and leave her feeling purged. Then perhaps she would have some idea of what she wanted to do. At the moment she had none, except to see Samuel's murderers brought to justice.

The suspicion, and later the certainty, that she was pregnant concentrated her mind. It was just possible that the child was Samuel's, but it was more likely that it had been implanted by one of the murderers. She was revolted by the probability. In England, most towns had women who, for a price, would relieve sufferers of their burden, but Amity doubted if the tiny white community at Fort Selkirk boasted such. And even if it did, secrecy would be impossible. Only one other option presented itself: to leave Fort Selkirk now, before her condition became apparent, and establish herself elsewhere until the baby was born. Then, if it bore no resemblance to Samuel, she would smother it.

She had lived here long enough to know the difficulties of constructing a shelter capable of seeing herself and David through the winter, of heating it, and of supplying herself with enough food to prevent starvation. But it was possible. Many prospectors overwintered in substantial tents equipped with a stove, and in winter, game could be kept indefinitely.

When Sergeant Woolacombe discovered her plan to leave, he tried to discourage her.

"No, Sergeant," she said. "I know it seems foolhardy, but I cannot stay here all winter. I'm a parasite here, and I don't like the feeling."

"Where do you intend to go?"

"I don't know. I can only tell you that you won't find us back at Samuel's claim, and I'm not going to Dyea."

Once he was convinced that Amity could not be persuaded to change her mind, Sergeant Woolacombe helped her by obtaining for her a second canoe to carry her equipment, which soon included a tent, a small stove and its chimney, and supplies for the winter. The fact that she paid for all these things with nuggets of pure gold caused no little stir. She shrugged when Mr. Mauldon commented.

"My hus— Samuel had been in the north a long time. He picked up the odd piece here and there. Where others would have rushed to spend it, he preferred to depend on his trapping. This was nothing but a small reserve, just in case."

She took care that no one saw the precise size of the small reserve, but even so, there was much whispering in corners, and it was not forgotten that Samuel York had filed a mineral claim on his stretch of the creek. As soon as the thaw came . . . People kept thoughts such as these very much to themselves, but they laid their plans with care in the hopes the pickings would be big.

AMITY and David sped down the Yukon River with no thought of leaving it until they had passed the sharp bend where the Stewart River entered it from the east. For reasons which she had not attempted to analyze, she was heading for the Alaskan border. They therefore went west, up a sizable tributary creek.

Her knowledge of the region told her that sooner or later the creek would narrow and become too fast for her safely to be able to negotiate it with the second canoe in tow. It therefore became a matter of some urgency to select a place to settle. She found it at last—a sheltered place where the bank shelved and led to a cleft between timbered hills. Amity hauled the canoes out of the water and looked about. "I think this is it, Davy," she said.

Amity was touched by how hard the child worked to help her bring everything ashore and to assist his mother with the tent. The stove had to wait. She would need to make a small sled to get it in place, but there was plenty of dry timber around and a fire was soon burning in front of their new home.

"Isn't this exciting?" Amity said, as much to encourage them both as an expression of her own opinion. David stared at her with wide-open eyes, and she thought he nodded, but he said nothing.

In the days that followed, Amity watched the sky anxiously and sent up prayers of gratitude that her years with Samuel York had not only taught her the skills needed in this harsh land but had also hardened her enough to put them into practice even in her present condition.

JAKE Treviscoe's arrival was unexpected. Amity's initial delight at seeing him step ashore and beach his canoe was diluted by the certainty that there would be questions to answer.

"So it is you," he said. "I thought it might be."

"Why should you have thought that?" she asked.

"I've been up to the Throndiuck and saw the ruins. The Indians told me you'd gone to Fort Selkirk. I wasn't so sure. Saw the smoke and thought I'd investigate."

"The Indians were quite right," she told him. "It was too . . . restricting, so we came away."

"Must have been bad to drive you off so close to winter," he commented. When Amity made no reply, he went on. "Need any help? Don't mind chopping wood if it gets me one of your stews."

"Chopping wood would be perfect," she said. "I've been despairing of getting enough together to see us through the winter."

He pitched his own small tent close by hers and took his axe into the woods. That evening he looked around him approvingly as he tucked into the promised stew. "You've picked a good spot, Mrs. York, though you'd have done better to overwinter in Fort Selkirk."

"Jones," Amity corrected him.

He looked bemused. "I don't follow."

"Jones," she repeated. "I've discovered Samuel already had a wife, so I'm still Amity Jones, but I prefer 'Mrs.' for David's sake."

"So you discovered that, did you?"

"You knew?"

He sounded apologetic. "We all knew. That's to say, we knew he had had a wife and she left him. We thought you were a wife left behind in England, and that the marriage to Edda was the bigamous one. She was gone, so why upset you?"

Amity considered his words. "Samuel had been here for fifteen years. How could I possibly have been a wife left behind?"

"Been in Canada that long, had he? He'd been in the north for only four, maybe five, years when you came out. It would have made you a very young bride, but we weren't to know your age."

"But later, when I told you I had been a mail-order bride, you must have realized."

"It occurred to me," he admitted. "But if I'd told you there was a strong chance you weren't married then, when you were expecting David, would it have made your life any easier?"

"No," Amity agreed.

"How did you find out? Is that why you burned the place down?"

He was so wide of the mark that Amity laughed. "I was in complete ignorance of Edda York until I went to Fort Selkirk. I assumed David and I would inherit Samuel's claim. That's when I discovered we didn't—and why."

"So the grave is Samuel's?"

Amity nodded. Reluctantly, then, she told him what she'd told the police. He'd been a good friend, and if anyone ought to be told, it was he.

He listened without comment until she had finished. "Was it gold or pyrites?" he asked when she was done.

She hesitated briefly. "Gold."

"You know what that means? If you go Outside with what I presume you've got, this territory will be overrun within the year."

"Then you'd better file your own claim first," she said bitterly.

"Maybe I will at that, but not just yet." He looked about him. "Is this where you intend to settle?"

"I don't know. Why?"

"You couldn't have picked a better place if there is a rush. If my reckoning is correct, Alaska is just across the creek. You're just about on the border between Canada and Alaska."

"The gold we found was in the Throndiuck, not here."

"If there's gold worth taking on the Throndiuck, this whole place will be saturated with diggings. I'll guess there's gold in this creek, too. You could start that lodging house after all."

"I think I'll concentrate on getting through this winter," she said.

Jake Treviscoe looked at her consideringly. "Let me at least start you a cabin," he suggested. "If I start building it round the tent, it'll afford a little extra protection even if it only gets to four or five logs up before winter. What do you say?"

Amity hesitated. It was a generous offer, but she was unsure what it implied about his future intentions. She had come here to have an unwanted child in seclusion. The last thing she wanted was anyone around to prevent the execution of her plan after it was born.

"You must have more pressing things to do," she said.

"If I had, I wouldn't have offered." He glanced at her shrewdly. "Don't worry. You've only got to say the word and I'll be gone at any time."

Amity smiled hesitantly. "In that case . . ."

"Good. It's settled."

He was as good as his word, and a small cabin grew up slowly round the tent. After about a week he disappeared for several days without saying good-bye. When he reappeared, he had acquired a small sled in need of repair and three half-starved huskies.

"Throw-outs," he told Amity. "They didn't thrive during the summer, so they were going to be killed to feed the ones that did. Most villages have a few like this every fall. Feed them and they'll do."

"And the sled and harnesses?" Amity knew very well that no one would have thrown such valuable items in with the dogs.

"I did a deal. When you're running your lodging house, you can let me lodge free in return."

The dogs were pretty poor, but Jake proved right about the effects of feeding them. At first Amity was worried they would eat her out of house and home, but gradually, as they filled out and sleekened, their appetites became more normal and they looked less of a liability.

She and Jake Treviscoe were sitting by the stove one evening after David had been put to bed. Jake glanced across at the small figure.

"I don't think I've heard that child speak since I've been here."

"He hasn't spoken a word since Samuel was killed. He just follows me around all the time."

"Doesn't it worry you?"

"Of course it worries me!" she snapped, betraying the depth of her anxiety. "He was a chatterbox, if you remember. Now, nothing. It's odd, too. I don't think he's shed so much as a tear for his father, yet they were very close. I sometimes wonder if it would be better if he *did* cry."

Jake threw another log in the stove. "And have you grieved?"

"Of course. Not a day has passed when I haven't missed Samuel."

"That's not quite what I meant."

"You mean have *I* cried? What good would it do?"

The question was so obviously rhetorical that Jake made no attempt to answer it. After a while he said, "Whatever your motives for coming here, it's my belief you grew very fond of Samuel York."

"We got along."

"It was more than that, I think," he said gently.

Amity thought about it. "I suppose so. At least it was after that childish escapade when I ran away. Somehow it seemed to make things better. Do you know, Samuel never once asked for an apology. All he ever asked was whether I came back of my own accord."

"He was always a man to work out what was really important."

Amity had never thought about him in those terms, and she realized Jake was right. Samuel had always known what really mattered. For a brief moment tears pricked the corners of her eyes. She put up an impatient hand to brush them away and found a large square of linen being put in it. She smiled weakly. "I'm sorry. I'm being silly."

"Never apologize for being human," he said.

"You see, Samuel's death was such a . . . a waste." The tears were more difficult to control now, and the handkerchief was more necessary. She looked up at Jake. "Why did it have to happen? And why to him?"

He put his arm round her and turned her towards him. It was a caring, tender gesture that raised the floodgates. Amity clung to him while the grief that had been hidden for months came bursting to the surface, racking her body with great, heaving sobs.

"I'm behaving like a ten-year-old," she said eventually.

"You're behaving like a woman who's lost her husband in the most appalling manner," he corrected her.

Amity sniffed again, sobs shaking her shoulders. "But that's just it. He wasn't my husband. He was somebody else's."

"But he regarded you as his wife. Surely that's all that matters?"

"I suppose so," Amity said doubtfully. "But why did he do it?"

"Marry you bigamously, you mean? I suppose he was lonely. At least he went through a form of marriage. Most men up here wouldn't have bothered."

"But I wouldn't have come out here if there hadn't been a marriage."

"Would marriage to your butcher have been preferable?"

"You remember that?" Amity was surprised. She considered his question. "No, I don't think it would have been."

"So Samuel's little deceit gave you a better life than you might otherwise have had. It can't have been too reprehensible, can it?"

"I suppose not."

Jake put his finger under her chin and kissed her damp cheek. "I reckon you'll sleep now," he said.

WHEN Amity awoke next morning, she felt more refreshed than she had been for a long, long time. Over the next few days she realized how great a difference the capacity for tears had made to her spirits. She still found herself weeping a little from time to time, but each bout was short-lived, and she felt better afterwards.

Soon the first thin fall of snow covered the ground, and after that, there were few nights without snow. Now another worry replaced any old ones Amity might have had. She was very aware that her girth was increasing. She had no desire to spoil the pleasant understanding that seemed to exist between her and Jake, but she did not want him to know of her condition, since she had a shrewd idea he would insist on staying with her. Had she been sure the child was Samuel's, there was no one she would sooner have with her. Instead, she had her own plans for this child, and she suspected Jake would be appalled if he learned of her intentions.

As she became increasingly conscious of her size, she became convinced that he suspected something. She was sure she caught him glancing at her speculatively, and found herself trying to devise a way of asking him to leave without offending him. Finally, reluctantly, she decided that it would be best to waste no more time before broaching the subject. She chose suppertime.

"You'll be wanting to be gone, Jake," she said.

"Will I?"

"If you don't go soon, you'll not get down the creek before winter. And it's wrong to keep you here when you could be about your own business."

"You're not keeping me. I don't stay anywhere if I don't want to."

Amity frowned. It was as if he were deliberately not understanding her. "It seems to me this would be a good time for you to go."

"Are you telling me to get out?"

The one thing Amity had hoped to avoid was telling him anything quite that bluntly. "In a way, I suppose I am," she admitted.

"Then why beat about the bush? If you don't want me, I'll go." He paused and looked at her. "But if you think you may need me, I'll stay. You've only to say the word."

When Amity remained silent, Jake said, "All right, I'll be gone in the morning." He got to his feet. "Then I'll turn in. There is just one thing. You won't forget our deal?" He jerked his head towards the door. "The team out there. Free board and lodging when you've a lodging house."

Amity laughed self-consciously, unsure to what extent he was to be taken seriously. "I shan't forget," she said.

Chapter Nine

PANDORA—Amity recalled Sergeant Woolacombe's comment, and the name seemed appropriate—was born in a whiteout, with the temperature nudging thirty below. Her birth, like David's, was mercifully straightforward, but the weather thwarted Amity's plan to set her son some task outside the tent when her time came. He helped with the hot water and blankets, then sat, silent and wide-eyed, throughout the labor.

After the birth she wrapped the baby in a warmed blanket and looked down at the bundle in her arms, feeling none of the repugnance she had anticipated. Of one thing she was sure: this was no child of Samuel's. The hair was fair and the eyes a deep sapphire blue. Although she had done nothing to encourage the infant to breathe, it appeared to be breathing quite normally. "Get me some warm water, Davy," she said, and she unwrapped and bathed the child. As it wriggled and gurgled in her arms, the child stirred instincts Amity would rather have left unstirred. She unfastened her parka and the shirt beneath and held the child to her breast, all thoughts of smothering her gone. Amity could not envisage loving a child conceived as this one had been, but the child itself was innocent. Come the thaw, she would take her Outside and find an orphanage to take her. In the meantime she would do the best she could.

She smiled across at David. "This is your little sister," she told him. "We shall have to look after her well in this cold weather."

David, still as silent as ever, became Amity's right arm. It fell to him to keep the family supplied with rabbits and other animals small enough to be caught in snares. It sometimes seemed to Amity that he was becoming old before his time, especially when she saw him sitting by the stove, his serious little face watching gravely as she attended to Pandora. Amity tried to involve him in the simple games she played with the baby, but he seemed to have lost the gift of play along with that of speech, and moved like an elder statesman.

Thus she was startled one afternoon to see him running as fast as his little fur-clad legs would carry him out of the forest and into their clearing. Amity snatched up the rifle and ran to meet him, wondering what could have induced this uncharacteristic rush.

He grabbed the bottom of her parka and dragged her back into the tent, looking fearfully over his shoulder.

"What is it, Davy?" she asked.

There was no reply of course. Amity put her head outside the door flap. There was still no sign of anything to account for David's agitation. She uncocked the rifle and stood it against the canvas side before taking David in her arms. "There's nothing there, my love."

David shook his head, peering fearfully at the entrance.

It must have been some ten minutes later when their three huskies gave the kind of roar which heralded the arrival of strangers.

Amity looked out. A man was stumbling out of the trees. He wore one snowshoe and was supported on a crudely made crutch. Without a second thought she pulled up her parka hood and ran towards him.

A few feet from him she pulled herself up short, her stomach lurching sickeningly. Something about him was familiar. His straggling beard and mustache were encrusted with ice, and his drawn cheeks bore the telltale white patches of frostbite, but it was the eyes that looked out from beneath the fur peak of his muskrat cap that transfixed Amity's attention. They were pale blue, watery and abnormally prominent. One of Samuel's murderers. One of the men who raped her. Even, possibly, Pandora's father.

Amity shuddered and backed away. "Go away!" she shouted. "Go back. You can't come here. We don't want you. Go away."

It was obvious he didn't recognize her. Indeed, she was unsure whether he even heard her, for he didn't falter in his stumbling progress. Amity continued to retreat from him. She could see now that one leg was fractured. The foot was almost certainly frostbitten, and if it thawed out, it would become gangrenous. Amity realized with savage satisfaction that the man was as good as dead.

They were almost at the half-finished cabin wall now, and Amity caught sight of David in the doorway. She turned to tell him to go back inside and realized that his terrified eyes were fixed on the visitor and that he had dragged the loaded rifle from the tent. She knew then that what had terrified the boy in the forest was not the sight of an injured man stumbling towards him. He, too, had recognized the man as one of Samuel's slayers.

"I don't want that, Davy," she said, thinking he had brought the gun out to her. "Take it back in and look after Pandora."

David appeared not to have heard. It took him both hands to

cock the weapon, and then, that accomplished, he pointed it firmly at his father's killer. "No, David!" Amity screamed. She lunged towards him, but she was too late. He fired, and the recoil forced the gun out of his hands. A sudden cry was wrenched from the stranger, and he fell into the snow.

She rushed over to David and caught him in her arms. Should she praise him for having taken revenge on so foul a beast? Or should she reprimand him for killing anyone, however deserving?

She did neither, but gently led him into the tent. For a long time she sat on the edge of the sleeping platform with her arms round her son, rocking him as she had done when he was a baby.

Finally she released him. "David, I want you to stay here with Pandora. I've got to do some . . . some tidying up outside."

She pulled her hood over her head and went out into the cold. The body would probably have stiffened already, she thought, but it must be moved. The last thing she needed was scavengers near their home. She must drag the body off and cover it with snow.

When she came alongside the body, she noticed a superficial wound at the top of the thigh of the unbroken leg. David's bullet could not possibly have killed the man. Presumably, in his weakened state, the impact had knocked him over. The cold and his previous condition had been enough to do the rest. She couldn't help but feel savagely glad that he was dead.

Amity took a deep breath and started to work. She harnessed the small team to the sled before loading the body. Then she leaped on the sled's runners and sent the team charging into the forest.

When she returned to the tent two hours later, she put her arms around David and gave him a hug. "The bullet hit his leg, Davy. He was already dying. You were very brave to defend us. Now we should get some sleep."

A FEW days after this traumatic event, Amity heard her name being called. She reached for the rifle and went outside. A man was coming towards her with a dog team, though he was still far away.

"Amity!" he called. "Amity Jones!"

Between his fur-trimmed hood and beard, it was impossible to make out his features, but something about him was familiar.

"Amity?" There was no mistaking the voice this time, and Amity dropped the gun and ran towards him.

"Jake? Oh, Jake, you can't know how glad I am to see you," she cried. It did not seem the least bit strange that as she reached him, he leaped off the runners and his arms opened out to enfold her. She clung to him, weeping, for several minutes, and he held her close without a word. Only when she glanced up at him, with tears on her cheeks, did he comment.

"Funny way to show it," he said.

Despite the pent-up strain she had been under for the past few days, Amity chuckled and half sobbed.

Jake's lips brushed the hair escaping from her hood. "That's better," he said. "Now tell me what it's all about."

Briefly Amity did so.

"Are you sure he was one of the three men?" he asked.

"Oh yes. I wasn't mistaken, and neither was David."

"No, I suppose that's to be expected. Tell me about the baby."

"What do you know about a baby?" she asked.

"For heaven's sake, woman, do you imagine I hadn't realized you were increasing when I was here in the fall? You kicked me out then, remember? I had a strong suspicion it was because you didn't want me around when it was born."

His voice was harsh, and it frightened her a little. She wrenched herself from his arms. "Come and see for yourself," she snapped. She led the way to the tent, where they found David and Pandora safe and warm.

She kissed the boy warmly. "I've a nice surprise for you. You remember Mr. Treviscoe?"

Jake rumpled David's hair. "How are you, Davy boy?" he asked, and then, ignoring the absence of an answer, "How do you like your little sister?"

David said nothing and clung to Amity's caribou-clad legs, but he peeped over his shoulder with the ghost of a shy smile. This was more than Jake had expected. He had already admired Pandora.

"I don't recall when I last saw hair that color," he said.

"Babies rarely stay that fair," Amity told him.

"I can't see much resemblance to either of her parents."

Amity had prepared herself for that comment. "Neither can I. It's my guess she takes after her grandparents. She's got my mother's eyes, but I've no idea to what extent she takes after Samuel's parents."

"These things do sometimes skip a generation," Jake agreed, and dropped the matter. Amity, engaged in preparing the baby for bed, failed to catch the quick speculative glance he cast her.

Jake crossed the tent and undid his backpack. He picked up a candlelike object wrapped in paper and handed it to David.

David unwrapped the paper, and his face lit up with pleasure at the long golden twist of barley sugar that was revealed.

"You've been to Dyea!" Amity exclaimed.

"And Juneau. Did you know word had got out about the gold?"

She stared at him. "Nonsense. It can't have. Not yet."

"Well, it has. You wouldn't recognize Dyea. White men outnumber Indians now. They're congregating at the foot of the Chilkoot Pass and plodding their way up it in single file. They say the North-West Mounted Police have established the border at the top, and they're not letting anyone over who hasn't got a year's supplies with him. I took one look, asked a few questions, and quit."

"For Juneau?"

"Right. Lots of boats waiting in Juneau to bring more prospectors out here come the thaw."

Amity shook her head. "I can't believe it's happened so quickly."

"Why not? It only needed one person to write one letter from Fort Selkirk telling a friend to get up there by spring and they'd make their fortune. How many friends do you think would be able to resist the temptation to let someone else in on the secret?"

Put like that, it was all too likely. "But why did you go on to Juneau?"

Instead of answering, he rooted around in his pack until he came up with a flat packet wrapped in oilskins. "Open that," he told Amity.

She did and found a large envelope containing some papers. She seemed bemused by the contents. "Jake, I don't understand."

"I've registered your claims to this land on both sides of the creek, both as a settler and as a prospector. This side you're in Canada, and over the creek it's Alaska. You can prospect it yourself, you can charge a toll for those who want to use the river, you can work the land, or you can wait till the strike is at its peak, sell up and retire to England a rich woman."

"You did all this in Juneau?"

"Of course not. Only the Alaskan claims can be registered there. I filed the others in Fort Selkirk."

"Where, like Samuel, you never go."

He fingered his beard. "I took a chance no one would know me."

Amity looked at her name on the certificates. "I'm very grateful," she began. "You've been to a considerable amount of trouble." She glanced at him. "Are they legal if someone else obtains them?"

"I signed as your agent. Besides, I filed on my own behalf as well, in Juneau, which quietened any suspicions there might have been. I was disinclined to give my name in Fort Selkirk."

Amity studied the Canadian certificates. "It says here, 'John Biscoe, his mark,' " she said quizzically.

He grinned. "Suddenly discovered I'd never learned to write. I had to give them some sort of name," he explained apologetically. "It's not my fault if the clerk got it a bit wrong."

Amity rewrapped the certificates before putting them away.

"What do you intend to do now, Amity?"

"Since discovering you've filed claims for me? It's hardly had time to sink in."

"May I make a suggestion? You've got a head start on all those hopefuls dragging themselves over the Chilkoot. Why don't you work your claims on both sides of the creek? I'll show you how to pan. If you strike gold, you'll be able to put away a useful nest egg. Then, if you want to, you can sell your claims and leave."

"And if I don't strike gold?"

He shrugged. "You'll be no worse off than you are now."

Amity considered. "I'll think about it."

She lay awake most of the night doing exactly that, and when morning came, she told Jake she would follow his advice.

"You won't mind if I hang around till the thaw?" he asked.

"I'm banking on it. You're going to show me how to pan."

"Right. First we dig," Jake told her. "We dig as much muck out as we can, and then when the rivers are flowing once more, we'll sift it through a rocker and see what we've got there."

Amity stared at him. "How do we dig through frozen soil?"

"Thaw it first."

Day after day they lit fires on the ground. Amity discovered that after twenty-four hours of burning, the ground beneath the fire could be dug to a depth of about a foot. The earth was piled up, and a new fire lit in the hole to thaw out the next foot or so of dirt. David was given the task of minding the fires. A number of these rudimentary mines were dug in various places on both sides of the river.

Jake did most of the digging and also constructed a sluice box and a cradle, which would be used when there was running water once more to wash the gold out of the dirt. Amity helped whenever she could, but Pandora, and cooking for them all, occupied her fairly fully.

The days became noticeably warmer, and when the thaw began, Jake taught Amity and her son how to take a shovelful of river silt, tip it into something that looked like a large, handleless frying pan, add river water and then circulate the water to wash the lighter soil over the rim. The heavier gold would remain behind.

David's interest soon waned, and the work fell largely to Amity, while Jake operated a sluice and rocker. David looked after Pandora and sometimes fished at a quiet spot upstream of the claim. It was from here that he came running back to Amity, shouting excitedly and holding his hand out in front of him. "Mummy, Mummy, look what I've found!"

Amity dropped her pan and Jake his shovel, and they rushed over to the boy. They stared in disbelief. In his hand David held nearly a quarter of an ounce of raw gold.

The gold was not the only reason for their disbelief. Amity swept David into her arms and kissed him. "You clever, clever boy," she said, tears running down her cheeks. And if David thought she was referring to his find, Jake knew her delight was due primarily to the sound of her son's voice.

"You've done well, Davy," he said. "Show us where you found it."

David led them upstream to the spot where he had been fishing. Just emerging from the bank, beneath a thin layer of stone fractured by the frost, was a yellow band nearly half an inch thick.

Jake knelt down and lifted the topmost slab. The vein was six inches across. He looked up at Amity, standing behind him with her arm round David. "We've done it," he said softly.

"How far back does it go?" Amity asked.

"We'll soon find out. Even if this was all there were, we'd be rich. I've never seen anything like it."

"How come David only just found it?" she asked. "We were here in the autumn, and I know he fished from that same spot."

"My guess is that it took this winter's freeze to split the rock." Jake stood up. "We can pan it to start with, but I'll move the sluice and the rocker closer. Let's keep our fingers crossed and work this as long as we can."

She chuckled. "With our fingers crossed? Won't that hold us up?"

Jake stared at her blankly for a moment; then he picked up a handful of snow and pressed it into a ball. As Amity saw his arm lifted to throw it, she picked up her skirts and ran. The snowball hit her between the shoulder blades, and she stumbled on the uneven ground. As she put out a hand to save herself, she felt her other hand grabbed by Jake and her fall arrested. She straightened up, laughing.

"Thank you," she gasped.

"For the snowball or the helping hand?" Jake still held her and was looking into her face. He drew her to him and kissed her, briefly at first and then, when she made no attempt to draw away, more lingeringly. She responded with an eagerness that took her by surprise.

His lips became more urgent and demanding, and there was no reluctance in Amity's response. She had an inner warmth, an excitement, that was entirely new to her. She knew only that she longed for it to go on and on.

It was David who broke the spell. He tugged at his mother's skirt. "Pandora's crying," he said.

She was, quite loudly, and Amity withdrew reluctantly from Jake's hold. "I must go," she said, smiling shyly.

"Of course you must. We've no need to hurry."

The comment flustered her, because she thought she knew what he meant, but was unsure what her own reaction should be. She was glad of the need to run back to Pandora and feed her.

Amity and David spent the afternoon panning, while Jake moved the heavier equipment closer. David chatted the whole time, talking partly to himself and partly to his mother. But Amity's mind was far away. The warmth of Jake's embrace remained with her, casting a shimmer of rosy light over everything she did. Did she love Jake? Equally important, did he love her? If he did, why had he never given the slightest indication of it before? Besides, Amity reminded herself, all Jake had done was to kiss her.

When supper was over, Pandora sound asleep and David tucked up snugly, Amity ducked out from the tent and joined Jake, who was perched on the half-built wall of the cabin.

"I ought to finish this," he said, patting the logs. "That's what I came back to do, you know."

"Is there much point? It's not as if we were planning to stay. Now that we've found a rich vein, let's take what we can and get out."

"I've a hunch the vein may cross the river," he told her, "and that's filed in my name. When we've taken what we can from today's strike, I'd like to work my own claim for a while."

Amity was aware of a little tinge of disappointment. It began to sound as if Jake would do whatever he wanted, even if it meant they went their separate ways. "No reason why you shouldn't finish the cabin for your own use," she suggested.

"I thought you intended to sell your claim on the basis of all the gold we've found here."

Amity thought about that. "Yes, but surely I can sell the claim and leave you with some sort of squatter's right to the cabin?"

"Maybe. Right now we need all our time to work the claim. If it begins to peter out, I'll think about the cabin again."

"We need to do some hunting, too," Amity told him. "I'll take Pandora with me tomorrow and see what I can get."

"Hunting's a man's job."

"So is loading mud into a cradle, and I can tell you which of the two I'd rather do." She laughed. "I expect David's asleep now. I am going indoors."

Jake sprang down from the wall and followed her. "One way or another, you're quite a determined woman," he said.

She glanced at him over her shoulder. "I don't think the other sort lasts long up here. Do you?"

Inside, David was sleeping as soundly as his sister. Jake went over to the small bundle of fur with the fair hair not quite hidden. With one finger he gently lifted some of the fur away from Pandora's face. He smiled and turned to Amity. "If she keeps that hair, she'll turn a few heads when she's older."

"I don't know that turning heads is anything to be proud of," replied Amity harshly, and turned to make coffee. She had become fond of Pandora, but she still resented the baby's existence and found it quite unacceptable that any child conceived the way she had been should provoke compliments.

Jake looked surprised. "As you will," he said, and came back to the stove, took the coffeepot out of her hand and replaced it on the stove lid. "Later maybe," he said, taking her in his arms once more.

Amity needed no encouragement to raise her lips to his to receive kisses which, while they began tenderly, soon became demanding and urgent as his hands caressed her body.

She clung to him with a desperate longing, every fiber of her body crying out to him. As his hand unfastened the buttons of her bodice, her eyes fluttered open, and over Jake's shoulder she caught sight of David's horrified eyes staring at them.

All passion and desire fled. With a strangled cry she pulled away. Jake let her go. "What's the matter? My love, what's wrong?"

She glanced past him. "Davy," she whispered.

Jake turned and saw the boy's expression before he buried himself back under the furs. Jake frowned. "You all lived together in the one room up on the Throndiuck," he said, puzzled. "Did he see Samuel force himself on you?"

"No! I don't think it's that. It's just . . ." Her voice trailed away.

Jake dropped her hands. "Perhaps we'd better have that coffee."

Amity poured out two cups and handed one to the man now sitting among the fur blankets on the floor. She made as if to sit opposite him, but he put out a hand to her.

"No, Amity. Sit close to me. I won't touch you, but I'm going to be here for quite a while and it's important he sees we're still friends."

Amity longed to feel Jake's arms around her. She longed also to be able to explain. But how revolted would he be if he learned the truth? Most men would have expected her to go to almost any lengths to resist Samuel's murderers—certainly to have told them what they had wanted to know. Telling them about the gold would have been tantamount to committing suicide, to say nothing of ensuring David's death as well. She had played for time and had gained enough for Samuel to reach home. The tragedy was that that had not been sufficient. Would Jake—would any man—believe that? She would have to be very sure of him before she could tell him the full story.

They sat, mostly in silence, until it was time for Amity to curl up under the blankets with her children and for Jake to get into his bearskin bag on the floor by the stove. The incident was not referred to again by either of them. Things continued as before except that Amity felt conscious now that there was—had always been—something missing from her life. These were feelings she disguised under her usual brisk practicality, and she tried not to feel hurt by the fact that Jake seemed to have put the incident out of his mind altogether.

The vein which David had discovered gave generously of itself for over a week, but as they worked their way back, away from the river, it became thinner and narrower and then intermittent.

They discovered another pocket of gold, though the vein leading to it would require real mining skills. "It seems to me that between us, we're sitting on a goldfield," Jake said. "Do you want to change your mind and stay?"

Amity thought about it. "No, I don't think so. I'll stick to our original plan and leave. Do you want to buy me out?"

Jake considered her offer. "I'll buy your mineral rights on both sides of the creek," he told her. "And I'll take the use of the cabin, but I'll not buy your claim to settle the land on either side. I've got a feeling you'd be better off keeping it."

"It won't be much use without the mineral rights."

"True enough, and I sure as hell don't intend to leave anything in the ground that I can get out. Want to change your mind?"

Amity shook her head. "I can't see any reason to change my mind. Let's empty this pocket and divide it. Then I'll be gone."

Chapter Ten

THE rush of meltwater that turned the Yukon into a raging torrent every spring had subsided by the time Amity's laden canoe nosed into it from the creek, but it was still a powerful force to have to paddle against, and she knew she had a strenuous journey ahead before she reached Fort Selkirk.

She was mildly surprised to see another canoe rush past her, headlong downstream towards Fort Selkirk. Canoes were the sensible means of summer transport, though she couldn't recall ever having actually met another one. But by the time she decided to stop for the night, five more craft of one sort or another had passed them, and every day until they reached Fort Selkirk they passed more boats. This, then, was the gold rush both Samuel and Jake had predicted.

She scarcely recognized Fort Selkirk. A tented township had grown up around the palisaded settlement. With difficulty she found a mooring for the canoe and filled her fur sleeping bag with everything movable. With Pandora in one arm and assisted by David, she pulled the bag along the small wharf and into the town. The crowds and the intermittent summer rains had churned the streets into a quagmire. Eventually they reached the police post.

Sergeant Woolacombe looked distinctly harassed, but not so much so that he did not instantly recognize Amity. "See what you've started, Mrs. Jones?" he said grimly, ignoring the press of people demanding his attention.

"I can hardly believe it," she told him. "The town out there—it's beyond imagining."

"And this is only the beginning. News of the strike has hit the papers all over the States and Canada, and as far as Europe, too."

"Well, I can bring you one tiny bit of good news," Amity told him. "One of Samuel's murderers is dead. At least that's one less to look for." She told him the circumstances and agreed to write it down for the record. Then she asked him to record Pandora's birth.

He did so and then brought down another file and riffled through it. "You settled on Sixty Mile Creek, I gather?"

"Is that what it's called? I didn't know."

"A man came in and filed on your behalf. Tall, with a beard. Illiterate. Made his mark. Said his name was John Biscoe."

"That's right. I gave him shelter for a while. He figured it would be a good idea if I had a title to the land I was living on."

"So what are your plans now?"

Amity looked about her. "It had been my intention to go back Outside, but now, seeing all these people, I'm not so sure. You think they bring in the barest minimum of supplies?"

"If you're thinking what I think you are, Mrs. Jones, you're right. There's a fortune to be made providing them with what they can't bring in or what they run out of, but it will take capital."

"Can you find me lodgings for a couple of nights?" Amity asked.

"I daresay someone will find a bed for an old acquaintance. There's still some of the Klondike gold left, I take it?"

Amity smiled, wide-eyed and innocent. "Something like that."

AMITY'S return to Fort Selkirk with a daughter who bore little resemblance to her mother and none at all to Samuel York aroused intense curiosity.

Almost as interesting were Amity's intentions. She was buying enough flour to feed an army, not to mention sugar and coffee, molasses and oatmeal, salt and pepper, tins of butter, sides of bacon, sacks of dried fruit, yeast, a small barrel of vinegar, and even live chicks and a goat.

There was far more than could ever be transported in one canoe, so she hired Indians and canoes. She guessed there would be speculation that she was spending more than her original hoard of gold and that her claim lay in Sixty Mile Creek. Inevitably, word would soon get out to the hordes of prospectors, who would find it easy enough to head off up that river instead of going on to the Throndiuck, or, as Sergeant Woolacombe was now calling it, the Klondike. What mattered was that she should get there before they did.

THE procession of well-ballasted canoes made excellent time down the river, the canoeists' skills enabling them to pass many vessels that had set off before them.

If Jake was surprised to see her back, he gave no sign of it, though he watched with raised eyebrows the freight being unloaded.

"Expecting a siege?" he asked.

"That's right." Amity straightened up. "You've finished the cabin!" she exclaimed. This was better luck than she had hoped for.

She paid the Indians and watched them disappear downstream. They could scarcely have missed the sluice box and the rocker and might sell some cheechako, or newcomer, the information that he needn't go so far as the Klondike to find gold. It would suit Amity well if they did, but she doubted Jake would be happy about it.

"What brought you back?" he said eventually. "I thought you were going Outside?"

"Jake, they're coming downstream in droves. Some of them are still dressed as they were when they got off the train at Vancouver. Fort Selkirk is a sea of mud surrounded by tents. The price of everything has shot through the roof. It made me think. Remember what you said about my opening a lodging house?"

"Vaguely," he admitted. "Is that what all this is for?"

"Exactly! It's only a matter of time before they start investigating this creek. They'll need somewhere to sleep, somewhere to eat. So I'm following your advice."

Jake seemed less than flattered. "How many men do you imagine you can cram into that cabin?"

"I don't intend them to actually stay very long. I'm more interested in providing them with food. They can live in their own tents, but my guess is they'll be glad to be saved the trouble of cooking. If there's much demand, we can build another cabin to extend this one."

"No, Amity. Not we. You."

She stared at him. "Me? I can't build a cabin on my own."

"Then perhaps you should have considered that before you went to so much trouble."

"Are you refusing to help build it?"

"Listen, Amity. I built this cabin because I thought—I hoped—you'd want to stay here. When you decided to go Outside, I was disappointed, but I understood. I didn't bargain for this."

"Neither did I. It was seeing the people flocking in that gave me the idea. It's a way of getting rich without the hard labor of digging."

"It'll still be hard work, make no mistake about that. Personally, I'd rather dig. Just about the last thing I want is every Tom, Dick and Harry pockmarking this valley with their little pits."

"You'd rather it was pockmarked with yours," she snapped.

"Right. At least they'll be dug in silence and I shan't be continually watching my back for the quick knife blade."

Amity was obliged to concede that Jake had a point. "We both know they can't be stopped and that it's only a matter of time before they reach here, so we may as well turn it to what advantage we can," she said defensively.

"You turn it to your advantage," he said curtly. "I'll dig for gold."

THE brief arctic fall was well under way when David reported seeing strangers in their valley. The next day, Jake took a gun and left before dawn to see for himself.

"Cheechakos," he said disparagingly on his return. "They've pitched their tent, and they've started panning in the creek. Doesn't look as if they're making any preparations for winter."

"How many of them?" Amity asked.

"Four. It's a good number because there's always someone to fetch game or timber, but it doesn't look as if that's occurred to them."

Three days later a wide-bottomed, inelegant but solidly built craft hove to in midstream just opposite their clearing.

"Mind if we visit?" one of the two rowers called across.

"Come ashore," Amity called. "There's coffee on the stove."

They took up the invitation with alacrity, devouring freshly made bannocks as if they hadn't eaten for a week.

"Why haven't you gone on down to the Klondike?" Jake asked.

"Have you seen it lately?" one of them asked. "There's barely a square foot of diggable ground that's not been filed on, so we decided to try here. It looked unexplored." He laughed self-consciously. "Seems we were wrong. You've filed, I take it?"

Jake nodded. "Both sides of the creek, in Fort Selkirk and in Juneau."

The man's eyes narrowed. "You must have been very sure of gold."

"No. Mrs. Jones and I just like to have everything neat and tidy. Saves misunderstandings later. You see, she lives here. I'm just passing through."

Amity stared at him. That was news to her—unwelcome news. She wondered to what extent her decision to welcome prospectors had affected his intentions.

"I take it there'd be no objection if we moved up and dug adjacent to your claim?" one of them asked.

"Depends on who you're asking," Jake said. "Mrs. Jones here can't wait for people. She aims to open a lodging house. I'd rather you stayed where you are. Legally there's nothing to stop you."

The man turned to Amity. "You'd put us up for the winter?"

"Just so long as you can afford to pay. It might be wiser to provide your own accommodations and eat here."

"Sounds a good idea. We'll get back and talk it over."

When the two men returned with their companions, Jake had erected a rudimentary fence along the edges of their combined claims. The four men, who had come from Tennessee, set up their tent downstream. One of them went back to file, while the others tried to find their arctic feet.

By the time winter had settled in for good, another dozen claims had been filed along Sixty Mile Creek, and their owners were sitting out the long winter, digging in preparation for the spring sluicing and spending too much of their small stakes on Mrs. Jones' excellent grub. When one or two prospectors ran out of ready money, Amity still fed them, but instead of accepting IOUs, she suggested they should be calculated in terms of labor to be utilized in the spring. It occurred to none that time spent laboring for Mrs. Jones was time not available for prospecting.

By the time the inconvenient fact had dawned, Amity had a substantial cabin and the beginnings of what she hoped would become a store. The problem was stocking it. When she broached the subject with Jake Treviscoe, he was as angry as she had ever seen him.

"You have more gall than any woman I've ever met," he told her. "Do you reckon me to be some tame sheepdog to be sent off on errands when it suits you? Get this straight, Amity: I started your cabin because I knew it wasn't something you could do yourself, especially not in the condition you were in. I finished it because I thought you'd gone and I might as well have somewhere decent to live. It suited me—it suited us both—to join forces in prospecting. When you came back, I thought— No, it doesn't matter what I thought, but it never crossed my mind that some lighthearted remark I only half remember making would bring you back here to play your own part in raping this land."

Amity stared at him, so angry that she quite missed the underlying hints of a deeper feeling. "And you have had no part in this? At least when Samuel found gold, he tried to forget about it. He really did love the land."

"Yes, he did, and I'll admit to my own self-interest. But not this. I'll not be used, Amity. You'll have to solve your problem another way. I'll make my mineral claims over to you. I'll cash in what I've got and find another unspoiled place if I can." Then, without pausing, he turned on his heel and strode out of the cabin.

Amity felt drained and realized she was shaking. She would see him in the morning when he'd had time to calm down. She'd apologize to him, and everything would go back to normal again.

In the morning Jake Treviscoe was gone.

HIS departure left Amity in a quandary. She desperately needed stores, but it was out of the question for her to get them herself, and there was none among the prospectors whom she was inclined to trust. She was beginning to despair when a familiar figure walked into the cabin. It was the old Russian prospector.

She ran to greet him, wiping her floury hands imperfectly on her apron as she went. "Mr. Kislov!" she exclaimed. It occurred to her that he represented a possible solution to her problem.

She bided her time for a few days, then broached the subject. To her delight he declared himself very willing to get her stores, provided she paid him in gold, and he undertook to get them back to her before winter arrived again. Amity heaved a sigh of relief, knowing there was no one she could trust more, either with her gold or with succeeding in his mission.

HER TRUST WAS NOT MISPLACED, but she was surprised, when he returned, to find that he had bought far more than she had asked for and had additionally taken it upon himself to hire Chilkats to help transport it.

"Dyea's black with would-be millionaires, and they say Skagway's the same," he told her. "I reckon come spring, you're going to need all this." He paused. "D'you want a piece of advice from an old man who's going to put as much distance as he can between himself and this place just as soon as he's rested up?"

"I'll always listen to your advice, Volodya," she told him, using his nickname.

"Start thinking of this place as a town—one that straddles the border. Finish your store. Start employing men. Pay them well enough and they'll be honest. There'll be the odd bad apple, of course, and when you find one, get rid of it. But if you choose with care and treat the men fairly, by and large you won't have much to worry about. And get yourself an assayer."

"For a man who stays away from men, you know them well."

Kislov dandled Pandora on his knee. "That's why I stay away," he said.

During that winter Amity grew rich both in labor from those who had not yet struck it rich and in gold for food and other supplies from those who had. She drew the line at calling the new town that grew up the next spring after herself, as the prospectors wanted, but finally agreed to the compromise name of Friendship.

The town developed along one street, which stretched along the dry valley where she had originally set up her tent. She soon discovered among the men many craftsmen who now perceived that riches from the gold strike were to be made by pursuing the very crafts they had vowed would never again soil their hands.

The cabin was extended yet again, and a board over its door proclaimed FRIENDSHIP HOTEL, EMPORIUM AND ASSAY OFFICE, with the words CLAIMS REGISTERED underneath. This last, Amity was able to bring to fruition when Sergeant Woolacombe decided it was time he checked on the new border town under his jurisdiction. He knew that his own work would be considerably relieved if she was able to process claims, though she would have to get rid of her own claims to avoid any complaints of conflicting interest. The sergeant conceded that it was sufficient to transfer them to her children.

In the spring, for the first time, there were women among the new arrivals. The first, a Scot called Bessie Sauchrie, took on the job of washerwoman. Then two other women arrived. They were named Maud and Enid, and neither of them was in the first flush of youth. They rented a plot from Amity on the Alaskan side of the creek, where they erected a substantial tent with a wooden façade on the street. Their arrival puzzled Amity, since they called themselves seamstresses, a profession for which there was no call in Friendship. Amity expressed her doubts to Bessie, who roared with laughter.

"God bless you for an innocent, Mrs. Jones," she said. "The closest they'll come to dressmaking is taking those high-buttoned dresses off, and there'll be plenty to pay them to do it, too."

It took a moment or two before the implications of what Bessie was saying sank in. Ever practical, Amity decided to raise their rents.

A fourth woman came to Friendship that summer, and to Amity's mind, this one fitted the description of a demimondaine far more closely than either Maud or Enid. There was an indefinably brazen quality about her. Of moderate height but with an ample bosom and hips that made her look shorter, she had striking straw-colored hair that Amity knew could not have been natural. Her costume was old and worn, but it had been expensive, as had her button-boots. Her suitcase and carpetbag were carried into the hotel by the young man who had rowed her here.

"I need a room to myself," she told Amity.

Amity smiled, but without enthusiasm. This was not a woman to whom she warmed. "I can manage that, but it will be a small one. What brings you here?"

The woman looked at her, surprised. "Gold. What else?"

"I think you'll find most of the land's already been claimed."

The woman chuckled. "Don't worry, sweetheart. My claim's rock-hard. I've a lawyer's opinion on that."

Amity pushed the register across the desk and said, "Perhaps you'd sign here. Just your name and address."

The woman signed. "This is my address, at least for the time being," she said, writing "Friendship Hotel, Friendship" in the address column. She pushed the book back to Amity, who smiled a little at the address. She didn't smile at the signature, though. The woman's name was Mrs. Edda York.

Chapter Eleven

AMITY'S stomach lurched. She had no intention of introducing herself. She wanted some time to think over the implication.

She handed Edda York a key. "Along that corridor there, Mrs. York. You'll find it towards the end, on the left."

As soon as she had gone, Amity took a deep breath. What had brought Edda York to Friendship? Gold, she had said. But she didn't look like a woman who was prepared to grub in the dirt. Had she heard that Samuel was dead? That he had had a "wife" at the time of his death? Had Edda assumed that Amity had illegally sold Samuel's claim?

Edda spent two or three hours looking around Friendship, talking to people and crossing over to the less developed Alaskan side of the creek to chat there, too.

When Edda returned, Amity was in her emporium. "You're Amity Jones," the woman said, in a voice that was somewhere between a question and an accusation.

Amity nodded. "That's right."

Edda looked her up and down critically. "I'd never have guessed. We need to talk. Is there somewhere we can go?"

"The office will be quiet." She led the way, then closed the door behind them. "You'd better sit down. You've the look of someone with a lot on her mind."

Edda York sat down. "You know who I am?"

"I think so. You tell me."

"I married a certain Samuel York a long time ago. So did you, I gather, only more recently. Although I left him, we were never divorced. So you married a man who had no right to get married."

Amity flushed. It wasn't a story she enjoyed having spelled out quite so baldly. It was true, however, so she nodded.

"That was a dirty trick he played," Edda said, not unsympathetically. "I suppose he figured you were too far away from civilization for anyone ever to find out."

"I don't know," Amity said sharply. "I didn't discover it until he was dead. All I do know is that he was very lonely."

"You've got children, I believe."

"Yes."

"Pity they're not entitled to the name—or the property."

Now we're getting to it, Amity thought. "We're doing well," she said. "It bothered me at first, but I think we'll make out."

"I'm sure you will. You've got a nice little thing going here. I gather you got it all started on Samuel's gold."

"No, Mrs. York. Samuel's gold was locked up in his claim. I've never had that. I won't deny I expected to have it, but it's yours—the rights to minerals and the trapping rights. They ought to make you a very rich women if you've a fancy to work them."

"Which I haven't. I already sold those claims at Fort Selkirk. Unfortunately, the gold claim has been jumped, so the price wasn't anything like what I had hoped for. That's what I've come to see you for."

"I can't imagine why. You already know all there is to know."

"Including the fact that you paid for all your supplies with raw gold when you left Fort Selkirk. That gold must have come from the Throndiuck, from Samuel's claim. That gold should be mine."

"No, Mrs. York," Amity said firmly. "That gold was collected either by David or by myself. Samuel knew about it. He didn't approve of it, but he let me keep it for David's future. It is what set us up here. The gold was never Samuel's."

"That's more or less what they told me at the police post," Edda agreed. "Still, I wasn't content with that, so I spoke to a lawyer, and he says it should have come to me. That's why I'm here. I want the gold that's due me, and since you've had the use of it for a couple of years, I want interest—or a share in the profits you've made so far, which by my reckoning are pretty substantial."

Amity had no intention of handing over any part of her hard-won riches to a woman who had abandoned Samuel and only reappeared when there was something to be got out of so doing. "There's the door, Mrs. York. You're welcome to spend the night here at my expense. I'm sorry you've had a wasted journey."

Edda stood up and smoothed her mud-bespattered skirt. "If I go back to Fort Selkirk, it will be to pursue the matter through the courts. It will take time, but I'll win."

Amity stayed deep in thought for a long time. Then she went out into the store and across to the little office from which her assayer, George Dowsby, weighed ore and recorded claims on her behalf.

"George, cast your mind back a few months. Didn't you tell me one of the men on the Alaskan side had once been a lawyer?"

"That's right, Mrs. Jones. Dougal Kehelland."

"I take it he is prospecting and isn't setting up in practice here?"

"Ah, well, I think he had a bit of bother in Canada. That's why he's on the other side. Something involving clients' money."

Amity groaned. "A crooked lawyer. Just what I'm looking for! I don't suppose there are any more lawyers hereabouts?"

"Not that I know about. But why not speak to him? After all, his knowledge won't be affected by the fact that he's got sticky fingers."

Dougal Kehelland and his partner were sluicing ore when Amity trudged through the mud to their claim. "Mr. Kehelland? May I have a word?" Amity asked.

"Why not. It's a free country—this side of the creek at any rate."

"With all due respect to your partner, I'd like to talk in private."

"Look after things here, Abel. We can use my tent," he suggested.

Two packing cases served as seats. Amity settled herself down on one. "George Dowsby tells me you're a lawyer," she began.

He hesitated. "You know I'm not practicing now."

"That can't alter the fact that you still have your legal knowledge."

"There's a good lawyer in Fort Selkirk, I hear."

"So do I, but I want an opinion now."

He nodded. "Very well. For what it's worth, I was always pretty sound on the law."

Briefly Amity explained the circumstances relevant to Edda's claim. "Could she succeed, do you think?"

He pursed his lips. "Could do, and probably for the wrong reasons. You say she left York after only a short time together. Can you prove that?"

"Not personally. It's what I was told. And there were no neighbors on the Throndiuck, Mr. Kehelland."

"Exactly. No one who could testify to any aspects of their marriage except that it took place and was never dissolved. If she appears in court as the impoverished widow, while her husband's mistress grows rich from a claim that his brutality drove her from—"

"No!" Amity exclaimed. "Samuel was never brutal."

"That's irrelevant. What matters is how it would appear in court. Your great advantage is that despite the shock of finding that you were not legally married and had no lawful entitlement to York's claims, you made no attempt to overset the opinion of Sergeant Woolacombe. You'd have no difficulty proving you acted in good faith."

"If she won, would I have to hand everything over to her?"

He considered. "Unlikely, I think. There's no doubt that your present success is due to your own efforts, but you could lose half."

"Over my dead body," Amity said. "What do you suggest I do?"

"Frankly, I'd avoid at all costs letting it go to court. Quite apart from the length of time involved and the doubtfulness of the outcome, it would be horrifyingly expensive. But remember, a prolonged court case is hardly in her interests either. If you send her packing with nothing, you've got as long as it takes her to reach Fort Selkirk to pull all your gold together, sell up and get across the creek to Alaska. The alternative is to do some sort of deal with her."

Amity stood up. "I won't pretend I like your advice, Mr. Kehelland, but then I didn't come here to be told what I wanted to hear." She brought out a small pouch from her pocket. "Regard this as fee plus a retainer," she said. "I may want your advice again."

That night after supper Amity invited Edda into her office to talk. "I've been considering the conversation we had earlier," Amity said, placing a tray with coffee on the table between them.

"I thought you might," Edda York replied smugly.

"I have absolutely no doubt at all about the justice of my claim," Amity told her, "though you'd say exactly the same. The point is, there's a good chance we'd both have to settle in the end, and I don't doubt you've been advised, as I have, that going to court is going to be a lengthy and expensive business."

Edda leaned forward, her face serious, her eyes hard. "I think we can deal together, Mrs. Jones. What have you in mind?"

"Whatever the rights and wrongs of my initial grubstake, the fact remains that it has been my efforts that have turned it into a thriving business. I've got my children to consider. Nothing I've put by up to now is on the table. I'm prepared to deal you in on what I've put together here, but you'll have to work for it. I'm interested in no sleeping partners. Agreed?"

"Agreed. I can work if I have to," Edda told her.

"I have title to land on both sides of the creek. It's my judgment that this gold rush has only just begun—at least as far as the Alaskan side is concerned. At the moment, this side is doing best, but that's only because the Canadian end got started first.

"Now, if the Alaskan side develops as much as I estimate it will, it's going to need more than one person to control it. I'm not sharing title, but in every other respect I'm prepared to go into partnership with you. We'll share the costs and the profits of both sides of the river, but I'll have overall charge on the Canadian side, while you have it on the Alaskan. The actual implementation, including the hiring and firing of any workers, is entirely up to the partner concerned. How does this strike you?"

"I need time to think about it."

"Take all the time you need," Amity told her.

Edda York was not somebody with whom Amity would ever have chosen to go into partnership. She suspected that the older woman wouldn't hesitate to cheat her. It was up to Amity to ensure that any agreement was as watertight as it could be made.

At breakfast the next day, Edda sat by Amity. "I did a lot of thinking last night," she said.

"I thought you might," Amity said, echoing Edda's words.

"Sounds like a good idea to me."

Amity nodded. "If you're sure, I'll get something drawn up."

Amity decided to be in no great rush to visit Kehelland. Edda could stew for a little bit. She left the table and went through into the store.

There was only one customer there, and she recognized one of those original cheechakos, now a seasoned northerner. They exchanged greetings and passed the time of day.

"You knew the old Russian, didn't you?" the man asked.

"Do you mean Kislov?" Amity smiled, recalling the old man with his endless stories and his protestations of wanting to make the biggest strike ever, yet leaving the places where it was most likely to happen because he didn't like the crowds or the staying put. "He's a good man. I daresay he'll be back in a year or two."

"Not this time, he won't. You haven't heard, then?"

Amity stared at him in dismay. "Don't tell me he's died."

"He was killed. It seems he'd had quite a successful season on the lower reaches of the Yukon. They say his skull had been staved in."

Amity shuddered. "Poor old man. I hope someone gave him a decent burial."

"I reckon they did," her informant told her, as much because it was what she wanted to hear as because he knew it to be true.

Amity visited Kehelland later that day. And when she returned, she found Edda had introduced herself to the children. She had given Pandora a brightly colored bead necklace to play with and was teaching David to play a card game called snap.

She looked up as Amity came in. "Your children do you credit, Mrs. Jones. It's odd. There's something faintly familiar about Pandora, though I can't put my finger on it. She's a pretty little thing."

Nothing she said could be taken as more than politeness, but she made Amity feel uneasy. Amity dreaded someone else discovering the truth about Pandora, and she would have been happier to find some excuse to keep the children away from Edda.

IT QUICKLY became apparent that Amity and Edda had very different ideas as to the manner of Friendship's growth on the Alaskan side, but Amity certainly couldn't criticize the vigor with which her partner put them into operation. It was Edda's philosophy that they should take full advantage of Friendship's unique location by ensuring that the Alaskan side provide what the Canadian side lacked, namely, alcohol. It was the perfect place, in Edda's estimation, for a saloon, with all the facilities such places offered. Canadian Friendship should—at least for the time being—have the monopoly of the assay office and the registration of titles.

There was no doubt that Edda's schemes were popular. Every night Canadian Friendship emptied and the lights blazed along the opposite bank of the creek until the early hours. But Amity stood firm against the establishment of any lodging house on the Alaskan side.

"If they cross the border to file their claims and get their gold assayed," she said, "they can cross the border if they want good food or a comfortable bed."

She and Edda had been going over the books together and were leaving Amity's office when Jake Treviscoe entered the store. Amity's expression of pure delight was fleeting and brought quickly under control, but not before Edda's glance caught it.

"I didn't expect you to come back," Amity said to the newcomer.

"I heard about this place. It sounded as if it had grown a bit." He looked at Edda. "I've seen you before somewhere," he commented.

"This is my partner, Edda York," Amity told him, knowing the name would tell him all he needed to know.

Edda frowned. She didn't normally forget men's faces, particularly not when they were so striking. "Were we introduced?"

"It was a long time ago, and you were getting on a boat at Dyea. Someone pointed you out to me because they knew I knew your husband. I'm Jake Treviscoe, by the way."

Edda smiled. "I may not remember you from then, Jake, but rest assured, I'll not overlook you next time." She turned to Amity. "I'll be off to Alaska. You old friends will have things to talk about." She cast him a provocative glance. "I'll see you again, Jake."

There was a brief silence until she left the building. Then Amity said, "You've never mentioned having met her." The remark sounded accusatory in a way she hadn't meant.

"No reason why I should have, is there? Besides, it wasn't a meeting—more of a sighting."

"If you had seen Edda, you must have wondered why he married me," Amity said defensively.

Jake looked puzzled. "Why should you think that? She's blowsy and almost certainly available. You're less obvious and almost certainly not. Would you prefer to be blowsy and available?"

"No, of course not." She decided to turn the conversation into less personal waters. "What has really brought you here, Jake?"

"Curiosity—and hunger. The food here has become a legend across the North West. Wherever I go I meet men who dream about your venison stew with dumplings. Besides, I'm broke, and I seem to remember a promise of free board and lodging if you ever started your own lodging house, which was my idea in the first place, as I recall."

Amity laughed. "Free board and lodging for as long as you need," she said, "but for old times' sake, as one friend to another."

"I hoped you'd say that," he said, smiling, and Amity's heart skipped a beat. "How are the children?" he went on.

"Fine. Pandora's hair is beginning to darken, so you may not recognize her. And David's growing into quite the man of the house."

"I'm glad he gives you no cause for concern."

"Not in himself, but I'm worried. Edda York has made something of a pet of him. He takes himself over to Alaskan Friendship, and she teaches him card games."

"Amity, I doubt if David can even hold a pack of cards properly."

"It doesn't stop him trying. Jake, she runs the saloon."

"Ah, I see your problem. Like me to keep an eye on him?"

"Would you? He adores you, you know."

"I'll do what I can." He looked at her. "If you sold up and took him Outside, you'd remove him from her influence."

"I've thought of that, but I'm not quite ready to move on."

He took her by the shoulders, his face very serious. "Will you ever be ready to move on?"

Amity laughed nervously. "Of course I will. But not just yet." She looked up into his gray eyes, a mutely vulnerable appeal in her own. "I don't intend ever to be poor again, Jake Treviscoe, and that's why I'll stay."

He shook his head. "Make your fortune by all means, but don't let the making of it stand in the way of enjoying it."

He bent over and deposited a quick, disappointingly chaste kiss on her cheek. "You have a room for me?" he asked.

DAVID was delighted to see Jake again and insisted on taking him to his favorite places. Amity would have been happier had more of these been on the Canadian side and had Edda York not found quite so much time to join them. Jake might have called her blowsy and available, but he seemed happy with Edda's company, which gave Amity no small pang of jealousy. He only returned to Canadian Friendship to eat and sleep or to spend time with David and Pandora. Both children patently adored him.

Amity caught herself wondering what Jake's attitude to Pandora would be if he knew the truth, and she shuddered. For her part, she was beginning to love the child and was even able sometimes to dissociate her daughter from her conception, but she believed it unlikely that a man would be able to do so.

The onset of winter saw Jake still in Friendship. Amity did not begrudge him his board and lodging, but she did wonder whether he was doing anything to put a grubstake together. She was several times on the point of asking him about his future plans but refrained. Their last parting had driven a wedge through their previous companionable accord. They were still friendly, but not quite friends, and she had an uncomfortable feeling that that was unlikely to change while Edda was still around.

Amity had hoped that the onset of a hard winter would send Edda on her way again. It seemed, however, as if a great deal of money and an abundance of admiring men were adequate compensation for waking up to find icicles hanging from the ceiling. Besides, the men spent more time in her saloon in winter, spending what the summer had put in their gold pouches.

The assay office, though, was less busy in the winter. Most of

Friendship's residents used the winter to dig the muck that they would sluice in the spring, so it was during the spring and summer months that they brought ore in for George Dowsby's expertise. Winter brought men from farther afield, those who had spent the summer panning the hundreds of creeks that crisscrossed the vast territory. It was a reasonable guess that many of them had come by their gold through methods other than sheer hard work.

Such was George Dowsby's assessment of a lumbering great bear of a man who rolled though the door of the Friendship Emporium one day. The huge newcomer hesitated and looked around him, then thrust his bearded face at the assayer's cage. "I want this assayed, and I want a price for it," he said, pulling out a substantial poke bulging with gold.

George took the poke and emptied the contents onto his scales. As the tiny nuggets tumbled into the pan, he caught sight of the initials B.M.K. tooled into the leather of the pouch. He glanced across at the stranger. "I can assay it for you, but it's Mrs. Jones who does the buying. It'll all take some time." He wrote the weight down on a piece of paper and handed it to the man, who stuffed it into his pocket. Then George asked the emporium's assistant to ask Mrs. Jones to join him in his testing room. The request was so unusual, Amity went at once, entering the little cubicle directly through the door that connected it to the hotel's office, where the safe was kept.

"Take a look at that," George told her, handing her the pouch.

Amity shrugged. "It's someone's poke: 'B.M.K.' "

"I've seen that poke before, Mrs. Jones. Remember the old Russian, Kislov? It's his."

Amity examined it more closely. "No," she said. "His first name was Vladimir."

"That's right, and his full name was Vladimir Mikhailovich Kislov. Only the letter V is B in Russian. I know because I asked him about it once. The point is, this is without a doubt Kislov's poke, and we know Kislov was murdered, don't we?"

"Don't let's jump to conclusions," Amity said. "This man might have come by it legitimately."

"I wouldn't bet on it. I've seen him, Mrs. Jones."

Amity peered round the door, through the cage. There were three people in the store. Only one of them was a stranger, and he

ASSAY OFFICE
CIGARS
FRIENDSHIP
HOTEL

had his back to her. She turned back to George. "Is he a big man?"

"Like a grizzly."

She looked again, but this time the object of her gaze turned round, and Amity's stomach lurched. She had to steady herself against the testing counter. "Close the door," she told George, and he obeyed. "George, I know that man. I don't know whether he killed Kislov, but he certainly had a hand in murdering my—Samuel York."

Like most people in Friendship, the assayer had heard something of Amity's history, although this was the first time he had ever heard her refer to it. "What do we do?" he asked.

"We need two or three men to arrest him and take him to Fort Selkirk," Amity said.

"I'll get some men. D'you want me to mention Mr. York?"

Amity shook her head. "Just say we think he killed Kislov and he's been identified as having killed another prospector."

George snatched up his coat and dashed out of the hotel and over to a nearby group of men. Mention of Kislov's pouch was all the incentive they needed—every prospector in the north dreaded the attack of such vultures. The group raced to the hotel in the assayer's wake, shouting to all who could hear, "Kislov's killer's in the store!" and soon they had a sizable following.

Amity heard the approaching hubbub and groaned. Couldn't George have been a little more discreet about it? However, it didn't occur to the stranger that he was the object of the high feelings until the door burst open and the little mob stood just inside, rendered suddenly silent by the sheer size of their prey.

The huge man did not possess the keenest of intellects, but his sense of self-preservation was well honed. He lowered his head, like a bull moose, and charged at the group, which was so taken by surprise that it let him through. Almost immediately they realized what they had done and raced after him.

Like many big men, this one was surprisingly light on his feet, and he gradually pulled away from the crowd, heading towards the frozen river that would take him into Alaska. He was beginning to congratulate himself on having outsmarted his enemies when a cooler head picked up a rifle, took aim, fired and watched the running man fall. "Don't reckon he's alive, but someone had better check," the shooter said laconically.

Jake Treviscoe appeared close behind him. "You're a good shot," he commented. "Good enough to have dropped him without killing him. That way at least he'd have stood trial."

The man shrugged. "Why waste public money?" he asked, and went forward to inspect his handiwork.

"Who says that was Kislov's killer?" Jake asked another man.

The man jerked his head in the general direction of the store. "Dowsby. Something to do with the Russian's poke."

The assayer produced the leather pouch and handed it to Jake, who turned it over. "That's Kislov's all right. I've seen it many a time. Doesn't prove this was the man that killed him, though."

"Mrs. Jones said this was one of the men who killed York."

Jake strode off in search of Amity. He found her in her room, sprawled across her bed, sobbing into the pillows. Jake sat down on the edge of the bed and lifted her, so that her head rested in the hollow of his shoulder. "Tell me about it," he said.

It was some minutes before she could respond. "There was a man," she began.

"I know. A big man who had Kislov's pouch."

"Did they catch him?" She looked up at him anxiously.

"You could say that. Someone shot him, so we'll never know exactly how he came to have the pouch."

"He was one of the men who . . . who killed Samuel," she whispered. She clung to him, and a fresh wave of sobbing swept over her as she remembered the sheer brute size of the man as he attacked her.

His enfolding arms tightened, and he dropped a kiss onto her head. Her behavior confirmed a suspicion he had long held that there might be more to Samuel's death than anyone had been told. He longed to ask her to recount it, but he sensed that Amity must come to this on her own. All he could do was to make it clear that he was the person in whom she could safely confide.

He stroked her hair. "It's over, Amity. He's dead. I'll make sure they bury the body on the other side."

She shook her head. "It's not that. Jake, he's the second of the three to arrive here. Once I'd moved away, I didn't think I'd see any of them again. Now I'm waiting for the third."

He held her close. "It was sheer chance that brought them here. Maybe it's divine retribution. Neither stood trial, but both are dead."

"They killed Samuel," Amity objected. "They should have been convicted in a court." She looked up at him, her eyes swimming with tears. "If Samuel had been killed by a bear or if he'd died in a whiteout, I could have borne it. Those are the risks we run up here, but life is too hard to have it snatched away for nothing more than greed. Jake, Samuel is dead, and I don't want him to be." She buried her head in his shoulder, and her sobs burst forth anew.

Jake continued to hold her close, but he felt the icy hand of desolation clutching at his heart. He had expected her love for Samuel to have drifted quietly down to a pleasant memory. Now he began to think that she had loved him more deeply than perhaps even she knew. If that was so, it was going to be a long, long time before she would consider anyone else in his place.

Chapter Twelve

WITHIN a week Jake had gone, without warning or explanation. Both children were upset.

"Mr. Treviscoe is a free man," Amity explained. "He may come and go as he wishes. We can't tell him to stay."

"But I thought he liked it here," David went on. "And Pandora misses him, too. He used to tell her good stories."

"I know he did. You'll have to tell them instead. She'll like that."

"Will he come back?"

I wish I knew, Amity's heart cried out. Aloud, she said, "I've no idea. We'll have to wait and see."

Edda didn't learn of his departure until the next day, when a sulky David poured out his woes in her room in the saloon. She was furious. "When's he coming back?" she demanded.

"I don't know. Nobody knows," David told her tearfully.

"Hmm." Edda pursed her lips. There weren't many men in the goldfields that matched up to Edda's estimation of what she was looking for, but Jake Treviscoe came close.

That evening Edda had some questions to put to her partner. "David tells me Treviscoe's gone," Edda said as she tucked into a bear steak at the hotel. "What drove him away?"

"I don't know that anything 'drove' him. He doesn't seem to stay anywhere very long."

"But to go without a word! You must have said something."

"I can't recall anything," Amity said truthfully.

Edda glanced round the dining room. It was full of interested eavesdroppers fascinated by a topic of conversation that differed from the usual. A row between partners would not be good for business, so she let the matter drop until supper was over. Then she followed Amity to her office and closed the door behind them.

"What did you say to Jake?" she demanded.

Amity turned, surprised. "I told you—nothing that I can recall."

"There must have been something," Edda persisted.

"Such as what?" Amity demanded, irritated.

"Well, you don't like me, for a start, do you? You've never forgiven me for being Samuel's legal wife. And having cheated me of my inheritance, you now drive away the one man who could replace him."

"Aren't you a little confused?" Amity said, trying to keep her tone reasonable. "Far from cheating you, I went into partnership simply because we both knew the cost of settling the dispute in court. As for driving Jake away, if he were as taken with you as you seem to wish him to be, I find it hard to believe that anything I said could possibly send him from your side."

Edda flushed angrily. Amity's remark was too close to the truth to be welcome. She had to admit that Jake had proved rather adept at avoiding her more ingenious lures.

"I certainly don't know what you said, little Miss Innocent," she snapped, "but I don't believe he left for no reason."

With that, Edda swept out of the office and the hotel to sparkle over the gamblers in the saloon. With Jake gone, she would be better employed finding someone to take his place than sighing at the window like some moonstruck calf.

There were few remotely suitable candidates in Friendship, and visitors in winter were few and far between. Edda was assuring herself that things would change with the thaw, which would bring the new year's prospectors through, when a visitor arrived to restore her faith in natural justice.

Mungo Speen was distinguished by having a larger-than-average team of larger-than-average dogs. There were fourteen of them, and they drew an admiring crowd when he left them outside the saloon. Their driver—a tall, thin-faced, clean-shaven man with graying hair in need of a trim—strode over to the bar. "Whisky?" he inquired.

Something familiar about the voice caught Edda's attention. She stared at him for several moments, but she couldn't immediately place him. When she did, a few seconds later, she came out from behind the bar, her face wreathed in smiles, her arms stretched wide. "Mungo Speen! I almost didn't recognize you without your beard." She turned to the barman. "Bring the bottle into my office with a couple of glasses, Tom. Mr. Speen and I are old friends."

Once in her office, she helped him out of his full-length lynx coat, worn northern style, with the fur on the inside. She smiled. "You seem to have been doing well for yourself since I saw you being kicked across the border all those years ago."

"I can't complain," he said. "Did a bit of prospecting up on the Klondike before the rush started. Did all right, too, until the police came snooping around. But they can't touch me if I stay this side of the border. I'll stick to Alaska now." He looked about him. "If this is yours, you ain't doing too bad, my girl. Not bad at all. Perhaps we can do business together."

"I have a partner," Edda said cautiously. Mungo Speen was not a man in whom to place unguarded trust.

"Don't tell me that trapper you married set up all this?"

Edda laughed. "No. He's dead. That's how I got a grubstake together. The man was fool enough to marry again without divorcing me. My partner is his other 'wife.' She cut me in on this place."

"Sounds like a woman after your own heart."

Edda grimaced. "Not at all. As a matter of fact, he was about the only thing we had in common. I run this side of the creek. She runs the Canadian side. That's where the hotel is, and the assay office."

"And the police?"

"Sometimes. You'd marvel at the number of men who come over here when one of them drives in."

"I wouldn't be surprised at all. Are you telling me there's no lodgings over here?"

"That's right. That's our agreement. But there's nothing in it to say I can't have a friend visit for a few days. For the time being, it suits me. But if I could see a way to get hold of madam's interest, I'd take it."

"Easy enough. There must be plenty of men here unscrupulous—or desperate—enough to oblige one dark night."

Edda shook her head. "Not with the police at Fort Selkirk, and it's not in my interests to kill the goose. Besides, she's got a couple of children everyone dotes on. If anything happened, they'd not be too particular about where the border was. No, there must be a way of getting at her through the business."

"If I can come up with a scheme, will you cut me in?"

"I might," Edda said. "It would depend on the scheme."

"Give me a few days to see how things work."

Amity rarely went into Alaskan Friendship; it wasn't her sort of town anymore. Even so, it took very little time for the news to reach her that Edda York had found herself a fancy man to help her over Treviscoe's departure. David had met the man and at first had seemed uneasy about him. But the boy came round, and Amity had a pretty shrewd idea that a combination of barley sugar and the team of huge dogs had something to do with it. David referred to him as Mungo, and Amity wondered what sort of a face fitted so peculiar a name.

When they went through the week's takings from both sides of the creek, Edda told her partner she had something to discuss. "There's a lot of gold coming out of Alaska now, and I think we ought to open another assay office on that side," she said.

Amity schooled her features to disguise her unease. But the suggestion was inevitable, and perhaps the only real surprise was that it had not been made sooner. The assay office was the most profitable activity of the partnership. "I suppose George Dowsby could train up someone by the thaw," Amity said.

"No need to wait," Edda told her, a hint of triumph in her voice. "We've got an assayer now. An old friend, Mungo Speen."

"I heard he's a prospector—quite a successful one, by all accounts. Why should he want to work as an employee?"

"He's done his share of prospecting—and trapping, too, I daresay. He says there are so many people flooding into Alaska nowadays that it makes more sense to get in on the other end of the process—providing services for the prospectors."

"Can this man be trusted?"

"You trusted George Dowsby on a far briefer acquaintance."

"Maybe you'd better invite him over here for supper. I'd like to meet him. If my opinion of him coincides with yours, there's no reason why we shouldn't give him the job."

Edda flushed angrily. "I see," she said, her face grim. "I'm your partner—supposedly—but I'm not judged capable of choosing an assayer. I can employ my own bartender and my own piano player, but I can't be left to employ an honest man to assay gold."

Edda's charge was just. No matter what her private opinion of Edda might be, the woman had never given Amity any reason to mistrust her where business was concerned. "You're right," she admitted. "The decision should be yours. All the same, I'd like to meet him."

"I'll tell him he's got the job," Edda said. "But you'll have to come to Alaska to meet him. He steers clear of Canada."

This statement did nothing to relieve Amity's unease. "Why?"

Edda had realized almost as soon as her words were out that they would have been better left unsaid. "Some silly misunderstanding. The gist of it was that Mungo was in partnership with a man who ran out on him, leaving Mungo to face the music. They put out a warrant for Mungo, so he fled, too. It wasn't his fault. I think we should give him the benefit of the doubt."

"I don't think we should take the risk. Maybe we do need another assayer, but let's leave it to George to find someone."

"No," Edda said, her mouth set in a firm line. "I'll vouch for Mungo. If you're determined not to have him, then we split up. We divide up what's in the safe and go our own ways."

Amity would not have been sorry to lose her partner, but she knew that Edda's suggestion would operate in her own favor, since there were already signs that the Klondike goldfields were saturated, and an assay office on the Alaskan side of the creek might soon prove more profitable than one on this. Edda had been benefitting from the Canadian profit. Amity saw no reason to forgo a share in the Alaskan profit.

"What happens if your trust proves misguided?" Amity asked.

"I'll make good any loss to you that's attributable to Mungo."

Amity considered the offer. If anything went wrong, she would be bound to acquire some of Edda's assets. "All right," she said. "On those terms we'll give him a chance."

When Edda had gone, however, Amity's unease returned in increased measure as the days went by. Only by meeting Mungo Speen would she rid herself of it, and so she decided to cross the creek and make his acquaintance.

The pretext she needed came when David did not appear for his afternoon reading lesson with Mr. Newport, a prospector who had previously been a teacher. The man earned himself two or three good meals a week by teaching young David to read and write.

Amity told him she thought she knew where David would be. She got Bessie, her laundress and occasional cook, to mind Pandora. Then she headed straight for the saloon.

She found David sitting at a table, his feet dangling beneath a chair that was too high for him. He was engrossed in a game that involved shuffling three walnut shells about on the tabletop. Edda was standing opposite him, and beside him, his back to Amity, stood the man she took to be Mungo Speen.

"No," Edda said. "I saw that." She leaned across and turned one of the shells over. "It's this one." A dry pea was lying on the table.

Amity reached across and swept the shells off the table. She glared at Edda. "How dare you!" she exclaimed. "How dare you teach my son to gamble!"

Edda looked genuinely taken aback. "He's not gambling, Amity. We're teaching him a skill that he'll find very useful in the future."

"So that he can fleece idiots with no more sense than to be taken in by his sleight of hand? No, thank you, Edda. Right now he's missing his afternoon's lessons, and I'm taking him home." She turned to her son. "As for you, young man, if you sneak off once more, I shall ban you from coming over here ever again."

David, suitably shamefaced, slid off his chair.

"Now that you're here, you might as well meet Mungo Speen, our new assayer," Edda said. "Mungo, this is Amity Jones."

She turned to acknowledge the introduction and felt as if the ground had given way beneath her. He was better dressed than he had been before. His lank hair had been trimmed, and he no longer wore a beard, but the cadaverous features and the pale, cold eyes were unforgettable. The last time she had seen them, they had been just inches away from her face while he inflicted the ultimate degradation upon her. And then he had fired the bullet that had killed Samuel.

She drew back. So clearly was the memory of that appalling day etched in her mind that she found it inconceivable that he would not also recognize her. He must, even though several years had elapsed. And then what could she expect? A bullet when she was off guard? Mungo Speen had only to flee back across the creek to be out of reach of Canadian law.

If he had recognized her, he hid it well. "Mrs. Jones? Pleased to meet you." An ingratiating smile divided the lower half of his face, but his eyes remained cold and calculating. "Hope you'll be satisfied with my work," he added.

"Not very likely if you extend it to teaching my son skills no decent man has need of," she said sharply. She saw him frown, as if something in her words had rung some distant bell. Amity reached down for David's hand. "Put on your parka, Davy. We must get back. Mr. Newport is waiting for you." She turned to the assayer while David did as he was told. "Good-bye, Mr. Speen. I'd have preferred to meet you in a less contentious situation."

Speen frowned again as the woman and her child left the saloon. There was something about her that he knew, but he was damned if he could place it. There had been so many women in so many different places. But something about this one struck a chord.

Amity was glad to have escaped. If her guess was right and Mungo Speen had not yet recognized her, she was safe so long as she stayed in Canada. The interesting thing was that David had so far not recognized him, despite meeting him several times.

She handed David over to Mr. Newport with an exhortation to the teacher to make up for lost time, then retired to her room. The previous summer she had indulged in a small potbellied stove so that the room could be kept warm in winter. That, and the addition of a bentwood rocking chair to replace the wedding present that had been burned with the cabin, made this room a pleasure to sit in.

She fed the stove and sank into the chair, gazing at the flames through the stove's open door. What should she do now? Perhaps Sergeant Woolacombe would be able to spare a trooper to use Friendship as a base until Speen could be lured across the border on some pretext or other? That way he would be brought to trial. This time she would like justice to be seen to be done, she thought savagely. Convicted of murder, Speen would hang. But then something occurred to her. He was sure to hang only because there was an eyewitness. What better way of discrediting her testimony than by admitting not to a rape, but to being caught by her husband in the most delicate of situations? That would open up all sorts of other possible explanations for Samuel's death, all of them to Speen's advantage.

As she turned these perturbing thoughts over in her mind, the door opened, and Pandora came in. She reached up her hands to be lifted onto her mother's lap. As Amity bent over to do so, she found herself looking into disturbingly familiar eyes. The deep blue of childhood had changed a long time ago to a pale blue, which confirmed Amity's opinion that Samuel had not been the girl's father. There was nothing cold or inhuman about Pandora's eyes—quite the reverse, in fact, for she was a laughing, happy child. All the same, they were without a doubt the eyes of Mungo Speen, and with that realization came a revulsion that almost made Amity push her daughter from her. But as she looked at the child, she knew that Pandora was the least to blame. So instead, Amity drew her daughter to her in so forceful a hug that Pandora struggled to free herself.

EDDA was not sorry that Amity no longer crossed the frozen creek. The less opportunity Amity had for seeing what went on, the better. Besides, Edda had not been entirely happy at something in Mungo's eyes when he had looked at her partner.

Then one day Edda received a nasty jolt. Pandora, well swaddled in cozy furs, had made her way across the ice in the wake of her brother. Amity had been too sensible to make Alaska more attractive to David by banning it. Instead, so long as he had finished his chores and made no further attempts to skip his lessons, he was free to do as he wished. Pandora was now big enough to make the short journey under her own steam, and tagging on to her big brother was the most important thing she could think of to do.

The assayer's cage had been constructed at the end of the bar, and Mungo stepped out as David came into the saloon. "Brought your sweetheart with you?" he asked teasingly as he saw Pandora waddle in behind him.

David looked round with some disgust. "That's not a sweetheart. That's my sister," he declared scathingly.

Mungo bent down to pick her up. "My, but she's a pretty little thing," he said. "She may not be your sweetheart, but she'll sure break a few hearts when she's a bit older."

Edda came out of her office at the precise moment that Pandora glanced in her direction, and the two heads were both facing the same way. She saw with devastating clarity what Amity had seen. There was absolutely no doubt in Edda's mind that she was looking at father and daughter. Nor was there any doubt that neither of them was aware of the relationship.

She cast her mind back to her original discussion with Amity about employing Mungo. She was quite sure the name had conveyed nothing to her partner, though Mungo Speen was unlikely to be the only name by which he was known. Try as she would, Edda could not convince herself that her partner had shown the slightest sign of recognition—and neither had he. Had Amity become so very adept at disguising her feelings? Or had the association been so brief as to leave no recognition at all on either side?

It was a fascinating enigma.

Edda smiled. "Fancy you coming all this way to visit us," she said, chucking Pandora under the chin. "I think that deserves a reward, don't you? What would you say to some candy?"

Chapter Thirteen

THE Alaskan assay office did well from the beginning. More than once Amity found herself wishing she had agreed to set it up before. But when the Alaskan side of the assaying business began to outstrip the Canadian side, she became worried. Had it been midsummer, when business customarily increased, this would not have struck her as odd, but it was winter and a particularly harsh one at that. Few men brought in all the season's raw gold during the summer, keeping some back to pay for the provisions they now depended upon Amity's store to provide. There was therefore always a steady trickle of gold during the winter months. Since the Alaskan office opened up, that trickle had become a steady stream, but always through that side of the town. She mentioned the phenomenon to Edda, whose only surprise was that Amity was surprised.

"What did you expect?" she said. "I've been telling you it would be worthwhile to open up on my side. There are people who prefer the less rich pickings out of reach of the law. It will tail off eventually."

But it did not, and Amity discovered, on checking the ledgers, that the Alaskan takings amounted effectively to the Canadian shortfall. She drew George Dowsby's attention to this.

"I know, Mrs. Jones. I can't explain it. I can't ask the prospectors a direct question, because I work for you, and they wouldn't tell me."

Matters got no better. Indeed, there was a gradual falling off from the Alaskan side, too. Then one morning George sought Amity out in her office. "A word, Mrs. Jones?" he asked.

"Of course, come in. Sit down."

He glanced around outside the door before closing it carefully, and spoke in a low voice. "I heard something last night. Just a whisper. It didn't altogether make sense, and I've spent a good part of the night trying to see how it fits together."

"Go on."

"The Alaskan assay office is offering a higher rate for its gold."

"That's ridiculous!" Amity exclaimed. "Mrs. York is as keen to make profits as I am, so why should she pay more? The books certainly don't show it. I could understand their paying less and pocketing the difference, but this just doesn't make sense."

"I wondered at first whether the intention might be to bankrupt your business as a way of forcing you out and enabling Mrs. York to have it all. But that almost amounts to cutting off her nose to spite her face. However, if they raised the price and at the same time fixed their scales so that the gold appeared to weigh less than it really does, they would be luring the prospectors away from you *and* acquiring more gold than they're paying for. That's very profitable."

"But we share the profits, and I see the books each week. If you're right, I should be receiving my share of this deception."

"With respect, Mrs. Jones, you're being naïve. You see a set of books that shows the amount of gold indicated by the rigged scales—a smaller amount than is actually assayed—being paid for at your rates. Now, if the extra paid is just a couple of cents but the scales are fixed to give an advantage of, say, four cents' worth of gold, then someone pockets an additional two cents, and it doesn't seem to be you."

Amity considered this theory in silence. No one likes feeling deceived, and she sought the flaws in his hypothesis with some desperation until finally she thought she had found one.

"But George, prospectors all have their own scales. They'd query the weight."

George shook his head. "Everyone knows prospectors' scales are inaccurate. So long as the difference isn't too much and remains constant, they'd never question it."

Amity knew he was right. "So you think Mungo Speen has set up this scheme?"

"I'm inclined to think so. He couldn't have carried it out on his own, though. Do you think that Mrs. York would have had anything to do with it?"

"Since we're being frank, I'd say she'd jump at the chance."
"What will you do about it?"
"I don't know. I suppose the first thing to do is somehow check for ourselves whether the story is true. Perhaps we could find a trustworthy prospector who would be willing to get some gold assayed on our behalf over there and report back."
"I've got an idea," George said. "Old Habakkuk Bronlund is due in around now. What do you think about asking him?"
"He's more reliable than most. Won't it look odd, though, if he comes here first and then takes his poke across the creek?"
"If he's agreeable, maybe we can stage a disagreement over the scales. Everyone knows he can be cantankerous. They'll not assume there's any substance in his complaint."
"You'll have to be careful how much we tell him before we've got his cooperation," Amity warned. "We don't want him trotting over there to put them on their guard."
There was nothing more to be done until Habakkuk Bronlund put in one of his rare appearances, so Amity and her assayer carried on as before, watching with alarm the continuing decline in their business. It was a remark of Edda's that caused Amity to revise her assessment of her partner's involvement in any scheme.
They had been going through the books. Edda studied them and then said, "Things don't seem to be improving this side, do they? Look at the books. It's still tailing off. Our side's dropped a bit, too."
"Any ideas why?" Amity asked.
Edda looked at her in wide-eyed surprise. "Goodness, no. Maybe we should put our minds to it, though."
Edda's remark puzzled Amity. She had never liked Edda, but she had never had reason to mistrust her until the arrival of Speen. Couldn't he be carrying out his scheme without Edda's knowledge? Surely the fact that she drew Amity's attention to the situation was, if anything, evidence of her ignorance of what was going on. The more Amity thought about it, the more she was inclined to think the other woman was as much a victim as she was herself.

HABAKKUK Bronlund was a prospector in the same mold as Vladimir Kislov. He had been in the north a long time and knew its ways. He did a bit of prospecting, a bit of trapping and avoided his fellowmen whenever possible. When it wasn't possible, he threw himself into their company with gusto, and nowadays that meant he stayed at Amity Jones' excellent hotel.

It therefore turned out to be a simple matter for George Dowsby to engage the old man in conversation. Later, over a friendly game of dominoes in George's cabin, Habakkuk agreed to cooperate. Indeed, he felt that he might quite enjoy storming out of the office and across the creek the next morning. There was no need for Mrs. Jones to provide him with gold to be assayed; he had his own, already weighed and lodged in her safe.

"But get this clear, young un," he warned George. "I can't storm out of here and then not sell over there, and if what you say is true, I'm going to lose on the deal. What're you going to do about that?"

"Mrs. Jones has agreed to make up the shortfall."

The next morning the handful of customers in the store were treated to one of old Bronlund's more memorable displays of ire as he insulted the assayer with such impressive terms as "perfidious shyster" and several more down-to-earth expressions. The consensus was that you couldn't help but admire the way Dowsby kept his temper, simply handing the old man back his poke and advising him to take it elsewhere.

Habakkuk spit on the floor. "I'll do just that," he declared, and stomped out of the store and across the creek to Alaska.

He slung his poke onto the bar, and Mungo looked at him through narrowed eyes. "Don't think we've seen you here before," he said.

"Not likely, since you weren't here before," Habakkuk retorted. "I'm not sorry to see Mrs. Jones has got some competition, because the woman just tried to cheat me out of my due."

Mungo Speen longed to ask more but was shrewd enough to hold his tongue. "Well, you won't have that trouble with us."

Habakkuk watched him with hawklike eyes. He made no comment when he was told the weight, but raised his eyebrows at the price. "That's better than I was quoted elsewhere."

Speen smiled. "This is Alaska," he said.

Habakkuk winked. "Suits me."

"I thought it might. Want to sell all of it?"

"Might as well. Don't suppose you'll object if I spends a good part of it in your saloon."

Speen grinned. "It'll be our pleasure."

When Habakkuk Bronlund rolled back to the Friendship Hotel, he wasn't nearly as drunk as he appeared.

Amity went to greet him. "I'm sorry you had a little altercation with George Dowsby this morning, Mr. Bronlund. I've had a word with him, and he's ready to apologize. I hope you'll accept it."

Habakkuk waved one arm in the expansive gesture of the inebriate. "I can afford to be mag . . . mag . . . nanimous, Mrs. Jones."

"Then why don't you join me in a nice strong cup of coffee? It will show there's no hard feeling. What do you say?"

"I say, Mrs. Jones," he replied with the carefulness of one whose words were not emerging in their intended form, "I say that you are a remarkably fine woman, and a cup of coffee would be a pleasure."

Once the door of Amity's office closed behind them, the pretense was dropped, and he reported what had happened. "Your suspicions were correct," he concluded. "It weighed out at considerably less. The price was better, but not better enough to leave me richer."

"Were all your dealings with the assayer?" Amity asked. "Was Mrs. York there?"

"No—only the assayer."

Amity calculated the shortfall and added it to Habakkuk's poke. "Thank you for your help," she said. "There'll be no bill for your stay here. Just don't mention to a soul that this was prearranged."

"Wouldn't cross my mind." He grinned.

THE confirmation Habakkuk had obtained came as no surprise to Amity, but it seemed to prove that Speen was acting on his own initiative and, presumably, for his own profit. Edda needed to be warned. But if she was as besotted with him as Amity was afraid she might be, it was unlikely Edda would believe her.

After a sleepless night Amity went to seek out Edda. She nodded at Mungo Speen as she passed his cage. It pained her to have to do so, but it was important he should see nothing untoward in this visit. She knocked on the door to Edda's quarters. She found Edda sitting in an upholstered armchair with a fur rug round her legs.

"There's something we have to discuss," Amity began, perching on the edge of Edda's bed. "Edda, how sure are you of Speen?"

The question was entirely unexpected, and Edda was not able to disguise either her surprise or the wariness that swiftly replaced it. "Absolutely sure. Why?"

"How well do you actually know him? You know he doesn't dare set foot in Canada. Doesn't that make you wonder?"

Edda shrugged. "Is that all? Lots of men make up such stories about the North-West Mounted Police chasing them, particularly if they want to impress a woman. Why have you suddenly taken a dislike to the man?"

"I haven't, though I'm bound to say that I don't share your high opinion of him. Edda, I think he's cheating us." Quickly Amity told her partner her suspicions.

"This is preposterous. You're making it up," Edda said sharply when Amity had finished.

It occurred to Amity that Edda was less upset than she should have been. "No, I'm not. I sent someone I could trust over here to test it out. He brought over some of his previously weighed gold. It was assayed and sold here. Then he reported back to me."

"He must have quite a soft spot for you if he's prepared to lose money like that just to confirm your suspicions."

"I made good the shortfall."

"Ah, now I understand. Having explained it all to this trusted soul, you didn't realize you'd given him the very means by which he could exploit you. You've no proof beyond his word that he was paid over the odds or given false weight." She laughed. "Poor little Amity. It's you who have been deceived."

Amity cursed herself for not having foreseen that argument. There was nothing for it but to tell her about Samuel. "That isn't all. His story about not setting foot in Canada wasn't just perverse bragging. That man is Samuel's murderer. I recognized him."

Edda looked shaken. "You let me employ a man that you now claim had murdered my husband—*my* husband, not yours—and you said nothing? Just how gullible do you think I am?"

"When I agreed to his employment, I hadn't seen him. After we'd met, I didn't know what to do. The authorities can't touch him here, and I've no wish to be murdered in my bed. He hadn't recognized me, so I stayed away. Maybe it was cowardly, but that's what I did."

Edda was out of her chair now, pacing up and down. "That's not the reason at all, is it? The last thing you wanted was for the police to step in, because once they did, the real story would come out."

Amity stared at her, bewildered. "What do you mean?"

"Maybe Mungo did kill Samuel and maybe he didn't, but I'm not a fool, Amity, and I'm not unobservant. Do you imagine I haven't seen the resemblance between Mungo and your daughter? It's my belief Samuel died because he came home and caught you together. If Mungo shot him, you were an accomplice."

"No!" The word was a cry wrenched from her heart.

"What I couldn't understand was why Mungo didn't recognize you," Edda went on relentlessly. "Now, why should that be? There was you, stuck in the back of beyond with a dreary husband, who was away from home as often as not. Along comes a stranger, makes a few charming noises and you were seduced. You'd remember him because it was one bright light in a dreary life, but he wouldn't remember you, because you were neither the first nor the last. Now you decide to come to me with this story that he's been cheating us. Why? Are you sour because he hasn't remembered you? Or are you jealous because he prefers me?"

Amity was shaking her head. The only possible refutation of Edda's malicious theories was the plain, unvarnished truth, but there was so much spite in the conclusions Edda had drawn that Amity could not bring herself to disclose any more. Her visit here had been futile.

She crossed the room and hesitated after she had lifted the latch, half inclined to tell Edda the whole story, but her instinct won. That brief hesitation was all Mungo Speen needed to nip smartly back behind his cage. Amity strode across the saloon without a glance to right or left. The assayer had not heard all the conversation, but he had heard Amity's allegation about Samuel's murder, together with Edda's conclusions, and he put two and two together.

His immediate reaction combined fear with fury, and he resolved that Amity must be silenced. But as the conversation progressed, his resolve eased. He found Edda's suggestion that he had represented excitement in Amity's life an appealing one. Then there was the child. What could be more natural than that Amity had not given him away, because he was the father of her child and Amity had not been entirely averse to his attentions?

He knocked on Edda's door and stepped inside without waiting for a reply. "To what did we owe the honor of that visit?" he asked.

Edda smiled. "She came to warn me that you're cheating us as well as the prospectors. She sent someone over here after having weighed his gold, so they know about the difference in weight and price. But as long as she goes on thinking you're deceiving me as well as her, she'll tell me about any steps she intends to take."

He nodded. "Sounds reasonable. Was that all?"

"Isn't that enough?"

"I'll get back to work, then."

So Edda wasn't mentioning the murder charge. Why? Either Edda hadn't made up her mind whether to believe Amity or not, or else she was dreaming up some deeper scheme, which might not be to Mungo Speen's advantage.

The revelation that Amity had caught on to their little ruse was not as unwelcome as it would have been had he not made the discovery about Pandora. He would have to play his cards carefully, but if he was successful, he could win Amity over—the thought of acquiring a ready-made family held considerable appeal, especially when the woman involved was wealthy enough to ensure a comfortable life. The assayer decided to continue to operate his present scheme but with a subtle change of emphasis: it would be Edda who would be gradually bankrupted out. The beauty of this little alteration was that she would continue to believe the situation was unchanged, so she would not be likely to question his actions.

It wasn't difficult to persuade David to bring his little sister with him to visit the Alaskan side, though Mungo was careful to stress to the boy the importance of not missing his lessons. Pandora was always glad to go. Mr. Speen seemed to have an inexhaustible supply of sweets.

AMITY viewed the whole situation with distress, lying awake at night wondering how best to drop the association with Edda.

"I've had a word with Mungo about the price we're paying," Edda said when she next visited. "It seems he misunderstood. Something I said made him think we were paying more than we should. He insists, however, that his scales are right. It seems your informant knew when he was on to a good thing."

"It certainly looks like that," Amity agreed. There was no point in drawing Edda's attention to the fact that the price recorded in the ledger was the correct one and that, if the assayer had believed the higher one to be right, he would have recorded it accordingly. Both Edda and Amity would have picked it up as soon as they went over the books at the end of the week. Amity could not have been given a clearer indication that George's assessment had been the more accurate. Now she knew that Edda had known what was going on. The price had been put right, but the prospectors would still be cheated on the scales.

A far greater worry was the fact that though Edda had appeared not to believe Amity's murder charge against Speen, it was reasonable to assume Edda had told him of Amity's accusation. Once he knew who she was, her life could not be worth much.

Almost more than the revelation of her identity, Amity dreaded Speen's being told of Pandora's paternity. She had no idea how a man of that sort would react. At present he was being very kind to both children. Perhaps there was nothing incongruous in such a violent man liking children, but she would rest easier when the creek thawed and Pandora would not be able to cross it unassisted. The time had come to tell Sergeant Woolacombe who Speen was, but she dared not risk driving to Fort Selkirk now. She would have to wait till the thaw. Then she could travel with those prospectors who decided to go Outside at the end of the winter. She would take the children with her, and they would remain close to police protection until something had been done about Speen.

Amity felt beleaguered by a partner she could no longer trust and an employee who would kill her if it suited him. She felt totally isolated. Consequently, when a familiar tall figure stomped snow all over the mat inside the hotel door, she almost ran to meet him.

"Jake, you're back! I thought you'd gone for good!"

Chapter Fourteen

"Now that is *not* the sort of welcome I was expecting," he said dryly. When she was within reach, he drew her to him and kissed her.

"It's more than you deserve," she retorted, her eyes laughing up at him. "Whatever happened? One day you were here and the next you'd gone. The children were very upset."

"Only the children? I'd hoped their mother might have been, too. Tell me, does the offer of free board and lodging still hold?"

Amity drew back, unable to hide her disappointment. "So that's it," she said lightly. "You've run out of grubstake. Yes, Jake Treviscoe, it still holds, if only because it's good to see a familiar face again." She hesitated. "Jake, I'm glad you're back."

He looked at her enigmatically. "Good—and sometime I want to have a serious talk with you."

"What about?"

He glanced around. "Not now. I don't want to be overheard."

"It sounds intriguing."

The children's delight in his appearance made David and Pandora forget all about visiting their "friend," Mr. Speen, and Jake spent the evening telling them stories about his adventures. He seemed to have spent a lot of time encountering Indian deities, who pointed him in the direction of dinner or shelter or the right trail.

Pandora, sitting on his knee, was wide-eyed. David was unconvinced. "How come we never see these spirits?" he asked.

"Because they've been driven away from places like Friendship. Friendship is built on gold, and the men who are greedy for it come here with nothing else in their minds. Only in the stillness of the wilderness will you find the old spirits."

Amity smiled sadly. "You sound just like Samuel. I've never been quite sure to what extent you shared his view of this country."

"Samuel's view was simple, direct, and time is proving it to be true." He put Pandora down on the floor. "David, you and your sister should be in bed and asleep." He led the children to a cozy box bed behind a curtain in their mother's warm room and tucked them in.

"Now, what's all the mystery about, Jake?" Amity asked when the children were settled and the bed's door was closed.

He took her hand. "Amity, why don't you get out before all this comes crashing down? The Klondike fields are about dug out now, and next season may be the last. Sell up and take the children back to England. Make their future your excuse, and you should get a good price for your share of the business."

Amity knew he was talking sense, but she knew, too, that if she sold out, she must first offer her share to Edda, who would be bound to discuss it with Speen, and Amity could not see him letting the one eyewitness to his crimes walk away. Now, if ever, was the time to unburden herself to Jake, but she still could not tell him the truth about Pandora. She shook her head. "Not just yet."

"The gold has really got hold of you, hasn't it?" Jake said bitterly. "Very well, perhaps I can offer a more appealing suggestion. Come with me to Nome. It's on the west coast of Alaska. There's placer gold in the sands there. I've seen it for myself."

"The coast must be frozen solid. How were you able to work it?"

"What makes you think I've been working it this winter? I've known about it for years, but it will be discovered by the end of next season, most likely. Let's get there by the thaw, pan for a summer and quit. We could take a boat to Seattle or San Francisco or back to England if that's what you want. Then David can have that education you were always talking about. Pandora, too."

"I suppose," she said reflectively, "if the sands of Nome are as rich as all that, there'd be no need to sell up here. I could just take what's in the safe and go. Still, I'll have to think about it."

Jake frowned. Amity would have little difficulty selling her share of Friendship, and for a good price. Why on earth should she contemplate not bothering to? It wasn't in character at all.

Amity went to bed that night with much to turn over in her mind. She wished he had been more explicit about their own relationship. Whenever she had begun to think they were reaching an easy understanding, he had simply disappeared, for no apparent reason and with no later explanation. It was almost as if he were afraid that the easy understanding would develop into something more. Thus she knew that the one question she longed to put to him would be precisely the one that would send him away for good.

She saw little of Jake the next day as he trudged round the township with the two children at his heels. She was aware, however, that he did not cross the creek to see Edda, and her spirits lifted.

When supper was over and most of the diners had left, Jake said to Amity, "I've had a good look around. The signs tell me there's just one more clear season here. Delay and you'll lose it all."

Amity looked at him curiously. "For someone who only does a little prospecting, you speak with remarkable authority."

He grinned. "I'm a miner by training."

"Cornwall, as I recall, but that can't have been for gold."

"No. Tin. But a worked-out vein is a worked-out vein, no matter what the metal is. Prospectors are careful what they tell a stranger, but the clues are there. They're getting less gold to the ton than they used to."

Amity looked at him curiously. "So where did you learn about working with gold?"

"Australia," he said.

"Australia," she repeated. Several things that had troubled her began to slip into place. "I see." She recalled Jake's reluctance to set foot in Fort Selkirk and that he had used an assumed name when he did go. Had Jake been transported from Cornwall to Australia to work the mines? If he had somehow then escaped from Australia before his time was served, he had taken some big risks on her behalf.

Jake was silent for some time. Then he said, "I've been hearing gossip. Seems Edda York's got herself a fancy man."

Amity looked at him sharply. "Her assayer. Do you mind?"

"Why should I?" Jake sounded genuinely surprised at her question, and Amity was conscious of a quiet satisfaction. "You said 'her assayer,' " he went on. "Does that mean he's not employed by both of you?"

"A slip of the tongue," Amity replied. "We both employ him—technically—but he was Edda's choice, and he never comes over here."

"You don't like him? Am I right?"

Amity hesitated. The temptation to unburden herself was almost overwhelming, but at the same time all the arguments against telling him returned in force. She avoided his eyes. "I just find him . . . unappealing."

"Just as well, I'd say, if Edda's got her hooks into him," he commented dryly, but he noticed the evasion. For a moment he had felt that he was holding the key to all those unexplained facets of Amity Jones, which made him unsure how much of his own feelings he could wisely reveal. But the moment had passed.

The next day Jake extended his inspection across the creek. Apart from the absence of a store, the signs of prosperity in Alaskan Friendship were marked. More people now lived in cabins than in tents, and some of the cabins had false fronts that gave the illusion of two stories.

He stepped through the narrow door of the saloon to be met by the welcoming blast of hot air from the potbellied stove in the middle of the room. He glanced at the man inside the assayer's cage. There was something familiar about him, thought Jake, although he was sure he had never met him before. He knocked on the door of Edda's office and went in without waiting for any response.

She looked up and instantly smiled. "Jake Treviscoe!" she exclaimed. "I thought you'd gone for good. When did you get back?"

"Day before yesterday."

"Why didn't you come to see me before?"

"I wasn't sure I'd be welcome. I'm told you've a new fancy man."

She laughed. "Old friends are always welcome, and if the new ones don't like it, then that's their misfortune. Mungo won't mind."

"Who's this Mungo?" Jake asked.

"Mungo Speen, my assayer."

"I saw him as I came in. Maybe I should meet him sometime, but right now I want to talk to you about Amity's children. They were the reason I came back."

Edda looked surprised. "Why? They're not your responsibility."

"I've known them for a long time, and I'm fond of them. I don't feel this is the place for them. I'd like to persuade Amity to sell up and take them Outside, maybe even back to England."

Edda stiffened. This looked suspiciously like interference with her business. "Why mention it to me?"

"Because you'd get first refusal on her half of the business. If I know you're happy to buy her out at a good price, it will be easier to persuade her."

"If she wants to go, she'll have to take what she can get," Edda retorted. "She couldn't expect top price."

"She might get it elsewhere if you weren't interested, and you might have another partner foisted on you. It wouldn't surprise me if several prospectors got together to buy her out."

Edda pursed her lips. New partners delving into her system was not something she relished. Her plan had always been to get Amity's share for herself, but she had not expected to have to buy her out at full market price. "You'll have to give me time to go over the figures." She regarded him speculatively. "I suppose your motives are entirely altruistic. Or is it that Amity would then be very rich?"

"If that's what you want to think, I can't stop you."

"And you can't stop me planting the suspicion in Amity's mind."

"No. But if Amity suspects my motive, she'll sit tight. Another strike on the Canadian side, and then you'll never shift her."

Edda's eyes narrowed. "Is there likely to be another strike?"

"That's what the word is. Can't say I've seen any sign of it, but if I can't persuade Amity to go, I'll have a shot at it myself instead."

"Let me think it over."

Jake got to his feet. "Fine, but don't be too long."

Edda rose, too, and led him out into the saloon.

When he was gone, Edda spoke to Speen. "Lock up your cage and come to the office."

When he joined her a few minutes later, she gave him the gist of her recent conversation. "It's not quite what we planned, is it?"

"No reason why we shouldn't turn it to our advantage," Mungo told her. "But if Treviscoe's story about another big strike is true, then why is he anxious to get your partner and her children away? Why not stay and make the strike?"

Edda smiled knowingly. "Much easier to batten on a woman who's made herself a fortune in the last couple of years."

He nodded. "I suppose that makes sense. Maybe if the price is right, you could do worse than approach her."

"I'd much rather have forced her out for nothing," Edda said.

Edda had given Mungo much to think about. If she was right, then Treviscoe was on to a scheme which Mungo could only regret not having thought of for himself. He had hoped to ingratiate himself with Amity and to turn the tables on Edda. Unfortunately, Amity's failure to visit Alaskan Friendship and his own reluctance to set foot in Canada prevented his advancing that scheme. He had to persuade her to listen to him, and that meant he must find some way of speaking to her away from the influence of others.

AMITY knew that the children's affection for Jake would not keep them at his side indefinitely. Therefore, so long as David's lessons didn't suffer, she tried not to mind that they began once more to spend time across the creek. But when she learned that David had not appeared for his lesson, she made her way angrily to the saloon.

Edda looked up as Amity stormed in, and seemed genuinely surprised. "Aren't they back yet?"

"Back from where?" Amity demanded.

"I haven't the slightest idea," Edda told her. "Mungo took them for a drive. You've no need to worry. They'll be perfectly safe with him."

"Are you out of your mind? Edda, I told you about that man. I don't want my children's throats slit."

"Now you're being silly." Edda put a hand on Amity's arm. "Mungo's fond of those children. They will be all right."

Amity calmed herself with an effort. "I'm sorry," she said. "When they get back, will you make sure they come straight home?"

"I'll bring them myself," Edda promised.

When Amity reached home, she went to her office. She had been there barely five minutes when a man she knew only by sight tapped on the door. He handed her a note. "I was asked to give you this," he said.

Amity slit it open and glanced at the signature. It was Mungo Speen's. "When were you given this?" she asked sharply.

"Can't say, exactly. Sometime after breakfast."

"Why didn't you bring it straight to me?"

"I was paid not to. 'She'll be around after lunchtime,' I was told. 'Don't give it to her until she's back to Canada.' "

As soon as the door closed behind him, Amity read the letter:

> I have your children, both your son and my daughter. They are well and unharmed. If you want them back and in that condition, you will meet me at the place indicated below, bringing with you the contents of your safe, both gold and money. An escort would be inadvisable.

The words did not seem to register at first. The shock was too great. Not only had her children been kidnapped by a cold-blooded murderer, but he also apparently knew all about Pandora.

Now, more than ever, Amity needed Jake's advice and help, even if that meant telling him all the circumstances surrounding Samuel's death. Her children's lives were far more important than Jake's opinion of her. But Jake had gone hunting, and she had no idea when he would return.

She studied the rudimentary map at the bottom of the letter. She knew the rendezvous. The dry valley following the main street out of Alaskan Friendship fed into another, promisingly wide, dry valley. The promise was deceptive, for this valley narrowed quickly and ended at the sheer face of a mountain. At its foot stood the cabin of a long-dead trapper, kept in a modest state of repair by anyone who needed to use it, but which was deserted most of the time. Amity had visited it once or twice. All the same, she tore the map from the letter and stuffed it into her pocket. Then she took a deep breath and left her office, her plan made.

She had no difficulty assuming a worried expression as she emerged into her store and crossed over to the assayer's cage. "George, will you keep an eye on the store for me? I've had a cryptic note from Habakkuk Bronlund asking me to send some supplies. I know where he is, and it will be easiest if I go myself."

George looked uneasy. "You're sure it's from Habakkuk?"

"Oh, quite sure. I know his hand," she lied. "I'll get through quicker if I do it myself. Some flour and sugar, coffee and beans—that ought to serve the purpose." She loaded the sacks of goods onto a trolley and pushed it into the office. There it was a simple matter to replace the food with the gold and coin from the safe. Then she harnessed her dogs to her sled and brought them round to the front of the store. As a precaution, she strapped a rifle, an axe and a shovel to the sled. The stores were soon loaded up, and in a very short time Amity and her team were making their way down to the creek.

NIGHT had fallen by the time she reached the cabin. The door was closed and the one window shuttered, but through chinks in the log walls, thin lines of firelight flickered.

By the time she had finished tethering her team, Speen was standing in the open door. "Thought you'd make it," he said smugly. "You've brought the gold?"

"First I see my children," she replied, disconcerted that neither of them had rushed to greet her.

"You'd better come in." He stood aside to let her pass, and she walked into a room which was empty except for a pile of blankets. "Where are they? What have you done with them?" she cried.

He put a finger to his lips, stepped across to a small door tucked into the darkest corner of the cabin and opened it. Since her last visit, someone had extended the eaves at the back of the cabin to form a small room. Here both children slept snugly under bearskin rugs. Speen closed the door gently.

"It's the only part of the cabin where the logs have been properly chinked," he told her. "That's the warmest place to sleep."

"How considerate of you," Amity said acidly. She turned towards the door. "I'll fetch the gold. Then we're going home."

He was at the door before her. "I've a better suggestion."

Amity's insides twisted sickeningly. Oh, please, no, she thought. Please, not again.

"Sit down," he told her. "I want to talk."

Warily Amity sat on an upturned box by the fire, while Speen crouched on his heels on the other side, looking up at her across the flames. "You recognized me at once, didn't you?" he said.

"In the circumstances, I was unlikely ever to forget your face."
"I didn't recognize you at all."
"Why should you? I don't imagine I was the first woman you'd ever raped, and I'm probably not the last."
"Oh, come now. It wasn't as bad as that. Anyway, in my book the fact that you wouldn't tell us where the gold was suggests that you were looking forward to a bit of excitement."
"There's nothing exciting about pain," she snapped.
"No? Not everyone would agree with you. Still, why argue? The proof's in there. Pandora's mine, and if it was as repugnant to you as you're trying to suggest, why should you have kept her?"
Amity paled. "What makes you think you're her father?"
"I don't think. I know. I have this nasty habit of listening at keyholes. I heard what you told Edda. You had me running scared for a time there. I thought you'd send for the police, but you didn't, did you? And why not? Because deep down you'd enjoyed it all."
Amity could barely bring herself to look at him. "You disgust me. Take the gold and let us go, and I'll pray we never meet again."
He shook his head. "I've a better idea. We'll take the gold, yes, and I'll persuade Edda to buy you out. Then we'll get married and take the children and go. We'll become a proper family."
Amity's mouth fell open in disbelief. "No!" she cried, but before the cry had died away, David, who had been listening quietly at the cubbyhole door, burst into the room and hurled himself at Speen. Amity saw to her horror that he was clutching a hunting knife. "No!" she shouted again.
Speen easily disarmed his assailant and pushed him aside. As Amity opened her mouth to protest again, Speen grabbed her wrist and pulled her towards him, the point of David's knife pressing at the side of her neck. "If you refuse me, I'll leave you and the boy lying here in a pool of blood, and I'll take the gold and my daughter and I'll bring her up *my* way."

Chapter Fifteen

THE early arctic twilight had almost faded into night by the time Jake Treviscoe drove back into Friendship, the carcass of a bighorn sheep loaded on his sled. He unhitched his team, hauled the day's catch into the icy storeroom and entered the hotel.

There was no immediate sign of Amity. George Dowsby had already closed up the store and was in the process of locking his cage.

"Is Amity around?" Jake asked.

"No. She went out with the team well after noon. I don't imagine she'll be back until tomorrow. Said she'd had an urgent request from old Bronlund for some supplies."

"Why didn't she send someone?"

"She said she knew the trail and it was easier to go herself than to try and explain to someone else."

It was odd, Jake thought. If Habakkuk had been in difficulties, why didn't whoever brought the message help him out instead? Still, peculiar things did happen up here.

He had barely closed the door of his room when there was a tap on it. George Dowsby stood there, the office keys in his hand. "There's something I think you ought to see, Mr. Treviscoe."

Jake followed him to the office. When the door was closed behind him, George went on. "When I came to put away today's gold, I found the safe unlocked. This is what was inside." He swung the door open to reveal tins of butter, beef, milk and marmalade. "These are some of the supplies she had ready for Bronlund. She loaded the whole lot onto that little trolley she uses and left it in here while she hitched up her team."

"I take it there was gold in here?" Jake asked.

"It was pretty full—everything we've taken this winter, ready to go out with the thaw."

"That's what I thought. Did she take the children with her?"

George shook his head. "I don't see that she could have. They went out this morning and didn't come back in time for David's lessons. Mrs. Jones went storming over to Alaska to fetch them, but she returned without them and made no further reference to the matter. Half an hour later she said she'd had this message from Bronlund."

"Who brought it?"

George shrugged. "No idea."

Jake caught sight of a piece of paper beneath Amity's desk. As he picked it up, his eyes caught the signature "Mungo Speen." He read the message and knew at once why Amity had disappeared. He also thought that he had found the unpalatable answer to several unanswered questions. He pushed the letter into his pocket.

"She's gone to collect the children," he said.

"And the gold?"

"Use your imagination. They've been kidnapped, but I'd suggest you don't spread that around." He would have preferred not to have to reveal even that much, but needed Dowsby on his side.

"Do you know where they are?"

"No. But they certainly won't have been taken deeper into Canadian territory, and there's only one trail out of Alaskan Friendship, so that's where I'll begin. Who's got a fresh team they can lend me?"

"Bill Conniston's got one," George suggested.

"Ask him if I can have the use of it. Tell him he can use my dogs in the meantime. But don't tell him where I'm going or why. If ever there was a gossiping old woman, it's Bill Conniston."

George grinned. "Don't worry."

Bill Conniston, though puzzled, willingly accepted Jake's team as surety for his own dogs. The fresh team was fastened to the sled, the lantern was lit and Jake set out across the creek and onto the trail through Alaskan Friendship.

The team pulled well together, but the need to find Amity's tracks meant that speed was out of the question. One thing worked in his favor. Once he was well away from the settlement, he saw that only two sets of dogsled tracks had used the trail since the last light snowfall. It was a reasonable guess that Mungo Speen would conceal himself and the children in one of the smaller valleys that cut into the mountains off the main trail. Jake knew of one particular valley that had a cabin. That would be the ideal place for Speen's purpose.

Jake noticed the dogs were making rather heavier weather of the journey than expected, then realized the runners were biting rather deeper into the snow than was usual. The snow was no harder than if it had just fallen, yet it should be frozen solid. He hoped the temperature would soon fall again.

Jake had plenty to occupy his thoughts as he urged the dogs on. Most on his mind was Speen's assumption that Pandora was his own daughter. Jake had always recognized that the child did not resemble Samuel or her mother. But now that the idea had been put in his mind, he could see there was quite a striking resemblance to Mungo Speen.

There had been something familiar about Speen when Jake first met him. No wonder Amity was reluctant to leave Friendship. He thought that she disliked the man, and she had virtually said as much. Perhaps what she really disliked was his liaison with Edda York.

Amity had seemed shattered by Samuel's death, yet how could she genuinely have mourned a man when she must so very recently have played him false? Now he knew why she had always withdrawn from any advance he had made. She preferred Mungo Speen.

A disappointed and resentful corner of Jake's mind advised him to leave Amity to sort out her own mess. But he dismissed it. No matter how one looked at it, right now she was being shamefully used, and Jake could not stand idly by. He urged the dogs on.

AMITY tried to back away from Speen, but the grip on her wrist was too tight and the knife too close to her neck. He glanced over at David. "Don't you try nothin', boy, or your mother's the one that will suffer. Just like she did before. Remember?"

"Do as you're told, Davy," Amity said, striving to keep her voice calm, trying to stall for time.

"In my pocket you'll find some strips of rawhide," Speen told her. "Take one out and tie that little hellion's hands behind him. I can't keep my eyes on both of you."

Amity hesitated before doing as she was told.

Speen grinned. "Sensible woman." With David no longer a threat, he marginally relaxed. "Tomorrow we'll head west and find a preacher to tie the knot. A wife can't give evidence against her husband, so once I'm married to you, I'm safe."

Only until I poison you or the carving knife slips, she thought.

"Meanwhile," he went on, "I've no intention of staying awake all night just to watch you and that son of yours." He felt in his pocket and brought out more rawhide. "Put him back in the cubbyhole and tie his feet. Tell him not to try anything. I'm a very light sleeper."

Amity pushed David gently towards the door. "Try to sleep, Davy. Things won't look so bad in the morning." She wondered, though, what improvement in their situation could possibly arise in the night.

She closed the door of the little room and, as she turned from doing so, cast her eyes rapidly round in search of weapons. Speen still held David's knife, and the hilt of his own was just visible in its sheath beneath his knee. His rifle was propped up in one corner.

But fleeting as her quick survey had been, it had not escaped Speen's notice. "You, too," he said. "Come here."

Amity did not at first understand his drift. As soon as she was within reach, his arm shot out and grabbed hers again, this time twisting it round behind her back till she thought it would break. He held it there until he could tie her hands behind her back. That done, he threw her down onto the pile of blankets and used his muffler to tie her ankles together.

"Thought I didn't see you looking for something to use," he said with relish. He was kneeling beside her now. Amity could feel his breath on her face, and the memory of their first meeting returned with frightful clarity.

He grinned and lightly ran the knife blade down the front of her bodice. "It's a temptation, but I can wait till we're married."

He bent closer, and her whole body became rigid with revulsion.

At the precise moment that Speen's mouth descended on hers, Amity heard the cabin door burst open. Her assailant's back was to the door, but over him she saw Jake, his rifle raised and cocked.

Jake was devastated at the scene that he thought he saw before him. He had not bargained to find Amity and Speen in any embrace. He blanched, then lowered his gun just as Speen rolled over towards his own gun. Jake realized at once that Amity had been in no position to repel her assailant. Caught off guard, Jake was only sufficiently alert to duck as Speen cocked and fired. He was not fast enough to stop Speen from running past him and out into the night.

Jake stifled his impulse to give chase in the necessity of freeing Amity. "The children?" he asked.

"They're all right. I'll see to them. Go after him, Jake. He's the man who killed Samuel—the one who pulled the trigger."

If Jake had been devastated before, he was stunned now. "And Pandora?" he asked. "Is he her father?"

Amity's tormented face looked up at him. "Yes. And I had even less choice about it then than I would have had just now."

Jake became very still. He rested his hand briefly on her shoulder, a gesture that spoke volumes. "Go back to Friendship in the morning. I'll return there as soon as I can."

Amity shook her head. "We'll stay here until you get back," she said. "There's food on the sled. We'll not starve."

He nodded. "Don't wait longer than three or four days for me. Then go back. Agreed? Things may not turn out as we'd wish."

"Agreed."

SPEEN PAUSED ONLY LONG enough to remove the easily identifiable sack of gold from Amity's sled. This he heaved onto his own sled before unstaking the team. Not only were his dogs bigger than those of the other two teams, they had also had several hours' rest.

Still, the transfer of the gold cost him precious minutes, and when Jake finally emerged, he was in time to see Speen disappear down the valley.

Amity's team was fresher than Jake's own, but he would first have to unload her sled. His team, tired as it was, would be the better bet.

He let the dogs set their own pace. There was no need to keep the other man in sight, for he knew that when Speen hit the main trail, he was unlikely to turn back towards Friendship.

But which trail would he take? Jake pondered. His only feasible alternative to passing through Canadian territory was to head across to the Copper River, where, come the impending thaw, he'd be able to trade his dog team for a canoe trip to Juneau.

Jake knew he was on the right trail when he glimpsed Speen as he passed across a patch of moonlight some distance ahead. Jake decided to rest his team for the few remaining hours before dawn.

The wisdom of this became apparent several hours into the new day, when he sighted Speen and his team only two or three miles ahead. No longer driving his dogs, Speen was walking with them to lighten the load. Obviously he had not been prepared to risk resting them on the trail, and now he was paying the price. Jake smiled to himself and checked his rifle.

Not far beyond Speen, Jake could make out a broad expanse of ice where the frozen river widened out into a lake. He guessed the other man would use this unobstructed stretch of ice to push his team harder, and Jake now pressed his own dogs to cut the distance between them.

By the time Speen had reached the lake, Jake was half a mile behind. The yip-yip of Jake's dogs alerted Speen, who glanced over his shoulder and realized how close his pursuer was. He raised his whip to force his team on.

Jake could see how reluctant the big dogs were to step onto the ice—a sure sign that they sensed its instability as a result of the imminent thaw. Speen appeared not to be taking this into consideration. It was a foolish man who thought he knew better than his team. Jake pressed his own dogs forward until he was within hailing distance. "You can't make it, Speen," he called. "Give yourself up."

He had no idea whether Speen heard him, for the man continued to lash his dogs onto the ice. The leader stepped gingerly onto the frozen surface. Then, finding it supported his weight, the dog continued with added confidence, the rest following. Speen gave a whoop of triumph and took his place on the runners. Jake brought his own team to a standstill and watched Speen drive his team on across the lake.

The big team had gone less than fifty yards when a crack, like a rifle shot, rent the air, followed almost immediately by another. Jake saw the ice crack under the sled. Seconds later the undertow pulled the floes apart and the overladen sled slipped into the black water.

As Jake watched from the bank, the dogs, their instincts more finely honed than Speen's, managed to haul themselves farther onto the ice while their load dangled behind them, too heavy to be dragged up behind them, but not yet heavy enough with ice to drag them back down.

By the time Speen realized what was happening, the rear of the sled was already slipping beneath the surface. Too late to leap from the sinking runners onto a stable floe, he sank slowly into the icy water, his mukluks filling as he submerged.

His head went under and then surfaced. Desperately he reached for the sled, but he was not strong enough to counter the undertow.

Jake snatched up his shovel and ventured onto the ice, spread-eagling himself across the surface, shovel in one hand, knife in the other. He pushed the handle of the shovel toward Speen. "Grab it, man. Grab it, and I'll haul you out somehow."

But it wasn't urging that Speen needed now. It was strength. He reached towards the shovel. His fingers, frozen numb in their sodden mittens, came within half an inch of their goal, then slipped slowly and inexorably away. As Speen realized he wasn't going to make it, the desperate determination faded from his face, to be replaced by wide-eyed fear as he went down for the last time.

Jake watched in horror, knowing there was nothing more he could do. He wished no man a death like that, but he thought of Amity and Samuel, and David's muteness after his father's death, and wondered whether there might not be divine retribution in the murderer's end.

He had not finished here yet, however. There might be nothing more to be done for Mungo Speen, but his exhausted team was still struggling against the weight of the sled. Jake crept cautiously over to the dogs until he could reach out and sever the traces that held them to the sled. As they leaped, relieved, for the firmer ice of the shore, he followed them and freed them from their harnesses. It was no cruelty to turn them loose in this territory. Dogs such as these were more than capable of fending for themselves.

He returned to his own team, strapped the shovel back onto the sled, then turned the dogs and headed back. They all needed a rest, but not here, at the lake of despair.

IT WAS getting late when Jake finally approached the little cabin. His heart lifted as he saw light flickering through the unchinked logs. He hammered on the door. "It's Jake," he called in warning, and opened the door.

Amity stood up as he came in, her arms round her children. "Where is he?" she asked warily.

"Don't worry. He's dead. The fool forced his dogs onto ice they knew wasn't safe. The ice broke and the sled went down. I tried to fish him out, but he couldn't make it. I'm afraid your gold's gone, too. It was on the sled."

She nodded. "I suppose I'm as addicted to gold as the next person, but I can afford to lose one season's takings."

"If you can say that, you're not addicted." Jake sniffed. "Do I smell food?"

Amity was suddenly flustered. "I'm sorry. Of course, you must need something to eat."

Half a spit-roasted hare and a large spoonful of beans soon took the edge off Jake's hunger. He became aware that David did not take his eyes off him.

"When are you going away again?" the boy finally asked, almost defiantly.

Jake looked taken aback. "I don't know," he said. "I wasn't reckoning on going away at all."

David glanced around the cabin. "You won't be very comfortable here."

"That wasn't what I had in mind," Jake told him gently.

"You're coming back to Friendship with us?" the boy asked.

"I'll do a deal with you, Davy," Jake said. "If I go anywhere without you, I'll give you plenty of warning. That's a promise. Now, why don't you and Pandora take yourselves off to your snug little cubbyhole and go to sleep."

"You won't be gone in the morning?"

"Definitely not." He could see that David was not convinced. "Tomorrow I'll go shoot something big enough to feed the dogs and us. I'd be happy if you'd come with me. How does that strike you?"

David's face was wreathed in smiles. "Mighty well," he said. "Come on, Pandora. I'm going to need my sleep tonight."

When the door had closed behind them, Amity poured some coffee. She, too, longed to know exactly what Jake had meant, but she felt inhibited about asking.

They sipped in silence, and Jake frowned as he watched Amity. Her eyes were downcast, avoiding his, unlike her usual forthright gaze. He finally decided to break the silence. "I don't know what you plan to do, but the offer about coming with me to Nome still applies."

Amity glanced at him. "You're an honorable man, Jake Treviscoe, and I'm grateful for that, but the circumstances are different now. I don't think you've had time to reflect fully on all the implications."

"What on earth do you think was going through my mind during all those long hours of tracking Speen? Amity, you packed a real sledgehammer of information into those few brief moments before I left here." He reached across and covered her hand with his own. "Why did you never tell me the full story before?"

She looked at him almost fearfully. "We seemed to be good friends. Once, I even thought perhaps you were a little fond of me. I didn't want to risk losing that friendship. I dreaded seeing repugnance in your face when I told you the truth."

He frowned, puzzled. "It would have been repugnance for the crime, not the victim."

"Are you sure?" she asked bitterly. "Wouldn't the question have been at the back of your mind whether I'd invited it in some way?"

He shook his head. "No. You've let it fester till it has warped your judgment. I'm sorry you didn't feel you could trust me."

She smiled wistfully. "I came close to telling you once or twice, but the opportunity seemed to slip away."

"I've had a similar sensation myself from time to time," he admitted. "But none of this explains what you feel has changed."

She colored and looked down at her hands. "I thought that once you knew the full story, you would no longer want our company."

"You are quite wrong, and I am not just being honorable."

"If you're quite sure about that, I think Nome would be a good idea. It would get both the children and me away from Friendship."

"I'm glad to hear it." He cupped her face in his hand to bring it close to his. When his lips descended upon hers, her response was unhesitating. The silence in the little cabin was as deep and satisfying as the kisses they exchanged.

"It seems we have lost time to make up for," he whispered.

Amity's reply did not need to be expressed in words. For the first time in her life she experienced the joy of being loved by a man who knew how to use a lover's caresses to unlock the sensuality in her.

Afterwards they lay in each other's arms in quiet contentment.

Jake pulled a bearskin over them both and dropped a tender kiss on Amity's forehead. "Does this mean you're coming to Nome?"

She snuggled up to him and said, "I should think so."

"Do you want to go back to Friendship first? There was the little matter of selling your half to Edda."

"Let her keep it." Amity giggled. "Besides, a good part of its value is sitting at the bottom of a lake in a flour sack, so she might just as well keep what's left."

Jake raised himself on one elbow and looked down at her, an affectionate smile on his lips. "We'll give the dogs a day's rest and then leave. With luck we'll get to Nome just before the thaw. With even better luck we'll find some gold-panning preacher man out to increase his worldly goods who'll take time off to marry us. Or would you rather wait till we can be married properly in a church?"

"You don't already have a wife tucked away somewhere—in Australia, for instance, or Cornwall?"

"Absolutely not."

"Then I'll trust it to a gold-panning preacher man."

ABOUT THE AUTHOR

Janet Edmonds has two great loves, her writing and her dogs. Originally a teacher in her native England, she decided that writing was more fun. "I'd been watching a television program on writing romantic fiction and thought, I could do that." She began with the sort of books that she enjoyed reading—historical romances—and gave herself five years to get into print. She'd just published her first book when, in the mid-1980s, she was offered the chance to take early retirement. She leaped at it and has been writing ever since.

Janet Edmonds

Besides writing romantic fiction, Edmonds also enjoys the intellectual challenge of writing crime novels. "My hero is always a vet and the stories usually revolve around the dog world." As a top-class breeder, exhibitor, and dog-show judge, Edmonds knows the canine world well. Her home in England's Cotswolds is crowded with her favorite Alaskan malamutes and German spitzes.

The inspiration for Amity Jones came in part from the author's grandmother Bessie McKay. In 1887, at age seventeen, Bessie left her family for Canada to make a new life. For ten years she worked her way across the continent as a cook, and was in Vancouver at the height of the Klondike gold rush. There she met and married a British naval officer and returned to England. "My grandmother rarely spoke of the past," Edmonds says. "But when she saw my first Alaskan malamute, the floodgates opened. I was struck by what an enterprising young woman she must have been, and I've wanted to build a story around her pioneering character for many years. Now I think I've done it."

Grandmother McKay, we are sure, would be pleased with the result.

PHOTO: MARC HENRIE

NEWBURY
GENERAL STORE

Sometimes trouble comes to the nicest places.

HARDSCAPE

by Justin Scott

To a landscape architect, hardscape is the rock behind the shrubbery.

To an artist, it is the skull behind the face.

To Ben Abbott, hardscape is what his sleepy New England town becomes the day Rita Long drives up in her Jaguar. She is beautiful and alluring—and she probably means trouble. But is she also capable of murder?

Somehow Ben Abbott is not at all sure he wants to find out.

1

I HAD a gut feeling that Alex Rose had not really driven his Mercedes all the way from New York City to buy a weekend home in Newbury. It had been a while since I'd been a New York player, but, like my Armani suits mothballed in the attic, I had kept the instincts. I disobeyed them and offered to show him the Richardson place, hoping he was real. With the recession still twined around Connecticut, stubborn as poison oak, and the country-house crowd pondering fair-share taxes and hourglass loopholes, I had time on my hands and fifty listings for every buyer.

I drove him in my Oldsmobile, singing the praises of Main Street. Our homes are set far back. A sweep of green grass separates curbs from sidewalks, and hundred-year-old elms and sugar maples arch overhead. Customers love it. It's the street they had in mind back in kindergarten when they crayoned their first house with smoke squiggling from the chimney, a flower, and a picket fence.

Rose sat silent as ice sculpture, blind to snug Colonials, elegant Federal mansions, snow-white churches, even our famous flagpole.

The only commercial structures in sight were the barn-red Newbury General Store, the Newbury Savings Bank—housed in a structure as conservative as its lending policies—and the picturesque Yankee Drover Inn. There was my BENJAMIN ABBOTT REALTY shingle and a couple of shingles belonging to my competitors. And that was about it, thanks to my grandfather, who wrote the zoning laws, and my father, who enforced them.

Modern conveniences, I explained, like the Grand Union, video rental, gas station, and the White Birch—the bikers' bar—were hidden at the bottom of Church Hill Road. Rose grunted. I told him our flagpole was the tallest in Connecticut. He didn't seem to care.

He was a big man who led with his belly—a well-fed forty-five or so, health-club tanned and burly, with soft brown hair fertilized by Rogaine. He studied me with busy, hooded eyes.

He was dressed like a house hunter outfitted for "the country," in Bean boots and a corduroy shooting jacket. He also looked like he could afford to buy, judging from the S-class land yacht parked at my office. So I kept driving and hoping.

Out of town, Route 7 runs along the river, matching it bend for bend. Four miles south of town, past the Calvary Horse Farm, I turned onto Academy Lane and, after a mile, onto a dirt road named Richardson Street, which was lined with ancient decaying maple trees. They made a grand tunnel between two of the loveliest hayfields in the county.

"This used to all be Richardson land, but it's been sold off. The house has six acres, with another fourteen available."

Rose's silence doomed his charade. Any buyer worth a mortgage would ask whether the open land would be developed.

The neglected though elegant farmhouse was relatively new by Newbury's calendar—built thirty years after the American Revolution. New wings and Greek Revival detail had been added on as the Richardsons prospered. It had been maintained as an exquisite country home from the 1920s into the early 1960s. When we got out of the car, I directed Rose's attention to the faint lines of brick paths through the thorn-tangled gardens. A cherry tree grew out of the clay tennis court, and the skating pond was reverting to marsh.

"Adlai Stevenson used to visit his mistress here. Or so they say. Her estate was out there, through the sycamores."

Rose turned a full, slow circle, confirming we were alone. I pulled out my big ring of keys.

"There's a beautiful brick keeping room that overlooks the skating pond. I swear, on a winter day you can still smell the hot cocoa."

"Do you know a lot of people around here?"

I told him I'd been born in Newbury.

"You know the Longs? Jack and Rita Long?"

I knew who he meant. And I knew about the thirty-seven-room stone house they had built just across the Morrisville line, which people called the Castle. Fred Gleason had sold them a hundred acres and celebrated that winter in the Caribbean. The Longs had built in a Victorian turreted style, with crenellations and, for all I knew, a moat of alligators.

"Friends of yours?" I asked.

Rose pretended not to hear me. "He's about my size, dark hair, mustache. A little overweight. She's a terrific-looking brunette."

"I don't know them."

It was none of Rose's business that I had met Jack Long briefly and seen him in action at a land-trust meeting. He had a firm handshake and looked you over real quick, pigeonholing you and assessing your worth. I thought he was a little pushy.

Rose wouldn't let it go. "They come up on the weekends. Maybe you've seen them in town buying the *Times.*"

I was tired of the game. "I'm sure I'd remember meeting a terrific-looking brunette. Are they the reason you're looking for a house in Newbury?"

"Tell me about yourself." The hooded eyes opened wide, hardening his big, blocky face.

I said, "I've got a better idea. Why don't you tell me what you already know about me. You've dragged me out here under a pretext to talk about these Longs, which means you want something from me because you think you know something about me."

Rose planted his feet and folded his arms. His new shooting jacket looked a little silly. I was wearing my basic Realtor's uniform—chinos, an old tweed jacket, and penny loafers.

Rose gave me a smirky wink that made his big face go lopsided. "You asked for it," he said, and to my surprise recited my dossier. "Benjamin Abbott the Third. You were born here, went to grade school here. Your old man ran the real estate office. He was also first selectman, which is sort of like mayor. You attended the Newbury Prep School as a day student, then the United States Naval Academy at Annapolis. You served in naval intelligence, then went to work on Wall Street. Am I right so far?"

He had missed twelfth grade, when my father packed me off to Stonybrook Military Academy—ostensibly to prepare me for Annapolis but mostly to keep me from getting into trouble with my cousin Renny. Renny was considered a bad influence. Only Renny and I knew it was the other way around.

Rose treated my silence to another smirk and headed for the good parts. "On Wall Street you made a bunch of money—running mergers and acquisitions—got nailed in the Michigan Machine insider-trading scheme and went to jail."

"I didn't break the law."

"But you did time."

"I sure did." I felt invaded. He had slid a knife under a scar.

"When you came home, you took over your father's business. His contacts put you first on line with old money and the big estates."

I wondered how a bloody nose would look on his shooting jacket.

"Don't you want to know why I'm telling you this?"

Of course I was curious why he'd driven a hundred miles to annoy me. "Not as much as you want to tell me."

He surprised me again. "I'm a private investigator."

I had pegged him for a lawyer, from his bad manners and his car. I knew he wasn't a Wall Street guy; they're friendlier—salesmen at heart. I was a salesman at heart. But I wasn't feeling friendly. "Who's paying you to dredge up my past?"

"I'm offering you a job. Mr. Long is my client. I want you to shoot a video of Mrs. Long in bed with her boyfriend."

I laughed. "I thought there were professionals who did that."

"There are, and were she sleeping with this guy in New York, I would employ one. But I don't know anyone I can trust to go rooting around up here without getting caught by the cops. The Long house is way out in the boonies. I need a local man. I'll pay you two thousand dollars for a half hour of clear videotape."

"Two thousand? I'll introduce you to a local who'll do it for two hundred." I had in mind one of the Chevalley boys.

"I don't want some damned redneck swamp Yankee."

He was mixing his regional slurs. I let him, just as earlier I had not interfered when he mispronounced Newbury like the fruit instead of the cheese. Neither a berry nor an event in a graveyard, we are, properly, Newbrie. "I'm not a cameraman."

"It's just a Sony camcorder. A kid could use it."

"I'm not interested in taking dirty pictures." Actually, I was intrigued. I could certainly use two thousand dollars, and playing detective sounded like fun, provided one didn't break one's neck falling off the lady's roof. But I had enough troubles reputationwise without it getting around town that Ben Abbott was a Peeping Tom.

"Three thousand dollars."

I walked to my car. "I've got to get back, Mr. Rose."

He got in and we drove out of there, and it was my turn to be silent. Rose got talkative. He remarked on the trees, the river, the horses, even the car. "What kind of car is this?"

"Oldsmobile." Cars I would talk about.

"I didn't realize they were so powerful."

"Caddy engine. Eats BMWs for breakfast— Damn!"

"What's wrong?"

I slowed down and pulled over, my mirrors sparkling like the Fourth of July. Trooper Oliver Moody—who should have been down at the high school at this hour instead of hiding behind a utilities truck—swaggered out of his state police cruiser, already writing a ticket. He danced me through the procedure, enjoying every moment, and advised me I could pay the fine at town hall.

Rose said, "I thought they didn't ticket locals."

"We're not friends."

Oliver burned rubber out of there with an ironic salute, and I continued driving silently into town.

At the flagpole, Rose said, "Four thousand dollars."

The money was sounding better and better. I couldn't deny I could use it. "I ask you again, why me?"

Rose exploded. "You want me to paint a picture? Mr. Long goes first class. He believes he gets what he pays for. He doesn't question my fees. He only expects me to get the job done. He can afford it."

"You bill him cost-plus."

"Exactly like you when you ran leveraged buyouts."

"And I'm first class because I went to prison?"

"The word is, you did time because you wouldn't rat on your friends. Loyalty's valuable. The fact you got out alive says you learned to handle yourself. That's an asset, too."

"Tell your boss if he ever finds himself in a similar position, treat it like Outward Bound."

"The jail thing is my opinion. What Mr. Long likes is your navy intelligence background. He ate that up—fought in Nam."

I still wasn't quite sure why Rose wanted me. And I had a feeling if I opened the door without speaking, he'd up his offer.

I opened the door.

"Five thousand."

THE WILDEST THING MY FATHER ever did in his good and orderly life was marry my mother, Margot Chevalley—bastardized from "Chevalier" in New England, where folks never needed black people to dump on, because they already had the French.

Centuries before the railroad, Newbury had a wrong side of the tracks, named Frenchtown. Mother's people farmed outside of Frenchtown on a hodgepodge of swamp and cold north slopes. After my father died, she moved back to the farm, leaving me the big white Georgian house on Main Street with the shingle out front, an office in a glass porch, and a red barn in the backyard.

At my father's old desk, Alex Rose, P.I., wrote a check for five thousand dollars and extended it with a flourish. He opened a leather shoulder bag he had brought in from his Mercedes and took out the camcorder and some tapes. "It's real simple to use." He demonstrated, then handed the camera to me.

"What's that red light?"

"Indicates you're taping."

"You want me to shoot through a window at night while hiding in the woods. What if Mrs. Long glances at the window and sees this little red light in the woods?"

"Okay, put some tape over it."

"Terrific." I was loving this whole concept less and less. It seemed I'd gotten caught up in negotiating a price instead of questioning the deal—an old '80s habit that apparently died hard.

"You know, I don't get the point of this. New York and Connecticut are both shared-property states. What does Mr. Long get out of a video of his wife cheating on him? She still has the protection of equal distribution. She won't lose it all for getting caught."

"Divorce law is a little more complicated than that," Rose said.

At that second a scrawny eleven-year-old girl with a shy, crooked-toothed grin darted into my office like a muskrat. "Mom wants to know if you'll have supper with us tonight."

"Tell your mom I would be delighted. This is Mr. Rose, up from New York, looking at houses. This is my neighbor Alison Mealy."

Alison saw his camera, and her eyes grew big. I handed it to her. "Go take some pictures of your mother cooking supper."

Rose blanched as his camera sped out the door. He watched Alison run down the driveway. "She's taking it into the barn."

"She lives there."

Rose said, "Do you own a gun?"
"Why?"
"This guy Mrs. Long is seeing might get a little violent."
"You mean like if he gets ticked off because he sees a man in the woods taking his picture?"
"Obviously, the best thing is, don't get caught."
I slid his money across the desk toward him. "I feel well advised to turn down the job. Thank you very much. If you're ever in the market for a home in Newbury, please call for an appointment." I stood up and extended my hand.
Rose looked appalled. "Wait a minute. We have a deal."
"You put money on my desk, then tell me I need a gun. There was no gun in the original deal. So we don't have a deal. You got the wrong guy." I felt relieved. The more I thought about taking pictures of some poor couple making love, the more it sounded like a lousy way to earn a buck. Even five thousand bucks.
Rose looked sick, like a guy who had blown a really big deal. That was puzzling, because what were we talking about but a silly little job anybody could do? In fact, he seemed so upset that I got curious. "Are you Long's investigator for everything or just the divorce?"
"Anything he needs."
What I was beginning to understand was that Rose was a high-priced gofer. He'd get the video and dig up other stuff in New York and *then* carry the evidence to a shark divorce attorney, who'd hint that maybe Mrs. Long would forgo her half of the stock option.
Rose proved to be a shrewd, high-priced gofer worth his fee. He grinned. "Your little neighbor needs braces."
"What?"
"The little girl who lives in your barn needs her teeth fixed before she grows up ugly."
He was right. Alison made a cute tomboy, but she would end up hiding her smile as she got older. "So?"
"I got a client who's the absolutely number one orthodontist in New York. You do the job, I'll take care of the girl's teeth."
"Who is this guy that Mrs. Long is sleeping with?"
"A guy the Longs have known a long time. Just do the job, take the money, and give little Alison a break. She'll thank you the rest of her life. We're talking thousands here, fella, if you had to pay for it."
Rose knew I was beaten. He said, "They'll be at the house tonight."

"Then I'll do it tonight."

"That's the spirit."

"Spirit's got nothing to do with it. The moon's getting full. Any brighter and they'll spot me."

I walked Rose to his car and ran his money over to the bank.

I had accepted Alison's mother's supper invitation with no illusions. Janet Mealy was the daughter of generations of hardscrabble New England farmers—a thin, pale, weary country girl of twenty-six, old beyond her years. She had borne Alison at fifteen, trading a drunken father for a drunken husband. She had waited tables in a diner up on Route 4 and had had a few factory jobs—a wolf-at-the-door existence where all could be lost with a single missed paycheck.

For a brief interlude her husband had driven a Newbury snowplow, only to get jailed for stealing parts from the township garage. It had been a quick tumble to welfare and homelessness.

I'd come across her and Alison last spring, hitchhiking out on Route 7, hoping to find work in a New Milford motel that I had already heard was going out of business. I was definitely not in the market for roommates. But the sight of Janet Mealy's stringy hair turning dark in the rain, the plastic shopping bags at her feet, and her bone-white arm wrapped fearfully around Alison's shoulder pretty much eliminated any options in the matter. I took them home and put them in the barn, which had a crude whitewashed apartment last lived in by my great-grandfather's stable hand.

Janet always addressed me as Mr. Abbott in deference to my family and the social gulf that stretched between us. She expected me to call her Mrs. Mealy to honor her marriage and her hope that Alison's father might one day come home sober. Alison, of course, called me Ben, but the quaint titles of courtesy her mother and I shared allowed "Mrs. Mealy" and "Mr. Abbott" their privacy and dignity.

Talk around town ran the gamut nonetheless. Gossips said the barn was a front and Mrs. Mealy actually slept in my own four-poster, while busybodies with a Marxist bent claimed that she worked as a slave, cleaning the empty houses I tried to sell. The truth was, it had been her idea to clean them.

So I had no illusions about supper. Mrs. Mealy inclined toward prepared foods. We ate frozen baked potatoes and fried preformed hamburger patties. Dessert was Cool Whip on Jell-O.

After supper we trooped to my house and popped into the VCR

the footage Alison had shot of her mother cooking. Janet Mealy hid her face in her hands when Alison said, "Mom, you look great."

I left them to watch the tape again. I was anxious to get over to Morrisville while there was still daylight enough to get the lay of the land. I loaded a fresh tape into the camcorder and changed into jeans, a dark sweater, and my Swiss climbing boots, which I had purchased for a junk-bond seminar in Aspen. Then I took a couple of pocket flashlights from my night table. My father's .38 was in the drawer. It was a fine old piece—ideal weight to pack while filming lovers from the woods—but I left it. I am next to helpless with a handgun. If Mrs. Long's fella came gunning for me, the best defense would be to bolt into the dark or politely raise my hands.

Route 349 runs east from the flagpole, over the hill to Morrisville. North of the road lies Frenchtown; south is a long, rolling hill, home to big estates and horse farms, a section divided by an invisible Newbury-Morrisville line. The Castle was just east of it, down a dirt road with woods on one side and pasture on the other.

It was immediately apparent that the Longs were not suffering from the recession. Money had been spent and was still being spent on upkeep and expansion. Before I reached the house, I passed restored barns and silos that made a postcard picture, catching the golden light of a soon-to-set sun. Then the woods on the left began to sheer up the slope, opening to broad meadow that blended into a wide lawn that rose to a stone fantasy straight out of *Ivanhoe.*

It really did have a turret—up one corner rose a round stone tower with a conical roof and narrow windows suitable for sheltering archers. Though a good sixty feet high, the turret worked nicely, even with no moat. The house had been rendered romantic, not by the silly crenellations or the turret, but by being placed perfectly on the edge of the woods. To the south, the upstairs rooms would enjoy wonderful views of the hill rambling down to the river. But the back rooms, I imagined, would feel like a tree house, the sloped forest looming, kindly and mysterious.

I saw a problem right away. The lady's bedroom was probably in front, to take advantage of the views, while my best shot would be shooting down from the woods. I drove back to 349, cruised around until it got dark, then stashed the car behind one of the Longs' decorative barns and walked. I had rerigged the camcorder's shoulder bag so I could strap it around my waist, leaving my hands free.

The few dimly lit windows in the Castle were on the second floor, hinting that Mrs. Long and her boyfriend were heading for bed. I cut across the meadow to the lawn and circled behind the house, hugging the woods as I climbed the slope.

A figure—it looked to be a man—passed across a second-floor window, thirty feet from where I was catching my breath after the steep climb. The house was tucked so close to the woods and the slope was so steep that I was literally standing above the second floor, looking down through the back windows.

He came back the other way, carrying a pair of wineglasses. He had apparently come up a back stair from the kitchen, and the window I saw him in seemed to light a hallway. I headed left along the woods, paralleling the direction he had gone. At the end of the house an odd square structure bulked up out of the pitched roof. It was a big dormer.

White light exploded in my face. I dived into the woods, thinking that they had seen me and turned on the security floods. I banged into something solid—a huge tree—and scrambled behind it.

But no one shouted. No attack hounds bellowed up the slope. I peeked around the tree and saw that the light source was not security floods, but a wall of glass lit from within. The dormer housed an artist's studio—a lofty, bare white room. A huge canvas was propped on an easel, draped with a bedsheet. Next to it a small easel that held a blank sketch pad faced a low platform.

A pair of shadows leaped on the walls. For a moment I was back in a darkened theater in Manhattan, waiting for a play to begin.

2

NAKED, the boyfriend looked like a guy who enjoyed working out. His shoulders, broad chest, and upper arms were heavily muscled, his waist and hips model trim. He was not, however, a professional model. He mounted the platform a little clumsily, threw his arms apart in a self-conscious way, and grinned.

He looked very happy—a young, happy, clean-shaven guy with white-blond hair. I was reaching belatedly for the camcorder when Mrs. Long strode into view, her back to me, and fully clothed in a long, flowing silvery blouse over jeans. Only her feet were bare. Rose had called her a brunette, which hardly conveyed the Oriental splendor of the inky black hair that fell shining down her back.

Mrs. Long went to work with a pencil. Practicing zooming the lens over her shoulder, I could see the drawing clearly. With uncommon skill she quickly established the bulge of his chest muscles and worked her way down his flat belly. I panned the sketch, unzoomed to take in her standing before the easel, swept the studio, then zoomed in on the sketch again, in time to see her hesitate.

Suddenly she went for the face. I let go the trigger. He had a broad, almost round face, but on drawing paper, only his pathologist would ever know him. Instead of his face, she sketched his skull. She drew cheekbones, but no cheeks; brow ridges, but no brow; no hair; no eyes, only their sockets. She did his teeth in jagged strokes, a bony jaw, and the short, split bone of a fleshless nose. I shivered.

Mrs. Long put down her pencil and started toward him. By now my camera was dangling from one hand. He smiled with an anticipation he might not have felt had he seen how she had rendered his face. I was beginning to wonder about Mrs. Long, but her boyfriend had no doubts. He jumped down from the platform, scooped her into his arms, and kissed her, which I dutifully recorded. They broke at last, and I could see by his expression that he probably wouldn't care what she sketched.

She pushed him back onto the stage, gestured that he should spread his arms again. I fired up the camera, anticipating her next move. Sure enough, slowly unbuttoning her blouse, she let it slither off her shoulders. Mrs. Long had round white courtesan shoulders like Rubens painted. How she looked in front could be assumed by her boyfriend's eager "Yes, yes, yes," clearly audible through an open casement window.

She laughed and did a little shimmy. Her shirt slid off her back—a smooth, very beautiful back. She stepped closer. Her hair blocked the camera, but there wasn't a divorce court in the nation that wouldn't get the picture. Her boyfriend reached for her. She pushed his hands back in position and whirled back to the easel.

It was my turn to cry out—a gasp of astonishment at my first glimpse of her face. I had never seen a woman so beautiful or so happy. She had a heart-shaped face with a high brow, wide-set cheekbones, a strong nose, and enormous blue eyes. Her lips were full, and when she laughed, she radiated joy.

I ripped the video cartridge from the camera and threw it into the woods. I felt redeemed for a fraction of a second. I had come too close to doing a terrible thing to a couple of happy people, and I saw Rose's spy job for the dirty job it had been all along.

Then the tape hit a tree—with a surprisingly loud bonk—and bounced onto the lawn. The cartridge was made of black plastic, except for the white label on the face, and sure enough it landed face up, gleaming in the light from the window.

I heard Mrs. Long say, "What was that?"

I scrambled after the cartridge, hugging the woods. I was nearly to it when she cried, "Raccoons! Raccoons. Turn on the floods."

Fortunately, it took him a moment to find the switch, during which time I slid down the slope, grabbed the videotape, and scrambled for cover. My head and shoulders were in the dark space between two bushes when suddenly the backyard was bright enough to land helicopters.

"It's somebody hiding in your woods. Hey!"

Deep in shadow at last, I glanced back. He was leaning out the window. She was pulling him back. "What if he has a gun?" Then she acted like a smart city girl. She ran to a security keypad on the wall and pushed the panic button on her burglar alarm.

More lights. They blazed down from the roof and lit three acres, while a siren began whooping like a klaxon straight out of *The Hunt for Red October.* I wouldn't doubt that it sounded in the alarm company's New Milford office, where they would dispatch a car and alert Oliver Moody that someone was housebreaking on his turf. Oliver would respond first, armed and dangerous. I ran, tripped on a fallen limb, and fell face down, crunching my knee on a piece of granite ledge.

I have felt real pain in my life, but nothing like what I felt then. I ground my teeth and dragged myself deeper into the shadows.

Mrs. Long strode back to the keypad and punched in a code that stopped the siren. Then she put on her blouse and went to the window where her boyfriend was peering intently into the dark.

"Lock yourself in our room. I'll deal with the cops."

He protested.

She said, "Don't worry. I'll be fine. Here they come. Now go!"

I heard it, too—across the hills the urgent scream of a police siren and the spectacular roar of a Plymouth Fury flat out.

Even if I ditched the camera and the tape, what possible explanation could I offer for trespassing in Mrs. Long's woods in the middle of the night? And even if Oliver didn't arrest me—fantasy, because he had waited years for the opportunity—my name would be wrecked again, which would put me out of business. You can't make money selling houses without listings. A number of strait-laced people had been very kind when I came home. But two strikes and I was out. This stupid lark was about to finish me.

I stood up, took a step, and fell down. It hurt like hell, but I knew nothing was broken. Oliver's siren got loud, and his lights came bumping across the Longs' meadow as he careened into their driveway. I backed up the wooded slope, pulling myself from tree trunk to tree trunk, getting nowhere fast. A huge tree loomed, a red oak. Its lower limbs were enormous, barely clearing the slope behind. I got my hands around one, swung, and tugged myself up onto it. Then, clutching the main trunk, I climbed another limb and perched precariously, fifteen feet above the forest floor, some twenty feet in from the floodlit lawn. I peered around the trunk.

Oliver had gone in the front door, and now he came out the back. He was wielding a five-cell Mag-Lite about two feet long, the type that comes with instructions from the maker that it is not to be used as an "impact" instrument. "Stay inside!" he commanded Mrs. Long.

He started up the slope. He held the light in his left hand. His right hovered near his holstered gun.

Resident state troopers are a special breed—part Lone Ranger, part schoolyard bully. Oliver Moody, who stood six five and weighed two hundred and sixty pounds, came up the slope like an armored personnel carrier. He was ten years older than me, but I suspected that in a footrace up the hill, he'd be waiting for me on top with his impact instrument.

I sat tight and watched. He moved cautiously through the undergrowth, playing the flashlight on the shadows. To my relief he was looking at man height, not tree height.

Oliver stopped. He aimed his light at something on the ground. He picked it up and pocketed it. I couldn't see what he had found.

Then something yowled in the treetops, crashed through the leaf canopy, and landed on the end of the limb I was sitting on. When it turned toward me, I saw in the moonlight the masked face of a raccoon. Oliver came pounding up the slope.

I was not unaware of the comic nature of the preceding events, but I wasn't laughing. Raccoons don't fall out of trees unless something is wrong with them, and we were in the thick of a rabies epidemic. When the raccoon saw Oliver's beam darting between the trees, he backed away, closer to me. Finally he sensed me and growled. I pointed the camera at him. He retreated back from where he came, only to get hit square in the face by the flashlight.

He was a horrible sight; he had clawed his own stomach open in his agony. He bared his teeth and growled down at the state trooper, who had come to a halt a few feet below.

From the house, Mrs. Long called, "Are you all right, Officer?"

"Found your prowler," Oliver called over his shoulder. "Rabid raccoon. Go get a plastic garbage bag."

I pressed like bark against the tree, praying he wouldn't see me and hoping he wouldn't splatter rabid raccoon all over me with the cannon he wore at his waist. Then Oliver glanced back, making sure Mrs. Long couldn't see him, and reached down and pulled a little Beretta .22 from an ankle holster concealed under his pants. In all the years I had known him, I never knew that he carried a backup weapon. You learn something every day.

Holding his light in one hand and the gun in the other, Oliver caught the raccoon's attention by talking to it and telling it everything would work out fine. Then he shot the animal neatly through the head. It fell at his feet.

"Bring the bag," Oliver called.

Mrs. Long ran up her grassy slope; Oliver met her at the edge of the woods. Taking care not to touch the animal with his bare hands, he worked the bag around it and tied it shut. Then he sauntered down to the house, trailing the bag.

"What are you going to do with it?" asked Mrs. Long.

"Landfill." He walked around the house, slammed the Fury's door, and drove off as the burglar-alarm company's van raced up, with a funny little blinking light on the roof.

As I drove down deserted Main Street, the town-hall clock bonged eleven—amazingly early, considering my night so far. Once inside the house, I went straight to the bourbon. Then I put the tape in the VCR and erased it. I wondered whether erased video recordings could be restored by computer enhancement. What if Rose suspected I'd shot some footage, and spent Mr. Long's money on a rocket-scientist hacker? But I couldn't trash it. Recycling's very big up here, and a discarded video cartridge would be just the thing to catch the sanitation officer's eye. So I hid it. A big old house has more stash holes than a maze.

NEWBURY celebrates Labor Day the third Saturday in September, mainly because the bigger towns have huge parades that siphon off the crowd we need to buy tickets to our fire department cookout. The morning after my exploits at the Longs' dawned warm and sunny as August.

Alex Rose called. "So how'd it go?"

"Lousy."

"How lousy? You get caught or something?"

For all I knew, he had tapped the Longs' phone, in which case he would know the alarm had gone off. I told him the truth. "I've decided against a rematch. I'll mail you your camera."

"Hold on."

"And your money," I said, and hung up. I bought a blank videotape, wrote Rose a check, packed the camera and the spare tapes in a box, and walked the whole thing down to the post office, where I mailed it. Then I went home and cleaned my grill and my long-handled spatula, and took them to the lawn behind town hall.

They had wheeled out the fire engines for the kids to climb on and had hung a banner that read NEWBURY ENGINE COMPANY NO. 1, FOUNDED 1879. Someone had rigged a forty-gallon corn boiler, and the ladies of the Newbury Engine Auxiliary were spreading paper plates, ketchup, relish, and mustard on folding tables.

We arranged the cooking grills in order of splendor. First was Rick Bowland's gas-fired, volcano-stone, hooded monster that had enough dials and gauges to monitor a public utility. In the middle was Scooter MacKay—my neighbor and the town's newspaper publisher—at his thirty-six-inch charcoal-burning Weber. Last was mine.

Rick Bowland nudged Scooter. "What is that thing Ben's got?"

"This is a triple-length charcoal grill for cooking meat, chicken, and vegetables out of doors," I said. "It's based on a hibachi design. I bought it on sale at Caldor's down in Danbury for nine dollars and expect old friends to toast marshmallows on it beside my grave."

"Nine dollars?"

I said, "We need a plan. Rick, why don't you toast rolls and cook the dogs? Scooter and me'll do the burgers."

"Hey, this thing's great on burgers," Rick said.

"We'll do the burgers," said Scooter.

He's an excellent newspaper publisher but too free with the Weber's dome, so I said, "I'll do rare, you do medium and well."

The next hour was a blur of hands thrusting open buns in my direction. I was just holding my own—rare, but not raw. Beside me, Scooter was smoking them medium, raising his dome with billowy flourishes to general applause. Then I had a little fire, which I was knocking down with a water-spray bottle when I heard a harried Scooter say, "Rare? See my colleague at the nine-dollar grill."

I looked up into the smiling face of Rita Long, who said, "They tell me you're a rare man."

Hard to know how long I stood staring at her.

She asked, "Wha'd I say?" and the fire I'd just put out flared up between us, prompting shouts from Scooter and Rick.

"Rare," I said finally, spatula-ing my best burger onto her bun with my left hand while extending my right to introduce myself. "Ben Abbott. I don't believe we've met."

She had a Diet Pepsi in her other hand, but she extended an elbow with a grin, saying, "Rita Long. We're new in town."

"Oh, yes. Fred Gleason found your property."

"Are you a Realtor, too? Right, right. I've seen your sign. You have that lovely Georgian house near the flagpole."

I like newcomers. They don't say hello thinking, Bertram Abbott's kid. The one who . . . She just took me as the guy who lived in the Georgian house near the flagpole. She was beautiful, as I had seen last night, but now, dressed in pleated khaki pants and a faded work shirt, very much the married lady—friendly, but not flirting.

She asked, "Do you do appraisals?"

"Same as Fred. We're not bank appraisers, but we can recommend a price range. Do you have a friend looking?"

Before she could answer, a greasy hand thrust a hamburger bun between us—my cousin Pinkerton Chevalley, Renny's big brother, availing himself of thirds. I dripped hot grease onto his thumb, but it apparently didn't penetrate the calluses. Mrs. Long backed away and wandered toward the ketchup table.

I saw her look across the lawn with a secret smile, followed her

gaze, and there was the boyfriend, munching a hot dog, glancing repeatedly in her direction as she moseyed about.

He looked maybe a little older than he had in the buff. He wore chinos and a pin-striped shirt with the sleeves rolled up, and had an air of being very much in charge of something. He reminded me of a hotshot manager working a buyout. Only this one was smiling, like he'd already closed his deal. Once, when he looked across the lawn at her, she was watching some kids, and his face practically melted. He was nuts for the woman, which I found understandable, and she seemed nuts for him, too. I wondered if they had any inkling that her husband knew.

Mrs. Long came back.

"Another?"

"No, thanks. That was great. Listen, do you have time to come out today and give me an appraisal?"

"*Your* house?" I had more time than a retiree, but fair was fair and friends were friends. "Well, Fred Gleason is—"

"I'd like a private opinion."

I decided that the only way to talk to this woman was as if I had not seen her with her boyfriend the night before. What was a private opinion? Well, it was not the first time I'd been asked by one side of a marriage to appraise the honeymoon cottage.

"I'll have a look. I can make it out there by five."

"Perfect. I have to run down to the mall. I'll make it back by five. After you look, it'll be time for a drink."

As I'VE said, there was nothing flirtatious about Rita Long. Even so, drinks at the Castle was the best offer I'd had in a week.

I showered the smoke out of my hair and put on my uniform, tweed jacket over my arm in the warm afternoon. I was about to get into the Oldsmobile when I thought, What the heck. Last warm day for a while. I pulled the cover off the Fiat. It was a '79 Spyder 2000 roadster, British racing green, that my father had bought new for my mother's sixtieth birthday. My mother felt it was too flashy, and when she moved back to Frenchtown, she left it for me.

By daylight the grounds of the Castle were something to behold. The driveway paralleled a serpentine pond complete with snowy egret. The hardscape surrounding the house was splendidly conceived and brilliantly executed.

Hardscape is a word coined by landscape designers to distinguish elements constructed from those that are grown—masonry from nursery, cobblestones from coreopsis. Hardscape is what you see in winter when the flowers are dead and branches bare. It forms the character of a house, like the bones behind a face.

I had heard that the Castle's granite walls and flagstone terraces had been built by Italian stonemasons who usually worked down in Greenwich. It showed. There was a polish to this work rarely seen north of Long Island Sound. Walls that looked like dry stone had been cemented by an artful hidden-mortar technique.

"I love your car," Rita Long greeted me.

I told her how I got it from my mother, and complimented her landscaping and the quality of the stonework.

She explained that they had owned a big place in Greenwich. "When we decided to build here, Jack said we should use the workmen we knew. I felt a little funny, cutting out the local guys."

"Tough call," I agreed. "Who's the architect?"

"It was Jack's plan. I drew it, and then we paid an architect to work out the structural details."

"Nice. Who did the outside?"

"I did."

"Really?" I looked again. I don't care how talented an artist is, only one in a million retains a sense of scale outdoors. The sky is simply not a ceiling. I glanced up at the turret. "There's a rumor around town that you shoot deer from your turret."

"Jack did. Once last year, during hunting season. I told him I'd shoot *him* if he did it again. Are you ready to see the inside?"

We went in and wandered the rooms, most of which were still unfurnished. A central staircase lit by skylights was magnificently paneled in rosewood. The spotless kitchen had the latest everything.

The house did not have quite the rumored thirty-seven rooms, but there were three beautiful guest suites upstairs and a spectacular master bedroom, with a fireplace and his-and-her baths.

I could not resist asking, "What's down that hall?"

"Just my studio."

"Do you want me to look at it?"

She hesitated. "Sure. Just a second." She ran ahead, and when she called, "Okay now," I walked into the white studio and saw she had draped the small easel as well as the big one.

"So? What do you think?"

"I think you have a lovely house."

"If you were handling the sale, what would you ask?"

"Well, I'm not handling the sale, but if I were . . . four million."

"And what would you advise me to take?"

"We're just talking, but you ought to know that the lowest number you allow your Realtor to mention is very likely the number he'll bring you in the end."

"Okay."

"I wouldn't take a penny under three million. And I'd fight like hell for three five."

"Thanks. Come on. We'll have that drink."

We got down to the kitchen, and she said, "Any objections to champagne?"

"None." I smiled, thinking I couldn't imagine a lovelier end of the day—or beginning of the evening.

She filled an ice bucket and dunked the bottle. Then she got a pair of flutes and said, "Grab that bucket, if you don't mind." She led me down a hall and through a massive oak door, to the foot of a narrow spiral stair that led up into the turret.

I smelled gun smoke. "Mr. Long been shooting deer again?"

"No. He set up some paper targets last weekend."

It smelled more recent to me.

Up and up we went, round and round, higher and higher, until right under the conical roof we came to a little round platform just big enough for a couple of chairs and a table for our glasses. I put the bucket on the floor and sat down when she did.

"Would you open it?" she asked, handing me the bottle.

I freed the cork with a modest pop and filled our glasses. She touched hers to mine and met my eye. Her expression was clear—open and content. "Isn't this great?" she asked.

Directly in front of us was an opening wider than the bowmen's windows. Through it we could see for miles, a view like a Dutch or Hudson River School landscape—hills and trees and meadows, all in the fading light of a September evening.

I asked, "How could you sell it?"

I regretted asking, because suddenly she was not content. She stared into her glass and said, "Everything's a trade-off."

It occurred to me that the Longs might have gone broke. The

Castle wouldn't be the first great house to mask its owners' private desperation. But knowing more about her than I had any right to, I figured she was more likely considering leaving the husband—and the money—for the boyfriend. I wanted to warn her that her husband knew.

I looked at her, and she looked away and stood up and moved to the opening in the wall. She stared out. I drank champagne.

Suddenly her whole body stiffened. She thrust her head and shoulders through the opening in the stone, straining to see. "What's that?"

I stood up beside her and looked. The sun had deserted the meadow but for the eastern edge along the woods, and there, in the last rays, something gleamed white. It was quite a distance away, and yet I could sense it shiver when the wind riled the grass around it.

"Looks like a deer's white tail," I said. "But they don't lie down in the open, and certainly not at this hour. It's feeding time. You've never seen it before? Maybe your husband shot another one."

"No," she said impatiently. "He's away, in Washington, D.C." She turned to the stairs, worried, and said, "I have to see what it is."

She started down the steps fast. I left my glass and followed—my hurt knee locking—through the big door, down the hall, and out the back door. On the lawn she broke into a run.

She crossed the meadow exactly where I had trod last night, and went up the slope toward the woods. Suddenly she stopped and put her hand to her mouth. I caught up. The white thing blowing in the wind was hair. Blond hair. Her boyfriend was sprawled on his back with a brick-size exit wound where his muscular chest had been.

3

THERE's truth in the cliché that people seem to shrink when they die. My father's body had looked hollow at Butler's Funeral Home. Mrs. Long's boyfriend was different—robust—drinking in the sky with wide-eyed wonder.

His name was Ron; she kept calling him Ron as she knelt and took his body in her arms. I reached to comfort her and lead her away, until I thought, Wait, this isn't television. Let the poor woman grieve. I backed off and stood at a distance.

It could have been a hunting accident. Some damned fool

poaching out of season, spotting the white flash of Ron's hair, mistaking him for a whitetail deer. It happens both in season and out—high-powered weapons, low IQs, and plenty of booze. But poachers tend not to have hunting accidents. They are, in their way, professionals and usually treat guns with the respect they deserve. I'm not saying that a Chevalley boy or one of the Jervis clan would never have an accident poaching, but it's less likely. Still, Oliver Moody and the state police investigators would be combing the woods for evidence—as soon as I called them.

I wished I hadn't smelled the gun smoke in the turret.

I went back to Rita and said, "Mrs. Long, I'd better call the police. Are you all right here or do you want to come with me?"

"I can't leave him here. Help me get him inside."

"We shouldn't move him. The police have to investigate."

"He's dead. It doesn't make any difference. There'll be animals at night. It's getting dark. I don't want him hurt any more."

She took my heart again. I wished to heaven I could make things right for her. "I'll call the police, and I'll come right back with a blanket and flashlights, and we'll stay with him until they come."

Halfway to the house, I looked back. She was dragging him through the grass. "No!"

I ran to her. The damage was done. She'd gotten her hands under his arms and had somehow moved him ten feet from where the bullet had killed him. She was breathing hard, gasping with each step, an expression of total concentration on her face.

I knelt, worked both arms under him, and carried him, cradled, through the grass, the blood trailing down his pin-striped shirt. Rita held his hand, letting it go only to open the front door. At her direction, I laid him down on a couch in the living room. It was upholstered with a silk brocade, but I knew enough not to suggest a towel. She arranged his arms and legs as if he'd dropped off for a nap; then she knelt on the Persian carpet, put her head on his shoulder, and wept.

I went into the kitchen and telephoned Oliver.

"What do you want?"

"A guy's been shot at the Long place. Dead."

"Who shot him?"

"I have no idea."

"Don't touch a thing."

ANGRY, OLLIE LOOKED EVEN bigger. He stood close, muscles gathered, ready to throw a punch. "I told you not to touch anything. You moved the body. You're impeding an investigation."

"You told me too late. It's done."

"Done, hell. I'll charge you."

"You want me to show you where we found him?"

He did. We walked across the lawn and through the meadow.

"We found him there."

"Stand back." He strung yellow crime-scene tape in a fifty-foot circle around Ron's blood. It had looked to me when I first saw the body that Ron had fallen dead there. Now who knew? Rita and I had flattened the grass.

Oliver scanned the woods. "What were you doing out here?"

"Appraising the house."

He took off his mirrored glasses and fixed me with his pale gray eyes. I had always preferred him in sunglasses. His eyes were reptilian: cold and stupid. Komodo dragons are stupid, too, but they eat mammals. "Did you know the guy?"

"No."

"Did she?"

"She didn't say." I supposed I'd be wise to cover myself in advance by relating last night's fiasco—bring it up before they backtracked to Alex Rose through Mr. Long, but that reeked of snitch.

The state police major-crime unit arrived. A young couple in plainclothes who looked like poster children for the FBI—Sergeant Arnold Bender and Trooper Marian Boyce—listened to Oliver's report, then ordered him to rig lights at the death site. The woman, Boyce, went into Rita's house; Bender came to me.

"Why'd you move the body?"

"It was getting dark."

"So what?"

"Animals would eat it."

"Are you trying to be funny?"

"We've got raccoons, crows, turkey buzzards, weasels, and rats." I was winging the weasels; I had no idea if they ate dead meat, but everything else did, which I wanted to establish before this moving-the-body thing led to charges.

"You shouldn't have moved the body," Bender said. "Do you remember how the body looked before you moved it?"

"I saw a huge hole in the guy's chest. His eyes were open. He was on his back, staring at the sky."

"Curled up? Spread out?"

"Spread out."

We walked to the site. Bender shook his head at the crushed grass. "Mr. Abbott, did it look like he crawled there wounded?"

"No. I got the impression he hit the deck dead."

"Which way was he lying?"

"Head up toward the woods."

"Did you hear shots?"

"No."

"How'd you happen to find him then?"

I turned around and pointed at the tower. "We were in the top of the turret, looking out that window. Mrs. Long saw his hair. It was shining in the sun. We went to investigate. I thought it was a deer lying dead."

"What were you doing in the tower?"

"Drinking champagne."

"You got a thing going with the lady?"

"No."

"Trooper Moody tells me you're covering for her."

"Trooper Moody should stick to speeding tickets."

Bender was half Moody's size, but he had the state police stare, which he gave me full force. "Moody tells me you did time."

"I served my time. I'm not on parole. You are way out of line."

"I got a dead man, apparently shot. You moved him. My lieutenant's going to ask, Why didn't you bring the jailbird in?"

"My false-arrest suit against you will be based on two facts: First, I was charged with a white-collar crime. Second, when whatever happened to that poor guy happened, I was grilling burgers for three hundred people at town hall."

An elderly diesel Mercedes chugged into the drive, decanting Dr. Steve Greenan, who served as one of the part-time assistant medical examiners for Plainfield County. Largely retired, he was a tall, white-haired, handsome man. He trudged our way, seeing the yellow tape; Sergeant Bender ran to intercept. I followed, passing Oliver, who was stringing extension cords from the house.

"Ben," Greenan called.

"How you doing, Steve?"

"I was busting my back planting bulbs for Mildred. This call saved me." He turned to Bender. "Okay, sonny," he said, "where is it?"

I followed them into the house. Yellow tape cordoned off the living room. Ron lay there alone. He seemed to be getting smaller.

Steve stepped under the tape. "That's it for this couch," he said.

The cops had a private word, after which Bender headed upstairs, where his partner had left Rita with a female officer. Trooper Boyce took me into the dining room—a vast, high-ceilinged, partially furnished hall.

She was a nice-looking woman, wearing a knee-length skirt, running shoes, and a crisp white blouse under a blazer. She had short hair, a wide, friendly mouth, and a take-charge manner. Her trooper eyes were gray and wise. She played it soft at first.

"I'm going to ask you many of the same questions Sergeant Bender asked, just so we can gather as much information as you can recall. Okay, Ben? Is it all right if I call you Ben?"

"Sure."

She indeed asked every question Bender had, including the jailbird jibes, couched in the careful manner of a graduate student polishing her thesis: "I understand you served time in prison."

Her partner's "jailbird" had rankled more than I should have let it. I said, "I was rehabilitated."

She got unnice very quickly. "Are you trying to be funny? We've got a dead man here."

"*You* have a dead man here. I didn't kill him. I didn't know him. I just found him. If I sounded like I was wisecracking, it was because I'm irritated that you're wasting time on my past while whoever shot the man is probably in the next state by now."

"What makes you think he was shot?"

"Something came out of his chest with great force. Unless they're filming *Alien 4,* I'd guess he was shot in the back. Probably with a 12-gauge deer slug. I'm sure Steve will fill you in."

"Steve?"

"Dr. Greenan. The assistant M.E."

"He's your doctor?"

"He delivered me."

Trooper Boyce frowned. "How well do you know Mrs. Long?"

"Met her this afternoon at the cookout. She wanted a burger. Then she wanted her house appraised."

"Just like that?"

"Happens all the time. People at a party ask Steve about their allergies. They ask me what their houses are worth. I'll bet they ask you how many miles over the speed limit they can get away with."

I got a smile at last. "So why'd you move the body?"

"I've been through this with Sergeant Bender."

"Go through it with me." No smile.

"We thought it best to move the body indoors before dark."

"What if I told you Mrs. Long said you suggested moving it?"

I didn't believe her. "Mrs. Long didn't say anything of the sort. Trooper, at worst we made an error in judgment. Are you investigating how the man got killed or are you building a case against me and Mrs. Long for screwing up the evidence?"

"How the man died could explain who killed him," she said. "I can't decide if you're a wise guy or you're hiding something."

I inventoried what I was hiding: Rose and the videotape and the gun smoke I'd smelled in the turret topped the list. But I could not believe that the joyous woman I'd seen last night had shot her man. I said, "I didn't see anything. Looks to me like a hunting accident."

Doctor Steve barged in. "I'd look for a deer slug if I were you," he said to Trooper Boyce. "Probably what did him. Right in, and out the other side."

"What range?"

"Close as you'd get to a deer. Fifty, sixty yards."

I let loose an internal sigh. If that were the case, Ron hadn't been shot from the tower. His body had fallen more like eighty yards from the tower. Whatever I had smelled up there had nothing to do with it. It was probably a hunting accident—some hunter either didn't know he'd shot him, or did and was running like hell, with nightfall on his side. Now all Bender and Boyce had to do was find the slug, match it to a gun, and make a charge. Of course, if the poacher was smart—which ruled out all the Chevalley boys and most of the Jervis clan—he'd toss his gun in the river, and the troopers would never find it.

Then Sergeant Bender walked in, calling, "Doc, you want to give Mrs. Long a shot? She's getting hysterical." Steve didn't answer. He was staring at the shotgun Bender was carrying by a wire hanger through the trigger guard. The sergeant said, "Marian, take a powder analysis on Mrs. Long's fingers. Do one on the jailbird, too."

"Where'd you find that?" Steve asked.

Bender smiled. "In the turret. Been fired recently."

Steve hurried out to help Mrs. Long.

Oliver Moody came in, holding a flashlight in one hand and a plastic Ziploc bag in the other. "Found a slug," he announced.

I had one friend in the house, and that was Steve. Bender and Boyce got distracted when more cops arrived, and I took advantage of the interruption to buttonhole the doctor when he returned. As a medical examiner, he was in charge of the crime scene.

"Can I see her?"

"I don't think they want you to. You got a thing going with her?"

"No such luck."

Steve cracked a little smile. "She's in a guest room. First right at the top of the kitchen stairs."

"Thanks." I cut through the kitchen and up the back stairs. I was afraid they'd hear if I knocked, so I opened the first door on the right and shut it behind me.

Rita lay on an elaborately stitched down quilt. She was on her side, staring into the cold fireplace, curled up like a question mark. Her black hair shone in the light from the night table. When I was a child, my mother's hair had been almost as long and black; nights, sometimes, she'd let me help brush its hundred strokes.

I moved around the bed into Rita's vision. She looked confused and seemed to be fighting Steve's tranquilizer.

"Can I do anything for you?" I asked.

She shook her head. Tears trickled down her cheek into the corner of her mouth. She said, "He was so wonderful."

"Ron?"

"Just wonderful. . . . *We* were wonderful."

"I'm really sorry," I said, adding lamely, "You poor thing."

"Yeah, I'm a poor thing all right. A real poor thing. . . . Poor Jack. It's so ironic. We tried not to hurt him. Keep it from him while we tried to figure out what to do. And now—now he's going to know."

I had to tell her that her husband knew already, but it could wait.

"Why did they keep asking me why we took him inside?" she asked. "I told them it was my idea, by the way. I said you only helped. Why did they keep asking?"

"It has to do with their investigation. We didn't follow their procedure, so they're upset. Don't worry about it."

"Why did they test my hand?"

"They found a gun in the turret that had been fired."

Her eyes flashed. "Idiots. Jack and I were shooting last week."

"And they found a deer slug in the grass."

"Must have been a poacher. We caught one last month. And last night there was someone in the woods."

"Did you tell the cops?"

"They came out here and shot a raccoon. Said it was the prowler."

"Do the police know who Ron is?"

"Of course. I told them. What's to hide? It's all going to come out. There's no way Jack's going to believe Ron was here for any other reason than the very obvious."

"You can't tough it out?"

"When you stop sleeping with your husband, and one day his former partner turns up at your house while your husband's in Washington, he's going to get the picture."

"Former partner?" I echoed, surprised that Alex Rose, P.I., had neglected to mention this startling leg of their love triangle.

"Jack bought him out," she muttered. She was trembling.

I said, "Would you like me to call a friend for you?"

"Ron was my friend, my best friend."

"Can I do anything? Some tea? Coffee?"

"No, thanks. . . . Tea. Yeah, tea might be a good idea. The doctor gave me this shot. My head is like oatmeal."

"I'll make tea."

CIGARETTE smoke hung thick downstairs. There were cops everywhere, gawking at the lavish rooms.

"Excuse me." I shouldered between two giants with their hats on, filled a kettle, and set it to boil on the eight-burner Garland range. There were matching Sub-Zero refrigerator-freezers. The first held beer and wine. I found milk in the second. I located the tea in an airtight cabinet.

Upstairs in the guest room, Rita had dozed off. I put her cup on the night table. I sat in an easy chair, sipped my tea, and studied the room. They'd had a fire in the fireplace last night—it had to be "their" room—and candles on the mantel had burned to stubs. There was a pair of empty wineglasses in the bathroom. It was funny how casual they were about their room. Why had they left all this night-of-love evidence around? I would have thought they'd have scoured the place before Ron left.

Maybe he hadn't left. Long was in Washington. Maybe Ron had been planning a round-trip to New York and back tonight. Then it dawned on me: in order to get shot, he had to have left the cookout ahead of Rita and come back here first.

I heard a car door slam. I got up and looked out the window. A Newbury volunteer ambulance was pulling down the driveway, doing double duty as a morgue wagon. I sat a while longer watching Rita sleep. Suddenly a whole slew of car doors slammed. I looked out again. This time state troopers were streaming from the house, running full tilt to their cars. Sirens whooped and gravel flew.

Rita stirred, but did not wake. I went down to the kitchen. Steve was on the telephone, hurriedly explaining to Mildred that he was going to be late. Then he ran for the front door with his black bag. It was heavy, and he was not young, so I grabbed it and ran alongside. We passed a rookie state trooper at the door, who looked put out that he'd been left behind.

"What's going on?" I asked Steve.

"Plane crash," he said, climbing into his car. "You coming?"

Rita wasn't likely to wake up, and the trooper had the house secured, so I got in. A shooting and a plane crash in one day was more action than we'd seen since the Hawleyville Tavern burned down.

"What's the big deal? Why'd the plainclothes go?"

"The plane was found on Al Bell's strip. When Al drove up to see if the pilot was okay, the cockpit looked like a snowstorm. The troopers suspect it's not baking powder."

"Oh." We don't get all that much dope action in Newbury. Little wonder that every state trooper at Rita Long's house was howling through the night in the direction of Al Bell's private airstrip. Careers were in the making. Suspicious death on a rich man's estate offered promise, but a plane full of coke crashing into northwest Connecticut's exclusive hills guaranteed a media feeding frenzy, with sound bites for all.

Without Trooper Moody to lead the way, it would have taken the state police all night to find Bell's airstrip. We climbed Morris Mountain on a dirt road, took a number of turnoffs, then ran through a deep woods that opened suddenly on two thousand feet of mowed pasture. At the far end, the police cars had clustered. We bounced across the grass. They'd aimed their roof lights at the plane, a white Cessna, which had smacked its nose into a tree. A trooper hurried over and asked the doctor to have a look at the pilot. I went with Steve, carrying his bag. Oliver Moody was guarding the entrance to the cordon. He saw me and said, "Get outta here."

I gave Steve his bag and went back to the car.

The doctor returned shortly, looking grave. "Ben, I'm sorry."

"What's wrong?"

"It's Renny Chevalley."

4

MY COUSIN Renny was the only Chevalley boy ever to fly.

Chevalley women did all right, but the men just didn't fit in. They tended to tumble out of the school system around eighth grade. They were great with a chain saw, they were born to the seat of a bulldozer, but they hadn't the entrepreneurial skills to acquire their own machines. They made good truckers until they drank too much. When they drank, they fought, and when they fought, normal people called the cops. They got better as they got older: my mother's brothers made wonderful uncles.

Renny stayed in school. In seventh grade Mr. Tyler, the shop teacher, taught him how to turn metal on a lathe. When the rest of us brought home our little wooden water-pump lamps, Renny gave his mom a gleaming polished aluminum ship's helm lamp. When I started prep school, Renny rebuilt a Pontiac GTO, which his big brother Pinkerton raced to victory on dirt tracks as far away as Maine. When I got accepted at Annapolis, Renny cracked up the GTO. It was the night before he was to go to Hartford to receive first prize in a statewide shop-project contest—for a chrome version of the ship's helm lamp—and he nearly died. When he could walk again, he rebuilt a wrecked Piper Cub and learned to fly.

I thought then there'd be no stopping him, a hope confirmed when he was accepted into the air force. But though his scores were high and no one could outfly him in a trainer, Renny was suddenly discharged. He wouldn't talk about it until years later. Boot camp was the first time he'd ever slept farther from his bed than my house on Main Street. He told me he had simply gotten homesick. But he still wanted to fly for the airlines.

Acquiring flight time was a long, expensive process without air force backing. He had worked as a flight instructor, an occasional charter pilot, and a "freight dog." Freight dogs fly at night, shuttling between small airports to deliver bank checks to central clearinghouses. I rode along with him now and then; it was magnificent droning through a dark sky peppered with stars.

Gradually he had given up the dream of being an airline pilot. Some of it had to do with one of the Butler girls, whom he married on her eighteenth birthday. Along came a baby, and a second. His father decided to retire, and the logical thing was to take over his Frenchtown garage—a dank, greasy establishment with a surly dog on a chain that scared most customers off to Jiffy Lube. Renny discovered a flair for business. He cleaned up the garage, invested in some modern tools, initiated a free towing service for his startled customers, and turned the place into a going enterprise.

I told Steve I had to see Renny.

"Coming through," growled Steve Greenan. He walked me past a grimly smiling Oliver Moody and right up to the plane. "You okay?" he asked me.

"I don't know." We climbed onto the hood of a police car they'd driven close to use for steps. Its roof lights illuminated the cockpit. The windshield was shattered. Renny sat buckled into his seat. Blood had trickled down his face and dried, marring his dark, lean good looks. He was wearing a leather bomber jacket. It was open, and it and his shirtfront were dusted heavily in white powder.

"I don't believe this," I said. "Is that coke?"

"Tastes like it to me," Steve said.

"Renny wouldn't fly dope."

The doctor's silence said that he, like most of Newbury, wouldn't put anything past a Chevalley boy.

"Steve, he didn't need this. He had his business."

Steve said, "I'm just telling you it tastes like coke."

"Well, it's not his."

"That might have been the problem," Steve muttered. "Look at him."

I saw that the cockpit was intact but for the shattered windshield, and the plane was barely scratched. Renny's seat belt had held, and it looked to me like he hadn't even hit the glass.

"What killed him?"

"He's been shot."

"Shot?" I reached to touch Renny's face.

Steve stopped me with a gnarled hand. "You don't want to see the back of his head. Come on, Ben. Let's get out of here. I told the cops I needed you for a positive I.D. I'll drive you home now."

I walked from the plane in a daze, barely aware of anything but the smile on Oliver Moody's face. From his point of view, dead Chevalleys and Jervises represented little victories. And in general I can't say I blamed him; he was the guy who had to break up bar brawls and pull violent men off their women. But it wasn't fair to Renny, and I would never forgive that smile.

"You want your car?" Steve asked when we got to Route 361.

"I better get it. I left the top down. I'm sorry, Steve."

"Don't worry about it."

The Longs' floodlights were all blazing, and the young trooper was still guarding the door.

I put the top up and led Steve back to Newbury. Back home, I lit a fire and had a couple of Jack Daniel's. I thought of driving over to see Renny's wife, but I knew the whole huge clan would be there looking after her. The third bourbon sent me reeling. I staggered upstairs, got into bed, and lay awake a long time trying to come up with a plausible reason why a thirty-five-year-old businessman with two babies would fly cocaine.

No doubt he owed plenty on his business. Turning a rathole of a fix-it shop into a seven-bay wonder of computer diagnostics costs plenty. He had been into me for a few grand, part of which he had paid by shoehorning the Caddy engine into my dad's old Olds. But the bulk of his money would have come from banks.

On the other hand, Chevalley Enterprises was booming. Nothing like a recession to convince people they could eke a few more years out of the family cars instead of trading them in. Chevalley Enterprises treated them better than the dealers, fixed it right, and kept it reasonable. The last time I'd been in for an oil change, all seven bays were working, and Renny'd been talking about adding two more if he could get the financing.

Oliver Moody's smile floated before my eyes. The trooper's pleasure in Renny's death was not general. He hated two people in the world: Renny and me. His smile had said, One down, one to go.

THE TELEPHONE WOKE ME. I should have let the machine take it, but I croaked a dry-mouthed, bourbon-fouled hello, and the voice of my great-aunt Connie said, "I hope I didn't wake you."

"No, no, Connie." I found the clock. Seven.

"You've heard about Renny, haven't you?"

"Last night."

She was on the "Fish Line," a telephone circuit used by older people who called each other in the morning to check that no one had fallen and needed help. It helped those alone to stay in their own homes rather than move to retirement communities, and it spread news faster than CNN.

"I'm sorry for you. I know you liked him. I must call on the Butler girl. Would you like to come with me?"

Connie was a forthright ninety, but her manner of speech required decoding. "The Butler girl" was Renny's wife. Everyone else called her Betty Chevalley, but Aunt Connie tended to remember us as children; also, she had no truck with Chevalleys. As a Christian, however, she must call on anyone in need. "Would you like to come with me?" was her way of asking if I would drive her. She would drive herself, but the sight of her peering under the rim of the steering wheel would scatter the few who hadn't already taken cover at the sight of her black Lincoln. So if I were to oblige, she would take the sensible course. But she would not ask.

I said, "I'd like very much to go with you, thank you. I'll drive if you'll let me."

"Half an hour?"

"It's early, Connie. Maybe we'll give them a little time. I'll come over at nine."

I WALKED across the street to Connie's. Her house is a Federal era mansion, the grandest in town. She's bequeathed it to the historical society, and if she ever dies—which doesn't seem likely—Newbury will possess one of the most lavish museum houses in New England, chockablock with pre-Revolutionary antiques, Persian carpets, and Chinese porcelain. I went around the back. She was waiting at the kitchen door with her coat, gloves, and hat on. Good posture and thick curly white hair fooled strangers into thinking she was only eighty.

"I've started the car to warm it," she said, adding tartly as I offered her my arm down the steps, "We should not stay for lunch."

"Of course not."

"We will go to church at eleven." Sunday. I'd forgotten my tie.

The stable was choked with fumes. The sun spilled in on a 1960 sedan, black as midnight and bright with chrome. "Connie, please remember, don't start the car before you open the door."

"Let's go."

She barreled in, waving the fumes with her pocketbook. I helped her with her seat belt and drove out of the stable, stopped to close the door—no electronic door openers in this house, thank you very much—went down the drive, and turned onto Main Street.

"What happened to Renny?" she asked. "Why did he do it?"

My question exactly. When I didn't answer immediately, Connie said, "You are aware he was smuggling cocaine?"

"I don't believe it."

"Why not? They said the airplane was crammed full."

"I saw."

"You were there?" She looked at me sharply, her bony face and snow-white curls frozen in sudden astonishment. For one second I could see her thinking, Oh, Lord, Ben was in on it.

"Steve Greenan took me to identify the body."

"What for? He's known Renny since he was born."

"He knew I wanted to see him."

Connie nodded, relaxing back in the seat. "Stevie Greenan was always a very thoughtful boy. Is it true Renny had been shot?"

"Yes."

"So why don't you believe it?"

"Connie, Renny's not a criminal. He was a businessman."

"Businessman? A Chevalley? Come on, Ben."

"Connie, he had seven mechanics working for him, two tow-truck drivers, and a secretary. He became a businessman."

Connie was no fool. "Where did he get the money for all that?"

"Banks."

"Perhaps he was having difficulty paying them back."

"Maybe. But I just don't see him doing that. Some people are naturally honest."

"Some people are brought up properly."

She had never approved of Renny as my friend. She was behind the decision to send me to the Newbury Prep School and then off to Stonybrook Military. She had interceded personally to get my senatorial appointment to Annapolis. And she'd attended every day of my trial, taking up residence at the Carlyle Hotel.

"Do you suppose," she asked, "that there is a connection?"

"Between what and what, Aunt Connie?"

"Between the two killings."

"Oh. You heard about the man at the Long place."

"I heard he was where he shouldn't be."

"How so?"

"*Mr.* Long was away. *Mrs.* Long was entertaining." Connie glanced at me. Most of the elderly blue-eyed people I know get watery-eyed as they get older. Not Connie. Hers were sharp enough to cut. "You're a connection."

"Me?"

"Well, I hear you found the poor man's body. And now you tell me you and Stevie found Renny."

"Al Bell found Renny."

"Ben, should I be worried about you?"

"No, Connie. It's just a lousy coincidence. I'm sorry if you have to hear more embarrassing gossip."

"Ha!" She laughed—a reminder that when it came to society in this corner of New England, Connie Abbott set the standards.

We descended the long slope to Frenchtown, past Chevalley Enterprises, which was shut for Sunday.

"Do you know Mrs. Long?" Aunt Connie asked.

"Very slightly."

"If she's the girl I saw chatting you up at the cookout, she's a great beauty."

"Yes. Rita Long is a great beauty."

"I was reminded of your mother."

"The hair."

"And that woman who testified against you."

"Same thing," I answered sharply. "Her hair."

"I always thought you were a fool for women."

"Not all women, Connie."

Ahead lay Renny's neat little ranch, built down the road from his parents' ramshackle farmhouse. Trailers up the hillside housed brothers and sisters. The drive and the lawn were scattered with pickup trucks parked at urgent-looking angles. A gang of men with caps pulled over their long hair were hanging around the front door, sipping coffee from containers and morning Buds from cans.

Caps flew, and the gang at the door melted with a mumbled chorus of "Good morning, Miss Abbott." She greeted each by name. There wasn't a man among them who hadn't raked leaves for her at some point in his boyhood. I got my usual allotment of "Hey, Bens." Pinkerton Chevalley stood off under a tree, looking like he would kill someone if he could only figure out who.

Inside were women, coffee, and cakes. Renny's mom, my aunt Frances, hugged me and shook hands with Connie. Aunt Frances was a Jervis, with just enough Butler blood to bring her indoors. Still a looker—with her taut French cheeks, dark hair, and meet-me-in-the-hayloft eyes—Frances wore the rigid smile of a woman who did not yet believe that she had lost her son.

Aunt Connie took Frances' hand in both of hers. "I'm sorry, Frances." She had a gift for making the simple phrase "I'm sorry" sound as if she grieved for Renny's mom from the bottom of her heart. Her presence was balm; her words were wisdom. "May we see the widow?" she asked after a proper interval.

Frances ran ahead to alert Betty Butler Chevalley. I trailed Connie into the bedroom, where Betty was sitting with a bunch of her sisters, all as redheaded and round as she. They were stabbing out cigarettes and rising nervously for Connie, who trundled in, waving them down with her pocketbook. She went right to Betty and took her hands and spoke quietly and urgently for a moment.

Betty, who was twenty-three, looked like a child who had lost her pet. She'd been crying. Her fair skin was blotched; her eyes were swollen slits. She turned to me when Connie let go of her hands.

"Renny didn't do anything."

"I know."

"The cops searched here. They handcuffed Pink. They scared my kids. And Oliver Moody said they'll be back to search the garage."

Renny's mom asked if Connie would like some coffee. She started to say no but noticed the Butler girls eyeing her like the grande dame from their favorite soap opera, and said, "Yes, thank you. Would it be possible for me to sit down here?" Girls leaped. A chair was offered, and they gathered around.

I went outside and joined the guys. Joey Meadows got a cold one from his truck and pressed it into my hand. I said, "Here's to Renny," and drained half of it in a bourbon-sluicing swallow.

"Anybody know, was that his plane?" I asked.

Gary Nello said, "I hear it was rented."

"You saw him?" Pete Stock asked me.

"Yeah. He never felt a thing."

"So how'd he crash?"

"I don't know," I said. "I don't really think he could have tried to fly. Doc said the whole back of his head was gone."

"So he crashed and then he got shot—unless the guy who shot him crashed the plane."

I said, "There was coke all over everything. Like a bag broke. Who would bring coke by plane?"

Several men looked off at the woods. Someone mumbled, "I hear they drive the stuff in, same as grass."

Pink wandered over from his tree and fished a fresh Bud out of his truck. "This whole thing don't make no sense."

"Did you know he was flying again?" I asked him.

"Told me he was flying some charter jobs. Taking rich people out to Block Island. The bucks were good. Needed the bucks."

"Was he doing it a lot?"

"Once, twice a week most of the summer."

"Where'd he get the plane?"

"I don't know."

I slipped a hand around Pink's thigh-size biceps and walked him back to his tree. "Pink, do you think he was flying dope?"

"I don't know," said Pink, looking away.

"Come on, Pink. It's me. Was he flying dope?"

"I know it's you. I don't know. I ain't his nurse."

"So who would know?"

"Maybe Gwen Jervis."

"*What?*" I was astonished. Between my real estate business and my far-flung family, there wasn't a whole lot going on in Newbury that I didn't know about. "Gwen Jervis?"

"You got a problem with that?" Pink, never far from looking dangerous, began to look very dangerous.

"Well, she's his cousin, and— I'm just surprised. I thought things were great with Betty."

"Long as Renny had Gwen, things were great with Betty," said Pink. "You don't know squat about life, do you?"

THERE ARE FOUR CORNERS ON Main Street at the flagpole, and three churches. The fourth corner is the Yankee Drover Inn, in whose cellar bar I would ordinarily be reading the Sunday *Times* with a Bloody Mary. Instead, I was across the street sitting next to Aunt Connie in the front pew of the Episcopal church, listening to a hastily written sermon on the Sixth Commandment. While our two killings had occurred too late for the morning papers, Reverend Owen had risen to the occasion. He asked the congregation to join hearts with our neighbors in the Catholic church across the street—Renny's church.

As we shuffled out after the benediction, Connie asked me, "Where was your mother? I thought we'd see her at Renny's."

"Aunt Frances told me she had just left."

"Well, sometime this week it would be nice if you would drive over there with me. I've not seen her in some time."

"I'll call her. Maybe we could drive over Wednesday."

Oliver Moody was directing traffic as the Catholic, Congregationalist, and Episcopal parking lots emptied simultaneously. He held everything up for Connie to cross the street. Whatever he held for me in his gaze was hidden by his sunglasses. I walked Connie home, and wandered back up to the general store for a paper and into the cellar bar of the Yankee Drover. I ordered a Bloody Mary and a burger, and settled into the cool dark. Tony Franco, the owner, set down my spicy, straight-up Bloody and said, "There's a guy in a booth asking for you."

I watched in the back bar mirror as he emerged from the shadows. He had exchanged his country clothes for a Sunday-best suit, neatly tailored for his ample frame.

"Home at last?" said Alex Rose, taking a stool next to mine. He looked smug as a CNN correspondent in a brand-new war.

I said, "Your camera's in the mail."

He said, "They're gonna arrest Mrs. Long for murder."

Renny held a monopoly on my emotions, and at first the strongest feeling I could rouse for Rose's news was surprise that the New York P.I. knew his way around my town better than I.

"Where'd you hear that?"

"I bought a friend in the Plainfield state trooper barracks. Tipped me off in time to get Mr. Long up to the house with a limoload of lawyers, including Ira Roth." Ira Roth was *the* criminal lawyer in the county. Nobody could remember the last time he'd lost a case.

"Shouldn't you be holding their coats or something?"

Rose's beefy face got hard. "You got a problem with me?"

"I got a problem with everybody at the moment. I just lost a friend. If you don't mind, I'd rather drink alone. Even if you do mind."

"Your cousin Renny. I'm sorry, fella." Then Rose said, "Rita's innocent."

"You don't have to convince me."

"I want to know what you saw when you found the jerk. They're basing the case on the M.E.'s opinion of the angle of entry."

"He wasn't a jerk. He seemed like a decent guy."

"That why you didn't do the videotape? You liked them as a couple. I'm not surprised. I had a witness in New York, a waiter, raving on about how romantic they were."

I raised the paper, trying to read the political cartoons.

Rose said, "Let's get back to when you found the body."

"Why are they charging Rita?" I asked through the paper.

"Her shotgun. Her fingerprints."

"Powder test?"

"Passed it. But she could have scrubbed or worn a glove."

"Anyone suggesting a motive?"

"Lovers' quarrel. Old reliable. Juries do love the lovers' quarrel."

"That's bull," I said. "Long's standing by her?"

"One hundred percent."

"Why? I thought he wanted a divorce." I lowered the paper.

"Hey, just because he's rich doesn't mean he's smart," Rose said. "Maybe he loves her."

"Who was Ron?"

Rose looked surprised. "You don't know?"

"Nobody told me. I just know he used to be Long's partner, a fact you neglected to mention."

Rose didn't apologize. "Ronald Pearlman," he said. "Sold his father's furrier chain before the fur market crashed. Bought a Hong Kong chip factory and merged with LTS—Long Technical Systems."

"Rita told me Long bought Ron out."

"He hates partners. Ron had brought him excellent manufacturing capability, but once he had those offshore factories, it galled him that Ron would split the profits."

"Did they fight?"

"Over what? Ron goes from, let's say, ten million bucks from his father's business to two hundred and fifty million bucks for his Hong Kong operation. The guy's thirty-eight, with enough money to buy Rhode Island. He's got it all."

"Except his own wife."

"Some guys are greedy."

I wondered why, if Rita wanted to run off with Ron, she had wanted to sell the Castle—when Ron had a quarter billion bucks in the bank. "How'd he parlay ten million into two fifty?"

"First you answer my questions. Then I'll answer yours. What did you see when you found the body?"

I told him everything I'd told the state police. Then Rose asked, "So you still think he was shot from the woods?"

"Hey, I didn't do the autopsy. I heard Steve guess it was close range. The woods were about fifty yards off."

"How far was the tower?"

"Eighty yards."

"They think she shot him from the tower."

"That will be a tough one to prove."

"They don't seem worried."

"So how'd Ron Pearlman multiply ten million dollars into two hundred and fifty million?"

"He was well connected in Hong Kong from his old man's fur-coat factories. The government gave him grants to expand. Hot operation. The chip factory had some new process. A bunch of different American outfits wanted to control it for their own exclusive supply. They got in a bidding war. LTS won."

"Connected, smart, and lucky."

Rose agreed. "I'd be envious if he weren't dead."

"I don't buy the lovers' quarrel."

"I'm hoping you'll tell that to the jury."

"What?"

"You saw them together, right?"

"Briefly."

"Well, it's too bad you blew the taping, but at least you saw them playing around together. No one else has. They were really careful in New York. I've got waiters who'll testify they had lunch together. But in you I've got a well-connected local guy who can persuade the jury that Ron and Rita were deeply in love."

"Wait a minute—"

"I know you don't want to stand up in court and admit you were sneaking around the woods taking pictures. But you were."

"You're forgetting my rep. The prosecutor will eat me for breakfast. He'll discredit me to discredit my testimony."

"Oh, he'll try to destroy you. But he can't discredit your testimony; the jury will get that those two adored each other."

"I don't want to be destroyed here. This is my home."

"Sorry, fella. You want that woman to sit in jail for the rest of her life for something she probably didn't do?"

"Probably?"

Rose shrugged. "Whether she blew him away is not the question. The question is: Will she serve time for it? Now Mr. Long is up there with four of the top lawyers in New York to answer no. And I'm out hustling witnesses to answer no."

I started to protest. Rose cut me off. "This is not debatable. We'll subpoena you. You'll testify for the defense."

"And if I refuse to testify?"

"Look what happened last time."

I would have decked him right there, but whether I wanted to testify wasn't the issue, because I'd seen something at the Castle that Rose had not. Rita's spooky drawing would steamroller any sympathy I could build for the loving couple.

So instead of knocking him off his barstool, I said, "I'll do what I can to help her. But anything I say won't help one bit the second the jury gets a load of one of Mrs. Long's drawings in the studio."

"Which one?"

I described the figure of Ron, naked with skull. "At the trial they'll show that picture. Any twelve jurors will take one look and say, Yup, a woman who'd draw a picture like that would shoot a man. They'll make me testify I saw her draw it, and it'll hang her."

Rose took a notebook from his jacket and opened it to the first page. "Bear with me a minute. Just checking the police warrants. . . . No. There's no such picture mentioned in the warrants. I was just up there in the studio. The big one was a landscape—"

"The little one. On the smaller easel."

"No. That was a landscape, too. I don't know what you saw, but it isn't there now."

"You took it."

"No. I wasn't there yesterday. Just you and her and Ron." He closed his book and pocketed it with a satisfied smile.

"You think she killed him, don't you?"

"The jury won't care what I think."

"Does Mr. Long believe his wife killed her lover?"

"He doesn't confide in the help." Rose got up from his stool.

"If I testify, I have to testify I saw her drawing."

"I thought you said she's innocent."

"She is. But I can't lie for her."

Rose said, "With a friend like you, she won't need enemies."

I switched to bourbon old-fashioneds. I'd had enough tomato juice, and felt like something sweet.

5

On Monday my mind was clear despite a ferocious headache. I had coffee in my office, paid a couple of bills, and balanced my checkbook. August is always a slow month. This year September looked worse. At nine thirty I telephoned Trooper Boyce. "Would you like to have lunch with me?" I asked.

I believe she was so surprised that she said yes before she could say no. I suggested the Hopkins Inn, overlooking Lake Waramaug. We agreed on twelve thirty. I booked another ad in *The New York Times* for the Richardson place. One of these days it was going to sell, and I intended to be at the closing. Then I walked over to the general store to see what the paper had on Renny and Rita and Ron.

The Danbury *News-Times* gave what they called the death plane front-page treatment, with an equal-sized headline for Rita's arrest. She was described as a "wealthy weekender from New York City." Bail hearings were Monday morning, which meant the poor woman had spent the night in jail despite her hotshot attorneys.

Trooper Boyce arrived at the Hopkins Inn looking flustered. I had the definite feeling that some small female-kid part of her wanted lunch to be a date, so I was flattered. She looked kind of cute, in a brown suit, with a handbag big enough for an automatic, and her hair all fluffy.

"Sorry I'm late," she greeted me.

"Bail hearing?"

"Denied." She studied my reaction. I was surprised. I had figured Long's legal muscle could spring Rita on bail.

Trooper Boyce said, "Should we order a drink or should I open my notebook?"

"Coffee for me. What would you like? And you're going to need two notebooks."

She spread her hands on the table. "Two?"

"I want to talk to you about Rita Long, and I want to talk to you about Renny Chevalley. Renny first."

"I'm going to read you your rights."

"No need."

She read them anyway, in a low voice, by heart, while holding a menu. "Do you understand your rights?"

"Yes, dammit. This isn't a confession. Are you ready?"

"Go."

"Renny Chevalley would not fly coke into Newbury."

"How come?"

I told her all about my cousin. She listened, taking notes. When I was done, she said, "Your opinion is noted."

"No. You don't get it. What everyone thinks happened up there, didn't happen. If Renny was flying dope, he was tricked into it. Maybe he discovered it and tried to stop them. Maybe that's why they shot him."

"We've considered that. But why would they leave the coke?"

"The bag broke."

"Maybe. But it would have been worth the trouble to stuff it in their pockets. Thousands of dollars."

"Where did the plane come from?"

"Your cousin rented it in Danbury." She saw my disappointment. "Tell you what: I'll follow up the facts you've laid out about your cousin. Whatever he did, *someone* shot him. I'm investigating a murder here. Two murders, actually. Now, what do you recall about Mrs. Long?"

"She didn't do it. I still think it was a hunting accident."

"The coroner doesn't agree. He was shot in the back from the turret. The slug struck him at a high angle."

"The woods slope up sharply. Thirty yards inside the trees, a hunter would be standing as high as the top of the tower."

"We found no sign of a hunter," she said.

"Mrs. Long told me they had a prowler the night before."

"Turned out to be a raccoon. Trooper Moody shot it."

I said, "You've probably figured out that they were lovers."

"No kidding."

"Has it occurred to you that her husband might have shot Ron?"

"Mr. Long was in the Rose Garden of the White House having his picture taken with the President of the United States. Do you have any more information?"

I had no information and, with Jack Long off the hook, only one theory. "If I find a hunter—a poacher—who shot him by accident, can I come straight to you?"

"Fast as you can dial 911."

"I'm trying to tell you she didn't do it."

"You've got the same problem with your cousin: you're not telling me why."

"I just know it. She could not have killed Ron."

"Why?"

"She loved him too much."

"Wait a minute. You said you met her at the cookout. And you went to appraise her house. Then you drank a glass of champagne in her turret. If that was your total contact with the woman, how do you know she loved her boyfriend too much to kill him?"

I was close to telling her about the video and the couple I saw they were. But I was afraid it would lead to more misery for Rita, so I said, "By the way she held his body."

"I hope the food here is worth the drive." She put away her notebook. "So tell me, what's it like to grow up a rich kid?"

"I wasn't a rich kid."

"Trooper Moody said your father was mayor. Mine pounded a beat in New Haven. To me you're a rich kid."

"Well, in that case, it was very pleasant growing up in Newbury. A little boring, but we made our own fun."

"I heard the guys at the barracks laughing about some fun you made with Trooper Moody."

I couldn't stop the grin that jumped onto my face. "When you see Ollie, watch how he always walks behind his car before he gets in."

"Wha'd you do? They wouldn't tell me."

"Why not?"

"One thousand state police. Fifty women."

I got the impression that being tough enough to handle bigotry didn't mean she didn't get lonely. So I said, "Renny helped."

"Is that supposed to be a character reference?"

"Yes, as a matter of fact, because he was backing me up. Trooper Moody had done something pretty awful to me. I was a teenager. It seemed like a big deal at the time."

"Did he humiliate you in front of your friends?"

"How'd you guess?"

"I'm a cop. So wha'd you do? Don't worry. As long as you didn't murder somebody, the statute of limitations is up." She flashed her pretty smile.

I told my story. "There was a dance at the Grange hall. Renny and I sneaked a double-barrel twelve-gauge out of my father's gun case and hid it in the field behind the hall. Then we borrowed a hundred-foot logging chain from Renny's brother, Pink, and wheelbarrowed the chain to the Church Hill Diner. When Ollie drove up and went inside for his coffee break, we tied one end around that maple out front and the other around his rear axle."

"You're kidding."

"Renny ran back behind the Grange hall to fire the shotgun in the air. Both barrels. Kaboooooom! You can imagine how it echoed on a still summer night.

"Ollie came out of the diner like someone had fired him from a cannon, leaped into his cruiser, hit lights, siren, and ignition all at once, and floored the beast. He took off, *screaming* up Church Hill. He hit forty before the chain fetched up. All of a sudden—bang!—rear wheels, axle, and differential were bouncing at the end of the chain, but Ollie kept going. He slid a hundred yards in this huge spray of sparks and smoke before he finally scrunched to a stop in the middle of Church Hill Road."

"Rotten kids."

"Long time ago. . . . Marian— May I call you Marian?"

"Yes, Ben. Of course, call me Marian."

"We were both 'rotten kids.' Me worse than him. But he was never a kid to smuggle coke. You gotta know that."

"And Rita Long's not a woman to shoot her lover. You know something? You're a romantic guy, Ben. Got a girl?"

"Nothing that's going anywhere. Which is fine with me. How about you? Got a fella?"

“Two at the moment,” she answered, volunteering nothing more about her love life as she picked up the menu. “What do you recommend?”

“The view.”

She perused the menu, noticed me frowning, and leaned over the table. “Hey, you’re kind of pent-up about your cousin right now. Why don’t you give yourself a couple of days to rethink all this?”

“I knew Rita Long didn’t kill her boyfriend before I found out about Renny.”

Trooper Boyce sighed. “I checked you out, Ben. I know your background. Put yourself in my place. Remember what you thought of hunches when you were in naval intelligence?”

“I remember hunches that led me to facts.”

She smiled her pretty smile. “Hunches are nice. Facts are better.” She took a card from her bag and scribbled with a smile. “Call me when you get some facts.”

We had trout. It was great. As for the purpose of lunch, it was a disaster. After coffee, Marian signaled for the check.

“No, my treat,” I protested.

“You get the next one, when it’s not business. Call me.”

I drove straight back through Newbury, on toward Danbury.

Two propeller planes droned around Danbury Airport. One flew for the highway patrol. The other plane, painted Chinese red, belonged to Sky Rentals. The owner was practicing approaches apparently, touching down on the runway, skipping away, touching down again, and wobbling back up. I waited beside a hangar.

At last the red plane came down and trundled up to where I was stationed. A man climbed out of the plane. “You waiting for me?”

“If you’re the Roy Chernowsky who rents planes.”

“Sorry I took so long. I was checking out a renter. He didn’t pass. What can I do for you? Looking to rent?”

“I’m Ben Abbott. Renny Chevalley’s cousin.”

“Renny’s your cousin?” Chernowsky glanced around, frightened.

“Relax,” I said. “I’m just trying to figure out what happened. I don’t believe he was flying coke. Do you know whom he was flying with?”

“Just a cat. It belongs to this doctor. The doc’s got a house on Block Island. She goes out for a week at a time. The other day she couldn't find the cat, so she went without it. Then her housekeeper finds the cat. The doc says, 'Great. Tell Renny to fly it out here.' "

"The doctor knows Renny?"

"Sure. Renny runs her out regular. So the housekeeper gets hold of Renny, who hires my plane and flies the cat out to Block."

"So how does this turn into coke?"

"You tell me, cousin. He's supposed to be back here by one in the afternoon. Instead, he telephones and says he's keeping the plane late. I say, 'How late?' He says, 'Home by dark.' Fine with me. Comes dark, no Renny. No plane. No calls. Till around ten, when a trooper shows up waving a search warrant, takes my books, and informs me they're impounding my plane."

"Who's the doctor?"

"Zelda Schwartz."

"Got her number?"

"I think it's private."

"Never mind. I'll call her office. What time did he call you from Block Island?"

"Cops asked the same thing. About eleven in the morning."

"So from eleven to dark, let's say, how far could he have flown?"

"You're talking about nine or ten hours' flying time. That's a fast plane—nearly two thousand miles, minus fueling time. Toronto, Montreal, Washington, Philly. Anyplace east of the Mississippi."

"Did he file a flight plan?"

"Didn't have to. He could stay out of the patterns. The way I heard it, he flew from Block to La Guardia."

"Where'd he go from there?"

"No one knows. Flying at the unrestricted eight hundred feet, he could have gone anywhere."

I found a pay phone, lost a quarter, and decided finally to buy a car phone. I found a discount outlet in the Danbury Fair Mall, paid a hundred bucks, and joined the late twentieth century.

Dr. Schwartz's nurse agreed to ask the vacationing doctor to call me. I was nearly home when my new phone buzzed and a gravelly-voiced woman asked for Ben Abbott.

"Dr. Schwartz?"

"My nurse said you're Renny's cousin. How can I help?"

"I don't believe Renny was smuggling cocaine, Doctor."

"I don't believe it either, but I don't know any facts to the contrary. He was a pleasant, shy man, punctual, a confident pilot, and polite—none of which would prevent him from doing what the police say he was doing."

"When did he leave Block Island?"

"He was still at the airport when my caretaker picked the cat up."

"So you have no idea how long he stayed."

"Mr. Abbott, all I know is that my caretaker gave him a telephone message and he said he would see me next week to fly me home."

"Someone left a message for him?"

"It sounded like a flying job. 'Pick up Mr. Smith at two thirty.' "

"Smith? Where?"

"Just the name and the time. Anything else, Mr. Abbott?"

"Thanks for calling back."

Pick up Mr. Smith at two thirty said nothing. Renny had filed a flight plan to La Guardia from Block Island. He could have picked up Mr. Smith at La Guardia and flown him anywhere in eastern America. Or "Mr. Smith" could be code for a bag of coke.

That night, I was sitting in the deep silence of my library, watching applewood burn orange in the fireplace. What had Marian Boyce called me? A romantic without the facts. Yet maybe their facts just *seemed* like facts. It *looked* as if Renny had had a falling out with a partner while smuggling coke. He had cracked up in Al Bell's field. There was cocaine in the plane. Renny was shot. And Renny had had plenty of time to pick up a partner and dope somewhere between Block Island and Al's landing strip. There was no way that I alone was going to find out where else my cousin had touched down.

I needed a partner—a professional who could work his contacts in and out of the law. A sleaze in a Mercedes. I didn't like Alex Rose, but at least I could afford him. I found his card and called.

"What's up?"

I said, "I want to deal. Testimony in support of Mrs. Long."

"There's no deal. You got to testify."

"You will do better if the jury likes me."

"True," Alex Rose conceded. "On the other hand, the prosecution's going to ask whether you've been paid to testify."

"I don't want money. I want two things. Alison's teeth—the orthodontist."

"No problem there. What else?"

"Help me find the guy who murdered my cousin."

"Whoa! That's a tall order."

"Long can afford it. Put it down as a consulting fee."

Rose was silent for a while. Then he said, "You got to find some fact that'll help me believe before I get involved."

"Like what?"

"Somebody believable who has reason to think that Renny Chevalley had no intention of landing dope in that field."

"He was just a businessman, not a drug runner."

"Prove it."

"That's what I'm asking you to do."

I WAS sitting at the kitchen table when the phone rang.

"It's Rita Long" came her soft, low voice. "I have to talk to you."

"You're home?"

"Bail. Can you come over?"

"I'll be there as soon as I can." I asked if I could bring anything.

"Milk," she said. "I just got home. There's nothing here."

"Have you eaten?"

"They let me out before dinner."

I hung up the phone, wondering where the hell her husband was.

I drove to the Grand Union, shopped, and arrived at the Castle with two bags of groceries and a bottle of wine. I saw her sitting on the front steps as I drove up. The steps were oversized, and she looked like Lily Tomlin's little girl on a giant set. She had her hair pulled back in a sleek ponytail and was wearing jeans and a thick Irish sweater. Her hand was freezing.

"Getting cold?" I said.

"You know what it's like to be outdoors after being locked up?"

"I remember," I said. "I brought some basic eats. There's wine. Like a sip?"

She hesitated. The daylight would linger another hour. I said, "Stay here. I'll make some tea and bring it out."

"Thank you. You have wine, if you like."

I made two teas, and while the water boiled, I unpacked chicken breasts, chopped veal, greens and carrots, a loaf of bread, and a quart of milk. I found her where I had left her—on the front steps, drinking in the sunlight on the lawn, which was striped in long shadows. She wrapped her hands around the mug.

"Heaven," she said after a moment. "Thank you."

"You're welcome."

"Alex Rose, my husband's detective, said I should call you. He said you could help me."

"Did he say how?"

"He said you'd explain a few things. What's going on?"

I stood up and walked down the steps and kicked the gravel in the motor court.

Rita said, "I don't understand your connection. It was just coincidence you were here when we . . . found Ron."

"It was," I agreed. "Sheer coincidence." In actual fact I had to admit I had been wondering how much coincidence it was. She had invited me to drink champagne in the turret. She had spotted Ron. She had moved him. She could have established me as a sort of witness to the discovery. But she had invited me *before* Ron was shot. Had she set the whole thing up? Cold-bloodedly decided to kill him and cold-bloodedly planned our discovery? No way, I thought.

"He said you'd explain." She was insistent. "Well?"

I kicked some more gravel. "You're not going to like this."

"I haven't liked anything since last Saturday." She had a bleak look in her eyes and now a hard edge in her voice.

"Your husband already knew about you and Ron."

She blinked, stood up, and stammered, "What do you mean?"

"Hasn't Jack told you?"

Rita sank to the steps again and put her head in her hands. "We left it unspoken that Ron was here for the obvious reason. Jack was very forgiving, very supportive. He said it was his fault for being too busy. He *knew?*"

"A lot's been going down," I said. "Where is he now?"

"New York. He said he needed time to think. He'll be back for the next meeting with the lawyers, whenever that is. I'm not allowed to leave Plainfield County. What's your connection?"

"Alex Rose is the connection. Your husband ordered him to collect evidence of your affair with Ron Pearlman. He followed you around New York."

"That slimy fat skeeze. So where do you fit in?"

"I was the raccoon."

"You lost me." But not for long. She jumped to her feet, dropping her tea mug, which cracked. "You were spying on me?"

"Yes. Rose hired me to shoot a video of you and Ron for the divorce lawyers."

"You're kidding. Jack was going to *divorce* me?"

"Rose thought so."

"I was going to divorce him."

"Were you?"

"I don't know. I didn't want to hurt him." Standing a couple of steps up, Rita Long looked down at me as if I were a snake that had just slithered off the lawn. "You had a camera? You took our picture. A video. You disgusting—"

"I erased it."

"You saw me and Ron? Where?"

"In your studio."

Her eyes cast back to that night. "Oh, no."

"You were fully clothed."

She cast back again. "No. I took off my blouse."

"I saw only your face. I stopped the camera and threw away the tape. It fell on the lawn, and you heard it. I ran out to get it, and when I got home, I erased the tape and hid it. All I gave Rose was his camera and blank cassettes."

"Get off my property."

"It wasn't like that. *I'm* not like that. It was a stupid thing to take Rose's job, but I didn't know you."

"And now you *know* me," she echoed scornfully.

"I knew you that night. That's why I stopped filming."

"What did you know?"

"I knew you were happy."

Rita Long stared, her mouth hard, until her eyes filled with tears.

I said, "I was happy for you both. And I was head over heels in love with you."

"Through a window?"

"I never felt so close to anybody in my life."

She gave a baffled groan. "What kind of game is Rose playing?"

"I don't think he's playing a game. He thinks that if there's a trial, it will help your defense if I testify you and Ron appeared to be a gentle, loving couple. That's what he wants you to talk to me about."

"They want to indict me. It's unbelievable. Would you go now?"

"Would you answer a question first? Where's the picture of Ron you drew that night?"

"It's in my studio."
"Rose says it's not there and that the cops didn't take it. Would you check?"
"All right." She ran up the steps and banged the door behind her. I heard her pound up the central staircase to the second floor. She came back, looking wary. "It's not there."
"Was it there when I came to appraise the house?"
"I don't know."
"But you ran ahead into the studio to cover it."
"No. I always cover my work. I just went to make sure I hadn't left my panties lying around."
"So the easel was covered when you ran ahead?"
"Yes."
"Somebody took your picture of Ron. Who could get into the house?"
"Just Ron, when he came back."
"What about your husband?"
"He was in Washington."
"Rita? Can I ask why you drew the skull?"
"What do you mean?"
"I mean, that picture could give jurors in a trial an impression of . . . strangeness."
"For heaven's sake. It's a foundation technique. You start with the bones and add muscle and flesh and skin. Any art teacher could explain it," she said impatiently, as if the skull was the least of her problems. Perhaps it was, but I couldn't help feeling that jurors might wonder, like I did, what else was in her head the night before her boyfriend was murdered.
"When I came over to appraise the house, where did you think Ron was?"
"He said he was going to drive to New York and come back late. But when I got home from the mall, the Jag was in the garage. I couldn't find him in the house. I supposed he had gone running. Would you please go away now?"
"I'm sorry for what I did."
"You've got to live with it," she said. "I'm going in." She turned and headed up the steps.
I ran up behind her. "Could your husband have killed Ron?"
"Jack was in Washington."

"I know. But if he weren't, could he?"

I thought she was going to tell me to hit the road again. Instead, she answered reflectively, "I asked myself that a thousand times, sitting in that cell. Could he pull the trigger? I don't know."

"Or have hired a killer to shoot Ron?"

"I don't even know the answer to that. I wonder how well you know somebody if you can't answer such a question."

"How long were you married?"

"Nine years. I always had a funny feeling that Jack . . ." Rita looked at me and said, "Why am I telling you this? Good-bye. Oh, and you can take your testimony and shove it."

She plunged inside, slamming the door.

I walked down to my car and called her on the phone. On the fourth ring, the machine picked up. I said, "It's Ben Abbott—"

She broke in. "What?"

"What were you saying? A funny feeling that Jack . . ."

"I was just thinking about how Ron and I met."

"How'd you meet?"

I figured she'd hang up on me. Instead, she groaned aloud, then sighed. "Do you want some more tea?"

"Thanks." I walked back to the house.

"This has got to be the weirdest relationship," she said. "Voyeur and object."

"I am not a voyeur. You are not an object. And this is not a relationship."

I followed her into her beautiful kitchen. She looked around like a stranger. "Are you hungry, by any chance?" I asked.

"Suddenly. Maybe there's some cheese."

I opened the refrigerator. She gaped at the interior, bright with greens and meat packages. "What's this?"

"Groceries. The receipt is on the counter."

She picked it up and read the printout. "What about the wine?"

"On me. How about a veal burger?"

There was a splendid spice rack beside the refrigerator. I worked tarragon, anise, caraway, parsley, and salt and pepper into the ground veal, and formed patties. I sliced the French bread, washed the arugula, and threw some garlic into a lean oil-and-vinegar mix.

I heated the smallest pan I could find—just big enough for the two thick patties—salted the bottom, and tossed them in.

"Don't you want oil?" she asked.

"The salt keeps them from sticking."

I seared both sides, turned the heat down, and let them cook a moment longer. I opened the wine, and we sat on stools at the kitchen worktable and ate. "That's good," she said. "You just buy veal and do that?"

"Your spice rack gets the credit."

"Thanks."

"You can do something similar with the chicken breast I left you. Just lightly coat the pan with butter or oil first."

"Yeah, right."

"You never cook?"

"We have a cook in New York. I just haven't decided if I want one up here."

She finished her salad. I passed her the bread and refilled her wineglass. "How old are you?"

"Twenty-nine."

I was surprised. It wasn't that she looked older. It was the way she handled herself. "You were twenty when you got married?"

"Yes. And I don't want to talk about it."

"Sorry. You were going to tell me how you met Ron."

"Yes, I was, wasn't I? Right after Jack made the deal to buy Ron's factory, I gave a celebration dinner—just us and the lawyers and a few accountants. Anyway, that afternoon, before the dinner, Jack called from New York. He said Ron had just flown in from Hong Kong and was wiped, so he was sending him on ahead. Could I set up a guest room? A few minutes later the limo arrived. Ron had fallen asleep in the car, and he got out all woozy, looking about fourteen. I thought, Oh, wow. Gorgeous. You gotta know, Ben, I did not play around. Ever. Anyway, I sent him upstairs with the housekeeper. An hour before the dinner, Ron came down and we sat and talked. By the time Jack got home, Ron and I were friends." She fell silent.

"Then what happened?"

"Jack went to Washington. When he left, he invited Ron to stay at the house."

"When was this?"

"Just last year. We were still finishing this place. Jack and I stayed in the Greenwich house until this was done."

I nodded.

"So Ron stayed in Greenwich," Rita continued. "All on the up and up. I took him to dinner and sailing with friends. Jack flew out to Hong Kong. And one morning Ron and I ended up in bed."

I emptied the wine bottle into our glasses. She sipped hers and said, "The thing is, looking back, it was almost like Jack wanted us to have an affair. He made it very easy."

"Were you and Jack getting along?"

"Oh, sure. We always got along. I mean, we didn't fight. We didn't love much either, but we didn't fight."

"Maybe he's having an affair?"

"I don't think so. When I got out today, he said he wants to work things out."

"What do you want?"

"I want Ron back alive." She started crying.

"I'm sorry."

"Thanks for cooking dinner. I'm tired. I want to go to bed."

I said, "I will testify for you if it will help."

"I don't want to think about it now."

I got up and headed for the door. "I'll find my way."

"I'm sorry about telling you to shove your testimony."

"I'm sorry I did what I did." I wished her good luck.

6

EARLY next morning, Wednesday, I took the remote phone out to my cutting garden and moseyed barefoot on the cedar mulch. The garden was still producing mums, roses, snaps, and some weary cosmos. Aunt Connie telephoned at seven to remind me of our lunch date with my mother.

"Shall I drive?" asked Connie.

"Oh, I'll drive."

"Would you like to drive my car?"

I told her that I'd be delighted, cautioning, "If you warm it first, Connie, please remember to open the stable doors."

"I'll remember. You told me that Sunday. I'm not an idiot. I'm just old. What are you bringing your mother?"

"White roses." They were her favorite—hybrid teas. "What are you bringing?" I asked Connie.

"There's a pie in the oven. My russets are almost ripe."

I suppressed a groan. Her Roxbury Russet apple trees were enormous, and the thought of her on a ladder . . . "I'll pick you up at eleven thirty."

"Now listen to me," she said. "I'm told your mother is very upset about Renny. This latest event will only make things worse."

"What event?"

"It's all over town. You've been calling on the Long woman."

The Fish Line was bottom trolling. I said, " 'Calling on' implies a connection that isn't there, Aunt Connie. People should mind their own business."

"People should also obey the Ten Commandments, but they don't, so we accommodate reality. The point I am making, Ben, is that you ought to try and put your mother's mind at ease."

I went back to my flowers.

CONNIE had started the Lincoln, backed it out of her stable, and closed the doors herself. She was sitting in the passenger seat wearing a cardigan over a summery dress, and a Lilly Daché hat. Her pie sat on the back floor, swathed in tinfoil. I laid my roses on the back seat and climbed behind the wheel.

"Drive," she said.

I drove.

Just as Connie had always regarded my father as the son she never had, my mother was in some similar way the daughter. But my mother was a Frenchtown girl. As much as she loved Connie, she could never feel comfortable in her presence. Typically, when we arrived, Mom was fluttering up the dining-room walls, convinced that something was wrong with the table setting. She was seventy-five herself, but today she was the eighteen-year-old that Bertram Abbott had brought home to a stunned Main Street.

Connie, who had her blind sides, said, "Oh, let's eat in the kitchen. Dining rooms are so gloomy in the daylight."

I saw my mother start to die, and intervened.

"Let's eat here. The table's set." My mother had probably set it the night before and reset it again in the morning.

"Mom, can I help carry?" I asked as she headed for the kitchen.

"No. You talk to your aunt Connie. I'll be all right."

"He already bored me in the car," said Connie. "Come sit with me, Margot. Let Ben serve."

It worked. My mother gambled that I was able to shift her chicken potpie and salad to the dining room without dropping them.

After lunch Connie sat with her in the kitchen while she washed up, and I went out and wheelbarrowed some firewood from the shed to the kitchen porch. There was a nip in the air. Sometimes I wondered why my mother had come back out here. But on a fall afternoon, there is no place like it. One woman's dank swamp is another person's teeming marsh. The water draws the migrating birds. The sumac and red maple that thrive on moisture turn red early. The air is thick, damp, and full of life.

My mother came out carrying two mugs of coffee. She's a tiny little thing, blessed with those dark Chevalley eyes. "Connie's napping," she said. "Are you warm enough?"

"I'm fine."

I sat on a stump, she in her favorite Adirondack chair, which I carried down from the patio.

"I missed you by five minutes at Renny's," I said after a silence.

"I was too upset to stay. I kept thinking, It could have been you."

"How so?" I asked carefully.

"He was your age. You used to be like two peas in a pod. His poor mother." Sisters-in-law separated in age by more than twenty years, my mother and Renny's had nevertheless become like sisters.

I said, "Don't believe the stories. He didn't do anything wrong."

"I'm sure he didn't. If it were Pink or one of the others, I'd say I wasn't surprised. But not Renny."

"I feel the same way."

"I'm sure there's an explanation for everything, even the money."

"What money?"

My mother looked distressed. "Frances called this morning. The police searched the garage. They found forty thousand dollars."

"What?"

"In cash. In a shopping bag in back of a closet."

I was stunned. Where the hell would Renny get forty thousand in cash? And why would he hide it in a closet? I glanced at my mother. She was hanging in there for her family, but the look on her face forced me to admit that she, too, had lost faith.

She looked at me, blinking rapidly. She dabbed her eyes with a Kleenex. "Were you involved?" she asked coldly.

"With Renny? No."

"What about this woman who shot her boyfriend?"
"I was only there doing an appraisal."
"I couldn't bear for you to get in trouble again."
"I won't."
"Promise me."
"I promise."
"It killed your father, and this time it will kill me."

I took a deep breath, stood up, and walked rapidly down to the swamp, which started at the edge of the lawn. It spread for acres, spiked with the bleached gray trunks of dead trees. The water table had risen, and the swamp was much closer to the house. I did not kill my father. But she thought I did, which was almost as bad.

I felt her eyes on me. I took another deep breath and walked back, a light comment on my lips. "I swear, if the swamp gets any higher, you'll have to swim back to Newbury."

"*Never,*" she cried, startling me with her vehemence. "I will never go back to Main Street. I don't ever want to see that house again." Her jaw was working, and she was twisting her fingers like a nest of worms. I was terrified she would cry next.

"But you lived most of your life there."

"And I was very happy. It's a lovely house."

"It's your house."

"Not anymore." She gazed past me at the ugly little farmhouse she had grown up in. "Down here, people don't turn up their noses. Everyone's got someone in their family who's been to prison."

Stung, I fired back, "That's because they're easier to catch."

"It's not funny. All my so-called friends on Main Street—I knew what they were thinking. Ben's Chevalley blood came out. My blood. Your father never would have had such a son if it weren't for Margot Chevalley."

"Oh, Mom—"

"You erased fifty years of slowly getting accepted."

"I didn't mean to."

"I don't mind," she said, fingers flying. "I never fit in. They knew it. I knew it."

I stood there shaking my head, helpless to unravel the strands of hurt. There was a core of truth in my mother's thinking. The women she had called her friends—the wives of my father's school chums and neighbors—were, by and large, prisoners of their neat, orderly lives, and hostages to their belief that good stock was all. Good seed will out. Bad blood will out. I was the tainted product. Proof that Margot Chevalley couldn't escape her fate.

No wonder she had suspected me of flying coke with Renny. The poor thing thought it was her fault.

"I'm sorry," I apologized. I had survived the public censure of the court, survived the fines that took every penny, survived prison. It had not occurred to me, back when I was standing up for my own principles, that I wouldn't be the only one to pay.

AFTER I drove Connie home, I stopped by the drugstore and ran into Al Bell, who had found Renny on his airstrip. The old pilot was inquiring loudly if his hearing-aid batteries had come in. They had, and I helped him load them into his hearing aids. Al screwed the amplifiers into his ears, fiddled with the knobs, and shouted, "Say something."

I said something, and his face lit up. "Now you're talking. Been deaf for a week."

Walking out to the cars, I asked him, "How'd you happen to hear Renny's plane land?"

"Didn't. Car went by the house like a bat out of hell. Later I got to thinking maybe some kids were messing around. I drove up to check my plane."

"You saw a car? What kind of car?"

"Like I told the cops, all I saw was his dust through the privet hedge. Sorry about Renny. Tough way to go—getting shot."

"Must have been a shock finding him."

"I didn't realize he was shot. I thought he'd cracked his head on the windshield. Took his pulse. Dead as a rock. Poor kid." He climbed into his Jeep and roared off.

I went home and telephoned Trooper Boyce. She was out, and returned my call around five. "What's up, Ben?"

"What's the story on the cash you found in Renny's garage?"

Marian was silent for a while. Then she surprised me. "Take me to dinner. Maybe I'll fill you in."

"It's lobster night at the Yankee Drover."

"You're on. I can make it by six thirty or so."

I got there early and ordered a glass of white wine. I was halfway through it when she arrived in blue jeans and a sweatshirt. I looked her over, wondering where she'd stashed her gun. Her bag was too small and her clothes intriguingly snug. "Ankle holster," she said with a friendly smile.

Wine in the cellar bar. Lobster upstairs at the Wednesday night all-you-can-eat $21.99 special. Not a bad life. Particularly in the company of an attractive, sure-of-herself brunette.

So it wasn't until after dinner that I said, "You were going to tell me about the forty thousand dollars cash they found in Renny's garage."

"Officially?"

"I'd like the official take and then your take."

"Okay." She pushed back her plate and said yes to coffee. "Officially, you can see how it looks to our investigation. We got a garage mechanic murdered in a plane full of coke. We find major cash hidden on his premises. We conclude that he did not earn this money replacing ball joints."

"Do you read it that way?"

Marian hesitated. "You understand, I can't discuss cases with civilians."

"Not to mention felons."

She smiled. "Now don't quote me, but it's too pat." I waited. She took her time. "I'll buy your cousin running coke. Why? Means: the plane. Need: heavy debt. Connections: felonious relatives. And I don't mean your kind of felonious—I mean heavy hitters."

I said, "Chevalleys aren't that heavy."

Marian gave me her thinnest smile. "Ben, you know I'm not talking about Chevalleys."

I knew she meant Jervises. "Sorry. I know the relatives you mean. So you think Renny had the means, the motive, and the connections to run coke. Where's the *but*?"

"But I walked through his garage. He could serve his own lobster night on the floor, the place is so clean. I go into his machine shop. It looks like diamond cutters work there. This isn't a man who stashes forty thousand dollars in a shopping bag in the back of a closet."

Before I could respond, little Alison Mealy came running into the restaurant, spotted me, and pounded between the tables as only an eleven-year-old can pound in sneakers. "Ben!"

"Hello, Alison. What's up?"

"Ben, there's a man sneaking around inside your house."

"What?" I jumped up. "Marian, do you still do simple burglaries?"

"Sit down, Ben. If someone's in your house, call the police."

"You're the police."

"I've had three glasses of wine. I can't even drive home, much less walk into your house with a badge in my hand."

"Well, excuse me. I'm going over to see who the hell is in my house. Alison, you stay here with Trooper Boyce."

Marian said again, "Sit down, Ben."

I headed out the door and ran down the sidewalk. I stopped at the foot of my driveway, and I heard Marian running up behind me. A shadow moved across one of the lighted windows in my office.

I charged up the drive and threw open the office door. There were two men. One was deep inside the closet. The other, who was rifling my father's desk, reached inside his Windbreaker.

I slammed the closet door and dove for the guy at the desk. He was short, broad, and very fast. He chopped at my jaw, but I kneed him, and he doubled over. I tore his hand out of the Windbreaker. He held a badge. "State police," he gasped.

"What?"

Sergeant Bender pushed out of the closet, waving a search warrant.

"What's going on?" I was utterly baffled.

Marian Boyce crashed through the door. "What took you so long?" she said to Bender.

"Jailbirds know how to hide stuff."

I looked at Marian. To her credit, she couldn't meet my eye. "What stuff?"

Bender handed me the warrant. I skimmed a blur of print.

"What are you looking for?"

"Cash," said Bender. "In a shopping bag."

Alison hovered at the door, bewildered. "Are you okay, Ben?"

"I'm okay. Go home, hon. Go on. Everything's fine."

"Frisk him," Bender ordered.

I backed up a step. "Let the child go first. Go on home, hon. It's okay."

Alison ran like the wind.

"Spread 'em," said Bender.

Boy, did a pat-down bring back a lot of memories. The pat-down is a humiliating example of the guard's power and the prisoner's lack of it. Bender knew full well I hadn't gone armed to dinner.

"What did you do, Arnie?" Marian said. "Stop for supper?"

"We found guns upstairs. He's got an arsenal."

"All permitted," I said. "They were my father's."

"Gun permits for a convicted felon? Let's see 'em."

I had applied to renew my father's gun permits under my own name. His old desk was my physical connection with him, more than the guns; but in the first months outside of prison, the right to keep them had seemed very important.

Holding the permits to the light as if suspecting a forgery, Bender growled, "Look, the jailbird is licensed to carry."

"Marian," I asked, "why the charade? Why not just knock on the door with your warrant? I'd have let you in."

"You called *me*," she said. "Remember? The warrant came through, and I took the opportunity to conduct a clandestine search. Sometimes it works better that way."

She was explaining, but not apologizing. I said, "I presume you know by now you struck out."

"We're not done," growled Bender.

"If you want to stay up all night to make a stupid point, I can't stop you. I'll be in the library." I went in and closed the door. I couldn't bear to see them pawing through the rooms. An hour later Marian stuck her head in. "We're done."

"Close the door on your way out."

"I had a nice time at dinner," she said, and smiled. I didn't. She said, "Good night." I didn't.

THE next day, I sat in the sun at the table in front of the general store, drank some coffee, and brooded. One misery led to another: poor Renny, the cops invading my house, my sinking business and nonexistent earnings. Scooter MacKay, the local *Clarion*'s publisher, lumbered by with a bundle of newspapers on his shoulder. Scooter maintains an old tradition of the publisher personally carrying the new issue to the general store.

He tossed a copy on the table. "Hot off the press."

There was a photograph on the front page of Jack Long with the President. The headline on the accompanying article read

LOCAL RESIDENT JOINS OTHER PROMINENT BUSINESS LEADERS FOR D.C. LUNCH WITH PRESIDENT.

Scooter himself had the byline.

> Morris Mountain weekender and land-trust advocate Jack Long flew to Washington, D.C., Saturday for a lunch with the President at which meaningful views on the economy were exchanged in an atmosphere marked by informal cordiality.

Scooter came out with a cup of coffee, sat beside me, and said, "You look like hell, Ben."

"It's been a rotten week."

"It can only get better, right?"

I started to say wrong when a silver Jaguar pulled up, and Rita Long called, "Hello there."

Black hair swept back into a ponytail, black sunglasses, onyx earrings—she looked as mysterious as the night and very beautiful. I introduced Scooter. Rita took off her sunglasses and complimented the *Clarion*'s photography. Scooter preened. As he left, he muttered to me, "Told you it would get better."

I told him quietly to go to hell.

"Terrific-looking car," I said to Rita.

"Come for a ride."

I got in. Sank into delicious leather. It was the V-12 model—a deluxe rocket ship. At the controls, a superdeluxe pilot.

She looked rested and artfully made up—still in jeans but topped with a black cashmere sweater.

She tooled out of town along Route 7. Fall was coming in with a bang, and the colors were exquisite, with red maples, birches, and ash leading the parade. We enjoyed it silently for a few miles. When we got to Academy Lane, I said, "Turn right." Then it was right again at Richardson Street and down the sugar maple tunnel.

"Where are you taking me?" asked Rita.

"My favorite house."

She glanced over at me. "Is it for sale?"

"Perpetually."

"What's wrong with it?"

"I don't know. Ellie Richardson died four years ago. It's been on the market ever since. Wait till you see it."

"Business is still that bad?"

"Mine is. The driveway's right up ahead. Watch the potholes."

The Jaguar bucked and bounced, and then we were within the yard.

"Oh, it's lovely," said Rita. But to my disappointment, she gave the neglected grounds a cursory glance.

I was feasting on the steep gables that spiked the sky. "Adlai Stevenson visited his mistress near here."

Rita looked puzzled.

"Ran for President," I explained. "Back in the '50s. Around the other side are beautiful walks and rose gardens. Clay tennis court."

She smiled. "And you're hoping for a buyer who'll restore it."

"Somebody's going to fall in love with this place." I laughed, a little nervously. "Your friend Alex Rose pretended to be house hunting, so I drove him out here. He didn't get it."

"He's not my friend."

"Well, he's on your side."

"How long can you wait to start selling houses again?"

"Financially? Who knows?"

"Do you have big expenses? A mortgage?"

"My house really belongs to my mother. I pay the taxes and whatever upkeep I can afford. If I can't afford it, I try to fix it myself. Why are you asking me this?"

"I'd like to offer you a job."

I laughed again. "What is it about this place? Last time I was here, Rose offered me a job. Now you're offering me a job."

"Rose works for my husband. I'm second on his list. I'm afraid the state's attorney will indict me. I would feel better if I had someone on whose list I was first."

"Well, I hear you've hired Ira Roth for your defense. You'll be number one on his list."

"My husband hired Ira Roth. I want you to help me."

"I'm not a lawyer."

"You were an investigator with naval intelligence."

"Rose tell you that?"

"He told Jack. I checked you out. I know it's true. I want you to be my Alex Rose. Find out who killed Ron."

"Rita, I did one murder investigation in the navy. It wasn't in the real world; it was the rarefied world of the service."

"Newbury isn't exactly the real world either," she argued.

She had me there, but I said, "It is to me."

"Perfect. I need a friend who's 'real' here. Somebody murdered Ron. Please help me find him."

I shook my head. "I'm sorry, Rita. If I'm going to play detective in my hometown, it'll be to find out who killed my cousin Renny."

"Ben, you'll need expenses to chase Renny's killer, right?

"We've already established I could use the money."

"I understand private detectives up here ask twenty-five dollars an hour. I'll triple it, plus all expenses. Ben, will you help me?"

I didn't say I would, though her money would make it easier to chase Renny's killer. All I said was, "Two questions."

"Go."

"Did you shoot Ron?"

"No." What was she going to say? Yes? Still, I believed her. Not only because of what I had seen of her and Ron, not only because she could charm my socks off, but because I didn't see the violence in her. Rita was not a killer. I'd stake my life on it.

"What's your second question?"

"Do you have a suspect?"

"Yes."

"Going to tell me?"

"Going to take the job?"

I thought of three reasons to take the job: the money to pursue Renny's killer, the opportunity to spend some time with Rita, and that sensation that killed the cat. I said, "Yes, with one condition."

"Which is?"

"I want Renny's name cleared. I want his killer. I won't charge you for that time, but Renny comes first."

"Deal."

We shook hands.

"Who's your suspect?"

"I don't know how he did it, but I think it's Jack," she said.

"I just saw Jack's picture in the paper, shaking hands with the President. It said he went for a luncheon. And stayed for dinner."

"I still think it's Jack."

"You mean he hired a killer?"

"However."

"Why? Jealousy?"

"Why not? Check him out tomorrow night. Jack's coming up. I'll have a supper party—you, me, and Jack."

7

JACK Long met me at the door in a flannel shirt and jeans. He invited me into his rosewood-paneled, skylit foyer, looked me in the eye, shook hands, and recalled the land-trust meeting.

Alex Rose had tagged him a little overweight; actually, I thought, Long was built more along burly lines. His jeans were stiff, and his shirt a muted red check—your basic country-life-catalogue ensemble mail-ordered by the wife of a guy too busy to shop. He wore a bushy black mustache and funny running shoes.

"Oh, take off your tie," Rita said as she breezed in from the kitchen. She looked lovely, with her hair swept back in a French roll.

I unknotted my tie, and we rolled merrily toward the living room. Jack asked what I would like to drink. I looked to see what Rita was drinking. White wine in a near empty glass. Jack had set a red wine, similarly drained, on the coffee table. I wanted a few moments alone with Rita, so I asked for a bourbon old-fashioned.

Long covered his dismay and hurried off to the kitchen.

I said to my hostess, "This is bizarre."

"Go with it." The living-room couch where we had laid Ron's body was replaced by a new eight-thousand-dollar Henredon.

"What does Jack think you're thinking?"

"It's never concerned him before."

"But this is—"

"Jack! Do you need help?" she called.

From the kitchen came an insincere "I'm all right, darling."

"Excuse me, Ben. He doesn't know where anything is." She took both wineglasses with her.

Jack eventually returned from the kitchen, bearing my old-fashioned. Rita fluttered behind him, carrying their wineglasses filled to the brim. I said, "Cheers."

"How's the drink?" Jack asked.

"Remarkable." It tasted a little of barbecue.

"So how's the real estate business?"

Oh, it was going to be a wonderful night. I explained to this titan of technology that things were a little slow in the real estate business. Surprise, surprise. I answered a half-dozen questions. And how, I wondered, were things in the electronics business?

"Gangbusters!" said Jack.

"When's it going to filter down to the rest of us?"

"Don't hold your breath."

"Oh, Jack. Don't be such a pessimist," said Rita.

"I'm not a pessimist," he replied. "Ben's no fool, and with his background he knows what I mean. I'm talking about efficiency. And I know you know the price of efficiency."

I took a second hideous swallow, wondering how he had screwed up a simple cocktail. I had the weirdest feeling that they had both forgotten Ron. But I soon discovered that I was wrong.

Long said, "My poor partner—former partner, the guy you found—had a big problem understanding that. His father had made his bucks in the fur trade and had long ago ditched his American factories. Ron just couldn't get that the employee you pay in Hong Kong is going to spend his paycheck in Hong Kong."

I had yet to meet a successful entrepreneur who didn't sooner or later develop a deep philosophical explanation for what was wrong with the world. I couldn't resist asking, "Are you moving your operations back to the States?"

"Damned right."

"Jack's very patriotic," said Rita.

"Patriotism has nothing to do with it," her husband fired back. "A homegrown workforce spends its salary at home. But the bind is that to compete with overseas labor, you have to increase productivity, which *eliminates* jobs."

Rita yawned. Jack didn't notice. "Could I have a refill?" she asked.

Long's gaze locked on my glass, still three-quarters full.

"Good heavens!" He leaped to his feet. "Worcestershire sauce! I put Worcestershire sauce in your drink. It's supposed to be bitters, isn't it?"

"Traditionally," I admitted.

"I'm sorry. Let me fix you a new one." He snatched my glass and went off, trailed by Rita's enigmatic gaze, which swung toward me when he disappeared through the door.

"Well, what do you think?" she said.

"I think you're both pretending nothing happened."

"It's how we live. We hardly ever see each other, and when we do, the personal stuff gets pushed in the corner."

I got up and looked out the window. There was a thick autumn haze in the fading light.

Jack brought my drink in, and it was excellent. He watched intently as I tasted it. "How is it?"

"Excellent."

"Good. Sorry about that. I feel like an idiot. Rita, we gonna eat?"

"Soon. Excuse me, Ben. I've got something on the stove."

"Brace yourself," Jack warned me, loud enough for her to hear. "Rita's taken up cooking."

"She told me you designed this house."

"Rita did. From a picture in a children's book. I ran it through some architecture software and voilà!"

"Did you train as an engineer?"

Long smiled into a practiced routine. "I'm an electrical engineer from M.I.T. But now that software's the hot thing, I'm a windjammer captain of a steamship—if you know what I mean."

"Like a bowman with a shotgun."

Long flashed me a fast, hard, you're-messing-with-the-wrong-guy look. "Speaking of shotguns," he said bluntly, "what's your take on this mess?"

"I think from your wife's point of view it's damned serious. I wouldn't want to go to trial in her position. You're outsiders. You're wealthier than any jurors they'll empanel. And you represent a world many local people find distasteful."

"Maybe we should go for a change of venue."

"Not a bad idea. But hey, with any luck there'll be no trial. Everybody agrees they've got a thin case."

Long rubbed his face. "I hope you're right. I've got my absolute top people on it, but I'm scared."

"I hear you hired Ira Roth. Good move. He's never lost a case."

"So he told me," Long replied dryly.

"What does he think about the ballistics conclusions?"

"He's hired an expert who swears the shot came from the woods."

"What do *you* think about the ballistics? I gather you're a shooter. Could the shot have come from your tower?"

"*I* certainly couldn't have scored a bull's-eye at eighty yards from the tower," Long said.

"What about Rita?"

"She's a fair shot. But the state's attorney is talking about some pretty fine gun work."

"Who do you think shot Ron?"

"A deer poacher is my guess. Shot at movement or sound, realized what he did, and faded into the woods."

"That's how I read it," I agreed.

"I'm glad to hear that." Long rubbed his face again. "If Ron had been just an ordinary houseguest, that's how the state police would have seen it, too. But, dammit, Rita spilled her guts to that woman state trooper. Thanks to her big mouth, Ron jumped from houseguest to millionaire's wife's boyfriend."

"And a millionaire in his own right."

"Yeah, right," Jack conceded bitterly. "Born with a silver spoon in his mouth. His old man gave him the money and told him what to do with it. He was the quintessential preppy airhead. Too dumb to be a doctor, so Daddy bought him an electronics factory. Ron was always a momma's boy."

"I'm getting the impression you didn't get along."

Rita hurried in with high color in her cheeks. I couldn't tell whether she was flushed from cooking or had overheard Jack's low opinion of Ron. "Dinner," she said. "In the dining room."

"I'm hungry," said Jack. "I'll open some more wine. You want another of those, Ben?"

I told him wine would be fine, and followed Rita into the cavernous dining room, where stood a card table set for three with a linen cloth draped halfway down its spindly legs.

"Light the candles, Jack," said Rita, racing out to the kitchen.

"You got a match?" Jack asked me.

"No."

As he went in search of matches, Rita pushed through the swinging door, carrying a platter. She put it down, stood back tentatively, and wiped her brow. "What do you think?"

"Beautiful." Whether she could cook was still an open question, but she was an artist and had arranged the chicken breasts, baked potatoes, and string beans in a parkland of parsley.

Jack came back with the matches, complaining, "I can't find a damn thing in this house."

Rita and I took our places, and Jack lit the candles and poured the wine. Then we fell on the chicken, which was cooked rare.

I said, "I think I'm familiar with this recipe. You've got a nice touch with herbs."

"The builder gave us a spice rack," Jack explained, then, a bite later, "This is really good, hon."

"Thanks, hon. Ben, did you say you cook?"

"Yes."

"Do you think these same spices would work with veal?"

"Ground veal," I replied, and got a secret smile.

"I'm told you used to be a genius at structuring debt. Did you ever think of getting a job?" Jack asked. His superior tone did not inspire me to admit that occasionally I did long to get back in the action.

"No," I answered. "My business keeps me busy."

His gaze alighted inquiringly on me. He was wary—maybe even rethinking what I was doing in his home. "I'm always looking at new acquisitions. I could use a man with that talent."

I replied, "Keep in mind, Jack, when I worked on Wall Street, debt was the *goal.* I doubt that's your position now."

"You telling me you're too old to adapt?"

"I have adapted."

"What are you, thirty?" Jack scoffed.

"Thirty-five."

"That's not too old to change—"

"Ben is saying he's already changed," Rita interrupted. "He's gone from Wall Street to . . . Main Street. Haven't you, Ben?"

"Right. If you're offering me a job, Jack, I'm flattered. But I'm not interested in that sort of work anymore. Wheeling numbers is for the young and dumb. Pass the time, make a ton of money."

"You've got plenty of time on your hands not selling houses, and damned little money, from what I can see."

"Jack," said Rita, "that's no way to talk to a guest."

"Relax, hon. Ben and I understand each other. Don't we, Ben?" Fully on the attack now, he hunched over the table, probing for any ambivalence he could turn against me.

"You probably understand me better than I understand you," I answered. "What do *you* want to be, Jack?"

"Nothing I'd waste time thinking about. I just do it."

"Why bother? Aren't you rich enough already? Why not bank it, move full time to Newbury, and grow flowers Rita could paint? What are you trying to prove?" No way to talk to a host I barely knew, but he'd set the tone. Nor did he seem to mind.

"The fight's not over, man. That's all I'll say. Look, Ben, I'm offering to put you back in the game. Think about it."

I wondered whether he had guessed I was working for Rita and was trying to buy me off. Rita seemed to wonder, too. She looked worried, so I said, "I've thought about it, Jack. I'm a country boy, back home where he belongs."

"Country boy my foot! I know a player when I see one. Guys like you don't sell houses. You sell towns."

"Not anymore. At least when I sell a house, it's the beginning of something. When I ran takeovers, people got fired."

"They should have been. The bloated payrolls were killing us."

"We used to tell ourselves that at the celebration dinner—improving efficiency, raising productivity, streamlining."

"You know what I'm hearing?" asked Jack. "I'm hearing that you lost your money in the crash and got religion."

"No. I got rich in the crash. I'd moved all my ill-gotten assets into bonds."

Jack Long stopped sneering abruptly. "You did?"

"Followed my gut. Made out like a bandit."

Jack looked at his wife. "You see why I want this guy on my side? Don't say no now, Ben. Keep my offer in mind."

After dessert we withdrew to the drawing room.

"I saw your picture in the paper," I said. "What's it like meeting the President, Jack?"

"Less expensive than it used to be under the Republicans. He shakes your hand, speaks your name, gives you a big hug. This guy's smart, and he listens. What worries me is whether he can rise above the people helping him. They're very young. But you should have seen his inner circle that night. One of them did the Larry King show. King massacred the puppy, but they sat there telling him what a great job he'd done. Total fantasy."

"What does it cost to meet the inner circle?"

"A whiff of cordite."

"Jack was a war hero," explained Rita. "That always goes down big with the Beltway crowd. No matter who's in office."

Jack laughed. "I was young and dumb. I joined the marines as a teenager. Went to Nam. Two tours, and I was back by '64."

"He won a Silver Star," Rita said with genuine admiration. "Tell him how, Jack."

"I'd trained as a helicopter mechanic. When we had a chopper down with a blown engine, I jumped in with some parts, installed them, and flew the thing out."

In, I gathered, meant into the Vietcong's jungle. I was impressed and said so.

"You do what you have to do." Jack shrugged. "Brandy?"

"No. I got to drive."

"Oh, don't worry about that," said Rita. "Stay the night."

"Sleep here," Jack echoed. "We got an extra bedroom furnished upstairs. No one's using it now. Right, Rita?"

"Stay. Jack, pour Ben some brandy. I'll have some, too."

"You've twisted my arm."

Jack opened a Chinese lacquered cabinet, came up with three snifters, and cracked a new bottle of sixty-year-old Napoleon.

VERY late that night, tucked into the guest room where Rita had tucked Ron, it occurred to me that I still had no idea whether Jack Long had been jealous enough to kill his wife's lover and then cold enough to let her go to prison for it.

The main subjects on his mind seemed to be money and debt. It probably meant nothing, but if there was one thing we learned from Robert Maxwell and Donald Trump, it was that they were never as rich as their bankers hoped.

I heard a knock at my door. I sat up and called, "Come in."

Jack walked in with a couple of brandy snifters. "Kick me out if it's too late, but I can't sleep, and I really hope I didn't mouth off at you too hard. I like mixing it up in conversation, and then later Rita tells me I've been acting like a jerk."

This was a different, extremely apologetic Jack, and I hardly knew how to take him. "Relax. I had a great time."

He handed me a glass and sat down in the armchair. He was wearing a silk paisley robe. Where Cary Grant would have knotted his cravat, Jack had bundles of chest hair.

He turned out to be in a confessional mood.

"Ben, let me tell you, this is crazy time. I was up to my eyeballs buying another Singapore operation. Then Rose calls me and tells me there's a dead guy on my property. Then he calls back and says it's Ron. Then it turns out Rita's sleeping with him. This is not my idea of a marriage. But instead of wanting to shoot her, which would seem reasonable, I'm worried sick about her trial. I got Rose lurching around like a loose cannon and a bunch of farmers hoping to crucify my wife. That's why I can't sleep. And if I got out of line at dinner, I apologize. I've been under a lot of pressure."

"Why is Rose a loose cannon?"

Jack scratched his chest. "Al's all right. He's doing a crackerjack job backing up my lawyers. He stays on top. He got to me before the cops."

"I don't follow."

"I pay so that I'm not surprised. When the cops called to tell me there was a dead guy on my land, I was already heading up here."

"Rose told you?"

"Sure. That's what I pay him for."

"How'd he find out?"

Jack peered into his brandy. "One thing I learned: when people bring you information, don't ask. It's like sausage. You don't really want to know how they make it."

He struggled to his feet, gathering his robe. "Hey, you're passing out, Ben. Get some sleep."

"Thanks for the drink."

"Don't mention it. Anything you want in the house is yours. Except my wife." He smiled as he pawed open the door, but if it was a joke, it didn't quite work, and I felt sorry for him.

AT DAWN I heard a car crunching down the drive; I fell asleep and awoke in daylight to the smell of coffee. Rita tapped lightly at the door and entered with a cup and saucer. "Good morning." She looked all fresh-faced, as if she'd been walking.

"Good morning."

"Jack's gone to New York. He had a good time last night. He said to say good-bye."

"I had a good time, too." I sat up in bed and arranged the blankets to make room for the coffee.

She perched on the deep windowsill. "So? What do you think? Am I crazy? Or is he a killer?"

"I don't know."

"What did he say about Ron?"

"He didn't like him much. Called him a momma's boy."

"Momma's boy?" She smiled a secret smile that said she had a different opinion. "Momma's boy is Jack's lowest put-down. He's a little strange about family. What else?"

"He came by with more brandy after we went to bed. Apologized for mouthing off. Said he was under pressure—buying a new Singapore operation. Is Jack in debt?"

"Of course. How could he do business and not be in debt?"

"I mean really in debt."

"I don't think so."

"You'd know his financial situation, wouldn't you?"

Rita looked out the window and considered her answer. "Until a year ago Jack didn't make a move without talking to me."

I doubted that Jack's young wife had played as big a part as she thought. LTS wasn't exactly a family grocery store.

"Do you want breakfast?" she asked.

"You're getting pretty sure of yourself around the kitchen."

"I've been reading up on toast."

She swung her pretty legs off the windowsill and hurried out the door. I called after her, "Hey, how'd you meet Jack?"

"I was a bicycle messenger."

"Beg pardon?"

She came back. "I dropped out of Columbia University to study at the Art Students League. My parents wouldn't pay for it. I was supposed to be a lawyer. My father had a hardware store, and he wanted me to be something special, which to him meant a professional. So I worked as a bicycle messenger."

"Jack's limo ran over your bike?"

"No. I delivered blueprints up to his office one night, late, and he was alone. And we talked. He was fat and funny-looking, but I was so glad to be in the air-conditioning. It was August, and muggy. When I got down to Sixth Avenue, they'd stolen my bike. It had been the worst day, and I was standing there crying when Jack came down with his blueprints. He bought me a new bike, and then he bought me dinner. Three months later we were married."

"How'd you go from bicycle messenger to business adviser?"

"Jack saw I had a head for business. He'd been on his own almost twenty years. He hates partners. But he began to feel he needed a sounding board. He got in the habit of laying out a plan, and I'd play devil's advocate." She turned to go. "We had a lot of fun, Ben. We were very busy. And I was very young. . . . I still am."

I lay in bed awhile thinking about Jack. Fat and funny-looking, Rita had thought at age twenty. Not exactly aphrodisiac.

Smoke drifted up the stairs. I climbed quickly into my pants. "It's okay," I heard Rita call. "It's just the toast." Blue haze hung in the kitchen. She looked flushed. "The second batch is perfect."

"Did you love Jack?"

"He was my best friend until Ron."

"Would you call him passionate? I mean, no offense, but he doesn't seem passionate about you. Not enough to kill for you."

"He'd kill to win. Didn't you see that in him?"

"No. I saw a guy too happy in his work and too smart to risk the second half of his life in jail. I think when he found out about you and Ron, he wrote you off."

"You're wrong. Jack knows I never ran around on him before. He wants me back. And now he's probably got me."

"Sounds like you've made a big decision."

"Not if he killed Ron."

So that was my job. I worked hard at keeping my poker face, but I was shocked and dismayed. Rita wasn't as worried as she should be about her trial. She was looking ahead, past an acquittal, hoping I could confirm that her five-hundred-million-dollar husband and friend would make a proper partner for the rest of her life. Maybe she had left herself an out: If it all hinged on Jack's not murdering Ron, who safer to prove that he didn't than an amateur?

I THOUGHT about it all weekend. I wondered some more about Jack's financial situation. But the weekend was no time to gather business gossip; I'd been out of the loop too long to bother people at home. So I posed a question: If Jack didn't kill Ron, who did?

How about Alex Rose, the man in the middle? Security man. Intelligence gatherer. Was he a rich man's indulgence or a shrewd operator who protected Jack's back? Did he leap when the boss hinted how happy he'd be if Ronald Pearlman disappeared?

By Sunday morning I was all over the map. It was possible, regardless of the lack of evidence, that some damned fool Chevalley had accidentally blasted Ron from the woods. My cousin Pink might have heard by now. But he'd never tell me.

Sautéing a plate of mushroom-stuffed cappelletti Sunday night,

I found myself focusing on Jack again. Maybe it was because money was what I knew best, but I just couldn't ignore the possibility that Jack Long might be in serious debt.

Six o'clock Monday morning I unlimbered my old Rolodex and started working the phones. I got some very wary hellos until I assured my former colleagues I was not looking for a job. That they took the calls at all was less a matter of friendship than fear. It was widely known that I had declined to cooperate with the Securities and Exchange Commission. But people wondered what I knew, and if I had changed my mind about spilling it. So they took my calls and promised to keep their traps shut about my questions. Unfortunately, they didn't have much in the way of answers.

LTS was privately held, so Jack Long was legally permitted to play it very close to the vest: no prospectus, no SEC filings, no analysts' reports. A full morning's work on the phone—sixty calls—got me the names of several institutions that *might* act as Long's bankers. Finally Bob Mayall, a savvy investment banker who was more of a friend than most, asked *me* a question.

"Why don't you call Leslie Harkin?"

"I doubt she'd take my call."

"She owes you at least a call, Ben."

Back when Leslie Harkin, my former love and protégée, had frolicked by my side in the rust belt, there wasn't a machine shop in the state of Michigan she hadn't put into play at least once. To many a trade unionist she was the she-devil incarnate. And since I'd been her boss, they lit bonfires the night I went to prison. I did not want to confront Leslie, and yet she looked like my best source. "Is she vulturing on her own?"

"You never heard of Harkin and Locke?"

Before I could comment on that grim alliance, I heard a scream from the barn.

8

FOUR seconds after ripping a pocket on my kitchen doorknob, I burst into the barn. The Mealys' apartment was up a rickety interior staircase. I took the wooden steps three at a time. Their door was smashed open, sagging on a broken hinge. Through the little living room I could see into the kitchen—Mrs. Mealy crawling across the floor, a large man rearing back to kick her, Alison clinging to his leg, screaming, "Don't, Daddy!"

Tom Mealy had won parole.

He faced me as I came through the door. When he recognized me, he balled his fists. "You're sleepin' with my wife," he slurred.

"No," moaned Mrs. Mealy, dragging herself over the linoleum.

He whirled on her, aiming another kick. He was tall and broad, but he was drunk, so I took a chance and went straight at him to do quick damage to his gut. Tom tried to bear-hug me. I butted him until he stopped trying, and kept on hammering his belly. His anger turned to shock, then bafflement as his legs gave way.

Alison flew at me, her little body all desperate bone and muscle, clutching my leg, pleading, "Don't hurt him, Ben."

Adrenaline was popping through my skin, and I was breathing hard. Tom eyed me blearily from the floor; then he sagged back as he closed his eyes.

I looked at the big, inert form on the floor and tried to figure out some way to protect his family. One thing was for sure: I wasn't going to New York that afternoon.

I said, "Alison, take your mother to my house. Can you walk, Mrs. Mealy?"

"I'm okay. I'm okay."

Janet Mealy was, in fact, white as the kitchen wall. There was blood on her lip. I insisted that Steve Greenan look her over. "No," she whispered, explaining that the doctor would tell Trooper Moody, and Oliver would arrest her husband.

I looked at Alison and saw that this warped logic made sense to her. "Ben, don't you understand? They'll send him back to jail."

That struck me as a terrific idea. "Maybe that would be better for a while, until he calms down. They can help him there."

"Detox didn't work last time," said the eleven-year-old.

"All right," I said. "Go to my house. I'll talk to him."

"Ben, don't hurt him. Promise," Alison demanded.

"Don't worry. I'll just sober him up and get him out of here."

They went at last, with fearful glances.

Tom opened his eyes. "They gone?"

"They're gone. When'd you get out, Tom?" I asked.

"Last month."

"Took you a whole month to come home to beat up your family?"

He said nothing.

"Where you living, Tom?"

"By the river."

I had heard that somewhere ten miles downstream the homeless were camped. He was too drunk to reason with, but maybe I could scare him. I said, "Tom, I'm sorry, but I've got to call Trooper Moody."

He sat up. "No. They'll send me back for violating parole."

"Maybe we can get you into a program."

"No way. I ain't going in no program!" he shouted.

I was getting nowhere fast. "Tom, if I give you a hundred bucks, will you get on a bus and go to Florida for the winter?"

"For a lousy hundred bucks?" he asked with a crafty smile. "*Five* hundred."

"I don't have five hundred."

"Then I'm staying."

That tore it. I yanked him to his feet and marched him out and down the stairs before he realized we were moving. "What are you doing?" he whined.

"We're going to Trooper Moody."

"No." He dug in his heels. "If you let me go, I'll tell you something about the guy who shot Renny Chevalley."

"*What?*"

"You gotta give me the hundred bucks, too."

"*What?*" I shouted again in amazement. "What do you know?"

"You let me go."

"Only if you leave the county."

"I'll go to Massachusetts. I got a buddy up there."

"Fine." I would have preferred a more distant state, but he held the cards now. "So, what guy are you talking about? Did you see him?"

"Buddy of mine did. On Morris Mountain Road."

"Where is your buddy?"

"By the river."

"Take me to him."

"First the hundred bucks."

"When he shakes hands with me. Not before. Get in the car."

He climbed into the Olds. I opened the barn doors and drove out. After I swung by the bank to withdraw a hundred dollars, Tom

Mealy gave me directions to his piece of the river; then he fell asleep—reeking, and snoring loudly.

A few minutes later I spotted the overgrown logging road that Tom had instructed me to look for. I nudged him hard in the ribs. He woke up and eventually remembered why he was in my car.

"Right past that oak."

We stopped in a small clearing.

"Now what?"

"We gotta walk."

I followed Tom Mealy into the woods on a deer path. Ahead, the tree canopy thinned, marking the bed of the river. The deer path descended steeply until we found ourselves on the open bank.

Tom gave a low whistle. At an answering whistle, he said, "Come on," and headed down the bank, ducking low limbs. A hundred yards of that brought us to a meadow where a twelve-by-twelve blue poly tarp was pitched lean-to style. Three people were sitting under it.

A fourth was trying to start a fire. "Who's this?" he asked.

I was wearing my tweed jacket. Old as it was, it looked a little out of place. The men and woman under the tarp were wearing dirty blue jeans and hooded sweatshirts. The guy building the fire—who looked oddly familiar to me—was upscale by comparison, with cleaner blue jeans and a bright green nylon Windbreaker.

"He wants to talk to you," Tom told him.

He was about forty-five, with a walrus mustache and a gentle but weary look in his eye that reminded me of Mrs. Mealy. He finished piling squaw wood and lighted the fire with the last match in his book. It flamed instantly. He looked up with a lopsided smile and said, "I didn't do it, Officer."

"I'm not a cop. Could I have a little of your time?"

He considered that gravely.

I walked away to the river. He bent his head in discussion with Tom a moment, then joined me. "Tom says you're paying him a hundred bucks for me to talk to you."

"I'm paying him to go away and stop beating up his wife."

"Tom's a menace," the man said quietly.

"I'm Ben Abbott, by the way." I stuck out my hand.

"Oh, I know you, Mr. Abbott," he said as he took my hand.

"I'm sorry. You look familiar, but I can't place you."

"My name's Ed Hawley. I cook at the Church Hill Diner. You come in for breakfast now and then."

"Of course. Oh, yes. But what are you doing here? I mean, why are you living outdoors when you have a job?"

"Security deposit and first and last month's rent up front," he answered. "I'm still getting it together."

I must have stared. I thought I knew something about the ways of the world, but I hadn't put much thought into the fact that a guy with a job couldn't rent some little apartment someplace.

I said, "I don't have it with me, but I'll certainly slip you a hundred if you tell me what you know about my cousin."

"I'd appreciate that very much. But I didn't see much."

"What did you see?"

Hawley explained that to supplement his short-order-cook income, he tried to get daywork. A farmer on Morris Mountain had offered him five dollars an hour to drive fence posts. Hawley had taken it, but near the end of the day the farmer refused to pay him all the money, because he hadn't sunk enough posts. Hawley contended that the stony land had slowed him down. It had turned into a shoving match, and when the farmer threatened to call the police, Hawley had run for it without any money at all.

"Anyway, I'm walking down Morris Mountain Road—"

"What time?"

"It's three thirty. A little white plane comes in low, looks like it's going to crash in the trees. Disappeared. I didn't hear a crash or see any smoke, so I figure he made it. Ten minutes later I hear this car screaming down the road. Guy goes by me at sixty."

"What did he look like?"

"I saw sunglasses and a baseball cap."

"You saw nothing of his face?"

"Not behind that fancy smoked glass."

"The sunglasses?"

"And the car windows."

"What kind of car?"

"Old muscle car. Camaro maybe."

"Did you see the license?"

"Connecticut plates," he answered. "Something H-A-L. Three numbers and HAL. I remember the HAL because that was the name of the computer in *2001*."

I was sure that the three numbers preceding HAL could be found in Marian Boyce's computer.

"I really appreciate this, Ed."

"Yeah, well, he was your cousin."

"I'll bring your hundred in the morning. Soon as the bank opens."

We walked back across the clearing, where Tom Mealy stuck out his palm for his hundred dollars. I drove him to New Milford first, to put him on the Pittsfield bus. I told him not to come back drunk, and if he wanted to visit Alison sober, to call me first, and I'd set something up. I gave him the money and he lurched up the steps, belching and grumbling.

I passed the bus on the first short straight and tore across the county to see Marian Boyce.

TROOPER Marian welcomed me to the Plainfield barracks with a big handshake. "What brings you to Monster-woman's Lair?"

"I got a partial license number from a car leaving the airstrip the afternoon Renny Chevalley was shot."

"From whom?"

"Homeless guy walking down the road."

She invited me in. The detective room was bright and snappy, and Marian's office could have belonged to a C.P.A. On her desk were a pencil, a phone, and a notepad. A computer waited.

"This guy have a name?" Marian asked.

"Why don't we check out the number first?"

Marian gave me a wintry look. I gave her one back.

"H-A-L. Old Camaro probably."

Marian shrugged, poked her computer, and punched HAL into it. "Sit," she said. I sat. Marian frowned as blocks of information scrolled up the screen. She touched a key, and the scrolling stopped. "You're not going to like this. We've got one 1973 Camaro, navy blue, 337 HAL."

"Who owns it?"

"Chevalley Enterprises. It's Renny's car."

"No. He doesn't drive a Camaro. He leased a four-door Blazer when the kids were born."

"He registered the Camaro two weeks before he was murdered."

"Oh, no. One of his restorations."

She made some notes. "Okay. Let's have the witness's name."

"Ed Hawley. He cooks at the Church Hill Diner in Newbury. Don't screw it up for him."

"Contrary to what you may think, I am not in the business of getting witnesses fired from their jobs. If you don't mind, I'd like to discuss with Mr. Hawley anything else he might have seen. At least this suggests your cousin expected to land at that strip."

"And the guy who shot him stole his car."

"Could have happened. Thanks for coming by. Appreciate the witness." She gave me a good-bye look.

"Show your appreciation. Answer one question."

"What?"

"Did Renny's plane crash into that tree landing or taking off?"

"Taking off."

"Was he shot through the windshield?"

"No more questions. We're even."

I left, thinking that the existence of Renny's car at the airstrip—which suggested that Renny had planned to land there—sort of fit Marian's drug-delivery theory. But he had crashed taking off. Trying to escape? Or to return the plane to Danbury, leaving his passenger a car to drive away in? So why was the coke aboard the plane? It made no sense to unload it at Danbury in front of Chernowsky. Why not in the privacy of Al Bell's hilltop airstrip?

I was curious how Renny had gotten the Camaro up there, so I swung through Frenchtown on the way home and asked at Chevalley Enterprises whether Renny had towed the Camaro the day or so before he died. He had not. So if he hadn't towed it up Morris Mountain, who had given him a ride back when he dropped the car?

I had a feeling I knew who, though prying it out of her might be impossible. It meant putting off my New York City trip again. Another day without seeing Leslie. With luck, Jack, Rita, and Alex Rose would all confess to Ron's murder and I'd never have to go.

THE wise man calls on a Jervis woman when her father, sons, and brothers are away. The safest bet is the first day of hunting season. I couldn't wait till then, so I tried twelve noon—time, I hoped, for Jervis men to be down at the White Birch for their morning beer.

Gwen's branch of the clan lived in a crowd of trailers circled like prairie schooners in the deep woods, far beyond Frenchtown, on the edge of the Housatonic Reservation. In the center area of beaten earth, children fought. Beyond the trailers were cars and trucks up on blocks. Women called their children inside as I parked beside Gwen's rust-eaten '79 Ford pickup. My Chevalley connections were worthless here. Jervises drew no distinctions between Frenchtown and Main Street.

Gwen's tin door had buckled at the lock, and someone had bolted on a couple of two-by-fours to straighten it out. A fair-sized crack remained between door and frame, stuffed with a pink towel. I knocked a few times. "Gwen, it's me. Ben Abbott."

"I know why you're here," she greeted me. Her old bathrobe would have looked ratty on a woman with a lesser body, but at forty Gwen was still all curves and angles—full-breasted, narrow-waisted, long-legged. To describe her as sullen would ignore her sadness.

"I'm real sorry, Gwen. I miss him, and I know you do, too."

She'd hung in at school until tenth grade. Puberty had propelled me in her direction with a six-pack of Bud that Pinkerton Chevalley had bought for me. She wasn't sullen back then—just a big, warm, open girl-woman. She'd lived a hard twenty years since.

"I've really got to talk to you, Gwen."

"About what?"

"Renny. I'm trying to find out who killed him."

She just stared.

"He wasn't running coke, was he?"

"Cops think so. Busted into the trailer. Trashed my door. Oh, they had all their papers. Left real disappointed, though."

"Renny wasn't running coke, was he?" I asked again.

Gwen stared some more. Then she said, "Take me for a ride. I'll get dressed."

She came out in tight jeans and a loose sweatshirt, and she'd run a comb through her thick red Jervis hair. We got into the Olds. "Where would you like to go?"

"The mall."

I knew she meant the new minimall down Route 7. The Danbury Fair Mall was as intimidating to her as Fifth Avenue.

"How'd you hook up with Renny?" I asked.

"My truck stalled over on Route 349. Renny happened along in his wrecker. Jumped me," she said with a smile. "After that, we jumped each other every chance we got."

"Wha'd your husband think?"

"Last I heard, he was on an oil rig in the Persian Gulf. What do you want to talk about?"

"Did Renny have any problem with your brothers?"

"Pete ran him off the road, but I spoke to Daddy, and he ordered a truce. Said I'm old enough now to run around with who I want."

"That sounds uncharacteristically mellow of your father."

"Daddy's got arthritis. He's slowing down."

"Pete taking over?" I didn't say "the business," but she knew I meant the cigarette smuggling, the distribution of uppers and downers to the truckers, and the fencing of stolen goods.

"Little Bill," she answered. "Pete's got a drinking problem."

"Good choice," I said. Little Bill Jervis had beaten a triple-murder rap back in 1978. Some Hell's Angels from Derby had tried to cheat him in a drug deal.

We finally reached a blacktop road. I hated to admit it, but part of me had to wonder whether Old Man Jervis had intervened in the Pete-Renny dispute for business reasons, such as protecting a valuable coke-flying pilot.

"So what do you want to know about Renny?"

"The stuff he'd tell you and no one else," I said. "I'll bet he would have told you if he was flying coke."

"He wasn't."

"Are you sure?"

"Positive."

"What if he were working for your father? Would he tell you?"

"Why not? Daddy and me get along fine." I glanced over at her. She was regarding me with mild puzzlement. My problem was this: she might be telling the truth; but if Renny had been working for her father, she might be lying. She didn't owe me anything.

We got to the mall. It had a grocery and a drugstore, a toy store, a video rental, a liquor store, an ice-cream shop, and a lot of unrented space. While I went to scout out some coffee, Gwen ran ahead. I found her in the toy store. We strolled the empty drugstore, the grocery, and the video shop. I asked her if I could buy her anything. She said she had everything she needed. While I bought a used video, Gwen wandered.

Back in the car, as I drove away, she said, "Look, Ben."
I looked. She lifted her sweatshirt. Out tumbled a videocassette, some pricey shampoo, perfume, and a teddy bear.
"Hey, you stole—" I turned the car around.
"Where you going?"
"Back to pay for that stuff. My money."
"No. If you don't turn around *now*, I'm jumping out of the car."
She opened the door. The road roared by at forty. I saw she meant it. I pulled over and stopped. "Jump."
"If you pay, I won't tell you about Renny."
"Tell me what?"
"Take me home." She picked up her shampoo, opened it, and sniffed. "Oh, wow. You gotta smell this, Ben."
I headed back to Newbury. "Tell me about Renny."
"What?"
"Dammit, Gwen."
"Okay, okay. You should see your face. You're so serious."
"I am serious about Renny. I thought you were, too."
"Ben, your cousin was your friend. He was a lot more than that to me. Okay? Let me be sad the way I want to be sad."
"I'm sorry, Gwen. I'm really wired about this."
Silence the rest of the way to Newbury. Silence all the miles to the junction with the Jervises' dirt road.
"Stop."
I shut off the engine. A shotgun echoed in the hills. Someone jumping the season. Gwen grimaced. "Deer meat till April." She gazed into the deep woods.
"Gwen, give me a break. All I'm trying to do is clear Renny's name."
"What for? Who cares? He's dead."
"He cared," I said. "He worked like a dog for respect."
"He worked for money. He wanted to be rich."
"Of course he wanted money. But he wanted respect, too. So I'm going to clear his name and also get the guy who killed him."
Gwen touched my hand. "Tell *me* who," she said matter-of-factly. "I'll take it from there."
"No, thanks. I'll take it to the cops. But first I have to find him," I said. "Which is why I need your help. Did you give Renny a ride back when he dropped the Camaro at Al Bell's field?"

"We met up there Friday night."

"And you left his car?"

"Yeah."

"Did Renny say why he was leaving the car?"

"No."

"Well, didn't you ask?"

"I don't ask men their business. I wasn't raised that way."

As if to emphasize her point, the hemlocks on the edge of the dirt road parted and out stepped a Jervis teenager—wild and lanky as a coyote—carrying a shotgun. Gwen waved. The kid was trailed by old Herman Jervis himself.

"Oh, no," Gwen whispered. She jumped out of the car and approached her father warily. That she was his favorite did not exempt her from the occasional backhand swipe of a bony hand if he was crossed.

Well into his seventies, Herman Jervis slouched in a wide-legged stance, baggy green pants sliding down his skinny hips. A red scar slanted down his face from temple to jaw, and his eyes brimmed with cold intelligence and contempt for everything he saw.

He jerked his head at the kid, who handed him the shotgun and slipped back into the woods. Then he addressed Gwen, who listened, head down. I couldn't hear what he was saying. When he was done, Gwen came back and leaned in the window.

"He shot a buck. Wants you to run it back to my place."

"Oh, great." I could just imagine Oliver Moody cruising by me, with an out-of-season deer on my roof. Not, I could see, that I had a lot of choice in the matter. The boy staggered out with the deer on his back and heaved the carcass up, bouncing the Olds on its springs. Old Man Jervis approached, pulling a rope from one of his pockets as blood trickled down my windshield.

"Here. Pass it through." He shoved a rope end in my window and indicated I should pass it to Gwen. We passed it over the deer a couple of times until the old man allowed it would hold.

"Get going. When you get to my daughter's place, you lend her a hand hanging it."

"My pleasure. I'm Ben Abbott, by the way, Mr. Jervis."

"I know who you are."

"Can I ask you something, Mr. Jervis?"

Gwen, who had climbed back into the car, gave a little inward hiss of alarm, but it was too late now. Her father broke open his ancient double-barrel, inserted fresh loads, and snicked it shut.

"Like what?"

"Would you know if my cousin was flying drugs?"

"Yup."

"Was he?"

"Nope."

"Thank you. I'll get your buck home."

"Sonny, you ask the wrong man questions like that, he'll blow your head off." Trailed by the kid, he plunged back into the woods.

Gwen exhaled. "You are out of your mind. You are crazy."

"We understood each other."

Gwen snorted. "You didn't even hear the warning."

"What warning?"

"Don't ask Bill."

"Your brother? Does that mean Renny might have been working for Bill and your dad didn't know?"

"He said he'd know, and he said Renny wasn't. Which I told you all along. You asked two of us now. Go look someplace else."

"Gwen—"

"Your car's getting bloody. You better take me home."

I drove her home to the trailers and parked under a tree that had a hook and chain hanging from a low limb. I took off my jacket and shirt and wrestled the carcass onto the hook.

Gwen returned from her trailer with paper towels for the blood and a cold beer. "You better get going before the boys get home."

I cleaned off, dressed, and drained the beer. "Thanks."

"No more questions?"

"You told me not to ask." I got into the car.

"That never stopped you before."

The edge of anger that had underlaid her mood all afternoon was gleaming in her eyes. "Ask," she said.

"All right. Renny left his car because he knew he was flying into Al Bell's field. Did he tell you who his passenger would be?"

"No."

"But you think it was someone in your family."

"One of my people," Gwen confessed.

"And you're caught in the middle. You'd never tell who."

"I don't know who. If I did, I'd kill him."

I started the engine. "You're wrong, Gwen. It wasn't your family."

"Are you kidding, Ben? Soon as they learned Renny and me were running around, they went for him like flies on honey. A real live pilot! They were tickled pink, except for Pete, but I told you, he drinks. I swear, if my husband had come home from the Gulf, they would have drowned him in the river."

"No," I said. "Renny played it straight."

"They would have given him anything."

"No. He hated being at a disadvantage. I lent him a few bucks for the garage. Drove him crazy. Finally insisted on giving me a new engine. No way he would have let your people get control over him by doing something illegal."

Tears slipped from Gwen's eyes, down her face. "Are you sure what you said—that it's not my people?"

"Positive. Partly for the reason you just said. If Renny had flown coke—which I'm sure he didn't—they wouldn't kill the golden goose, would they? It had to be a paying passenger, Gwen. Somebody local he'd leave his car for. Somebody he trusted."

9

THEY had a long memory at Le Cirque, and a table ready. I noticed a higher percentage of ladies lunching at the restaurant since the Drexel Burnham mob had dispersed.

Otherwise the New York I saw on the walk from Grand Central Terminal didn't seem all that changed. Traffic was dense as ever. Madonna naked couldn't have nailed an empty taxicab. But the women definitely looked younger.

Alex Rose arrived for lunch glowering suspiciously. In his pin-striped suit he looked like a truculent lawyer. Perfect.

I myself was resplendent in an Italian midnight-blue double-breasted suit vaguely redolent of mothballs, and a Dunhill shirt. I wore a gold Piaget moon watch I should not have accepted from an arbitrageur. Alison could have had a week of boarding school for what I had paid for my tie.

"I don't get this," Rose said, looking around the lavish room. "Wha'd you hit the lottery?"

I didn't tell him it was Rita's lunch tab.

"Like I told you on the phone. I got nothing new on your cousin."

"I figured that after we talked, you might have made a call or two," I said.

"Well, I did talk to a guy at La Guardia."

"And?"

"Renny Chevalley took off at two fifty that afternoon."

"Thank you."

Ed Hawley had seen the plane at three thirty. Forty minutes to Newbury, nonstop. Thank you very very much.

We ate a sumptuous lunch—*écrevisses, ris de veau,* and *crème brûlée.* I pumped him a little about the detective business and learned a lot. Rose was mystified as to why I had invited him, but he was an ebullient talker once he got wound up. By dessert he'd packed my brain with the latest P.I. basics, especially telephone bugs he'd installed at the Castle. He was, however, no fool and had noticed people watching us while we ate. When I had paid the check, he said, "You used me for cover, didn't you?"

I denied it, of course. We left the restaurant.

"How'd you happen to tell Jack Long that Ron had been shot before the troopers called him?" I asked him.

"I pay the security company. They know that if I don't hear everything to do with Jack's house, I hire a new alarm company."

"How'd they find out? There was no alarm."

Rose's cockeyed wink hardened into an unpleasant squint. "They got a radio scanner. They monitor the state police channels. You ought to buy one, Ben. Keep in touch."

MY NEXT stop was the midtown offices of Harkin & Locke—Buddy Locke, my second protégé. I had phoned for an appointment and been told that Ms. Harkin's schedule was booked for a month. I had told her secretary I was coming anyway.

Harkin & Locke's reception room had a stunningly beautiful blond greeter, a heart-stopping view of Central Park, and a single article of Japanese sculpture that, if I knew its owners, had probably been looted from a Kyoto monastery.

"Oh, Mr. Abbott. Ms. Harkin has just gone into a meeting."

"That's okay. I brought a book."

When the receptionist interrupted me an hour later to tell me Ms. Harkin was still in the meeting, I expressed my gratitude. It was approaching five o'clock when she interrupted me again.

"Mr. Abbott? Ms. Harkin is expected at the Downtown Athletic Club at six, but she can squeeze you in for a moment right now."

"Terrific." I followed the blonde into Leslie's office. Leslie was on the telephone, her back to me, looking out the window.

"She'll be with you in a minute," whispered the receptionist.

Leslie spun her chair and hung up the phone. "Thank you, Doreen." Doreen went out the door.

Leslie had my full attention. I hadn't seen her in the five years since the trial. To say that she strongly resembled Rita Long would be to say that all raven-haired beautiful women looked the same. Both women radiated their personality, but what shone through their beauty was quite different. Need a guide across a foreign city, ask for Rita Long. Need an escort through a hostile one, hire Leslie Harkin. Leslie was leaner. She was a few years older than Rita and looked it—too much jet travel and too many nights of shorting sleep. Her most compelling feature was her strange violet eyes.

I thought I had developed partial immunity to the Leslie Look after she plea-bargained me into the U.S. Attorney's lap. But my heartbeat—which had revved at the sight of her familiar silhouette—redlined when she faced me. I had been nuts for her in bed and awed by her ferocious intelligence. If that wasn't love, she still stirred my soul, and I knew in an instant why I hadn't had much success in trying to hate her.

"What do you want, Ben?"

"I'm chasing some information. Everybody says to ask you."

"Ben, I'm busy. Ask your question."

Before I could, the telephone buzzed. She answered it without apologizing and talked machine-gun style for five minutes. She hung up, looked at me, and it rang again. Another five minutes, this time in Japanese. When she hung up, I said, "I'm impressed. When'd you learn Japanese?"

"What do you want to know?"

As I opened my mouth, she looked at her watch. "I gotta get downtown. Come on. We'll talk in the car." She left, firing orders at secretaries and assistants, trailed by a vice president who held papers for her to sign, and me.

We settled into her limo, and the cell phone tweeted. She picked up—again without an apology—and singsonged in Japanese. At Houston Street, she hung up with a hearty "Banzai!"

"Ask," she said to me, writing a note in her datebook.

I said, "What do you know about—" and the phone rang. That conversation was still going when the car stopped dead in heavy traffic at Canal Street. A homeless guy approached, rapping the window with a battered paper cup. I lowered the glass.

"What are you doing?" asked Leslie. I took her phone, gave it to the guy with the cup, and closed the window.

"What? That's a two-thousand-dollar telephone!"

"I'll give you mine. Now will you answer my question?"

"You gave him my phone."

"I'll give him your datebook next. Will you shut up and tell me what's going on with LTS?"

She said, "I hear you're trying to put LTS into play."

I must admit enormous satisfaction in manipulating Leslie. It had occurred to me over the weekend that she wouldn't give me the time of day if I came on as an amateur detective and simply asked whether Jack Long was riding as high as he claimed, whereas a deal in the works would make my questions potentially valuable—especially if it sounded like a deal she could move in on.

It had been a safe bet that some sort of rumor would get around after last week's Rolodex party. I had engineered today's conspicuous lunch with a mysterious stranger at Le Cirque to give plenty of ammunition to the two-hundred-phone-calls-a-day crowd.

"Well," I said, "don't believe everything you hear."

The phone was forgotten. "What do *you* hear?"

"You first."

"Okay. Get this, Ben: Jack Long goes to Salomon Brothers, like maybe he's interested in floating a high-yield bond."

"That's not exactly news."

"Oh, yeah? How about the fact that he's approached the Flying Dutchmen?"

"Come on." I winged it again. "He's been in bed with Holland Brothers forever." Interesting. It sounded like Jack Long was looking to borrow hard money. Be it junk bonds or a private loan from the usurious Holland Brothers, he would pay the high interest that businessmen paid only when no one else would lend at normal rates. Maybe—just maybe—LTS was suffering.

This was like shooting fish in a barrel. Could I get her to spill again? I debated appealing to her vanity, and chose, wisely, greed.

"I'll hop out here," I said. "I'm meeting a guy." Her car was creeping past Trinity Church at the foot of Wall Street.

"Wait. What are you doing, Ben? I didn't even know you were back. Did they lift your ban?"

"Nice talking to you. Say hello to Buddy. Driver, stop here."

"No. Ride down with me. Please, Ben. We should talk."

I shot my cuff and looked at my Piaget. She looked surprised I hadn't hocked it. "Okay. I'll ride along. He'll wait."

"So what are you doing?"

"It's just exploratory. No big deal."

"You want money? You name it, we'll raise it."

I said nothing.

"What set you off?" she asked. "Long's Hong Kong deal?"

She was watching my reaction intently now. I assumed she meant Ron Pearlman's factory. But I didn't know the electronics field like she did, didn't know what other big deals Jack Long was juggling, didn't know diddly.

"The Hong Kong deal sounded expensive," I ventured. "Made me wonder how badly it exposed him."

"Big question," Leslie said. "What's his payment schedule?"

"One of the big questions," I replied too vaguely. She smelled a rat.

"Wait. Didn't Ron Pearlman get killed up where you live?"

"Shot."

"That's what started you?" Scorn stalked across her face.

I laughed at her. "Yeah, right. The idea popped into my head two weeks ago."

"Do you know his payment schedule?"

I looked Leslie straight in her violet eye. "No, I don't. And neither do you."

"Want to bet? I have a source."

"You know rumors. It's a closely held company. Your source doesn't know. Jack Long is not the kind of guy to share that with anybody."

"You know Long?"

"Sure. We had dinner the other night. Straight shooter. Probably wouldn't tell his own wife what he owes or when he owes it."

"December thirty-first—less than three months away. Eighteen months after they closed the deal. Notes. Something like two hundred twenty-five million."

Bingo, I thought. I said, "He doesn't seem worried. The man's talking expansion into Singapore."

Leslie beamed. "I *knew* you were running a deal," she said triumphantly. "You're putting him into play. Let us in on it, Ben. We'll spook his bankers."

"I don't think so, Leslie. I'm not looking for partners."

"Because I testified against you?"

I gave her an unsmiling look.

"You want revenge. You hung this deal in front of me to make me feel bad I can't be part of it. Well, let me tell you something, Ben. Buddy and I will leave you in the dust."

I had to remind myself we were discussing a fantasy. I had no deal, no plan to take over LTS. It would be funny if Harkin & Locke destroyed LTS trying to make my fantasy happen. Not so funny if my name got attached; technically, just sitting in Leslie's limo violated my SEC ban. Not at all funny if Jack Long was innocent. "Drop me here."

Her limousine raced off—in search of a pay phone so she could call Buddy Locke and start raking Long's bones.

I went down into the subway, wondering if I had created a monster. I telephoned Jack Long's office from Grand Central. Jack greeted me in a country-neighbor voice.

I said, "Try to keep my name out of it, but you ought to know that my old playmates Harkin and Locke might make a move on you."

He waited half a second too long to laugh. "I'll eat their lunch."

I GOT home thoroughly depressed. I'd done well in New York, and I should have felt elated, but I felt old and out of it.

I supposed I should report to Rita, but it was likely that she could have told me half, at least, of what I'd learned from Leslie. Strange she hadn't told me that Jack was scrambling.

I wandered into my office and checked the answering machine. There was a message from Rita, and she sounded depressed, too, saying, "Ben, please call. Anytime. I'll be up late."

"Hi. I just got back from New York."

"Have you eaten dinner?"

"No. I was just getting hungry. I had a big lunch."

"Would you bring a pizza?"

"Okay. You don't sound so great."

"I had a very depressing visit from Ira Roth. They're really going to indict me. He's worried."

"I'll be there in an hour."

THE Castle was lit up like The Plaza Hotel—windows blazing, spotlights scouring the lawns, fairy lights winking on the walks. "Up here," Rita called from the turret. "The door's open."

I carried the pizza up the steps into the cold tower. She was in the observation room, dressed in a wool shirt and down vest. "I can't stand going indoors tonight. Okay to eat out here?"

"If you don't mind ice on your pizza."

She made room on the table for the box and handed me a beer. "How'd it go in New York?"

"When people talk about Jack's Hong Kong deal, do they mean Ron's chip factory?" I asked her.

"Probably. It was the biggest and the most recent."

"Did Jack pay two hundred and fifty million to buy Ron out?"

"Yes."

"With a big note due?"

"Yes."

"With something like ten percent down, with the remainder due in eighteen months? December thirty-first?"

"I think so. I wasn't in on the final details. But December thirty-first sounds about right. Hey, you're good, Ben."

I opened the box, cut through the steaming cheese with my penknife, and lifted out a slice. "Do you have a copy of the contract?"

"Not here." Rita bit into her pizza.

"I'd like to read it. How's Jack going to pay Ron's family?"

"He was hoping to pay cash—to buy him outright."

"If Jack couldn't raise the money, would he lose the ten percent?"

"All twenty-five million dollars."

"Have you read the contract?"

"I read the deal memo. We agreed to pay Ron two hundred and fifty million dollars for his Hong Kong operation, plus a two-and-a-half-million-dollar management fee yearly for five years."

"What?"

"What's so strange about that?"

"Jack made a big point of saying Ron was a pampered dilettante. Why would he want him for a manager?"

"Ron insisted. It was a deal breaker. He wanted to keep his Hong Kong connections. It's a hot city. Who knows what'll happen after the Chinese take over in '97? Ron intended to run the operation while he scouted out new opportunities."

It struck me that a dead Ron meant that Jack not only got his wife back, he also got rid of a thorn in his side.

"I want to see the contract."

"I'll get someone to fax it to me. I can't leave the county."

"Don't let Jack know."

Rita smiled. "I have friends."

SHE called me at noon the next day. "Got it."

"Be right there."

I sat at Jack's own desk and read the ten-page document word for word. I made one note. When I finished the last page, I read the entire document again. Then I took a head-clearing turn around the lawn and read it a third time. I found Rita in the kitchen, staring blankly at a copy of Julia Child.

"Did you read it?" I asked her.

"As it came off the machine."

"Did you see what I saw?"

"Yes. The bastard murdered him."

Assuming he was broke, the contract gave Jack Long a powerful motive. If—said a little escape clause on the last page—Ron Pearlman was unable to accept his five-year management contract, LTS could cancel the deal and get its ten-percent deposit back.

With Ron dead, all bets were off. His heirs—his father, presumably—still owned his piece of LTS. But Jack was off the hook. He didn't have to pay two hundred and twenty-five million bucks on December 31.

Jack knew that if he had failed to make his payment to Ron, his banks would have taken a closer look at his entire indebtedness, disliked what they had seen, and called his loans, retiring him to the same hands-tied limbo to which they'd sent Donald Trump and Robert Maxwell.

Rita looked sick.

"You didn't know about this?" I asked.

"He must have negotiated it after the memo I read."

"But how did he shoot Ron from Washington, D.C.?"

"He paid Rose to shoot him," said Rita. I had to agree that was probably the way it went down. "Who do we tell?" she asked.

"First your lawyer," I said. "Give him something to fight with."

TWENTY-FIVE years older than I, Ira Roth was rich, vigorous, and driven. He wore splendidly old-fashioned three-piece suits, florid neckties, and a trademark gray fedora. He kept his main office in Plainfield, by the courthouse, and lived on a splashy western-style horse farm on Morris Mountain, not far from Rita.

"First of all," he said when we called at his home, "what is Ben doing here?"

"He's with me," said Rita.

"He's a witness for the prosecution. He saw the body. Ben, I can't see you."

"Rose threatened to force me to testify for the defense," I told Ira.

"I know. That was the dumbest idea Long's so-called lawyers had."

"He stays," said Rita. She looked at me.

I said, "We have a theory that Mr. Long hired a private detective to kill Ron Pearlman."

"In a fit of jealousy?" the lawyer asked scornfully.

"No. To nullify a contract."

His eyebrows rose a fraction. "To nullify *what* contract?"

"Ron Pearlman dead means Long doesn't have to pony up a heap of money. There's an escape clause in the Hong Kong buyout contract, and it looks like Long might be in fiscal trouble. If he had had to honor the contract, his banks would have shut him down."

"That's very interesting." Ira turned to Rita. "It's a tricky tactic, Mrs. Long. If the jury thinks you're trying to weasel out of this with smoke and mirrors, they might conclude that you conjured up a far-fetched tale because you have no other defense. In other words, guilty. Next case."

"Isn't this worth pursuing?" she asked.

"Look at it from the state's attorney's point of view. He has a choice of convicting you—discovered on the scene with a gun and fingerprints—or your husband, who, sadly, does not project the image of a jealous fiend and who happened to be shaking the President's hand in Washington, D.C., the day the victim was shot."

"What about a hired killer?" I asked.

"Ben, do you mind my asking your interest in this?"

"I think Rita's been set up."

"Is there something between you two I should know when I'm pleading your case, Mrs. Long?"

"We'll keep you informed," said Rita. "Come on, Ben. Let's go."

Roth stood up. "Ben, a word with you, please?"

"I'll catch up," I said to Rita, who pushed through the door and hurried down the porch steps to her car.

"Ben, I implore you to be careful. This is a very delicate case. Perception is all. If the prosecution gets wind of you running around accusing her husband, they'll paint pictures of multiple infidelities that I will not be able to keep out of the trial. It's going to be a circus anyway. Try to avoid joining the animal act. By the way, Ben, have you told anyone about that videotape stunt Rose paid for?"

"Only Rita. But Ira, Rose knows. And if he's protecting Long to protect himself, what's to stop him from blabbing it to send Rita down the river?"

"Look at the bright side," Ira said grimly. "That would pretty much validate your theory that Long hired Rose to kill Ron Pearlman."

"Very funny. Ira, how bad are Rita's chances?"

"About as bad as yours were when you went down. Always wondered why you didn't call me. I'd have gotten you off."

"Maybe I didn't want to get off."

"But you were framed. You didn't break the law."

"I know, Ira, but I broke the spirit of the law. I plundered. I deserved to go down."

"That is your crazy aunt talking Puritan claptrap."

"Clean slate, Ira. I'm not guilty anymore."

Rita huddled in the car with her arms crossed. "I'm scared."

She said she was scared, but she acted more like mad. Flooring the Jag, she treated me to a blistering critique of her lawyer all the way home—his taste in furniture, his Wild West ranch house.

When Rita finally noticed I wasn't responding, she screamed at me, "Would it be too much trouble for you to investigate where Rose was the afternoon Ron was murdered?"

"My next step," I assured her. Wondering how I would go about doing that, I picked up my car at her house and drove home.

TROOPER MOODY WAS WAITING in my kitchen, out of uniform. He wore heavy boots, jeans, and a commando sweater stretched tight around his chest. I liked him better in trooper gray.

"Who let you in?"

"Jailbird, you've got problems." He kicked my feet out from under me, picked me up, and threw me into the dining room.

10

I SKIDDED across waxed chestnut and crashed into a heap of chairs. Oliver loomed in the doorway. He had me by half a foot and one hundred pounds. I looked for a weapon.

It stood on the mantel—a heavy brass candlestick. I mapped a route to it under the dining table and looked elsewhere before he noticed.

"Don't get up. You just lay there and listen."

"I listen better on my feet."

"Remember what happened last time you got up when I told you not to?"

Like yesterday. "You made me cry in front of my friends." We were hacking around on a Saturday night—Renny and me and Scooter and the Butler boys—and suddenly, there was the new resident state trooper on the Grange hall porch. He was twenty-five, fresh out of the military police, and knew how to inflict savage pain without leaving a mark.

"Remember what happened to your vehicle?" I said.

Oliver Moody went red. I got ready to roll under the table. But then, to my surprise, he regained control of himself and whipped a flat, silvery object out of his pocket.

"Recognize this, jailbird?"

"Looks like a TV channel zapper, Ollie," I answered, concentrating on not looking at the candlestick, and worrying how hard to hit him with it.

"It's a remote control for a Sony camcorder."

"So?" *That* was what he had found in Rita's woods. It had fallen out of its nest on the camcorder. I hadn't noticed it was missing and neither, apparently, had Rose when he got it back in the mail.

"It's from a camcorder purchased in New York City at Grand Central Camera by a private detective named Alex Rose."

"So?"

"Two weeks ago Alex Rose was in your Oldsmobile when I issued you a summons for speeding."

"I was showing him a house. But I don't recall introducing you."

"His Mercedes-Benz was parked in your driveway."

"Oh, I get it," I said from the floor. "Rose dropped his remote control while you were giving me a ticket. You found it and ran a license check on his car to find his address in order to return it. And just to be sure it was really his, you went all the way to New York City on your day off to confirm the serial number at the store where he bought it. I'm impressed, Ollie."

"*You* dropped it, jailbird."

"Me?" I looked at him like he was nuts.

"*You* dropped it in the woods behind the Long house the night before Mrs. Long's boyfriend got shot."

"Ollie, if the remote control belongs to Alex Rose, wouldn't any normal human being conclude that *Rose* must have dropped it?"

"Rose was watching the Sox on Lori Match's TV."

Lori Match owned Matchbox, on Church Hill Road, one of the last old-fashioned tourist homes in the area.

"Rose stayed in Newbury?" I asked. "Stayed the *night?*"

"Never left the house. I noticed the Benz parked there and checked with Lori."

"I thought he was going back to New York."

"So tell me, Ben."

"Tell you what, Ollie?"

He pulled a black leather-covered sap from his jeans. "Tell me you went back the next day and shot the boyfriend."

"Are you out of your mind? For heaven's sake, Ollie. It's the '90s. Cops don't beat up white people in their own homes."

"It's my afternoon off."

I got scared. Ollie may have been stupid, but there was nothing quite as frightening as a bully with a plan.

"I figure it went down like this," he said. "First Rose pays you to videotape his boss's wife playing around."

"Why would I do that?"

"You're broke. So you tape 'em, but they spot you and call me and you run off in the woods. So Rose says, 'You screwed up. I won't pay you unless you shoot the guy.' You figure, what the hell.

The money's good. You don't know the guy. You sneak in the house and steal one of their guns."

"It's got burglar alarms like Fort Knox."

Ollie smiled. "Maybe somebody *gives* you the gun. Anyhow, you shoot the guy like it's a hunting accident." He switched the blackjack from his right hand to his left and reached back into the kitchen and produced an artist's sketch pad. He flipped the cover, revealing a penciled landscape. "See this signature?"

"Can't see that far from the floor, Ollie."

"It says 'Rita Long.' See?"

"Where'd you get it?"

"Found it in a mini Dumpster of construction garbage belonging to the Longs."

"Did someone happen to give you a tip?"

"Check this out, jailbird." He flipped back the landscape and there was the sketch of Ron Pearlman—naked, with skull.

"What's that supposed to be?"

"Chest and legs remind me of the boyfriend."

"Could be anybody."

"Look at this thing. She's nuts."

I tried to keep it simple for the man with the blackjack. "The picture isn't finished, Ollie. She didn't draw his face yet. That's all."

Ollie didn't buy it for a second.

"Nuts. Wacko. This proves it. I think they had some fun and games. Think it got out of hand. She waits until he turns his back the next day and blows him away."

He sounded so damned sure that even I found myself wondering, Did Rita shoot Ron?

"Kind of lets me off the hook, doesn't it?"

"Not if she gave you the gun."

"No," I said. "Something's wrong here. Ollie, what do you want?"

"I want you as a witness."

"Witness to what?"

"To her sleeping with her boyfriend. To being weird enough to kill him. What are you protecting her for?"

"You looking for a promotion, Ollie? Is that why you're playing detective?"

"You think I can't move up?"

"It never occurred to me. I thought you liked it here."

The fear that flickered on his face looked as out of place as a McDonald's on Main Street.

"That's it," I said. "The budget." He wasn't stupid; he was desperate. And in his desperation he had surrendered the moral high ground.

I stood up slowly. He watched me carefully, but made no threatening move. "Am I right?" I asked.

"This damned town. Worked here twenty years. Now they want to save a couple of bucks on my house."

I almost felt sympathy for him. Connecticut's budget was a mess, forcing the towns to slash school programs, ignore potholes, and raise dump fees. Another way to save money was to stop paying for a resident state trooper. It had happened in neighboring towns already. Ollie would lose his town-supported house and be transferred to some godforsaken part of the state.

Much better for Trooper Moody to help the state's attorney crack a big murder case. Get promoted. Up his pay. Increase his pension.

I said, "You haven't shown Bender and Boyce that remote control or the picture yet, have you?"

"Not yet. I'm still building my case."

"Ollie, you're taking a hell of a chance withholding evidence. They're the investigators. You're the donkey."

"Shut up."

"You're also so far off base you're in the skybox. Rita Long didn't kill Ron Pearlman. Neither did I. First you say I killed him for Rose. Then you say *she* killed him. You can't have it both ways, Ollie."

Oliver Moody put down the sketch pad and switched his blackjack back to his right hand. "I'm not worried. You'll clear things up for me."

"How you going to explain the bruises?"

"That car of yours is going into a tree. It won't kill you."

I hit the floor, rolled under the table, and came up beside the mantel, candlestick in hand. "I hope you get a desk job out of this, Ollie. You'll have trouble walking when I'm done with your knee."

Again he switched hands with the blackjack. He reached down and drew his ankle gun. "Put it back, turn around, and face the wall."

"No."

"Ben, I'll kill you."

"In my own house? Out of uniform?"

I began to sense that I had misunderstood him all these years. He was much more dangerous than a bully. He was a sociopath in uniform who needed his badge and gun like I needed air. After twenty years, how much could he still hate me for the logging-chain caper? Plenty, I feared. After all, the memory still made *me* smile.

My expression rattled Ollie. I think it began to dawn on him that maybe he wasn't the only crazy in the room. "Ollie," I said, "you can shoot me and wreck your career. Or you can let me help you."

"Why would you help me?"

"We can help each other. Put the gun down. Here." I returned the candlestick to the mantelpiece. "You know I didn't shoot Pearlman. I know Rita didn't. 'Cause I know who did. Just give me a couple of days before you turn in that drawing. I'll give you the killer, and you can take him to the state's attorney's office."

"Why would you help me?" he asked again.

"We're even," I lied. In truth, he still owed me for his smile at Renny's death. "Want to put down the gun, please?"

He holstered the gun, pocketed his blackjack, and strode to the mantel. He snatched up the candlestick, twisted it like a paper clip, and threw the ruin on the table.

"Twenty-four hours."

THE White Birch, Newbury's biker bar, is not as scary inside as it looks, because the owner, Wide Greg Wright, is even scarier than *he* looks. Every day, from noon opening to two a.m. closing, he's a firm host, sauntering among his guests, chatting, smiling.

As I entered, an argument broke out at the pinball machine. Greg asked the tattooed disputants was there a problem. Both men were much taller than Greg, but it developed there was no problem. I found space at the long bar and ordered a beer. Eventually Greg came by and asked how I was doing. I told him I wished the real estate business was half as good as the bar business.

Then I said, "I'm looking for a guy named Alex Rose."

"I tend not to remember names," said Greg.

"I was just talking to Lori Match. Alex Rose stayed at the Matchbox, night before the cookout. Lori said he wandered over here next morning."

Wide Greg looked genuinely surprised. "I don't get much trade from Lori."

"I'm not surprised." Though diagonally across Church Hill Road from the White Birch, the Matchbox's clientele tend to be elderly, middle class, and sedate.

"I showed him a house the day before the cookout. I thought he liked it. But he never got back to me, and I lost his number. Big guy, barrel chest. Looks like he's been around."

"Doesn't ring a bell."

"Shoot. I figured cookout day would have been kind of quiet for you. I thought you might have noticed a stranger."

"Ben, you see, the thing is, many of my customers have made a personal decision to maintain their privacy. They count on me to hold up my end."

"Wait a minute, Greg. The guy doesn't ride. He's a private detective from New York. I'm just curious how long he stayed."

"A private detective? In my place? Wha'd you say his name was?"

"Alex Rose. Expensive clothes. Face like a boxer."

Wide Greg chuckled to himself. "His name isn't Alex Rose."

"What do you mean?"

"Al *De*Rose. French name, he said. He rides a bike down in New York. Showed me pictures. Custom-built Harley."

"You sure it wasn't just a picture?"

"No. He fit right in. Talking with a bunch of the guys. He had a ball. Drank your cousin Pink under the bar."

"Wait a minute." Something didn't compute. I had seen Pink at the cookout around two o'clock—stone sober—while Lori Match told me that Rose had read the morning papers on her porch until the White Birch opened at noon.

"Was he in and out?"

"Never left. Opened the joint and shut the joint."

"You say he came at noon and stayed until two in the morning?"

"He left about midnight actually. 'Scuze me a minute."

Wide Greg homed in on a conversation that had been heating up down the bar and walked someone to the door. I couldn't believe it, but believe it I had to. My prime suspect had a perfect alibi. No way he could have shot Ron Pearlman.

I was quietly going nuts. This made no sense at all. Why had Rose stayed overnight in Newbury? Why had he spent the day in the biker bar? Why, when we spoke on the phone that day, did he not mention he was right around the corner in Newbury?

Wide Greg returned.

"Did Rose make any phone calls?"

"Oh, yeah. The man was wired like NASA. Beeper. Cell phone. Of course, the cell phone didn't work down here at the bottom of the hill. He kept asking for change—checking in with his answering machine."

HURRYING up Church Hill Road, heading home from the White Birch to inform Trooper Ollie that Alex Rose was our man, I had to admit I had almost believed that Rose owned a custom-built Harley-Davidson motorcycle. There is a gold-plated gang of rich New Yorkers who cruise in the mythic wake of Malcolm Forbes. But I had stopped believing when I learned about the phones. Alex Rose had stood by to help the killer.

Okay. Alex Rose hadn't shot Ron Pearlman personally. But he had waited close by to back up a professional killer he had hired on Jack Long's orders. If the murderer got in trouble, Rose was there to help him out. Maybe even provide the getaway.

My logic was impeccable—so long as I assumed Alex Rose was stupid. If *I* accepted a job from Jack Long to kill Ron Pearlman, would *I* take the risk of hiring somebody else and then hang around Newbury until the job was done? No, I would not. And neither would Alex Rose. We would have the good sense to avoid a conspiracy by doing the deed ourselves.

And why, if Rose didn't need an alibi, did he go to the trouble of establishing an alibi? Why had he stayed at the White Birch all day and all night? Why do business by beeper and pay phone?

Attaining the crest of Church Hill, I waited to cross Main Street. On the other side was the Yankee Drover. Now, there was a bar to spend the day in. Quiet. Decent food. High on the ridgeline of Main Street—a great place to use a cellular phone.

Of course cell-phone calls are expensive—charged by the minute, incoming as well as outgoing. But Rose didn't count pennies. Unless, of course, he did not want incoming telephone calls recorded on his cell-phone bill.

Rose was Jack Long's gofer. He was loyal and obedient, but not stupid. What if his *boss* ordered him to stand by in Newbury? What if he is sort of innocent? What if he suspects a killing might be on Long's agenda? He obeys orders. He stands by. But he covers his backside at the White Birch—an alibi *and* an excuse to his boss: Sorry, boss. The cell phone musta been out of range. I checked my machine in New York in case you tried to call me.

And what would happen if I asked him, Long hired his own killer, didn't he? You were afraid he'd involve you if something went wrong. The private detective would laugh in my face and say, Successful businessmen don't hire killers. To which I might add, Especially businessmen who hate partners.

I KNOCKED on Scooter's back door. His wife, Eleanor, answered and told me he was sneaking a cigarette behind the barn. She did not allow him to smoke indoors. I found him sitting on the woodpile gazing dreamily at the smoke. It was nearly dark.

"Can I see your files?"

"What files?"

"Press releases for the issue before last."

"Which ones?"

"Could I just see them without telling you which ones?"

"What's in it for me?"

"I don't know. You want to scoop the dailies?"

"Not really," he answered. "But it would be nice to know I could. . . . Come on. I'll walk you over to the office."

Scooter's father had computerized the *Clarion* while the *Daily News* and *The New York Times* were still setting Linotype. By now his computers were third or fourth generation. Hard to believe, as the *Clarion*'s quaint barn-red clapboard building with its white shutters and double-hung windows looked more like a used-book store than a newspaper office.

"Tell me who wrote the story, and I'll point you to their files for that issue," said the publisher, leading me into the editor's room.

"You did."

Scooter grinned. "You're looking up Jack Long, aren't you?"

"Do I have to answer that?"

"There's the file. Use my desk. Coffee down below."

The White House press releases were written in a breathless style preceded by a stern warning not to release the information early. There were photographs of a striped luncheon canopy and a whole slew of pictures of Jack Long shaking the President's hand.

A second release included a photo of Long surrounded by bright young men and women in sweatshirts—"the President's closest advisers"—watching television that evening in a book-lined study. They were eating—I swear this is true—TV dinners on trays. It did not say what they were watching. Nonetheless, I almost broke a finger in my haste to dial the contact number on the cover sheet.

"P.R.," answered the person at the White House.

"Donald Dodson, please," I asked, naming the contact listed.

"Dodson here."

"Mr. Dodson, I'm Scooter MacKay of the Newbury, Connecticut, *Clarion*. We're writing another story about a visit to the President two Saturdays ago—"

"Got a file number on that release?" Dodson interrupted. I gave it to him. "Who we talking about here?"

"Jack Long. Supper with the close advisers."

"Right."

"They're watching TV."

"Yeah?"

"What show are they watching?"

"Gee, I don't know."

"Our readers might wonder why Mr. Long went all the way to Washington, D.C., to watch television."

"Well, it was something political, you can be sure. People don't sit around here watching sitcoms. Hang on."

The minutes ticked by on Scooter's phone bill.

"Sorry it took so long. The supper ran from about nine to midnight. They were watching a special edition of *Larry King Live*. Zack Bowen was King's guest. The group watched, and then Zack returned from the studio and joined them for coffee."

"Thank you very very much. By the way, what went on between lunch and supper?"

"What do you mean?"

"Well, Mr. Long lunched with the President and supped with his advisers. What did he do in between?"

"It looks to me like he went back to his hotel and changed."

"How do you figure that?"

"In the photos I'm holding, he's wearing a different tie at supper."

I laughed. "Boy, you'd make a great detective." Though hardly in the class of my great-aunt Connie, I thought. Perched beside me—alert as a blue jay on our drive to visit Renny's widow—she had fancied there might be a connection between the two killings.

I wasn't surprised I had missed the change in neckties. I was getting cold inside.

"Anything else?" the P.R. man asked.

"Yes, one question: What time did the President leave lunch?"

"Oh, that's easy. He was outta there by twelve twenty."

"Twenty after twelve. Did the guests stay much longer?"

"They were free to go once he said good-bye."

"Thanks," I said, and hung up.

Colder still, I had one more question for one more person.

AFTER dark was a hell of a time to call on Gwen Jervis. I would have preferred driving a tank instead of the Olds. And a bulletproof vest instead of down. When I reached the end of the long, dark trail through the woods, I turned on the interior light, kept both hands in plain view, and parked slowly beside Gwen's pickup truck.

A bright light on a pole in the center of the trailer circle switched on. The woods beyond its glare were black. I got out slowly, sure I was being watched, and knocked on Gwen's door.

She opened it and stood there swaying drunkenly.

"Can I ask you a favor?"

"Try."

"Tell me who Renny's airplane customers were."

"The doctor with the cat was the main one."

"Right. Danbury–Block Island. Who else?"

"A stockbroker in Roxbury. Renny landed right in his backyard. And a guy who had horses over in Pawling."

"Who else?"

"The new guy in the Castle. What's his name? You know, the guy whose wife's boyfriend you found. The one who got shot."

I should have listened to Connie. I was ready to kill, but I didn't want Gwen doing it for me, so with my last ounce of rationality I said, easing toward the car, "Who else?"

"Oh, I don't know, Ben. Hey, where you going?"

"Gotta go, Gwen. Talk to you soon." I started the Olds and drove home, counting for the hundredth time the hours it took to travel from Washington, D.C., to Newbury, Connecticut, round-trip.

11

One-o'clock shuttle hits La Guardia Airport before two. Fifty minutes to find Renny and take off in his rented plane. Three thirty, land on Al Bell's field. Shoot Renny. You are now the only person in the world who knows you are in Newbury.

Rev up the plane and run it slow into a tree. Scatter a plastic bag of cocaine, indicting a kid from the wrong side of town for drug smuggling. Drive down Morris Mountain in Renny's Camaro. Park behind the barn and sneak into your own house. Take your wife's gun, wait for her boyfriend, shoot him in the back. Put back the gun and get Renny's car at four thirty, before Rita gets home. Drive two hours to La Guardia Airport, where you catch the seven-o'clock shuttle to Washington and arrive in Washington in time to shower and change in your hotel and return to the White House for TV dinners with the President's men.

I continued driving home and called a number I had entered somewhat optimistically in the car phone's memory.

Rita answered sleepily. I said, "Go to the guest room where you made love with Ron. I'll call you right back."

"Why?"

I hung up, gave her a moment to walk to the guest room, and dialed again.

"Jack killed Ron."

"Can you can prove it?"

"I'm waiting on one more piece. Day after tomorrow I can tell the cops."

Jack Long called me nine o'clock the next morning.

"Ben? Jack Long. Hope this isn't too early."

"At my desk, paying bills." Barefaced lie. I'd been staring at the telephone since seven, praying that Alex Rose still checked the bugs he had installed for the Rita-Ron gaieties.

"Listen, Ben. Rita and I don't think we can go on living in that house—because of everything that happened there."

"Sounds like you're putting it on the market."

"We are. We'd like to give you an exclusive, but we feel obligated to Fred Gleason."

"Understood."

"We'd like you to share an exclusive."

"I'll have to talk to Fred."

"You do that. In the meantime we're going to need a place to live. Alex Rose told me about an old estate you showed him."

"The Richardson place."

"Sounds interesting."

"Jack, it's a nice house, but it's not a thirty-seven-room stone mansion on a hundred acres."

"Rita and I want to downscale a little. Maybe we need a simpler life. A place we could manage alone."

"Would you like to see it?"

"How about this afternoon? Around three?"

"The light's real pretty around three."

HE ARRIVED at my office at ten after. To my surprise he had brought Alex Rose. Rose was back in his shooting costume. Long wore a Windbreaker and a baseball cap that almost made him look local. Both men looked nervous.

"Sorry I'm late. Pickup truck almost ran us off the road."

"Where's Rita?"

"I wanted to look myself first."

I glanced at Alex Rose, and Long said, "We had stuff to discuss, so we drove up together. You want to wait here, Al?"

"I'll come along. If it's okay with you, Mr. Long."

Long replied, "Suit yourself," as if he couldn't care less.

We got into my car—Rose in the back seat, Long in front beside me. As I pulled onto Main Street, they checked the traffic.

"You guys okay?"

"Yeah," said Long. "I swear that truck was following us. Gone now, looks like."

There were no pickup trucks on my agenda. I figured they'd annoyed a drunk who'd taken a dislike to Rose's Mercedes.

Eventually we reached Academy, headed down it and onto Richardson Street. It hadn't rained for a week, and we churned up a huge dust cloud. The maples had turned a soft amber gold.

"This used to all be Richardson land, but it's been sold off. The house has six acres, with another fourteen available."

"Think I could buy what's been sold off?" Jack asked. "I don't want someone building in my front yard." He gazed around appreciatively. "The views aren't as good as ours, but this is a nice piece of land. Hey, Al, isn't this great?"

Rose was peering out the back window. I'd been watching, too, but I had not seen any pickups.

"Oh, wow! This is great. Look at that house," Long said.

We got out of the car. I pulled out my keys. "There's a beautiful brick keeping room that overlooks the skating pond," I said. "I swear, on a winter day you can still smell the hot cocoa."

"Ben, we gotta talk." Long was watching me intently. Rose had wandered back toward the road, still watching for the phantom pickup truck.

"You can't make a bid without seeing the inside," I said.

Jack called, "Al, why don't you wait in the car? Ben's going to show me the back of the house."

"You sure?"

"Yeah, wait here. Come on, Ben, show me the skating pond."

We walked up the overgrown brick front walk. It split at the front steps and continued around both sides of the house. I forged ahead to the left-hand path and led Jack Long between the sunroom and the overgrown rose gardens. We continued around behind the house and stopped on a slate terrace between the keeping room and the silted-up skating pond.

"That used to be the tennis court." I indicated to the right.

"Ben, let's talk."

"All right, Jack. I gotta be frank."

"I agree. Cut the bull."

"I represent the estate."

"What? What estate?"

"Ellie Richardson's estate. Her heirs have no interest in this land. They just want some money. So I have a chance to sell you property at a very reasonable price."

"Don't try your head games on me, kid. We gotta talk. And you know damned well what we gotta talk about."

I turned away from him and walked closer to the house. He caught up and took my arm. "You know, Ben, you do a lot of deals, you never know which one's going to bring you down. You don't even think about it. You can't operate if you think that way, right? You know what I'm talking about. You've been there."

"Where?"
"Taking chances."
"Yeah, I've been there."
"All those balls in the air—one falls, so what? You toss another. Then one day you reach for another, and it's not there. I still cannot believe that of all the deals I cut, Ron Pearlman's factory would bring me down. You know what I mean?"
"I know one thing, Jack. When businessmen spout philosophy, they're through. You drop the ball, you pay the penalty."
"You do what you have to do," Long shot back. "Let's talk."
"About what? Shooting your partner in the back?"
"He was sleeping with my wife."
"That's not why you killed him."
"Oh, yeah? Why'd I kill him?"
"The payout. Like you just said, the deal was bringing you down. You didn't have the money you owed him."
"So what do you care? I did what I had to do."
"You left your wife holding the bag."
"She'll get off. Rita's tough. She can handle a trial."
"You killed my cousin to cover your tracks."
"For heaven's sake. I didn't know he was your cousin. I didn't know you. He was just a pilot. Dime a dozen. Hey, I'm not saying things didn't get out of hand. They got out of hand. That's why I'm explaining to you. I'll make sure his family's taken care of. Scholarships for the children, you name it. Set up trusts. You'll be the executor. And it goes without saying, name your own price, too. I assume you're the only one who's put this together, right?"
"Rita has a fair idea of what you did."
"I'll deal with Rita."
I looked at him. He looked me straight in the eye. "Last chance, Ben. What do you want me to do?"
All I had wanted him to do was say out loud that he had murdered Ron Pearlman and Renny Chevalley, and he had pretty much done that.
"Renny Chevalley was a good man."
Long reached into his Windbreaker and came up with a gun. Surprise, surprise. Then around the house came a real surprise—Alex Rose running flat out. "Hey, you said you were going to pay him off. What are you doing with a gun?"

I said, "He can't pay me off."

"Ben, the man's holding a gun. Hear him out," Rose said. "Mr. Long, this is getting out of hand."

"Go wait in the car," Long said to Rose.

"Mr. Long, you're making a mistake."

"I'm only talking to him. Go wait in the car."

Rose shifted from foot to foot, like a worried bear.

"Now!" Long's voice cut like a whip.

Rose stepped back. "Okay. I'll wait. See you guys in a minute."

Oliver Moody, who had finally heard enough, stepped out of the keeping room, both hands wrapped around his automatic. In full uniform and Smokey Bear hat, he looked nine feet tall.

I HAD neglected to warn Ollie that Jack Long had been a marine, while Ollie, who should have known better, made the mistake of thinking rich men were soft. Long launched his burly frame into a flying leap, hit the terrace rolling, and came up shooting with remarkable accuracy. The state trooper got off a round that went wild as he pitched forward, blood spraying from his neck.

"You shot a cop!" yelled Rose.

I was stunned. Oliver Moody down was an impossible sight.

"That didn't happen," said Long, eyeing me as he knelt coolly and picked up Oliver's pistol. "What happened was a shoot-out between our resident state trooper and his old enemy, the Realtor convict." He turned to me with the smile of a man who knew that a very messy situation would be contained.

I looked to Rose. No help there. He wasn't smiling, but he looked relieved. Long's story would sell.

Long aimed Ollie's gun at me. I felt my legs shaking and couldn't stop them. "I thought you hate partners, Jack."

"You lost me there, Ben."

"You kill me, and you've formed a lifelong partnership with your tame detective. He'll have this on you forever."

"No problem," Long agreed. "Al got caught in the cross fire." He raised Oliver's gun, and it boomed like a cannon—twice.

Long's first shot surprised me as much as it did Rose, whose jaw dropped when the bullet sent him reeling backward. The second shot tore through the detective's arm, spinning his body in a circle before it landed. I dove on top of Oliver Moody. It was the trooper's ankle gun or nothing, provided I could extract it from the holster and figure out how to disengage the safety.

I got one break. Long mistakenly assumed I was hiding behind Oliver's body. He took a second to step closer and aim, and in that time, I got my hand up Oliver's pants leg and around the Beretta before Long caught on. He snapped a shot. The slug whanged slate chips in my face, and then I was jerking on the Beretta's trigger.

At Leavenworth NRA meetings, all members agreed: Shoot. Shoot. Shoot. Don't aim. Just keep shooting. My mentors would have been proud. Bullets sprayed all around Long. One of my shots finally caught him in the arm. He cried out, turned, and ran.

Before I could get to my feet, Jack Long was around the house. I charged after him and saw him running for my car. Suddenly he skidded to a stop as a rusty '79 Ford pickup burst between the hedges that screened the road and roared up the rutted drive.

Jack Long ran. The pickup truck veered, cut him off, hit him with an enormously loud boom, and threw him thirty feet across the weed-strewn parking lot.

Long hit the ground rolling. The truck spun on a dime, spewing dust and gravel. Long tried to stand, screaming as the truck knocked him down again and ran him over. Red brake lights flared, then backup whites, and the truck backed on top of him and stopped.

Gwen Jervis jumped out. Ignoring me watching from the corner of the house, she knelt under the truck and gazed silently into Long's face.

I heard a desperate cry from the back of the house. "Ben!"

I ran back to Ollie. Blood spurting, he struggled to stand. I gentled him down in my arms, found a terrible gouge in his massive neck, and tried to squeeze it shut.

Movement. I looked up. "What—"

"Saw your dust." Gwen Jervis, who had not been quite as drunk as I had thought the night before, took in the scene.

"Grab the phone in my car. Call for an ambulance," I said.

Instead, Gwen knelt. "I'll do him. You call." Her hands clamped surely on the wound. "Make it two ambulances. There's a guy out front got run over by a pickup truck." There was dead calm in her eyes. "Fell right under my wheels. Twice."

I ran to my car and telephoned 911.

Thirty feet down the drive, Jack Long sprawled under Gwen's truck like a scarecrow blown off its pole. Newbury answered. I told them they had better bring the Morrisville and Frenchtown ambulances, too. Then I knelt for a closer look at Long. His eyes flickered with light for a second—pale, dim, and fading fast.

His chest was crushed. His voice bubbled—thin and bloody. "Why'd she run me over?" he asked, bewildered.

I told him she did what she had to do, and I went back to Oliver.

THE body count had dropped a full basis point in my absence. Alex Rose was sitting up. Ever cautious, the detective had worn a bulletproof vest under his fancy shooting jacket. His arm was going to hurt a long time, but he was not dead. In fact, he was hoarsely gasping a story he thought we ought to present to the cops. I told him to make up his own story.

"Hey, I didn't know he offed Ron."

"Not a clue?"

"Okay, so maybe I suspected."

Gwen looked over. "Ask him about Renny."

"I didn't know anything about Renny."

"Didn't you wonder why Jack told you to stash forty grand in Renny's closet?"

"I didn't do that. I swear it. Jack must have."

I exchanged a look with Gwen. We must have looked dubious, because Rose protested indignantly again. "I never touched the money." Too indignantly, I thought. So did Gwen.

"Then what are you lying about?" she asked.

Rose thought a moment. We heard a siren on the wind. "Jack asked me to buy him a few grams of coke. That's all I did."

I looked at Gwen, who shrugged.

The Newbury volunteer ambulance arrived first. They were afraid to move Ollie, so they radioed for the Life Star helicopter, which lifted him out before dark. By then we had a lot of state police on the Richardson place, including Bender and Boyce.

Gwen answered their questions with practiced ease, saying that she had just come down Richardson Street to pick apples from the abandoned orchard, and this guy ran out in front of her truck. "Hit him, threw him, and ran over the poor bastard." She probed between her teeth and reflected. "It was a terrible experience."

The cops looked at me. "That what you saw?"

I wasn't a liar. I looked at Gwen, who was as fearless as a hawk that soared on instinct. She gazed back, asking nothing. Like I told Jack Long, you drop the ball, you pay the penalty. I had made mistakes. I had paid the price. I paid for principle, paid willingly. Though in my heart I had to wonder if I had spent coin that wasn't only mine.

"Ben?"

"I had my hands full with Trooper Moody. I thought he was a goner until Gwen came running and got the bleeding stopped."

A state police captain who had battled Jervises his entire career asked dryly, "You've had experience with gunshot wounds, Gwen?"

"Hunting accidents," Gwen confessed.

DARK set in, and we all adjourned to town hall, where the police set up a temporary HQ. The state's attorney himself came down from the county seat. Ollie had choked out a statement on the flight to the hospital, confirming the essence of Jack Long's confession. Now Ollie was tubed and trached in recovery, and his doctors would permit no more interviews until tomorrow. Alex Rose had either been on the wrong side of the house or unconscious in the grass. That left me as the state's attorney's best witness to the events that appeared to turn his case against Rita Long into low comedy.

He was not a happy man. Nor was he pleased when Ira Roth bustled in, in full three-piece regalia, assuring me sotto voce he was working pro bono.

The state's attorney said, "Let me get this straight. This man claims—"

"My client asserts," Roth interrupted.

"Your client asserts that Jack Long shot Ron Pearlman in order to nullify a contract that would have ruined him financially. He further claims—asserts—that to maintain the illusion that he was in Washington, D.C., all day the day of the murder, Jack Long shot your client's cousin, Renny Chevalley, the pilot who flew him to Newbury, and made it look like a drug deal gone bad."

"Where'd the coke come from?" asked Sergeant Bender.

"How could my client possibly know about cocaine? He had had only a passing acquaintance with Mr. Long at what I recall was a land-trust meeting. Is that right, Ben?"

"That's right. We shook hands."

"You're asking the wrong man," Ira continued. "Just as you're trying to stampede a grand jury into indicting the wrong woman."

The state's attorney swore.

"Give thanks to Ben Abbott, Counselor. Better now than getting laughed out of court." Ira turned to me without even asking the state's attorney's or the police's permission and said, "Ben, may I offer you a lift to your car?"

"It's impounded," growled Marian Boyce. "I'll drive him."

"Where to?" said Marian once we were in her car.

"The Castle."

"I thought so, Mr. Romantic."

"Does she know yet?" I asked.

"I told them to hold off. You'd tell her."

THE front door was open, the house dark but for a single light atop the turret. I climbed the stairs. Rita was in the observation nest, seated at the little table. Beside her sat a bottle of champagne on ice and two glasses. An Ithaca Deerslayer lay across her lap.

"Jack?" she asked as I reached the top of the stairs.

"Ben."

Her shoulders sagged. "Did you kill him?"

"No. Renny's girlfriend ran him over with her truck."

"Did he suffer?"

I recalled his scream. "Briefly."

"He deserved to."

"Yeah, right. What's the gun for?"

"He said we had to talk."

"Who's the champagne for?"

"A man I used to love. Want some?"

"I'll pass. Maybe I can bring a new bottle one of these days."

"Not too soon."

I started down the stairs. My aunt Connie was right. I was a fool for women. But this one would save me from myself.

"By the way, there's a wiretap on your guest-room phone."

"I disconnected it."

"When?"

"When you told me about the video, I realized that Rose must have installed a tap."

"But I called you on that phone last night, and—"

"I figured you were sending Alex Rose a message, so I called him up and told him."

"Why?"

"I knew you were bluffing about proof. That meant you were bluffing Jack. To force him out in the open. Right?"

"You knew he'd come after me?"

"Obviously, you had a plan."

"What if I didn't?"

She patted the Deerslayer. "I did."

CONNIE and I gave an orphans' Thanksgiving. We invited Ed Hawley, the cook at the Church Hill Diner; Alison and Mrs. Mealy; my mother; and Rita.

Connie had insisted on cooking the turkey, so I hustled across the street to give her a hand. Last night we'd set the table and arranged the flowers.

Alison and her mother tried to hide in the kitchen. Poor Janet Mealy was absolutely overwhelmed by Connie's mansion, while Alison had already informed me that her new braces made her smile look like the front of my Oldsmobile. Connie chased them into the drawing room. There, sitting with a simple elegance in a Salvation Army thrift-shop suit, was Ed Hawley, who addressed Janet as "Ma'am" throughout the afternoon.

Rita Long arrived late, flushed from the cold, as beautiful and exotic as a Russian princess. She presented Connie with an enormous basket of glacéed fruits. Connie thanked her courteously, even as her back stiffened at the extravagance.

At the table, however, Connie warmed to Rita, admiring how she drew Mrs. Mealy, Alison, and Ed into the conversation. Twice Connie cast me unusually approving glances, and once I caught her nodding at my mother. Rita charmed her, too, of course.

After dinner Rita was the last to leave. At the door she said, "Will you take me house hunting tomorrow? I've decided to stay, but not in that house."

"Do you know what you want?"

"Something nice and cozy."

I'd believe that when I saw it. She was a wealthy widow, sole heir to Long Technical Systems, which had a good chance of surviving Jack's death thanks to Ron's canny father and some managerial people I'd recommended. I promised to show her a few places in the morning.

I HAD prepared a list of "cozy," and we spent Friday morning going from one cramped cottage to another; then we visited some bigger places in the afternoon. I was about to invite her home for a drink when she said, "Show me the Richardson place again."

"I don't want to go there."

"He was my husband. Nobody you loved died out there."

"*I* almost died out there."

"Show it to me."

I headed out Route 7 fast, because the days were getting very short and we'd lose the light by four thirty. Rita was sitting with her head back on the seat, hair shimmering like black lacquer.

"I like your house," she said suddenly.

"Not for sale. Besides, you wouldn't want to live on Main Street. You can't run around naked with the shades up."

"But at least you don't get raccoons making videos."

"Sometimes they come in the house. Slip down the chimney."

Ahead a quarter mile, someone had parked a hay wagon on the shoulder. I got a little warning tingle in my scalp and hit the brakes.

"What?" she cried, thrown against the seat belt.

"Speed trap."

We eased by Ollie at forty-four.

I waved. One finger.

ABOUT THE AUTHOR

"Most young people who decide to write have a bad moment telling the family," says Justin Scott. But when Scott announced his decision, he had no qualms. Both parents were themselves seasoned novelists. "The advantage of being born into a family of writers," Scott explains, "is that the people you love and admire agree that writing fiction is a respectable way to earn a living." Scott recalls that when he broke the news of his writing ambitions, his father simply looked up from his typewriter, said "Congratulations," then continued typing.

Justin Scott

However, there can be disadvantages to growing up in a literary household, says Scott. "Fewer people write for a living than carve gargoyles," he points out. "Children of writers grow up a little disconnected from the real world that writers are supposed to write about." Scott made up for this shortcoming in numerous ways. Before deciding to write full time, he drove trucks, built beach houses, tended bar, edited an electronic-engineering journal, and throughout pursued a lifelong love of sailing. He has continued to nurture this connection with other worlds by extensive traveling and research and by trying his hand at different kinds of books: mysteries and sea sagas, psychological chillers and international thrillers. "I've resisted repeating myself," he says—a tall order, considering he has published fourteen novels.

Now, with *Hardscape,* Scott has inaugurated a new mystery series, featuring amateur sleuth Ben Abbott. The setting is a world close to Scott's heart: small-town America. Newbury is a composite of his Long Island hometown and the Connecticut town where he and his wife, a landscape designer, now live. For Scott, Newbury is such an irresistible place that Ben Abbott is likely to have a good many future adventures there.

PHOTO: LORI MARCH TAUBMAN

ILLUSTRATORS

George Sharp: *A Dangerous Fortune*

Don Daily: *The Select*

Neville Dear: *Rivers of Gold*

Sal Catalano: *Hardscape*

The original editions of the books in this volume are published and copyrighted as follows:
A Dangerous Fortune, published at $23.95 by Delacorte Press, a division of Bantam Doubleday Dell Publishing Group, Inc.

The Select, published at $22.00 by William Morrow and Company, Inc.

Rivers of Gold, published at $18.95 by St. Martin's Press

Hardscape, published at $19.95 by Viking Penguin, a division of Penguin Books USA Inc.

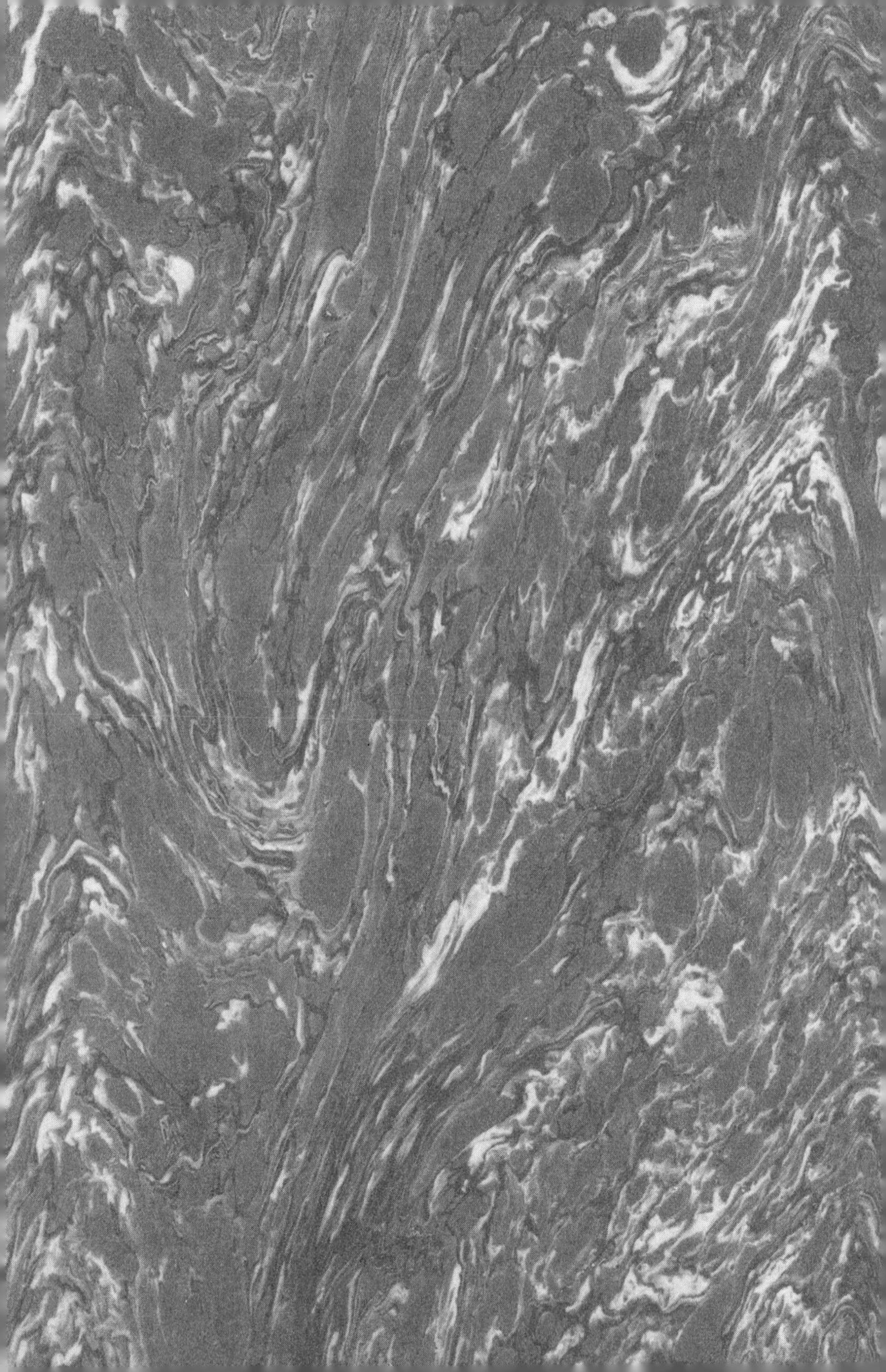